A Slow Burning

Stanley Pottinger has had successful careers as a lawyer and an investment banker and has also written for a number of magazines including *The New York Times*. He lives in New York.

Praise for A SLOW BURNING

'Ingenious, ambitious and sprawling medico-racio-psycho thriller ... if you have a taste for violence and complicated high-tech surgical thrillers ... your reward could be a gripping read'

Daily Mail

'Pottinger proves he is a master of the art of the medical thriller ... The action bounces around like machine-gun fire in a dark alley ... This kaleidoscopic thriller is marvellously complex, charged with emotional impact and resounding ethical questions'

Publishers Weekly

Also by Stanley Pottinger

The Fourth Procedure

A Slow Burning

Stanley Pottinger

CORONET BOOKS
Hodder & Stoughton

Copyright © 1999 Stanley Pottinger

First published in Great Britain in 1999
by Hodder and Stoughton
A division of Hodder Headline

A Coronet Paperback

The right of Stanley Pottinger to be identified as the Author of
the Work has been asserted by him in accordance with the
Copyright, Designs and Patents Act 1988.

10 9 8 7 6 5 4 3 2 1

A CIP catalogue record for this title is available from the British Library.

ISBN 0 340 69592 7

Typeset by Palimpsest Book Production Limited,
Polmont, Stirlingshire
Printed and bound in Great Britain by
Mackays of Chatham PLC, Chatham, Kent

Hodder and Stoughton
A division of Hodder Headline
338 Euston Road
London NW1 3BH

For Joni

Sine qua non

Many things in this book have already happened.

All things in this book could.

Whop, whop, whop, whop . . .

Look at that. Here comes one now.

The third-graders on the summer school field trip stood on their tiptoes and peered out the windows in the Statue of Liberty's crown, watching a red, white, and blue SK-2 hover over the harbor. The morning sky was glistening and squeaky-clean, freshly washed of July soot by an all-night rain. Boarding the ferry, their teacher had told them to count the methods of transportation that matched the pictures in their social studies reader. So far they'd found a boat, a train, a car, a truck, and an airliner gliding toward LaGuardia. And now this. A helicopter.

Whop, whop, whop.

The kids jostled for position at the windows to watch the plane's silhouette. Instead of slicing past them, it stood still, like a hummingbird with blurry wings.

Now, they noticed, appearing a bit larger.

The kids pawed each other – Let me see – It's my turn – *Stop it*, Jimmy, or I'm gonna tell. Come on, kids, the teacher said, it's time to go.

Some of the children grabbed the stainless-steel hand rail and started down the staircase while others clung to the brass frames around the ports. The helicopter raised its nose slightly like a horse being reined in and, about fifty yards away, made a graceful quarter-turn, revealing a large open door on the side. A man sat on the floor, feet dangling, his hands holding a camera.

1

Crabbing sideways, the helicopter moved closer. The man lifted his camera.

A boy waved at it. Don't do that, Steven, the teacher said, they might be making a movie.

The sound of the popping blades was lost in the din of a powerful engine cranking out five thousand revolutions a minute, straining to keep a ton of metal hanging in the air. The chopper was so close now they could see the photographer's hair whipping in the wind, the color of his goggles, the microphone curled in front of his mouth and the brass clips on his safety harness. With his camera chest high, he spoke into his microphone and punched the air with his finger, move in closer.

Isn't he a little *too* close? the teacher said.

The helicopter inched sideways, now only twenty yards away. The kids pressed their foreheads to the glass, entranced with the high-pitched whine and sight of a huge metal bug actually flying. Looks like a Commanche, one of them said, speaking of his favorite video game.

Suddenly, a stream of black oil shot out of the engine and puffed into a swirling cloud in the rotor downdraft. Black mist covered the chopper's bubble canopy and sprayed the statue's windows, turning them into light-brown filters.

The helicopter made a small jiggling motion, shivered, and rolled toward the statue so steeply they could see the tops of the rotors, the feathery yellow circle made by the warning stripes on the blades.

Cool, one of the boys said.

The man in the door dropped his camera and gripped the hook on his safety harness and tried to scramble backwards into the cabin. His eyes locked onto the kids' faces.

The teacher screamed. The ear-splitting noise drowned her voice.

The deafening roar was broken by the *chunk-ka-chunk* sound of the blades hitting Miss Liberty's left cheek, just below her forehead where the children stood. Bits of copper and steel shrapnel exploded into the hollow behind her eyes. Some kids squealed and ran, others stood and watched without blinking.

The air inside the crown filled with smoke and the high-pitched sound of an eight hundred horsepower engine stripping the teeth off its gears as it cranked broken rotors, most of which were already fluttering in shattered pieces toward the grass.

The kids watched the helicopter nose over and drop out of sight, leaving a trail of steam and smoke like a dying roman candle. It hit the stone base near Miss Liberty's feet, bounced off, and fell farther onto the New Hampshire marble platform below, a harmless, smoking toy.

Wow, one of the boys said to his stricken, speechless teacher. I wanna see this movie! That really looked *real*!

ONE

There is always one moment in childhood
when the door opens and lets the future in.
—Graham Greene

Fragments from
Three Childhoods

FRIDAY, *November 22, 1963*

He had seen a cross like this once before, in the field behind
the barn where he'd been sleeping on a hot summer night. But
this one was different. When the torch light hit it just right,
it looked as if it was upside down, and instead of being plain
and white, it had bands around the beams, like strips of paint,
or cloth, or rope. Or something.

Hunching down, he reached out and carefully parted the
thorny blackberry bush, afraid that the hooded figures could
see his puffs of breath hanging in the cool November air. The
white-sheeted figures seemed huge and unreal, powerful in the
way they moved, mysterious like ghosts. Maybe they *were* ghosts.
Maybe they didn't need to see him at all – maybe they could
catch his scent or feel his presence. The thought of it dried his
mouth and numbed his lips. Get out of here, his legs said, but
his eyes held him tight. He was witnessing something large here,
like the sinking of a ship or a wrecked train, and no one, least of
all a nine-year-old boy, could be expected to run from that.

He let go of the berry bush and lay on his back behind its
camouflage. His eyes were open, the stars brightly lit, his mind's
eye reconstructing the cross he'd seen the summer before. He
remembered waking to the sound of strange voices, then peeking
through the cracks in the hayloft wall to see phantoms in white
robes lifting the Mississippi pine into place, hand over hand, as if
it was a barn post. He remembered watching them use ax heads
to pound stakes around the base, then douse it with gasoline
and touch firebrands to it and make it quiver beneath a film of

floating yellow heat. He could still picture the flames licking its skin, arching a halo across the velvet-black sky. He could still feel the shock of seeing the symbol of Jesus rising like charred flesh into heaven. At first he'd thought they'd stolen the cross from the Baptist church in Hardy and were just prankin', but then he understood who they were. These were the men his parents described as 'Satan's children', the nameless, faceless ones he saw in nightmares standing unburned in rings of fire, tall steeples of cold, white stone. Seeing them that summer night was the first time he'd grasped his parents' warnings that it was the brutes, not the angels, who held power over the earth. At least, if you were black.

One of the men in the distance cursed, stopping the boy's heart. After scrunching up, he lifted his head and found the cross through the leaves. Why had they turned it upside down? He tried to make out what they were doing and saying, but he was too far away; he'd have to circle around to the trees and crouch in the cotton stubble and watch from there. Quiet and invisible. Brave.

His heart pounded in his throat. Brave? He was so scared his lungs ached. What he *really* needed to do was run back to the farmhouse and tell his father and brothers to get the dogs and the shotgun and—

What's that?

Two white robes moved toward the base of the cross, torches blazing. There was something on the other side of the vertical beam, as if it was lashed to a mast.

The doctor closed his eyes and tried to imagine the girl they were talking about, but he was upside down, and blood had pooled in his head, threatening to black him out. Despite the stench of kerosene-soaked torches, he could smell the man's fetid breath, rancid with rotting hush puppies and cheap liquor. His upper eyelids fell open. A foot away from his face, two

10

inverted heads covered in white leaned forward from a kneeling position to get a closer look. Behind the ragged holes he could see their eyes, one pair clear and cold, the other pair blinking nervously.

'Tell me you did it and we'll leave you be,' the cold-eyed man said.

'Elsewise,' the blinker said, 'we gonna hurt you bad.'

He's the weak one, the doctor decided . . . the coward with a spine of booze and an unhinged tongue . . . talks tough when the action's high . . . vomits when it's over.

The doctor listened to his pulse pound in his ears. St Peter . . . crucified . . . on an inverted cross. *Dear God . . . if you can hear me.* His toes were turning cold from hanging upside down, and from the bindings on his ankles.

'We know you did it, Doc,' the cold-eyed man said. 'She done told us. Alls you gotta do is admit it and you kin go home.'

'Did . . . what?' the doctor said.

'Aw, shit,' the nervous blinker said, taking an angry swipe at the grass. He stood up.

Cold Eyes didn't move. 'Is that what you want? To hear the words?'

Toeing the sod, the nervous blinker said, 'You ain't never gonna hear it come outta my mouth.'

The first man bent a little closer, speaking quietly in the intimate tone of a friend. 'She ain't my girl, Doc, so it don't make me no never mind whether I say the words or not, but you know what we do to niggers who mess with our women, so what's the point?'

The doctor pictured the young white girl on the floor of his clinic, her eyes staring blankly into space, her cold, taut body quaking in an epileptic fit. He remembered kneeling beside her, holding her arms down with one hand and using the other to pry loose the tongue that had collapsed into her throat. He hadn't treated a white patient for years, but this was an emergency. Her panicked sister didn't know where else to go; he was the closest doctor she could find; naturally he would help. Of course, the girl had said nothing about her sister being pregnant, much less being raped. He'd explained that to the Klansmen over and over, from the first time they'd called him at the clinic and threatened him, to only an hour earlier, when they'd dragged him to the pebble pasture and tied him to the cross. But none of it did any good. Telling them again would only mean another blow to his head, which was already the size of a melon. It might shake loose the watch, too, and if things didn't go right – *Lord, help me* – he'd need the watch.

He turned his head to the side, searching for a way out, and felt the adhesive tape stretch the skin on the side of his neck. The watch fob was still there, but how was he going to get to the case? *Should have thought of this . . . missed my chance to open it when they grabbed me.* He saw three more white sheets standing off to the side, each clutching a torch.

'Don't look away from me!' Cold Eyes barked.

Turning back, the doctor saw two hooded men on the other side, one standing still, the other rocking back and forth like a little boy trying not to pee his pants. There were five of them in all . . . maybe seven.

The ringleader stood up and pulled two men aside and talked to them in a low voice. The doctor watched, trying to keep his mind alive. Their white costumes reminded him of something . . . Halloween . . . his five-year-old daughter in her little cat suit, pulling off her whiskered mask because it was too hot and sweaty, too hard to breathe, too stupid to wear. Now these men . . . overgrown children without the wits of five-year-olds . . . too hot and sweaty to breathe . . . too dumb to take the hoods off.

The leader returned to the stake. 'Listen to me,' he said. 'I'm gonna give you one more chance.'

The doctor, dizzy and swollen, refused to speak.

Cold Eyes reached under his robe and withdrew a bone-handled knife. *Shick-clunk* – a gleaming blade appeared from nowhere.

Stay awake. The pocket watch is there . . . but no good unless you can reach it. Stay awake.

The boy sneaked onto a bed of pine needles and curled into a ball. He was no more than seventy-five feet from the cross now, hidden from view on one side by a pile of fir logs too full of pitch to be used as firewood, protected on the other side by the night. He decided to lie still and make sure he was invisible before lifting his head to see what was happening. Brave enough? For what? He wanted to know without knowing.

'The baby looks just like you, Doc. Just like you.'

'I . . . never . . . touched . . . the girl.'

'Then why's she say you're the one? Tell me, Doc. Why would she say a thing like that?'

The doctor tried to shake his head slowly.

'You expect me to take the word of a nigger over the word of a innocent, fourteen-year-old white girl?'

'Let's check him out,' someone said. 'She told us how to prove he's the one.'

'Shut up!' the ringleader said. Using his fingers and thumbs, he pressed the cloth of his hood into his eyes to wipe away the sweat, then exhaled a long, defeated sigh. Holding the switchblade across the doctor's neck, he drew its flat edge against the grain of the old man's day-old growth with the sound of a soft zipper. When it reached his chin, he lifted it, stood up, and placed the sharp tip of it into the doctor's pants near his knee.

The doctor trembled and closed his eyes. Laboring to breathe, he said, 'Watch.'

'Watch what?' the Klansman said. 'You the one needs to

watch.' He grabbed the old man's pant leg at the shin and drew the knife downward toward his crotch, cutting his trousers open clean as a seamstress.

The other white sheets stood still, hoods pulsing in and out at their mouths, eyes fixed on the knife, some blinking, some not.

He placed the blade under the elastic band of the doctor's undershorts and flicked it upward, cutting them loose. Then he stuck the knife under the cloth from the waist to the leg hole and cut it in half.

'Watch,' the doctor said again.

'Look at that,' the nervous one said. 'Didn't I tell you? She said he wuddn't circumcised!'

'You dumb son-of-a-bitch,' the ringleader said. 'Ain't ten old niggers in the county been circumcised.'

Another one said, 'Got to be hospital-born to git circumcised.'

The ringleader squatted down and once again brought his face close to the doctor's. 'Last chance, Doc. Why'nt you just admit it and git it off your chest?'

The doctor heard a popping metal sound. *I know that sound.* He murmured something. The hood bent down closer.

'My . . . watch,' the doctor said in a raspy voice.

'Your watch? What about your watch?'

The doctor's outstretched hands curled back toward his chest as if he were reaching for something. *I know . . . that sound . . . the popping of sheet metal cooling . . . like a tin of water . . . or a can of gasoline.*

A cat walked down his spine. It had been years since lynchings were commonplace in Mississippi, not since the late twenties, early thirties, but there was trouble in Mississippi now, civil rights workers coming around, angry marchers and torch-lit mobs and church bombings, and when that kind of trouble reared its head, he knew the whitecaps would pick up the torch. Fire was what the Rocky Ford mob had used on a family in Vicksburg, and it was how a mob had killed the mulatto gambler named MacIntosh. Fire was their favorite way in Mississippi. Wasn't that long ago that a six-hour lynching – what whites called 'a slow burning' – brought out ten thousand citizens, including the sheriff and his family, on a Sunday afternoon. After roast chicken dinner. After Sunday morning church. After readin' the Bible and prayin'. Couldn't let a lynching interfere with lovin' God and prayin'.

The hood looked at the doctor's wrists but found no watch. He stood up. 'He's talkin' crazy again. He ain't gonna admit nothin'.'

'Let me try,' the nervous blinker said. 'I gotta right, she's my girl.'

The ringleader stood looking down at the old man's face, fingering the enormous switchblade, deciding what to do. After a moment he took a step backward and let the girl's daddy take his place.

With his head up and his gaze fixed, the boy's spirit drained out of him like syrup off a spoon. He knelt in the bed of pine needles, a legless statue, open-mouthed and wide-eyed in a dream. The object on the cross was a man, someone hanging upside down, his feet tied at the top, his arms outstretched on the horizontal beam. And someone in a sheet was doing terrible things to him – punching him, yelling at him, hitting him in the face, the stomach, between his legs. He could see the victim's feet curl forward each time a blow landed, see bits of corn meal shaken loose from his pants cuffs. He could see his shoes trembling . . . a pair of high-top farmer's shoes with long laces tied around the ankles and back to the front in a bow.

Exactly the way his father tied them.

The obvious washed over him. He became disembodied, unable to feel the ground beneath him, unaware that he was standing up or walking out into the open. Only the sound of his own voice yelling 'Dad!' brought him back to reality.

That, and the vice grip of a man's hand on the back of his neck.

The whitecaps at the cross looked up through their saggy holes and watched as their lookout steered the boy toward them.

His father's eyes were swollen closed, but Cush could tell that his dad knew what had happened: his nine-year-old son had been captured. A shot of adrenaline surged through his veins making the ropes moan against the cruciform. He tried to speak, but his voice box was smashed and swollen, allowing only a whisper.

One of the hooded men said, 'What the fuck you doing bringing that kid over here?'

'He seen us!'

'Seen what? What the hell you think we wearing these hoods for, you dumb son-of-a-bitch?'

'Everybody shut up!' the cold-eyed ringleader said.

Cush dropped down to his father's head. 'Daddy!' he said, hanging onto his father's battered face and neck.

'Run,' his father whispered to him. 'Run, run . . . run!'

Cush heard him but didn't move. 'Dad!' he pleaded, as if this man who saved other people's lives had the power to save his own.

'My watch,' his father whispered. 'Open it.'

The boy didn't understand.

'Take . . . my watch.'

Cush fumbled at his father's torso, searching for the big pocket watch he'd seen him pull from his pants many times before. He felt it in the center of his chest. With his hands shaking, he unbuttoned his father's shirt and found the gold circle dangling on a fob that had been taped to his smooth skin.

'Hey, boy, what you got there?' the nervous blinker said. He reached down and swatted the nine-year-old onto his haunches, then took the timepiece in his hand and lowered his hooded face for a closer look. 'Where'd you get this, nigger?' he said to Cush's father, and pressed the latch that opened the gold cover. A small, black capsule dropped onto the ground. 'What's that?' the blinker said.

'Leave him alone!' the boy cried.

Paying no attention, the nervous man knelt beside the doctor's face and pawed the grass for the pill. 'You fixin' to git outta this with cyanide, old man? Before I'm done with you?' He tugged at the watch again, but the taped-down fob held fast. He turned his head up to the ringleader. 'Gimme the knife,' he said.

'Fuck the knife, just take it.'

'It ain't the watch fob ah'm fixin' to cut.'

The ringleader flicked open the blade and laid the handle in the nervous hood's outstretched palm. He turned it around and pushed the sharp tip against the doctor's neck, indenting the skin. 'Hold the boy,' he said. 'This'll learn him a lesson he won't never forgit.' With his other hand, he tugged at the watch fob and felt it hold fast. 'Shit,' he said, and in a violent rage, ripped it off the man's chest.

As the watch fob pulled away from the skin, the whitecap's knife hand jerked forward no more than a quarter inch – but enough to puncture the swollen jugular.

Blood spurted out of the bulging vein in a geyser, squirting in pulses onto the Klansman's white robes, spewing under the enormous pressure of gravity and a desperate heart.

The Klansman yelled, 'Ah, shit!' and scrambled backwards, shaking the blood off his outstretched hands, head bent down toward the stream of red.

The other men froze.

'Jee–zus,' one of them said.

The boy stood still, disbelieving. '*Run, run, run,*' his father had said. Cush grabbed the watch off the ground and bolted on liquid feet toward the ravine.

'Get the kid!' someone yelled.

'I cain't run in this goddamn thing!' another answered.

'He ain't seen no faces!' a third said.

'Shit!' the killer said, shaking his dripping hands, gawking at his red-soaked robe.

One of the Klansmen raised a rifle, took aim at the fleeing boy, and fired a single shot. 'I got him! I got the kid!'

'Let's get outta here!' the ringleader said. Someone splashed gasoline onto the cross, the doctor, and the ground.

The first torch set the place ablaze, then everyone tossed in their own, end over end like juggler's pins. Like an awakened dragon, the crucifix roared its voracious split-tail flames into the air, sucking everything into a consuming vortex – leaves, oxygen, breath, madness – inflating itself with a guttural growl that stunned the Klansmen and scattered them into the night like frightened maidens running with their skirts held high.

The pyre continued burning without an audience, cauterizing the air and cleansing the earth, transporting a human spirit into the ether. With its work finally done, with yet another Mississippi killing field sanctified, the fire slowly receded into a cool, crinkled ash, transforming itself from a raging inferno into a dignified cocoon, removing the last remains of the doctor from the beauty and scum of the world, ensuring, at last, that nothing – not a torch or a hand, not a curse or a breath, not even the adoring gaze of his children or the gentle rays of the morning sun – would ever touch him again.

As young Cush Walker approached the steps of the church dressed in his Sunday best, even though it was Saturday, he saw a newspaper pinned to the side of the dilapidated newsstand on the corner. His mother let go of his good hand – the other was in a sling from a bullet wound in his shoulder – and embraced a woman in a black straw hat, one of the doctor's patients who'd come to pay her respects. Cush wandered over to the shed and read a one-word headline on the bottom half of the folded paper that spoke of the earth-shaking events of the night before. SLAIN! it said and, beneath it, a line that said after November 22, 1963, the world would never be the same.

Cush stopped to ponder what he saw, impressed that the white people who printed newspapers had heard about his father's murder so quickly. He wanted to see a picture of him on the pages inside, the faces of his killers without their masks, the doomed expressions, the slouched figures sitting on metal bunks in the jail behind the courthouse. He asked the vendor if there were pictures of his daddy inside. When the man finally understood what he was talking about, he unfurled the newspaper and showed him the headline above the word SLAIN! PRESIDENT, it said.

President slain? The story was about the killing of the President?

The sense of betrayal was instant. Tears welled up in Cush's eyes, but his mother's white-gloved hand reached down and took his own and tugged him toward the church. Soon he was in the midst of flowers and sad music and a sanctuary filled with black folks dressed in their Sunday best just like him.

Assassination?

The rest of the world might think the day before was about the death of a president and white folks' problems and all the other terrible things going on up north, but Cush knew better. The day before was about his father, Dr Calvin Walker, and what white men did to blacks. He knew because he'd seen it with his own eyes, witnessed first-hand how they went crazy with a hate so hot it burned up the air itself. Maybe the newspaper people didn't understand this, but he did. So did his father. So did God.

Considering what he wanted to do, that would probably be enough.

The organ finally went silent and the preacher took the pulpit to comfort the living and bury the dead, but Cush wanted no part of it. He sat fingering his father's pocket watch, hearing nothing the minister said, staring at endless bunches of hideous blue lilies.

He turned the watch over and read the inscription: *Death is but crossing* . . . There had been more words following them, but they'd been sheared off years before.

Cush read them, thinking about hot cider on cold nights and the stories his father saw flickering in the fireplace flames. He pictured him in the immaculate white coat he wore at the Calvin Walker Clinic for Negroes and smelled the pills that filled the huge brown bottles on the shelves in his office. Then he saw his father hanging upside down on the inverted cross, his face swollen beyond recognition.

He looked at the words on the watch again, *Death is but crossing* . . .

Someone was crying at the pulpit, but Cush Walker was dry-eyed and concentrated, no longer thinking of the past but staring into the future.

November 22, 1963, a day of death and outrage.

When the newspapers said the world would never be the same, they had no idea what that meant.

No idea at all.

THURSDAY, *October 29, 1929*

The young girl hurried across the street in quick, deliberate steps, paying no mind to the oppressive heat of the day. October in New Orleans was like the devil's pied piper, gathering the gullible behind the promise of autumn one day, marching them back to a summer swamp the next. Calendars be damned, the town was baking as if it was mid-July, with street tar as sticky as filé gumbo and steaming bayous hot enough to cook their own crawfish pie. Sweating men in undershirts unloaded trucks in slow motion, and damp-skinned women took afternoon breaks on wrought-iron verandahs, legs set apart and skirts pulled high, fanning themselves with sheet music or church programs, moving the languid air as thick as black bean soup. On a scorching day in New Orleans, time moved at the pace of a tired horse while everyone waited for the hell-yellow sun to burn itself out and give them the softer gift of night. The seedy, dreamy night, when the scorching sun was down and people's appetites were up, giving the French Quarter its fragrant soul.

Maybe for others, but not for Camilla Bea. In her world, sunset meant the end of the day, not the beginning. At fifteen, with strict patrician parents and a family name to uphold, evening time consisted of dinner at the huge Queen Anne table, reading or catching fireflies with her cousins, playing the piano in the recital room for cotton merchants or linen-suited bankers or bishops and Southern politicians. Then it was early to bed, where she'd write an obligatory passage in her diary, endure a loving homily from her black nanny, and turn off the lights.

Dreams there would be of distant, candlelit places as she tenderly explored her own body, but the real thing? The flesh-and-blood goods of life? Not at her age, not in this house. That she would have to continue discovering secretly, in the afternoon heat, while the rest of New Orleans endured and waited.

Camilla Bea passed by the chemist on the corner of DeMuth and Lessay and turned into the recessed doorway beyond a black iron gate. The heavy wooden door to the building closed behind her, leaving her standing before a long stairwell, looking up at a cut-glass window with a leaded crucifix in the center. She closed her eyes and filled her lungs with scents of clove and citrus. It was always the same when these doors went closed, this moment of transformation.

She climbed the steps one at a time, smoothly, like a spotted fawn. Reaching the top, she stood on tiptoe to see through a peephole in the door, then knocked gently.

The door opened and a man in his early thirties, the finest piano teacher in the French Quarter, stood with his arms outstretched, smiling. He wore an open-necked shirt with billowing sleeves, the foamy surf of fine white Egyptian cotton splashing over velvet, copper skin. With his light features and an aristocratic bearing, his friends assumed he was a distant offspring of the nineteenth-century *gens de couleur libre*, New Orleans's 'people of free color' who, depending upon the genes they'd inherited and the lies they told, passed for either black or white. In the two years she'd known him, Camilla thought of him as a golden god.

'Hello, Camilla,' he said in a resonant voice, unexpectedly deep for his slender build. He closed the door and led her by the hand to the practice room, a small, high-ceilinged library dominated by a polished Steinway mirroring the afternoon light. After seating her on a tufted leather couch, he walked to the kitchen and returned with two tall glasses of freshly brewed ginger tea, each garnished with mint and rimmed with brown sugar.

'You look wonderful,' he said. His long, elegant fingers rose to her face and laid back a wisp of her honey-blonde hair. He brushed her pink cheeks lightly with the back of his hand. 'It's too warm to be running.'

'I didn't want to be late,' she said.

'You're never too late.'

He took her hands in his and inspected them, first the backs, then her palms. Then her eyes. 'Are you ready to play?'

The word 'play' tickled her blood. 'Yes,' she said, this time feeling the blush in her cheeks. 'That's why I came. To play.'

The late afternoon light descended the wrought-iron balustrade and infiltrated the room between the shadows and the blinds. Above the bed, a ceiling fan stirred the flesh-fragrant air, cascading a light breeze onto their naked bodies. Camilla lay on her side with her head on her teacher's chest, eyes closed, hair strewn over his neck and arms as if freshly washed and drying in the sun. He twirled a lock of it in his fingers.

'Camilla?' His tone was soft as petals.

'Mm?'

'I'm afraid it's time to go.'

'Mm.' She summoned the strength to move her lips. 'But I don't want to.'

'Your mother will start wondering, and besides, I have another student coming.'

She waited a moment – he did not push her – then dragged herself to her elbows. Scratching her head, she turned herself into a blonde Medusa. 'But I haven't played the piano.'

'We'll do it next time.'

She bent down and kissed his nipple and laid her chin on his chest. 'I can't go quite yet. I have a present for you.'

He looked amused. 'What kind of a present?'

'Do you know why I was late today?'

'No, why?'

'I stopped to see Miss Emily.'

Now perplexed. 'Miss Emily?' She said nothing. 'On Pinellas Street?'

Yes, her eyes said.

He sat up. 'How do you know Miss Emily?'

She was mildly insulted. 'I have friends in the Quarter, you know.'

'Camilla, stop it. What are you telling me?'

She kissed his smooth, hairless chest, waiting for him to guess. When he didn't speak, she said, 'You're going to be a daddy.'

He laid his head back against a bolster and stared at the ceiling fan. She rested her cheek on his breastbone, once again fanning her hair over his neck. This time, he didn't twirl it in his fingers.

'When?'

'I don't know. Five or six months from now.'

He closed his eyes. Oh, God.

'I kind of knew a few weeks ago,' she said, 'but I was scared to find out for sure. That's why I asked Miss Emily to, you know, examine me.' She balanced her chin on his chest, waiting for his reaction, but he said nothing. 'It's true,' she said, as if perhaps he didn't believe it. She took his hand and opened it and ran her index finger along his lifeline, wondering what lay in his silence. 'I'm a little scared,' she said. She'd known another girl in her situation: sixteen, Catholic, white family. Before her 'problem' became obvious, the girl had disappeared to her grandmother's house in Iowa without even saying goodbye.

He took a deep breath and held it as if under water, then let go, exhaling grandly. 'Well,' he said mostly to himself, 'what's done is done.' His voice struck her as distant now. 'Your family will be – Lord, what *will* they be?'

'Shocked,' she said. 'Daddy would be furious if he knew his little flower is blossoming.'

Sebastian blinked slowly. 'He still calls you his little flower?'

24

'Always,' she said. 'He says I was named after one.'

'Good Lord,' he scoffed. 'That's a *camellia*, not a Camilla.' He stroked her hair lightly. 'Leave it to an uneducated cotton merchant not to know the difference between a flower and a Roman warrior.'

She pulled back and sat on her haunches. 'Camilla was a warrior?'

He reached for a cigarette and a tortoiseshell holder on the round marble table next to the bed. 'According to Roman mythology, she lived with the shepherds who taught her how to hunt. When she grew up, she led maiden warriors into battle against Aeneas.'

There it was again – that sophistication from being an artist and living in Europe and knowing music and wine and food and other marvelous things. He was deep and worldly, not superficial and conventional like her white friends. 'That's *wonderful*,' she said. 'For the first time I absolutely *love* my name.'

'Yes, well, don't tell your father,' he said, working the end of the cigarette into the holder.

'Daddy's not a bad person, Sebastian.'

'Of course he isn't.' He stroked the cigarette between his fingers. 'He's just so fucking bourgeois.'

She waited a second, digesting his comment. 'But he loves his family more than anything in the world,' she said. 'If he knew I was pregnant, it would absolutely kill him.'

'Not to mention me.'

She touched his cheek. 'Your color won't make any difference to him.'

'You really have had a heatstroke, haven't you?'

'It absolutely won't, you know why?'

Sebastian closed his eyes, he couldn't imagine.

'Because he's never going to know you're the father,' she said.

He put the cigarette holder in his mouth. 'Don't be naive, Camilla.'

'He's not, I swear. I'll never tell either of them who it is. Never.' She stared at him intently. He had no rebuttal. 'And I'm not naive, Sebastian,' she added. 'I'm a warrior.'

'That's good,' he said, rising from his pillow. 'Before this is over, you're going to need to be.'

They dressed in silence. When she dallied, he removed the cigarette holder from between his clenched teeth and pointed it at a mahogany clock. 'When are you going to tell them?'

Buttoning her dress, she said, 'I'm going to tell Mother tonight, before I start to show.'

Trying to appear nonchalant, he reached out and placed his hand on the gentle curve of her belly. 'Of course. You have to.' He struck a match, touched it to the end of the cigarette, and drew in smoke. 'What will she say?'

'I don't know.' She stopped buttoning and reached for his cigarette, looking for a drag to dizzy herself. He held it back; the smell on her breath would give her away. She frowned. 'She'll be furious,' she said. She considered his face. 'You aren't angry with me, are you?'

He looked a little miffed. 'Why would I be angry?'

'I don't know. You seem kind of strange.'

'I'm just surprised.'

'Me, too.' She slumped under the weight of it. 'What are we doing to do?'

'I have to think about it.'

'I know!' Her eyes brightened. 'Let's run away to Paris!'

'Paris?'

'Of course! It's your home and I've never been.' She looked up at him. 'What's it like?'

He raised his eyebrows. 'It's the most beautiful city in the world – graceful, green in the summer, full of life and poetry and music. Except for the goddamned Eiffel Tower, it's perfect.'

'What's wrong with the Eiffel Tower?'

'Oh, it's hideous – an iron monstrosity with no art or soul.'

'Then we won't look at it.' She closed her eyes. 'We'll erase it from the sky!'

He smiled at her and brushed her cheek. 'Do you know how wonderful you are? So full of possibilities.'

She placed his hand on her belly again. 'So full of you.' She threw her arms around his neck. Their kiss was warm. He opened the bedroom door and extended a hand.

She said, 'I'll come back tomorrow morning and tell you what happened, and we'll make plans.' She looked up at him. 'If it's a boy, I want to name him after you.'

He lifted her hand and kissed her palm tenderly. 'Come early, little lamb. We have many things to talk about.'

She smiled. 'And then you can tell me what that word means.'

'What word?'

'Boohj-wah.'

Camilla Bea entered the grand foyer of her antebellum house, and like a kid sniffing boiled spinach, knew immediately that trouble was afoot. There was a quiet hush of crisis, the heavy air of dread. She stood waiting. Who could have told them?

Her nanny entered the room with her finger at her lips and quietly pulled the drawing-room door closed.

'What is it?' Camilla asked nervously.

'I don't know, Miss C, 'cept they's saying the stocks crashed and it's bad, real bad.' She underlined the point with a scowl that said, you best mind me on this one, chile.

Camilla started up the winding staircase to her room, then stopped. 'Tell Mother – better tell Mother I need to see her.'

Nanny looked worried. 'Now don't you be makin' trouble for your mother today, you hear?' She wiped her hands on her small white apron. 'Not today, honey, hmm-mm.'

$\star$ $\star$ $\star$

Camilla's mother sat on the chintz-covered chaise in her daughter's room, her back straight, her eyes fierce and level. Camilla was on the edge of her bed with a white cotton coverlet pulled over her lap, as if for protection. She picked at the lace fringe, eyes on her fingers.

'Who's the father?' her mother asked.

Camilla said nothing. Her mother waited. Finally, Camilla said, 'I'd rather not say.'

'You – what did you say?' She was incredulous.

'It doesn't matter who it is. I'd rather not tell you.'

Her mother's cheeks reddened. 'If you think for one *second* that you can sit there and . . .' Her voice trailed off and her hand rose to her mouth. 'Oh, my God. You had a piano lesson today.'

Camilla looked up, slightly stricken. 'So what if I did?'

Her mother touched her forehead. 'Good Lord, how could I have missed it?'

Camilla watched her set her lips grimly, as if words were not permitted to pass, her eyes blue with frost. She knew. Her mother *knew*. The silence stretched so long Camilla lost track of time. What was she thinking?

A knock on the door and the nanny's face appeared through a crack. 'Mister say he need you in the drawing room right away, ma'am. He's fixin' to leave for New York.'

Her mother stood up. 'I'll deal with this when I come back.' She opened the door. 'If you see your father, say nothing about this, do you understand? I'll tell him when the time is right.'

Camilla faced her. 'It doesn't matter when the time is *right*, Mother, and there is nothing to *deal with*. I love Sebastian and he loves me. I'm sure he'll want to marry me.'

Her mother walked over to her and examined her as if she'd never seen her before. The girl stared back defiantly.

Her mother said, 'You disgrace your family with this vulgarity, and now you have the gall to stand there and pretend you're going to disgrace us with a *marriage*? Have you forgotten who you are? Do you think I don't know who *he* is?'

'Who is he, Mother?' she hissed. 'Go ahead and say it! Who is he?'

Her mother clenched her teeth and slapped her daughter hard across the face.

Camilla's hand rose to her cheek in disbelief. In one instant, everything familiar disappeared – love, hate, time. Watching her mother return to the door, Camilla leaned forward and wailed her fury. 'I don't care what you think, Mother! He's beautiful and he loves me!'

She heard the door lock click from the outside, making her a prisoner.

'I hope my baby is black as coal!' she screamed. 'You're not going to stop me! *I love him!*'

WEDNESDAY, *July 13, 1977*

The sandy-haired boy stood at the front window of the fast-moving subway car pretending to be an astronaut in Stanley Kubrick's *2001*. He loved every minute of that movie – the apes, the space walks, the computer named HAL – but most of all he loved the scene when the spaceship reached a distant planet and had to fly through layers of onrushing color and lights. No matter how many times he saw it, it still took his breath away, dazzling him with the sensation of speed and flight. That's what the subway tunnel reminded him of with its cross ties fluttering beneath his feet, its green and white lights whizzing past his ears, the shiny tracks slipping beneath his spaceship like a pair of endless, silver arrows. It was the perfect start, a great beginning.

Staring through the window, Nat Hennessy paid no attention to his reflection in the glass. At eleven, he was still more dead-end kid than adolescent, taken with the world of adventure instead of mirrors and pimples and the first broodings of adolescence. He loved summertime nights like this, walking down the street toward the subway entrance with his father, breathing in thick, humid air that smelled of river scum, warm cement, and the sweet stink of overcooked sausages, then speeding along toward Yankee Stadium.

He turned from the window and looked back at his father sitting with his coat off and his tie loosened, staring across the car blank-faced and preoccupied. Nat knew what was on his mind: he was yearning for his wife, Nat's mom, cursing the cancer that had taken her. But having choked it down for so long, Nat was ready for a break from it, a moment of rebirth, a taste of normal life doing normal things with his dad. Tonight, he sensed, was the official start of their future life together.

They had made this trip to the Bronx before. In past summers, he and his father, sometimes with his Uncle Jim, had trekked off to see the Yankees play on Bat Day, when kids were given a free baseball bat for the price of admission. This year they'd missed the game when his father had been forced to tend to a crisis at the office, but Nat's Irish luck hadn't run out: to make up for it, his father had arranged with a friend in the Yankees' front office to give them a private tour of the stadium while the team was on the road. Tonight Nat would see things other kids could only dream of: the club's locker room, Reggie Jackson's at-home uniform, the dugout where Babe Ruth, Mickey Mantle and Joe DiMaggio had once sat, the mound where Don Larson pitched his perfect 1956 World Series game. Died and gone to heaven is what Nat had done. He could feel the angels in the air.

At 116th Street, in the middle of Harlem, the train took on three boys about Nat's age, and soon each took a turn dancing in the aisle while the other two set the beat with clapping hands. Because it wasn't a game night, Nat and his father were the only white people on the car, but Nat didn't care. He liked the way these kids moved, admired their audacity and street-smart style. When one of the boys came to the front of the car with an up-turned cap, Nat's father dug into his pocket for change, after which the boy thanked him and returned to his seat.

That made Nat proud. He left the front window and sat next to his dad. A lean man of forty-five, his father smiled and tousled his son's hair, then wrapped his arm around him and pulled him tightly to his side. Slightly embarrassed but loving the hug, Nat sat with his cheek against his father's shoulder, smelling his warm suit and the aroma of spent cigars, the faint blend of musk cologne and evening perspiration. He loved these tangs of his father's strength and prowess, these scents of King Arthur and leather shields and men storming a musty cell to free the Queen. That's who his father was to him now: a modern knight, lonely, but loving and strong. With no brothers or sisters and his mother dead, Nat needed him like oxygen.

The train sped beneath Harlem toward the South Bronx, traveling north through the crusty bowels of the city. When it pulled into the 125th Street station to exchange passengers, Nat stood up and returned to his place at the front window.

Only three more stops to go.

The train left 138th Street and was speeding along nicely when all the lights in view – track signals, bulbs on the walls, the interior lighting in the car – flickered in a unified, cosmic blink – and died.

The train's brakes jolted, bringing the cars to a shuddering halt. All sound disappeared: the motor, the air fans, the passengers and squealing of steel on steel.

Voices behind Nat rose in curiosity – 'What's happenin'?' Nat felt stuffiness and uncertainty closing in around him. Suddenly, what had been a magic capsule was now the inside of a pitch-black closet with the doorknob missing.

Nat raised his hands in front of him like a sleepwalker but couldn't see them. 'Dad?' He began inching forward when the battery-powered fluorescent lights blinked on, spreading a funereal glow through the car. He reached his father and pressed himself against his knee. 'What's wrong?'

'I don't know. Sit tight and we'll see.'

Fifteen minutes later, the conductor entered the car waving the beam of a flashlight and walked to the sliding doors. After lifting a seat, he reached down and pulled a large handle and opened the doors manually. 'Listen up, everybody. The power's gone out and we're going to have to walk the tracks to the next station. Stay in line behind me. I don't want nobody near the third rail, the power could come back on at any minute.'

People grumbled and stirred. Three older boys, excited by the chaos, jumped down and ran ahead, heedless of the motorman's warnings. Older people shuffled forward, held on to the sides of the door, and with the help of the conductor's hand, stepped cautiously onto the filthy, wet ground.

As Nat's father started out the door, the conductor, a black man, stopped him with a hand on his biceps.

'You know where the Forty-fourth Precinct is?' he said quietly.

'Is that the one on the other side of the stadium?'

'That's it. When you get to the street, go straight for it.' He looked at Nat's father squarely. 'You're in the middle of the South Bronx, you understand what I'm saying?'

Nat's father nodded and stepped down, with Nat following.

Once on the ground, Nat got a firm grip on his father's hand and waited for the conductor to lead the way. A few minutes later they were stepping over ties and around puddles, plodding behind the conductor's beam of light toward the station a half mile away.

'What did he mean back there?' Nat asked softly.

'He was just being a friend, that's all.' His father's voice was seamless and comforting, showing no trace of concern. Nat never saw his father worry about things.

By the time they reached the 149th Street station, the fun had already begun.

They climbed the steps and came onto the street to the sounds of broken glass and distant sirens and the whooping of boys in fishtailing cars. Nat and his father stepped into the middle of the Grand Concourse and looked down 149th Street toward Manhattan. The city they knew had disappeared into the asphalt as if it had been stepped on by an enormous shoe.

Whole skyscrapers, flattened. Queens and LaGuardia Airport, gone. Billboards on the Major Deegan, missing. Traffic lights, time-and-temperature boards, street lamps – the ordinary veneer of civilization – all disappeared. Suddenly everything was altered, not just what was visual, but the night itself, as if when the lights had gone out, so had the rules. In a matter of minutes, the town had become a roadside saloon reeking of spilled beer, bad music, fuck-you eyes, and tattooed muscle itching to be tested.

Nat flared his nostrils like a jungle cat at an unfamiliar watering hole. No longer did he appreciate the scents of the city – these odors of sulfur flares and burning rubber and men sweating danger. No longer did he find the street romantic.

'What happened?' he asked his father.

'It's a blackout,' he said. 'All the electricity's gone.'

Nat heard steel wheels on cement and turned to see a flashlight beam coming at him, a surfer on a skateboard rocketing down the sidewalk. Just as Nat stepped back, the boy reached out and lifted Nat's baseball cap off his head, then sailed on, hooting and waving it like a scalp.

Nat touched his head to make sure the hat was really gone. His father touched his shoulder. 'You all right?'

Nat stood with his lips parted, then nodded yes.

'Come on,' his father said, taking Nat by the hand. 'The police station's only a few blocks away.'

They walked up the Grand Concourse at a fast clip, past the post office and Cardinal Hayes High School. When they reached 153rd Street they stopped in the middle of the intersection to get their bearings. Ahead was a siren-burping ambulance caught in a parade of slow-moving automobiles . . . headlights illuminating a geyser from a hydrant, people dancing in the spray . . . bottles streaking down from atop tenement buildings before splattering on the street. It was the way to the station house, but it was also a gauntlet.

They looked to the left down 153rd Street. At the bottom of

the hill cars were moving along the Major Deegan Expressway.
'Let's go to the highway and catch a lift,' his father said.

'You think somebody will take us home?' Nat asked.

They hadn't walked more than ten yards when they saw a
flash of T-shirts and people running, then heard a full-throated,
unmuffled automobile engine revving up – then tires screeching,
metal cranking, and the loud crash of a tin roll-down cover being
ripped off a store window. People ran toward it, and within
seconds the street was filled with splintering plate glass, more
yelling, and the car dragging the gate away.

Nat's father stopped and turned in a circle. They were
trapped.

'This way,' his father said confidently. They stepped onto the
sidewalk and started back up the Grand Concourse, but it was
now a hallway of flying bottles and fire hydrant geysers. They'd
walked half a block when the outlines of a hill loomed on their
left behind a waist-high stone wall. A few more steps and they
came to a concrete park bench with its wooden slats ripped off,
and next to it, a sidewalk entrance angling past a sign that read
Franz Siegel Park.

They stopped. Nat watched his father consider the risk of an
unlit park. What *was* the risk of an unlit park? Nat had no clue,
but it didn't matter. He had his father.

They heard the whoop of a police siren down by the looted
store, then a police bullhorn – 'Clear the street or you'll be
locked up!' And the answer – 'Fuck you, pig!' A floodlight
from the cruiser burst onto the looters, scattering them like
roaches.

They heard what sounded like firecrackers.

'Are those firecrackers?' Nat asked. He could hear his own
breathing now.

A car careened around the corner and headed directly for
them. Something came flying out a window – a glint in the
air – the sound of an open beer bottle cooing like an owl.

Glass smashed on the sidewalk, spraying shards against Nat's legs and chest.

His father pulled him up the ramp-like sidewalk into the pitch-black park.

When they reached the top of the hill they looked down toward the street below and saw the glow of a bonfire, then caught the smell of burning garbage. Descending the path, they heard voices up ahead. Men's voices. Nat's father stopped and listened. 'Be quiet,' he said. The two of them continued moving toward the sound. In the distance, where the path met the street, they could see a group of men gathered in a circle lit by a fire in a wire trash basket, sitting on boxes or standing, their eyes focused on something in the center of a ring they formed as if they were shooting craps or watching a fight. Whatever it was, Nat knew his father didn't like it.

'We have to go back,' he said. He took Nat by the hand and turned around.

A flashlight beam hit them between the eyes. Nat's father blocked it with a raised hand.

The beam dropped to the sidewalk, revealing two men standing behind it.

'What you lookin' at?' a large man in an undershirt said.

Nat's father waited a moment, then said, 'Maybe you fellows could give us directions. We're looking for the stadium.'

Both men laughed. 'Ain't no Yankees game tonight,' the one with a stick and a bottle of whiskey said. 'Game tonight be on the *street*.'

Nat's father pulled his suit jacket off his shoulder, flipped it over his forearm, and tugged at Nat to follow him past the men.

'Wait a minute,' the man with the bottle said, stepping in front of them. 'You jus' got here.'

Nat's father stood quietly, looking at him.

The drunk turned to his friend. 'Jus' like white folks, always be *rushin'* around.' He tapped an imaginary watch on his wrist and extended his lips in mock seriousness. 'Got me a meetin' to go to,' he said like the Kingfish. 'Got to go down to the *bank* an' *with-draw* a million 'fore it *close*.' He bent forward at the waist and took a drink of whiskey.

'Maybe he want to tell the po-lice what he seen down there,' the man in the undershirt said.

Nat's father looked toward the bonfire and back. 'Sorry, guys, but we weren't close enough to see anything.'

The drunk stepped closer and placed the stick he held against Nat's father's suit coat, touching it lightly. 'Hmm,' he said, inspecting the garment through a pair of imaginary bifocals. 'Maybe he want to go 'cause he don't like our *company*.' He took another swig of whiskey.

'I've got no problem with you fellas,' Nat's father said.

The large man in the undershirt said, 'You lookin' for Yankee Stadium, you got to go this way.' He pushed Nat's father on his chest, toward the bonfire.

Nat had never seen anyone do that to his dad before, and the sight of it momentarily jolted him. Nat felt his father's hand form a fist by his side, then relax. They turned, as instructed, and continued down the path, leaving their two friends on the path.

As Nat and his dad approached the bonfire again, the walkway widened, and through the leaves Nat could see candles and flashlights in tenement windows on the other side of the blacked-out street.

Walking a step ahead, his father stopped abruptly and placed a hand on Nat's chest to keep him from going farther.

That's when Nat heard the voice.

At first it was no different from other voices yelling and whooping it up on the street, except that this one was higher pitched – the voice of a woman. A voice that was not celebrating so much as yelping. Or pleading. Or crying.

Now, shrieking.

Nat's father turned around, still blocking Nat's view of the bonfire.

'Who's that yelling?'

His father didn't answer. 'We have to go back,' he said, once again taking Nat by the hand.

'But those guys won't let us,' Nat said, hoping he was wrong.

He wasn't. His father didn't move. Nat thought his dad's large, engulfing hand was unusually moist now, not entirely from the hot night air.

They heard another sickening moan.

His father turned around and looked down the path toward the voice. Nat stepped around him and looked too.

On the sidewalk below, three dark-skinned men stood to the side of a burning trash can, its dirty, sparky smoke casting an orange light onto the sidewalk in place of the unlit street lamps. Between the men Nat could see a young, brown-skinned girl on her hands and knees facing the trash can, her body lit enough to show her dress pulled up over her waist. A muscular man with a towel over his bare shoulder and a pair of flowery, baggy beach pants around his calves kneeled behind her, pulling on her long, shiny black hair as if it was a bridle, yanking it as he moved his hips back and forth against her backside. The girl was crying, her head pulled back, her cheeks glistening with tears.

A shirtless, skinny man sporting a mustache, torn jeans, and heavy work boots took a drink from a can wrapped in a brown bag. Then, holding it off to the side, he bent down and said something into the girl's ear while the man behind her continued his motion. Nat had never seen anyone having sex before and it took him a moment to get it. He swallowed involuntarily. The scene terrorized and mesmerized him at the same time.

A fat man wearing a cut-off tank top unbuckled his pants, dropped them around his ankles, and stepped out of them. How weird. How embarrassing. He wasn't wearing underpants.

The muscular man with the baggy pants around his calves let go of the girl's hair, allowing her forehead to drop to the ground. As he backed away from her, the man with the mustache and brown bag put his hand on the girl's neck to keep her from crawling away.

The muscular man behind her stood up, pulled up his baggy pants, and leaned down and picked up a baseball bat from the sidewalk.

The fat man in the tank top stepped behind the girl, went to his knees, and took the muscular man's place. Looking down, he groped at his midsection a moment, then grabbed the girl's flanks and began moving against her the way the first man had.

Nat felt his heart straining against his chest.

While the fat one undulated against the girl, the muscular man in the baggy pants kneeled next to her, resting the baseball bat against his leg, and gathered her hair into a pony tail like a stalk of celery. The other men said something, then laughed and slapped their thighs.

The girl cried in big sobs.

Up on the path, Nat's father stooped in front of his son.

'Now listen to me,' he said. 'If something happens and we get separated, I want you to run down that street and turn toward the highway at the first corner.'

'Why are we going to get separated?' Nat's voice verged on panic.

'We're not, but if something happens, that's what I want you to do, OK?'

Nat felt his throat muscles tighten.

'Do you *understand*?' His father's voice was almost scolding.

'Yes,' he said. 'But Dad—'

His father raised his hand to quiet him, then handed Nat his suit coat. 'Remember what I told you,' he said, reaching for his son's hair. Instead of tousling it this time, he smoothed it down gently, finger-combing it the way Nat's mother used to do when she tucked him into bed. His father used to watch her do that, but he'd never done it himself.

'Wait here,' his father said, then turned and walked down the path toward the group of men. By the time he arrived, the three had become four, then five.

Nat stood still, watching without understanding, shivering in the heat. He saw his father step into the middle of the men and stand next to the girl. She craned her neck upward to see who he was, then grabbed his leg and held on. He didn't bend down to help her, but kept his eyes on the muscular man with the baggy pants who was still holding her hair in a bunch.

Seeing Nat's father, he seemed surprised at first, then angry. He reached down with his free hand, lifted the baseball bat, and pointed it at the intruder.

Nat laid his father's coat on the ground and watched. His father was talking to them, but Nat couldn't hear what he was saying.

The skinny man with the mustache, work boots, and brown bag put his nose in Nat's father's face. 'Hey, brother,' he said, 'who you be, telling us who we can fuck?'

'You in the *wrong* neighborhood be talkin' that shit, Jack,' another man said.

Nat's father glared at the man with the brown bag, then bent down and put his hands under the girl's arms to help her to her feet.

The muscular man in the baggy pants squeezed the bat handle as if he was at home plate and Nat's father was the pitcher. Then, without warning, he swung the bat in a small circle, smashing it onto Nat's father's arm. The blow weakened his knees and closed his eyes in a grimace. He bent over, holding his bashed arm with his good hand.

Up on the path, Nat's heart stopped. *Hey – you hit my dad!*

'You want the girl, motherfucker?' Baggy Pants said. He pulled her ponytail hard, raising her to her knees, holding up her head like a rabbit by its ears.

The other men moved in closer.

Nat took a step down the path toward his father.

The girl looked up at Nat's father with pleading eyes.

'Come on, honky,' Baggy Pants said. 'You want the bitch, come and get her.'

The fat man in the tank top pushed Nat's father in the center of his back, making him stumble toward the girl. He raised the palm of his undamaged hand, trying to calm them. 'Take it easy,' he said. 'I'm not looking for trouble.'

'You sure's hell found it,' a man said.

'Just let her go and we'll get out of here,' Nat's father said.

The man with the baggy pants and the bat cocked his head to the side, all attitude. 'I told you, come and get her.'

Nat's father was breathing hard now, nursing his damaged arm against his stomach as if it was in a sling.

The fat man pushed him from behind again. 'You heard him, go 'head.'

Nat's father waited.

Baggy Pants gripped the girl's hair in one hand and held the baseball bat in the other, tapping it against the sidewalk. 'How many times I got to tell you?' he said.

Nat's father wiped the sweat out of his eyes with his forearm. No one moved. He took a step toward the girl, keeping his eyes on the bat. Baggy Pants's fingers worked the handle like a string of worry beads.

Nat's father bent down slowly to help her up again.

The man lifted the baseball bat and swung it, this time bringing it down onto Nat's father's shoulder so hard that his legs buckled and his body crumpled onto his hands and knees.

The girl turned back to see the hitter raising the bat for another blow.

'No!' she screamed.

Baggy Pants stuck his foot onto her chest and pushed her backwards.

Nat found himself running toward the men, crying and yelling in someone else's voice.

The fat man who'd pushed Nat's father now kicked him in the side, making a whomping sound with his foot.

Good idea, the man with the brown bag nodded. Standing in front of the downed man, he did a small hop and kicked him in the face with his steel-shanked work boot. Nat's father's nose snapped to the side and his mouth split into four lips. Blood spewed in all directions.

Running down the sidewalk, screaming, Nat rammed his head into the stomach of the kicker, stunning him without knocking him down. Carried beyond him by his own momentum, Nat hit the ground and skidded across the sidewalk, splitting his chin with a pebble-filled gash.

Rising to her knees, the girl beat Baggy Pants with her fists, yelling incomprehensible words from a contorted, furious face.

Nat got up from the sidewalk, blood dripping from his chin, and ran back to his father who was on his hands and knees spitting pieces of broken teeth and red goo to the ground.

He pulled at his father's neck to help him rise. 'Get up, Dad!'

His father coughed. In a gurgling voice, he said, 'Highway.'

The man placed the end of the bat on the woman's collarbone and rammed it forward, sending her sprawling onto her back. Then he raised the bat in both hands like an ax.

Nat saw the bat poised in the air, but had no idea why.

The man brought it down in an enormous blow onto the back of Nat's father's neck. His body flattened onto the ground, extending his arms out to his sides as if he was trying to embrace the whole of mother earth.

Nat's eyes paralyzed him.

The man in the baggy pants raised the bat and swung it again, this time landing the sweet spot on the back of Nat's father's head. The blow crushed his skull and sent chunks of hair and bone into the air, some of it against Nat's face.

He didn't blink.

His father didn't move.

'Ou-*wee*,' the brown bag man said of the sight. 'That peckerwood be *daid*.'

Nat sat in a catatonic gaze, one hand suspended in space.

That can't be. That didn't happen. That *can't be*.

Stepping up to the body, muscles rippling, Baggy Pants poked at his victim's gaping skull with the end of his bat like a golfer playing with a divot. As the other men stared at the carnage, the half-naked girl scooped a wallet off the ground near Baggy Pants's feet and crept backwards into the darkness.

'What about the kid?' the man with the brown bag said.

He looked at Nat, then gripped the bloodstained bat in both hands again.

'Hold his head out,' he said to the fat man in the tank top. 'Don't get too close, this could be messy.'

Nat stayed at his father's side, eyes dry and unblinking, reaching out slowly to gather up the pieces of his father's head that lay scattered on the sidewalk.

Back together . . . got to put him back together . . .

The fat man in the tank top placed his hands under Nat's arms and lifted him to his feet and placed his hand behind his neck and bowed his head forward onto an invisible chopping block—

BAM . . . *zing!* They heard the sound of metal bouncing off concrete.

The fat man looked up. 'Huh?'

BAM . . . 'Ouch!' The fat man grimaced and let go of Nat and grabbed his shin and danced on one foot. 'Fuck – I been shot!'

The men looked up and stared into the anonymity of a blacked-out tenement and a vigilante who was shooting at them.

The girl didn't care. She ran up behind Nat like a cat, grabbed him by the hand, and pulled him into the middle of the street, trying to make him run.

BAM, *zing!* More bouncing lead, more men crouching and ducking. Suddenly, the air was full of a new menace, the ink hiding someone else.

BAM, *thwock*. A bullet splintered a piece of the bat in Baggy Pants's hands and ricocheted into his right jaw, tearing off a piece of flesh and bone. He dropped the bat and grabbed his face, grimacing. Blood oozed between his fingers and ran down his hand and wrist. He pulled his palm away and looked at it. 'Shit.' His eyes were raving.

BAM, *zing!*

The men scattered.

A few yards away, Nat saw the jagged wound on Baggy Pants's jaw, the blood and the volcanic, searching eyes. They found Nat's freckled face. The girl yanked his hand and he stumbled in the direction she pulled him, still dazed and unanchored, propelled by high-twitch muscle, disconnected from reality.

The highway . . . the highway . . .

The girl and Nat were running without direction now, streaking blindly into the stenchy night beyond the reach of them all – soulless maniacs and bat-wielding killers, rescuing snipers and dumbstruck voyeurs – beyond fever and insanity and everyone they saw, trusting nothing but the cover of night and their instincts to survive.

TWO

'It's powerful,' he said.
'What?'
'That one drop of Negro blood – because just one drop makes a man coloured. One drop – you are a Negro!'

—Langston Hughes

She's descended from a long line her mother listened to.

—Gypsy Rose Lee

The Present

A half dozen men stood in hardhats, heads tilted back, shading their eyes from the sun. The chief engineer focused his binoculars to get a better view of the gash on Miss Liberty's face. With the noise of a construction company helicopter hovering overhead and the roar of a truck's diesel engine nearby, it was hard to hear.

'How's it look?' he yelled into his headset microphone at someone in the helicopter.

'Like a mess,' a voice cracked over the din of the Sikorsky's engine. 'There's paint on the skin where the fuselage hit, mostly red, a little white and blue, and it looks like some kind of liquid's been sprayed across her neck and bust.'

'Can you see what color it is?' High-octane fuel, oil, hydraulic fluid, there were several possibilities.

'I got the telephoto lens on it, but I can't tell,' the voice from the 'copter said. 'If we move in a little closer—'

'For Christ's sake, don't get any closer!' the engineer yelled. Crazy damn pilots, always pushing the envelope. Didn't he know that's how the other one went down this morning? Two men killed over a lousy advertising agency picture?

The diesel engine on the truck's winch revved up with a loud blat, lifting the carcass of the morning's wrecked chopper off the plaza floor.

'Finish up with the long lens and get the hell out of there!' the chief engineer said to the inspector in the chopper. He lowered his binoculars and found a young assistant standing nearby reading architectural drawings as if they were the Sunday *Times*. 'We're going to need a climber to do the close-ups!' he yelled at the kid. 'Get on the horn and call Camilla!'

It was either late that night or early the next morning, depending on whether you were a day or night person. The last few detectives were departing Delolio's at 39th and Broadway, a garment-center bistro where guys from Midtown South drank, swapped stories, and sometimes got together on special occasions. Tonight's was a bachelor party for Nat Hennessy, a thirty-something detective third grade who was three days away from marrying the love of his life, thirty-three-year-old Camilla Bissonette. The party was a dying duck now – glasses stuffed with napkins on Formica tables, cigarette butts clogging tin ashtrays, Sinatra crooning, a handful of cops in a huddle talking shop, their backs turned to girls sitting at tables, bored and sleepy.

The party would last awhile longer for the hard core, but Nat was ready to go home. Camilla had to get up early to inspect the Statue of Liberty, damaged that morning when a helicopter had drifted into her head. Newspapers and television reports had been showing the crashed helicopter and the statue's mangled face all day.

'So long, old buddy,' a young detective said, extending his hand.

'You make it sound like I'm about to die,' Nat said.

'You're already dead, you just don't know it. But don't worry, it'll kick in somewheres around your first anniversary.'

Nat nodded wearily and turned to find Amerigo, the squad commander and his boss, to say goodnight. He found him standing in a huddle with four detectives working the night watch, the guys who covered major crimes from midnight to six. Midtown South covered one hundred and twelve square blocks, and although it had only seventeen thousand permanent residents, there were two and a half million commuters and tourists who passed through it twice a day going to or from Grand Central Terminal, Penn Station, Madison Square Garden, the Port Authority, Times Square, the garment center, the theater district, and some of the tallest buildings in the city. It was not only the largest but the busiest precinct in New York.

'I'm out of here, guys,' Nat said, turning his rum and Coke glass bottom up.

A beeper sounded and the men reached for their belts like cowboys in a shootout. Lieutenant Amerigo read the message on his pager and left to find a telephone.

Nat thought, that could be trouble, better get moving. After shaking hands with the guys and taking the last of their tribal ribbing, he backed away, making his escape.

Joe Amerigo cut him off at the door. 'Get your coat,' he said.

'I don't have one, and I'm not working night watch.'

'Doesn't matter, you're first up in the morning.' Amerigo knew everybody's assignments at all times, day or night. 'Besides, if this is what I think it is, you're going to want to catch this one.'

Nat and Lieutenant Amerigo walked across Bryant Park toward Grand Central Terminal, four blocks east. The night air was cool now, the sidewalk benches deserted and lonely, no longer warmed by crackheads and junkies as they had been a few years before.

'The fellows who know your bride seem to think she's quite a catch,' the lieutenant said. He was tall and thin and gray-haired with deep lines in a tan face that made him seem somewhat gaunt and older than his fifty-some years. He was wearing civvies tonight, but in his midnight-blue uniform with his shiny-billed cap pulled low and his decorations striping his uniform, he cut an imposing figure. It was one of the reasons he'd been elected to the Superior Officers' Council, a group drawn from the sergeants', lieutenants', and captains' police unions, and why he had been tapped as a leader to fight the City Council over a proposal to test police officers for racial bias. 'I gather she's an artist of some kind?'

'Camilla's an architectural restorer,' Nat said. 'Repairs monuments, historical buildings, bridges, that sort of thing. She's going out to the Statue of Liberty this morning.'

'To do what?'

'Climb around her face and check out the damage to her skin. A few months ago, she was all over George Washington's nose at Mount Rushmore.' Nat himself was Jimmy Stewart in *Vertigo*. He got sweaty palms just thinking about it.

'I guess that's what a combined degree in fine arts and engineering from Columbia will get you,' the lieutenant said.

'Exactly,' Nat said. How did Amerigo know about that?

A block from Grand Central, the lieutenant said, 'How long you been on the force, Nat?'

'Twelve years, five on patrol, seven as detective.'

'You ought to be coming up pretty soon.'

'I'm ready when you are,' Nat said. It was still early to make detective second grade. What did Amerigo want?

They reached the corner of the terminal at Vanderbilt and 42nd Street and stood near a lamppost. Three blue-and-white radio cars were parked at the curb along with a station wagon marked CSU, for Crime Scene Unit. Patrolmen milled around on the sidewalk, talking and waiting for instructions.

'Listen,' Amerigo said, 'I haven't got much time if I'm gonna make the train to New Rochelle, so let me get to the point.'

Finally.

'Couple of weeks ago I overheard some of the guys on the

squad talking about Camilla,' he said. He shook a cigarette out of a soft pack, his last one, and crumpled up the container and tossed it toward a wire wastebasket, bouncing it off the rim. 'Don't get me wrong,' he said, 'they had nothing but good things to say about her.' He lit up and exhaled out the side of his mouth, staring Nat in the eye.

'And?' Nat said.

'The subject of the doctor came up,' he said. 'Dr Cush Walker.'

Nat looked at him without speaking.

The lieutenant said, 'I gather she used to go out with him.'

An invisible hand punched Nat in the stomach. He saw Amerigo searching for a reaction and told himself not to show that he didn't know. 'Yeah,' he said, 'I think it was a while ago.'

'With this BIAS stuff coming at us—'

A good-looking hooker wearing tall boots, a tight, silver-lamé skirt, and a well-filled black halter walked up to Amerigo and interrupted him mid-sentence. Her hair was wild and red and appeared to be her own, not the usual hooker's wig. She hiked up a shoulder bag strap and stroked Nat with a pair of deep brown, you-know-you-want-me eyes.

'Sorry, babycakes,' Nat said, 'not tonight.'

The hooker turned to the lieutenant and looked at him as if to say, tell this guy the time of day, OK? Lieutenant Amerigo said, 'Not now, my dear.'

The hooker looked back at Nat and started to speak.

'We're cops,' Nat interrupted. 'Take a hike.'

She gave him a fuck-you stare and turned and walked proudly toward the side of the building.

'The place is swarming with uniforms, and she comes on to us?' Nat said, knowing she could hear him. 'She trying to act stupid, or can she just not help it?'

Lieutenant Amerigo took another drag on his cigarette. 'I'll deal with her in a minute. Right now I'm interested in what Camilla knows about Dr Walker that could be *useful* to us, if you know what I mean.'

Unfortunately, Nat did. Amerigo was looking for a way to checkmate the great Dr Walker – neurosurgeon, biochemist, talked-about candidate for a Nobel Prize for his work in the field of brain cell reconstruction, and a threat to every white cop on the force. As the head of NeuroPath Laboratories, Walker had designed a brain scan called the Biochemical Index of Antisocial Syndromes – or BIAS – a test that supposedly measured a person's predisposition to prejudice the way a polygraph gauged someone's emotional reaction to telling a lie. According to Walker, it could identify a police officer's potential for blowing up and losing control in situations where race was part of a dangerous conflict. Liberals inside the department and elsewhere loved the idea. The mostly white police unions had another view.

When the press first heard of BIAS two years earlier, it had been treated as a bit of a joke, spawning cute headlines and editorial page cartoons. But then the press discovered that for two years the NYPD Health Services Division had been quietly testing BIAS in a program called Operation Screen Door, and that it had predicted police misconduct with a high degree of accuracy. After the usual political infighting, the City Council was preparing to vote on legislation that would mandate the use of BIAS not only with new recruits, but with veteran officers.

It was the veteran thing that tore it. Suddenly, the politics of race and the criminal justice system had flipped: the American Civil Liberties Union was calling BIAS no better than an illegally mandated lie-detector test, and the mostly white unions were sounding like carbon-copy minority groups protesting college admission exams, IQ tests, and 'artificial barriers' to the workplace.

Amerigo was coming to Detective Hennessy for help. Nat

was young, good-looking, and decorated for bravery under fire, which made him a potentially effective mouthpiece. But more than that, he was going to marry the former girlfriend of the big-name scientist who'd invented this cockamamie test. Someone who might have some 'goods' on him, whatever that might mean.

Nat put his hands in his jacket pockets and stood with his feet apart, a soldier at parade rest. 'Let me understand this,' he said. 'You want me to ask my fiancée to rat out her former boyfriend?' The word 'boyfriend' felt like lead in his stomach.

Lieutenant Amerigo blinked slowly, his way of objecting to Nat's artless characterization. 'Now listen, Nat. If we don't find some way to take this guy down a peg or two, he and the bleeding hearts are going to wreck the careers of guys like you and me.'

Nat heard him but wasn't exactly moved. At Amerigo's urging, he'd taken the BIAS test the week before and wasn't worried about it. 'I don't like tests and never have,' he said, 'but it's not *that* bad, Lieu.'

'Not that bad? Let me put it this way, son. I couldn't pass it, and neither could you.'

He didn't get it. 'What do you mean?'

Amerigo shook his head and raised his eyebrows. 'Scores came in this afternoon. You flunked.'

Flunked? Jesus Christ. He felt like a third-grader who'd just been told he was being held back. He hadn't thought that much about it, but maybe Amerigo was right. If BIAS became law, and they didn't grandfather the senior cops who flunked it, he really would be kicked off the force. He pictured one of the videotape scenarios they'd shown him while he was wired to the machine: a black man grabbing his wife to use her as a shield, then a white man doing the same with his wife. He'd had the same emotional reaction to both situations – hadn't he?

The lieutenant looked at his watch. 'I gotta run. Walker's

meeting the union reps tomorrow to talk about this thing. Why don't you come and take a look?'

'No thanks, Lieu. I'm not into department politics.'

Looking around, Amerigo spotted the redheaded woman and wiggled his finger at her. She pushed her shoulder away from the terminal and walked over to them.

'This is Officer Sally Shaw,' Amerigo said as she joined them. 'She's been working the Public Morals Division for the last two years.'

'They call it Vice now,' she said, looking straight through Nat.

Nat felt his face redden. Knowing she was a cop suddenly put her in a different light: her red hair wasn't quite so wild, her boots not quite so cheap. In a uniform, he imagined she'd cut a pretty serious figure. Pretty and serious. 'You look like you must be good at it.'

'*Was* good at it,' she said.

'She was reassigned to Midtown South this morning,' Amerigo said, backing toward the door to the train station. 'She's going to be your new partner for awhile. Show her the ropes, Nat. She could be good.'

Amerigo nodded at Shaw to join him as he walked, which she did. Nat followed.

'You asked if he's got any quirks you needed to know about,' Amerigo said to Shaw, not realizing that Nat was within earshot. 'Only one I can think of is, when you're shooting the shit about your personal lives, lay off the subject of his father, OK? I'll explain some other time.' Amerigo hustled down the ramp toward the trains, leaving Shaw a couple of steps in front of Nat.

Nat stopped and rubbed his forehead. Fuuuuck, what'd I do, *what'd I do*? It's one in the morning, I catch a case at my own bachelor party, I find out my bride-to-be slept with the enemy – a big-time black doctor with a genius IQ – I'm told I flunked his bullshit race test, and unless I snake some nasty shit about him out of my fiancée, I lose my job. And for a kicker, the Lieu assigns me a police department hooker as my new partner. Thanks a lot, Joe. Next time, save your breath, I'll just bend over and grab my ankles.

'Got a headache, Detective?' Officer Shaw asked as they started walking down the ramp toward the crime scene.

'Not yet. You expecting to give me one?'

Nat walked into the ladies' room a few steps behind his new partner, saying nothing to the *New York 1* television crew that seemed to show up at night-time crime scenes faster than the police. Flashing his shield at a uniformed cop, he entered the doorway and stopped to survey the room and see what the killer had seen only an hour before. The bathroom had been recently remodeled with gray-and-white speckled floors, white tile walls, framed mirrors, and toilet stalls with stainless-steel doors that had already become dented, by what instruments and for what purpose he had no idea. The light cans in the ceiling hummed a monotone tune.

The room was already crawling with official representatives of the criminal justice system: the forensic guys from the Crime Scene Unit – 'Hey, Nat, I hear we busted up your bachelor party' – lifting prints, bagging hair, combing the floor for the breadcrumbs they hoped would lead them out of the forest. A photographer had shot the area once, and a uniformed sergeant – 'Who'd we get off your face, a blonde or a brunette?' – stood nearby with a female duty captain, a patrol sergeant and his driver, and two Metro-North Railroad detectives who were talking and watching. A uniformed cop waited to begin searching the body. As the detective in charge, Nat would direct the search and tell him what to do, but like all detectives, he'd do his best to avoid custody of the evidence. In a post-Miranda world, whenever you touched something it meant paperwork and time in court.

'What have we got here?' Nat asked Shaw, who'd been here earlier and scoped out the situation.

She pointed at a toilet stall in the middle of the row of doors. 'She's in there.'

Nat walked toward the door with an open hand extended toward one of his forensic pals who laid a pair of latex gloves in it and gave him a personal warning: 'Love lasts a night-time, but marriage lasts forever.' Pretending he hadn't heard, Nat pulled on the gloves and continued walking. 'It's already been dusted,' the man added.

Nat reached the stall and gently pushed open the door.

Lying on the floor on her left side was the form of a woman, late twenties, early thirties, white skin, one hand extended over the toilet bowl, the other tucked under her cheek like a sleeping child. A splay of thick, blonde hair obscured her face except for a pair of lips that were open in a relaxed gasp like the mouth of an asthmatic child. A crumpled miniskirt had been pulled up around her waist and the leather straps on her chase-me-fuck-me pumps were still tightly wound around her ankles. Blood puddled neatly beneath her body, rich and black like the remains of a blown-out oil well. The stall reeked of cheap perfume.

Nat lifted her hand from the toilet to examine her fingers. Even without the passion-pink fingernails, he could see that they were firm and veiny and long enough to palm a basketball. He leaned forward to catch a look at her crotch but couldn't see it. Reaching out, he lifted the synthetic hair off the right side of her face. The eyes, open and shiny, were a girl's, but a telltale sign of the male species – the Adam's apple – gave her away. What was left of it, that is. It had been split into two pieces by a deep, crescent-shaped slice that ran across her neck and disappeared under the hair Nat was holding. He pulled her mane back farther to see where the cut ended. Where the ear should have been was a red hole that looked like a morning glory with half its petals missing.

The lieutenant was right. He wanted this case.

'Angel Rico,' he said.

Shaw leaned forward and looked down at the face. 'Doesn't look like an angel any more. What a mess.'

'Very good,' Nat said. 'First thing a detective should see is the obvious.'

Ignoring him, Shaw said, 'Wait a minute, I know this girl. She's a trannie named Tangerine, not Angel Rico. Works Forty-second Street between here and the Port Authority.'

Nat straightened up. Angel Rico wasn't the name of the victim. Angel Rico was the name of the killer. Was it possible he was already on the street? Let's see: a voluntary manslaughter plea, time off for good behavior, a break from overcrowded prisons and a limp-wristed parole board, done three out of five to fifteen. Yeah, of course he was out.

'Where's her bag?' Nat asked, sticking with the female pronoun. Transvestites and transsexuals might have male anatomies, but when they were in drag and on the street, Nat always referred to them by the gender they preferred. It was frequently the only official respect they got.

'Over here,' Officer Shaw said. They walked across the room toward a diaper-changing table that had been lowered from the wall into a makeshift counter for the technicians.

Nat said, 'I take it you've known Tangerine for a while.'

'Everybody did. Her fifteen minutes of fame came from giving an arresting officer a blow job in the back seat of a radio car while they were taking her downtown,' Shaw said. 'She testified in a narcotics case a couple of years ago to stay out of jail.'

On the table they found the prostitute's large leather bag with its contents already laid out: the usual cosmetics, a bottle of water-soluble lubricant, a phone book, quarters for pay phones, a half dozen lottery tickets, a beeper, and a rolled-up sweater and a pair of stretch pants in case she got arrested and hauled off to the tank. She-males didn't want their asses to be hanging out of a short skirt when they went before a judge, even less when they were thrown into the men's cell for the night, as queens always were. The criminal justice system might have made progress since Charles Dickens's time, but not enough to give perps in drag their own holding cells. According to the system, you peed standing up or sitting down, end of story.

'Was she carrying drugs?' Nat asked.

'A little heroin.'

That was for recreational use, not sale. 'Cash?'

'Two hundred dollars.'

Rico must have done this in a hurry. Ordinarily he left nothing on the table, least of all drugs or money. After all, he would have reasoned, what good were those pleasures to someone he'd just killed? If you had the balls to commit murder, Nat had discovered, you became a kind of Superman, breaking through the walls of the law and leaping over moral buildings. The feeling was homicide's 'high', its dirty little secret. But of course there was also that small fly in the ointment called getting caught. That tended to cool most people's homicidal heat.

Nat lifted the items and replaced them carefully, sniffing the air. 'What kind of perfume was she wearing?'

Shaw shook her head.

A uniformed sergeant approached Nat. 'There's a reporter out here who says he'd like a couple of minutes when you're free.'

'Who's he with?'

'I don't know, the *Times*, I think. He's covering the BIAS hearing and wants to talk to you about the union's views. Says Amerigo told him to ask.'

Nat turned away. 'Tell him not to wait, it's gonna be awhile.' He walked over to a washbasin and pulled off the latex gloves and dropped them into a waste can.

Shaw watched. 'Who's Angel Rico?' she asked.

'A pusher and a pimp who killed someone exactly the same way.'

Shaw looked surprised. 'Doesn't he know an MO is a sig-nature?'

Another obvious discovery, good for her. This time he looked at her eyes instead of her long legs. 'If he thought about it at all, which I doubt, he knows it's tough to convict on an MO alone, especially if you've got an alibi, which I'm sure he does.' Still, it wasn't a bad question. He had once seen a Mafia boss convicted of conspiracy to murder a numbers runner based on nothing more than a woman's testimony that she saw the boss get up from a restaurant table, take a call on a pay phone, and nod to a guy who turned out to be the hit man. Not much, but enough.

But that was then, and this was now, and he knew they'd never nail Angel Rico with nothing more than a repeat style of killing. Nat was used to seeing crime where everyone on the street knew who did it but you couldn't prove it. Still, every now and then it grated on his nerves. Call it the law, call it the rules, the Constitution, the system – he didn't care what you called it, as long as you didn't call it justice.

'Any witnesses?' he asked.

'That old guy standing out there in the hallway says he saw Tangerine walk in here with a man behind her.'

'Can he make him?'

'Brown skin, black hair, medium height, medium build. Can't be more than a million guys like that in New York, right?'

Rookie inexperience he could take, but not rookie humor, not at this hour. He watched Officer Shaw shrink at his deadpan reaction. Christ, he remembered when he was as buff as she was, asking big-eyed questions and giving naive answers. It had felt good, actually. Being fresh and ambitious.

'How old are you?' he asked.

'Twenty-seven,' she said.

God, that *was* depressing. He was only seven years older than she was but it felt like seventy. He leaned toward the bathroom mirror and pulled down a lower eyelid, checking out the red cracks in the white underbelly.

Shaw said, 'Maybe they'll lift a print.'

'Maybe they'll lift a hundred prints, but none of them will be Angel's. Jesus, my eyes are puffy.'

'So how do you know so much about this guy?'

'I put him away three years ago.'

'For the killing?'

Nat nodded.

'Who'd he do?' she asked.

'A runaway teenager from Minnesota named Debbie Duzzit.'

'And he's out in three?'

'Yeah, how about that?'

'What was he, her pimp?'

'No, he did it for her pimp, to pay off a debt.' He patted his eyes with his fingertips. 'You married?'

'No, are you?'

'Two and a half more days. After you're married, does your wife tell you when you look like shit?'

'Mm, my impression is not in the first year, but after that, anything goes.'

'How do you know?'

'Oprah. Listen, would you do me a favor?'

'Nothing's impossible.'

'I'm not overly sensitive, OK? I'd like to be treated as a cop, not a girl.'

Nat let go of his lower lid and turned on the cold water tap. Bending over the sink, he raised handfuls to his face, then straightened up, water dripping down reddened cheeks, and pulled a brown paper towel from the holder.

'It's Shaw, right?'

'Sally Shaw, but everybody calls me Shaw.'

Nat drew the paper towel over his face. 'Being a cop and

having feelings are not mutually exclusive, Shaw. Have you ever worked a homicide case before?'

'No.'

'Then why do you want to start now?' He tossed the crumpled towel into a waste can.

'I want to be a detective,' she said.

He looked at her. She gave him a committed stare. 'Let's see how you feel about that after you've searched the victim,' he said. He walked back toward the toilet stall.

She said, 'How are you gonna find Angel Rico?'

'How would you find him?' he asked.

'His parole officer should know his address, right?'

'Sure, and after you find out it's his mother's apartment and she hasn't seen him for five years, where do you go next?'

She thought about it.

'Let me give you a hint,' Nat said. 'He's from the Dominican Republic.'

She raised her eyebrows. 'Call the embassy?'

He smiled. That was good. Call the embassy. Cute.

'Not the right answer,' she said.

'The answer is if you're a Dominican in New York, chances are you'll be in Morningside Heights or the South Bronx.'

The sergeant came into the room again. 'The guy from the *Times* says he doesn't want to interview you about this particular homicide, he's interested in your opinion about racism as an underlying cause of crime.'

Nat felt his cheeks tingle. What a cliché. He found the duty sergeant across the room. 'Hey, Sarge, my new partner here wants to be a homicide detective – what do you say we let her do the search?'

The sergeant nodded, and Nat stepped back to the stall. He pushed open the door and held it, a gentleman waiting for Shaw to step inside. 'Sure you can handle this?'

'No problem,' she said casually, focused on the body. 'Does it bother you?'

'Not any more,' he said. He pulled up his trousers and tucked the cuffs into the top of his socks to keep his pants legs from touching blood splatters on the metal partitions or the side of the toilet bowl. What bothered him most these days was not the blood, but no longer being bothered by the blood.

A uniformed cop came to the stall and gave Nat and Shaw each two fresh pairs of latex gloves. After putting both pairs on, one on top of the other, Nat told her to begin with the shoes, untie the binding up the legs and remove the high heels and see what was beneath the insoles.

The sergeant came over. 'The *Times* guy says he'll be back in a little while.'

Fine, you come back real soon, and bring along one of your pipe-smoking editors who wants you to write about racism as the underlying cause of crime. Nothing ever changes.

'Don't overlook the inside of the garters,' he told Shaw. She straddled the victim's body and, without hesitating, carefully lifted an elastic band ringing a smooth, shaved thigh. Nat watched, impressed with the way she went for it. 'What were you, a medical examiner's daughter?' he said.

'My father was an undertaker,' she said, returning the victim's leg to the messy floor, then lifting the other one. 'How about—' she caught herself before saying, 'yours?'

'My father?' he said.

She changed the subject. 'Seeing all those funerals must have got me ready for this.'

Nat watched as the body was touched and searched and violated by the hands of the state even before it was lifted out of the pool of its own coagulating blood. Yeah, come on back and take a close look, boys. Put down your notepads and pencils and step inside the real world for a while. Take a look at this thirty-year-old drag queen lying dead on a toilet floor.

Check the size of the gash in her neck and the hole where she used to have an ear, and when you're done with that, I'll run the newsreel in my head back a few days to another touching moment of reality, the girl I found with a nine-millimeter slug in her temple. Feel her neck for a pulse while it's still warm and listen to her mother screaming in the next room.

'Check the bruise on her hip.'

And if you're not impressed with that, fellows, come inside the tenement I worked last month. Learn how to step around the evidence on the kitchen floor – the broken bowl of spaghetti slithered across the linoleum by the arm of a woman fighting for her life, the vomit she added to it while she was being raped, the puddle of urine her husband couldn't hold before his throat was slit. You'll find that it's not a normal thing, people vomiting and urinating on their own kitchen floor. First time you see it you feel kind of confused, like watching a film snap in the middle of a movie and hearing the actors gurgle and seeing sprocket holes jump across the screen. It takes a second to realize what's happening. Even if this dead trannie no longer startles you or breaks your heart the way it should, it's the real thing, not some abstract statistic about racism being the underlying cause of crime.

'Careful with the bra,' he said. He stood calmly directing the search, not so calmly imagining the crime. Or Angel Rico. His first big collar. Angel's brown face – part black, part Hispanic – jump-started the demon in his psyche.

For some reason, he pictured a newspaper photo of Cush Walker.

Take it easy, he told himself. The reporter and his editors are just doing their jobs.

'Check the pads and watch out for needles,' he said.

But it was too late to take it easy, he could already feel the racial heartburn starting up his throat the way it did whenever he saw a crime like this. Or when he read a newspaper story about kids dying in Rwanda. Or saw coverage of the Yankees on opening day. Or was asked a simple question from a well-meaning reporter. He didn't let it affect the way he did his job – he was pretty sure about that – but deep down where there were no public politics to worry about, no need to lie to himself, no need to censor himself, he let it rip.

Nat said, 'Those are needle marks.' Shaw gave him a look that said, no kidding.

Sure, fellas, come on in and play homicide detective for awhile. Get a good whiff of what it's like. Pretend you're standing behind Tangerine's naked ass the way poor, deprived Angel Rico stood here awhile ago. Assume the position he assumed, think the thoughts he thought, go through the movements he went through, then make the kill. And if that doesn't give you some valuable journalistic insight, try playing Angel Rico when he was fucking Debbie Duzzit seven years ago. Do what he bragged to his cellmate he did. Put her on her knees and look her in the eye and listen to her plead for her life before you make her blow you one last time. Cock your finger like it's a gun and lay it on her head and tell her after you shoot your duck butter you're gonna shoot her brains out, and when she starts to cry, give her a laugh, make her feel at ease, tell her you're just kidding – it's just a finger, not a gun – and then turn her around and put your knife to her throat and draw it across her neck so hard you take off an ear while you're at it.

'Take the wig off slowly, it's gonna be pinned on.'

Come on inside, scholars, take any case you want. Play the role of the perp real slow and tell me you get no click, no recognition of humanity, no sense of right and wrong. Tell me the moment you squeeze the trigger or draw the knife or unzip your pants you're not a human being with a choice, you're just a poor, pathetic victim of racism, an innocent, misunderstood child whose criminal life was destined by systematic abuse, institutional neglect, and a half dozen other fifty-cent descriptions of helplessness. Tell me there were so many uplifting books you never read and so many decent meals you never ate and so many white people who didn't love you, how would you know killing someone is wrong? Tell me your mother never taught you about no motherfucking golden rule, you never even picked up a *rumor* that killing is wrong – never saw it on the news, never heard it from a preacher – how could you be expected to know about that?

'Right over there. What is it, a broken fingernail?' She picked it up and dropped it into a glassine bag.

Go ahead, Mr Reporter. Stick your head in the sand and tell me everybody commits crimes – white people, Hispanics, Chinese, Eskimos, Indians – everybody, so why pick on blacks? Put me in your perfectly beat-up '89 Saab and take me someplace and show me what you're talking about. I want to *see* Eskimos shooting crack and having kids when they're twelve years old and wearing green hair and earrings in their noses. I'm a detective; I need evidence, like prosecutors and judges and juries. Drive me around town and show me what you got, and when you can't show me that everybody who commits a crime is a victim first and a criminal second, then go ahead, go back to your office and fuck me with a typewriter.

He felt his RPMs. Oh, man. I need a vacation.

'Bag each ring separately.'

Shaw stooped down low and gently lifted the girl's leg to the side, revealing, at last, the male genitals that had been cinched back and tucked out of sight by a nylon thong.

'Do a cavity search next,' he said, expecting her to flinch. He watched her hand disappear between the victim's legs and saw her do the job without blinking. Maybe Amerigo was right. Maybe she had the right stuff. After finishing, she pulled the top glove off her examination hand, turning it inside out, then felt around the edge of the body and the floor.

'What have we here?' she said. Grimacing, she pulled her hand from Tangerine's back and held up a small bottle of cologne with the bottom broken out. She lifted it toward the open door to catch the light and turned it right side up to read the label. A small amount of liquid that had been trapped in the top spilled onto Nat's pants leg.

'Oh, damn, I'm sorry,' she said, and pulled a line of toilet paper off the roll and brushed at his shin.

'Forget it. What's on the label?'

She held it up to the light. 'Looks like Cheetah,' she said.

'Smells like they bottled the wrong end of the animal.'

'Wait a minute,' she said, turning over the container. 'There's something written on the back. It says . . . "Dolly. 555–6986."'

'Who's that?'

'I don't know,' she said, standing up. She looked perplexed. 'She's not on my beat.'

'You personally acquainted with every hooker in Mid South?' Nat asked.

'Quite a few,' she said.

Nat pulled his pants legs up, popping the cuffs out of his socks, and took a step out of the stall. 'Bag it and let's go home,' he said.

'OK. I'll be with you in a second.' She pulled out a pad and pencil to write down the name Dolly and the telephone number.

Standing outside the stall, Nat brushed off the bottom of his trouser leg and was preparing to leave when he glanced back and saw Sally Shaw still leaning over the victim's body. He watched her pull the transvestite's tiny skirt down over her naked hips, then lift her wig from the toilet's flush handle, hold it up to find the front and the back, and gently place it back on the dead girl's head, tugging and adjusting it until it fit almost as well as it had when she was alive. She touched Tangerine's face gently, closing the eyelids and mouth, then stood up to leave.

She shouldn't have done that before the photographer finished his second shoot – Nat would have to tell her about that later, but not now. Right now he preferred to watch how she treated the victim, the regard she showed. He'd planned to bitch at Amerigo in the morning and ask for a new partner, but now he wasn't so sure.

She straightened up and took a deep breath. It was hot in the room, and her long red hair was beginning to curl. Small beads of perspiration sparkled on her forehead and upper lip. She was top heavy from a large chest and slim hips and long legs made longer by her four-inch heels. No wonder johns liked her on the street. He wouldn't be surprised if they liked her off the street, too.

They walked to the sinks where he checked his watch. It was two in the morning.

Shaw dabbed at her face with a tissue. 'Does it worry you? A guy you put away for a homicide being out in three years?'

'It's not the first time.' He thought about the money and drugs left in Tangerine's bag. 'Hey, Rodney, send me a copy of the ME's autopsy report, would you?'

'Do guys you put away ever threaten you?' Shaw asked. 'You know, like, when I get out, I'm coming after you?'

'Sometimes.' He pictured Angel Rico standing in court speaking to Nat with his eyes, *I'm gonna hurt chu, man, real good*. 'You don't think about it.' He waved goodbye to the sergeant as he exited the room.

'I'll try to find Dolly – is that OK?' she said.

'That's the idea,' he said absent-mindedly, going out the door. Tangerine and Dolly were already fading from his attention. He stopped walking and turned around. 'Hey, Shaw,' he said, catching her eye. She looked back at him, standing tall in her knee-high boots. 'Nice job.'

She gave him a half-lidded, Lauren Bacall smile.

He walked toward the yellow cabs on 42nd Street. Cush Walker and Camilla . . . Cush Walker and Amerigo . . . Cush

Walker and BIAS. He'd never even met Cush Walker, and yet the guy was tromping around inside his head like he owned the joint.

He jumped in a cab, gave the driver his address, and leaned back for a ten-minute nap. Cush Walker and Camilla. Cush Walker the neurosurgeon. Cush Walker the genius.

He wondered: if he took the BIAS exam again, could he pass it?

Not tonight, man. Not a chance.

Piercing eyes and a lascivious tongue greeted Nat as he walked through Camilla's darkened, downstairs studio. He covered the gargoyle's ugly face with his jacket and walked softly toward the kitchen, trying not to wake his bride-to-be in the bedroom at the top of the spiral, wrought-iron staircase. It was nearly two thirty, and the glow of SoHo's night air drifted through the loft's large windowpanes, powdering the room with a soft gray light that allowed him to navigate around the work bench and tools and broken artifacts strewn across the floor.

He passed an old Italian doorframe, a cracked bust of an ancient poet, a chipped fountain, a Greek column. Stepping around a pair of light stands, he followed the smell of brushes and pots of paint and open jars of linseed oil, two-part epoxies, turpentine and thinner – there was always the smell of thinner down here. And white and gold paint. Speckles of it on her fingers, reminding him of the first time he'd touched her earlobe.

They'd first met when Nat joined a sidewalk crowd watching a woman in climbing gear descend the face of a building on East 42nd Street. Feeling a tinge of his own acrophobia, he was amazed that anyone had the nerve to do that, even more so that it turned out to be a good-looking woman. When she reached the ground, he'd used his shield to enter the roped-off area and struck up a conversation with her, ending it with an invitation to join him at a corner coffee shop. When she said, thanks but no thanks, he said, but every climber of city buildings should know a detective, as if she was supposed to follow the logic of that, even though he himself had no idea what it meant. She said, maybe so, but she had a perfect record of not knowing detectives and saw no reason to spoil it. Oh, he said, it's too late for that. Fifteen minutes later they went for coffee.

It was a disaster.

She was an upper-class girl from a wealthy New Orleans family, he was a regular guy who'd grown up in New York City. She had a masters degree in fine arts and engineering from Columbia, he had a bachelor's degree from Fordham. She asked him what he thought of the controversy over BIAS, which had been in the newspapers, and he said it was a load of political manure. She said she thought it was a good idea, long overdue. He said being a good cop was a good idea long overdue, not tests. She said, how would you know unless you took it yourself? He said it wouldn't matter if he had, he'd put no stock in the results. Wow, she'd said, she'd learned three new things in the space of a short half hour: how to meet a detective, why she didn't like northern rednecks, and where to find a cup of bad coffee.

He said he wasn't a redneck and deeply resented being called one. She said maybe she'd spoken too hastily, she was sorry. He said he'd accept her apology only if it was over dinner. She said she'd give him an apology in skywriting if that's what he wanted, but dinner was out of the question. He waited three days and called her anyway. Despite herself, she later said, she'd been thinking about him and his persistence. They made a date.

A few nights later, over salmon and penne, they finally discovered something they had in common: an interest in family histories, his involving his father, hers involving her grandmother. In both cases, there was unfinished business involved, someone from the past who needed to be rediscovered. Of all the mysteries in the world, he said, there was none more compelling than your own. When he was honest with himself, he had to admit that it was probably one of the reasons he'd become a detective, but when she asked him to explain, he changed the subject.

At evening's end, standing at her front door, he wanted to kiss her, but thinking better of it, he reached out and gently pinched her earlobe instead. She looked at him a moment, surprised, then kissed her fingertip and touched it against his lips. That's when he saw the first speckle of gold paint on her hand, giving him an excuse to hold it up and point it out. Funny, they both thought, how the simplest gestures were often the most affecting.

The next night, after dinner, they found a second thing they had in common: kissing. They were good at it, and even though she should have known better, it led to another date.

Weighing a shower against hunger, he opted for the bathroom and picked his way back through the studio to the spiral stairs and climbed them as quietly as he could. When he reached the top, he was surprised to see light slipping through a crack beneath the bedroom door. He knocked once and opened it.

Camilla sat cross-legged in the middle of the bed in a pair of cut-off jeans and a sweatshirt, barefoot. On the floor next to her was a spilling stack of documents, and spread out on the quilt cover were file folders, papers, photographs, and letters. Flattened new cardboard storage boxes leaned against an ottoman, bound by plastic strapping tape, waiting to be opened and assembled. The low-volume television set was showing *Star Wars* with Luke Skywalker, Princess Lea, and Camilla's all-time favorite bad guy, Darth Vader. Paying no attention to it, she was bent over a worn, leather-bound diary with little red flags sticking out of the margins, deeply absorbed in what she read through a pair of horn-rimmed glasses. A pencil rested lightly in her hand, and a notebook with her own fresh jottings was open at her knee.

His eyes caught the frayed denim at the edge of her shortened jeans lying like feathers on her smooth, tan skin. Then he captured all of her. Full of mysterious energy. Unique. He couldn't imagine loving her more.

She lifted her eyes. 'Hi, baby,' she said.

'Hi,' he said. 'I thought you'd be asleep by now.' He crossed the room to the other side of the bed and with a knee on the mattress gave her a warm hug and a long, complicated kiss.

She pinched his earlobe. 'Was it a good party?'

'The usual,' he said, disengaging. He took off his coat.

'I smell cigarette smoke and cheap perfume.'

'It's called Cheetah, from one of my ladies of the night.'

'With your good looks, I expect you to do better than that.'
He took off his shoes. 'I caught a homicide tonight.'

'Who was it?'

'A trannie hooker. What's all this stuff?' he said, unbuckling
his belt.

'Mother's papers and things. They finally came today.' Her
mother had died two months earlier after a long bout with
coronary disease. 'You wouldn't believe it. That whole thing'
– she pointed at a polished, rosewood box – 'was filled with
papers she inherited from my grandmother Camilla Bea.'

'Anything interesting?' he asked, stepping out of his pants.

'I'm just getting into it. There's all kinds of letters and photographs and legal documents. Look.' She held up a photograph of
her grandmother and her family posing for the camera. 'Here she
is,' she pointed, 'and this is her father, my great-grandfather.'

'The one who lost his fortune in the crash.'

'There's a better one of him here.' She pawed through some
papers and found a partly burned black-and-white photograph of
him standing beneath a rain tree in Africa, his hunting rifle on
his arm, a large man next to him with the bizarre name of the
Hammer scribbled beneath. 'But look at this.' She held up the
tattered book she was reading. 'It's my grandmother's diary.'

'What's in it?' he said, unbuttoning his shirt.

'When she was fifteen years old she got into a hot love affair
with her piano teacher, a guy named Sebastian.'

'What was his story?'

'I don't know yet, except get this: she got pregnant by him
with my mother.' She waited. 'My mother was a love child,
babe. Isn't that cool?'

He gathered up his clothes and carried them to a hamper across
the room, then returned to the ottoman, stark naked, and opened
a new cardboard banker's box. Holding the flattened casing in
one hand and the unassembled drawer in the other, he quickly
folded, bent, and slipped the tabs and slots together without

consulting the directions, creating three perfect containers in a matter of seconds. He had no idea why, but he'd always had an uncanny gift for spatial relations. After placing her loose papers neatly into a cardboard drawer, he headed for the bathroom.

'You've got a nice bottom, you know that?' she said. He didn't answer. 'Fifteen years old and my grandmother's going to have a baby.'

'Happens all the time,' he said through the open bathroom door.

'Wait, it gets better.' She lifted the diary and pushed her glasses up the bridge of her nose. 'She wants to marry this guy Sebastian and run away to Paris, but her parents find out she's pregnant and make her a prisoner at home. Let's see.' She turned back a page in the diary. 'Here it is, listen to this . . .'

Camilla Bea appeared at Sebastian's door holding a small cloth bag and a straw hat with a pink ribbon trailing behind, her cheeks flushed with the heat of the sun and a pumping heart that had, at last, come back to life. It had been a week since she'd last seen him; despite her promise to return the next morning, she had been required to contend with the petty, mean-spirited concerns of her parents' bourgeois hearts, the meaning of which she now understood all too well.

The morning after the market crash her father had left New Orleans for his office in New York City to deal with the financial crisis. On his way out of the house, he had walked past Camilla's bedroom door in stunning silence – no 'How's my little flower this morning?' Not even a knock. Considering the special sweetness of their relationship, the snub was a dagger in her heart, a final, telling revelation of what mattered to him most when she needed his love and understanding.

By noon that day, she had discovered her own bootstraps and, following her father's oft-stated advice, pulled herself up by them. But she also discovered the relevance of another one of his favorite clichés: that a bird cannot fly until it's left the nest. There was nothing she could do about his turning away from her except leave. In that searing moment in her room the night before, when she'd fought with her mother, a torch had been passed, separating them forever. Consoling herself at the end of the day, she decided that she had not lost her parents so much as found the love of her life to take their place.

Her mother remained in New Orleans the week after the crash to face what she called 'the problem at home', employing the arsenal of personas mothers keep in store for such trying times. One day she wore the mask of the master, venting her wrath; the next day she appeared as a dove, suing for peace. One moment she was a surgeon, slicing up her daughter's longings for Sebastian; the next she was a nurse, tending to her wounds. And always, without exception, she was the sheriff, holding her daughter under house arrest, away from her lover and everyone else. Everyone, that is, except for the family doctor, whom Camilla was required to visit under the trustful, watchful eye of her nanny. Trustworthy the old woman was, too, having been with Camilla's father for over thirty years. Still, Camilla knew, that wouldn't be enough to stop a determined fifteen-year-old girl from making her escape.

It happened after the doctor's visit, when Nanny took her to Hoffman's apothecary for an ice-cream cone. Ice cream, for God's sake, as if she was a little girl. Licking the cone and watching people, Camilla finally made her break – strangely, as it turned out, with the cooperation of her nanny – and arrived at the wrought-iron gate to Sebastian's building at exactly the time reserved for her weekly piano lesson. She knew he'd be waiting. She knew.

Entering the foyer, she closed her eyes at the bottom of the stair and let the violet, citrus-scented aura welcome her back. For the first time in seven days – seven winters was what it seemed like – she felt alive, safe, and at home.

After climbing the stair, she stood on tiptoe at the apartment door and looked into the peephole and saw something so strange she thought she must be on the wrong floor. Sitting in the dusky light were packing boxes and litter, and where the grand piano had been, nothing but empty space. Stepping back to check the number on the door, she saw an ecru envelope pinned to the jamb with her name written in the center in Sebastian's distinctive, willowy hand. She pulled it off and opened it.

The words '*My dearest Camilla*' penetrated her eyes. She read: '. . . *was not meant to be . . . perhaps in another life . . . forgive me, but I must leave New Orleans . . . for Paris . . . to join my wife and child.*' Wife and child? *Wife and child?* By the time she reached '*But I will love you forever*', another winter had already set in.

At the bottom of the page, jiggling through her tears, she saw the line of a poem he'd apparently written in the hope of linking the two of them forever. '*They that love beyond the world cannot be separated by it.*' No matter how many times she read it, it was so anemic and baffling she found it impossible to understand how it could have been his.

Having read the letter over and over, having searched for an escape from its cold, unmistakable message, she finally relented. Clutching the piece of paper, she dropped everything else she was holding – her hat, her dreams, the empty envelope, her innocence – and left Sebastian's door.

Six months later, as expected, Camilla Bea gave birth to a healthy baby girl. Despite being unmarried, it was an occasion for quiet celebration among friends and family, marred nearly as much by her father's absence as by her missing lover.

After reading the goodbye letter Sebastian had pinned to the door, Camilla Bea heard nothing more from him until now, a few weeks after the baby was born, when a second envelope arrived from Paris.

Her heart beat fast as she opened it, then slowed when she

withdrew the first item: a beautiful etching of the Eiffel Tower. He had despised it so much, her first reaction was to think he was trying to hurt her.

Then a letter. The handwriting was in the beautiful, distinctive strokes that were uniquely his, but the message was surprisingly formal, short, and all too appropriate. Friends in New Orleans had told him of her baby's birth – *their* baby's birth, he should have said – but he was, of course, unable to be there for the event. He thought of her often. He hoped she was well. He hoped 'the baby' was in good health, strangely making no reference to her as a girl. He remembered their time together 'with great fondness'. He was 'living happily with his wife and son'. There it was again, a reference to the gender of his other child but none to his new daughter. The letter gave no explanation for the Eiffel Tower etching either, and for some reason, she now noticed, the page was undated.

Reading on, she noticed no return address, only the stiff sentiment that he wished he could hear from her but thought it better that he didn't. But he would always remember her 'with warmth', he said, once again ending his letter, '*They that love beyond the world cannot be separated by it.*' He signed it as he had the first one, too: '*Take care, little flower. Sebastian.*'

The damnably kind tone, the cryptic line of poetry, the indifferent references to his own child, the etching of the Eiffel Tower, the use of the term 'little flower' that he hated – all conspired to insult her deeply and make her heartsick over his betrayal. But later, in the quiet moments when she recalled his words, his eyes, his touch, she knew that she still loved him. And that compelled her to look for other explanations for his behavior. Of course he should have told her about his wife and child, but not even that duplicity could obscure a larger truth: just as she loved him, she knew that he still loved her. Each awful thought about his departure, each cold sentence in his two letters was dissected by her powerful female instincts.

Perhaps he had no choice about leaving New Orleans for Paris. And surely he would never deliberately insult her with a sarcastic gift or response. Never. No, there had to be other reasons.

Late one night, tired but faithful to her diary, she lifted a pen to write her daily entry. She had been deeply hurt by her lover, but she was still alive and had a beautiful daughter and had learned something valuable about herself. Sebastian had stolen her innocence, but not her spirit. She would be more cautious with her life, more insightful and wise, but she would never become cynical. And she would remember him just as he would remember her: always. *They that love beyond the world cannot be separated by it.*

Two days later, at the library, she found the poem.

The next night, she awoke with a start, sitting up in bed with perspiration dotting her face. Suddenly, as she'd dozed, every question had been answered, every circumstance made clear. At last, she understood why Sebastian had left her. Without a doubt, she knew.

Her skin turned cold with the realization.

She turned on the lamp next to her bed and opened the nightstand drawer and took out her diary and pen. After finding the last page, she wrote: *'What happened is too painful to bear. I cannot write of it. Ever.'* Then she closed her diary and placed it back in the drawer and turned out the light.

And never opened it again.

Camilla Bea married no one, and had no other children. Neither she nor her daughter, Danielle – a beautiful woman with fine aristocratic features, almond-white skin, and soft brown hair – ever saw Sebastian again.

Twenty-five years later Danielle married a handsome young man from a fine New Orleans family – Dr Carroll Bissonette, a psychiatrist – and on the eve of their wedding, Camilla Bea gave her daughter Sebastian's love letters and her own diary, including the pages that recorded the circumstances of Danielle's birth. After reading them, the young bride placed them in a drawer under lock and key, not out of disgrace, but to keep them private and safe.

In time, Danielle and her husband had a child of their own, a beautiful little girl with bright blue eyes, ebony hair, and a feisty, independent disposition that mimicked her grandmother Camilla Bea's as surely as if it had been passed along in the milk. In honor of her spirit, Danielle and her husband gave their daughter the only name they could imagine, the one that personified the vitality they hoped she would never lose.

Camilla is what they called her. Camilla Bissonette.

She continued talking to Nat through the bathroom door. 'So Camilla Bea escapes during a doctor's visit and goes to his apartment, but when she gets there she finds a Dear Camilla letter pinned to the door telling her that her lover has a wife and baby and has gone to Paris to be with them.'

'Nice guy,' Nat said. He turned on the water at the sink.

'I've got the letter right here,' she said, lifting a heavy piece of ecru stationery.

'What did she do when she read it?'

'I don't know. That's where I was when you came in.' No answer. 'You listening?'

'I hear you,' he said over running water and moving toothbrush.

Camilla turned back to a page she'd marked with a flag in the diary. 'Something about this doesn't make sense,' she said. 'Listen to what she wrote after she ran off to meet him.' She got off the bed and walked to the bathroom door to read.

On our way back from the doctor's office, Nanny and I stopped in at Hoffman's for an ice-cream cone. Wanted to throw up, but didn't say anything because this was my chance to get away. Nanny wasn't supposed to let me out of her sight, but when she turned around to pay, I just up and walked out the door! She never could have caught me, but as soon as I got outside I thought, I can't do this. She's been with me since I was born. If I walk out now, Daddy will fire her for sure.

*I came back inside the store trying to think up another way
to leave, and that's when she did the most amazing thing. She
finger-combed my hair and gave me some fold-up money and
said, Go to him, Miss C. Big tears in her eyes. Where she got
the nerve to do that I'll never know. What's even weirder is when
Daddy called from New York and found out what I'd done, he
didn't ask how I got away or say a harsh word to her.*

'Why,' Camilla said, 'do you suppose Camilla Bea's father
didn't jump down the nanny's throat for helping his fifteen-
year-old daughter run away to Paris?'

'Probably because she didn't do it,' he said.

'But that's not the point. The nanny had no way of knowing
Camilla Bea's lover had already left town. Camilla herself didn't
know until she got to his apartment and found the letter.' She
heard the sound of the shower. 'Something about it doesn't seem
right,' she said, turning the page. After reading a moment, she
raised her voice over the splashing water. 'Are you hungry?'

'Are you making something?'

'I'm in the mood for scrambled eggs,' she said. 'Want some?'

'Be down in a minute.'

She picked up the diary and a folder marked TRUST
AGREEMENT, then slipped her feet into a pair of moccasins
and headed for the kitchen. As she descended the steps, she
opened the folder and read the first page. It was dated October
30, 1929, the day after the great stock market crash. She knew
at once who had written it: Camilla Bea's father.

Camilla Bea's father sat in his New York office in the heart of
Wall Street. The room was filled with the trophies of success and
the trappings of Roaring Twenties wealth: Oriental rugs, supple
leather chairs, and the exotic wood grains of Africa, Asia, and
the Americas. Water buffalo horns mounted on polished brass
cradles adorned the walls, along with sepia-toned photographs

of men on safari, groups of them standing tall and courtly, guns resting on forearms, khaki jackets rolled to the elbows.

He sat in his favorite place, a small, luxurious office off to the side of his larger one, nestled deep into a green leather chair wrinkled from years of use. The room seemed strangely listless now, drained of energy, as if a sad story had finally come to an end. Spread out on the ottoman at his knees was a newspaper with the names of great companies headed for bankruptcy, their stock prices circled in fresh red ink that bled into the porous paper as if from a rich man's veins.

The telephone call would tell him what to do next. He waited for it like a verdict, nervously but with resignation. He'd already made alternative plans, regardless of what he heard. Either way, he was ready.

He set his empty Scotch glass on a Biedermeier table beneath an unlit brass lamp and lifted a framed photograph to his rimmed, watery eyes. Three men stood facing the lens beneath a great African rain tree: his partner, Jedediah Stone, a roguish trader with a stogie between his teeth and an Irish grin wicked enough to spring him from an Englishman's jail; in the middle, himself, twenty years younger and full of beans, no hint of the face he wore today; and the other man, the third leg on the stool . . . the pot-bellied man who hunted big game with a smile on his face. The New Orleans Chief of Police, called the Hammer.

Camilla Bea's father laid his head back on the chair and closed his eyes. After a moment he roused himself and walked across the room to a large window. Parting the white curtain liners, he squinted eastward toward the Atlantic Ocean and drew himself back to wind-swept decks on tramp steamers, to night watches in the crow's nest and the sound of the bow churning up the foam . . . If he could do it all over again he'd do it pretty much the same – a twig here, a quicker move there, maybe – but most of it no differently. Except, of course, for that one big mistake. But he couldn't do any of it over. Least of all that.

He looked back at the telephone. It sat there as silent as the guillotine. Ring, he told it. Ring.

He turned back toward the window. Life's long knives were smooth and quiet even when they severed a pumping artery. He could withstand angry markets, face a charging water buffalo, tame litigating lawyers, even lose a first child to a fever and still survive, move on, prosper. Those were enemies you could look in the eye, take aim, and give your best shot, but not this. This mistake had come out of the tar pits of emotion, the irrational, wily, bubbling pot of passion. It was ironic enough to make him smile. After all the dragons he'd slain – after all the industry and intelligence and nerve and technology that had got him where he was – to be undone by something this simple was hard to believe.

Being a rational man, he knew what he had to do.

He got up from his chair and walked to the window and lifted it an inch or two to breathe in the scents of the city, a rich blend of roasted chestnuts and horse manure and pungent smoke stacks and dead fish floating in the East River. He wrapped the white curtain liner around his hand and drew it to his face, holding it to his nose as if it was a perfumed lover's scarf. Then, suddenly irritated by it, he dropped it and closed the window.

He carried the photograph of the three men on safari back to the chair, sat down, and methodically tore off the back of the frame. Without looking at the picture again, he rolled it into a column and stood it in the center of a crystal ashtray among bits of burned tobacco scattered across the bottom.

The telephone rang. He reached for it a little too quickly.

'Hello? . . . Yes, it's me . . . Mm-mm . . . Mm-mm. But that's what the deed and the stock were for, to solve the problem – now you're telling me it's not enough? . . . No, no, no, I *have* considered it, and there's nothing more to give you. It's not called a stock market crash for nothing . . . I can't give you that, I have a family to consider . . . No, *you* listen to *me*. Then pour yourself a whiskey and think about it and call me back.'

He hung up the telephone and sat in perfect quiet, his eyes lit like a candle at its peak, pondering the contingency plan that sat on his desk in the main office. There was no way he'd allow himself to be beaten by a corrupt, tin-star crook. Not a chance. Decent men always beat the bums. It was their duty. And if they did it right, their pleasure.

All you had to have was enough guts.

He took a deep breath through his nose. There was nothing more to consider. If he had the nerve, the plan would work. He listened to the sounds on the streets below: the horns, a siren, the hum of city commerce. After a while, he got up from the chair and walked through the door into his larger office and stood at his desk.

He opened a manila folder. Inside was a document marked TRUST AGREEMENT. He turned the pages quickly, skimming its contents . . .

such documents as are contained in said safe deposit box to remain privileged and confidential for fifty years from the date of this instrument, *provided that*, in the event the maker of this trust should be accused of a felonious crime by any *bona fide* legal authority during said fifty years, such documents shall be removed by Trustee and distributed to the following individuals, governmental offices, and newspapers . . .

Turning to the last page, he touched the blue-ink signature he'd affixed earlier. Then he placed the document in a large envelope addressed to his lawyer across town and dropped it into his secretary's leather basket.

It was on its way.

Opening a second manila folder, he found a tissue paper copy of the same trust. After checking to be sure all the pages were in order, he placed it inside a large envelope and sealed it with a lick of his tongue. This one, too, he held above the leather basket – checking to be sure that the address of Chief Vernon Hammer, New Orleans, Louisiana, was right – then dropped it into the basket.

There was one more envelope to be launched, a large one already sealed and addressed to a lawyer in Paris, France. His fingertips traced the outline of its contents and his instructions. After positioning the envelope in the leather basket, he patted the stack once.

He was done. He was ready.

The first step – the last step – was utter magic, the instantaneous transformation of stifling pain into boundless relief. Because he'd been living in numbness for the last few days, it surprised him that his evaporated senses could return so acutely: the sound of the wind piercing his ears; the cold air tasting rich and clean; the ashen skies, soft and welcome; the bricks whooshing by in a waterfall of red. He closed his eyes and listened to the rapping sound of the curtain liner fluttering behind him like an unopened parachute. All at once he was a baby tossed into the air by his father – arms out, stomach churing – waiting to be caught by his warm, strong hands.

Or the ground.

Splintered ideas crackled through his head at lightning speed. Regret. Forgiveness. His wife and son. Camilla Bea, her baby, her shame, his shame – his own insurmountable *shame*.

They said there'd be no pain. Only blackness.

He started to cartwheel slowly, a scarecrow in a wind-storm, limbs extended, eyes wide – sky-buildings-ground, sky-buildings-ground – wrapping himself in the curtain like a burial shroud. His thoughts ripped through his head faster than he fell, as if time had slowed.

They'll think the crash made me do it.

Reaching terminal velocity, the on-rushing air began to suffocate him.

Hammer knows the truth, but when he sees the trust he won't be able to talk about it.

Would his grandchild be a boy?

For a split second he wished he hadn't done this.

He'll have to cover it up.

They said there'd be no pain, only blackness.

There were automobiles below – no horns, only the sound of the curtain liner – the sight of windows blinking by in the fading five o'clock light. Was it already over? No, no, not yet, he could still see light and they said there should be nothing but blackness.

No one will ever know—

He caught a glimpse of a flag ripping by – blurred red, white, and blue – the American flag on the building – he was passing the third-floor library – French windows – ficus tree – needs water—

A split second later he found what he expected.

No pain.

Only black—

Camilla stirred the eggs slowly as she continued to read.

Saddest day of my life. Sebastian gone, Daddy dead. Knew when the telephone rang it was something bad, then Momma came in with teary red eyes. He was by himself in his office and he fell out a window, she said. But I know better.

Her left hand continued stirring the eggs.

He jumped because of me and Sebastian. He was too embarrassed . . .

She laid the rubber spatula down.

. . . that his little girl is going to have a baby out of wedlock. Not any baby, but one he can't show off. Oh, but Daddy, if only you knew Sebastian and what a gentle, beautiful man he is! If it was his color that mattered so much, why didn't you meet him first and see for yourself?

Color? The eggs were slowly burning. She read more.

He passes everywhere he goes.

Passes? What was her grandmother talking about? Maybe I'm reading it wrong.

She read on, forgetting to stir.

I know why you killed yourself. Mother told you I hope my baby is . . .

She turned the page.

. . . black as coal.

She read it twice.

'Hey, what's burning?'

She heard Nat speak at the same moment she smelled the eggs. Closing the diary with one hand, she quickly pulled the skillet off the burner and tilted the pan over an empty plate and scraped out the drying eggs.

'Oh no, they're ruined,' she said. *Black as coal?* My grandfather – Grandma's lover – Sebastian the piano teacher – was a black man?

'Nothing a squirt of ketchup can't fix,' Nat said, pinching a piece of egg from the plate. He put it into his mouth and casually reached for the diary.

'Hey!' she said, laying her hand on top of it.

He stopped. 'What'd I do?'

She picked it up. 'I . . . don't want to lose my place.' She asked herself why she'd said that. Why does it matter if he reads it?

He carried the plate of bone-dry eggs to the center island and sat on a high stool. Having already set two places, she poured them orange juice and carried strips of bacon to the island and sat.

'What else did you find out about your mother?' he asked, taking a bite of toast.

'Nothing.' The diary entry was still working its way into her consciousness. 'Tell me about the case you caught tonight.'

'Remember I told you about a girl named Debbie Duzzit?'

'The one killed by her pimp?'

'The one killed by her pimp's hit man, Angel Rico. I think he did the trannie at Grand Central.'

'How do you know?'

'Same MO, a throat slashed from behind and the right ear taken off.'

'Good God,' she said.

'I'll find him,' he said. He took a bite of ketchup-soaked eggs. 'How come you're not eating?'

'They're too dry,' she said. Amazing. If she had it right, this made her part black. So romantic, so interesting, so . . . what? What else? She couldn't see the boundaries yet.

'I'll cook you some more,' he said.

'This is all I want,' she said, lifting a piece of toast. She sliced some butter off a stick and spread it. What would Nat think? That's the problem: it's not clear. So why guess? He's sitting right here next to you. Ask him.

'Nat?'

'What?'

'Did you ever go out with a black woman?'

He looked at her for an explanation. 'What makes you ask that?'

'Just curious.'

He looked at his plate and poked at his eggs. 'No.'

'Why not?'

'I don't know, I guess I never had the opportunity.'

'That's hard to imagine. There must have been attractive black women in college and on the police force.'

'There were and there are,' he said.

'Then why didn't you go out with one?' She was sounding slightly accusatory.

He set his fork down and wiped his mouth with his napkin. 'What is this, some kind of pre-nup political correctness test?'

She gave him a look. 'Forget it.'

'No, no, whatever you want,' he said. 'Pass the jam, would you, please?'

She handed it to him. Sebastian and Camilla – my mother – and now me. Part black. She ate in silence. *So why am I not telling him?*

'But I gather you have,' he said.

'Have what?'

'Dated somebody black.'

She felt a speed bump in the road.

He said, 'Somebody on the squad said you used to go out with Cush Walker.'

Oh, my God.

He looked up from his plate. 'Does silence mean yes, or are you taking the Fifth?'

'Why should I take the Fifth? You think dating a black man is self-incriminating?'

He returned to his plate of eggs. 'Only if you feel you have to keep quiet about it.'

She felt a chill. 'What's that supposed to mean?'

'You used to go out with one of the most powerful men in the country, the same guy who's busting the department's chops with BIAS, and you never even *mentioned* it?' He took a piece of toast and tore it in half and stuck it into his mouth without butter or jam.

'I didn't know it was such a big deal.' Actually, that wasn't true. She'd deliberately avoided telling him, hoping the subject wouldn't come up.

He picked up the ketchup bottle and squirted another dollop onto his eggs. 'Jesus,' he said. 'A Nobel Prize-winning black stud scientist is no big deal?'

'He hasn't won a Nobel Prize yet,' she said, deliberately not rebutting the stud part. Better to let him think she hadn't told him because of sex instead of – the other thing. 'Why are you looking at me like that?'

He poked at his plate. 'Just wondering.'

'Wondering what?'

'Why you kept it a secret.'

'Going out with Cush Walker isn't a secret. It's private. There's a difference.'

He chewed a piece of bacon.

She said, 'Don't be so jealous.'

'It's the mystery of the thing that makes a person jealous,' he said. 'Once you know what's going on, you couldn't care less.'

'But there's nothing going on! My God, it was three years ago – two years before I even met you!' Her cheeks flushed. 'If it means this much to you, I'm sorry I didn't tell you, but believe me, there's nothing to tell. OK?'

They ate without talking.

'How long did you go together?' he said.

'Oh, for God's sake, Nat.'

'What's wrong with that question?'

'It's not the question so much as where the question is leading. We went together for about six months.'

'So you slept with him, right?'

'No, he tried to kiss me goodnight once but I wouldn't let him.' Her fork clattered on the dish as she laid it down. 'We spent six months together; of course I slept with him.' More silence. 'So what do we do now, talk about positions?' Better that than the truth.

He took a moment to consider that. 'Yeah, why not? Was he good?'

She gave him an I-don't-believe-this look. 'What is *with* you tonight?'

'I'm trying to figure out why you didn't tell me.'

'No you're not, you're comparing dick sizes.' Orange juice up, orange juice down. 'I already told you why I didn't tell you. It wasn't important. I didn't think about it. Present sex lives are basic, past ones are baroque. Who cares?'

'I do.'

'Obviously.'

'So sex wasn't the reason you didn't tell me?'

Uh-oh, don't get started down that road. 'I don't even *begin* to understand why sex before I knew you is so important.'

'Yes you do, give me a break. The darker the berry, the sweeter the juice. You know the stories.'

'I don't take sexual myths seriously, and neither should you.'

'If it *is* a myth,' he said.

Click, click, forks on plates.

'So, were you in love with him?'

Yes, she'd been in love with him, and he'd been crazy in love with her. If half of what he'd professed was true, he probably still was. But say that? She shot him a cold eye-dagger instead. 'There's no answer I can give that won't need explanation, so I don't want to *talk about it*!'

'This is just great,' he said, wiping his mouth with a paper napkin. 'Men are always being accused of refusing to talk about their feelings, then when we show some, women don't want to talk about them. Just tell me why you broke up and I'll leave it alone.'

'Sweetheart?'

'Yeah?'

'Leave it alone.'

He ate his eggs. 'Must have been something,' he said. 'I mean, you're going out with an older man—'

'He was only forty-four at the time.'

'Old enough. Sophisticated, rich, smart. And cool, right?'

'You mean black.'

'I mean cool.' To himself he said, 'Black, cool – they mean the same thing.'

'You know,' she said, sitting up straight, 'now I remember the reason I didn't tell you.'

'Why?'

'Because I knew you'd go nuts.'

'With all due respect, Cam, you're missing the point. When I fell in love with you I fell for the whole package – your childhood, your attitude, your successes and mistakes – not just who you are after the day we met.'

'Mistakes? What mistakes?' She held up her hand to stop a rebuttal. She said, 'What about the other guys I went out with? Why don't we talk about them?'

'I already know about them,' he said. She didn't respond. 'Don't I?'

'Mostly.'

'Mostly?'

'Nobody else that matters.'

'What's that mean?'

'Nobody else that matters.'

'Oh, great, who'd we miss – Denzel Washington, Brad Pitt, or Harrison Ford?' He salted his eggs for the third time. 'You've got to admit that going with somebody of a different race is a little unusual, isn't it?'

'Oh, please.' Another chill.

'What did you see in him?' he asked.

'I asked the same questions about him I ask about any man. Do I like him? Does he make me laugh? Is he a good cook?' She waited a beat. 'Does he like to dance?'

She saw his reaction all over his face: low blow, Camilla, you know I can't dance. If they were at a party he didn't mind her dancing with other men – up to a point – but he himself, as she put it, didn't possess the rhythm of a dog. It was an unlikely defect for a man who was a good athlete, but there it was.

'So, was he a good cook?'

'The best.'

'Did he make you laugh?'

'Occasionally. When he unwound.'

'And did he like to dance?'

'All the time.' She was saying it now to distract him and get under his skin.

'Dirty dancing?'

'Every kind you could think of.'

'Including in bed?'

'Here we go again.'

He rolled his eyes. 'Was he good in bed?'

'I take the Fifth.'

His eyes said, Christ, that's worse than a yes, it leaves so much room for speculation. 'I guess that answers that.'

'Wait a minute, I took the Fifth – that's no answer at all.'

'Only in court. In real life, everybody knows the Fifth is a confession.' He carried his plate to the sink. 'You didn't say whether you were in love with him.'

'Fifth.'

'Consider marrying him?'

'Fifth.'

'Do you still think about him?'

'Fifth. No, I take that back. I'd say that over the last three years I haven't thought about him half as much as I have in the last ten minutes.'

'If you loved him, why not?'

She growled cutely. This was never going to end. Maybe she should just tell him and get it over with. Then she thought: are you kidding? The way he feels about the doctor? The personal jealousy, the professional threat? Who knows how he'd use what she could tell him?

Don't paint a detailed picture, just give him enough to get him off your back. And don't mention that you're going to NeuroPath Labs tomorrow. Even though there's no chance of

98

running into Cush – she'd already confirmed he wouldn't be there. Given Nat's state of mind, it would only be trouble.

'You keep thinking it's about sex,' she said, 'but you're wrong. It's about something else.'

'What kind of something else?'

'If I tell you something a little vague and general, will you leave it alone?'

'How can I say no to that?'

'When I was going with Cush, I saw something happen that – unnerved me.'

'Unnerved *you*? The high-wire artist? The human fly?'

'That's good. So now we can leave it alone, OK?'

He left it alone for, oh, all of twelve seconds.

'Cam?'

'Leave it alone.'

'I have one other question.'

'Leave it alone.'

'Is it anything that puts you in danger?'

'Only if we talk about it. So let's leave it alone, OK?'

He frowned. 'What a great way to start a marriage. A secret the size of Mount Everest.'

'Nat—'

'OK, OK,' holding up his hands, 'but don't expect me to leave Walker alone.'

'Why?'

'Amerigo has dragged me into the union fight against BIAS.'

She knew it. 'That's just great.'

'You see a problem with that?'

'Not for me,' she said. 'Not for you, either, if you don't mind siding with the bigots.' How strange: the word 'bigots' came out with more emphasis than usual. She sat pretending to read the newspaper, thinking about her grandmother while Nat cleared the island and began cleaning and stacking the dishes.

What did it mean, having black blood in your veins? She felt as if she'd opened a gift at a surprise party but couldn't tell what it contained. Why the special curiosity, the irritating touch of disorientation? This wasn't the *Mandingo* fifties. If she'd just learned that her grandfather was Irish instead of French, she'd be interested, but not like this.

She turned the page and straightened up on her stool. Why hadn't her mother told her? Or her grandmother? Probably because they considered it a 'delicate situation', the thought of which suddenly miffed her. If Sebastian had been a full-blooded Cherokee, the whole family would have happily laid claim to those romantic roots long ago. Why shouldn't it be the same with someone black?

She spread her fingers and looked at the back of her hand, searching for a sign of something she'd never noticed before – a clue to the past, a shade of melanin that revealed something new. Her skin looked exactly as it always had – or did it? Of course it did. She closed her fingers.

Although, come to think of it, she did tan easily.

Seeing her, Nat said, 'You freaking out imagining how it will look with a wedding ring?' His tone was light-hearted, as in, is the argument over with now?

She carried her glass to the sink and stood behind him as he washed it. She was proud of her roots. Or was pride what she was *supposed* to feel, not what she really felt? She placed her hands on his shoulders and laid her cheek against his back.

It's silly. It's history. It's no big deal, not even for a girl from New Orleans. *Least* of all for a girl from New Orleans. So tell him.

'Our first fight,' she said.

He turned around and put his hands around the small of her back and lifted her off the floor. 'No, it isn't,' he said. 'We fought about getting a dog, remember?' He wanted a dog to keep her company when he was working nights, but she'd said they were too busy to take care of it.

She hopped up and wrapped her legs around his waist and pulled his face into the base of her neck. 'I sort of like it that you're jealous.'

'Sorry I badgered you,' he said.

She stroked his hair. 'It doesn't really bother you that I went out with Cush Walker, does it?'

'Christ, no, Cam, I wouldn't care if you'd gone out with a goat.'

She pulled her face back. 'Is that how you think of him?'

'No, no, no, I was just trying to make a point,' he said.

She pulled his face up to hers and kissed him. You're kissing a black woman now. Would it matter if you knew? She had no proof that it would, but her viscera – this new blood she'd discovered in her veins – wanted the answer. When they finished, she knew how to get it. 'Does it work in reverse?'

'What do you mean?'

'Should I be jealous if you told me you'd been involved with a black woman?'

'I don't know, should you?'

'Easy enough to test,' she said.

'You want me to go out with a black woman?'

'I'm not crazy about that, but I have a better idea.' She put her feet on the floor and stood in front of him, one hand around his neck, and brushed her lips against his cheek. 'I've got a new climbing harness. I should adjust the fit before I leave in the morning. Come with me to the studio and we'll try it on.'

She was on her back on the old chaise longue. The newspaper clippings and magazines had been laid onto the floor, and a nearby candle flame danced in the air, casting shadowed light across her skin. He was facing her, saying nothing, letting his motion convey the message, reminding her of rhythmic waves lapping the hull of a boat.

Never mind that. What was he thinking?

She couldn't tell. They often played games in bed – word games, touching games, fantasy games that were tender or hot, generous or self-indulgent, whatever interested them. Nothing serious, no test of prowess or taste or character. Just games.

Until tonight. Now the dice were loaded.

'Know what I want?' she said into his ear.

'What?'

'I want you to think of me as somebody else.' She felt him pause.

'Who?'

He started up again, catching the rhythm of the music she'd put on the stereo, a quiet, steady thump like a heartbeat from inside the earth. A sexual sound, an African sound, even if thinking of it that way was a cliché.

'Somebody . . . black.'

He didn't answer. She turned her head toward the candle and imagined Sebastian, lean and handsome with long, delicate fingers . . . young Camilla Bea sneaking into his room at night to make love by candlelight. She imagined the air as hot and thick,

New Orleans in the twenties . . . no air conditioning or excuses, no second chances or abortion . . . just daring love flung against the world. The thought of Sebastian's blood running through her . . . the rhythm of the music . . . the feel of Nat against her carried her along.

She wrapped her legs around him and stretched her hands out to the sides and let his imagination cook. After awhile, when the time seemed right, she began talking to him, shaping *his* fantasy, egging him on with whispered taunts and the peppery heat of the smallest word in the sexual vocabulary: *It*. Take it. Feel it. Do it. Work it. Words she'd said to him before, but that came out now as if spoken by someone else. Herself morphed into a new woman.

Was he into it? Did he imagine a different person stretched out beneath him? Someone of a different shade, color, or essence? That was the test. She knew from experience that the male sexual psyche was fragile, not robust; that locker room bravado was mostly a fig leaf covering a narrow range of genuine, unreserved desire. Male lust was a steam engine made of glass, ignited or turned off by the smallest, most irrational images imaginable. Stockings or bare skin, dark nipples or light, full cheekbones or chiseled – these and a thousand other impressions were impervious to conscience or learning or politics, billowing or wilting desire regardless of what the civilized, socialized man might think he should want. Thomas Mann had said it all: the curl of a woman's mouth was enough to ignite one man's passion and kill another's. That's what she was after, the emotional truth that lay deep inside Nat, beyond his control, asserting itself regardless of what he'd say or think about her blackness once she told him. She didn't want to talk him into acceptance. She wanted to see his sentiment unvarnished, the one she would have to live with for the rest of her life.

He started to raise his head above hers to kiss her and talk to her, but she ran her fingers into his hair and held his face against her neck. She didn't want to show herself right now. She wanted his eyes shrouded to make it easier to imagine someone else and show the thing that would give him away – a sign of desire or curiosity. Or, she feared, a sign of disrespect.

He was rising like dough. She could feel it in his movement and hear it in his breathing. He normally painted word pictures when they made love, but not tonight. Why? Was her game censoring him? What was he thinking?

'Tell me, baby,' she said over the music. 'What's it like?'

He didn't answer.

His movement turned intense, no longer supple but desperate the way he got when the end was approaching. With his face still buried in the chaise, he reached down and took hold of her hips. He'd held her like this before, but now she had a different sense of it . . . an image of herself as a horse with its haunches being stroked. Was that what he was thinking? That she was a mule?

'Baby, are you making love to me . . . or are you just . . . fucking me?'

He spoke between breaths. 'Whatever . . . you . . . want . . . baby.'

At least he called her 'baby', not 'bitch' or 'ho'.

Jesus, Cam, now who's the racist here?

This game was distracting her from her own pleasure. Forget the inquisition, get into the lovemaking.

Too late. He was teetering on the brink. She decided to go for it. Arching her back, she said, 'Come on, white boy – show me what you've got.'

He held on . . . saying nothing. Then he went over the edge.

A moment later they lay side by side, damp and spent. He put his arm across her back but didn't speak, creating a vacuum she filled by imagining herself as a lesser object. No, that wasn't it: a *permanent* lesser object. Playing sex object from time to time was fine with her because when the game was over, so was the role.

But blood was different. Color was forever. Black or white, you didn't change it.

When the time was right, she said, 'Are you OK?'

His answer was a gentle massage in the small of her back. No words. Just fingers.

She continued filling in the blanks. It must have been good. It must have been bad. Who knows? What a dumb thing to do, turning your lover into a Chinese wall poster you couldn't read, holding out on your own climax, holding back a piece of information and infusing it with superstition like some voodoo priestess. What in the world had she been thinking?

She relaxed her muscles and laid her hand across his back and tried to wash away the silence, but no matter how hard she tried, she knew the question wasn't, what in the world was she thinking? but what she'd been asking from the start:

What in the world was *he* thinking?

Nat sat on the edge of the mattress and looked back at Camilla, making sure she was still asleep. He stared at the clock: ten after four, so late even the fluorescent hands were dim.

He walked to the door, then down the spiral stairs, keeping his feet near the center pole where the weld was strongest and the creaks less loud. After reaching the bottom, he picked his way to the kitchen, found the telephone, and dialed a number he knew by heart.

The telephone at the other end of the line rang a minute, then a recorded voice told him that he had reached a voice mailbox, leave a message after the tone.

'Lieutenant, it's Nat. About that union meeting on BIAS? I've changed my mind and I'll be there.' He paused, wondering how much he should say on the machine. 'I've got an idea concerning our friend, the doctor. If you meet me in the squad room at nine thirty, I'll explain.'

He started to hang up, then pulled the phone back to

his ear. 'Make sure you round up Hart for the meeting.' Sergeant Hart was as out-there racist as you could get. 'And there's a piece of equipment we'll need to sign out of the cage.'

'Is this Dolly?' Sally Shaw said into the telephone. She sat at her desk in Midtown South drawing five-pointed stars on a pad of paper with the name Dolly next to the telephone number she'd found on the bottle of Cheetah perfume.

'Who's this?' a suspicious female voice said.

'This is Officer Sally Shaw with the New York Police Department. I'm looking for a woman named Dolly.'

'What do you want her for?'

'Are you her?' There was no answer. 'If this is Dolly, I'm calling because your name was found on the body of someone who was killed last night, and I need to ask you a few questions about it.'

'Who got killed?' the voice asked.

'A woman – a man – named Tangerine. Do you know her?'

There was no answer. The distrust on the line was thick enough to clog it.

'Look,' Shaw said, 'you're not a suspect, but I have to talk to you. I have your telephone number, which means I can find your address, so we can either do this over the phone or I'll come up and see you anyway.' No reply. 'Is this Dolly?'

'Yeah, this is Dolly, but I don't know anything about a killing.'

Shaw put a large star next to the number on her pad. 'Do you know who Tangerine is?'

There was another silence.

'Does the name Angel Rico mean anything to you?'

No answer. Then the woman said, 'How do I know you're really a cop?'

'Take this number down,' Shaw said. 'Got a pencil?'

'Go ahead.'

'My name is Officer Sally Shaw, and my partner's name is Detective Nat Hennessy. You can reach either one of us at Midtown South, 212–239–9811.'

'I'll call you back.'

'That's fine,' Shaw said. 'I'll be waiting.'

She stood on the observation platform in the center of Miss Liberty's brain, just above the inside of the lady's eyes, looking down through a ragged gash in her cheek where the helicopter blade had made its cut. What a mess. And all for a photograph. The slash from the blades could be repaired more easily than removing the paint and oil-based stains from her copper skin.

Before taking the ladder up to the torch, she took a moment to look out the statue's crown and imagine ships a hundred years earlier passing through her line of sight. All those hopeful immigrants looking up at these opaque copper eyes. It must have been more than a face to them. More like an open door.

Except for the ones who'd come earlier. The ones in chains.

'Ready upstairs, Camilla,' a team member in a blue jumpsuit said. He opened the gate to the cramped passage inside the statue's right arm and led the way up the steel ladder.

She emerged from the narrow stair through a small hatch door and stepped onto the circular platform around the base of the flame, thirty stories high. She'd been here fifteen years earlier during the centennial restoration of the statue, as a student at Columbia who'd researched ways to remove the old paint and coal tar that had been layered inside the statue in an effort to seal out the rain. Having dreamed up the idea of using liquid nitrogen to freeze off the paint, turning it to dust that more or less fell off, she'd been brought onto the restoration team as a consultant at the tender age of nineteen, the youngest of the group.

The scene today was no less breathtaking than it had been in the mid-eighties. Standing on her copper perch, she had a perfect, 360-degree view of New York Harbor. Directly below, on the apron around the enormous stone pedestal, were members of the inspection and restoration team – personnel from the Ellis Island–Statue of Liberty Foundation, engineers, contractors who would make repairs, National Park Service staff, and a crew repairing scrapes on the marble plaza caused by the downed helicopter. All of them were looking up, waiting to see what she was going to do.

Among them, she hoped, was someone from NeuroPath Labs who would accompany her back to the hospital lab where she could deliver her samples for examination under a powerful scanning electron microscope, known as an SEM. When the chief engineer had told her the SEM at New York University was tied up and he'd arranged to use the one at NeuroPath Labs, her face had apparently dropped. Is there a problem with that? he'd asked. No, she said, and arranged the visit. Regrettably, Cush's secretary said, he would be out of the office attending a police union meeting in Queens. Too bad, she'd said, good deal, she'd thought. Especially considering Nat's 'thing' about the man.

She gave herself a short lecture, telling herself to push everything out of her mind – Nat, Cush, the game she'd played the night before – and focus. It was time to climb.

She pulled her wind-blown hair into a knot, tied it back, and stuffed it under a red helmet, then pushed her gray, polarized sunglasses into place and tucked the braided cord attached to the temples down the collar of her khaki jumpsuit. A wireless earphone transmitter fitted snugly beneath her head gear. She adjusted the curved microphone tube to the front of her lips.

'Can you hear me, Jim?' she said.

'I hear you,' he answered.

'OK in the crown,' another team member said.

Her climbing harness was comfortably tight. She checked the buckles again – all set – and fed the end of a braided nylon line through the loop on her harness, just below the small knot that was forming in the pit of her stomach. Like all climbers, her pulse quickened the moment she tied in with a double figure eight. There'd be no D rings or carabiners on this primary line: the fewer links in a chain, the fewer that could break. As it was, she'd have to use carabiners on the other support ropes as she reached them.

She tested the main line by pulling hard. The knot tightened on itself and held. She snapped two padded equipment bags onto the sides of her harness – a tin snipper on her right hip, a 35mm camera and Pentax 30X telescope on the left. After wiggling her fingers into a pair of tight-fitting chamois gloves, she positioned herself on the north side of the torch platform above the statue's uplifted forearm and right shoulder. Viewing the tip of Manhattan, she paused to breathe in the sun-baked scent of algae and ozone.

There was one last item to strap on: the Thermos-sized canister of liquid nitrogen she'd use to test the red, white, and blue paint on the skin. One of the crew members lifted a stainless-steel bottle with a scarlet warning triangle on the side and held it up to the wind. The liquid inside was 340 degrees below zero, so cold it would freeze virtually anything. One of her favorite tricks was to take a fresh banana, dip half of it into a pool of LN-2, use the frozen end to pound a nail into wood, then peel the other end and eat it. She also knew what liquid nitro could do to human tissue. Her arm had once accidentally caught a layer of the gas; it had blistered like hot grease.

The crew member holding the canister called out a warning – 'Venting!' – then pressed a lever at the top of the cylinder, bleeding off the excess pressure in a small whoosh of freezing fog. Properly housed, the chemical remained in a sub-zero state for a month or so at a time, but the inevitable, slow leakage of ambient air into the bottle converted some of it into a slowly expanding gas that propelled the fluid out of the wand. The excess pressure was automatically released every few hours through a spring-loaded pressure valve, often surprising bystanders with a rude, flatulent screech. As a precaution against startling her while she was climbing, the crew member was clearing the valve.

Camilla threw one foot over the railing. 'All set, guys.'

A team member lifted a brake handle and played out a few feet of line from a large spool anchored to a rubber-coated chain around the base of the statue's flame. He and another man placed their hands under Camilla's arms and lifted her over the edge of the platform railing, lowering her a few feet until the slack in the line to her harness had been taken up. She dangled a moment before her extended foot touched the statue's wrist.

'Lower me a couple more feet,' she said into her microphone, looking down. The statue's copper skin, heavy and substantial to the eye, was only as thick as a penny, pliable enough for its French artisans to hammer three hundred sections of it into shape. She would have to be careful not to step willy-nilly across the surface, placing her weight instead on lines of rivets supported by carbonized iron armature bars.

She looked down and found a rivet line in the center of the arm. If she stepped too far on either side, her center of gravity would swing her out into the open. The rope would hold – she assumed – but it would still be a failed repel on a sheer cliff: a heart-stopping fall, a split second to wonder if this was it, a twirling crash into the side, and a helpless dangle. Usually harmless, always embarrassing.

She placed one foot on the surface, then the other, keeping most of her hundred and twenty pounds on the harness line. 'More slack. I'm going down.'

As they fed out the line, she continued setting her soft-soled climbing shoes carefully, keeping her balance and lowering herself on the statue's massive right arm a few feet at a time until she reached the sculpted copper sleeve bunched up on the biceps. She moved down the enormous raised shoulder toward the neck until she was able to reach a second rope dangling across the statue's face from a window in the crown. After snapping the carabiner onto her harness, she moved across the figure's copper clavicle, stepping lightly on the folds of the Greek gown, steadying herself against the underside of the lady's enormous chin, moving toward her other side until she reached the third rope dangling from another window.

She snapped the D-ring onto her loop and looked up. There it was: a gash running from Miss Liberty's left earlobe across her cheek to her nostril. From inside it had appeared abstract; out here, on this great woman's face, it was sickening.

Camilla removed her camera, slipped its loop over her wrist, set her feet, and began shooting. When she finished, she lifted her tin shears and cut a two-inch square of paint-blemished skin that had curled up from the impact. After dropping it into a plastic bag and stowing her gear, she adjusted her microphone.

'OK, guys. I've found a patch that's got a little bit of everything on it – yellow speckles, black spots, and streaks of paint. I'm going to try the LN-2 and see what happens.'

Pulling herself tautly against the line like a window washer, she lifted a clear, acrylic face guard from her chest and wiggled it into place. Then she unfastened the loop holding the canister of liquid nitrogen and raised it slowly, careful not to tangle the tether that would keep it from falling if she dropped it. Even though the liquid was insulated by two vacuum jackets, she could feel the coldness through her gloves.

She removed the foot-long wand from a clip and placed the trigger handle in her palm. The device was difficult to press down, ensuring that it would shut itself off automatically like a dead-man's switch on a welder's torch. She aimed the wand at the paint and grease, gripped the trigger, and squeezed. The freezing nitrogen shot out, evaporating into a white fog the instant it touched warm air. Looking like a steam cleaner, it blasted the copper skin and bounced off in all directions.

She let go of the trigger and looked. The copper surface was encrusted with white dust. She lifted her face mask. The red and white paint had become a light pink powder that she could brush away with her glove, and crater-like edges had formed around the small black dots of oil as if the cold gas had broken their bond to the copper. So far, looking good.

She found her camera and took more pictures. She'd have to examine the paint and stains under the electron microscope and see whether liquid nitrogen would do the whole job, or whether an abrasive substance like baking soda would have to be used as well.

'You finished?' a crew member asked over the wireless.

'I want to do it one more time,' she said, raising her protective mask and unsnapping the loop holding the canister. That's why they had hired her. That's why she was good.

They'd been waiting for twenty minutes, and you could feel the impatience. An audience of fifty people or so, mostly men, sat in a small auditorium on the sixteenth floor of the police building in Lefrak City, Queens, dressed in civilian clothes, talking about wives, husbands, and BIAS, the main reason they were there.

Representatives of the police unions – the captains' union, the lieutenants', the sergeants', and the largest, the street cops' Police Benevolent Association – were on hand. So were the fraternal organizations – the Emerald Society for the Irish, the Columbus Society for the Italians, the Guardians for blacks, the Shormrian for Jews, the Gay Officers Action League, the Asian Jade Society, a group for Hispanics, Germans, you name it.

Nat Hennessy sat on a chair near the back of the room talking to Lieutenant Amerigo. A sergeant looked at his wristwatch, exhaled impatiently, and said, 'Come on, where is this guy?'

The door opened and the yakking stopped in a ripple of silence as everyone turned to see who was coming. The first to enter was the man they'd all been waiting for. Tall and well dressed, he moved down the aisle with the kind of effortless authority usually shown by heads of state. They tried to size him up quickly the way cops do, but it wasn't easy. He was handsome enough – coffee-colored skin, great cheekbones – but his eyes were intelligent and determined, a serious combination. It was probably nothing more than his reputation preceding him, but walking to the front of the room, Dr Cush Walker seemed mysterious, a man capable of maneuvering in places most people didn't understand: the human brain. He was a man of science and medicine. Twilight zone stuff. They were skeptical of him but, being cops, they were also honest about what they saw, and they were impressed.

Following him down the aisle was the NYPD Chief Surgeon, a distinguished-looking man with white hair and ruddy cheeks and three stars on his dark-blue uniform. The audience watched as he ushered their guest to a folding chair behind a table. Instead of sitting, Walker lifted the chair and brought it out in front, leaving no obstructions between himself and the audience. They couldn't tell if it was a friendly gesture or in-your-face self-confidence. Or both. The Chief Surgeon held a couple of white index cards and patted his chest for his glasses.

Waiting for the introduction, the audience kept its eyes on the guest of honor. He sat regally, his hands resting in his lap, consulting no notes, appearing to be in control of himself and the room.

The Chief Surgeon looked up from his notes. With the auditorium turning quiet, Amerigo leaned over to Nat Hennessy and whispered, 'You get the cross, I'll get the hood.'

Jokingly, of course.

Cush sat and listened as the Chief Surgeon rattled off the highlights of their guest's résumé: born in Mississippi, educated at MIT and Yale Medical School, post-graduate work in neurobiology at Rockefeller University and Columbia, associate editor of *JNS*, the *Journal of Neuron Sciences*, now president of NeuroPath Laboratories in New York City and its lab in Hardy, Mississippi, where he grew up and still spent much of his time. Cush scanned the audience and read their faces, particularly the white men who made up the majority. Who is this guy? they were asking. Who is this black wizard who wants to get inside our heads? It was a mix of hostility, grudging respect, and that unmistakable electromagnetic force field that surrounded white people whenever they felt challenged by a black man with power. Never mind the form it took – money, muscle, fame, intellect – it always provoked this noticeable tribal instinct for self-protection. Having lived his whole life in a white society, Cush had learned to catch its scent long before whites recognized it in themselves. If they did.

Standing before the audience, Cush began by making fun of himself for being late, telling them it was no surprise he couldn't find the building, he had so many worn-out neurons – brain cells – he couldn't even remember what he had for breakfast. He'd learned long ago to put suspicious white audiences at ease with a self-deprecating quip. Some of his black friends worried that it amounted to a bit of a shuffle, but not Cush. Although he would never have said so, privately he saw himself as a general with an army of power and prestige and knowledge on his side. Showing consideration, as far as he was concerned, was nothing more than extending an olive branch from a superior force.

'I have been asked to explain what BIAS is all about,' he said. 'Considering the confusion that's in the air, I'm glad to have the chance. If you've been to the hospital recently, or watched *ER*, you know that recent medical technologies allow us to explore the workings of the human brain more precisely than ever before. In a nutshell, that's all BIAS is. It uses super-fast magnetic resonance imaging to create a live video of the brain as it functions. The rest of the test is like taking a polygraph, and even uses much of the same technology. It's non-invasive and takes about thirty minutes.'

He turned back to the table and found a pitcher of water and poured himself a glass.

'So what is this super-fast MRI videotape showing us? When a person thinks about something, relevant brain cells draw oxygen and sugar from the bloodstream to do their work. What the fast

MRI sees is this energy burning up, which, depending on the duration and intensity of the thought, appears on our monitors in different colors.'

He lifted the glass.

'What kinds of thoughts can we see?' He took a drink and watched their worried faces. 'Don't worry, not those.' There were some relieved chuckles in the audience. 'We can't see specific thoughts of any kind, only their location, particularly if they are emotional. For example, if you use the super-fast MRI on someone who's looking at a photograph of an attacker's face, you can see how and where the viewer's brain reacts to it. This has been done for a few years now, in what are called cognitive activation studies. What BIAS does is refine this process by measuring a person's emotional reaction to race and color and ethnicity in situations that are likely to come up in your work as police officers.'

The audience sat impassively until someone cracked, 'You shittin' me?' which made everyone laugh.

Cush smiled and set down his glass of water.

'When it comes to race, all of us are to some degree innately suspicious of people who look different from ourselves. In other words, in some measure – and how much or how little is precisely the point of BIAS – a defensive impulse is triggered by facial features, language, skin color, voices, and other sensory information that's "foreign" to the viewer. I've scanned hundreds of people, and I have yet to find anyone of any background who didn't reveal some awareness of other people's physical differences. According to the evolutionary guys who study this stuff, a certain amount of fear and suspicion of outsiders became hardwired over time as strategies for survival, but in a sense that's beside the point. It's what we do with this suspicion that matters.

'Let me give you an example. A few years ago, a skinhead was tested as part of a volunteer prisoner study and showed hate for other racial and ethnic groups at levels so high they would have scored nearly a hundred per cent on the BIAS scale. A few months after he got out of prison, he accidentally killed one of his own children with a gun. The experience shook him so deeply he underwent a kind of spiritual conversion, and before long he'd left the skinheads and was touring the country speaking out against the Klan and racism and bigotry even in the face of some nasty threats from his old buddies.

'About a year later, we did another scan on him and found that deep in his hippocampus – the seat of human emotion – he was still reacting to African-Americans in ways he had in prison. In other words, when he was confronted by photographs and scenarios reminiscent of what had shaped his learning as a boy, parts of the same brain cells activated in his prison hate-mode lit up again. At some deeply visceral level that's slow to change, he was, and probably still is, a fearful, race-aware guy, and yet on the conscious level where he now lives and makes choices, that's no longer true. Later, when we did a BIAS scan – which measures not only his innate, slow-to-change responses, but his conscious, deliberate attitudes as well – he scored quite low, which means he showed little racial prejudice. Not that I'm proposing to make him a cop.'

Some rustling in the audience, some folding of arms.

Cush said, 'There's pretty good evidence that in time, even deep neurological systems become modified by thought and experience, so that a person is not necessarily stuck in a lifelong battle with his own bias, assuming he wants to change. But that's not the point I want to make today. What's important is that neurological systems, however they're formed, whether hardwired at birth, learned, or a combination of both, are subject to being reshaped and countered by other influences, like learning, experience, and drugs. Personality is not inflexible even when it's antisocial. Change may not come easily, but brain cells are plastic. What we think of as judgment and free will still count.'

Some of the men had their elbows on the backs of the chairs in front of them, cheeks in hand, listening intently. Others slouched with their arms folded across their chests and calves across knees, feet bouncing. Cush appeared relaxed.

'So, what does this have to do with the New York City Police Department?' he asked.

'I was just wonderin' that,' a cop near the front of the room said, louder than he intended.

'Almost two years ago,' Cush said, 'after we'd taken BIAS as far as we could go in the lab, we tested it on the street in a confidential program called Operation Screen Door. Officers volunteering for high-risk undercover assignments were given the exam along with the usual battery of psychological tests measuring fitness for dangerous work, and so were some detectives. Some of you here apparently took the test; I know because I saw a nod or two when I was describing how it works.

'The department didn't use these test scores to disqualify anyone from an assignment, but it monitored the test takers and followed their performance to see how well the test predicted. What we found is that in the vast majority of cases, subjects who had high BIAS scores accumulated five times the number of race-related complaints of misconduct as those who scored in the lower range. Three of the most celebrated excessive force cases in New York City in the last two years involved officers who scored in the ninety-fifth percentile or higher. Had we known then what we know now, the department might have screened them out and retrained them and kept these incidents from happening. And before you jump to the conclusion that this is denying somebody a job, ask the victims *and* the offending police officers if they'd like to turn back the clock. BIAS could have spared all of them and their families a lot of pain and suffering, and the city a lot of expense.' Cush unbuttoned his jacket and sat on the edge of the table, one foot on the floor.

'Those are the basics of BIAS. It has been used and it works. It isn't spooky or paranormal, it's merely an indicator of a police officer's predisposition to let racial or ethnic sentiment cloud his judgment in ways that are dangerous.' He took another drink of water and assessed the audience. At the moment they looked more like victims than cops.

'I could go on with the description, but why don't I answer questions at this point.' There was no applause.

'What is the cutoff point?' a sergeant asked. He was white, a little overweight, and slightly pink in the jowls.

'What score makes you ineligible for police work? That's up to the department, but if the test is used, I'd recommend that they start cautiously and allow only high BIAS scores to disqualify a candidate. Yes?'

A skinny young white cop stood up. 'Is this test gonna be given to everybody on the force or just us historic white discriminators?' Someone behind him applauded. He turned around, took a small bow, and sat.

Cush smiled at the show. 'White guys are not the only historic discriminators,' he said. 'Operation Screen Door identified non-white, non-European officers as bad risks who proved its predictions right too.' He pointed. 'Yes?'

'This thing smells like quotas somehow.'

'Actually, it's just the opposite of quotas because it's letting real job-related qualifications determine who goes on the police force instead of irrelevant things like race or sex or ethnicity. In that sense, it's really no different in concept from what white employers and universities and unions have been using for years: aptitude tests, entrance exams, and all those other objective predictors of performance.'

He saw a dumbfounded look on most of the faces in the audience. For years whites had argued that testing preserved merit, and that it was racial preferences that screwed them out of jobs by disregarding their generally higher scores. So let's hear it for tests, they said – except now they were looking at one that was going to cut them *out* instead of in. Cush found the irony of it momentarily fun, although it wouldn't last long.

'Did you take this test?' a white man asked.

'Yes, I did,' Cush said.

'What was your score?'

'Higher than I wish.'

'So why doesn't that disqualify you?'

'If I were trying to be a cop, it probably would.'

Camilla was stepping out of her harness when she saw a young man in a white jumpsuit crossing the plaza toward her, undeterred by a limp.

'Hello, there,' he said, and stuck out his hand. 'I'm Spider Murphy.' He was a large fellow in his twenties with unruly light-blond hair of the kind that made everything about him seem washed out – skin, lips, even, somehow, his eyes, which were albino-blue. Although young, his face had the worn quality of a weathered farm boy who smoked and drank too much.

'Camilla Bissonette,' she said, shaking his hand. 'Are you from NeuroPath?'

'Yeah, how'd you guess?' He let out an *isn't-that-something?* laugh. 'Looks *really* scary up there. Is it?' His tone was naive and boyish for his age.

'It is, but you get a great view,' she said.

She lifted a clear bag from her side, opened the zip lock, and lifted out the cut sample of the statue's skin, careful not to bend it or crack off the green patina. 'This is what I want to put under the microscope.'

'Oh, that's neat,' he said. 'Can I see?' A little boy again.

'I'd rather you didn't touch it,' she said, holding it in her palm.

'Wow,' he said. He looked up at the statue's face. 'Can you fix it?'

'Yes, but not in time for tomorrow.'

He looked puzzled. 'What's so special about tomorrow?'

'It's the Fourth of July, remember?'

He looked at her blankly, as if he'd never heard of the holiday. Then his smile returned and he opened a mesh bag holding some fresh fruit. 'Want some?'

'Thanks,' she said. Reaching in, she saw a tattoo on his right hand between his thumb and forefinger, a small black spider web with a tiny black cross at the apex.

She pulled out a Granny Smith apple. 'What's your job at the lab?' She took a bite.

'Eating wires and lighting fires.'

She stopped chewing. 'How's that again?'

'My favorite job is feeding the monkeys,' he said as if he hadn't heard his own answer. He lifted a banana out of the bag and clipped the empty mesh to a ring on his jumpsuit, then turned the banana upside down, stem to the ground, and snapped it open.

Maybe the altitude had made her dizzy. 'How'd you get a name like Spider?'

'I don't remember.' Holding the banana upside down, he pulled a strip of yellow skin from the bottom to the top. 'I think I got it in high school.'

In high school, and you can't remember?

He pulled the last strip of banana peel from the bottom to the top, turned the banana right side up like an ice-cream cone, and took a large bite. With his mouth full, he said, 'Dr Walker told me you know him.'

'Yes, we're old friends.'

Spider's grin showed banana pudding in the making. 'He's my friend too.' A happy child.

She bit into her apple. 'So when can we take a look at the sample?'

'Soon as you want,' he said.

'Then let's do it now.'

He finished wolfing down the banana and turned and found a trash container behind him. After tossing in the peel, he limped back, wiping his hands on the front of his jumpsuit. 'Ready when you are.'

'Do you always do that?'

'Do what?'

'Peel a banana from the bottom up?'

He looked down at his empty hands, then back at her with a blank face. 'I don't peel bananas any ways at all. I don't even *like* bananas.'

Cush Walker had thanked the union reps for coming and was preparing to leave with the stragglers when he saw three men still sitting in their seats near the front of the auditorium, waiting.

'Do you have a question?' he asked.

One of the men said, 'Yeah, Doc, I do.'

Cush backed up to the table and sat with his legs crossed casually at the ankles. He could feel the hostility in the room rising, sense it on his skin like a barometer.

'Since we're a small group,' he said, 'perhaps you'd be good enough to introduce yourselves.' Exchanging names, he'd discovered, often had a civilizing influence.

'Detective Sergeant Hart,' one of the men said in a loud voice. As the others gave their names, Cush noticed two men standing at the back of the room near the door with their backs turned toward him, heads lowered, talking quietly. After a few seconds, they faced front and walked down the aisle. The first was a tall, older man with salt and pepper hair who straightened his tie and pulled his sport coat down with a jerk, removing its wrinkles. The other was younger, probably in his mid-thirties, sandy-haired and ruggedly attractive, also in a sport coat and tie.

As they approached the front of the room, Cush said, 'And you?'

'Lieutenant Joseph Amerigo,' the older man said, taking a seat in the second row.

The younger man followed and sat down two seats away. 'Detective Nat Hennessy,' he said, 'Midtown South.' He took off his jacket and laid it on the seat next to him. 'I have a question, if you don't mind.'

'Go ahead,' Cush said.

'I'm curious about where all this BIAS stuff is leading to.' He unfurled a copy of the *Journal of Neuron Sciences*. 'I've been reading about how you repair brain injuries by rebuilding damaged neurons, and it just seems to me that if you can put that technique together with this BIAS test, you have the power to change the brains of people who don't think the way you want them to. I'd like to know what you want us to think.'

Cush took another drink of water. He knew who the 'us' was, and it didn't refer to him and 'his kind'. 'There's nothing in the BIAS test or in neuron reconstruction that's intended to tell someone how to think,' he said. But wouldn't it be fun to try with this guy?

The lieutenant leaned forward with his head turned slightly to the side and his hand cupped to his ear as if he was having difficulty hearing. Cush assumed he'd had an ear injury, maybe from a gun fired too close.

Sergeant Hart spoke before being acknowledged. 'What we're driving at, Doc, is whether this BIAS thing is a way for you people to get even with us people for what you people think has been a history of white supremacy and discrimination which guys like you think guys like me were responsible for even though we had nothin' to do with it.'

Oh, yeah, there it was: the cutting edge, even if somewhat humorously delivered. At least with cops it was out in the open, not hidden beneath an uptown, velvet cloak of contempt. Still, it made Cush's skin itch – but then, so what? Without an itch you couldn't scratch, and sometimes scratching felt good.

He looked at his watch. Only eleven o'clock. He took off his coat and laid it on the table, thinking, who knows? If he got lucky, maybe he'd get a chance to take off his gloves, too.

Sergeant Hart said to Amerigo, 'By the time he gets done with us, we'll be sending inner-city kids to summer camp and writing checks to the NAACP.'

'Not a bad idea,' Cush said, 'but it's not what BIAS does.'

Detective Hennessy said, 'But if you could identify racial prejudice and you had a magic pill or an X-ray or some scientific gizmo that changed the way people think, that wouldn't be such a bad idea, either, right?'

One of the guys said, 'I haven't even tried Viagra yet.'

'If fixing racism was that easy,' Cush saw Lieutenant Amerigo lean forward again so he raised his voice, 'if racism was that easy to fix, it would be great, but it isn't.' He added, 'At least not yet' – and immediately wished he hadn't. Fortunately, nobody picked up on it.

'Aw, come on, Doc,' Sergeant Hart said, 'the meeting's over, it's just us guys shooting the shit. After what you people have been through over the last two hundred years, if you could reverse the situation and put your own kind in control, you'd do it in a minute.'

Cush liked this guy's honesty and wanted to respond in kind. 'There probably isn't a black person alive who hasn't wondered what it would be like to live in America where blacks were in control, but—'

Hennessy cut him off. 'So you *would* like it?'

'Whether I'd like it or not is irrelevant because it isn't going to happen.'

'But what if it could?' Hennessy said.

Sergeant Hart turned to Nat and said, 'I'm telling you, that's where this thing is headed.'

What were they after? Cush felt a persistence, an agenda he couldn't quite figure out. They were trying to imagine the world upside down, with themselves at the bottom, but they had no idea what it would be like. The constant insults and suspicions, the liberal fawning that almost made everybody else's insults and suspicions feel good, the never-ending presence of color. Affirmative action? Compensation? Sensitivity? Jesus, most days he'd chuck them all for the blessings of simple indifference. But if these guys wanted to imagine a reversed world, why not help them?

'I'm curious about something,' Cush said, folding his arms and relaxing. 'What do you think would happen if the races did change places for a while?'

'It'd be a fuckin' disaster,' Sergeant Hart said.

'Why's that?'

'Because in my book black people aren't any better than white people, and if us white people are even *half* as bad as you black people say we are, I'd be fuckin' crazy to put you in charge of my ass.'

Cush had to smile, the man had a point. 'Not all white people with power are racist, Sergeant, and neither are all blacks.'

'But my friend here raises an interesting point,' Hennessy said. 'If black people were in charge, would they try to get even?'

There it was again, that goad.

'No doubt some would,' Cush said, 'but don't include me in that.'

'Oh, I wouldn't dream of it,' Hennessy said.

Cush felt heat prickles on his neck. It was more than a goad, it was a challenge. He felt like the performer in a comedy club he'd gone to one New Year's Eve where the guys in the audience with horns and paper hats were taunting the comic on stage with cracks like, 'Talk pussy or sit down!' and 'If it ain't dirty, we don't want to hear it!' Having taken all he could, the comedian finally ditched his routine and began telling them the dirty jokes they wanted, one after another, filthier and filthier ones until the women were covering their eyes and the men were staring silently at their beer bottles. He'd learned something interesting that night: sometimes the best thing you could give the assholes of life was exactly what they wanted.

'If the situation were reversed,' he said, 'I'd do exactly what decent white people do.'

The small group of men stared at him. 'What's that mean?' Hart said.

'It means I'd stop the black sheriff of Selma, Alabama, from using dogs and water hoses on you. It means I'd vote for legislation guaranteeing your right to eat in our restaurants, sleep in our hotels, and ride in the front of our buses. It means I wouldn't sit by and watch a black mob string you up to a tree for staring too long at a black woman.'

The men sat staring at him dumbly.

'It means I'd comfort you when you were castrated,' he said. 'And fight a civil war to free you from slavery.'

'I knew you weren't being serious,' Hart said.

'Let me tell you something serious, Sergeant. You couldn't find a black man who'd love you people the way I would.' *You people?* He'd actually said, 'You people.' Jesus, getting knee deep in pig shit was really easy – and kind of fun. 'Do you ever shoot hoops with your kids?'

'Sometimes.'

'There you go,' Cush said. 'A perfect example of your natural athletic ability.'

One of the men rose from his seat slowly and inched across the row and walked up the aisle to the door. Cush knew the guys remaining wanted to leave too, but like the audience in the comedy club that night, getting what they'd asked for had nailed them to their chairs.

'Yeah,' he said, 'I'd be one fine black citizen. Wars on poverty, civil rights, praying with whites in jail.'

129

Another cop got up and left, leaving Hennessy and Amerigo and Sergeant Hart and another cop behind. Watching the man go, Cush knew he should rein himself in. Insulting people, even jerks, was beneath him. But it felt too good to stop, and besides, they were cops, and cops could take as good as they gave.

'I'd lie in bed with my wife and watch sitcoms and wonder why black producers always seem to pick a fat white girl to be the star's sidekick. I'd organize prominent Afro-Americans to protest the lack of white actors in the movies and the constant portrayal of whites on the news as stupid, lazy, and criminal.'

Another policeman got up and left.

'I'd send our Betacams into the white suburban ghettos and show the country how the majority of white folks out there are just like us – hard-working, tax-paying, law-abiding citizens who want nothing more than a decent day's pay and a chance to ride around in their Winnebagos eating processed cheese and bowling and doing all those other wild and crazy things you white people like to do.'

He stared at the three men remaining. They stared back. Sergeant Hart said 'Fuck' under his breath and started to get up, but Hennessy put his hand on his shoulder and kept him in his seat.

'It's a fair question, Sergeant,' Cush said, 'wanting to know what it would be like being an honest-to-God, good black liberal in a powerful, black society.' He took another drink of water. Trapped like rats is what they were.

'I'd want to work for a presidential commission that studies the problems of race relations every ten years and comes to the same conclusions and issues the same reports. You have to do that sort of thing every few years because it gives you white people hope, and when you're at the bottom of the barrel, hope may be cheap but it means a lot.'

Hart had crossed his arms over his chest and sat red-faced. Lieutenant Amerigo leaned forward in his chair to hear better.

Hennessy sat back with his arm resting on the back of the seat next to him.

Cush knew he had to knock if off, but he didn't let up. 'I'll help you find your own white Frederick Douglass and Martin Luther King,' he said. 'I'll be in the front row in Oslo when the first white person in ten generations receives the Nobel Peace Prize for contributing to racial harmony. We need to give you that sort of award, not just for your sake, but for the sake of stability and continued black rule.'

The men sat apathetically, seeing, hearing, speaking no evil. Watching them, Cush thought what bugged him most wasn't their attitude, but what seemed to be their particular thick-headedness. Sometimes white people could be so incredibly, infuriatingly . . . *dense.*

He knew he was insulting them now, but screw it. He was going to put a small dent in their brain pans.

'I'd want to send a check to a white woman named Jessica Jackson to finance a tour around the country teaching whites that they *are* somebody. I'd really want to see that – white kids sitting in class chanting, "I am somebody."'

'That's it,' Sergeant Hart said. He got up and walked out of the room.

'How about interracial dating?' Hennessy said coolly.

'I'd be happy to see my six-year-old daughter bring home a little white boy and watch them play together,' Cush said. 'And when she's a teenager and wants to date him, I wouldn't tell her what she can and can't do, I'd just sit her down and warn her about the trials and tribulations that lie ahead and say, it's your decision, honey, and I respect whatever it is, and – oh, my goodness, what's this? A ticket to France for the summer? No, not for two, sweetheart, but Scott or Chad or Bruce or whatever the hell your white boyfriend's name is, don't worry, he'll be waiting for you when you get back.'

'And sex?'

'What about it?'

'Whatever.'

This guy Hennessy was really asking for it.

Don't do it. Don't say it. You've already gone too far.

What the hell.

'I'd march against the blacks who screwed your women like goats and broke apart your families and used you to build the country and then told you to kiss the black man's ass or go back to Northern Europe.'

Holy shit, talk about too far.

Damn, that felt good.

Detective Hennessy looked at his wristwatch and leaned forward in his chair with his palms on his knees, ready to rise. Lieutenant Amerigo raised his hands toward the ceiling in a relaxing stretch. A second later they both stood up and Detective Hennessy put on his sport coat. He stared at Cush and assessed him silently, man to man.

'Thank you for being so candid,' he said.

Cush was starting to cool off now, feeling his self-control and self-censorship returning. 'If I was *too* candid—'

'No, no, definitely not,' Hennessy said. 'The subject is too important not to be honest.'

The two cops walked up the auditorium aisle toward the door. Cush sat on his folding chair and felt his legs quake and his eyelids twitch as he watched them go out the door. Finally, he took a deep breath and calmed himself.

Free at last.

'This is the place.' Spider Murphy ushered Camilla into a small room with white, clinical walls and a radio playing softly. In front of her was NeuroPath Labs' scanning electron microscope, a putty-gray console about the size of a desk with a three-foot-high tube on top that shot electrons into whatever substance was being examined – in this case, a sample of the statue's skin. In front of the apparatus was a panel of dials, switches, and two large monitors and oscilloscopes. The room's lights were dimmed to make the screens easier to read.

'The guy who runs the microscope is Mr Rodriguez,' Spider said, 'but he's not here.'

Too bad. She had been under the impression he would be.

Spider checked his watch. 'Want to see my favorite place?'

She had wedding errands to run, but Spider was already out the door and moving down the hallway. She followed him, saying she had only a minute. He pushed open a door and she entered, instantly smelling the warm, stinky air of a zoo.

'This is where we keep the animals.'

'Oh, look at him,' Camilla said. Sitting in a cage on a table was a cute monkey with clear black eyes and a shiny brown coat.

'This is Cain,' Spider said. 'Say hi to our guest, Cain.'

The monkey waved his hand up and down.

'Well, aren't you smart?' Camilla said.

'That just means he wants something to eat,' Spider said. He lifted a large white tag dangling on the side of the cage. 'He's allowed to have a snack now.'

He limped to the refrigerator and took out two small, yellow-green bananas and brought them back to the cage, setting one on the table. Reaching through the bars, Cain grabbed the other one out of his hand, backed into a corner, and turned the fruit around and around, inspecting it. After a moment he raised it to his mouth, cracked open the skin at the middle, and dug the meat out with his fingers. Once he'd eaten it, he tossed the peel onto the floor.

'Dr Walker's in a meeting with the police,' Spider said.

'I'll see him another time,' Camilla said, partly disappointed, mostly relieved.

'Maybe tomorrow?' Spider said.

'I don't think so,' she said. 'Friday's the Fourth, remember? And the next day I'm getting married.'

'Wow. Who's the husband?'

'A detective with the New York City Police Department.'

He moved a coffee mug on the top of his desk. 'Does he like being married?'

She tried to understand the question. 'Does *who* like being married?'

'Your husband.'

'You mean my husband *to be*. We're not married yet.' She knew he had a head problem, but this was weird. She felt like a kindergarten teacher every time they talked.

Spider blinked once, obviously embarrassed, then looked at his watch even though he'd wound it only seconds before.

'I have to be going now,' Camilla said. She pulled the sling bag off her shoulder and took out the envelope of copper cuttings she'd taken from the statue. 'Would you mind laying these on Dr Walker's desk? He'll know what to do with them.'

'Sure,' Spider said.

She scribbled a note on a piece of paper. 'Dear Cush: It's been much too long, hasn't it? Thank you for doing this. Hope you're well. Warmest. Camilla.' After sticking it into the envelope, she handed it to him.

'Wait for me to come back and get you,' he said. 'You can't walk around here without an ek-sort – an eks—'

'Escort.'

'An ek-sort. It's a rule.' He left the room carrying the samples in the palms of his hands, like water.

She checked the time and dawdled, waiting for him to return. Looking at the monkeys, she wondered what kind of experiments they did on them. They certainly looked fine to her.

She wandered toward the cage by the refrigerator, checked her watch again and debated whether to leave or wait. *Come on, Spider.* She had to pick up her wedding shoes and make sure they'd been dyed the color of the ivory swatch. If they'd done it wrong, after one o'clock there'd be no time left to do it right.

She saw the banana lying on the table in front of Cain's cage. Across the aisle was another cage with a cotton cover over the top two-thirds of it. She picked up the fruit and stepped to the covered cage and looked at the tag hanging at the side. ABEL, it said. Isn't that interesting. Must be Cain's brother.

She lifted the cover and looked inside. A monkey sat quietly in a corner, less animated and cheerful than Cain.

'Hey, boy, what's the matter?' she asked softly.

He looked at her curiously. She held up the banana and made clicking sounds with her mouth, inviting him over.

He continued staring at her, his eyes going dead. Isn't that strange? It's like he's in a trance, trying to figure out who I am.

She was frozen with curiosity—

He sprang forward, teeth bared, voice screeching, spitting wildly – and snatched the banana out of her hand.

She fell back against the cages on the opposite table. Good God, what was *that* all about? Her heart was beating hard, fueled by adrenaline and the effects of fear. She brushed off the monkey's foamy saliva from her arms and chest.

Forget the ek–sort, she wanted out of there.

She walked to the doorway and, getting control of herself, stopped to decide whether to replace the cover she'd lifted off Abel's cage. He was in the corner inspecting the banana he'd snatched. After sniffing and feeling it, he brought it to his mouth and split the skin with his teeth, not in the center as Cain had, but at the top the way humans did.

She didn't move.

He held the banana at eye level, contemplating it, then turned the banana around, top down, and grabbed a tab of peel and zipped it upward – once, twice, three times – until the unsheathed meat was in his hand. Exactly the way Spider Murphy had done at the statue.

She stood watching. Wondering. Trying to speculate, but not knowing where to begin.

'Here I am,' Spider said, coming through the door.

She hiked her bag strap over her shoulder and started for the door. 'I gave Abel a banana,' she said.

Spider stopped, alarmed, then went to Abel's cage and consulted the feeding schedule on the large white tag. 'It's OK,' he said, obviously relieved.

Camilla opened the door and stepped into the hallway and waited for him to join her. Walking toward the elevator, she said, 'He peeled it upside down, you know.'

Spider showed no reaction.

'Did you teach him how to do that?' she said.

'Do what?'

'Peel a banana upside down. Did you teach him or did he teach you?'

Spider looked as if she was speaking a foreign language. 'What do you mean?'

Here we go again.

They drove north on Third Avenue toward the Willis Avenue

Bridge, one of Manhattan's links to the South Bronx, the location of Dolly's apartment. Once they crossed the Harlem River, their unmarked Chevrolet would announce itself as a police car, but only to the street-smart people who weren't supposed to know.

'Did she sound cooperative?' he asked.

'Not at first,' Shaw said. 'I asked her if she knew Tangerine or Angel Rico and got nothing, so I told her we had her address and were coming up to see her anyway.'

'That's what we should have done in the first place, show up unannounced,' Nat said.

'We couldn't. The phone number on the perfume bottle was a cell phone, which means I didn't have her address. I faked it.'

Not bad, Nat thought.

'I gave her my name and yours and our office number,' Shaw said. 'She hung up and I figured that was the last we'd hear from her, but fifteen minutes later she called back and said come on up, she had no problem talking.' She looked at Nat. 'Why do you suppose she changed her mind so fast?'

'Who knows?' Nat said. 'She's probably a flake.'

As Nat approached 96th Street he slowed and pulled over to the curb on the left side of the one-way street. Engine idling, he rolled down the window and waited, and in a moment a man wearing a zipped-up satin baseball jacket, nicely creased suit pants, expensive shoes and a cap pulled low on his forehead emerged from a tobacco shop and walked to the car. He obviously wasn't a street-corner kind of guy.

Nat reached beneath the driver's seat and pulled out a letter-size envelope and handed it through the window. There was no writing on it, but it bulged in the middle from an object about the size of a deck of cards. Saying nothing, the man took it and walked away. Nat rolled up the window, hit the accelerator, drove through a red light, and headed toward the Harlem River.

'What was that all about?' Shaw asked.

'Getting a watch fixed,' Nat said.

'Really,' she said. 'Looked more like a drug deal to me.'

Nat smiled. 'I guess it did at that.'

'I've seen that guy someplace,' she said.

He barreled through green and yellow traffic lights.

'It's the cap that's throwing me off.' She waited for a hint. 'I know, he's an actor on a TV show, right? Or is it the movies?'

Nat said, 'Let's stop at Louie's Diner for a sandwich and an egg cream.'

Camilla stood at the kitchen counter chopping carrots and snapping the ends off green beans, preparing an eleven o'clock dinner. Her raven hair was tied back with a strip of silk, smooth and shiny, and her cheeks glowed as if the kitchen was hot even though it wasn't. Over her jeans was a paint-speckled sculptor's apron. Her fingers were perfectly tapered, her often-broken, much-worked-on nails oval and clear.

She was preoccupied with a *déjà vu* that wouldn't reveal itself. Something stalking her from the shadows of her mind.

Nat walked in. 'Hi, sweetheart.'

He stopped at the center island which was covered with newspapers, lists of things to do for the wedding, swatches of cloth, unopened mail, a bowl of fresh fruit, spices, magazines, and place mats. After pouring a glass of red wine for her, he found a beer in the refrigerator, circled the island, and took the paring knife from her hand. Then he wrapped his arms around her and gave her a long kitchen kiss, the kind he remembered his father giving his mother.

He handed her the glass of red and guided her to the stool and sat her down, then took her place at the wok, slicing mushrooms on a board while she read her list.

The telephone rang and she picked it up. It was Lucy, her best friend, calling with a report from the wedding front. She'd decorated one of the tables in the garden of the Chelsea brownstone where they'd have the ceremony and the reception and it looked fantastic. Should the candles be lit in the daytime? she asked. The calligrapher had done a great job on the place cards, and the flowers – mostly white freesias – would look marvelous. Camilla listened to her with one ear while Nat whispered in the other. Pushing him away, she told Lucy she was in the middle of something, she'd have to call her back.

'What are you doing?' she said playfully, hanging up.

'I love the way you look,' he said. He'd stood against the counter, arms folded. His hands relaxed and he took a step toward her.

'Stay back!' she said, making a cross with her fingers. 'You're burning the mushrooms.' He chased her around the island. 'Nat,' she said, pleadingly, 'don't you dare.' Smoke rose from the wok. She pointed at it. He stopped pursuing and stirred the pan and lowered the flame.

She lifted a letter from the counter. 'Have you ever heard of a trust that held documents instead of money?' she asked.

'No, why?'

'Before Grandma Camilla's father died he created a trust filled with confidential documents to be released to the press. What do you make of that?'

'Have you seen any of them?'

'No, just this letter of instructions.'

He dropped cubes of chicken and vegetables into the metal bowl. They sizzled. He stirred. She read her magazine. He looked at his watch. 'Mind if I watch the eleven o'clock news?' he said.

Still reading, she picked up the remote control, aimed it at the TV set on the counter, and turned it on. Was it about the wedding, this free-floating anxiety she was having? Or was it about visiting the lab today, thinking about Cush and why she'd left him . . . what she'd seen in the field that night . . . the chill she'd felt when she'd read the first page of the memo she'd received by mistake.

She turned the page of the magazine and looked at an article.

Maybe it was about Nat. Their argument . . . the game they'd played on the chaise . . . the silliness of it. So what if she didn't know every detail about his psychological make-up? Who did?

She lingered on a picture of a chocolate-covered banana split.

But was his attitude about blacks really a detail? Sure it was. No, it wasn't.

Oh, shut up and relax.

She pushed a bowl of fruit aside to make room for the plates and picked up a fork. 'Have you ever seen somebody peel a banana from the bottom up?'

'What do you mean?'

'You know, from the bottom up, like this.' She mimicked it.

He shook his head.

'I saw a guy do it this morning,' she said. 'When I asked him why, he said he didn't know what I was talking about.'

'Who was it?'

'A guy named Spider Murphy.' She took a sip of wine. 'He works at NeuroPath Labs.' She waited for a reaction but heard nothing. 'I went there this morning to drop off samples of the statue's skin and saw a monkey do the same thing.'

'Maybe your friend Murphy taught him how to do it. Or vice versa.'

'Maybe, but he was so *strange*. He had a tattoo on his hand.' She doodled on the newspaper and lifted it up. 'It looked like this.' In the margin was the triangular spider web with a small cross at the apex.

'You saw that on his hand?' Nat said.

'Yes.'

'Between the thumb and forefinger?'

'Yeah, how'd you know?'

'That's the tattoo of Aryan Reign. Your friend is a skinhead.'

'A skinhead? But he was so sweet.'

'I'll tell you about sweet.' He carried the wok to the island. 'Four years ago a bunch of these guys beat up a Jewish couple so badly the man died and his wife was in a coma for two months. I picked up one of them at the Port Authority.'

She looked at her own drawing. 'A skinhead working in a world-class neurology lab? What's going on?' She served herself and speared a piece of chicken. 'Aren't you going to say something about my visiting NeuroPath?'

'What's to say?'

'Aren't you, like, a little curious about my seeing Cush?'

'Not in the least.'

How grown up. 'Why not?'

He turned up the volume on the television set. 'Tell you in a second.' The evening news was about to start. Dramatic music, helicopters, an announcer saying, '. . . Eyewitness News with Dave Jasper and Sandra Chin . . .'

The anchorman said, 'A controversial test to eliminate racial bias from the New York Police Department has been hit by a bombshell. Here with the exclusive report is Jay Daley live at City Hall. Jay?'

A reporter stood in front of a government building with a clipboard in his hand.

'Dave, after a tense meeting this morning between representatives of the various police unions – the majority of whom are white and *vehemently* opposed to the BIAS test – Dr Cush Walker, the president of NeuroPath Labs who invented the test, was secretly tape-recorded by someone during an unusually candid exchange of views. Apparently unaware that he was being taped, he made some *extraordinary* comments which are now threatening to blow apart the fragile coalition of council members.'

Cush was stepping out of the shower, reaching for a towel,

when he heard the word 'BIAS' on TV. Looking through the bathroom door, he saw words appear on the screen while a recorded voice played beneath. At first he didn't recognize it as his own. Then—

Oh, shit.

He scrambled for the remote and turned up the volume. It was him, telling the hangers-on at the meeting what it would be like if black people were in charge and whites were the minority. Played over an on-screen transcript, he heard his own icy, angry voice saying he wouldn't sit by and watch a mob of angry blacks string up a white man for staring too long at a black woman.

Good God, had he really said that?

That and more. He stood and listened.

A voice – his own voice – said he'd comfort white guys who were castrated.

Sweet Jesus.

He sagged on the bed next to the open suitcase he was packing for his return to Mississippi. More words appeared, some bleeped out because they were too raw for decent people's living rooms.

He raised his hands into the air in a spontaneous surrender. He wanted to turn off the set but he couldn't. The movie was rotten, but he was the star.

He heard his voice repeat other things he'd said, finally ending with his crack that he wanted to see white kids sitting in a classroom chanting, 'I am somebody.' It was the last self-inflicted wound they used, at least in this broadcast. Good Lord. They must have had it all – every cute, angry, profane, self-indulgent, articulate, race-baiting, ass-whipping comment he'd made.

There was a back-and-forth between the anchorman and the reporter about whether this 'dynamite' was going to 'blow up' BIAS, and that was it. He turned off the set and heard the crinkling sound of the cooling picture tube.

I really fucked myself this time.

He picked up a fresh shirt, and as he got dressed, played back the morning session in his head. It all made sense now – Detective Hennessy and Lieutenant Amerigo at the back of the room setting up their tape recorder and microphone, Amerigo's hand cupped to his ear as if he was hard of hearing so that Cush would speak up. Sergeant Hart, a good ol' boy who may or may not have been in on the deal – he would have spoken the same mind either way.

Cush finished dressing, grabbed his bag, and went out the door.

Mr MIT. Mr Smart Guy. Mr Cool Nobel Candidate. Taken to the woodshed by a couple of cops with a twenty-dollar tape recorder.

Hard to believe.

'I find it hard to believe,' Camilla said. 'It's just not like him to say things like that.'

Nat was still watching the TV set. 'He didn't say anything he didn't mean to say.'

'How do you know?'

'I was there.'

'This morning?'

'Yeah.'

'When those comments got recorded?'

'Heard them with my own ears.'

'No wonder you didn't care if I went to NeuroPath, you knew Cush wasn't there.' She swatted at him. 'How could they do this to him?'

'Nobody put the words in his mouth.'

'Yeah, but *come on*. He thought he was off the record, not making a speech.'

'Which is why it was honest instead of bullshit.'

'But out of context. How many times have you said the press kills the police with nine-second soundbites?'

He looked at his watch. 'I'm late.' He stuck an apple into his mouth and pulled on his sport coat.

She watched him. 'It wasn't you, was it?'

'Wadn't me whut?' he said through the apple.

'Who taped him?'

He stopped and looked at her a moment, then he opened his jacket, lifted his shirt, and showed her his naked midsection. 'Shee a wahr?'

No, she saw no wire, only hard abs. She watched him stuff his shirt tails into his pants, take a bite of the apple, and reach up to the ceramic chicken for his holstered .38 special.

She picked up the dinner plates and put them into the sink.

He took the apple from his mouth – 'I'll do those when I get back' – and ran his belt through the holster.

'When you get back, can we talk?'

'Sure, baby.' He buckled his belt. 'Anything in particular?'

'I feel like we need to clear the air about something, that's all.'

'Want to tell me what it is so I can worry about it needlessly while I should be focused on the job?'

'We'll talk.'

'OK.' He started to give her a kiss but she dodged it and gave him a patting hug instead. 'That bad, huh?' he said.

'We'll talk.'

Nat and Shaw drove their NYPD unmarked Ford up the East River Drive toward the Bronx, listening to the news at midnight.

'Do you talk to your partner about personal things, or are you all professional?' Nat said.

'I was a psych major and a woman, so I love to talk,' Shaw said. 'The woman part still holds true.'

'A psych major,' he said. 'Why didn't you become a shrink?'

'Not enough patience. Most people never change.'

They drove in silence, listening to news accounts: a mugging, a robbery, an assault, a fire.

Nat said, 'Have you ever done something really low and underhanded that made you feel like a first-class asshole?'

'Sure, who hasn't?'

'What did you do?' he asked.

'I secretly tape-recorded a prominent black neurosurgeon while he was talking to a group of cops off the record.'

He looked as if she'd just pulled down his pants.

'I own a television set, Nat. The guy you gave the envelope to yesterday was Jay Daley, Eye-Witless News. Hello?'

'Amerigo wore the wire, not me.'

'Oh, of course. How could you do that when you were sprouting wings?'

'Walker wasn't off the record.'

'Sure he was.'

'OK, he was.' Let it sink in. 'Fuck.'

'So which devil made you do it? Jealousy?'

'What does it matter? I'm hopeless.'

'It's worse than that. You're a guy.'

He drove two blocks without talking.

'I've got to get control of my life,' he said.

They listened to a news report of a woman who got caught hiring a man to kill her husband so she could collect his lottery winnings. The husband begged the judge not to put her in jail because he feared it would ruin their marriage. 'Love is a state of insanity anyway,' the man said. The judge gave her probation.

'You ever married?' Nat asked.

'Close but not quite. I take it this is your first?'

'Yeah.'

'You happy about it?' she said.

'I fell in love with her the minute I saw her.' He pulled out his wallet and opened it to a photograph of Camilla standing at a workbench in the loft, wearing denim and cotton.

'I love stories like that,' she said. She looked at the photograph. 'And I hate women like this. Anyone who looks this good in jeans and a T-shirt should be banned for life.' She handed back the wallet. 'Are you nervous?'

'About the wedding, no. About blowing it later, a little.'

'I thought the two of you were already living together.'

'We are, but everybody says marriage changes everything.'

'Not if you remember rule number one: eye contact. If you can look each other in the eye, everything will be OK.'

Right now he couldn't look a dog in the eye.

He drove up the ramp to the Willis Avenue Bridge. Approaching Yankee Stadium, the scene of his childhood battlefield, cleared his mental palate and made him nervous. He pushed it out of his mind.

'What are you supposed to own up to before you're married?' he asked.

'Very simple. If it matters, confess. If it doesn't, don't.'

'You actually paid tuition for that?' He turned left onto the bridge.

'I assume you're talking about who you slept with,' she said.

'What makes you say that?'

'The neon sign.'

They listened to the tires hum on the metal grating. Ahead of them was the Deegan and the Cross Bronx Expressway, two arteries built in the thirties that had severed the borough's beautiful old neighborhoods and left them to die.

'The rule on past affairs depends,' she said. 'If you slept with somebody and that's all, you don't need to confess it, but if you gave her a kid who's going to be knocking at your door looking for lunch money, you should probably tell her.'

He drove over the Deegan and entered a land of broken concrete sidewalks, steel window gates, potholes, and dirty brick tenements. Rolling down the window, he thought even the air smelled different here, full of stale French fries and smoking piston rings. There was a decrepit wildness about the place that still taunted him with memories of his father's death.

'What about something from your childhood?' he said. 'Something that still bugs you?'

'In order to give you an airtight answer on the level of a Dear Abby, I'd have to know what the problem is.' She glanced over at him. 'Trust me, I'm not asking.'

They drove in silence.

'Who'd you almost marry?' Nat said.

'A jerk.'

'Congratulations.'

'Yeah, I really dodged a bullet.' She leaned forward and turned off the radio. 'I seem to be a sucker for guys with good derrières.' She sat back and watched the skyline go by. To the window, she said, 'I gotta get over that.'

They drove the rest of the way without talking. They were so close to Yankee Stadium he could feel the weight of it pressing on his chest. He touched the scar under his chin and pictured it again: a July night just like this one, bottles crashing onto the pavement, the girl at the bonfire, his father, saying, wait here, I'll be right back. He could still see him walking down the path toward the man in the baggy pants, see the man pick up a baseball bat, hear the skinny man with the mustache talking to his father . . .

'Tell me what I should know about Angel Rico,' Sally Shaw said. They sat at the curb on a side street with the car's lights out.

'He'll roll over when you think you've got him, then slit your throat and walk away like it never happened.'

'Like he killed Tangerine.'

'Exactly.'

They sat in silence. 'So how's he out in three?' she said.

'You know how it works.' He wasn't interested in talking about the criminal justice system right now.

She let out a sigh. 'Look, all I want to know is whatever's going to help me do my job, OK?'

He looked over at her. 'You know, for a rookie, you sure got a lot of attitude.' She'd learn in time that he always turned quiet before making a collar. 'OK, here's the story. When Angel finally figured out I had enough to put him away, he tried to plead down from felony murder to manslaughter. The DA told him it was too late for that unless he had something good. Angel thinks about it and comes up with two stories, one about a drug dealer, which Detective D'Onofrio took, the other about this pimp he said he was working for when he killed Debbie Duzzit. I took that one, but it turned out the only thing he had to give us was the guy's telephone number and street name, Bambino. Perfect handle for a black guy from the Bronx, right?'

He reached into her stock of Reese's Peanut Butter Cups, took one out, and peeled off the wrapper. She ate so many of these things, he expected to see an elephant chasing her down the street one of these days.

'He sets up a meeting between me and this guy Bambino at a bar not far from here. Dede's,' he said, popping in the candy. 'We thought there was a pretty good chance Bambino didn't know we'd arrested his hit man, but we weren't sure.'

'So you had plenty of backup.'

'Yeah, lots of backup.' He looked at her. 'Seasoned guys.'

Her face said, thanks.

'So I go into Dede's pretending to be some slick guy from Newark with a pipeline of runaway girls I'm looking to put on the street. When I come in, my partner and two backups are sitting at the bar having a drink, watching a Knicks game. Should be OK, I think.' His eyes followed a kid walking across the street in front of the car.

'What happened?'

'The Bambino wasn't there, only a couple of his skells. The three of us go into the storage room where they keep the beer and peanuts, and right off the bat they don't like me. I look too straight. They smell a rat. So now I'm back there sweating bullets, waiting for my guys to come in and bail me out, but they aren't coming because I told them to sit tight and give me some time.' Nat was still scoping out the street.

'Did they come?'

'See that building down at the end of the block?' he said. 'The one with the busted fire escape?'

'Yeah?'

'If your friend Dolly isn't jerking us around, that's where Angel Rico lives.' He lifted his right foot off the floor and placed it on the gear shift console.

She stared at the building a moment, then pulled out her revolver. Chambers loaded, barrel rotating freely. 'So what happened?'

Nat retied the lace on one rubber-soled shoe. 'I bullshitted the goons long enough for my guys to come looking for me,' he said, lowering his right shoe, 'but it was too late, the guns were already out. There were thirteen shots fired. My partner, Ben Brown, took one in the stomach.' He dropped his foot to the floor and looked at her. 'You ready to go?'

'I will be as soon as you tell me what happened to Ben Brown.'

He looked at her skeptically. 'You asking out of a concern for him or yourself?'

'Myself.'

He smiled. 'I feel better about you already.'

He tucked the end of his necktie into his shirt beneath the third button down, a habit he'd picked up after seeing a guy in a movie get his tie caught in a moving gear that ground his face to hamburger. 'He took early retirement on full disability,' he said. 'Runs a little travel agency in the city and lives in Barbados in the winter.' He turned toward her. 'That's the trick, you know. Take a bullet that doesn't kill you but does enough damage to put you on the beach.'

She shook her head, no thanks. 'Did Rico set you up?'

'I thought so, but the story he gave D'Onofrio panned out, so he got his manslaughter two.' He opened his door.

'Wait a minute,' she said. 'If I'm your backup, how do I know how long to wait?'

Nat sat back with one foot out the door. 'Rule number one: never hit the panic button. The guys from the Forty-fourth would cream their Calvins if they could bail out a couple of cops from Mid South. Rule number two: when all else fails, check your ring.'

'My ring?'

His face fell. 'Don't tell me you forgot your glow-in-the-dark Sky King ring.'

She looked away, what have I done to deserve this?

He got out and closed the door. She leaned across the driver's seat to lock it and roll up his window. He walked around the front of the car and stepped onto the curb and waited for her to join him.

Looking down the sidewalk, he saw a man approaching in jeans, sneakers, and a shiny white silk T-shirt. A gold chain circled his neck and a black leather bag hung on his shoulder. When he was ten yards away, he slowed down and stared at Nat.

Nat stared back.

The man stopped, his face saying, *Uh-oh.*

'Angel Rico,' Nat said. 'Just the man I was—'

The man spun around and took off.

Nat ran after him.

Sally Shaw was still in the car rolling up the windows.

Rico ran to the corner and crossed the empty street and headed toward the tenement where Dolly had said he lived. Nat ran as fast as he could, keeping him in sight, but Angel was lighter and faster and quickly put twenty, thirty yards between them.

Nat drew his weapon and yelled, 'Freeze, motherfucker!'

Rico didn't. He turned the corner of the building and disappeared. Nat ran with his gun pointed forward, not upward the way they did in TV shows – you could shoot yourself in the nose that way – or downward – you could shoot something worse – ready to fire without needing to take time to level his weapon. God, he hated guns. He'd taken target practice only three days earlier and the noise was still rattling around inside his head. And for what? At fifty feet he couldn't hit a billboard.

When he came to the corner, he slipped his finger inside the trigger guard and peeked around the brick building. It was a service alley. At the end of it a side door to the building was just closing.

He ran to it, pulled it open before it locked, and stood back. Other than the sound of his own panting, he heard nothing. He stuck his head inside the doorway and jerked it back. No sign of life, no light. He waited, heart pounding, out of breath, hoping to hear a noise.

Nothing.

He listened for a sign – footsteps, a voice, a pair of lungs heaving like his own. Still nothing. Where are you, Angel? Rico's weapon of choice was a knife, but who knew what he was carrying in the bag?

He heard the sound of a door echo several floors up a stairwell.

That's where you are.

He pulled off his necktie, wrapped it around the outside doorknob, drew it across the latch plate to hold back the bolt, and tied the other end onto the inside knob. After entering, he found the steps and began climbing, eyes turned upward. The door behind him closed with the snap of a bolt into the metal strike. Damn, the tie hadn't held. Would she see the end of it hanging outside? Could she open the door if she did?

His eyes were adjusting to the blackness. He climbed the stair past the first-floor entrance and tried the door. No problem. It was open. No fancy steel fire doors in this building. He walked up to the second floor, trying to gauge the distance of the sound he'd heard, guessing it had come from the third or fourth floor.

Reaching the third, he opened the door. The hallway was lit by a single circular neon bulb, a halo in the center of the ceiling. Where was Rico? In the wilderness you had broken twigs and matted grass and footprints in the mud, but in the South Bronx you had nothing, not even sneaker marks on the floor. Damn city life.

The hallway felt deserted. At the end of it was a corridor that crossed it like the bar at the top of a T. He closed the door and climbed to four, the highest floor in the structure. Opening it, he found the same thing he'd found on three: annoying silence, the smell of garlic, a dim neon light that turned his skin sickly green.

He entered and walked down the hallway with his gun in hand, touching each door he passed to see if it was open. There were four apartments on each side of the hallway. He touched the first door – nothing – then did the same across the hall. Tight and quiet.

He moved to the second door on his left and placed his fingertips on the wooden surface, feeling for sound – a TV set, a stereo, a pair of feet, voices, anything that vibrated. He felt a steady thump, a bass on a stereo. He put his ear to the door and heard a Latin beat – salsa, merengue, tango? How the fuck was he supposed to know? He was Irish. Then the roar of a crowd on a television set – somebody having a beer and watching ESPN clips. Baseball at this hour? Yeah, sure. He wasn't in America now, he was in the Bronx annex of the Dominican Republic, a place where guys were known to walk out on their wives in the middle of labor just to catch a ninth-innings rally.

He turned toward the door and raised his hand to knock, debating whether he should wait for Shaw – assuming she could find him. Before his knuckles hit the door he heard a sound to his right, down the hall. He turned, crouched, and aimed – *I'm gonna take a bullet!*

The last apartment door on the right opened far enough to reveal a sixty-something black woman wearing a knee-length chenille housecoat, curlers, and a pair of matted pink slippers at the bottom of two Popsicle-stick legs. A cigarette dangled from her lips, its smoke rising incense-like from the tip. Her eyes remained unfazed even though she was looking at a gun pointed directly at her chest by a white cop.

Nat stood up slowly. The old woman stared back.

He pointed at the door where the TV was playing. She shook her head. He pointed at the door across the hall. She shook her head again. He frowned. Where then? She nodded once toward the end of the hallway. He nodded back, got it. She closed the door.

He moved toward the end of the main hallway where the top of the T crossed the corridor, hugging the left wall as he approached it, not knowing whether Rico was around the corner to the left or the right.

Reaching the end of the wall, he waited. There was no sound. Leaning forward, he glanced down to his right and quickly pulled back. He'd glimpsed two apartment doors near the end of the hall, and across from them grimy windows overlooking the street. He relaxed his gun hand, gripped it again firmly, and peeked around the corner to the left. No one there, either. He stuck his head out and looked longer. Twenty feet away at the end of the corridor was a partly opened door leading up some steps to a metal door to the roof.

That's where he was. Had to be.

He pictured the tenement as he'd seen it in the alley and didn't think the adjacent building was close enough for a rooftop leap. Maybe there was a working fire escape and Rico was long gone.

Then again, maybe not.

His gun handle was sweaty. He turned the corner and walked past a broken fire alarm box and vertical water pipes with crusty valves on the wall. Pushing open the inner door to the roof, he found the concrete steps. The ceiling above the stairwell was agape, as if someone had been working on it months ago and abandoned it. There were visible metal cross beams strung with cobwebs and a skewed handful of ceiling tiles on top of them.

He placed his foot on the first step and was raising his weight onto it when he felt something tap him on his left shoulder – *behind you!* He spun around but there was no one there. Then he felt it again – a ghostly tap on his shoulder. He glanced at his shoulder and saw bits of crumbling material falling on it.

He looked up just as Angel Rico jumped down.

Angel's foot hit Nat's gun hand first, knocking the weapon to the floor and Nat onto his back. Falling at an angle, Angel's feet hit the ground first, then his butt, back, and elbows. He scrambled to his feet holding a knife in his right hand.

Nat rose to his feet keeping his eyes on his attacker, not looking for his gun, trying to hold Angel's attention so he wouldn't look for it either. Both of them were breathing like horses.

Angel took a step toward him, slightly bent forward as if ready to spring, holding the knife with the shank protruding from the heel of his fist so it would slash when he took a prison yard swing.

Which he did.

Nat jumped back and sucked in his gut like a batter avoiding a brush-back pitch. The five-inch blade flashed in a horizontal arc and sliced through a buttonhole on his coat. Nat grabbed Angel's moving arm and spun him around, kicking his feet from under him and dropping him onto his back, then kicking at the knife in his hand, missing it, and smashing his big toe against the pipes on the wall. The impact spread the bones in his foot, lighting it up with pain.

He fell on his back, grimacing, and rolled onto his hands and knees. His gun – where was it? – had to be in that direction. He saw it lying on the floor about six, seven feet away, equidistant from himself and Angel. Angel was rising to his feet, still gripping his knife.

Nat saw him crouch, eyes focused and mean. Nat looked right, jumped left, and grabbed the gun before Angel saw it. Fumbling it, he turned onto his back and pointed the muzzle in Angel's general direction, searching wildly to get his finger inside the trigger guard and get the web of his hand off the hammer. If he'd had to fire, he couldn't have.

But Angel didn't know that. Seeing the gun pointed at him, he stopped and straightened up.

Nat cocked the firing pin and rose onto his left elbow. He nodded the barrel up and down – drop the knife – and Angel complied.

Nat rose to his hip, then to his knees, and motioned Angel to sit with his back against the wall. Angel moved like a creaky old man but dropped into place. In a quick thrust, Nat jammed the muzzle of his .38 special against Angel's forehead, dead center between the eyes. Even a bad shot like him couldn't miss from here.

'You fucking little prick.'

Angel's lungs were heaving and his eyes were so large and dry they made a clicking sound when he blinked. 'What the fuck . . . chu want with me, man?'

Nat pulled a pair of handcuffs from the back of his belt and clicked one onto Angel's right wrist, then slipped the other behind the peeling water pipe above a metal clamp. 'Up,' he said, and Angel raised his other hand for the second stainless-steel click. The 'fucking little prick' was now strung up like a slab of meat on a hook.

Nat pulled his gun away from Angel's head, leaving a dent in the skin, and wiped the sweat from his eyes. 'Last time you saw me you said you wanted a piece of me,' he said. 'Go for it.'

'Fuck you, man. I'm clean.'

Nat looked around and found the knife and picked it up, closed the switchblade, and dropped it into the side pocket of his jacket. Sitting still, breathing easier, he surveyed the hallway.

No one had heard the commotion – or, if they had, they'd decided not to come out. On the floor next to Angel was the black leather shoulder bag he'd been carrying, littered with bits of ceiling tile.

'Hey, cop, you got a warrant?' Angel said.

'I don't need a warrant, asshole, I got your invitation.' The pain in his foot was getting serious.

'What in-bitation you talkin' 'bout, man?'

'The one you left in the ladies' room at Grand Central.' He could feel his big toe swelling in his shoe.

He rose to one knee, keeping the weight on his heel, and grabbed the pipe to pull himself up. After hopping on his left foot to get his balance, he set his right foot on the floor to test it. The moment it touched the floor a bolt of pain shot up his leg. 'Shit,' he muttered, and sat down.

'I don't know nothin' 'bout no ladies' room, man.' Big scowl.

'Sure you don't,' Nat said. He could crawl to the corner and down the main hallway to the helpful old woman and use her phone to call in, or he could wait for Shaw to find him. Or maybe in a few minutes the pain would ease enough to hobble out under his own power.

He waited.

'What's in the bag?' he asked.

'Nothin', man, just some shit.'

Nat reached out and pulled it to him and unzipped it and turned it upside down and dumped out two cellular telephones, three pagers, and a UHF scanner used to steal security codes. The working tools of a hustler, dealer, and pimp.

'Who are you working for?' Nat said. 'Wait a minute – say Miranda before you answer that.'

'Miranda?'

'I just read you your rights. Who you working for?'

'Shit, man, I just got out.'

'Right, and you just happen to be getting your cell phones fixed at one in the morning.' Bastard. Out of prison one week and he was already back in business.

'Fuck you, *Henn*-uh-see. What chu want with me, man?'

'Did I forget to tell you? You're under arrest for the murder of a trannie named Tangerine.'

'I don't know no Tangerine, man. I was in my apartment last night.'

'Did I say it happened last night?'

Rico's jaw jutted out, righteous as a boxer. 'I got witnesses, man.'

'So do I,' Nat said.

'Bullshit, man. You ain't got shit.'

True. Nat looked at his wristwatch. It was ten after one. Come on, Shaw, where are you? He repositioned his leg to stop the pounding in his foot and leaned against the wall, trying to make himself comfortable. It felt good seeing this miserable piece of shit in cuffs, dangling like a fish on a line.

'While we're waiting,' Nat said, 'why don't you get it off your chest and tell me how it went down.'

'Fuck you, man.'

Nat smiled. Right to remain silent. 'Doesn't matter, I already know.'

'You don't know nothin,' man, you nothin' but a dick.'

'True, but I've got the story that's gonna put you away for life.'

Angel looked at him curiously.

Nat moved to a new position, and new pain. 'You want to know what the jury's gonna hear?' Angel wasn't saying no. 'Goes like this. You're a few days out of the can and so horny you can taste it, so you pick up this trannie named Tangerine—'

'I don't do no TVs, man.'

Nat raised his hand. 'Don't waste your breath. I saw her, she looked good enough to fool Dr Ruth. So you're on the street looking for some action and you find this drop-dead hooker hanging out near Grand Central, and pretty soon you're talking dirty and she says, "Hey, baby, the terminal's almost closed, want to go to the ladies' room and have some fun?" Nat watched Angel's eyes. 'You with me so far?'

Angel said nothing.

'Yeah, you're with me. So now you've got this babe in a stall bent over a toilet and you're doing her from behind, and you reach down between her legs, and – uh-oh, what's *this*? A basket? Fuck me, man, this isn't a *girl*-type person, this is a *boy*-type person! Thirty-eight months in the joint protecting my 'hood, and the first week I'm out I lose my cherry to some fucking *guy*?'

'You full of shit, man.'

'Pitcher, catcher, it makes no difference to you, either way this chick with a dick has turned you into a butt-fucking little fag!' He watched Angel squirm. Nobody was more insane about their precious manhood – their 'hood, as they called it – than these macho little fucks from Hispaniola. 'That's when you pulled out your knife and slit her.'

'Bullshit!'

'Bullshit nothing. You zipped her just like you zipped Debbie Duzzit – a knife under the chin and a curlicue finish on the ear. You think I forgot your MO?'

Angel's strung-up fists yanked forward, snapping a handcuff against the pipe. 'You got a big fuckin' 'magination, you know that, man?'

Nat enjoyed stuffing Angel's homophobia down his throat. 'Only trouble is,' he said, 'being in a rage, you didn't think about how it would look, did you? You didn't think killing a hooker the same way you killed Debbie Duzzit was like signing your name on the wall. You didn't think about how you can't cop a manslaughter plea this time because any kind of homicide now is going to get you locked up and the key shoved so far up your ass you can't find it with a flashlight. But maybe you like that now, huh, Angel?' He pinched his prisoner's cheek. 'All those buff boys back in the joint, waiting to tickle your tonsils from both ends at once?'

Angel leaned back against the wall, red-faced and sweating. 'What chu want, man?'

'I want you to spend a short life in prison and die.'

Angel stared at him, sweating, then oily nice. 'You want a girl, man? I got a girl for you – shit, man, she's clean as a fresh-split coconut, skin like velvet. Pussy so tight' – he winced in mock pain – 'it hurt you more than it hurt her.'

'Shut the fuck up.'

Angel tensed angrily, then slumped down, hung by his hands. Nat looked at his watch again. Shaw must be lost. He'd told her not to call for backup until she absolutely had to. Shit. Where was she?

'I got something big I can give you, man,' Angel said.

'Sure you do,' Nat said. He pulled his knees up – his foot throbbed with the movement – and prepared to crawl to the old woman's door.

'I can set up a hit for you,' Angel said.

'Just like you set up the Bambino, right?'

'I didn't set chu up at Dede's, man! No fuckin' way!'

Nat reached up and squeezed the one-way ratchet on the cuffs, digging them into Angel's wrists.

'Shit,' Angel said, licking his lips. 'The Bambino? He find out I set *him* up for *you*, man. He get so pissed he try to *kill* me.'

Nat rolled his eyes.

'You don't believe me?' Angel said. 'Take a look at my belly.'

Nat looked at him in wonder. Amazing, the bullshit these guys could shovel even when they were in cuffs.

'Take a look, man!' Angel said, eyes dancing. 'I ain't shittin' you, take a look!' He nodded at his stomach.

What the hell. Nat reached out and lifted Angel's T-shirt. On his right side was a six-inch-long crease with a deep hole at one end that had healed badly. He yanked the T-shirt back down.

'See?' Angel said. 'The Bambino done that to me, man.'

'And pigeons don't shit.'

'I'm telling you, man, he hire a con to kill me in prison! He know I send you to Dede's to bust his ass!'

'How'd he know that?'

'That's the way he is, man. J.J. like God – he knows *every-thing*.'

The two initials hit Nat somewhere behind his eyes.

'Who's J.J.?'

'The Bambino, man. J.J. Jackson.'

J.J. Jackson? He felt a shudder, the cool rush of a passing ghost. 'Who's J.J. Jackson?'

'I toll you, man, the Bambino.'

'Describe him.'

'Nothin' to describe—'

Nat grabbed Angel's shiny T-shirt and twisted it into a knot. 'I said, describe him!'

Angel's expression changed: hey, man, maybe I got me something here. 'Black dude,' he said. 'Not real tall, works out at the gym all the time. Lotta muscle.'

Nat felt it coming at him like a twister. 'His jaw,' he said. 'What's on his jaw?'

Angel's eyes showed his surprise. 'How you know 'bout that, man?'

'Know about what?'

'The scar, man.' He lifted his head and jutted his jaw out. 'Like a piece a *cheese* been cut out.'

Nat felt the air sucked out of his chest. It's him. Jackson Levander James – 'J.J. Jackson' – my father's killer. He'd been arrested the day after the '77 blackout – the wallet the girl had scooped off the sidewalk was his – but two old ladies had testified that he couldn't have been the killer, he'd been with them all night, and when the jury came in, he'd walked. Thirteen years later, on Nat's first day as a cop, he'd scoured the BCI files looking for Jackson Levander James. He'd found his file with no problem: arrested for numbers, gambling, and procuring, in and out of prison three times, including four years on a manslaughter plea that should have been murder. Lacking proof, the DA had cut the best deal he could get.

Then a brick wall. No rap sheet, no record. He'd tried the Department of Motor Vehicles, the voter rolls, prison lists, aliases, and people on the street. He'd asked the FBI, the DEA, Customs and every state and federal agency he could find. Nothing. It was as if Jackson Levander James had become invisible. Then it hit him. Other than death, only one thing could make a criminal disappear: the Federal Witness Protection Program.

A retired marshal he knew said an ex-con named Jackson Levander James had once given the Feds a bundle of racketeering indictments and then disappeared into the program. The marshal didn't know his new name – not that he'd tell Nat if he did. But over the years, Nat had noticed that even with the fresh identities these scumbags got from the government – a new social security number, a different birthday, a fake military record – they loved keeping a piece of their old selves, usually in the form of one or two original initials.

Jackson Levander James. He must have dropped Levander, the distinctive hook, and morphed the rest into J. J. Jackson. Was it really him?

'Why didn't you tell me his name three years ago?'

'I didn't know it, man.'

Nat could see him trying hard, working every angle. 'Where'd he get the name Bambino?'

'He play ball for the Yankees so they call him that, like Babe Ruth, you know what I'm saying?'

Christ, it made sense. It had to be him. The chin, the Yankees – *had* to be. Nat stared at Angel but he was seeing someone else now, feeling a new pulse in his neck, a slow burning in his veins. Nasty images were dancing in his head. Nasty, satisfying images.

A door closed in the distance, in the stairwell on the floor below. It was Shaw. She's here – time's up. J.J. Jackson was like a ripe apple on a tree, but there was no time to reach it.

Hearing the noise, Angel knew *his* time was up.

'Listen, man,' he said, 'you want the Bambino?'

Yeah, Nat wanted the Bambino.

'I deliver him to you, man,' Angel said.

Sure you will, and while you're at it, take a piss on his shoes. Even if Angel had the cunning to bring Jackson around – which he didn't – cutting a private deal with a con man was like paying good cash for a sack of shit. 'We been down this road before,' he said. 'Last time you said you'd set him up for me, it almost got me killed.'

'I ain't talkin' 'bout settin' him up,' Angel said. 'I'm talkin' 'bout *delivering* him. Know what I'm saying?'

Nat's mouth went dry. Yeah, he did. Angel wasn't just a con man, he was a killer. *A killer*. Nat tried to think, but his heart was pumping hot air into his head.

They heard the door at the end of the main hallway. It was Shaw, closing in, one step at a time.

'He cut me, man,' Angel said softly. 'I been dreamin' 'bout payback time three years in the joint. The bastard *cut* me!'

Nat figured he had about ten seconds before Shaw turned the corner.

Angel said, 'You know why I be carrying that blade? I was on my way to do J.J. *tonight*, man! If you don't stop me on the sidewalk, man, he be dead right now!'

'Bullshit,' Nat said.

Nine seconds.

Angel whispered, 'Take me downtown and what chu got, man? Nada. Zip. I be out in the morning. Let me go, you got the Bambino, man – on the end of a sticker!'

Nat shouldn't even have been listening to this garbage. But he was.

'Let me go, man. I do him for me *and* you.'

But there was no way to know he'd do it – no proof, no collateral, no recourse.

Six seconds.

Angel said, 'Why you want him so bad, man?'

'None of your fuckin' business.' Nat stuck his gun into his belt holster and struggled to get his good foot under him.

'Come on, man,' Angel implored.

Four seconds.

It was nothing but trash talk, and yet, when he thought about it, Angel was only asking for the chance to do what he wanted to do anyway. What if he really had been on his way to do Jackson when he stopped him? Why should a crummy little coincidence like that stand in the way of fate?

But it wasn't a coincidence. You came after him, and now you've got him, bail or no bail. 'Won't work,' Nat said. 'If you did Jackson, I'd still have to hunt you down for doing Tangerine.'

'No way, man.'

'No way nothing. I'd find you in two, three days most. I got CIs all over the South Bronx ready to rat you out the first time you order a Big Mac.'

'Don't matter, man, 'cause after I do Jackson, I gonna be gone.'

'Gone?'

'Back home to the DR.'

The Dominican Republic? Kill Jackson and leave the country? Angel said, 'What the fuck, man? You think I gonna do him and *stay*? Shit, man, he got friends – you think they gonna *arrest* me?' A guffaw. 'They gonna *kill* me!'

Christ. It sort of stacked up. Angel would have to get out of town. If he didn't, Nat would find him and bust him hard.

'Nat?' It was Shaw calling from the end of the main hallway.

Angel spoke softly, 'Come on, man! Take off the cuffs and let me do it! Let the street clean up this shit!'

Nat put his key into one handcuff and held it there. Amazing. He was actually considering doing it. Leverage? Maybe he had some after all. 'If I do this and you ever set foot in New York again, I guarantee you fifteen years in B Block Attica, know what I'm saying?' Every guy who'd done time knew what he was saying. When you got out of B Block – *if* you got out – you had three new orifices where the sun don't shine.

Jesus. He was talking Angel's game.

'Nat? Are you there?' The voice came from roughly the same distance. She wasn't moving fast, but she could start up any second.

There was no time. What was he: decent citizen or rogue cop? What was it going to be: another twenty years of rage or long-overdue justice? His head was saying, don't do this, Nat, but his churning gut was saying, what's to lose?

'Come on! Do it!'

Nat's fingers furnished the answer: they turned the key.

Angel dropped his hand into his lap with a look of pain, leaving the other hand suspended. 'I ain't got no money, man,' he whispered.

'Forget it,' Nat whispered back. He stuck the key into the second cuff but didn't turn it.

Angel's eyebrows lifted. 'How I gonna get home?'

Nat looked into his eager eyes and tried to sort truth from scam. 'Who flies to Santo Domingo?'

''Merican.'

'You do the job, there'll be a ticket waiting for you at the airport on the last plane out of JFK. When is it?'

'Five thirty p.m., man.'

They heard a rap-rap-rap down the hallway. Shaw was knocking on someone's apartment door.

'Wait a minute,' Nat said. 'How'm I gonna know you did it?'

'Nat?' Her voice was closer now. 'Are you there?' He pictured her moving cautiously, gun drawn, no more than fifty feet away.

Angel picked up one of the Airtel alpha-numeric beepers Nat had dumped onto the floor. 'I call you on this,' he said softly, handing it to Nat.

'And if I need to reach you?'

Angel lifted a second pager and turned it over, looking for a number.

'Quick,' Nat whispered.

'Call me at 555–3546,' Angel said, and stuck the pager into his jeans.

Nat let go of the key and wrote the number on the palm of his left hand. Then he opened the second handcuff.

Angel pulled away too fast, clanging the steel bracelet against the metal water pipe.

They both froze.

'Who's there?' Shaw said in a startled voice.

Nat shoved the cuffs over his belt and put his finger to his lips, *shh*. Gripping his gun in one hand and a rusty pipe in the other, he hoisted himself onto his good foot.

'Hey, man,' Angel whispered, 'how you want me to do him?'

Nat scowled, do what? I don't know what you're talking about. But then he couldn't help himself.

'With a baseball bat.'

THREE

Revenge is a kind of wild justice.
—Francis Bacon

He who seeks revenge must dig two graves.
—Confucius

THE SAME TIME, THURSDAY, *July 3*
1:30 a.m.

Where is that thing, anyway?

Waiting for Nat to come home, Camilla stood in the middle of the bedroom in a sea of wedding paraphernalia: her dress, hanging in a dust cover; clothes, passports, tickets, a transformer waiting to be packed for their honeymoon in Venice; the stuff she would take to the brownstone the morning of the wedding, like makeup, nail glue, extra stockings, shoes, safety pins, panties, needle and thread, a baby-blue silk garter, a hairbrush, and a change of clothes for after the wedding. But what she was looking for had nothing to do with that. It had to do with Cush Walker.

She stuck a piece of stale popcorn into her mouth, walked to her closet, turned on the light and pawed across the floor filled with sneakers, shoe boxes, and a broken tennis racket. Come on, where are you? Kneeling, determined, she found it next to a shoe rack stacked with winter clothes: a large manila envelope she hadn't seen for three years. She pulled it free and stood up.

Brushing a line of dust off the top, she walked to the bed, opened the flap, and pulled out a large, shiny negative with a one-page memorandum paperclipped to the top. Held up to the light, the negative revealed rows of photos of someone's brain, and on the margin, in gray letters, dates and medical terms. Her eyes moved to the word Patient. Next to it were the initials she remembered: RAD.

She pulled the memo off the paperclip and read.

CONFIDENTIAL – YOUR EYES ONLY

To: Dr C. WALKER
From: R. Rodriguez
Date: July 4
Patient: RAD
Ref: Scan Malfunction

The attached report is for your eyes only, when you are well enough to read it. As you requested, I have tried to write it as impersonally as possible.

We're looking at virtually the same conditions we faced in phase two of the Cain and Abel clinicals, except this time, of course, we're dealing with a human subject.

In a nutshell, here's what happened.

At some point during the transfer phase, a large number of Z-5s malfunctioned and went on a rampage. The majority of them migrated to unprogrammed locations in the brain, including the temporal lobes, and continued working on their own. We aborted and instructed them to withdraw, but they behaved like clawing viruses and refused to exit. Finally, about thirty minutes later, they went into 'pause' mode and stopped scanning. So far, they're still dormant and unthreatening.

That's the good news.

The bad news is MRI evidence that they attacked the anterior portions of the brain's temporal lobes with excessive heat. The same thing they did to Abel.

It's impossible to say how much brain damage they caused, or how long they'll stay dormant. As you recall, in the Cain and Abel trials, inactivity on the part of rogue Z-5s lasted anywhere from three hours to years. They could start up again at any time.

We've been over the procedure a hundred times and still don't know why this happened. I think synthetic organisms simply aren't that different from their natural cousins; they do what they can to survive and proliferate. Considering their ability to double themselves every 235 seconds, they can destroy the patient's brain in a matter of hours, once activated. It's the classic nanotechnology nightmare: uncontrolled synthetic viruses on a mission of their own.

The patient will have to be cautious, Cush. As we saw with Cain and Abel, electromagnetic activity, viral encephalitis, even a hard jolt to the head can bring them back to life. If that happens, given their present location, the patient faces a substantial risk of developing a case of KBS. I don't need to tell you what that means.

I'm in the process of looking at ways to

She turned over the piece of paper looking for page two, forgetting that she'd never had it. Instead, she found a note she herself had handwritten on her personal stationery:

Dear Cush:

Vestie Viney insisted I look at X-rays of her dead husband's head. She seems to be amazed to see a tractor bolt sitting inside it. (And thankful for your efforts to try to save him.) The enclosed memo and negative were somehow attached to the X-rays she showed me — mistakenly, I'm sure. (Perhaps it happened when she got her husband's X-rays from your lab?)

*At any rate, considering the 'Eyes Only' nature of the memo,
I thought I should return it to you along with the brain scan of
'Patient RAD'.*

Hope this finds you well. I miss you.

    Love, Camilla

P.S. I assume Patient RAD is your boy Roy Driggers. True?

But she hadn't sent them back. What she'd seen in the pasture that night had stopped her.

She stuffed the material into the manila sleeve, feeling the same queasiness she'd felt the first time she'd read it, and dropped the envelope behind the dresser. As an engineer, she appreciated nanotechnology as industrial science, but as experimental medicine? Procedures that left patients with high-tech bugs going haywire in their brains? Causing 'KBS' – whatever that was? What was he doing?

She hadn't wanted to know then, and she didn't want to know now.

She chewed on stale popcorn and continued packing. Did she need a box for her wide-brimmed black straw hat, or should she carry it?

She pictured Vestie Viney sitting in her living room telling her how her husband, Virgil, had died a few years earlier when a tractor had thrown a bolt from its engine. Sweet old Vestie Viney, as loopy as a carnival ride, treating the X-rays as if they were family photos.

Opening a hat box, Camilla decided she'd return the memo and negative to Cush when she got back from her honeymoon. At least then he'd know why she'd been scared away – although she wouldn't tell him what she'd seen, or what she suspected. That she had no reason to tell anyone, Cush included.

It hadn't been a graceful departure, giving him no explanation for why she was leaving, but what else could she have done? Tell him she'd walked across the pasture near Vestie Viney's house in the moonlight toward a pair of flashlights moving in the distance? Tell him she'd turned off her own light so that she could get close enough to see what they were doing? If she'd done that, what would she have done next? Ask him questions he couldn't answer? Ask him questions he could? No way. She cared too much about him to do that. If she knew too much, it would only endanger him, and she didn't want to do that. Ever.

She pictured the memo's words: *Cain and Abel trials . . .*

The names had meant nothing to her when she'd first read them three years earlier, but now that she'd actually seen Cain and Abel at the lab, they meant . . . what? What experiments had he tried on them?

Leave it alone. You don't need to figure it out.

One silk nightgown wasn't going to make it.

Patient: RAD?

That had to be Roy Driggers, the convict volunteer who'd jumped parole and gone AWOL from Cush's Mississippi clinic. At least that's how Cush had explained it at the time. The sheriff had accepted the story — so why hadn't she? Because her viscera knew better, that's why. Sometimes she didn't need more facts to know that she already knew enough.

Let's see, T-shirts, shorts, bathing suit.

Plausible deniability. That was the policy she wanted to maintain.

She laid her nylon bag of lotions, shower gel, and shampoos on the bed next to the suitcase and walked to the dresser. Reaching down, she took hold of the envelope and pulled it from behind the dresser.

Maybe she hadn't wanted to know three years ago, but why not now?

The body was cut in half in the middle, then drawn apart and propped up on large wooden blocks for everyone to see. It was two in the morning, and when the last cut was made, the two men turned off their acetylene torches and raised their welders' masks and let a couple of cold beers do the sweating for them as they admired their handiwork: another El Dorado sliced in two, ready to be welded back together with four extra feet of chassis in the middle. It would be J.J. Jackson's latest custom-made Caddy.

Jackson liked watching the torch men make their cuts – the red-hot steel, the blue flame and yellow sparks. In high school he'd enjoyed taking things apart: a frog, a squirrel, a fire alarm box in the hallway. He always thought if he'd been more patient with the books he would have made a good surgeon. Who knows?

The alarm on his wristwatch chirped. Time to go, his spinner was waiting at the club. Heading for the door, he saw the night manager stick his head over the railing outside the balcony office. 'Hey, J.J., you got a phone call.'

He didn't care. He wasn't working tonight, not even for Joe Romano, the man who made the stretch limousines, his best client. J.J. collected 'bad loans' for Romano, although 'collecting' wasn't exactly the term. By the time J.J. was called in, the debtor was usually beyond repaying, which meant Jackson had a license from Romano to do whatever he pleased to 'solve the problem'. He liked his work. He also liked driving. There was lots of cash, a new stretch every two years, and freedom to operate his own limo service on the side. He got a kick out of roaming the city with yuppie investment bankers, rich shoppers, turned-out hookers, and stylish pimps. The whole thing was a sweet arrangement.

He pictured the blonde he'd peddled to a bachelor party the night before. He could still pimp when he had to; he'd managed to get that act down cold. The look, the style, the rich and horny customers on late-night prowls – he knew the scene. He knew how to handle the girls, too – a tender touch here, a punch in the stomach there – screwing and babying and terrorizing them the way a good pimp did. Not that he ever messed up a girl's face – that was like shitting in your own hat. Besides, he didn't need to. He had an instinct for finding girls who came back to daddy regardless of the pain. Usually, anyway. Occasionally you had to make a point that a girl couldn't just bounce out of his stable whenever she felt like it, the way Debbie Duzzit had tried a few years ago. And Tangerine a few days ago. But large-scale pimping was a hassle – watching the cash, calming the petty jealousies, posting bond in the middle of the night. Fuck. It was almost as bad as running a restaurant.

'Who is it?' he yelled up to the night manager.

'Some guy named Angel,' he said.

Angel Rico? Jackson stopped, grabbed the railing, and climbed the steps two at a time.

Shit. What have I done?

It was nearly two thirty when Shaw dropped Nat at his loft and let him hobble inside. Regret had begun stalking him the minute he'd let Angel Rico go free. Second thoughts quickly followed by self-kicks in the butt. Shaw the rookie? Sure she was. Compared to what he'd just done, she was a pillar of wisdom and experience.

After cutting his deal with Angel, he had stepped out of the corridor into the main hallway, gun in hand, and made himself known to his partner. What happened? Shaw had asked, holstering her .38 to give him a hand. I whacked my toe chasing the perp, he said. Did you call for backup? No, I didn't, she said. Good, he answered.

Helping him down the stairwell, she said, why didn't you answer me when I called your name? He said, I wanted to make sure Angel didn't have a gun at your head, because if he did, and I answered you, he's got us both. Of course, she said, she hadn't thought of that.

Walking toward the car, she said, so I guess you didn't find him, huh? Yeah, he said, I found him. You did? What happened? Dancing on one foot while she opened the door for him, Nat grabbed the edge of the roof and lowered himself into the passenger seat. Once inside, he rolled down the window and said, he got away.

He took the elevator to the fourth-floor entrance to the loft, carrying the plastic bag of ice Shaw had picked up from an all-night Korean deli. After entering the studio, he set the bag on the chaise, then limped to the kitchen, draped his sport coat over a stool, and placed his holstered gun in the chicken on top of the refrigerator. Where were the crutches? Rummaging through a utility closet, he found a pair he'd used after twisting an ankle shooting hoops with the neighborhood kids and stuffed them under his arms. From there he hobbled to the bathroom and found a brown bottle of painkillers left over from the same injury. After grabbing a towel, he returned to the kitchen, collected a bottle of Scotch, a tall glass, and the telephone at the end of a long, kinked line, and carried them back to the studio.

He sat on the chaise and propped his foot up on a wooden bust of Shakespeare that Camilla used to hold hats. After reapplying the bag of ice to his foot, he lay back in the grayness. The room was remarkably quiet. Camilla must be asleep, which was good. Facing her now was not something he cared to do.

He leaned forward with a grunt, unwrapped the towel from his foot, and stabbed a hole in the side of the plastic bag. Lifting out a handful of ice chunks, he lay back and slid them quietly into the tumbler, then poured Scotch until he heard ice clinking against the side of the glass. He took a swallow – the first of his own particular twelve-step program – then, feeling better, wiggled his damaged toe. He had to get this thing well, and fast. Limping to the altar was not a statement he wanted to make.

He lifted the bottle of painkillers, shook one out, and downed it with another swig of Scotch. Step two. Were the pills too stale to work anymore? Better yet, was he? Christ, what had he done with Angel Rico?

He downed another pill for good measure, then lay back and looked at the ceiling, easing his pain but not his conscience. Angel Rico, hit man. Letting him go had been quick and impulsive, the kind of behavior he expected from a stupid felon, not a cop. He took another taste of Scotch. What was he thinking?

Relax. No way was Angel Rico going to kill J.J. Jackson. After he was done laughing at the thought, he'd grab the airline ticket and run—

The airline ticket. He forgot. He lifted the telephone – then set it back on the cradle. Leave it alone. Arranging a ticket would only make matters worse. Right now this was nothing but ridiculous, deniable talk. Buy Angel a ticket and you've committed an overt act in furtherance of a criminal conspiracy.

Head back, eyes closed. Then open again.

But what if Angel actually goes through with it and shows up at the airport? What kind of trouble was *that*? With no ticket out of town, what if he leaves the airport and gets caught? The last thing Nat needed was Angel Rico in New York, whether he hit Jackson or not.

Better cover that and figure out what to do afterward.

He lifted the handset and dialed a number. After a few rings a sleepy male voice answered.

'Ben, it's me. I got a problem.'

As a cop, Nat saw the world divided into two kinds of people: those who'd turn you in and those who wouldn't. Ben Brown, his former partner, wouldn't. Under any circumstances. Period.

'I need a prepaid ticket to Santo Domingo,' Nat said, 'American Airlines, no credit card number, I'll cover it with cash.'

Ben said, 'Whose name you want it in?'

Nat found himself not wanting to give the answer. 'Angel de Jesus Raul Rico Esperanza.'

There was silence on the other end. Ever since the blown bust at Dede's, Nat and Ben both assumed that Angel Rico had jobbed them. Now he was asking Ben Brown, the man who took the bullet, to help the guy who set them up leave the country. If his old friend slammed down the receiver, he wouldn't have been surprised.

Ben broke the silence first. 'You got it.'

Talk. Booze. Swagger. Music. Attitude. Smoke. Trumpets. Drums. Testosterone. Bongos. Calves. Lights. Movement. Dope. Smack. Heat. Laughter. Sweat. Dancers. Tits. Ass. Cool. Threats. Guns. Spinners. Eyelashes. Deals. Talk. Love. Talk. Anger. Talk. Trouble. Talk. Shrugs. Talk. Easy. Talk. Smiles. Talk. Talk.

The room was crowded, hot and dusky, with a Louis Guerra merengue rolling over a pulsating Latin bass, scattered red and yellow lights, rich plumes of secondhand cigarette smoke and the tang of overworked underarm deodorants. There was perfume in the air, the scent of silk and rayon, damp and warm. There was fresh lipstick and drying hair spray, Clorets cracked with every chew, broken swizzle sticks and patent leather shoes swiped clean with white linen napkins. It was Frank's Cabana in the South Bronx, the hour almost three. Prime time. Mellow time. Braless breasts time. Hands-on-thighs time.

And talk time. Voices competing with Victor Manuel and La India. That's what Angel Rico had come for. To talk.

He entered the main room and spotted Jackson sitting at a banquette at the side of the dance floor. On the table were glass tumblers and candles, a bottle of Pellegrino, a plate of chuchurillos and an ashtray, Marlboros in a hard pack with a matchbook cover in the shape of a tent. And lots of people, which made Angel feel almost safe. Still, this was J.J. Jackson's turf, and Angel knew he shouldn't have come here – not tonight, not so soon after the job he'd done on Tangerine at

J.J.'s direction. But he had information now, and if he handled it right, there was money to be made.

Sitting next to J.J. was an Asian girl small enough to sit in a peach basket – J.J.'s very own spinner – with straight black hair cut in bangs, green eye shadow, and natural lashes longer than the best fake ones pimp money could buy. Her cherry-red lipstick left traces on everything it touched, including the side of J.J. Jackson's neck. No doubt there were other traces in other places, but Angel wasn't carrying a flashlight.

He walked to the table hoping to catch J.J.'s welcoming eye and an invitation to sit. Jackson's right hand rested on his girlfriend's shoulder, his fingers fondling the back of her neck, his eyes glued to the impossibly small waist and haunches of a girl doing a salsa on the dance floor.

Angel stood waiting.

Jackson sat watching.

The girl continued dancing.

Angel would have undressed her, too, but Jackson had already done that, and besides, Angel was too nervous to be thinking pussy. When the girl finally disappeared, J.J. Jackson looked up.

'Hey, man,' Angel said with a forced smile, 'good to see you.'

Jackson looked at him a moment. 'Angel Hay-suse Rico,' he said as if they hardly knew each other, extending his left hand toward Angel's right. J.J. gave him a shake and pointed toward a chair.

Angel sat and ordered a Corona and lime and picked up a swizzle stick to play with.

'So you like to dance,' J.J. Jackson said. 'I don't recall that.'

'For a Dominican, I ain't real good, man,' he said.

J.J. smiled and stuck a toothpick into his mouth and patted the table and bobbed his head to the beat. His girlfriend pushed her hair out of her face and sipped a daiquiri through a straw. If Jackson wasn't going to introduce her, Angel wasn't about to ask.

'So what's the problem, Hay-suse? I don't like being seen with you so soon after a job, know what I mean?'

'It's like I tell you on the phone, man, I got some important-tay info-mation.'

'Let's hear it,' J.J. said.

Looking at the girl, Angel said, 'You want me to talk here, man?'

'Why not? My baby doesn't care about business, do you, baby?' He put his finger on her lips and pulled them apart and rimmed the glistening, smooth inside. She stared at him, letting him do what he wanted.

Angel watched her, thinking, shit, man, I could use some of that. 'It's about a cop,' he said.

Jackson sat with his finger in her mouth as if it were dipped into a bowl of icing. 'What about a cop?' His eyes stayed fixed on the girl's mouth.

'He want you, man,' Angel said.

J.J. smiled. 'Hear that, baby? A cop *want* me.' Then back to Angel, his tone unpleasant, his smile gone. 'What's he want me for?'

'I don't know, man, but he want you real bad.' 'Bout as bad as I want this little piece of ass.

Jackson withdrew his finger and leaned forward toward his spinner. 'You want me real bad, baby?' A kiss with open lips. Then back to Angel. 'How the hell's this cop know about me to want me, Hay-suse?' It was more accusation than question.

'From Dede's, man. The bust that went bad.'

'You telling me this is the same cop you sent into Dede's?'

'Yeah, man, that's what I'm telling you.'

'The one who got shot?'

'No, man, the other one, the white dude. He ask me, where's the Bambino? He want me to set up a bust of the Bambino.'

J.J. was getting interested. 'Why?'

'He didn't say, man.'

Jackson's expression said, this makes no sense. 'If he's a cop, he's gotta have something in mind. The thing that brought him to Dede's is too long ago.' He played with the swizzle stick. 'Did he say he wants the Bambino, or did he say he wants J.J. Jackson?'

Angel Rico's eyes twitched nervously. 'He use both names, man.'

'Both?'

'I don't know how he got 'em, but he use both names. Bambino and J.J. Jackson.'

'You don't know how he got 'em,' Jackson said.

'No, man, I don't know how.'

Jackson fiddled with the swizzle stick. Something was wrong with this picture, his silence said. He hadn't been busted since entering the witness protection program. His name should have been clean, no police record whatsoever. 'How'd this cop find you, Angel?'

'The Tangerine 'vestigation.'

'Tangerine?' Jackson said. For the first time, his voice showed a touch of anxiety.

'It's cool, man,' Angel said, 'he don't know nothing 'bout me doin' Tangerine, not for you or nobody. I show him the scar on my belly and tell him you do that to me for settin' you up at Dede's. He thinks you and me's enemies, man.'

Jackson checked Angel's face.

Angel said, 'He bought it, man, I'm telling you, he bought it.' He toasted himself with his beer, full of self-congratulation, like a prize fighter after a bout.

But Jackson wasn't finished. 'What made him think you did Tangerine?'

'He think I pick her up for nookie, man, and cut her when I find out she's a TV.'

'But why you? Any mack on the street could have cut her.'

'He say it looks like Tangerine be done the same way I do Debbie Duzzit.'

'Fuck, Hay-suse,' Jackson said, turning his head in disgust. 'You telling me you cut her the same way you cut Debbie?' Jackson hated seeing chickens coming home to roost.

'No sweat, man. He got nothin' on me. You know how I know?'

'Talk to me.'

'He let me go.'

Jackson hadn't thought of that. He seemed to like that.

'If he truly got something on me,' Angel repeated, 'he never let me go, right?'

Jackson sat back and watched the dancers, lost in thought. Persuaded.

Angel said, 'It ain't official business, what this dude want you for, man. He got something personal in mind.'

'In what way, personal?'

''Stead of wanting to bust you, he want you dead.'

Jackson listened. Dead? Why did a New York cop want him dead? As far as the cops knew, he didn't even exist. After thinking it over for a moment he said, 'Let's get out of here,' and pushed the table forward. Standing, he pulled his spinner to her feet.

Angel sat still. He wasn't ready to go someplace alone with Mr Jackson. Not yet.

J.J. pointed at a redhead in a short turquoise skirt dancing by herself. When she turned too fast, Angel could see that she wasn't wearing underpants. Looking relaxed again, J.J. bent down to his pal and said, 'Take a look at that – so hot it gives you the shivers, huh?' The music drove onward in an avalanche. Jackson lifted a napkin off the table and tapped it playfully against Angel's chin. 'You droolin', man. How long you say you were in?'

'Three years, two months,' he said, staring.

Jackson straightened up and whispered something to his

girlfriend, who walked onto the dance floor toward the redhead. Jackson said, 'Let's go,' but Angel was still afraid to move. 'Come on,' Jackson said in a reassuring voice. 'You did good, Hay-suse, everything's cool. Time you had a little fun.'

Nat turned on a small lamp next to the chaise longue, opened the palm of his left hand, and found the telephone number to Angel Rico's beeper. His eyes were bleary and his head spinning from the late hour, the Scotch, and the painkillers. He lifted the receiver and dialed. Two rings and an operator answered.

'Airtel, may I help you?'

'I'd like to send a message.'

'Go ahead.'

'Ticket at airport . . .'

The operator spoke as she typed. 'Ticket at airport . . .'

'Is job done? . . .'

'Is job done? . . .'

His next line was critical, the one that would call it off.

'If not,' he said – and waited.

'If not,' the operator said – and waited.

'If not . . .' He hesitated again.

'Nat?' It was Camilla, calling from the top of the spiral stair. 'Is that you?'

'Yes, it's me,' he called back. Into the telephone, he said, 'Send that out and I'll call back in a minute.'

'OK, sir, it'll go right out.'

Watching the redhead bend over as she climbed into the back seat, Angel ran his hand up her leg to the crease below her bare bottom. J.J. ushered his spinner to her usual place in the front seat, then circled to the driver's side and sat behind the wheel. After strapping on his seat belt, he rolled down the window and caught the eye of a parking lot valet, a tall, skinny kid smoking a cigarette, obviously not eager to let Jackson capture his eye. Once it happened, the kid had no choice.

'Come here, Disco,' J.J. said.

The boy tossed aside his cigarette and sauntered up to the limousine window and stood in a slouch, one hip cocked defensively, keeping his eyes on the Bambino. During Jackson's two-month stint with the Yankees he'd hit two-forty, including three doubles, then was sent back to the minors and never called up again. When he was traded to the Birmingham Sparks, his baseball career was over. Still, he loved to watch kids play in the parking lot across from Yankee Stadium, offering them tips on fielding and batting stances, smoothing out their swings, making the peewees in baggy pants choke up on the bat. As far as his pupils were concerned, J.J. Jackson was so cool he could have been Reggie's brother.

J.J. said, 'You got something for me?'

Disco looked down and shifted his weight to his other hip. 'Not tonight, I ain't.'

J.J. gave the kid a sympathetic nod. 'You know what I do when— Don't be backing away from me now, Disco,' he said, motioning the kid to draw closer. Disco stepped forward and rested his forehead against his arm above the car's window. J.J. reached out and cupped his hand behind the boy's neck and drew it in and spoke quietly. 'You know what I have to do when you don't cover, right?'

Disco's mouth turned sour. 'Yeah, I know.'

'Look at me,' J.J. said. The kid lifted his hound dog eyes up to J.J.'s. 'What's the first rule?' Jackson said.

'You wanna play, you gotta pay.'

'If you don't got the stash, you don't play the cash. You working days?'

'Yeah, delivering flowers. I had the money, J.J., honest – I had it but somebody picked it off me and—'

Jackson pinched the back of the kid's neck, cutting off

his words with a painful vice grip. 'What's the second rule, Disco?'

The kid squinted in agony and spoke through gritted teeth. 'Never shit a shitter,' he eked out.

Jackson let go of his neck and massaged it lovingly. 'So what do you think I should do in this situation?' he said.

The kid shrugged and looked down at his feet. 'I guess you can do anything you want.'

'Look at me.'

The kid looked up with hollow, graveyard eyes, glancing at the spinner in the passenger seat. 'You gonna cap me, J.J.?'

'Should I?'

The kid swallowed. 'You could.'

'Should I?'

'I'll have it for you tomorrow.'

'Should I?'

The kid leaned against the car and dropped his head between his shoulders, looking down at his feet again. 'Yeah.'

'Yeah, what?'

'Yeah, you should cap me.'

Jackson reached out again and laid his hand on Disco's shoulder, massaging it as if the kid had just heard that his mama had died. 'Go get somebody's car and relax.'

Disco's face rose up, his eyebrows arched in gratitude. He backed away. 'I'll have it for you tomorrow,' he said, 'no shit.'

J.J. adjusted the rearview mirror and looked at Angel sprawled in the back seat with a drink in one hand, his new girlfriend in the other, his face turned khaki by the television set behind the front seat. Worthless little shit. Before the night was over, he'd be good for something.

Nat hobbled over to the bed. She was lying on her side, her face bathed in filtered light from the large loft windows, the slightly irregular line of her nose revealed by a shadow. The small imperfection made her face interesting and gave it character, distinguishing it from the air-brushed look of magazine ads. Women in the nineteenth century had understood this trick of the eye perfectly, which was why they placed off-center beauty dots on their symmetrical, porcelain faces.

She rolled over onto her back and raised her hands to him with a slow, half-conscious determination.

He placed a knee on the bed and slid his hands beneath her and breathed in the fragrance of sleep-warmed skin and uncombed hair, making himself dizzy. The hour, the booze, the painkillers, the chase, the fight with Angel – all had taken their toll, but it was her arms that made him surrender. When her fingers stopped caressing the back of his neck, he kissed her and stood on his good foot and began undressing, dropping his clothes in a heap.

'Did you find Angel Rico?' she asked sleepily.

'Yes,' he said, pulling off his shirt. His foot hurt like hell. 'What'd you do?'

'Repaired Venus's lip.'

He finished undressing and lay on his side and reached out and ran his hand down the cool skin of her arm. 'Why don't you do her a real favor and give her a pair of these?'

She propped her hand against his chest and nestled her head into the pillow as if she was finished talking. Ordinarily when he came in late at night she'd turn on the lamp, toss her hair around her face like gorgeous black lightning, pad down to the kitchen for a Coke or a cup of tea, then sit in the middle of the bed and play Sherlock Holmes with his case. She was a natural-born detective: inquisitive, retentive, intuitive about people's motives, able to peel the bark off the trees without losing sight of the forest. Keeping secrets from her was not easy. Give her an inch of information and she knew how to enter it in a marathon.

'So did you arrest him?' she said.

There she goes, off and running. 'I had him trapped but he wiggled out.'

'How'd that happen?'

'I don't know. It wasn't my best night.'

She waited. 'How's your new partner?'

'She'll be OK.'

'Did she help?'

'Yeah, but I got too far ahead of her,' he said. He was saying nothing, but already it was more than he wanted. He felt a queasiness about the whole thing return to his stomach. 'You all set for Saturday?'

'I think so,' she said. She laid her head on her arm and stroked his chest. 'You must be exhausted.'

'I'm OK,' he said. 'Banged up my toe a little, but it's nothing serious.'

'What'd you do?'

'Kicked a steam pipe,' he said. He closed his eyes and folded his hands on his chest.

She stirred and said, 'Let me see.'

'It's no big deal.'

'I'll give it a massage and make it better,' she said.

Jesus H, the mere thought of touching it made it hurt. 'I'll do you first,' he said. Reaching down to the foot of the bed, he pulled the top sheet from under the mattress and peeled it back, exposing one of her feet. She didn't object.

'Seems like I've been standing all day,' she said.

Leaning toward the nightstand, he lifted a bottle of lotion and squeezed a dollop into the palm of his hand, warming it before laying it on her skin. 'Can I help you pack for the honeymoon?' he said.

'Why don't you wait till I'm done and tell me what I've forgotten.' Her voice was partly muffled by the pillow.

What a deal. He lifted her foot and slathered lotion up her ankle and onto her calves, noticing that her legs were perfectly smooth. Aware of it or not, she often shaved them in anticipation of making love. Maybe she'd forgotten whatever it was she'd wanted to talk to him about before he left. Or maybe she wanted to make up.

'That feels good,' she said. He liked the sensuous silence that followed. 'Can you believe it?' she said. 'Three days from now we'll be in Venice.'

He held the arch of her foot with his fingers – such a beautiful curve – and kneaded her sole with his thumbs. Except for the occasional clicking sound of lotion on skin, the room was quiet.

Now, too quiet.

His mind wandered to Angel Rico. He needed to send the rest of the message to his pager, calling the whole thing off.

'If we get married, that is,' she said.

Call him off before . . . if what? He slowed his massage stroke. 'Did you say, if?'

'I told you before you left I had something important to talk about.'

'Yeah, but you didn't say it was the A-bomb.'

She stayed quiet. 'I don't know,' she said softly. He worked the muscles in her foot. 'Sometimes I'm not sure I know you.'

'What you see is what you get,' he said.

'That may be the problem.'

He continued massaging her. 'It's about the game we played last night, isn't it?'

'Sort of.'

'Tell me what's on your mind.'

She stirred. 'You know what? Now that I've brought it up, I think it's too late to get started. I'm sorry.'

Bad news. Whatever it was, ten minutes of feel-good chatter and a foot massage wasn't going to fix it.

'I get moody sometimes,' he said, 'but it won't be a problem anymore.'

'Why not?'

'I got it out of my system.'

'You did?'

'Tonight.' Why'd he say that?

'How did you do that?'

'When you're about to get married, you clean house a little, that's all.'

'Which means?'

He kneaded her muscle.

She massaged his silence. 'Another mystery,' she said.

He worked her sole with his thumbs. Is that what he'd done with Angel tonight? Cleaned house?

'That's my thyroid you got there,' she said. She believed in reflexology, the theory that various locations on the foot were organically connected to locations in the body.

He moved his thumbs toward her toes. 'Where am I now?' he asked.

'Not where you think.'

Not to worry. He was so tired he couldn't have gotten it up with a car jack. 'What do you mean, "another" mystery?' he said.

'All day long I've been thinking about Camilla and Sebastian,' she said. 'I haven't figured out their story yet, but I'm getting close. I think you just hit my hypothalamus.'

'What's that do?'

'Controls appetite.'

'For what?'

'Not what you think,' she said. She turned onto her side. 'Cush Walker is the second mystery.'

He stopped massaging her foot and laid it down and pushed his damaged toe out in front of him to try to relieve the throbbing. After turning her onto her stomach, he picked up her other foot, bending her leg at the knee, and rested it against his shoulder while he squeezed out more lotion.

She lay with her eyes closed, her arms wilted. Even though she was relaxed, he could feel her thinking about something, mucking it around, compiling a list of missing parts.

'Where am I now?' he asked.

'The solar plexus.'

He stroked and squeezed her foot, sending ripples of pleasure up her leg. She reached down and wiggled her fingers in the air, looking for his hand. Reaching out, he locked their palms together, squishing cream between their fingers. Then he leaned forward and kissed her back.

'Now you've finally gone and done it,' she said softly.

He undulated his thumbs like a caterpillar up the center of her sole. 'Done what?'

'Touched my brain.'

'That's not what I was aiming for.' He could threaten with impunity. She knew he was too dead to follow up.

She turned onto her back and looked at him in the anemic light. 'Sometimes the way you massage me, it's like opening a peacock fan behind my eyes all the way to my toes,' she said. Then she raised her arms to him, inviting him in. 'I'd know your touch in my sleep.'

He ran his hands under her back and drew her to him. Holding her would be enough tonight, although what her kisses did to him proved he wasn't too dead to follow up after all. If she wanted him to.

Lazarus. That's who he must have been in a prior life.

The limousine pulled up in front of a gate topped with electrical lines and rolls of razor-tipped wire. J.J. Jackson raised a remote control and opened it.

Angel Rico uncoupled the redhead and sat up in the back seat. 'Where the hell are we, man?'

'Gotta drop off some tools and take out the trash,' Jackson said. 'You can give me a hand.'

Angel took a swallow of straight rum from a crystal glass on the back seat bar and watched. 'I don't do no trash, man,' he said.

Jackson pulled into a junk yard stacked with automobile carcasses, dirty tires, dented hoods, and blown engines, the refuse of Auto-rama America. 'Remember Sanford and Son?' he said, closing the gate behind them with a rumble. 'Those junk yard guys? Redd Foxx really cracked me up.' A light touch on the accelerator and the car started moving.

He steered along an oily path, turned the corner of a two-story stack of pick-up truck chassis, and headed toward a large garage door with a smaller door cut into it. The car came to a stop next to a pair of poles with high intensity spots lighting the area. He turned off the engine and found dance music on the radio, something with a hard, pumping beat. 'Be only a minute, Hay-suse,' he said, looking into the back seat.

Angel looked back warily, but before he could sit up the redhead had slipped her tongue inside his mouth and pushed him back on the black calfskin seat and undone his belt and unbuttoned his pants and unzipped his fly and Sweet Jesus, J.J. could stay in this dump as long as he wanted, no hay problema.

J.J. whispered to his spinner to get into the back seat with the redhead. She got out and walked around to the driver's side and opened the rear door and got in, pushing Angel's feet out of the way so she could sit down, leaving the door open.

J.J. pressed a button under the dash and popped the trunk, then walked back and pushed up the lid. Inside was an open wooden box, in it an acetylene torch, a scratched-up cylinder of fuel, a canvas jumpsuit, and a welder's mask, equipment from the auto shop. 'I saw Redd Foxx when I was a kid,' Jackson said in a loud voice, lifting it out. Before closing the deck, he reached deep into the trunk's space, grabbed a padlock hanging on a hasp, and pulled on it to make sure it held. Behind it, hidden by carpet upholstery, was the outline of a thin, rectangular box nearly as wide as the trunk itself. It looked as if it held something of value.

Carrying the welder's equipment past the open back door, he stopped and looked inside. Angel was lying on his back with his neck cradled on the passenger side armrest, his head bent forward so he could watch what was going on. The redhead was kneeling next to him on the shag rug floor, her head hovering over his midsection, her voice full of nasty promises. She pushed his silk T-shirt up. J.J.'s spinner was kneeling between Rico's ankles pulling his linen pants down his legs. She got them off and dropped them onto the step plate of the door.

J.J. set the tool box down and picked up the pants to toss them back inside, but just as he was about to let go, he felt something vibrating in the pocket. He reached in and pulled out a pager. Turning it up to the light, he read a message in the window: TICKET AT AIRPORT WAITING . . . IS JOB DONE? . . . IF NOT . . .

He stuck the pager in his coat pocket, picked up the wooden tool box, and walked to the passenger side of the car. After setting the box on the ground, he opened the limo's rear door. Angel's head fell backward; he looked up at J.J. with inverted eyes.

Jackson squatted down close to Angel's face. The redhead's tongue was gliding up and down Angel's favorite nerve endings and the spinner's mouth was lost somewhere in the same vicinity, her straight, black hair draped across his midsection. He groaned and lifted his head to look down again.

J.J. said, 'How much you want for the information?'

Angel stayed focused on the redhead. Her lips hovered above the tip of him, her pink tongue extended.

'Nothin', man,' he said. He closed his eyes. 'Shit, man, this bitch know what she doin'.'

'No cash?' J.J. said.

Angel opened his eyes again and focused on the girls. 'Maybe you make a little contribution to Uncle Tito's funeral, you know what I mean?' For some reason, con men like Angel always felt obliged to use a cover story to justify their take, even though everybody knew it was bullshit.

'Five hundred?'

'Aw, man, Uncle Tito don't wanna be buried in some fuckin' pine box.'

'A grand.'

'Five.'

'Two.'

The redhead buried Angel in her mouth. He groaned and said, 'OK, OK . . . two grand.' An octave higher, he added, 'You just make Uncle Tito the happiest man in town.'

J.J. stood up and took out his wallet. 'Next to you.' He held out a wad of bills and squatted down again. 'Now tell me. Who's this cop and why's he want me dead?'

'I told you, man, I doan know.'

'Then why did he send you to do the job?' He felt the pager.

For a moment J.J.'s words didn't register. Then Angel reached up and grabbed the hand strap above the door and raised his torso. 'What the fuck you talkin' 'bout, man?'

'Or were you just supposed to set me up for him the way you did at Dede's?'

'I doan have nothin' to do with settin' you up at Dede's, man. I set *him* up for *you*, remember?'

J.J. looked at him a minute, then tossed a wad of bills onto his chest and stood up.

Angel grabbed the bills in one hand and held onto the strap with the other. The spinner was still between his legs, her fingernails digging into his thighs, her eyes locked onto the horizon of his belly. Still kneeling beside him, the redhead continued bobbing to the beat of the music, bringing him along. Angel's eyes were wide, then squinty, his lips curled into a puckered snarl, ready for heaven to descend.

It came.

'Fuuuuuck!' he yelled, grimacing.

J.J. Jackson laid a leather strap around Angel's neck and yanked it backwards, pulling his naked, erupting body off the seat and onto the oily asphalt, skinning his back and elbows. The spinner looked up with confused eyes and swollen lips. The redhead stared at her empty hand as if she'd just dropped an ice cream cone.

Angel Rico was on the ground, pulling at the strap, his glassy eyes bulging, his hand still holding the money.

'You either talk too much,' Jackson said, 'or not enough.'

Nat closed his eyes and relaxed his muscles and felt the spikes of the night's conflict flatten and spread into a soft, blue blanket of snow. Lying quietly, he could feel their spirits drawing together like a pair of stretched rubber bands easing back. Soon the world would stop and he and Camilla could get off for the night. Any ... second ... now ...

'Nat?' she said softly. Her voice reached him gently, a rowboat drifting on a pond. For some reason she loved talking to him just as he was about to doze off.

'Hmm?'

'Who is Jackson Levander James?'

His eyes opened and his heart went back to work. 'Where'd you come up with that name?'

'When I was packing tonight I found a leather case in your sock drawer with an old security card in it.' She waited a second, then added, 'Are you pissed that I looked?'

'There isn't anything I own that you can't see.' Except maybe that.

'I just wondered who he is and why you saved his ID.'

Nat woke up another notch. 'He's a guy who used to work for Metro-North Railroad.'

'I know. The card says nineteen seventy-seven.'

197

Nat closed his eyes and pretended to be asleep. He could still see the ID, the name and photograph printed on it clearly.

'Sweetheart?' she said.

He didn't answer.

'He's not the man who killed your father, is he?'

His muscles tightened. Of all the nights she had to hit the bull's-eye, it would be this one. Jesus. What was he going to say? 'Can we talk about it in the morning?'

'Sure.' She laid her hand on his chest and rubbed it. 'As long as you're not in some kind of trouble.'

He took a deep breath and turned on his side to face her. 'No,' he said. He could feel her measuring his answer. She was a lie detector in a female suit. 'Maybe,' he said, hoping it would hold her.

They both lay still, neither saying anything.

'Want to tell me about it?'

'Yes,' he said.

Quiet.

'Well?' she said.

'In the morning.'

'This is the morning.'

He didn't answer.

'I'll tell you all about it this afternoon when we get to the statue,' he said.

'OK.'

They didn't talk again – at least not until she pulled the pin on a grenade of her own.

She said, 'I have something to tell you then, too.'

Get up and call it off.

Nat lay still and pictured himself getting out of bed, walking downstairs, turning on the light and sending the rest of his message to Angel's pager, telling him to reverse course. All it took was the will to rise, but doing it somehow remained distant in his head, as if he was lying in Kansas and the kitchen telephone was in Maine.

Want to talk about it? Camilla had asked. When he'd said yes, he'd meant it. He wanted to wake her up right now and tell her what he'd done, how he'd naively, impulsively drawn this rush of wild justice into his veins and sent a killer after a killer. He wanted to tell her who he'd become at that moment – a stalker, a felon, a payback man who knew that what he was doing was wrong, and that being wrong wasn't enough to stop him. He wanted to tell her that unless he got up and called it off, the whirlpool he'd created was going to take him down with his victim.

He waited. Any second now, when his heart stopped racing and the eleven-year-old child inside him could stop looking at his father on the sidewalk, he'd get up and make the call.

He waited. Just a minute. Then several more . . .

Jackson screwed the metal wand to the top of the bottle of acetylene, opened a valve, lit a match, and *bam!* He had heat.

'Pretty, isn't it?'

Angel Rico didn't answer. He was lying naked on his back, tied down with leather straps to the top of a huge metal bench next to vises and a lathe. A single light dangled above him beneath a metal shade, and above that was a void. Except for the sound of the welding torch, the vast garage was empty and quiet. No girls – they were outside in the limo – no music, no street sounds.

Jackson tuned the flame to a cold blue hiss that seemed disconnected from the end of the wand. His coat was off, his collar unbuttoned. He leaned closer and waved the torch in front of Angel's eyes.

'It's real simple now,' he said. 'You tell me everything, you live to see another blow job.'

'What chu want to know, man?' The heat of the flame

was barely perceptible on his face, but his skin was covered with sweat.

'Who is this cop who wants me dead?'

'I tell you what I know, man. I tell you everything.'

'You haven't told me shit, you greaseball turd.'

Angel's eyes were oozing a plea. 'I doan know nothin' more, man.'

'Who put the bug up his ass?'

'I doan know, man, I doan know.'

'It was you, wasn't it, Hay-suse?'

'No, man.' Angel's chest was heaving.

Jackson took the torch and held it above Angel's face. His neck muscles were straining, his eye's wild and soaring.

Jackson placed his free hand on his own groin. For some reason he liked this stuff, got a definite rise out of it. 'Now, tell me the truth, cocksucker!'

Angel's head rolled from side to side and tears ran down his cheeks. 'I tole you the truth, man, I tole you!'

'What about this?' He held up the pager.

Angel opened his eyes and batted his lids, trying to clear away the liquid. 'What's that, man?

'I already told you, it's your cop friend asking you if you've done the job yet. What job, Hay-suse?'

Angel's face took on the look of a killer about to be sentenced. 'I wasn't gonna do it, man, I wasn't gonna do it!' he cried. 'He tell me to do it, but I wasn't gonna do it!'

'Do what, Angel?'

'I tip you off, man! I tell you he want you dead!'

'Why did he tell you to kill me, Hay-suse?'

'I doan know, man, I ask him and he say, none of your fuckin' business.' Angel was crying so hard now he was difficult to understand. 'Doan burn me, man, Madre de Dios . . . doan burn me!'

'Were you gonna use your knife?'

Angel sobbed, his voice squeaked. 'I wasn't never gonna *touch* you!'

Jackson waved the flame over Angel's midsection. 'Look at that proud flesh now,' he said. 'All shriveled up like a roasted weenie.'

Feeling the heat, Angel began howling, arching his back and writhing, yanking at the straps with his arms and legs. Jackson pushed his own hardened flesh up against the edge of the table and brought the fire closer to Angel's skin.

'He doan tell me to use no knife, man!' Angel screamed. 'He tell me to use a bat!'

Jackson held the flame still. A bat? He pulled the torch away. 'Say what?'

Angel continued crying and moaning, flopping his head back and forth like a fish on the sand. 'A bat, a bat – a baseball bat!'

'A baseball bat?' Jackson said.

Gulping air between sobs, Angel said, 'He say, I doan wanna know how you do him, then he change his mind and say, use a baseball bat.'

'A baseball bat.' Jackson bent over Angel's face. 'What's this guy look like?'

Angel tried to stop sobbing and answer.

Jackson waved the torch. 'What's he *look like*, Angel?'

'Good-lookin' face.'

'Sandy-colored hair?'

'Yeah, man, sandy, sandy. He know 'bout your chin, too.'

Jackson straightened up. 'Well, I'll be damned.' He said it as if he'd just discovered a long-lost brother. 'Little Nat Hennessy, all grown up now. And a New York cop.'

'I tole you, man,' Angel said, sobbing and catching his breath. 'I doan know why he want you dead.'

'I do,' J.J. said.

Angel's sobs were punctuated by the sniffing and spasms of a little boy crying himself out. 'I tole you.'

'Yes, you did,' Jackson said. He turned off the torch.

'You gotta let me up now, OK?' Angel said.

'Sure,' Jackson said. He pulled a cellular phone from his pocket and laid it on the table. 'But first, you gotta do me a favor. Know what I'm saying?'

He heard the sound of a train whistle deep in the distance, a long, faint blast followed by silence, then another faint blast, then another silence. The whistle mutated into the chirp of a telephone – a chirping telephone coming down a railroad track . . . a railroad track downstairs . . . in the kitchen – *I'm dreaming*.

Nat opened his eyes and saw the night and felt his brain catch up with his pulse. Another chirp from the kitchen woke him a bit more. He turned and reached for the extension on the bedside table – the ringer was off – and lifted the receiver.

'Hello?' he whispered.

'My turn to wake you up,' a voice said.

Nat pushed for recognition. 'Ben?'

'Ticket's all set, one way from JFK to Santo Domingo, American Airlines.'

Tickets? Santo Domingo? Oh, yeah. Got it.

'I put it under the name of A. Esperanza. I thought Angel de Jesus Rico was, you know, a little obvious.'

'OK,' Nat said in a whisper. The fog had not completely lifted.

'You all right, Nathaniel?'

'Yeah.'

There was a pause. 'You sure?'

'Yeah, I'm sure.'

There was another pause.

'OK.' Click.

Nat laid the receiver in its cradle and looked over at Camilla lying on her side with her back to him, still asleep.

He dropped his head back on the pillow and listened to the rhythms of her breathing. His brain was staggering, his foot aching, his pulse pounding out a message he didn't want to hear.

Good God. Get up and call it off – *right now.*

Angel Rico saw a brown pig roasting on a spit, smoke rising from smoldering wood. Chuchurillos, barbecued pig skin cut into squares and eaten like potato chips. A gentle breeze blew the gray-white smoke into his face, turning the aroma of cooking meat into the stench of burning hair. He heard a familiar voice calling him, 'Angel . . .'

His mind corkscrewed out of the dream into a cloud of semiconsciousness. A sharp whiff of ammonia forked up his nostrils into his forehead, pushing him into another place. A present place. The here and now.

He opened his eyes and stared up at metal beams and unlit hanging lamps. Flashes of light sparkled against the corrugated roof like summer lightning, reflecting off greasy industrial surfaces. A haze of stench-filled yellow smoke hung in the air beneath a lamp, and there was this . . . *hissss.*

'. . . so Redd Foxx is on this train on his honeymoon . . .'

A nasal voice reached his ears through a stream of hissing air, a muffled voice, as if it came from inside a tin box.

'. . . and the train's all booked up, so he and his bride have to sleep in separate bunks across the aisle from each other, you know, the kind you gotta climb up to on a ladder . . .'

Hissss.

Angel tried to gather his hands at his sides and push himself up into a sitting position, but his arms wouldn't move. He tried to turn his head to the side to see what was holding them down, but a strap across his forehead held his skull in place.

'. . . middle of the night, Redd whispers across the aisle real

203

loud, "Hey, baby, come on over to my bunk!" And she sticks her head outta the curtain and says . . .'

Hissss.

Angel could feel his heart now, fluttering, fluttering, like the wings of a giant moth trapped inside his rib cage.

'. . . "I would, Redd, honey, but I got no way to get over there!"'

He could see light . . . hear a voice and smell a slaughterhouse, but his hands didn't feel right, they were zipping with electric tingles as if the circulation had been cut off.

'. . . so old Redd, he says, "Don't worry, baby, I got something long and stiff you can come over on!"'

The hissing stopped; the flickering on the ceiling ended. An eerie mask came into view as if sliding onto a movie screen and a voice behind a metal mask said, '"Yeah, I know, Redd, honey, but how am I gonna get back?"'

A hand cocked up the welder's mask, revealing Jackson's sweating face. Even with large pieces of white cotton stuffed into his nose, he looked amused.

'Get it?' he said, his voice no longer muffled by the mask. '"How am I gonna get back?"'

Angel Rico's brain skipped over grammar, structure, coherence. He closed his eyes and felt himself passing out again, falling back into a void. In the distance, he heard Jackson's voice saying, 'Don't do that, Angel,' and felt a cat lick his face with a cold, hairy tongue, startling him. His eyelids opened. Through a veil of swollen veins he saw a white, gauze-covered worm above his forehead . . . J.J.'s fingers squeezing it . . . breaking it . . .

. . . SNAP. Jackson popped another gauze-covered ammonia capsule and placed it under Rico's nose. The large, dripping paintbrush he'd wiped across Angel's face to revive him rested on the bench behind his head. Angel's pupils, framed in red, were beginning to focus again.

He was awake.

* * *

After a few rings, an operator answered with the same cheerful voice and asked Nat for his message.

He said, 'Change of plan . . .'

'Change of plan . . .'

'Forget about job . . .'

'Forget about job . . .'

'Page me to confirm.'

'Page me to confirm.' She finished typing. 'Is that all?'

'That's all.'

'Very good, sir, it'll go right out.'

He hung up and sat holding his head in his hands.

Fuck.

'Can you feel your legs and feet?' Jackson asked.

Angel's eyes were distant, unblinking.

'Can you hear me, Angel?'

Angel managed a grunt that sent white foam into the air like a puff of soap suds.

J.J. said, 'Wiggle your toes for me.'

Angel stared upward, unblinking.

'Work with me now, Angel, wiggle your toes. Here, let me show you how.' He raised Angel's feet and held them above his face. 'These are your toes, see? I don't see them wiggling, do you?'

Angel's eyes said, toes?

'Oh, my, here's the problem,' J.J. said. 'Take a look at this.'

Jackson lowered Angel's feet and unbuckled the straps, then slipped his hands under his torso and propped it up on welder's blocks at a forty-five-degree angle so Angel could look down at himself. Standing next to the table, Jackson put his hand between Angel's crotch and cradled his glutes in his palm. Then he lifted the severed lower half of the body upward, holding it in the direction of Rico's face. The innards below the plane of what had once been his waist were now charred flesh and charcoal-streaked nubs of hip and pelvis bone.

'This is you, Angel. You're looking down into your own bottom half like it's a pair of pants you're getting ready to put on, except, uh-oh – they're already filled up with your legs!'

Angel gurgled and his tongue spilled out of his mouth.

'I was reading about this guy who got cut in half by a train, you know?' Jackson said. 'He stayed alive for three whole days, but I think you can do better. I got the arteries pinched off, and the nice thing about the torch is the heat seals up all the veins.'

Angel exhaled a desperate wheeze. His eyelids quivered and his corneas disappeared into his forehead.

'You don't need your bottom half anyway, Hay-suse. Ever seen them guys without legs pushing themselves around on little skateboards? They get around OK, right?' He laid the lower half of Angel's body on the table below his still-living torso. 'You hungry?' No answer. 'How about some chitlins? I got plenty of heat, I got fresh intestines . . .'

Angel's head trembled and nodded from side to side almost as if he was saying no thanks. Seeing him escaping into a faint, Jackson broke out another ammonia capsule and stuck it under his nose.

'Don't pass out on me now, I still gotta finish writing the word HERE.' He relit the torch and applied the tip of it to Angel's chest.

Angel's clenched teeth sunk into his tongue, turning his lips red with his own blood. Once again the room filled with the smell of burning flesh.

'This is gonna look good,' Jackson said. He finished with the torch and turned it off and removed the cotton from his nostrils. 'Damn, you stink,' he said, making a face. Yellow liquid was oozing from huge blisters on Angel's chest, and tears and sweat covered his face. His eyes were becoming fixed on Jackson as if on a distant star.

'Hay-suse?' Jackson touched his neck. There was still a pulse. He checked the eyes. Bloodshot, wild, but still showing cognition.

Jackson looked at his watch. It was time to get his ass in gear.

He pulled a trash can over to the table and dumped the lower half of Angel's body into it upside down, like a tossed-out mannequin, then wiped a gloss of sweat off his forehead using the forearm of his jumpsuit. 'You say you don't take out the trash?' he said in a low voice. 'Motherfucker, you *are* the trash.' His eyes flashed and his fist swung like a baseball bat, whacking the back of Angel's head.

He placed his hands under the arms and set the severed torso up on the table as if Angel was the stooge in a magic show where the table had cut him in half. Angel's eyes were open, his downward-tilted face swollen, his arms limp and dangling out at his sides, his torso ready to topple over.

Jackson looked up and found two chains on an overhead track used to ferry engine blocks to the table. After pulling them into position, he went to work. When he was finished, he took off his jumpsuit, placed his tools in the wooden box, turned out the lights, and walked out the garage door. After locking it, he dumped his gear into the trunk and got into the limousine.

His two lovely passengers sat in the back seat watching a videotape of *Singing in the Rain*. He sat still, saying nothing, listening to Gene Kelly sing and dance. Soothing his nerves. Letting him think.

He'd give anything to know how to tap dance.

He'd give anything to nail Hennessy to a cross.

By the time the movie had ended, he knew how he was going to do one of the two.

Nat felt a tickle on his belly and woke up on the chaise longue. The pager that had slipped from his hand when he'd dozed off was vibrating. Must be Angel confirming the message to call it off.

He reached up and turned on the lamp. The message in the window read: NEED MORE MONEY. MEET ME AT A & E SCRAP METAL S. BRNX. ANGEL JESUS.

More money? What was he talking about? Blackmail, that's what. Or more time to do the job. Mopes like Angel always wanted something more, it was their style.

Whatever it was, the answer was simple: don't bite.

He tested his foot on the floor. It was still swollen and sore. He limped to the downstairs bathroom, sat on the toilet lid, and rigged up a splint from adhesive tape and one of Camilla's emery boards. A & E Scrap Metal? Whatever it was, he'd be crazy to go near the place. Gotta be a set-up.

More tape on the toes. He stood up and tested his medical handiwork. Not great, but passable.

Got to be trouble, that message. You're not a moth, so don't act like one. Go to bed and work it out in the morning.

He climbed the stairs quietly, found his sneakers, and brought them back downstairs. After cutting the toe out of the right one, he lifted his gun from the chicken and headed out the door.

Of course he wasn't a moth. But sometimes people couldn't help themselves either. Sometimes they, too, had to have the flame.

Hiding behind the tail fins of a rusting '59 Cadillac, he could see the open door across the lit junkyard apron, inviting him in. He turned his back to it and sat on the rusty bumper, resting his swollen foot and aching head. Why was reversing course always so tough? Why should undoing a screw-up be so costly?

He lifted his gun to check it. Ridiculous, these things. Trouble by definition. In seven years of work he'd drawn his weapon only three times, two of them tonight. Not a good omen for what lay ahead.

He ran through his options: A, go in. B, get the fuck out of here. B was the only sane course, but not an option. If he was going to get his life in order, the first step was here and now.

Let's see. If Jackson is in there dead, I gotta hope Angel grabbed the ticket and got out of town before getting caught, booked, and grilled. But Angel wouldn't get out of town, would he? He'd stick around to do business, knowing that if he *did* get arrested – and sooner or later, guys like him always did – he had a get-out-of-jail-free pass in the form of a Detective Nat Hennessy's ass. 'Detective Hennessy,' Angel would confess with those big eyes, 'he hire me to kill a man. Check it out.'

He put his weight on his bum foot. It hurt.

Wouldn't be that hard for Internal Affairs to confirm Angel's story. Jackson had killed Nat's father, which gave Nat motive as big as a house.

He leaned down and tightened the laces on his shoes the way he always did before a bust.

And how about the old woman in curlers and dirty pink slippers? She could put him in the hallway with Angel in a heartbeat. 'You got Rico trapped in a corridor,' a lieutenant from the IAB would be saying, 'your gun's loaded, he's got a knife, and he gets away? How is that, Detective?'

He stooped and looked at the door. He could circle left, hug the wall, and get close to it without crossing the lighted area.

And Angel's airline ticket – who did he think he was kidding, using Ben Brown, his trusted friend and former partner, to camouflage the purchase? Even though Brown would stay silent as a rock, the records would put the IAB on Nat's doorstep in about ten minutes.

He started moving.

And Angel's beeper. Christ, most pagers held the last ten messages they received – why hadn't he thought of that when he sent Angel his instructions? All the DA had to do now was look in the little message window and he'd have Nat's digital confession.

He crossed a junk-strewn path, limping slightly, head low. Gotta find this guy now and set it right. When he reached the side of the building, he stood in the shadows, nervous and dry-mouthed.

Where are you, Angel? He dried his gun hand. You too, Baggy Pants? You in there with him? Waiting to finish me off the way you tried twenty years ago at the bonfire? Or are you in there dead? The way my gut fervently hopes you are?

He picked up a dirty battery cable and threw it at the door, hitting the metal frame with a bang. And waited.

Nothing happened.

Level your gun and put your back against the bricks. Time to move toward the door.

He took one soft step after another until he was two feet from the open entrance, still unable to see inside.

It was *déjà vu* all over again. Once more he was stalking Angel

Rico in a blind alley – except this time he had no backup, not even Shaw coming in late.

He waited long enough to satisfy his instincts, then crouched low, gun extended. If his foot had been on fire he wouldn't have noticed, he was so focused. Take another look inside.

No light in there. No movement. No sound.

He stepped through the door and moved into the shadows cast from the outside lights. A recollection kicked in – *Look up!* – Angel likes to drop from the rafters, remember? But here the ceilings were twenty feet high, at least.

He moved into the camouflage of blackness and stood still, waiting for his eyes to adjust to the minuscule light, listening to himself breathing through a dry throat.

Stand still and wait. Don't move until you can see.

His pupils dilated, processing shadows . . . frosted windows across the room, ghostly equipment nearby . . . a table – right in front of you – the silhouette of a man with his arms raised—

'Freeze!' he yelled crouching, aiming, shaking.

The man's hands were lifted into the air, surrendering.

'Keep 'em high!' Nat barked.

He did. Saying nothing.

Nat reached out to his side and patted the wall – up, down, over, up, down, over – until he found a box with three switches close to the door. Must be the lights. OK, do this by the book: stay low, gun ready. One, two . . .

Lights on.

Huh?

He saw the back of a naked man standing with his hands held high in the air, holding onto a pair of chains – no, not holding on, tied to them – his head slumped forward, standing in a hole cut into the middle of the table—

Look again. There's light between the bottom of his torso and the table top. He's dangling above it. He's half a body.

Holy shit.

Nat looked over his shoulder for Jackson – a little late – but Jackson wasn't there. Then he turned and moved toward the back of the torso, and around it to its front. There were letters burned onto its chest: a B, an A, and a T. There were more letters below those – he saw HERE before riveting his attention on the man's head.

He reached out, placed the muzzle of his .38 under the man's chin, and lifted it.

A blistered, unrecognizable face – a swollen, protruding tongue – eyes closed beneath the signature widow's peak he expected.

Angel Rico's.

He felt his skin go clammy and a touch of stomach acid wanting to erupt. My God, what's hap—

He jumped back with an involuntary grunt, nearly leaving his skin behind.

Angel Rico had opened his eyes.

And blinked.

Time to play Let's Pretend.

Nat entered Midtown South wearing the same pair of cut-out sneakers he'd worn a few hours before. His toe was still swollen and sore, and he was walking with a limp, but that was good enough for him. An X-ray, he knew from experience, added nothing but a five-hundred-dollar bill and a bunch of forms to fill out. He hated paperwork. Detective, heal thyself.

He hobbled up the steps to the large common office on the second floor and found Shaw sitting at her desk typing a report, a rubber-bladed fan blowing air into her face. She spoke without looking up.

'Congratulations, that's one way to solve a crime.'

Now it begins. Look dumb and wait.

'Damn it,' she said, hitting the backspace button. 'Typewriters suck.'

'What crime?' he said.

She stopped typing and handed him a folder, still focused on the page. 'When the heck am I going to learn to use a computer?' she said. 'They found him this morning at a junkyard in the Bronx. Anonymous tip.'

That's me, all right. Mr Anonymous.

She handed him a folder of eight-by-ten black-and-white glossies shot by the CSU photographer. 'Ever see somebody cut in half with a torch?'

Only once. He turned off Shaw's battery-driven fan, opened the folder, and spread the pictures on her desk between a New

213

York *Post* and a coffee cup with a drawing of Snoopy lying on top of his doghouse. Angel appeared to be standing waist-deep in water, except the surface of the water was a bench top. Trick photography. Even now, it was mindbending.

Then a shot of a body bag. Guess he didn't make it after all.

He paused on a shot of Angel's chest. The burned-in letters said, BAT MAN, and beneath that, WAS HERE. Not even a scumbag like Angel deserved a fate like this.

'A whole new graffiti art form,' Shaw said.

'Any idea whose?'

'No,' Shaw said, 'but whoever it was, it looks as if he positioned Rico for a photographer.'

No, not for a photographer, for me. The bat in this BAT MAN was made of hard wood, not bony little black wings. Jackson must have tortured Angel into telling him everything, even the phone number of the pager. Which meant Jackson, not Angel, had sent the message to come to A & E Scrap Metal. Nat put the photographs back into the envelope.

So now Baggy Pants knows I sent Angel to kill him. So now the Bambino has a whiff of the long, slow fuse that's been burning inside me all these years. That's right, Mr Jackson. It's me. Son of the father. Cop and private stalker. Now it's your turn to sleep with your eyes open, wondering whether the next hand that touches your back is mine.

In spite of it all, Nat felt a spark of triumph.

But Jackson knew how to stalk someone too.

'What's the lab got?'

'The usual,' Shaw said. 'Footprints of everyone who ever walked through the place.'

Including some from the sneakers I'm wearing.

Shaw took her first long look at Nat. 'Remember when I said your wife won't tell you how you really look the first year you're married?'

'Yeah?'

'I'm not your wife. You look like hell.'

'Thank God for half of that news,' he said. 'Who's covering the crime scene?'

'We are. Car's out front.'

'See you downstairs in a minute.'

He left her desk and walked down the hall to the squad room and made a beeline for his metal locker. On his way in earlier, he'd placed Angel's Airtel pager on the top shelf behind his shaving gear. He grabbed it and stuck it back into his pocket so he could deep-six it in New York Harbor on his way to Liberty Island that afternoon.

After closing the metal door, he snapped on the lock and joined Shaw, who was waiting for him in the passenger seat of their police department Ford.

Camilla stood looking at the mess on her bed, pulling at her lower lip, trying to decide. The crown in the Statue of Liberty was closed for repairs – only the mezzanine floor museum and the island park were open to the public – but as a member of the construction crew she could take Nat up to the torch, show him the work they were doing, and spend some private time with him before the wedding. The rehearsal dinner would begin at eight, and from that point on, most of their time together would probably be a blur.

Let's see, what should I wear? She put on one of Nat's white button-down shirts with the sleeves rolled up, a pair of khaki shorts, and her favorite tan loafers, then walked down the spiral staircase to her studio and found a large canvas bag. What else? She dropped in a pair of yellow, rubber-coated binoculars, then went to the kitchen and added a chilled bottle of peach champagne, a reminder of bellinis from Harry's Bar in New York, where Nat had proposed. After wrapping champagne glasses in a cloth napkin, she checked her watch. She'd have to get started if she was going to finish her errands and meet him on the four o'clock ferry.

She put on her sunglasses and zipped the bag closed. Hoisting it onto her shoulder, her eye caught the red message light blinking on the answering machine. She really didn't have time, but . . .

She hit Play.

The first message had been saved from yesterday – same for the second and the third. Then came the new one.

'Hello?' It was Nat's sleepy voice.

'My turn to wake you up,' the caller said. Nat must have picked up the phone by the bed just as the recording on the kitchen phone had started.

'Ben?'

'Ticket's all set, one way from JFK to Santo Domingo, American Airlines. I put it under the name of A. Esperanza. I thought Angel de Jesus Rico was, you know, a little obvious.'

'OK.'

'You all right, Nathaniel?'

'Yeah.'

A pause. 'You sure?'

'Yeah, I'm sure.'

Another pause.

'OK.' Click.

She hit the Stop button.

Good Lord.

Nat roamed through the A & E Scrap Metal shop looking over the crime scene. He saw no hard evidence of Jackson's crime, but then, he wasn't really looking for it. He already knew the killer's identity.

He walked to the lathe table where the dissection had taken place. Shaw stood nearby finishing an interview with the junk-yard owner, a hairy-armed man with a long face sobered by the gruesome killing that had occurred in his shop. Nat looked at the table but didn't touch it. The lab guys had finished their work but the surface had not yet been scrubbed. He tried to picture the cutting, which was hard to imagine, and the pathological mind that had done it, which wasn't. He'd seen it in operation before. Up close in living color. Shaw approached him, jotting a note on her pad.

'He doesn't know anything about anything,' she said.

'How'd the perp get in?'

'Apparently he used a remote control to open the street gate and a Yale key on the shop door.'

'Who's got copies?' he asked.

'Half a dozen towing companies that drop off cars in the middle of the night. I'll run them down.'

'How's the owner keep from getting ripped off?'

'There's a night guard.'

'Where was he?'

'Out sick.'

'I'd check that out. Anything stolen?'

'No, but get this: none of the shop's cutting tools were used, which means the perp brought his own. Who do you know who carries around an acetylene torch at four in the morning?'

A maniac named J.J. Jackson. He probably carried all the tools of his trade. Guns, torches, whatever it took.

'It wasn't a case of random violence,' Shaw said, 'and it wasn't a robbery gone bad. Bat Man and Angel knew each other, which means once we figure out the relationship, we'll know who did it.'

Sally Shaw was good. Pretty soon he'd have to worry about that. A lot.

Nat and Shaw were driving south toward Battery Park when he felt the beeper on his belt vibrating. The message window's small liquid letters floated across like the news zipper in Times

Square: CITY ... COUNCIL ... KILLED ... BIAS ...
CONGRATS ... AMERIGO.

How about that? He'd nailed Cush Walker's test after all.

Nat turned onto Seventh Avenue and headed south toward
Battery Park and the ferry to Liberty Island.

It felt satisfying and, at the same time, depressing. Satisfying
to stop Walker, depressing to know how he'd done it. And
embarrassing, considering how much of it had been motivated
by personal jealousy instead of the good of the department.

What if Camilla knew? What if she knew he'd sent Angel
Rico to kill Jackson? He tried to sort out his screw-ups, but
they felt balled up like a bunch of cough drops in the palm of
his hand.

What a way to start a marriage.

A black limousine pulled into a public parking lot next to the
ferry terminal but Nat didn't notice it. Nor, with its windows
up, did he hear Oro Solido doing 'Maria Se Fue', or see the
driver's muscular fingers dancing the merengue on the steering
wheel. Limos were a dime a dozen in New York and he was
trying to put his detective radar to rest for the next ten days.

He pulled his pager off his belt and stuck it into his pocket
and felt it clack against the one he'd taken from Angel. Shaw
had dropped him off at the ferry early, giving him time to limp to
a florist nearby and buy a bouquet of lavender freesias. He walked
back to the boat in the afternoon heat, tie loosened, shirtsleeves
up, jacket over his shoulder on the hook of his finger, looking
nothing like a detective, which was how detectives preferred
to look.

He boarded the ferry, climbed to the top deck, laid his head
back on a wooden seat, and watched the sun illuminate the veins
in his closed eyelids. A few hours from now he'd be lying under
this same ball of fire somewhere on Lido beach, outside Venice,
and Camilla would be his wife.

What a funny phrase, 'my wife'. He drifted a little, picturing her lying beside him, her top off, her skin brown and velvet, that killer smile—

That killer smile. That killer— A shadow crossed his eyelids – someone was standing over him. His eyes opened just in time to see a head in the blinding sun coming down on him—

Jackson!

He saw her killer smile as he rose with a start.

'Did I wake you?' Camilla said as he propped himself on his elbows.

'Just daydreaming.' He stood up and set her canvas bag on the deck and wrapped his arms around her, kissing her. The engines started to rumble.

He handed her the bouquet of freesias. She brought them to her nose and breathed them in as if they were a new kind of air, a fresh start.

He'd told Shaw that detectives didn't think about bad guys trying to get even, and it was true, he never had. Until now.

The ferry horn sounded and they headed for Liberty Island.

For a moment it felt as if they were standing at the top of the universe, completely untouchable. The platform was thirty stories high with an unobstructed view, and laid out before them was the whole world: bustling New York Harbor, the sweep of Brooklyn, large eruptions of concrete at the tip of Manhattan, the forests of Liberty State Park, New Jersey's mighty cranes and refineries, Staten Island and the looming grace of the Verrazano Narrows Bridge, then full circle back to the sapphire Atlantic.

Camilla stood at the railing with a pair of yellow binoculars, roaming the view, her hair lifting and falling like a flag furling in a gentle breeze. 'Stunning, isn't it?' she said.

Maybe it was. First he had to look. Jesus, no wonder helicopters crashed into this thing, it was standing in the middle of the sky. The torch platform was smaller than it looked from the ground, about ten feet in diameter, the size of an ordinary kitchen with a large golden flame in the center where a cooking island should be.

He stepped next to her, cautiously.

'Keep your eyes on the horizon and don't look down,' she said cheerfully.

He immediately looked down. Everything appeared at a new angle: the spikes on Miss Liberty's crown, her Gallic nose, the huge tablet clutched against her breast, her sandaled toes on the immense stone pedestal. Below that, in the shrunken distance, was the white marble plaza surrounding the eleven-pointed star of Fort Wood, the massive, cement-filled base for the entire structure. Terra firma. Flat earth. People walking on it who looked like tiny little wind-up dolls, small, but sane for being there. He looked forward to joining them soon.

'If you lean out,' she said, leaning out, 'you can see where the rotor blades hit her face.'

He moved his neck maybe two inches, like a kid pretending to see something he didn't. A jagged gash on Miss Liberty's nose was all he needed to get the idea. He hated head wounds.

'Time to celebrate,' she said. She lifted her canvas bag from a pile of construction materials that had been pushed out of the way – climbing ropes, cans of solvent, tools – and lifted out the bottle of peach champagne.

Oh, good idea. We can get drunk and wobble on top of a flagpole.

He opened the champagne with a pop that shot the cork into the air, then caught the erupting froth in the glasses she held, wetting her hands.

Raising his glass, he said, 'To you, sweetheart. If I love you half as much in fifty years as I do today . . .' He didn't have a punch line.

'Then what?' she asked.

'I wouldn't be surprised.' Cool.

She smiled at him and cupped her palm on his cheek. 'To us, when together and apart.'

They drank and he wrapped his arm around her. Apart?

She kissed his ear. 'Want to fool around a little?'

'You serious?'

'It would be a first.' They were still at an age when firsts mattered.

He massaged the nape of her neck. 'I doubt that,' he said. 'One of those horny little Frenchmen must have beat us to it.'

'Maybe when it was on the ground getting made.'

'So to speak.'

'But not after it was erected.'

'So to speak.'

She reached out and took him by his necktie and pulled him toward her. 'Come here.'

'People can see us,' he said, not really caring.

'Not if we get down.' She undid his tie.

'What about helicopters?'

'If we do this right, who knows? Maybe we'll bring down another one.'

They heard a *hisssss* behind them that turned into a whine and a short bleat.

'What the hell's that?' he asked, turning.

'It's a liquid nitrogen canister bleeding off excess pressure. It's automatic. Pay attention to what we're doing here.'

They sat on the platform and drank champagne and got carried away and kissed each other on the lips and neck and other interesting places, and before long, with a touch of caution and a lot of abandon, they had managed to give the word 'engagement' its very literal, intimate meaning. Afterward, Nat rested on his back looking at a ceiling of blue sky, necktie entirely off, shirt unbuttoned. Camilla rested her head on his chest.

After a few minutes, he said, 'OK, I'm ready now.'

'For what?' she said, as in, again? So soon?

'Whatever it is you have to tell me.'

She sat on the platform with her legs crossed, he with his back to the torch. She was glad he'd asked. It was time to get this thing off her chest. 'You were right, it's about the game we played on the chaise,' she said, looking for a place to begin. 'I couldn't tell what you were thinking.'

'About what?'

'About me. The role I was playing.'

He laid his hand on her knee. 'It was just a game, sweet-heart.'

'Actually, it was . . . a little more than that.'

222

'In what way?'

She wanted to tell him why she'd been testing him, but she feared his reaction would be indelibly wrong. Not his spoken reaction, she knew what that would be – big deal, so you've got a black grandfather, who cares? – but the one she knew would appear on his face, from his soul, instant and unmistakable. Once she told him, he'd show disapproval or he wouldn't.

She didn't like the odds.

He rubbed her knee lightly with his palm. 'I'm curious about why you picked that particular game.'

'Pretending I was black?'

'Yeah.'

Because I am. She reached out and touched the back of his hand, then searched his eyes. 'I've got a confession to make, Nat,' she said.

'Good, I love confessions.'

Her mind circled Sebastian and her grandmother Camilla Bea and the subject she wanted to talk about . . . and landed elsewhere. 'When I was leaving the apartment I listened to the answering machine and heard a message from your old partner, Ben Brown.'

He stopped caressing her knee.

'He said he'd bought a ticket for Angel Rico to leave the country.' She saw him blanch. *See? His face always gives him away.* 'I've been wondering why you helped a killer leave the country.'

He leaned back.

She waited.

'It's complicated,' he said.

'Try me.'

'I don't think I can.'

He stood up and stepped over to the railing and rested his forearms on it. She got to her feet and joined him.

'I don't care about the legalities, if that's what you're worried

223

about,' she said. 'I'm just trying to clear the air between us before we get married.'

She watched him gaze at the plaza thirty stories below. Interesting, she thought, how he tends to lose his fear of something once he gets used to it. That was a sign of good character, wasn't it? Or was it just wishful thinking?

He said, 'I let him go because I thought he could help me find someone I needed more than him.'

'Who?'

'A criminal.'

She'd never heard of that. 'Is that kosher?'

'No.'

'Does anyone else know you did it?'

'No.'

'Not even your partner?'

'Not a clue.'

She didn't get it. 'What about Angel Rico? Aren't you afraid he might tell?'

'No.'

'Why not?'

'Because he's dead.'

Dead? 'My God, Nat.'

'He was murdered last night. It's in the newspapers.'

She hadn't seen one yet. 'Do you know who did it?' The message from Ben, the news of Rico's murder – it was adding up to something she didn't like.

He shook his head slightly. Does that mean he doesn't know, or he won't tell me? 'I gather you don't want to talk about it,' she said.

'Not at the moment.'

She didn't like that, either. More stonewalling, like last night. Leaning forward, she watched the people down below like a kid peering into a fish tank. 'There's something else I want to tell you,' she said.

'What?'

She looked at the cut on the statue's nose, not speaking. 'Now I'm the one holding back,' she said.

'Why?'

'Good question.'

'Come on.'

She didn't speak.

'Is it really that terrible?' he said.

'Oh, it's not terrible at all. At least, not as far as I'm concerned.'

'Then what's the problem?'

She raised her face to his. 'You are.'

'Me?'

'Let me put it this way: I'm afraid what I have to say will be important to you, and if it is, that's going to be a problem for me. Which means for us.'

'What kind of a problem?'

'I'm afraid you'll be . . . turned off in some way.'

'I can't imagine that.'

'Not deliberately. In a way you can't help.'

'Is this something about you and Cush Walker?'

He would think that. 'Not really.'

'"Not really" sounds like a hedge. What'd you do, remember something the two of you did together? Because if that's it, I don't need to know.'

'That's not it.'

'Does it have to do with why you left him? The secret you didn't want to tell me?'

'No, no, no, that's not it. I know why I left him, I just don't know all the details behind it.'

He reached down and picked up the bottle of champagne, and poured them both a glass.

'Oh, for God's sake,' she said, 'this is ridiculous. It's about Sebastian, my grandmother's lover, my biological grandfather.'

'What about him?'

'I didn't know until recently that he was part—' Her face froze. 'Oh, my God . . .'

He saw the color drain out. 'What's wrong?'

She set her glass down and touched her forehead. 'It just hit me.'

What did? Something about Walker, or something about her grandmother and Sebastian? Or was she on to what he'd done with Angel Rico?

He felt his pager vibrating in his pocket. 'Wait a minute,' he said, and reached in and pulled it out and looked down at the message window. That's strange, it's blank. He touched the off button but the humming continued against his leg. Christ, it was the other one – Angel's – the one he'd forgotten to throw overboard on the way out here.

He pulled it out of his pants pocket and turned off the buzzer and saw liquid letters scrolling across the message window: LOOK . . .

He felt Camilla's hand on his arm.

. . . TO THE NORTH . . .

'Oh, my God,' he heard her say.

. . . AT THE BOAT . . .

She squeezed him. 'Nat . . .'

. . . BY THE PIER . . .

'I know what happened,' she said.

'Know what happened what?' He leaned down and picked up the yellow binoculars and raised them to his eyes.

She put her hands on his cheeks beneath the glasses. 'Nat, listen to me.'

He found water, grass, the dock, and a boat sitting next to it, its bow pointed out to sea. There was a figure in the stern, a black man in a blue jacket and navy pants holding a pair of binoculars in his hands – looking up at the statue.

Looking at the torch.

Looking at them.

'Oh, Nat.' She stepped in front of him to get his attention. The light sparkled on her hair like crystals, obscuring his view through the lens. She said, 'I just figured it out.'

He lowered his left hand from the binoculars and placed it on the back of her neck and pulled her into a tight embrace to get her hair out of the way.

'Can you put those things down a minute and listen?' she said.

'Hang a second.'

He held the binoculars next to her ear, his eyes riveted on the man in the boat. Angel Rico was the only person who knew this pager number, but since he was dead, that meant—

'Nat, *please*.'

—his killer had it.

He heard her say something but his mind was focused elsewhere. Jackson was down there in the boat? Using a cell phone to call Angel's pager? What did he want?

She said, 'It's so clear now . . .'

I can't see what he's doing – he's got his back turned—

Her voice was insistent. 'Even if it wasn't premeditated . . .'

Wait a minute—

'. . . it was still the same as murder!'

—that isn't— Did she say *murder*?

He turned the focus knob and pressed the binoculars to his eye sockets.

That isn't a fishing pole he's holding. That's a—

A patch of smoke blotted out the man's face.

—rifle.

For an instant he actually saw the bullet bore a hole in the sky, black and vibrant against the puff of white. Traveling at 2200 feet per second, it gave his brain no more than a tick to comprehend what was coming.

It hit three inches from his eyes.

He heard a dull *thwock* and felt her head snap forward against his shoulder. Dropping the binoculars, he grabbed her as her knees buckled and her legs quit and her hands fell peacefully at her sides. Her head toppled backward, her lips frozen mid-word, her eyes staring through him as if he was dead, not her. The delayed report from the rifle pierced the air the way thunder follows lightning – *crack!*

Then the downward pull of her weight, the world collapsing in his arms. With his hand around her waist, he eased her onto the platform.

Kneeling over her body, his palm behind her head, he felt a warm trickle of syrup bathe his fingers. Blood ran down the bridge of his own nose as well, lowering a crimson shade over his left eye. Trying to clear it with his knuckle, he brushed away something that had lodged itself in his forehead. A distant memory shouted in his head: *you know what this is – this is a bit of skull – you've felt it before.*

He stared at Camilla's startled mouth and marble eyes, afraid to turn her head to see what was there, even more afraid to see what wasn't. Resting her head gently on its side, he withdrew his cradling palm and saw it was loaded with crimson – bits of hair, broken eggshell, wrinkled flesh – his, hers, he couldn't tell one from the other. Oh, Christ. He touched her neck with his oily red fingertips, searching for a pulse. Oh, Christ, no. *Not her head. Not Camilla.*

Not again.

Unable to find her heartbeat, he began yelling 'Fire!' knowing, as a cop, that no one responded to calls for help.

FOUR

Above thy deep and dreamless sleep
The silent stars go by.

—Phillips Brooks

When I make a mistake, it's a beaut.
—Fiorello H. La Guardia

THREE DAYS LATER, MONDAY, *July* 7

Black ice, hard and uncracked. No fire or reflection, no horizon or seams. No east or west, no up or down. Like a mariner's hull trapped in an early freeze, Camilla's consciousness lay splintered in a flow of swollen tissue, undirected by tide or compass, oblivious of the world.

Her head rested high on a pillow, mummified in bandages. A cranial bolt – a device placed through her skull – monitored the brain's slow delta waves and interior pressure. Only the click-clack of the respirator disturbed the soft hospital air – no fluttering eyelids, no rustling sheets, no legs curling the blanket to shape the nest. Sleep gathered its shaggy wool around her sentient mind and transformed it into a bed of tranquillity, quietly, magically, the way cold air turns rain into snow. She was at rest now, drifting through time and space with no beginning and no end, gliding on a boundless plane of black, crystalline ice.

Silence.

Out of nowhere, a lonesome brain cell, like a clarinet, wheezed its dry reed. *Nat*, it played, then fell silent. What is a *Nat*? the other brain cells asked.

A violin neuron with only one string quivered weakly in the air. *Angel*, it said, trying to connect itself to the others. Some heard, but few comprehended. None answered.

Silence.

An hour later, with no prompting, a bassoon brain wave burped out a *Cush*, and an oboe neuron answered with a recollection of the name: *dark, aristocratic, tall*. But then a piccolo added a *Spider* and a *banana*, confusing the song they'd started. The other instruments, trying to listen and pick up the tune, shrugged and returned to their snoozes.

And the violas – where were they? Gone, their chairs empty, as if a bolt of lightning or a hunk of lead had crashed through their midst and wiped them out. And what was wrong with the piano? Its keys moved, its hammers struck, but the strings stayed silent, as if they'd been disconnected from sound or thought, or were missing entirely.

Camilla Bea and Sebastian, a French horn crooned. So romantic, those horns, but who were they talking about? The other instruments tried to pick up the names and play, but having no score to read, they couldn't do it. The names meant nothing.

They fell silent.

After a while a pushy trumpet began playing solo. *Murder*, it wailed, prompting a cymbal to come crashing in with, *it was the same thing as a murder*. What was? the others asked. Who was?

Desperate to know, a group of frustrated brain cells began playing berserkly, sounding like pots and pans falling in a kitchen. Feeling stampeded, other neurons soon joined in, worsening the chaos, while still others tried to restore order, a beat, a rhythm, only adding to the mess. They were an orchestra out of control now, running up and down the scales like frightened mice, full of cacophony.

One by one the cells played themselves out. Exhausted, they waited for their conductor to step out of the cerebral cortex and lead them. They wanted that consciousness they called Camilla. They wanted to see her tap the podium, raise her baton, and do what she usually made them do, the thing they loved most: make music. They wanted coherence, melody, and memory. They wanted thought.

They waited, but no one appeared. The concert hall of the cranium remained quiet – not a cough or rustle to be heard. A bass drum mimicked the beat of her heart with a *ka-boom*, but the other neurons paid no attention.

They were depressed. Doesn't she understand? We need to exercise, we need to play. If she doesn't come out and lead us, we're going to die.

Seeing nothing, hearing nothing, the disheartened neurons turned cold and stony again, as lifeless as if frozen in a block of hard, black ice.

Having stayed at the hospital since the shooting, he'd been insulated from the public rituals of sympathy that had played themselves out in the aftermath of this wonderfully telegenic tragedy. He hadn't heard the anchorman bemoan the shooting or seen the wind-blown reporter at the Statue of Liberty speak of the irony of an architectural restorer, a giver of artistic life, being struck down on the very icon she was repairing. He hadn't read the headlines in the *Post*, MONUMENTAL SHAME, or *Daily News*, TORCH SNIPER HUNTED, or learned that this was the first time in memory that the statue had been closed to the public because of a crime.

He hadn't been home to hear the telephone messages that had filled the answering machine to capacity, or seen the E-mail on his computer. He hadn't picked up the notices of undelivered telegrams slipped under the door or been able to join friends who'd gathered at the loft of their neighbor, Robin Feld. He hadn't been to his desk at the station house to read the comments of colleagues circulated in the intradepartmental multi-use envelope.

But to those who'd come to the hospital visitors' lounge, Nat had been a generous emotional sponge, giving aid and comfort to would-be aiders and comforters. He'd spent his wedding day with Camilla's best friend, Lucy, letting her weep on his shoulder. He'd listened patiently to the members of the wedding party express their worry and grief, remaining graceful despite his own desire for solitude, while friends and relatives unburdened themselves of their pent-up sympathy. He'd listened to them all: the conveyors of greeting card clichés – we're thinking of you in this difficult time; the interpreters of Camilla's intent – she wouldn't want you to stay here all night without sleeping; the chipper optimists – something good will come out of this, it always does; the religious fatalists – God moves in mysterious ways; the narcissists – my mother was once in a coma for three months; the armchair doctors – they say if you hold her hand she can feel it; the patronizing stiffs – oh, you poor dear. As far as he was concerned, friends who gave the most comfort were those who offered the least, like silence, a touch, an unspoken prayer, or an old-fashioned promise to help if called. But he handled everyone nicely, knowing that for most people the art of giving sympathy was as difficult as receiving it.

Sally Shaw had come by the hospital and left a note for him at the nurses' desk, telling him that she was available to update him on the investigation, or just to be a friend. And Nat's old partner, Ben Brown, had arrived at Camilla's hospital room door and walked Nat to the cafeteria and said he assumed the shooter was the same person he'd read about in the *Daily News*, the one who'd killed Angel Rico. He wanted to know if he'd hurt Camilla by helping arrange the airline ticket, but Nat said no, just the opposite; if only Angel had taken the ticket and split, none of this would have happened.

Camilla's bridesmaids, Nat's Police Athletic League basketball buddies, friends, relatives, neighbors, and colleagues waited on the sidelines with offers of chicken soup and sympathetic body parts – ears for listening, shoulders to lean on, hands for helping. But now, three days later, the initial color of shock was already giving way to the pale necessities of people's daily lives, as if their grief and sorrow, like autumn leaves, were turning brown and fluttering to the ground.

Not for Nat. For him a black sun still burned in the sky.

He laid his head on the back of the hard-backed chair,

unshaven and exhausted, and closed his eyes. In front of him was Camilla, on her hospital bed, her face covered with gauze, tubes, and life-giving gear, a female astronaut napping on the moon. The respirator beat its tattoo with the relentless click–clack of a tugboat engine, the monotone sound of a cold machine pumping oxygen into a toy doll. It was three in the afternoon, uncharacteristically cool for the seventh of July, but he had no sense of the weather or outside world, no tentacled connections to steaming hot-dog stands or bicycle messengers or the life that resonated in the bones of New York City. The shades on the windows were drawn, merging time and space into a single monotonous line, the air in the room stale and dry with the faint aroma of antiseptic floors, pickle stems, dead tuna on white, and bacteria dancing in hidden places.

Wake up, sweetheart. Wake up.

Flaring his nostrils, he raised his watch to check the time, then squinted at the window. The afternoon rays were pale butter melting on the floor. Seventy hours since the shooting, and still no sign of life. He bridled under the slow, heavy clock that governed his life now, the endless waiting and watching, the threadbare uncertainty that Camilla's tomorrow would arrive.

If it doesn't come for you, babe, it doesn't come for me.

He stood up and walked to the window. Lifting the blinds, he peered into the ordinary world outside, a vaguely familiar place that had disappeared the moment the bullet had arrived. He raised the blinds, went to the bathroom to splash cold water on his face, and returned to the mold of his chair. The resident neurologist had said nothing could be done now, the wound was too grievous, all you could do was hope for a miracle, and if that didn't happen, pray for mercy. Nat knew what that meant. He'd seen the machine's plugs in the wall.

Come on, Camilla, wake up. Please.

He blinked away the hot, dry air that lay like sandbags on his eyes. I'm going to rest them for a second, and when

I open them, I want to see your hand in a different position.

His eyelids closed and before he knew it he was asleep. His inner ears scrambled their auditory sirens, but it was too late: his head fell forward, hitting the metal guard that kept patients from falling out of bed, *clong*.

He woke up. Slumping back into his seat, he looked at Camilla's hand. It hadn't moved.

A spider of warm blood crept over his eyebrow. Damn. He'd reopened the wound on his forehead.

He reached for a handkerchief from his back pocket and pressed it against the skin. The bedside call button brought a nurse named Virginia Punt, the one who'd given him a pillow and let him sleep in the room despite hospital regulations. He asked her for a bandage, but when she saw the wound, he didn't stand a chance. He was out the door and on his way to the ER.

Wait a sec, he said, looking up and down the hallway. He saw patients in green gowns and a few civilians, but no doctors. When the hospital neurologists examining Camilla had told him of the hopelessness of conventional medicine, he hadn't hesitated to admit her to the NeuroPath wing with its experimental procedures and ask Dr Schulman, the hospital's chief of neurosurgery, to consult on her case.

But where was the genius? This savior of humankind who everyone said was Camilla's only chance? Where was his bosom buddy, Dr Walker?

Dr Cush Walker entered the room to the quiet sound of a ventilator, low light, and the damped-down stillness of a funeral parlor. He moved to Camilla's side and stood quietly surveying her face, or at least as much as he could see of it through plastic, rubber, gauze, and stainless-steel gear.

Her chart indicated that the trauma team had followed the protocols for a bullet wound to the head: debridement of bone fractures, clots, dirt and tissue, a CT scan to see what had been scrambled inside, an emergency craniotomy to relieve pressure from swelling, and massive antibiotics to stem infection and pneumonia. With her skull opened up, they had inserted a tiny transducer into her brain to monitor the internal pressure. Then, like everyone else, they waited.

When the call came into the Mississippi clinic that she'd been shot, Cush had telephoned the hospital and arranged her admission to the NeuroPath wing, then flown back to New York to take charge. The Manitol had helped absorb cranial fluid into the bloodstream, but the pressure on the brain stem continued unabated, preventing her from breathing or swallowing. Even to his expert eye, her life now seemed suspended by little more than lines and hoses: a tube to give her lungs air, another to clear away fluids, small drains from her cranium, a pipe into her esophagus to keep her from choking, a catheter in her bladder, an EEG cable to her cortex, wires to a monitor showing her heartbeat, breathing, blood pressure, and temperature.

Cush checked the oscilloscope and saw the slow delta waves

of a coma, not the alpha waves of sleep. An EEG didn't measure the quality of thought, but at least she was cerebrating.

Using the ventilator controls, he increased her rate of respirations to avoid a build-up of carbon dioxide in her bloodstream that would dilate the vessels and increase her intracranial pressure. He made sure her head was properly elevated, then, even though her pulse beeped on the monitor, lifted her wrist to check it. After finding it beating against his fingertip, he found his own heart beating in the artery of his thumb. He waited for the two rhythms to cross, momentarily synchronized. Even in this morgue-like room he was aware of her life, her vitality. My God. He'd forgotten how much he missed her, how deeply he'd buried his feelings for her when she'd left. How much he wanted her. Now it was all bubbling back like a hot spring.

He flipped a switch, lowering the light on her face, then leaned forward, lifted her eyelid, and with a small penlight examined her retina for broken blood vessels. The pupil contracted with a small implosion, which was good. He saw no bleeding.

He stood up and looked at her. Being so close and yet so far made him feel like a prisoner behind a glass partition. He pictured the wounds beneath her bandages, the MRI and brain scan, the shredded tissue, the tangled, ruptured neurons that had once made her the person he'd fallen in love with, then lost. Now here she was, back in his life, a broken Humpty Dumpty. What a way to come back together.

If he could control the heat problem with his nanoscanners, if he had a blueprint of healthy brain tissue to work with, if she didn't develop pneumonia or post-trauma aneurysms – or something worse, like Patient RAD – if everything was three degrees different, he could try to put her back together again. But everything wasn't. Being so close and yet so far made him bridle with frustration.

The door to the room opened and Nurse Punt entered. 'Her fiancé is waiting,' she said.

He checked her vital signs and made a note on her chart. 'I'll be with him in a minute,' he said, concentrating. As she started to leave, he said, 'What's his name again?'

'I'm sorry, Doctor, I don't recall.'

He finished making his notes, remembering that Spider had said he was a detective with the police department. He wondered what kind.

Nat Hennessy sat at a large conference-room table, adrift amid portraits, glass, and mahogany walls. The wound on his forehead had been repaired with four stitches. His eyes were bloodshot but open, his idea of a second wind.

The door opened and Cush Walker entered carrying a manila envelope, reading a chart. Nat saw a navy suit, blue shirt, and a perfect silk tie worn by a man who looked taller and more elegant than he'd remembered from the union meeting. Approaching the table, Walker's eyes remained glued to his reading. What was this, a subtle insult? Proof of who's in charge here? Or was it – God, was it possible he didn't know who was waiting to see him? Nat clenched his teeth and waited.

Walker laid the envelope on the conference-room table and finally looked up. And froze.

Damn. Not a clue.

Walker tried to digest his surprise. 'Detective *Hennessy*?' The name came out like, mumps? Plague? Scurvy?

'Dr Walker,' Nat said, fortunately too far away to extend his hand and have it rejected.

Walker sat in the leather chair at the head of the table and leaned back and looked at his patient's fiancé. 'Detective Nat Hennessy,' he repeated in a tone of, well, well, well.

'I gather no one told you—'

Walker raised his hand, cutting him off. 'Before you say anything more, I have to ask a question.'

Nat's bloodshot eyes asked, what?

'Are you wearing a wire?'

Nat felt the fever in his cheeks. 'I didn't wear the last one.' It was lame and technical, the best that he could do.

Walker crucified him with a silent, dignified stare, his mahogany eyes covered with ice. Nat looked into them for as long as he could before reaching out and pulling a yellow pad toward him as a psychic shield.

'What do you want, Detective?'

'I want to know Camilla's condition.'

Walker paused as if deciding whether to answer him or tell him to go fuck himself. After a moment he reached out and drew the large manila folder toward him and carried it to a lightboard on the wall. Clicking on the fluorescent bulbs inside, he pulled out a sheaf of negatives and stuck them under metal clips. Nat got up and joined him.

Walker lifted a yellow pencil and pointed with the eraser.

'The bullet entered at the base of the skull here, then moved past the midbrain – this area – and corkscrewed through the left hemisphere and exited here, just above the hairline. You can see the path from these light-colored stripes.' The higher density of blood, bone, and swollen tissue appeared white or light gray in negatives. Even in cold, clinical images, the damage looked devastating. Nat stood saying nothing, and neither did Walker. Camilla had momentarily become bigger than both of them.

Walker raised his pencil. 'I'll give you the good news first. Unfortunately, it won't take long. The bullet missed the major arteries and veins except for one area, which I'll get to in a second. It also missed the cerebellum, which would have destroyed her coordination, and it missed the occipital lobe, here, which gives her sight.'

'So she can see?'

'Only if she wakes up.'

Nat felt a twinge of relief. 'And the bad?'

Walker surveyed the negatives again. 'Let's start with the

midbrain. It begins with the hypothalamus, this area right here, and continues down into the brain stem.' He pointed. 'It's what you might call the body's activation center. If it's been seriously damaged, she'll never wake up.'

'I don't see damage where you're pointing.'

'See this light-gray area? That's shear-force damage caused by shock waves from the bullet passing through nearby tissue. Collateral damage like this can be as devastating as the missile itself.'

Nat stared helplessly.

'Assuming it isn't fatal – and we don't know that yet – the next area of concern is the damage to the left hemisphere, especially this region, the superior temporal gyrus, or Wernike's area, and the left frontal lobe – here – where the bullet exited.'

'What's the problem with that?' Nat asked.

'I'd expect aphasia – speech defects – and amnesia, perhaps the loss of analytical thought, and some right hemiparesis.'

Nat was finding it difficult to swallow. 'What's hemiparesis?' he asked, hoping for a soft landing.

'Loss of motor function on the right side of her body. She's showing very little reaction to stimuli there, which means she'll probably have effects in her extremities.' He ran the pencil through his fingers. 'If she survives, she won't be doing more climbing, Detective.'

Nat waited in silence, fighting the facts, refusing to accept them. 'Is that it?' He was nearly begging now.

'I'm afraid not.' Walker placed another glossy negative on the view box. 'A common side effect of bullet wounds to the head is the weakening of blood vessels,' he said. 'See this?' He pointed to the left side of her brain. Light gray veins and arteries appeared like cracks in black marble. 'Now look at this scan taken forty-eight hours later.'

Three of the blood vessels showed small balloons.

'What are those?'

'Aneurysms.'

'Are they going to break?'

'I don't know yet.'

'And if they do?'

'It's not good.' Doctors had such obtuse ways of saying, you die.

'Is there any way to predict when it's going to happen?'

'Not precisely. We'll watch them with the MRI, and if we see a rapid decline we may do a nanoscan, which would give us a more precise picture of what's happening but is more taxing on the patient. Unfortunately, I've seen aneurysms go from undetectable to full-blown overnight.'

'What kind of treatment can you give her generally?'

'Until her brain stabilizes, there really isn't any.'

It amazed Nat, the havoc contained in these little pictures.

'We'll monitor her and try to get the swelling down and hope she gets back her autonomic functions like breathing and swallowing.'

'What kind of time schedule are we talking about?'

'The first seventy-two hours are the most critical. If she doesn't improve then, her chances of regaining consciousness are slim.'

'How slim?'

'Maybe twenty percent.'

'But we're at the three-day mark already.'

'It's not an exact measure,' he said. He picked up the large envelope. 'But we need to see some improvement soon if she's going to make it.'

'What about people who come out of comas after months or years?'

'It happens,' he said, turning off the lightboard. 'But don't count on it.'

He pulled the negatives down and placed them inside the large manila envelope. Nat watched, feeling the life drain out of him.

Walker put the envelope under his arm, looked at his watch, and walked to the door to leave. The relationship between them was clear now: Walker was the noble prince, Hennessy the scumbag serf.

'Doctor?'

Walker stopped and turned around.

Nat wasn't sure what he was going to say. 'Regardless of the outcome, I appreciate what you're doing.'

Walker looked at him a moment, and started back to the door.

Nat said, 'For what it's worth, I regret what happened at the union rep meeting.'

Without turning around, Walker said, 'So do I.'

So did he what? Regret his comments about white people, or regret that they'd been taped? Nat couldn't tell.

Cush Walker inserted his magnetic-striped security card in the slot at the door, waited for the electronic buzz, and entered, pulling the steel door closed behind him. The entire east wing of the fifth floor of the hospital was dedicated to NeuroPath, including offices, beds, two operating rooms, and laboratories. Entering a small computer room across the hall, he found Rodriguez working at a keyboard, wearing the lightly tinted amber glasses he used when spending hours in front of a monitor.

An impenetrable and brilliant young man, Rodriguez's baptismal name was Rodriguez Caesar Julio Hernandez Rodriguez, which had been reduced by the New York City school system to an Americanized first and last name, Rodriguez Rodriguez. From there it was an easy step to only one. When he was in high school, having a single name struck him as show-biz frivolous, like 'Prince' or 'Madonna' or 'Fabio', which bothered him because he was anything but frivolous.

But now, in his mid-thirties, he was beyond all that. Tall and skinny, with unruly hair, he had an intriguing face with ebony eyes that changed like the weather – soulful or threatening one minute, sunny and bright the next, but always intense. He resembled less the scientist he was than one of the ex-con buddies he'd grown up with in the South Bronx. Or, as they'd called it in his neighborhood, simply 'The'. As in, 'He's not from Brooklyn, man, he's from The.'

At age seventeen he had competed with the best junior science brains in the country to win a national Westinghouse Young Scientists award for inventing a homemade scanning tunnel microscope, known as an STM. It was ingeniously designed and surprisingly sophisticated for something constructed from off-the-shelf parts. To cushion it from vibration – the enemy of all microscopes – he'd mounted it on two rubber tires and a half-inflated inner tube he'd bought for ten bucks from Sal's Junkyard. And that was it. His future was set. Like all kids in the neighborhood, he'd hung out and had a couple of juvenile court appearances, but somehow he'd dodged the big bullets, both literally and figuratively. It still amazed him.

'How is she?' Rod asked without looking up.

'Bad,' Cush said, looking over his shoulder.

'How bad is bad?'

'Very bad. How's the new program look?'

Rod was simulating how their nanoscanners, or Z-5s, might operate if the impossibly tiny on-board computers that guided them were run by a different system of computation. The Z-5s were molecular-sized devices that could be injected into the patient's cortical spinal fluid, sent to the brain, and programmed to collect detailed information about blood vessels, cells, and the condition of the brain generally. When that phase was over, they could repair or replace damaged neurons not fixable by conventional neurosurgery. Although the nanoscanners were smaller than the sharp tip of a needle – tiny enough, in fact, to pierce the brain-blood barrier protecting a patient's cells – each one carried its own minuscule computer and communications system, allowing Walker and Rodriguez to control their work with microwave signals from outside the brain. By operating the computers with a more streamlined form of calculation called Reverse Logic, or RL, they hoped to reduce the amount of energy the devices used and thus the amount of heat they generated. Heat was the enemy of all brain tissue, as every mother who'd had a child with a fever knew. Enough of it and brain cells would shrivel up like crinkled matchsticks.

Rod hit some keys and waited, and in a few seconds a bar graph appeared summarizing the hypothetical performance of the Z-5s. 'Look at that. They're running ten, twelve degrees cooler.'

'Hypothetically,' Cush said. He was painfully aware of the gaps that existed between computer simulation and clinical reality.

'I'll start lab trials tomorrow,' Rod said.

Cush leaned in and took control of the keyboard. After typing some instructions, he stood up and waited for the computer to make another calculation. A few seconds later, a message appeared: *KBS effect: Unknown*.

Rod said nothing, and neither did Cush.

KBS was Kluver-Bucy Syndrome, a rare neurological disease that caused its victims to behave in gruesome ways ranging from trance-like states of passivity to indiscriminate sexual behavior to aggressive, maddened anger. And those were only some of its side effects. It was a subject they rarely spoke about, even in the privacy of the lab. They didn't need to – they'd seen it in action.

Usually he noticed her figure first – the legginess, the uniform shirt stretched laterally across her bust, the mane of red hair – but today he saw only her face, which was drawn and sympathetic. It was Monday evening, the waning of the longest day Nat could remember, and Shaw had insisted on picking him up, knowing it was his third day at the hospital with his comatose bride-to-be. They were getting into their car in the hospital parking lot when she spoke to him.

'How is she?' she asked.

Nat shook his head.

He climbed into the passenger side, wadded up a Reese's Peanut Butter Cup wrapper he found on the seat, and sat. Shaw pulled out of the lot and headed south. A few blocks later she gave him a report on the investigation.

'They've got three teams working the case,' she said. 'The guys in Major Case are coordinating with the FBI.' Major Case was the name of an NYPD squad that worked directly out of headquarters at One Police Plaza. Because the shooting had occurred on federal property, the FBI had primary jurisdiction.

'Has anybody come up with anything?'

'They found the boat at the Brooklyn marina,' she said. 'Belongs to a guy from New Jersey who docked it at the Park Service pier near Battery Park. The shooter must have been on your tail, and when he saw you and Camilla head out to the island, hot-wired a boat and followed.'

'What about the weapon?'

'Nothing yet,' she said. He assumed they'd never find it, not with the harbor so handy. 'FBI ballistics says the bullet fragments they picked up on the platform look like they came from a high-powered twenty-two.' That was interesting. It was a gun made for long-range killing.

Nat laid his head back on the seat and closed his eyes.

Shaw said, 'Can you think of anyone who wanted to hurt Camilla?'

'No,' he said.

'Anybody who'd want to hurt you?'

'Too many to count.'

They rode toward his downtown loft in silence.

'I think we're going to figure out who it is,' she said.

Figuring that out isn't the problem, Shaw. Figuring out how to keep you from figuring it out is the problem.

'Take a right here, would you?' Nat said. 'You can drop me at Fortieth and Fifth.'

She turned right. 'What's there?'

'The public library.'

She eased through an intersection and made an illegal turn left onto Fifth Avenue. 'I don't want to sound personal,' she said, 'but isn't this a strange time to be browsing for books?'

She picked her way through the traffic and pulled up to the left curb in front of the library annex, a block down the street from the two enormous stone lions guarding the entrance to the main building. Nat thanked her for the lift, got out and walked around the front of the car, stepping onto the curb.

Shaw rolled down her window. 'Want me to wait?'

'No, I'll see you in the morning.'

'Nat?' He stopped. She was obviously toying with another question he didn't want to hear. 'Get some sleep,' she said instead, lifting her foot off the brake. 'Seems like every time I see you, you look like hell. Nothing personal.'

'Seems like every time I'm with you, I feel like hell. Nothing personal.'

She pulled away as he entered the library.

Nat dreaded this moment more than he knew. It was his first time home since the shooting, and now that he was face to face with the door, he knew there was another reason he'd stayed at the hospital. He hated coming home without her.

Holding a book and a magazine article he'd printed out at the library, he drove the key into the lock and felt a coldness come over him he hadn't experienced since he was a child standing at his father's black and pewter casket. To this day, the mere sight of neat flower arrangements depressed him. He hoped Robin hadn't put a prim bouquet in the apartment.

The first thing he saw was the late afternoon light slanting through the window onto the chaise, spotlighting its emptiness. He left the door open as a kind of psychic escape. There were no flowers. Thank Robin for small favors.

He closed the door and stood still. A gargoyle with a grim, fixed face condemned him. He looked away and scanned the room. Nothing had been touched, nothing changed. Why would it be? Why would he even think it *might* be? Who, besides Robin, would have been here? There was no reasonable answer, only fuzzed up images of J.J. Jackson. Paranoia induced by guilt. He wanted the room to show a sign of life, a bolt of energy, Cam's sunny haunting, but of course it didn't.

He stood up straight and reminded himself that she was injured, not dead. 'OK,' he said aloud, and walked to the kitchen searching for normalcy, activity, make-work, small weapons of self-defense, like whistling in a graveyard.

You said cops don't think about the bad guys taking revenge. So don't.

He laid the library book on the kitchen counter along with the copy of an article from the *Journal of Neuron Sciences* edited by Dr Walker. His stomach was empty, his brain so tired it was bitching at him, but he didn't want soup, he wanted something to do. Something to delay his trip to the bedroom.

He pulled his leather holster from his belt and reached up to the top of the refrigerator and lifted the lid off the ceramic cookie-jar chicken. Laying his gun inside, he heard a metallic noise that sounded like the scraping of something against the side of the pot.

Lifting it off the refrigerator, he looked inside. Angel Rico's mother-of-pearl handled knife was lying in the bottom.

He took it out and examined it as if it was foreign money. He hadn't put it there. He never put anything there but his revolver. *Someone's been in the apartment.*

He sat down on a stool and retraced the chain of events. He'd taken it from Angel Rico, dropped it into his coat pocket, come home late that night, and laid his jacket on the chaise or kitchen stool. Which meant Camilla had hung it up, found the knife, and put it in the chicken.

She found the knife? Uh-oh. What was that gargoyle trying to tell him?

He laid the weapon back in the cookie jar and returned it to the top of the refrigerator. His appetite completely gone, he filled a tumbler with tap water and picked up the library book and article and carried them up the spiral staircase to the bedroom. May as well go ahead and get it over with.

He entered the open doorway and stood inside, scoping out the room the way he always did when he sensed something was wrong. But it was exactly as she'd left it, strewn with white tissue paper, clothes, wedding presents, half-packed suitcases, itineraries and glossy brochures of restaurants and hotels in

Venice. The feel of the place reminded him of Pompeii. Camilla's life was right here, frozen in the ashes. He told himself again: she's not dead.

He made himself busy turning on a reading light, putting the glass of water on the bedside table, pulling off his shoes, pushing aside bed-top clutter like clothes, plastic containers, and a large manila envelope with a note attached to the outside. He stretched out and laid the book on his chest and exhaled.

He felt it stalking him in a forest. Not Jackson, but the gargoyle. It knew what she knew, the ugly realization that had dawned on her when she'd found the knife.

'Angel Rico,' he said aloud.

That's it. That's what she must have figured out just before the bullet hit. Not the details behind why she'd left Walker, or some ancient mystery about her grandmother and Sebastian. She'd figured out the deal he'd cut with Angel Rico – how he'd made him a hit man, how it had boomeranged on him at the junkyard and got him killed. She'd figured out that the man she was about to marry and entrust her life to – her lover, her groom – had tried to kill a man and ended up causing the death of another. *Even if it wasn't premeditated . . . it was still the same as murder.*

An airplane did a loop in his stomach. He lifted the glass of water and took a drink. Wait a minute, wait a minute, slow down. Reconstruct *exactly* what she knew when she said that. She'd found the knife in his coat pocket after he'd told her that Angel had escaped. That's what she must have had in mind when she said she had something important to talk about. That and the security card she'd found with James Levander Jackson's name and photo on it. She wanted to know who he was. Then she heard Ben's message on the answering machine confirming Angel Rico's ticket out of town. Then later, on the statue, when he told her Angel had been murdered, she asked him who did it.

Jesus. The dots were so close you didn't need to connect them. That's why, when it hit her, she'd said, 'It's so clear.'

He needed air. He picked up his book and got off the bed and paced around the room. If she comes out of her coma, would she remember all this? Would she hate him? Would she even turn him in? My God, was that possible? He felt something wildly disorienting, a sensation he'd never felt before: fear of the woman he loved.

He exhaled, telling himself he was exhausted, his paranoia was running away with him. He opened the library book and blinked. Who knows what she actually figured out? It was probably a botched hotel reservation in Venice. Whatever it was, it wasn't the point. First, she needed to live. First, she needed a miracle.

He felt her absence again, the groaning weight of emptiness on her side of the bed. Think of something else. Make yourself useful.

He got up and went downstairs to the door and turned the dead bolt lock. Funny, he couldn't remember having done that before – the automatic button lock had always been good enough. He returned to the bedroom and lay on the bed.

He opened the library book and ran his finger down the table of contents. After turning to the chapter he wanted, he began to read. He didn't get far before he stuck his finger between the pages and closed the book . . . then his eyes.

Cush Walker laid the MRI films on his desk. Rodriguez stood across from him, waiting. Having consulted the hospital's chief of neurosurgery, they were trying to determine the rate of deterioration of the aneurysms in Camilla's brain. They couldn't.

Cush called for a fresh MRI and told Rod to compute a trend line. If necessary, they'd also do a more onerous nanoscan.

'When the damaged vessels have lost seventy per cent of normal strength, we're going to operate, regardless of her condition,' he said. 'I need to know when that's going to be.'

Nat slipped across the small bridge between sleep and consciousness, that place where the mind experiences a little of each but neither one alone. For a pleasant second his thoughts were uncluttered by Angel Rico, Jackson, Walker, or Camilla. Then, like a freight train, they all came roaring back.

What was that? That scratching sound?

The room was dusky. The book was still resting on his chest with his finger stuck between the pages. He turned his head toward the clock. The fluorescent hands read nine thirty.

He sat up fast, making himself dizzy. What had awakened him? A noise. Downstairs. Be quiet and listen. In the echo of his memory, it seemed to have come from the front door.

He swung his feet over the side of the bed, lowered his head and felt the blood rush in. Suddenly he was back on the starting line at his high-school track, fingers spread on the cinders, spikes in the blocks, heart pounding, waiting for the starter's gun.

He heard it. Not a bang, a *scraaatch*. The same one that woke him up: someone at the door. Maybe it was a good thing he'd turned the dead bolt after all – except, now that he thought about it, which way had he turned it? Maybe he'd absent-mindedly *unlocked* it instead of locking it.

The scratching sounded like someone sliding a credit card between the door and the jamb.

He got up in his tattered jeans, without shirt or shoes, and walked to the spiral staircase. His gun was in the kitchen. Damn. To get it he'd have to pass the front door so close he could touch it.

He walked down the steps the way he did when Camilla was asleep, keeping his feet near the center pole where the welds were tight. On the last stair step, the steel platform made a loud bang, stopping him mid-step, hand on the railing, eyes on the door.

There it was again, the sound of someone trying to enter.

Go for the gun.

He'd turned the corner and was barely inside the kitchen when he heard the buzz of the doorbell. He lifted the lid on the chicken, pulled out his gun, unholstered it, and walked toward the door. Another buzz. What is this? Can't break in, so you ring?

He stood off to the side, gun in hand. 'Who is it?'

'It's me,' a female voice said. 'Stop that!' it said lower, as if to someone else.

He put his hand on the doorknob and turned. It didn't open – the deadbolt was on after all. He unlocked it and cracked the door.

It was Robin Feld, his downstairs neighbor, standing in the hallway with a brown and white puppy cradled in her arms, his large black eyes fixed on Nat's.

'Jesus, Nat,' she said, her eyes on the gun. 'If I'm disturbing you, I can come back another time—'

'No, no,' he said, embarrassed, lowering his .38.

'I tied him to the railing to go back to the apartment for his bowl, and I heard him scratching to get in.'

'Come in,' he said, trying to sound normal. He stroked the puppy's head. 'What have we got here?'

They entered the studio and she sat on the edge of the chaise holding the dog in her lap. Nat sat next to them and rubbed the puppy behind his ears. 'Hey, boy,' he said. 'What's his name?'

'He doesn't have one yet.'

'When did you get him?'

'A week ago.'

'A week and still no name?' he said to the dog.

'He's Camilla's wedding present to you,' Robin said. 'She couldn't leave him at the shelter, so I agreed to take him until you got back from your honeymoon. Considering what happened, I thought, you know, I should bring him up.'

Nat reached for the dog and lifted him from her arms like a baby and sat him in his lap. The pup nuzzled his hand and wagged his tail in counterpoint to his hind end.

'Her wedding present?' The little guy climbed up Nat's chest and licked his chin. 'What am I going to do with a dog?' A small puddle warmed his lap.

'He's not completely house-broken,' Robin said.

No kidding.

She stood up and found a newspaper and spread it on the floor. 'He's just excited to see you.'

Can't have a dog, Camilla had said. Not enough time to take care of it. Then she gives him a dog. Faked him out.

'What is he?' Nat asked.

'Just a dog.' She put his little head in her palms and rustled it and kissed him on the nose. 'Looks like he's got some beagle in him.'

Nat put him down and let him roam the room, sniffing paint cans and table legs and wooden statuary, whatever was at nose level.

'You have no idea how excited she was about surprising you,' Robin said.

Nat leaned down and tapped his fingers on the floor. The puppy pounced on them and tried to pin them with his paws. Nat picked him up and rubbed his neck.

Robin said, 'If you house-break him, I'll look after him while you're gone.' Then a polite correction: 'Until Camilla gets back.'

Of course. Until she gets back.

Robin said she'd bring up the dog's things – food, a leather bone, and a stuffed parrot named Petey that he liked to shake in his mouth. Then she left.

Nat picked up the pup and climbed the stair to the bedroom

where he let him roam while he stripped off his clothes. Debating whether to wash or burn them, he finally headed for the bathroom.

After a hot shower, a shave, and a mouthful of foamy toothpaste, he came into the bedroom and found shreds of tissue paper all over the place and the puppy curled up on Camilla's sweatshirt. Nat lifted them both and breathed them in, the warmth of the dog and the faint smell of Camilla's perfume.

Still naked, he set the pup on the floor and wandered to the dresser for a shirt. The dog tried to catch a ride on his foot, so he lifted him again and set him on the top of the chest of drawers. By the time the pup had sniffed everything in sight – airplane tickets, a volt converter kit, himself in the mirror – Nat was dressed in blue jeans and loafers, without socks, and a blue blazer on an open shirt. He noticed that the circles under his eyes had disappeared. Having not eaten for three days gave his cheekbones a chiseled look.

He looked around the room for a shopping bag. Sorting through the things on Camilla's side of the bed, he found a large manila envelope with a note taped to it in Camilla's handwriting. 'TTD' was printed at the top, Camilla's shorthand for Things To Do. He read it quickly: items to buy, things to pack, calls to make, and a last item that said, 'Negatives – return to CW.'

Negatives?

He sat on the bed while the puppy pranced toward the pillow. The flap on the manila envelope was unsealed so he opened it and pulled out a large, colored negative similar to the black-and-white ones Walker had placed on the conference room lightboard. Clipped to the top of it was a note typed on white paper.

He held the film up to the light and saw a series of pictures of a brain. At the top were dates and medical coding. On the memo was the word 'Patient', and next to it, the letters, 'RAD'.

He heard a growl and the sound of tearing. The pup was at

the suitcase in a death struggle with another piece of tissue paper, holding it down and trying to eat it. No doubt he'd celebrate his victory by pissing on the bed. Nat carried him to the bathroom and set him down on the white oyster-cracker tile then placed the fireplace screen across the open door to keep him in.

He returned to the edge of the mattress and read the memo. It was addressed to Cush Walker. 'Subject: Scan Malfunction.' His eyes took in whole clumps of words. '. . . dealing with a human subject . . . Z-5s malfunctioned and went on a rampage . . . classic nanotechnology nightmare . . .' He read quickly but deliberately. '. . . even a hard jolt to the head . . . the patient faces a substantial risk of developing a case of KBS. I don't need to tell you what that means.'

Jesus, what was this?

He looked inside the envelope to see if there was anything he'd missed and found a note Camilla had handwritten to Cush – dated almost three years earlier – saying she was returning the documents. So why hadn't she? He saw the name 'Vestie Viney', Camilla's comment to Walker that she'd found the memo by mistake, and the postscript that said, 'I assume Patient RAD is your boy Roy Driggers. True?'

He shoved the documents back into the envelope and sat looking at Camilla's wedding dress hanging in a sheath on the back of the door. After a minute, he went to the bathroom and picked up the dog, leaving streamers of unfurled toilet tissue on the floor.

Who was Vestie Viney?

Who was Roy Driggers?

And what was KBS?

It was after normal visiting hours in the NeuroPath wing of the hospital, but Nat had a police officer's privileges, and given his personality, he came and went mostly as he pleased. Not that he minded the tight security of the place, particularly in light of news reports of the shooting and continuing coverage of Camilla's condition. But beyond that, hospital rules were suspect in his eyes, made as much for the convenience of the staff as they were for the patient's health and safety. Still, he'd obeyed the one prohibiting animal visitors and left the puppy with Robin.

An orderly nodded hello to him as he walked to Camilla's room carrying a white shopping bag at his side.

Approaching her bed, he heard the chatter of the wall-mounted TV set and reached for the remote control. The set had been turned on and left to run, a common practice in coma cases where spoken words and familiar sounds could sometimes spark neural activity. Nat turned down the volume. He had his own way of waking her.

He reached into the shopping bag and lifted out Camilla's sweatshirt and laid it on her upper chest close to her nose. The olfactory senses were supposed to be powerful hooks into a person's memory, the way cinnamon cookies and pine cones raised instant images of Christmas. He hoped her perfume might fire up her consciousness.

'Come on, baby. Give me a blink.'

He waited but there was nothing.

Moving to the foot of the bed, he pulled the top sheet from under the mattress and folded it back gently in a triangular patch, exposing her foot. After placing a pillow under it, he opened a bottle of lotion and poured some into the cup of his hand. When it was warm, he slathered it onto her arch and ankles and calves in a silky, semi-gloss sheen.

'Remember this?'

He began kneading the sole of her foot with his thumbs, the top of it with his fingers. 'This is the adrenal gland,' he said. His thumbs undulated in a slow, persistent rhythm. 'This is the energy spot.' When he'd finished there, he moved upward to the center of her arch. 'We're at the solar plexus now, remember? Reduces stress and improves your breathing.'

He worked his way slowly toward the ball of her foot, inside the invisible lines defining the connection to her heart. 'OK, Cam, this is it.' He massaged her with his hands and thoughts. 'Come on, sweetheart, time to wake up. Feel the peacock fan its tail behind your eyes.'

He pressed and kneaded and squeezed and massaged and worked and coaxed for half an hour or more. Giving his aching hands a break, he closed his eyes, and waited. Give me a sign. Give me some hope.

He sat for a long time, waiting for a miracle, but her coma was engraved in stone. The critical first three days were gone, but it might as well have been three years. She wasn't going to wake up.

A last-ditch idea occurred to him. Nat Hennessy – lapsed Catholic, street dweller, secular to the bone – decided to say a prayer. He hadn't prayed for so long it made him feel like a perjurer on the witness stand, but he did it anyway.

Here goes. I haven't called or written for awhile, God, and now when I do, here I am asking for a favor.

He took a breath of self-composing air.

Promises are cheap and deals frowned upon, I remember

that from catechism, so let me make a one-way, no-obligation, unconditional offer: if there's anything I can do to bring her back, let me know and I'll do it. This was my fault. Price is no object.

He kissed her foot and laid it on the bed and poured more lotion into his hand.

Whatever it takes, Cam, I'll do it, I promise. Whatever it takes.

Cush Walker stood behind the window in the control room with the Venetian blinds down and the louvers barely cracked, watching Hennessy massage his fiancée's feet. As a man of principle, spying was beneath him; as a human being, he did it anyway. Still, stealing Hennessy's private moment with his bride made him feel like the devil in church. He would watch them for only a moment, simply to give himself a professional insight.

Sure he would. Sure it was.

Holding the rod that controlled the louvers, he watched Hennessy touch her and felt the hair on the back of his neck rise in envy. He watched him hold her foot and close his eyes and sit still almost as if he was saying a prayer. He watched him tend to her patiently, searching for signs of life, immersing himself in her spirit without shame or self-awareness. It was powerful stuff, this groom's devotion to his bride, this patching together of broken dreams with delicate touches. It put the taste of metal in Cush's mouth, but he understood it perfectly.

He thought he'd gotten over her, or at least put her into that non-toxic place called perspective. Not so. He wanted her more than ever.

Hennessy held her foot against his cheek as she slept and spoke to her with words Cush couldn't hear but understood all the same, tender words that sliced through the glass window and tortured him.

She's his. She belongs to me but she's his.

He watched Hennessy fold the sheet over Camilla's feet, then reach beneath the white fabric and massage her leg rhythmically where Cush couldn't see his hands, making his cheeks tingle. What he was witnessing wasn't just sexual, it was *intimate*, the private fusion of two people in love. She and Hennessy together. Inevitable. Destined. Ordained.

He'd seen enough.

He rotated the rod in his fingers, tilting the Venetian blinds closed.

Wherever he walked, a small hush followed. Entering Midtown South, Nat received welcome-back greeting, soft pats on the back, and heartfelt clichés falling from heaven. 'Hang in there, buddy,' 'Everything's gonna come out all right,' 'She'll beat this thing, no question about it.' Like that. And from everyone, the momentary 'stare' that said, you're not the same guy we knew last week, you saw your lover's brains blown out – you're damaged, a media star, somebody *different* from us now – don't get too close, OK? He thanked everyone and looked for small sanctuaries of normalcy.

He could always count on Lieutenant Amerigo. Walking into his office, he found the lieu with his feet up on the desk reading a DD5, or 'Five', a detective's report of his or her official activities. His computer monitor was on, as usual, although like everything else that bored him, he was avoiding it. Nat liked his disregard. It felt regular.

'Feel like working?' Amerigo said without looking up.

'Sooner the better,' Nat said.

'The *Post* says our pal Walker is Camilla's doctor,' he said. 'Izzat true?' Amerigo was well known for criticizing people with this simple, derogative question, *Izzat true?*

Nat touched a bandage on his forehead that covered his stitches. No blood, no problem. 'I'd put Idi Amin on her case if it would save her.'

Amerigo dropped his feet to the floor. 'Well, if the press asks you how you feel about Mr BIAS working on your fiancée, would you mind giving them that answer? I like the comparison.'

Nat walked to his office and closed the door and sat at his desk. It was nine thirty before he had finished reading the *Journal of Neuron Sciences* article he'd copied from the library and the relevant chapters of the book he'd borrowed on nanotech medicine. When he finished, he stood up and poured himself a large glass of orange juice and drank it slowly, piecing together what he'd read. It was a long shot, audacious as all hell, but Camilla was out of luck now, and so was he.

He decided to go for it.

He picked up the telephone and made a one o'clock lunch appointment at the Oyster Bar at Grand Central Terminal. The restaurant was only a few steps from the ladies' room where Tangerine had been killed, the beginning of the chain of events leading to Camilla's head wound. He might have found this touch of irony irritating, but he didn't. He thought of it as an omen.

'Hello, I'm Cynthia Weber.' The young reporter from *Modern Behavior Magazine* stuck out her hand and felt Dr Cush Walker engulf it.

'Welcome to NeuroPath Labs,' he said. 'Care for a soft drink?'

'I'd love an iced tea if you have one.' She usually accepted an offer of something during an interview because it gave her a chance to look around and make small talk. The conference table held a model of the human brain with detachable segments in different colors; an artist's pad; pencils; a carafe of water; and a small vase of flowers to take the edge off the high-tech atmosphere. Dr Walker went to a small shelf at the side of the blackboard and picked up a glass. She was already impressed with his reputation, but seeing him in person was even better. He was handsome and graceful and powerful. Mysterious. And now this, the most impressive aphrodisiac of all: he was making her tea instead of having a flunky do it.

'You want to confirm the ground rules?' he said, scooping some ice from a bucket into a tall glass.

Walker rarely gave interviews, which added to his mystique, but she'd convinced him to talk to her about himself and the lab to help counteract the negative press over his comments at the union meeting. He'd said maybe she was right. Part of his job was to explain the program anyway – it helped the lab's reputation and funding – and he hadn't done a one-on-one for months. But he didn't want to talk about

BIAS, he said. He wanted to talk about nanotech medicine in general.

'Personally,' she said, 'I think BIAS has been covered to death anyway, although you have to admit it certainly did raise your profile.'

He pushed a button on a machine and drained hot tea into the tumbler. The cubes cracked.

'So does jumping off the Empire State Building.' He returned to the refrigerator beneath the shelf and got himself a can of Dr Pepper.

She rolled her notebook back two pages and read from it. 'Winner of the Merkle Prize for Nanotechnology, rumored candidate for a Nobel Prize in medicine, troublemaker for the New York City Police Department. Quite a record for a man of forty-seven.'

'Sounds spotty to me. What would you like to talk about?'

'I'm interested in a layman's description of how you repair neurons. As I understand it, a person's only got the brain cells he's born with, so once they're gone, there's no getting them back.'

'As a practical matter, that's still true. The human body repairs and replaces most of its cells quickly and routinely, but for some reason not in the brain, or at least not rapidly. Until recently, we didn't think it happened at all. But since you're born with a hundred billion neurons, you can lose a few without noticing.'

'What if you damage too many?'

'Practically speaking, you've got a problem.'

'Until now.'

'Until now only in a laboratory setting. We know how to mine the body's resources to build new brain matter, but we're still not at the point where we can do it safely and consistently.'

'But you're close, right?'

'We hope.'

'Tell me how it works.'

He turned the artist's pad toward him. 'The basic tool we use is a form of nanotechnology.'

'Which is manipulating cells at their smallest, most rudimentary level, like molecules and atoms?'

'Nothing wrong with that definition.'

'I read that in the cab coming over.'

'New knowledge is just as good as old,' he said. 'What we've learned to do is send molecular-sized devices called Z-5 nanoscanners into the brain to re-create the damaged brain cells that the body doesn't repair on its own.'

'Molecules. Can you give me some idea of the size of things we're talking about here?'

He lifted the pad and drew a circle the size of a cantaloupe with lines radiating out from it like legs on a daddy-longlegs. They represented a neuron's axons and dendrites, or the thin wires that connected one brain cell to another across tiny spaces between them called synapses, thereby forming the massive electrochemical network that made up the brain.

'Let's say this is a neuron.'

'Neurons and brain cells are the same thing?'

'The same thing, right.'

'How big are they?' she said.

'They vary in size, but I can give you a rough idea. One of the hairs on your head is about a hundred microns in diameter. A typical five-micron brain cell would be about a twentieth the width of that.'

She made a written note of the size and a mental note to pick up some hair conditioner on the way home.

'If this cantaloupe-sized circle were the body of an average neuron,' he said, 'again, let's say about five microns in diameter, then this dot' — he touched the end of his felt-tipped pen to the pad — 'would be the approximate size of a single Z-5 nanoscanner. Or to put it another way, if this conference room were the nucleus of a typical brain cell, a Z-5 nanoscanner would be about the size of a cricket.'

'And all this stuff is made up of molecules?'

'That's right, and molecules are made up of atoms. Once we get down that far, we're pretty close to the bottom of things.'

She took another note. 'And DNA? Where does that fit in?'

'There's DNA in the nucleus of every cell in the body, including brain cells. It's sort of like the software program that tells the cell how to grow and what to become – an eye cell, a fingernail cell, a brain cell, whatever.'

'What are the nanoscanners made of?'

'Silicon.'

'What guides them?'

'On-board biological computers.'

'Every tiny nanoscanner has its own computer?'

'Every one.'

She made another note and looked up. 'So what do these things actually do?'

'Their first job is to scan the brain and collect information about the neurons we want a record of – their size, shape, location, function – everything we can find. At this stage of the game we're talking about mapping healthy neurons, not damaged ones. Once we get that information from a scan, we can download it onto a computer and save it as a template or blueprint of the person's normal neurological structure.'

'And do what with it?'

'Proceed to the second stage, which involves the reconstruction of the cells after they've died or been damaged.'

'Like from a stroke or Alzheimer's or Parkinson's disease?'

'Like that.'

'Or the bullet that hit Camilla Bissonette.'

He paused. 'Theoretically.'

'How do they know where to go and what to do when they get there?'

'They're guided by electromagnetic signals to go back to the same place they did their scan, the way satellites guide ships and airplanes on the face of the globe. Except in this case, the Z-5s are moving around in your brain, and instead of being guided by satellites, they communicate with receivers and transmitters attached to a frame around the patient's head.'

'Wait,' she said, writing fast. She finished her shorthand and looked up. 'And this is the process that's called cell regeneration.'

'Strictly speaking, we're not asking the body to make new cells the way it repairs a cut finger. That's a DNA function neurobiologists will eventually get control of. Nanoscanners are more like construction workers. They collect the dead and dying cells, metabolize them as waste, and rebuild them according to their original profile, including the DNA.'

'Rebuild them out of what?'

'The same materials the body uses – glucose, nitrogen, oxygen, and carbon.'

'Carbon?'

'We augment the process with liquefied diamond dust.'

More notes. 'Diamonds in the bloodstream,' she said to herself. She loved that. 'How do you get the nanoscanners inside the individual brain cells so they can do this?'

'They're carried to the brain in a serum we inject into the spinal canal.' He got up from the table and picked up a small, sealed bottle of clear, pinkish liquid. 'There are about two hundred billion Z-5 nanoscanners in this little beaker. Once they saturate the cortical-spinal fluid, they penetrate the brain-cell walls by taking a ride on the glucose and salt that normally washes in and out of them.'

'Like surfers,' she said.

He looked as if he liked that. 'Tiny little surfers, catching a wave. Once the Z-5s are inside the neurons and record their positions, we signal them to start scanning. After they've collected information about how the brain cell is constructed – a static blueprint of its physical characteristics – they record how it behaves when it's functioning – a dynamic blueprint, so to speak.'

'And how do you get that?'

'We make the subject think of something specific or act in a particular way and scan the neurons while they're active. That way we know what neurotransmitters they're using during the event – how the receptors work – all the things that make thought and action possible.'

'Can you give me an example?'

'Got a favorite poem?'

'Uh . . . Hey diddle diddle, the cat and fiddle? The cow jumped over the moon?'

'Funny, I wouldn't have guessed that was your favorite poem.'

'Just goes to show you never know what's going on inside someone's head.' Like mine. Right now. Flirting with my kimono partly open. 'Can these things tell you what someone is thinking?'

'Not precisely,' he said. 'It's not a form of mind reading.'

'That's a relief,' she said, feeling her cheeks warm. Geez, Cynthia, why don't you get a little more obvious? 'It's not my favorite poem, it's just the only thing I can remember at the moment.'

'Nothing wrong with Mother Goose.' He took another drink. 'OK. When you said the words, "the cat and the fiddle", various parts of your brain had to go to work to put that thought together.'

'OK.'

'For the sake of discussion, let's say different aspects of this phrase are located in four different groups of neurons. One group gives you the visual image of a cat and a fiddle, one gives you the English words "cat" and "fiddle", one makes your lips move and say the words out loud, one acts as traffic cops to bring them together in a coherent way.'

'My God. I wonder what Einstein's brain looked like when he was thinking about the theory of relativity?'

'Fireworks,' he said, and let her catch up on her notepad. 'So now we have these different brain cells all operating at once. The nanoscanners record everything that happens in each location – the neurons that go to work to express a cat and a fiddle, the amount of sugar and oxygen they use, the timing of their firing in conjunction with other neurons, the size and composition of the electrochemical transmission, which receptors on the adjacent neurons receive them, how fast transmission occurs, the route it takes to the hippocampus – all that good stuff.'

'And the nanoscanners can handle it all?'

'Each Z-5 is capable of recording sixteen thousand functions simultaneously.'

'Really.' She wrote as she talked. 'How fast does a thought happen?'

'About two hundred miles a second, which is about a thousand times faster than the speed of sound.'

'That seems pretty fast.'

'There's an old story that during the French Revolution the crowds gathered around the guillotine to see if the victims blinked after their heads were cut off. They thought that after the blade fell, the brain still held enough blood and oxygen to give the prisoner a split second to see the world turn upside down as his head tumbled into the basket.'

'Is that true?' She was concerned.

He smiled, who knows? 'But to say that's fast depends on what you're comparing it to.' He finished his Dr Pepper. 'As quick as the brain is, it's not nearly as fast as a computer and it doesn't have nearly as much storage space or quick retrievability, which is why we love our hard drives. On the other hand, computers can only do one thing at a time, even though very fast, while the human brain can do hundreds of things simultaneously, which makes it far more complicated and in many ways more powerful.'

'I'm trying to think what the brain is like if it's not like a computer.'

'Every era has tried to understand the human brain according to ideas that interested people at the time. The Greeks thought because it was all wrinkled up it was a radiator that cooled the body. Monks in the Middle Ages saw it as clouds created by God. Eighteenth-century intellectuals tried to explain it as the wheels of a clock, and we got more of that gear stuff at the start of the industrial revolution. Now that we're in the space age, computers are hot so that's how we explain it. But none of them is right.'

'What is?'

'No single analogy does it justice,' he said. 'Some neurobiologists like to think of it as a complicated ecosystem, like a jungle with thousands of things happening at the same the time – plants growing, animals prowling around, communications going on through voice and stream and wind. Not bad.'

'What if part of the jungle is missing?'

'Depends on what it is. You may get less harmony and communication, or none at all.'

'Which brings us to back reconstructing damaged cells. I think we left off with the nanoscanners recording what was happening on their small plot of land while the brain was in the process of thinking. What happens next?'

'When the Z-5s have collected that information, we turn them off with an electromagnetic signal, guide them back into the spinal fluid, and extract them through a filter in the lumbar region.'

'Does it hurt?'

'No more than a blood transfusion.' He turned the page on his easel to a new graphic. 'After they're withdrawn we place them in an electromagnetic receptacle that downloads their data into a petaflop super-computer.'

'What-a-flop?'

'Petaflop. Peta means a thousand trillion, which is the number of operations the computer can do in one second.'

She looked at a machine at the side of the room about the size of a large copier. 'All that in there?'

'That's a terminal that communicates with a mainframe in Los Alamos. We just rent time on it. Once we've downloaded the Z-5s and sent the data to New Mexico, the mainframe is powerful enough to give us a four-dimensional picture of what we've scanned.'

'Four-dimensional?'

'Three dimensions of space and one of time.'

'In other words, a duplicate of the brain.'

'As much of it as we can get.'

'Why not everything?'

'We'll come to that in a second,' he said. 'With a dynamic blueprint of the beta tester's brain cells—'

'Wait a sec – what's a beta tester?'

'That's what we call a test subject patient, like a mouse or guinea pig or monkey. Once we have a static and dynamic blueprint of the beta tester's brain, we can send the Z-5s back to their original locations in the subject's head and rebuild damaged cells according to their original specifications.'

She wrote fast. 'Why can't you do this now?'

Cush leaned back in his chair. 'As I was saying before, we haven't solved all the problems that would let us do it clinically.'

'Such as?' She flipped to a clean page.

'Sometimes the Z-5s glitch out for no apparent reason, the way your desktop computer does. Sometimes the guidance system crashes and tells the Z-5s to rebuild healthy cells instead of damaged ones. We had that problem a couple of years ago.'

'What did that do to the cells?'

'It destroyed them.'

'Oops.'

'A very large oops. We had another problem when the Z-5s misread their software and reproduced themselves on their own.'

'That sounds like fun.'

'It's nanotechnology's classic bogeyman – molecule-sized devices going into uncontrolled self-replication, like a virus.'

'Couldn't you drain them out?'

'We tried, but once they escape their program controls they tend to behave like any other organism and do what they can to survive.'

'That can't be good.'

'That is definitely not good.'

'What happened to the test subjects?'

'The Z-5s clung together like a fast-growing tumor and forced the brain down into the stem.'

'Did that kill them?'

'It did.'

'Mice?'

'Mice and a monkey.'

Another note taken. 'What else bad can happen?'

'Sometimes they migrate to parts of the brain where they have no business and try to scan on their own.'

'What happens then?'

'We try to stop them and get them back.'

'And if you don't?' She saw that he was getting uncomfortable, his answers more measured. She'd hit some kind of pay dirt.

'That depends. In some cases, our signals put the Z-5s to sleep, sort of like putting a cancer into remission.'

'What if they've already done some damage? Can you send other Z-5s in to kill the rogues and repair the cells?'

'Not a bad idea, but so far we haven't been able to do that.'
He looked at his watch. A subtle hint.

'So those patients lived, but the nanoscanners stayed inside
them?'

'That's right.'

'Do they stay dormant forever?'

'Not necessarily. In some instances they stayed quiet for only
a few minutes, in others they've stayed quiet since the first time
it happened, which was about three years ago.'

'What are the symptoms of a beta tester who gets hurt by
rogue nanoscanners?'

'Unusual passivity, headaches and blind spots.'

She wrote that down. 'How do you know when a mouse has
a headache?'

'We watch how they behave,' he said.

Awfully bland answer. 'What do they do, run around looking
for aspirin?' He smiled in spite of himself. 'What else happens?'

'If they invade the temporal lobes, you can get some pretty
strange brain damage.' Before she could ask what that meant,
he said, 'We've solved most of these control problems by
programming the nanoscanners with a doomsday device that
automatically destroys them if they're not responding to directions for more than three seconds.'

'And that works?'

'For the most part, yes, it has.'

She watched him draw a pencil through his fingers smoothly.
Suddenly he was being so careful he seemed evasive, holding
back. There was something about these frolicking nanoscanners
he didn't want to talk about. 'So if you've solved most of these
problems, what's keeping you from making clinical repairs?'

'Heat.' He gestured toward the model of the human brain.
'Until we can control the heat that's generated by the scanning
process, using it on the human brain isn't feasible.'

'What causes heat?' she asked.

'Brownian motion,' Walker said. 'Molecules are constantly moving, movement causes friction, and friction produces heat. We can scan a brain for a few minutes, but then the accumulation of BTUs becomes too much and we have to stop or damage the subject's brain.'

'Can't you cool it?'

'We try, but it's like a Rubik Cube. Ever play with one?'

'I've tried.'

'Every time you solve one problem, you create another. If we lower the serum temperature too much it increases viscosity and slows the scanners. If we warm them enough to operate them smoothly, we don't have enough time to scan before they get too hot. We use a cryogenic blanket and liquid nitrogen, but the cooling patterns aren't spread evenly.'

'Which means some nanoscanners stay cool and others don't?'

'That's right. Until we find a system that runs them consistently cooler, we're limited in how long we can keep them operating.'

'How long is that?'

'At the moment, we can operate at acceptable temperatures for about ten minutes.'

'How do you define acceptable?'

'We don't want to exceed a hundred and five degrees Fahrenheit for more than five minutes.'

'I remember having a temperature of a hundred and six once,' she said. 'My mother put me in a bathtub full of ice water.'

'Good clinical practice.' He heard the telephone ring once and stop, his secretary's warning that his time was up. 'By scanning quickly, we've mapped small regions of monkey brains without hurting them.'

'When are you going to be ready to try it on a human?'

Walker doodled on a pad. Before he answered, the door opened and a tall Hispanic guy with an intriguing face stuck his head in. 'Suzy says I'm supposed to tell you you're late for your next appointment.'

Walker told Rodriguez to come in, and introduced him to the reporter. He offered to answer her questions and show her around the lab while Walker gathered up his papers and prepared to leave.

'Can I call again?' she asked Walker. 'If I have a question?'

'Sure,' he said, and shook hands goodbye.

Rodriguez said something to her but she missed it. She was too busy watching Dr Walker go out the door, wondering if she'd opened her kimono too little or too much.

Coromandels and Chiloes from Chile, creamy and smooth. Rilan Bays from the Pacific, briny and mild. Kumomotos from California, tiny, sweet, and deep-cupped. Moonstone Belons from Rhode Island, Permaquids from Maine – Wellfleets, Cotuits, Malpeques, and Blue Points – he loved them all. Chincoteagues weren't in season, which was good because they were Camilla's favorite. He decided he wouldn't have one until she could join him.

He had a plan to make that happen.

Nat sat in the Oyster Bar Saloon at Grand Central Terminal waiting for a cold beer and a second dozen oysters to arrive at his table. He checked his watch. It was one thirty. Half an hour late.

He picked up the menu and browsed down the long list. When he reached the Gigamotos at the bottom of the page, his eyes caught a pair of burnished cordovan loafers with two taupe cuffs breaking perfectly over their tops. He lowered the menu.

Cush Walker moved past him, a tall, slender pine that sat easily in a leather chair across the table.

Nat said, 'I was beginning to think you'd changed your mind.'

'Doctors are never on time,' Walker said.

A waiter appeared at the side of the red-and-white checkered tablecloth and Walker picked up a menu. His tailored suit was unwrinkled, his tie straight, his white, sea-island-cotton shirt a frame for a brown, athletic face. Nat wasn't insecure about himself, but Walker put him to the test. Watching him read, he saw traits he hadn't noticed during his bleary-eyed encounter with him at the hospital: the smooth skin, the hidden muscle, the graceful carriage that unsettled a white man's imagination. This guy's blackness was an asset, not a liability – an attractive quality that stood prejudice on its head. But a lot of him was also unavailable, hidden inside this dignified, self-contained shell. Fire beneath permafrost. A future Nobel Prize winner? That was fine with him, congratulations, go for it, no problem. What bothered him was what Walker held in reserve for Camilla, who was now quite literally in his hands. His hands. Nat looked at them holding the menu and saw the long, dexterous fingers winding their way through her hair. A fog of sexual paranoia descended.

This problem wasn't baroque, this problem was basic.

'I'll have an iced tea,' Walker told the waiter, handing him the menu, 'and a dozen oysters, your recommendation.'

'Any news?' Nat asked.

Walker reached into a bowl and picked up a single oyster cracker, avoiding Nat's eyes. Instantly Nat smelled trouble.

'We've been looking at her aneurysms.'

'And?'

'At the rate they're deteriorating, I'd estimate she has about seventy-two hours before one of them ruptures.'

'Christ,' Nat said, 'not another three-day countdown.' He wished he hadn't said that. They'd slipped past the first deadline without Camilla's dying, and he didn't want to kick a sleeping dog. He reached for a bottle of hot sauce, reflexively.

The waiter brought Walker's iced tea and plate of oysters, and another dozen for Nat. Walker speared a Caraquet with a small fork and dipped it into a paper cup of spiced vinegar. 'We'll have to operate and try to clip them off.'

'And the chances of success?'

'Not high.'

'How high is not high?'

'You're always playing the percentages, aren't you, Hennessy? The chief of neurosurgery puts it at one out of five, if we're lucky.'

'And you?'

'I think he's being optimistic.'

Nat shook hot sauce onto a Glidden Point, more than he wanted, then set it down. He looked at the doctor with accusatory eyes, as if Walker bore responsibility for the problem.

Walker was used to it – most doctors were – and waited for Nat's frustration to pass. 'What did you want to see me about?'

Nat turned over the journal he'd picked up at the library. 'I've been reading your latest article on nanotech medicine.'

Walker didn't need to see it. He'd written it only two months earlier, explaining the advances he'd made in the laboratory, the barriers he faced, and the neurological cures that would follow if they were hurdled. Some day in the future.

'If I read this correctly,' Nat said, 'you're close to replacing damaged brain cells in humans.'

Walker lifted an oyster and looked at it. 'And you want me to try it on Camilla.'

'Why not? You've done it with monkeys.'

'In small regions of the brain under highly controlled circumstances.'

'What's the difference?'

'Monkeys aren't people, and the laboratory isn't a hospital. In a controlled setting we can scan a monkey's healthy brain, scar a small section of it, and make a full repair. But we don't have a picture of Camilla's healthy brain.'

'I thought nanoscanners could build brain cells regardless.'

'There is no single neuron type. Without a blueprint of the healthy neurons we're trying to duplicate, we can't tell the scanners what to build or how to link them together.'

'Wait a minute,' Nat said. He flipped through the pages. 'Someplace in here you deal with that.' He skimmed through the sections he'd highlighted. 'You said that because people won't have templates of their brains on file for many years, what you'll have to do is rely on the plastic nature of brain cells to – here it is.' He read aloud: '"A template of another patient's healthy brain tissue might be used to make gross repairs to the same region of the patient's brain, with the expectation that these newly created neurons will form pathways on their own, much as they do when a child is learning basic skills." Doesn't that mean you can use the blueprint of someone's healthy brain to repair someone else's broken one?'

'That's speculation,' Walker said.

'Why not try it?'

'Because we don't have a healthy template of *any* kind to work with, her or anyone else's.'

'Why don't you get one?'

For the first time Walker showed impatience. 'Who's going to let us do that?'

'I don't know – a med student, a homeless person who sells his blood, a death-row volunteer?'

'You don't understand. Scanning enough living tissue to construct an entire model generates more heat than the neurons can tolerate. It *kills* the brain cells we're trying to scan.'

'Why not use a cadaver?'

'The brain has to be functioning when we scan it.'

'How much damage would the heat do to a living patient?'

'That depends.'

'On?'

'How long it takes to complete the scan, how well we cool the tissue, the general physiology of the test subject's brain. Many factors.'

Nat reached for a half lemon. 'Are you saying that if you had a healthy human model to work with, you might save her?'

'Let me put it this way. If we solved the heat problem long enough to complete a donor's brain scan, theoretically we could attempt to repair Camilla's damage – with highly uncertain results.' Walker speared another oyster. 'What's the point of this grilling, Detective?'

'I'm trying to decide if I should bring you one.'

'One what?'

'A subject whose brain you can scan.'

Walker didn't quite get the oyster into his mouth. He set his fork on the plate of shaved ice and leaned forward. 'Look, Detective, I want to save her as much as you do, but you can't just show up with a volunteer and expect me to put him at risk. You're grossly overestimating both the technology and my skills. It's dangerous.'

'If she's going to die anyway, why does dangerous matter?'

'Because . . .' He hesitated. 'Because there are some things worse than death.' Walker stuck an oyster into his mouth as if he wished he hadn't said that.

'Worse than death?' Nat said. 'What are you talking about?'

Walker ate his oyster instead of answering. 'Besides,' he said, 'doctors don't sacrifice one patient to save another.'

'Oh, don't give me that bullshit. Organ transplants, life-threatening births, emergency room decisions, battlefield triage – it happens all the time.' Nat downed a mouthful of beer. 'Anyway, I'm not talking about a volunteer.'

'What does that mean?'

'I've got somebody specific in mind. A killer.'

There was a slight change of expression on Walker's face, the kind a smart detective couldn't miss. Either he'd never thought about using a killer before – or he'd thought about it a lot.

'Even killers have rights, you know,' Walker said.

'Not this one.'

'Why not?'

'He's the guy who shot Camilla.'

Walker poked a tiny pitchfork into a Duck Island Petite,

then put Nat in his sights. 'Are you trying to set me up again, Detective?'

'I can't be wired today, Doc. I'm the one who's proposing this thing.'

Walker leaned back in his chair. 'I thought you were a cop.'

Nat felt his cheeks warm. 'I am, which means I know what I'm talking about. Here's option A: I arrest the man who shot Cam and turn him over to the criminal justice system, and they send him to prison for attempted murder. Result? A killer lives in the shitcan while his innocent victim dies.' He stopped talking to let someone pass by. 'That's the closest thing to justice the state can offer. Now let's consider option B, what you and I can do. I bring the sniper to your lab and you scan his brain and take your best shot at saving your patient. If we're lucky, she makes it; if we're very lucky, he makes it too. Now we're talking real justice, Doctor – a chance to make the bastard take back his bullet.'

'Interesting,' Walker said, 'but there's something else motivating you here, I can feel it.'

Not bad. The guy Nat had in mind also killed his father – which, when you factored in how he'd handled that, had led to Camilla's injury. Walker's intuition was good, and Nat hated an adversary with good intuition.

'I'm curious about something,' Walker said. 'When this killer shot Camilla, who was he aiming at?'

'Me, I'm sure. Who'd want to hurt Camilla?'

'How about someone who wanted to hurt you by hurting her?'

Actually, Nat had wondered about that. At first he'd assumed Jackson had hit Camilla by mistake, but then it occurred to him that maybe Jackson's plan was to torture him first by killing his bride in his arms, then get around to killing him later. Sort of a taste of what he assumed Jackson gave Angel Rico before finishing him off. Either way, Nat felt his face flush at having put Camilla in harm's way.

'Did I touch a nerve?' Walker said.

'Look,' Nat said, 'let's lay our cards on the table. We don't like each other, so what? We wouldn't like each other even if Camilla wasn't in the picture. But she *is* in the picture, and that means we've got to cooperate whether we like it or not. So why don't we cut the crap and get on with it?'

Walker squeezed lemon juice on his fingers and dried them with a napkin, then tossed it onto the table like a towel thrown into the ring. 'I'm not interested in your kind of cooperation.' He pushed back from the table and stood up.

Nat felt his hatred for Walker ripple from his collar to his shoes. What kind of a guy was this, anyway? A surgeon with the power to snatch the woman he loves back from death, and he wouldn't even try? An unempathetic healer? An unsympathetic black man? The arrogance of the man and the imbalance of power between them made Nat slightly crazy.

'Doesn't it bother you,' he said, barely controlling himself, 'knowing the man who shot Camilla is out there laughing about it?'

'I hate the bastard,' Walker said. 'I've thought about him a lot.'

Maybe he had. If so, now was the time to push this guy. Nat reached down and squeezed the large manila envelope by his side, preparing to take out the negatives and the memo and show them to Walker. But then his professional instincts kicked in: don't do it yet. You'll be playing your cards before you know what you're holding.

'Thanks for the oysters,' Walker said, and took a step away from the table.

But don't let him get away. 'She knows what you did,' Nat said coldly.

Walker stopped and stared at him, a mirror image of his own loathing. Plus something that Nat liked: curiosity.

'Beg pardon?'

'You heard me, she knows your dirty little secret.' He was bluffing – he didn't know what the dirty little secret was – but it was working enough to keep Walker's shoes nailed to the ground. 'She figured it out just before she was shot.'

Walker stepped back and sat down. 'I have no idea what you're talking about.'

Sure you don't, which is why you came back. Nat could smell it now: the anxiety, the focus, the exaggerated denial of facts that perps always made just before they tried to cut a deal.

'When we were up on the torch,' Nat said, 'she was telling me about why the two of you broke up, and suddenly her face turned white and she said, "Oh my God, I just figured it out. It may not have been premeditated, but it was the same thing as murder."' He took a drink of beer.

Walker sat down and stared at him a moment, then reached into his pocket and pulled out a bill clip. He laid some money on the table without looking away, then leaned forward, as if into a wind, and for a moment Nat thought he was going to go over the top of the table for his throat. Actually, he hoped he would.

Push him harder. 'Is that what's making you think twice about saving her?' Nat said. 'Your fear of what she'll remember if she wakes up?'

Walker looked ready to erupt. 'Listen to me—'

'No, you listen to *me*. You're no different from anybody else who does big, important things in life. You can't do them without picking up your share of skeletons along the way. So pay close attention to what I have to say. You're going to do what it takes to try to save Camilla because it's the right thing to do, but if you can't see that, you're going to do it anyway for the simple reason that if you don't, I'm going to dig up your private history and lay it out for everyone to see. It'll happen so fast you won't have time to kiss your lab and Nobel and arrogant ass goodbye.'

Cush Walker went into a barely controlled meltdown. 'Now you listen to me, you cocky son-of-a-bitch. I don't take threats from anybody, least of all some pasty-faced Irish prick who's responsible for getting my patient shot in the first place. That's right, Hennessy, you. I don't know how you did it, but I know she wouldn't be lying on her deathbed if it weren't for the kind of shortcuts guys like you love to take. It's written all over your face. Sure, you're a cop – one of the kind who thinks he's God. You live by the rules that suit you and make up the rest. Bringing me a killer instead of arresting him is just par for the course.'

Nat flushed but forced a smile anyway. 'I see we're finally communicating.'

'Go to hell,' Walker said, and stood up and left.

Nat sat there for a moment, finished his beer, then took money out of his pocket and laid it on his side of the table.

Pasty-faced Irish prick? That was definitely good. When a guy as dignified as Walker gave in to racial slurs, you could be sure you were getting somewhere.

'OK, everybody, that's it for now,' Cush said.

His New York staff sat around the conference-room table taking notes and downing coffee and Cokes at the end of their daily afternoon session. Like his Mississippi crew, they were divided into two teams, surgery and research. On the intangibles – dedication, professionalism, and excitement – to a person they admired Cush and took large satisfaction from being part of his work. As they broke up, he talked to the anesthesiologist about a new cooling blanket, then headed for his office. Passing Rodriguez on the way out the door, he gave him a sign to follow.

Cush entered his office, sat at his desk and pulled down his necktie, looking uncharacteristically beat. Rodriguez knocked once on the doorjamb and entered carrying a report in a red binder.

'I've got the results on the latest scan of her aneurysms,' he said, opening the binder. 'Take a look at page—' Cush was motioning to him to close the door.

'Have a seat.'

Rod closed the door and sat in a chair in front of the desk.

'I had lunch with Hennessy today and totally lost it.' Losing his temper and cursing was rare. His father had once told him that God understood why a man stole bread or fell in love with another man's wife, but swearing was letting the devil catch you on a dry hook.

'You mind my speaking frankly?' Rod said.

'Go ahead.'

'Fuck him.'

Cush's lips curled into a smile; his sentiments exactly. 'He's been reading books and articles on nanotech neurosurgery,' Cush said.

'So?'

'He wants to bring us a human beta tester.'

Rod hadn't expected that. 'Is he kidding?'

'No.'

Rod laid the red binder on Cush's desk. 'Who's he got in mind?'

'The man who shot her.'

'Jesus, Cush. That's—' He censored himself.

'That's what?'

'I was going to say, that's actually kind of interesting.'

Cush leaned back in his chair. 'Before you get carried away, there's something else you should know. He says just before Camilla was shot she figured out a secret about me.'

Rodriguez's face was not happy. 'Did he say what it was?'

'No, only that it had something to do with why we broke up, and that something I did was as good as murder.'

'Shit.' Rod stood up and leaned on the back of his chair. 'I told you it was only a matter of time before somebody got into this.' He drummed his fingers. 'I'm sure he doesn't know what he's got.'

'No, but he's threatening to find out and blackmail us into trying a repair.'

Rod paced. 'What have we got on him?'

'Nothing. My guess is he was the sniper's target, not her, but I don't know why, or what good it would do us if I did. But there's definitely something that's bothering him about why she was shot. You can see it in his face.'

'Maybe we should find out.'

Cush shook his head. 'He's the detective, Rod, not us.'

'I know another way to neutralize him,' Rod said. 'He can't blackmail us into doing something we've already decided to do.'

Cush said, 'Use the killer? You sound as desperate as he is.'

'We're that close, Cush. Once I've got the Reverse Logic program up and running, we've got a good shot at it.'

Cush tossed a bent paperclip into an In basket. 'But we're not there yet, and when it comes to surgery, close is no cigar.'

'I'll be ready to start trials in a few days,' Rod said. 'Problem is, even if I get it right, I'm not sure it's going to help Camilla. Take a look at this.' He opened the red binder to a line graph and turned it around for Cush to see. 'Her aneurysms are weakening fast.'

Cush picked up the report, and Rod walked to the door. 'Whatever you decide to do, Cush, I'm with you,' he said. 'Just try to keep one thing in mind.'

'What's that?'

'We've taken this risk before.'

'Shaw? This is Hennessy.' He stood at the pay phone at the Shell station, watching an attendant pump gas in the 'full' service lane. 'Two things. I need you to do a couple of name checks, one on a guy named Murphy – Spider's all I got for a first name – early twenties, white, member of Aryan Reign, volunteered to be a guinea pig at NeuroPath Labs while he was doing state time. I need to know what he was in for and what kind of medical experiment he got into.'

'The second?'

'Do the name check on a guy named Roy Driggers. That's all I got on him.'

'Anything else?'

'Yeah.'

'That'll be three things.'

The gas station attendant finished pumping gas and started back to the office. Nat pulled the telephone aside and yelled, 'You want to grab a sponge and take a swipe at the windshield?' He turned back to the phone. 'You get better service from the squeegie men on the street than you do at a station. Your friend Dolly.'

'What about her?'

'We need to pay her a visit.'

'What for?'

'She doesn't know it yet, but she's about to give the best performance of her life – as a hooker or a dancer.'

'Doing what?'

'She's going to give us the guy who killed Angel Rico.'

She didn't know how she was going to move him out of the room. He was becoming a fixture, staying after visiting hours, massaging her feet, fiddling with the volume on the television set, searching for movies he knew she liked, sitting in one of the two leather chairs at the side of the room reading beneath a gooseneck lamp, falling asleep with his head crooked to the side or stretching out on the floor. Nurse Punt wanted to give Detective Hennessy all the leeway she could, but if Dr Walker knew how much that was, he'd cut the detective's visitor privileges entirely.

There'd be no blanket and pillow for Mr Hennessy tonight. There'd be a kindly ejection.

She opened the door to Camilla's room and saw him sitting in a chair next to her bed, his back turned to her in the darkness. She knocked once. 'Detective Hennessy?'

He turned in the chair, startling her. It wasn't Hennessy, it was Dr Walker.

'Oh, Doctor – I didn't know—'

'Come in,' Cush said a little too quickly, stretching his arms as if taking a break from something tedious. Nurse Punt started to back out the door anyway, but he stopped her. 'Virginia?'

'Yes, Doctor?'

'I'm going home for a day or two, be back Thursday night, latest. Tell Rod if he needs me he can reach me at the farm, would you?'

'Of course.'

She closed the door, but not before noticing that instead of rising, he settled back into the chair and turned back to his patient.

Cush sat with her for a long time, trying to sort it out: what he'd do if she were someone else, which she wasn't; what he'd do if he ethically had a volunteer to work with, which he didn't; what he'd do if the cooling problem was solved, which it wasn't. And then there was Rod's parting shot reminding him that they'd taken the risk before.

He was in love with her, the only woman he'd ever really loved. How many times had he daydreamed of marrying her and having a family and living the part of his life he was missing – being ordinary and uncomplicated, not always some demigod of medicine? How often had he pictured her and him and the kids eating breakfast together, or lying in the grass at night listening to crickets? He didn't know how much of it was fleeting and how much was solid, but he didn't care. He wanted it. He wanted to make it happen. With her.

He had a difficult decision to make, and there was only one place he knew to make it.

Cush rolled down the back window of the taxi and breathed in the air heavy with green river water, slow sunshine, and overburdened crickets. In the last twenty years Mississippi had become a patchwork quilt of the old and the new, ranging from the shiny airport in Jackson to the aching smell of poverty still out here in the Delta, a vapor so thin and peculiar, only those who knew it could detect it, the way a coal miner's canary caught the first scent of gas. Cush got it.

Whenever he approached Hardy, the town near the farm where he had grown up, his mind went back to his childhood. Not that he and his family had been dirt poor, not growing up in the household of a doctor, but living with rural poverty, breathing it, being black in it, he knew it in his bones. Kids with spindly, bowed legs and ribs that turned outward, seven-year-olds with brown stumps for teeth – they had all been part of his early life, both in school and around his father's clinic, and the dull gaze seeping from their eyes would always be embedded in his memory. To this day he could spot a man who'd grown up in a Delta shack, no matter how well off he might have become: the slightly too-baggy pants, the way he cleaned his plate with a piece of bread, the momentary patience with a fly on his face, offering it a chance to leave under its own power before brushing it away with a slow wave of the hand.

Moving past a line of sparse elms, he glimpsed an old woman standing bent in front of her broken teal shutters, pumping air from an ungiving well, her face indifferent to the heat of the afternoon. Poverty in Hardy was by no means limited to black folks, but the short end of the stick certainly was. If you were poor but white, you could always find someone else to stand on – someone different, someone beneath you, someone *less* – and reach the edge of the basket to climb out. For a couple of centuries, black folks had served as that stepping stone quite nicely. 'If you ain't any better than a nigger, son,' the white farmer said in *Mississippi Burning*, explaining why he shot his black neighbor's mule, 'who are you better than?'

Cush's cab driver, a seventy-something white man known to the family only as Old Jimmy, drove him past the Hardy band shell to show him where a fire had broken out from a stray rocket on the Fourth of July, an accident Cush had not heard about at the farm. Seeing the scorched stucco, he pictured an evening of beer and hotdogs and the star-spangled banner and flags, some of them Confederate, although fewer than in years gone by. In the last decade or so, blacks had begun attending the town's Independence Day festivities, even in this part of the state where remnants of Mississippi's old plantation mentality were still alive. As a kid, Cush had loved watching fireworks – always at a black folks' distance – but the Fourth still felt too much like a white celebration to get him excited.

Driving past a strip mall, Old Jimmy pointed proudly at a banner announcing the construction of the latest monument to consumption, a new Price Club warehouse, obviously unaware that it dishonored Cush's memories of a harsher, more interesting and sinewy childhood.

Leaving the edge of town, he saw a rusting '56 Chevy sitting on cinderblocks, a redneck's pride, and instantly felt better. That was the Mississippi he understood best: a place of great beauty and rawness, of poetry and dissonance coexisting cheek by jowl. He'd always be ambivalent about this part of the world, the way a fallen Catholic was about the Church. You could escape it physically, but like the smell of incense, it was always lurking somewhere in the soul.

Getting into the cab at the airport, he'd decided to go straight to his grandfather's farm, where he'd grown up, and drop by his own house later. As they approached the turn onto a dirt road that led to the farmhouse, they came to a familiar row of pine trees standing as if waiting for Santa Claus, reminding him of his family reunion. He and his four brothers and sisters got together once a year and swapped stories over honey-fried chicken, bacon-fatted greens and corn bread so rich it fell apart on the plate. Once reunited, the five of them behaved toward each other with the same fondnesses, irritations, and disrespects they had show each other as children, as if their feelings had been hung in the smokehouse to be taken out when the holidays came along. They made their reversion to type unconsciously, knowing that to do otherwise would take them out of character and disrupt the family play. But having put their mother in the ground four years earlier, at least they'd finally stopped arguing about their places at the kitchen table.

Riding up the dirt road, Cush squinted through waves of heat wriggling off the dried, yellow grass to see the man he was coming to visit sitting on the old wooden porch: Dr Booker T. Walker, father of Calvin, grandfather of Cush. He knew he'd be drinking blackberry tea, cool but with no ice, moving in the sticky-thick Mississippi air just enough to keep the buzzards guessing.

What a wonderful man his grandfather had been, especially after Cush's father had died. As the oldest child, Cush had grown up with the usual advantages and burdens of the firstborn, replacing diluted parental love as each new sibling arrived with self-reliance and successes that distinguished him in his father's eyes. A few years after his father's death, when Cush was sixteen, his mother and grandfather had sent him to live on Martha's Vineyard with the family of a black doctor whose roots went back to Plymouth Rock and the textile trade, not Barbados and the slaves. There Cush had grown up fast, shaping the adult he'd become: a leader but slightly remote; remarkably accomplished but never self-satisfied; loose and light-footed physically yet emotionally intense, sometimes almost coiled. Most contradictory of all, he had a warm, infectious smile, a politician's dream, and yet rarely showed it. His brothers and sisters accused him of having run off with an unfair portion of the family's brains, but they admired him as they said it.

He got out of the taxi near the barn and walked across the grass to the porch, carrying his small commuter's bag. His grandfather sat in a wooden rocking chair wearing an immaculate white undershirt, faded tan cotton pants rolled up over his calves, and leather suspenders gathered around his waist. He was barefoot and, despite the heat, there wasn't a hint of perspiration on his face.

Cush said hello with his usual hug and went inside to wash up and take off his suit. A few minutes later he returned to the porch in a crisp blue shirt with the sleeves rolled up, a pair of beltless blue jeans and comfortable, worn-out moccasins he'd owned since medical school. He sat on the porch swing, moving in a carefully circumscribed arc, barely disturbing the stultifying July air.

'What brings you back so soon?' his grandfather asked. Cush had been there only a few days earlier, for the Fourth, and usually when he went to New York, he stayed a week or two, at least.

Cush glided, measuring his thoughts. 'I have a difficult decision to make, and this feels like the place to make it.'

His grandfather continued to rock, saying nothing, taking on the Yoda-like role Cush was looking for. Old friendship. Old wisdom.

'It's the neuron regeneration program,' Cush said, taking a pair of tortoiseshell eyeglasses from his shirt pocket. 'We've got most of the glitches out of the software, but heat is still a problem.'

His grandfather set his teacup down and lifted a pipe and a pick to clean out the bowl. 'Isn't that why God invented white rats?'

'Unfortunately, that doesn't solve this particular problem.'

'Why not?'

'In this case, the subject wouldn't be a rat. At least, not the four-legged variety.'

His grandfather continued cleaning his pipe. 'Who would it be?'

'Does it make a difference?'

'Maybe.'

Cush knew what he meant: how bad is the beta tester? What crime has he committed? Cush had used volunteer convicts before. 'I don't know who it is, except he's a murderer,' Cush said. 'The same one who shot my patient.' He wasn't ready yet to tell him who his patient was.

His grandfather continued cleaning his pipe. 'You know the risks involved in working with these men,' he said. 'You've been there before.'

'Problem is, I'm not sure how much of this would be for the greater good of human kind and how much of it would be for me.' He stood up and walked to the porch railing and leaned against it. 'Coming down today, I got out of the cab at LaGuardia and saw a sociology professor I recognized pulling a bag out of the trunk of his car, a big expert on race relations I was on a panel with a couple of years ago. When I saw him standing there I held out my hand and started to say hello. He put his suitcase in my hand and said he was late, I'd have to hustle if I was going to get it onto the plane in time.'

His grandfather rocked with a smile on his face. 'You got to stop wearing that red cap to the airport, Cush.'

Cush laughed and crossed his feet at the ankles. 'While he was digging into his pocket for a tip, I put the bag down and introduced myself.'

'What'd he say?'

'Oh, you know, he held his head in his hands and carried on. I let him off the hook as best I could, but we both knew what had happened. I'd become invisible.' He reached out and took a drink of his grandpa's tea. 'When I landed in Jackson, Old Jimmy picked me up as usual. There I was in my fancy gray double-breasted suit, and there he was, this old cracker with an eighth-grade education—'

'Fifth.'

'A fifth-grade education, no pension, a shack with holes in the screens and a bum ticker, but when we pulled up at the barn a few minutes ago he opened my door and lifted my bag out of the trunk and reminded me to tell you he asked after you.' Cush played with the teacup. 'Every night Old Jimmy falls to his knees and thanks God he's not black, but he behaves toward black folks with respect.'

'Up north they love the race and hate the individual,' his grandfather said. 'Down here they love the individual and hate the race.'

'Whatever it is, I'll take Old Jimmy over a politically correct professor who can't even see the people he writes about.'

His grandfather laid his head back. 'You got to be patient, Cush. It's one of the things we know how to do best.'

Cush sat listening to the crickets under the lattice-framed porch. After awhile he spread his fingers and examined the back of his coffee-colored hand. 'So whose white blood do you suppose is in this skin, Grandpa?'

His grandfather opened his eyes and lifted a book off the wicker table by his chair. 'I've been reading about the Walker family, but it doesn't say.' He handed the book to Cush, who turned the pages randomly. 'It's mostly about the slave trade,'

Booker T. said. 'Any idea how many slaves got sold in the eighteenth century?'

'Not a clue,' Cush said.

'About thirty million. Enough to put a dent in the African population.'

'How'd they all fit into Mississippi?'

His grandfather smiled. 'Lord, son, fewer than half a million came to the whole southern United States, only about fifteen per cent of all the Africans sold around the world.'

How weird. For some reason Cush had assumed they'd all come here. 'Where'd the rest go?'

'South America mostly. Brazil, the Caribbean, some to Asia, a few to Europe.'

'What'd they use them for?'

'Same thing, basically, although the system was a little different from place to place. Plantations down here raised slaves like cotton and beans and horses – bred them, broke up the families, and bred them some more. In Brazil they segregated them by sex and worked them to death and then bought replacements because they were so cheap.' He took back his cup of tea and finished it.

Cush closed the book and looked at his hand again. 'So who do you think it was? A slave master? Some redneck with the IQ of a mule?'

'Knowing you, Cush, I'd say it was probably a riverboat gambler.'

Cush smiled at the thought. 'I wouldn't mind if the reckless side of me came out of my white blood.'

'Why's that?'

'The irony of it. What goes around, comes around.'

Sally Shaw and Nat Hennessy were driving toward Dolly's apartment in the South Bronx when Shaw pulled a computer printout from her bag. 'Spider Murphy, member of a defunct skinhead gang called Aryan Reign, sentenced to prison for leading an assault on a Jewish couple in Monmouth Beach. Beat them up during some kind of initiation rite, husband died, wife recovered with permanent injuries. Let's see. He was released to Walker's laboratory program, turned in good behavior reports, was later paroled and hired as a full-time employee of Walker's lab.'

'Any indication what kind of experimental medicine he was in?'

'Nope.' She turned the page. 'The computer went down before I got to Roy Driggers, so I'll do it when we get back.' She closed the file and opened the window a crack.

Nat looked over at her. 'Carsick?'

'Happens when I read.'

'Eat a peanut butter cup. The sugar helps.'

She opened her bag, took one out, and took a bite. 'I eat one for every cigarette I used to smoke.'

'Must have been two packs a day.' They turned a corner and Nat looked for a street sign.

'So when are you going to tell me?' Shaw asked.

Nat kept peering at the street sign. 'Can you read that?'

She bent forward. 'Looks like . . . Ellison.'

'You've got pretty good eyesight,' he said.

'It's the peanut butter cups.'

'Tell you what?'

'Who killed Angel Rico?'

He'd known this was coming, he just hadn't known when. He could have said nothing, but if he was going to nail Jackson, it was clear that he needed her help. He decided to tell her as little as possible and hold back the bad stuff, like how Jackson had killed his father, and how he had let Angel go free to kill Jackson in return.

'His name is J.J. Jackson,' he said.

'Who's that?'

'He operates a limo service in the Bronx, apparently runs some girls. BCI's got nothing on him.'

'Why did he kill Rico?'

'Good question.' Dangerous question. Rule one on lying: if you have to do it, stick as close as you can to the truth. 'I think he may be the Bambino.'

'The guy you went after at Dede's Bar?'

'No, a different Bambino.' He wasn't usually snotty, but it kept her a little off track.

'What makes you think it's him?'

'Motive. When the bust at Dede's went bad and everybody got shot up, the Bambino must have known Rico had set him up. My guess is that the minute Bambino heard Rico was out of jail, he nailed him.' Not bad. Probably what Jackson had intended.

'You'd think Angel would have known that and been more careful.'

'Guys like him don't think that way.' He made it sound like the voice of experience.

They drove a half block. 'So how'd you find the Bambino?'

Careful now. 'When we were at A & E Scrap Metal doing interviews I found a locksmith across the street who was working late and saw a stretch come in. He got a piece of the plate.'

'You didn't tell me that before,' she said. 'Why didn't you tell me that before?'

Because I just made it up. 'What are we, spouses?'

'I'd rather eat ground glass.'

'Just thought I'd ask. I've been known to make some very bad commitments when I'm tired.'

She repressed a smile. 'So why didn't you tell me?'

'I just did.' Like a bloodhound, this girl. He turned the corner, careful not to run over a group of kids crossing against the light. 'DMV called this morning to say they made a match of the first three numbers to a limo owned by a guy named J.J. Jackson.' That part was true.

'Where does he live?'

'Who knows? I made a call to the address on his registration and it turns out to be a McDonald's on Jerome Avenue.' He pulled up in front of an apartment building and sat with the engine idling and the air conditioner struggling. 'We'll find him if Dolly gives us a hand.'

'Oh, she can do that, all right, if you get my drift.' She opened her notebook and flipped to a page with a paperclip on the side. 'Busted twice for prostitution, once in nineteen ninety-two and once in ninety-four. Since then she's been clean.'

'You mean since then she's been careful.' He turned off the engine and looked over at his partner. 'There's a difference. Keep that in mind and trust your nose as much as your logic, OK?'

'That mean you're not coming with me?' she said, opening the door.

'You'll do better on your own,' he said. 'You know the business so well. If you get my drift.'

Cush and his grandfather worked in the large farmhouse kitchen preparing a late lunch, or what old Southerners called dinner. Booker T. stared into the pantry, pawing at cans of soup sitting next to paraffin-capped jars of jelly, searching for sugar beets.

'What we need around here is a woman's touch,' he grumbled. He settled for butter beans he'd put up himself. 'How's your love life, Cush? If you want a family, you got to get moving.'

'The woman I want isn't available.'

His grandfather broke a waxy seal on the jar and smelled the contents. He didn't have to ask who Cush was talking about. When Camilla had left, Cush had been in a funk for weeks.

Cush wiped his hands on an apron. 'Where're the pot holders?'

His grandfather pointed at a drawer, then cut a piece of bacon off a slab, diced it, and dropped the pieces into a stir pot with the beans. 'Still can't make up with her?'

'Wouldn't matter if I could,' he said. 'She's in a coma.'

'Camilla?'

'Gunshot wound to the head.'

'Good Lord,' Booker T. said. Cush lifted a pot of boiling potatoes off the stove and set it on the counter. His grandfather stirred the concoction in the pot slowly. 'Can you help her?' He poured in a can of stewed tomatoes.

'Maybe,' he said. 'That's what I have to decide.'

His grandfather stirred the beans and watched them bubble. 'So that's why this isn't just about advancing the state of medicine.'

'You got it,' Cush said. 'This is a case of old-fashioned lust.' He picked up his beer and sat down in a rocking chair next to a potbellied stove that had been cleaned for the summer, then fiddled with the temples on his eyeglasses. 'If she was anyone else I wouldn't be tempted,' he said, 'but she's the only woman I've ever wanted, Grandpa. I was in love with her before I even met her.' He looked out the window into the yard and found the old water pump on the stone well. For a moment he could see her standing there working the worn steel handle, pumping up the cold, clear water, cupping her hands and drinking, wiping her chin with the underside of her arm. He wanted her so much it hurt.

His grandfather looked around the kitchen, taking stock of what remained to be done. 'Open that cabinet there and put out two glasses.' Cush got up and did it.

They sat at the large round table with an oilcloth cover.

'Tell me something,' Cush said, unfolding a napkin. 'Did it matter to you that Camilla was white?'

His grandfather looked over at him with a flat expression. 'Matter? Not to me. You think it should?' Cush didn't answer. His grandfather sprinkled his soup with salt, then, without a touch of irony in his voice, said, 'Nothing wrong with bein' white.'

Cush tried to repress a smile, but suddenly both of them were laughing and shaking their heads the way country folks do when they get an inside joke. When they'd finished, his grandfather took a mouthful of butter beans and bacon.

'If you do the operation on her,' Booker T. said, 'how you going to handle the transfer problem?'

'Better than the last time, I hope.' He shouldn't have said that. His grandfather didn't want to talk about that. All that was in the past, dead and buried. 'We're still trying to figure out how to control it. That and the KBS factor.'

'If you do get control of it, could you transfer what you want from one patient to the other?'

'Theoretically.'

'Where neither patient gets hurt? No KBS, just the clean stuff you send over?'

'That's the only way we'd do it.' He tore a hunk of black bread off the loaf. 'Why'd you ask?'

'Just wonderin',' his grandfather said.

They both ate quietly, imagining the unimaginable.

Dolly sat smoking a cigarette with her leg crossed over her knee and a foot dangling a strapped platform shoe from one of her talented toes. She held a picture of her brother, Daryl, who was also known as Tangerine. Or had been. She was crying. Sally Shaw sat quietly and let her spill.

'He took care of me,' Dolly said, wiping her cheeks with her fingers. 'He gave me money, and when I got sick, he stayed with me.' She pulled a tissue from a box and dabbed it at her red-rimmed eyes, then blew her nose. 'Why would Angel Rico kill him?'

Shaw shifted in her chair. 'Angel Rico just held the knife. Someone else did the killing.'

'Who?' she said.

'A man named J.J. Jackson.'

Her face went blank. 'Who is that?'

'A street hustler, pimp, and killer,' Shaw said. 'Your brother and Angel Rico were not exactly social acquaintances, Dolly. It was more of a, uh, business relationship.' She wondered: how'm I doin', Nat?

'What do you mean?'

'They both worked for J.J. Jackson.'

'Daryl? Doing what?'

Transvestite hooking – but why rub it in? 'Does it really matter? What counts is that your brother had a falling out with Jackson and he used Angel Rico to settle the score.'

Dolly wadded up her tissue into a moist ball. 'I hope you catch them both and put them in the electric chair.'

'One of them doesn't need catching,' Shaw said. 'After Rico killed your brother, J.J. Jackson killed Rico.'

'What?' Dolly tossed her head in confusion. 'I just hate it here,' she said. 'I hate New York, I hate the Bronx, I hate this life. I hate everything.'

'I'm sorry,' Shaw said. 'Detective Hennessy and I wanted you to know some of these details because we need your help.'

Dolly put another cigarette into her mouth and lit up. It stuck to her lips when she took it out. She exhaled long and wearily. 'What kinda help?' she said, picking the cigarette paper from her mouth.

'It has to do with your, um, business,' Shaw said.

Dolly's eyes turned cold. 'What business?'

'Hooking.'

Dolly glared at her. 'What is this, some kinda shakedown?' Shaw shook her head, but Dolly didn't let up. 'You can't entrap me, sister, I know the law. I haven't been arrested since nineteen ninety-four. You're a cop, look it up.'

'I'm not interested in laying a prostitution rap on you, Dolly, I'm working a homicide,' Shaw said. 'Frankly, I was hoping you weren't out of the business.'

'Why's that?'

'Because we want you to go to work for Jackson.'

Dolly's face turned long. 'You want me to go to work for the man who had my brother killed? Are you crazy?'

'It's the only way we're going to get the evidence we need to put him away.'

'If you know who he is and what he did, why don't you just arrest him?'

'Because right now the only thing we've got on him is pimping, which means he'd be out in an hour. I know, I used to work Vice.'

'You worked Vice?'

'Sure did.'

Dolly looked her over like a fresh piece of meat. 'I thought you looked kinda foxy,' she said.

Shaw looked away and lifted pencil to pad. *Foxy*, she doodled. Good thing Nat wasn't here after all. He'd have his nickname for her.

'We need your help from the inside,' Shaw said.

Dolly's leg started bobbing up and down. Good. She's interested.

'What's this guy's story?' Dolly asked.

'The only thing we know about him is that he's got a limousine and a few girls,' Shaw said. 'Does the name Bambino ring a bell?'

'No, but I wouldn't know, I don't work for tough guys. They have ways of messing you up.'

'Going to work for him would be dangerous, no question about it, especially if he found out you were Daryl's sister. And if you're not working anymore, I can't ask you to start.'

'I didn't say I wasn't working, I said I haven't been arrested.'

Score one for Nat.

Dolly drew on her cigarette, and Shaw saw a hooker's toughness beneath her bereaved exterior.

'What makes you think he's gonna want to turn me out?' Dolly asked.

'You're tall, leggy, and white, and no offense but my guess is you're good.'

Dolly's eyelids dropped to half mast: you don't know the half of it, sister. Shaw felt the coldness prostitutes reserved for johns who haggle over price.

'What's in it for me?' Dolly asked.

'For one thing, the satisfaction of nailing the man who had your brother killed.'

'Any money?'

'Uh, I can't authorize that.' Dolly's leg stopped bouncing. Damn, she should have eased into that. Revenge was a fine

308

piece of cake, but money was meat and potatoes and a working girl like Dolly had to eat and dress and buy perfume. 'We'll see what we can do.' Weak. 'You'll certainly get consideration downtown if you get arrested.' No response to that, either.

She'd blown it.

Dolly laid her cigarette in the ashtray and picked up her brother's photograph. 'I have no idea how to get the goods on somebody.'

'We'll tell you exactly what to do.'

Dolly stubbed out the cigarette. 'Where does this guy live?' she asked.

'That's the first thing you have to help us with. We don't know.'

'I wouldn't know where to start.'

Shaw had a brainstorm. 'Ever hear of Black Diamond Taxi?' Black Diamond was a telephone taxi company used by pimps to shuttle girls to outcall locations, pick them up when they were finished, and rescue them when they were in trouble. Having worked the street, Shaw knew that their dispatchers knew the score.

'I know who they are,' Dolly said.

'Let's start there.'

'I don't know.' Dolly was looking reluctant. 'The minute this prick starts up with that get-on-your-knees-bitch shit, I'll be out of there like Flash Gordon.'

'I don't blame you,' Shaw said. She almost had her. 'The second you smell trouble, you bail, no questions asked.'

Dolly walked to an end table and picked up a framed photograph of her brother when he was younger. Tears welled up in her eyes again. 'Daryl and I came to New York together,' she said softly. 'I was a dancer then, a Rockette.' Shaw could picture those legs in action. Dolly must have been a good inch or two taller than she was, and she was nearly five nine. 'He came to my shows all the time.' Her eyes stayed fixed on the photograph.

Shaw waited. 'Before you make up your mind, there's something else I have to tell you.' She didn't want to do this, but she had no choice.

'What's that?'

'We're running out of time, which means if you're going to help, it has to be now.'

'Like today?'

Shaw nodded at the telephone. 'Like right now.'

Dolly put the photograph back. 'I don't think it will work,' she said, 'but for Daryl's sake, I'll give it a try.'

Cush pulled off his tie and laid it on the porch banister, then loosened the button at the top of his shirt. He drew the gold stopwatch from his pants pocket and checked the time. The delicate hands said it was nearly six o'clock. He snapped it closed and rubbed his thumb over the bit of inscription that had escaped erasure. *Death is but crossing.* He'd already asked his grandfather what it meant too many times to ask again.

'I'm going to take a walk to the south pasture,' he said. 'Want to come along?'

'No, you go ahead,' his grandfather said. 'I'll clean up the kitchen.'

Cush started toward the wooden steps to the grassy yard, but his grandfather motioned him to come closer. When he walked to the rocker, the old man pulled him into an embrace. 'Tell him I love him,' he said, patting his grandson on the arm.

Cush squeezed the old man's shoulder, then stood up and headed for the killing field, a rolling pasture of grass and pebbles and weeds and damp air misting like steam in the late afternoon sun.

Walking past the barn, he remembered summer nights he'd spent there as a boy lying in the loft with his brothers and his dog. Continuing on, he reached the sloping hill with the crucible on the other side and felt his throat close in anticipation. The talk of family had cast another layer onto the things he had to think through. He saw his African ancestors, both the known and the unknown, as a mysterious force that ran stubbornly in his veins.

He was a man of logic and Calvinist hard work, and yet he believed that the mountain of heaped-up slaves who preceded him had contributed greatly to who he was, and he believed that in some silent way he could commune with them. When he turned private like this, he imagined their collective spirit still guiding him, much the way true believers followed angels, or the way agnostics believed in luck. Like most missionaries, he felt obligated to do something good, but unlike most missionaries he didn't have boundless forgiveness in his heart. Certainly not now, standing on this hallowed ground.

Perhaps, he thought, not ever.

There it was again: that haunting ambivalence, that flash of Mississippi lightning revealing purity and prejudice standing side by side inside him. It was a sweet and poisonous relationship, this combination of love and hate, setting him free one moment, burdening him the next.

He lost some of his breath climbing. Hope was what he wanted to think about now, because hope was the spiritual answer to his problems, the fuel that kept a black man moving toward his polar star. If he didn't think he'd succeed, he'd be lost.

When he came over the low-rising hill, there below him, standing in the distance, was the tall pine that had served as a boundary marker since he was a kid. The fire tree he'd called it, because of the dead needles at the top that glowed orange in the morning sun. They were gone now, leaving angled branches and a crusty bark in their place, but his eye could still see the line from the trunk that gave him a bearing on the headstone. Knowing his destination was in sight, he picked a handful of purple and pink meadow beauties and continued on. A few minutes later he arrived at the grave and laid the flowers on the rounded stone, then stooped down and touched the earth.

Father.

He wanted to remember him as the successful doctor he'd

been, the public man with special talents who'd built a hospital out of the rural clinic his grandfather had started in a church basement in the twenties. He wanted to think of the two generations of black doctors that preceded him, both waiting to see what he made of his life, but it didn't work that way. All he could think of was his father's suspenders and the times his father took him on house calls, and the end of the day when he carried him sleepy-eyed from the back seat of the car and laid him on his bunk bed and kissed him with warm lips and a scratchy, day-old beard.

He raised his eyes to the center of the bowl-shaped field where his father had been lynched and sought the inspiration he needed from that butchered November night. Tell me what to do, Father. Tell me what *you* would do. He waited but heard nothing. Then he understood why. He already knew what his father would do, and he knew it wasn't what he himself was contemplating. The silence in the air merely underlined their differences. Cush had come out here to consult his father's ghost, but now that he had, he wasn't necessarily ready to take its advice. But that, he decided, was OK too. You're on your own now, Cush, his father's spirit was saying, you've got to set your own course regardless of what I'd do. My life can offer you only so much. You're your own man.

Maybe I can get only so much from your life, Father. But oh, what a lesson I learned from your death.

He pictured it again, the burning torches, the gasoline can buckling in the heat, the inverted cruciform engulfed in flames twice its size. He remembered his father's gold watch, the nervous Klansman with the knife, the ruby liquid streaming out of his father's body, the sound of a gunshot and the sting in the shoulder as he ran wildly into the night, alone and disbelieving, as if God had bolted before him, leaving mortals to fend for themselves.

313

He continued to reconstruct the scene, focused and unblinking, saving his clearest eye for the wrinkled figures in white, the killers with stunted IQs masquerading as larger-than-life ghosts. Of all the things that had happened that night, he remembered them best of all. And now, on the oscilloscopes in his laboratory, he could actually see the stuff that made them crazy – the literal, phobic hate that oozed like lava in their heads, the fearful brain cells that sucked up oxygen from their bloodstreams the way the fire had sucked it out of the air that awful night.

He pictured the electrodes in his laboratory measuring the ordinary, daily anger his father's killers felt toward blacks as they went about their ordinary, daily lives. He imagined the thin, visceral loathing that warmed their veins whenever a black person walked by, their junky's need to see black men 'slickened' in the middle of the night, or black women stolen from their beds, or whole families consumed on whorling, burning stakes or at the ends of stretched-out ropes.

He pictured it again and again. Even now, after all these years, the images still put a knot in his gut.

He thought about his grandfather rocking in his chair, smoking his pipe and telling him to be patient. Patience and perseverance. We shall overcome. He'd heard those words for so long they'd become synonymous with blackness, but not for him. In a quick and technical world, understanding and forgiveness were the booby prizes for those who lacked the will to win. People talked about the progress blacks had made as if they'd stepped off bales of cotton onto gleaming social elevators. And surely many had – he himself was exhibit A, and glad of it. But the headway blacks had made was not the gift of a nation. It had to be taken the way white folks won the West, with strength and daring and risk-taking beyond the ordinary. He had the scientific skills to do his part. The question was, did he have the nerve?

He thought of his father again. Was he using his dad's death to justify something selfish? How much was this about his science, and how much about ambition and his need to capture Camilla? He didn't know. At the moment he didn't care. Regardless of how things balanced out, he would do his best to create a safe place where men like his father could never be touched. That was the message of this field, and if he could serve that purpose and save Camilla too, why shouldn't he? After all, the potential of his work wasn't narrow; like all scientific breakthroughs, success in one realm inevitably led to applications in another. That's how he could be true to them both – his father and the woman he loved.

If he took the risk. And if he succeeded.

After a while – he couldn't tell how long he'd been there – he stood up and began his trek across the pasture to the McCoy's farmhouse at the other side of the wood. When he arrived, he stepped onto the old porch – the slats were in need of repair, he made a mental note – and knocked on the door. There was no response; Vestie Viney must be out. No matter, he'd see her another day.

He walked to the outbuilding between the barn and the road, got his bearings, and paced off the steps to the edge of the pebble pasture. There he found another gravestone, this one flat and flush with the soil.

He stooped down and brushed the leaves and dead grasshoppers off the surface, then patted the stone as if to say thanks. Without lingering, he rose to his feet and started back to his grandfather's farmhouse, walking slowly, displacing anger with the pine and ironweed fragrances of his boyhood . . . the smell of burlap bags and his dusty dog . . . the perfume of the grape arbor near the stone well, the serenade of katydids and crows . . . the feel of red clay squished between his toes after a summer rain.

A sudden summer rain. A Mississippi cloud spilling its unrepentant tears. Whether it was the loss of his father, or Camilla, or another chunk of his own innocence, he didn't know, but all the way back to the house he opened up like a cloud during a sudden summer rain.

Whether he realized it or not, he'd made his decision.

'You want something to eat?' Nat said.

He was looking up from his bowl of soup, watching Shaw slip into the covered banquette across from him. She'd paged him with a message that she had big news, so he called and told her to meet him at the diner across the street from the hospital. She laid her bag on the seat next to her.

'Menu?' Nat said.

'In a minute. Guess what: Dolly found Jackson.'

She was right, that was news. 'How'd she do it?'

'Black Diamond Taxi.' Shaw shifted in her seat and made herself comfortable. 'She left a message for him and around six o'clock he called her. Now I ask you, do I know hooking, or do I know hooking?'

'Very good, Shaw. A little lucky, but good.'

'Lucky, my fanny. Give me some credit.'

'If this works out, I'll give you the Medal of Honor.' He opened a menu and slid it in front of her. Pointing his thumb at a man in the next booth covered with bandages, he said, 'Stay away from the pea soup.'

'There's more,' Shaw said, unable to contain herself as she closed the menu. 'He sent a car for her and brought her to his apartment. She's already inside!'

'Where's he live?'

'On Howe Street.' She handed him a piece of paper with the address Dolly had given her. 'The way she described it, sounds like a small fortress. We'll need a TAC unit to take him.'

A tactical team? Helmets and vests and rifles and swarming cops? No way. Take him like that and they'll haul him off to jail and he'll be useless. Nat had other plans for this guy.

'With a little help from Dolly,' he said, 'we're going to make the collar ourselves.'

'We are?' She loved the idea. 'You think we can do that?'

'Sure, we just need to figure out how. What's her frame of mind?'

'She sounds good. She must be putting on a pretty good act, she said he wants her to run his operation and build up his stable of girls.'

'When does she report to you?' The rule on snitches was basic: if they didn't check in exactly when they were supposed to, you cut them loose, instantly.

'I told her to call me every afternoon at four.' She pulled a piece of paper from her bag. 'I also pulled a rap sheet on Roy Driggers, AKA Sneezer.' She pushed the menu aside. 'You're gonna love how he got that nickname.'

Nat was more interested in confirming that his middle name began with an A, as in *Patient: RAD.*

Shaw read: 'Born in Mississippi, migrated to New Jersey, skinhead member of Aryan Reign. Let's see, yadda, yadda, yadda. Sentenced five to fifteen for participating in the beating of the Jewish couple Spider attacked and served three before being released to Walker's program.' She turned the page and continued reading. 'Two conditions of parole were to remain in Walker's custody and report to a parole officer once a week, both of which he did without fail. According to the custody reports, Walker found him to be, quote, highly cooperative.'

'Where was he when he jumped?'

She read the report in a quiet monotone, searching. 'NY parole . . . arrangements with Mississippi parole officer . . . Here it is. He was taking part in NeuroPath's program at Walker's clinic in Hardy, Mississippi, when Walker reported that he'd left the clinic for his weekly check-in at the parole office and never showed up. After that, there's nothing.'

'No contact with his family?'

'Not according to this.'

Interesting. An early release, an unblemished record of parole-office visits, no complaints by Walker, then gone without a trace.

'What's his middle name?' Nat asked.

She read to the end, turned back to the first page, and read some more. 'Doesn't say.'

'Everybody in the South has a middle name,' Nat said. 'Usually more than one.'

'Maybe BCI screwed up. One time, I pulled two different Bennetts and found the same information in both files.'

'What's the Sneezer story?'

'Seems when he gets – what should I say, sexually aroused? – he goes into a brief fit of uncontrolled sneezes. Usually five times, it says.'

'Now how the hell would BCI know that?'

'It came out of one of his parole background reports while he was in Walker's program. Some guy in Records who doesn't have a life probably thought it would be funny to stick it in.'

'They know a hard-on makes him sneeze but they don't know his middle name?'

'Well, you gotta admit, it's more interesting than a middle name.'

Nat finished his soup and laid his spoon in the bowl. He looked across the table at her, saying nothing.

'Jesus, Nat, I got so excited I forgot to ask about Camilla.'

'Or order your food.'

'I'm not hungry.'

He shook his head. 'She's no better.'

'What a nightmare,' she said.

Nat picked up the flimsy check lying on the table and slid toward the aisle. 'You ready for an adventure?'

'Depends on what you've got in mind.'

'If you have to ask, you're not ready.'

Her lids dropped to half mast. 'I'm ready. What is it?'

'A break-in.'

'Are we the perps or the cops?'

'The perps.'

'What's the target?'

'What's your preference?'

'Tiffany's.'

He slid out of the banquette. 'I like your style, but not tonight.'

'What is it then?'

'Someplace less expensive but more fun. A police station.'

Nat was in the chair at the keyboard, Shaw standing over his shoulder, keeping an eye on the door.

It was eleven o'clock at night, and they were inside Lieutenant Amerigo's office. From the hallway they could hear the business of the station house clattering on as usual. When Amerigo left for the day he routinely turned out the lights and closed his door but never locked it, knowing that no one had the temerity or stupidity to enter while he was away. Obviously, he didn't know Shaw and Nat. Not that they were interested in his files, only his computer. Problem was, they were computer neophytes – Frankie Avalon and Annette Funicello trying to surf the Net.

'He'll kill us if he finds out we've been in here,' Shaw whispered.

'So let's make sure he doesn't.'

'What are we looking for?'

'Something called KBS.'

'What is it?'

'If I knew, I wouldn't be looking.'

She pushed a button on the side of the computer case, triggering the appearance of an empty CD Rom drive.

'What's that?' she whispered.

He glanced down, then up. 'It's a cup holder. Push it back in.'

She did.

The screen said, **Access Denied. Please Enter Security Code.**

'We're boned,' she said.

Nat had never seen a security warning before and had no idea how to enter a code even if he'd had it, which he didn't. 'That probably locks his private stuff,' he said. 'We don't want that anyway.'

He clicked on various targets again. This time, the screen said, `Cannot detect HP II Printer`.

'I don't know what that means,' he said.

'It's obvious,' Shaw said. She reached out and turned the monitor toward the printer stand to the right of the desk. 'If it can't see it, it can't detect it.'

Nat's head flopped forward. 'That is the single dumbest thing I've ever heard,' he said. 'It doesn't detect it like it's got eyes. It detects it electronically. Digitally.'

A sign read, `Click Here for Search Engine`.

Clicking caused a small 'drop down' window to appear. Nat typed the letters KBS in it and hit FIND NOW.

They waited for the modem to haul digits.

In a descending wave of color, ten entries magically appeared on screen. The first two – the only ones visible – said, KBS: Beer Bottle Collection. The next said, Willkommen beim KBS, followed by a paragraph in German.

'That's no help.'

KBS Ecological Research, the next one said. Then, KBS Internet Services, and KBS Top Ten Rock. Not hardly. Then, KBS: the Korean Broadcasting System.

'We're getting nowhere fast,' he said.

'Says here we've only got seventy-eight thousand, six hundred and fifty-five more entries to go.'

Nat hit some keys to exit and try something else. A warning appeared: `You have performed an illegal operation.`

'Jesus, Nat, what have you done?' Shaw said.

'I don't know, but they can't arrest us, we're the police.'

He hit Enter and the screen flickered and showed a new message: `Strike Any Key to Continue`.

Nat examined the keyboard, fingers hovering, ready to strike.

'What are you waiting for?' Shaw whispered impatiently.

'I can't find the `Any` key,' he said.

'Oh, my God,' she said, 'that's the single dumbest thing I've ever heard.' She reached out and hit a key, any key.

OK, OK, so he was primitive. The screen returned to the search engine box. After reading the `Find` instructions, he typed `KBS + Medical + Science` into the window and hit Enter.

This time, there were only eight hundred entries.

He scrolled through them: Biosciences, Libraries, Navy Medical News, Maharishi Alternative Medicine. Descriptions in French, Danish, and Swedish. He was crawling around a haystack and didn't even know what a needle looked like.

He reached the end of the page and was ready to give up when he saw `Rhesus Monkeys`.

Monkeys? Really?

He clicked.

Key words appeared: `Neurological diseases. Bilateral Temporal Lobectomy. Kluver-Bucy Syndrome (KBS).`

OK, folks, we've got a winner.

They both read what they saw on the screen.

Kluver-Bucy Syndrome, the description said. A neurological disease occurring when the temporal lobes – a pair of organs in the brain just inside the temples – were damaged on both sides, 'bilaterally'. Injury could occur any number of ways – viral encephalitis, physical trauma like an accident, heat stroke, surgery sometimes used to eliminate severe seizures, among others.

They scrolled down the screen and read more.

The symptoms of KBS were listed in a long paragraph, and not even the unemotional, clinical nature of the description could mask the horror: psychic blindness – the inability to recognize things for what they were, whether a fork, a spoon, a friend, or

323

a spouse. Language agnosia – the inability to recognize words or sentences, rhyming and nonsensical gibberish similar to certain forms of schizophrenia. Amnesia – usually deep and long-term.

He clicked down for more.

There were two distinct and common symptoms of KBS. The first was the patient's oral exploration of the environment, like a baby trying to learn its surroundings by putting everything into its mouth. Examples included a woman who ate two rolls of toilet paper a day, another who ate her own feces, and a man who drank a bottle of liquid shoe polish during a medical examination.

Nat felt his dinner complaining.

The second typical symptom was sexual aggression. Nurses and orderlies reported having to stay on guard to keep patients from grabbing, kissing, and fondling them. One doctor compared the KBS patients she'd worked with to dogs humping other dogs. Normal sexual inhibitions such as time, place, prior acquaintance, or choice of partner were irrelevant.

They read more.

Other symptoms included the onset of general passivity, occasionally broken by quick, unexplainable bursts of physical aggression. Health care workers learned to recognize a 'prodromal stare' in the eyes of patients with severe KBS, a kind of deadness that preceded a violent lashing out. During a routine medical examination, a case study reported, a boy with KBS grimaced like a mad dog, foamed at the mouth, and bit his doctor.

Nat recalled Camilla's description of the monkey named Abel and his sudden, ferocious attack when she'd looked him in the eye and offered him a banana. Was it KBS? he wondered.

In severe cases, patients sometimes turned to self-mutilation. A paragraph discussed the case of a woman who had chewed off part of her own shoulder.

He hit **Page Down**.

Cures were something of a problem. Tegretol – an anti-seizure mood stabilizer given to schizophrenics and the criminally insane – sometimes helped, but generally speaking medical interventions didn't work. Unless KBS repaired itself naturally – and the article said spontaneous cures and remission did occur – rigidity of the muscles, Parkinson's-like tremors, and Pick's disease – an uncontrollable flailing of the limbs and jerking of the head – often followed. After a period ranging from a few weeks to years, victims with progressive symptoms typically dropped into an Alzheimer's-like stupor, experienced ever-lengthening seizures, partial paralysis, dementia, and death.

End of the first article. **For more, click here.**

'Good Lord,' Shaw whispered. 'When are you going to tell me what this is about?'

Nat chose a new entry and brought up a case study of a twenty-five-year-old girl who had collapsed with a heatstroke at the end of a marathon. Dehydrated, her core temperature at 103.1 degrees, she developed KBS and sank into a near catatonic existence, showing cognition and animation only in bizarre, animalistic behaviors.

Bilateral brain heat, the article said, was a well-documented cause of the disease.

Nat sat back in his chair. He'd never heard of anything like this. He wanted to read more, but they'd already been here too long.

'I need a copy of this,' he said. He clicked away, trying and failing to print the article on screen. The monitor read, **Place Disk in Drive and Shut Door**.

Shaw looked across the room. 'The door's already shut.'

Nat didn't say anything. He'd already proven himself to be in her league of computer illiteracy. He clicked on the icon of the printer to print out the document. When nothing happened, once again Shaw turned the monitor toward the printer stand.

There was a quick knock at the door and suddenly it was opening.

Seeing it, Shaw tilted Nat's head back and kissed him, keeping her back to the door.

The man's footsteps stopped in the doorway.

Shaw held the kiss, blocking the intruder's view of Nat's face. Her red hair she could do nothing about, except hope it looked like a bimbo's.

'Sorry,' the man's voice said, 'I didn't know you were working *alone* tonight, *Lieutenant*. I was just making the security rounds, but I can plainly see that you're not even here, *Lieutenant, sir*.' He closed the door.

'We gotta get out of here,' Nat said, standing up fast, a little dizzy from the kiss. Boy. He leaned down to hit the Off switch, but Shaw stopped him.

'Hear that?' she said.

The printer whirred and spat out pages.

Nat held his forehead. She'll always be convinced she made the printer work. He picked up the article from the paper tray.

Puffing out her glorious chest, Shaw turned off the computer and the desk lamp as Nat walked to the door and opened it a crack, waiting for an empty hallway to make their escape.

'Nat,' she whispered, coming up behind him, 'about that kiss—'

'Good thing it never happened,' he said. He opened the door wide. 'You heard what the man said. We weren't even here.'

Shaw pulled up in front of Nat's loft and parked at the curb, leaving the engine running. Finally, he grabbed the door handle and said, 'You want to come up for a beer?'

'No thanks. I think I'll write up my Five and hit it.'

He opened the door a crack, but his feet didn't move. He tried again. 'Sure you don't need the potty?'

'No, I'm fine.'

They sat watching a tree sprout white flowers.

'Boy, do I dread this,' he said.

'Dread what?'

'Going into the apartment.'

Shaw saw his face warmed by a New York street lamp.

'She gave me a puppy for a wedding gift,' he said.

'What kind?'

'One part beagle, two parts dog.'

'Has he got a name?'

'I thought I'd wait until she comes home.'

'You should call him WFC. Waiting For Camilla.'

'Yeah, WFC.' He stared ahead, thankful for silence.

'For what it's worth,' she said, 'everybody on the squad knows what you must be going through. Everybody thinks you're a really fine cop.'

'Real fine.'

'It's true. That's why I asked Amerigo to make me your partner.'

He didn't know she'd done that. The story poked him in the

gut. Undeserved respect on his left, an empty apartment on the right. He pulled the door handle and swung his feet onto the sidewalk, looking back at Shaw. 'Can you live without me for a couple of days?'

'I don't know. Masochism gets into the blood.'

'I'm going to knock off for awhile.'

'Good idea. Going fishing?'

Yes, but not for fish. 'I'll give you a call.' He got out and closed the door and rapped his knuckles on the window. She lowered it with a switch. 'One other thing,' he said, bending down. 'It kills me to say this, but you're a pretty good partner.'

'Take two aspirin and go to bed,' she said. 'You've got a fever.'

'Cush?' His grandfather woke him with a shake. 'You got a phone call from New York.' He left the telephone on the floor next to the sofa and walked out of the room.

Cush stirred and lifted the receiver. 'Hello?'

Rodriguez said, 'I just found a large envelope delivered to your office. I wouldn't have bothered you, but the return address says it's from Detective Nat Hennessy.'

'What is it?'

'I don't know, it's sealed.'

'Open it.'

He heard the rustle of paper. 'It's – what the hell is this? It's a Xerox copy of my cover memo to you on the RAD scan malfunction. And a paper copy of a scan negative.'

Silence. 'How did he get those?'

'Beats me.'

There was a longer silence on both ends.

'Read the memo,' Cush said. 'It's been awhile.'

Rod read the page. When he was finished, he said, 'If this is all he's got, I don't see a problem.'

'I do.'

'Wait a minute,' Rod said. More rustling of the envelope. 'There's a note inside that says, "Please return to the file of Mr Roy A. Driggers."' A pause. 'Jesus, where did he come up with *that*?'

'Simple. He thinks RAD equals Roy Driggers.'

'Oh, man. What kind of bad luck is that?'

'It's a *Columbo*,' Cush said. 'It's always the thing you overlook that trips you up – the unexpected, small coincidence.'

Rod exhaled into the receiver. 'I'm still not worried,' he said. 'He may smell something, but there's no way he knows what it is.'

Maybe so, maybe not. 'Is Camilla still stable?'

'Neurology says she is, yeah.'

'I'm coming back in the morning anyway. We'll deal with Hennessy then.'

'OK.' No goodbye. 'But don't you agree? If he had the goods on us he'd be knocking on our door instead of sending us Xeroxes?'

'I'm not sure,' Cush said. 'He's a smart cop.'

'Yeah, but he's a *New York* cop,' Rod said. 'What's he gonna do, quit his job to go nosing around Mississippi?'

It was Nat's first trip to Mississippi, which meant he noticed things he ordinarily wouldn't have. He wasn't happy being this far away from the hospital, but there was nothing he could do for her in New York, while here, if he got lucky, he might find what he knew would be helpful. After getting a report on her condition from Nurse Punt – no improvement, aneurysms status quo – he'd flown to Jackson, the state capital, picked up a Hertz rental, and started the ninety-mile drive west to Hardy, a small farmer's town where rolling hills and rising bluffs bunched up the flat, silted land of the Delta.

Driving the interstate and listening to the radio gave him a taste of the land of cotton, which, as far as he could see, had been replaced by the land of trucks. Everywhere he looked he saw pickup trucks, cattle trucks, and more eighteen-wheelers than he could find on the New Jersey Turnpike. There were trucks pulling U-hauls, tow trucks with their booms tucked away for speed, feed trucks parked in fields near watering holes and fertilizer tanks. There were moving vans and Ryder rentals, horse vans with chestnut tails whipping in the breeze, house trailers with rusty corrugated roofs dragged along behind ageing Winnebagos.

There were construction rigs, flatbeds with earth-moving equipment, trucks carrying motorcycles, timber, new cars, and beat-up carnival rides. Even when you looked away from the road you saw the signs and spoor of trucks – strips of black rubber thrown off re-capped tires, and dead animals along the shoulders

– possums, skunks, rodents and rabbits squashed or flung about from the singing wheels of trucks.

Nat heard a rat-a-tat-tat to his left and looked up and saw a yellow Steerman swoop low over a field of peas, pulled through the thick, wet air by a huge radial engine. It opened its tanks and laid a poisonous fog over the rows of green, trading bug deaths for human life, killing the hapless insects that, like the boll weevil, didn't stand a chance against Dow Chemical.

The airplane drew Nat's eye toward a tall, pointed radio aerial stabbing the ground, its flashing strobe lights and orange balls on guy wires warning planes and birds of its unlikely presence in the sky. Beyond it, held aloft by steel arms, were the power lines that carried the juice that kept the South's air conditioners blowing. On the radio, a female singer with a whiny voice sang about how it felt so good to be loved so bad, it hurt so good, don't do it some more, those and similar heartaches found as easily on Long Island or San Diego freeways as they were in the deepest of the deep South. He had thought he was in a place noticeably different from the rest of the country, but with every passing mile, he doubted it.

He came to a row of gleaming white tanks bordering a field of huge rectangular ponds. Catfish Farm, the sign said, producing a no-thank-you shudder down his spine. Ugly, gray, bottom-feeding suckers. His uncle had once told him that the only way to eat a catfish was to bake it eight hours on a piece of plywood, then throw away the fish and eat the wood. His sentiments exactly.

He exited the interstate and picked up a rural road to Hardy, searching for signs of a quaint, more distinctive Mississippi. A single hawk with wide, Spitfire wings soared above him without flapping, searching for mice. The terrain was mostly flat here, but the trees seemed to be lusher and the grass longer, its purple and brown tips still seeding.

He drove past fields of soy beans and rice and acres of

white cotton balls floating atop brown stalks, the closest thing Mississippi had to a speckled field of early New Hampshire snow. There were large stands of loblolly pines, their needles rich and green on limbs so low to the ground a cow could find shade and scratch her back at the same time. Standing in the middle of a pine patch was a single blue Port-a-John that had fallen off a truck, as if the trees and thickets didn't offer enough modesty in the heart of hard-shell Baptist Mississippi and you had to pee in a stall.

A few miles from town, Nat saw old farmhouses with paint-chipped bell posts nestled in watercolor hills, swamplands with toothpick-bare Cyprus trees standing in nature's stew, and rattling pickup trucks with dirty hubcaps and bright plastic daisies stuck on their radio antennas. Lying in the fields were rolled-up cylinders of hay that looked like the Jolly Green Giant's shredded wheat. At the edge of the fields were big red barns and low Swedish farmhouses and black mesh satellite dishes.

Off in the distance, he could see a water tower in the shape of a ball sitting in a champagne glass. The more he looked, the more he realized that Mississippi was about water as much as trucks. He'd noticed other water towers: single-pole buckets, twin-spired jugs, three-legged stools, and four-poster containers, all painted with the fading name of the town or the blazing logo of a fertilizer company. The whole state, like the Indian river it was named for, was in a constant battle over water: how to use it, drink it, divert it, swim in it, pray for it, contain it, and harness it before too much or too little killed you.

The evidence of it was everywhere: concrete pipes big enough for a man to stand up in, buttresses, conduits, run-offs, reservoirs, ponds, berms, aqueducts, channels, flumes, ditches, waterways, dams, dikes, sewers, grades, trenches, gullies, furrows, sluicegates, embankments, wells, irrigation works, and levees. Especially levees. There was something about levees that captured the soul of Mississippi. Levees made of red dirt, levees made of cement, levees lined with grass, levees for driving Chevies, My, My, Miss American Pie levees for burying civil rights workers, levees as the stuff of poetry, dreams, and songs. Even the rain clouds seemed different here, heavier and pregnant, waiting to burst against the levees.

Entering Hardy, he found the town an incongruent mix of the old and the new – frame houses set back from the street behind wrought-iron fences and bent stanchions, then half a block away, a glitzy Ace-is-the-place hardware store. He saw a drugstore with a modern sign out front, and next to it the county courthouse with its tall, graceful antebellum columns. It was a town like other small towns in America, still morphing from Norman Rockwell's Sunday afternoon roaster into Burger King's chicken nuggets and fries.

The courthouse. He made a mental note.

He folded up the road map with one hand – perfectly, quickly, and on the creases, another use of his otherwise worthless aptitude for spatial relations – and looked for a diner where he could get something to eat and find someone who could tell him where to find what he was after.

Ginny's Coffee Shop was on the corner of the wide main street, a little place with large windows and double glass doors. After parking his red Mercury Sable between slanted white lines, he turned off the engine and heard the air conditioner die, then stepped out into the hazy afternoon sun. It was dead-of-day, midsummer Mississippi, the air hanging heavy with a damp, invisible moss.

Wearing chinos and a short-sleeved shirt, he entered the restaurant and took a seat at the last booth where he could get a good view of the room. The air inside was cold and smelled of fried food. A waitress with blue-white hair and glasses with the temples in the shape of a Z brought him a glass of water, a hello, and said she'd be back in a jiffy to take his order.

He picked up a menu. Moving down a long list – he'd

noticed that the smaller the restaurant, the more it offered – he discovered another rule of the South: everything was deep-fried. Hush puppies, potatoes, grits, catfish, meatloaf, perch, chicken, pork chops, croppies, crawdads, peas, corn – nearly everything on the menu, and if it wasn't on the menu you could get it anyway, there was hot oil bubbling twenty-four hours a day, it was required by state law. He saw deep-fried cheese, and under the dessert heading, deep-fried ice cream and bananas. He saw chicken-fried steak, but no steak-grilled chicken. People in these parts even went out and picked green tomatoes – couldn't wait for the poor little suckers to ripen – and fried them up in smoking amber oil.

The waitress returned and said, 'What would you like, honey?'

Honey ordered two eggs sunny side up, silver dollar pancakes, a slice of Taylor ham – fried, of course – and iced tea. After she left, he picked up a bottle of Heinz ketchup with a missing cap and a red crust around the lip and played with it as he looked around. There was friendly noise all about him – pots and pans clattering from the kitchen behind the counter, the sound of thick white crockery and heavy forks that didn't bend when you leaned on them. Carl Perkins was crooning on the jukebox. A handful of people ate and talked.

Time to go to work.

In the booth across the aisle a fellow he guessed to be a store manager – narrow tie, short-sleeved white shirt, a plastic pen holder in his breast pocket – ate in silence, his eyes glued to the plate as if it was a television set. A woman with a puffy hairdo and an upper lip drawn onto her thin-lipped mouth sat across from him, matching his silence as she ate an apple dumpling. He looked elsewhere. He needed someone who talked.

A black woman with gray hair sat in front of him reading a book. Right age, probably knew the town, but how would he get into the subject with her? She looked too proper, too conservative, probably uncomfortable being approached by a stranger. He marked her a Maybe.

Walking toward an old NCR cash register with a metal slide that returned your change was a young girl with bleached blonde hair, tight jeans, a nippled T-shirt and smile that was just suggestive enough to make a man feel good to be alive. She was on her way out, though, and too young and pretty for a stranger to be chasing down the street.

Sitting alone at the counter on a swivel stool was a man in a work shirt and never-been-stone-washed denim overalls gathered around the tops of his mud-caked shoes. A farmer, Nat assumed. He and a black waitress behind the counter were gabbing happily, which made the man seem friendly. Looked like he was eating hash browns and eggs. Fried.

Nat got up and walked to the counter and sat down next to him.

'Mind if I borrow the ketchup?' he said.

'Help yourself,' the man answered. 'Help' sounding like 'hep'.

Nat reached for it.

'Where you from, you don't mind my askin',' the man said.

'New York.'

'Thought so. I could tell by the *ack*-sent.' He ate another mouthful. 'In town for business or pleasure?' It came out, 'bid-ness'.

'I'm here to visit a woman named Vestie Viney. You wouldn't happen to know where I could find her, would you?'

The man took a bite of potatoes, leaned forward and wiped his mouth with a paper napkin. He looked at Nat, or rather, looked him over. 'What's your name, son?'

Nat put out his hand. 'Nat Hennessy.'

'Duncan,' the man said, not making clear whether it was his first or last name. He shook Nat's hand.

'It's a friendly call on Mrs Viney,' Nat said.

Duncan took a bite of butter-drenched toast and a sip of coffee. 'You in the in-shurnce business?'

'Something like that.'

The man turned back to his plate and stuck his fork into a cube of fried potato, rolled it in egg yolk, piled on buttered grits and syrup and put it into his mouth. He wasn't talking.

Nat waited as long as he could. 'Look at those pies,' he said. In front of him was a clear case filled with coconut cream, banana cream, and mountain-high lemon meringue pies.

'You like black bottom pie?' Duncan asked.

'Don't know what it is.'

'You don't? Ginny? Git this man a piece a black bottom pie and put it on my bill, would you?'

Nat thanked him and returned to his booth and waited for his eggs and pie to arrive. A few minutes later the waitress with the Z temples set them on the table. Before she left he took a bite of the dessert and told her to tell his friend it tasted great, then returned the favor with a piece of cream cake and a cup of coffee.

Fifteen minutes later, Nat saw Duncan headed toward him with his check in hand.

The farmer said, 'You go eight miles north on Route 35, and just after the feed bin you take a left.' Nat wrote the directions on a paper napkin. 'It's on the Walker property,' Duncan said.

Right *on* the property? How convenient.

'When you git to the dirt road,' Duncan said, 'take it easy with that Hertz Sable you got out there or you'll tear the oil pan off it before you git halfway to her house.'

His Hertz Sable, Christ. The man probably knew how much gas was in the tank.

'And son, Vestie Viney is her first and middle name. McCoy is her last.'

Nat thanked him and decided to take his time finishing lunch. No need to hurry to the farm for a surprise visit. Even if he flew like the wind, Vestie Viney McCoy would know he was coming.

It was a long ride down a long road, but after bouncing the car's oil pan off the ruts and humps Nat finally came to a rise and saw a small frame house with a gingerbread porch. Across the dirt road in front of it was a shed, and a little beyond that an old, dilapidated barn showing the pentimento of original red beneath faded white. In front of the house, in need of pruning, was a spreading oak casting shade on the porch so perfectly it looked as if the house had been built there for that reason alone, which in fact it might have been. Coming closer, he saw a chicken coop with a gaping hole in the wire fence, its hens waddling around outside trying to get back in. Other than that, the landscape was spare: no bony livestock or rusting tractors or wheel-less cars sitting next to house trailers. And why would there be? This was Mississippi, not upstate New York.

He pulled onto a flat of weeds and brown grass and got out holding a large manila envelope. After standing by the car door a moment to make himself apparent, he walked to the house and up the creaky porch steps to the door. He knocked, and in a moment the inside door opened and an old woman stood behind the screen, thin and angular – 'rawboned' would have been the term had she been a man – with a bandana covering a pile of pinned-up gray hair he guessed had once been naturally blonde. Considering its length and the heat, she was obviously still proud of it.

'Mrs McCoy?'

'Yes?'

'My name is Nat Hennessy, and I'm a detective from New York City. Can I talk to you a minute?'

'Land-a-Goshen, you come all the way from New York just to see me?'

'I want to talk to you about your husband, Virgil.'

'He's dead,' she said.

'I know, I'm sorry.' In the South it was important to pay respects to the dead even if you didn't know them.

'Why you sorry? You didn't know him, did you?'

He shifted his weight onto his good foot; his right one was still sore. 'May I come in?'

'I ain't finished cleaning,' she said. 'But if it don't matter to you, guess it don't matter to me.' She pushed open the screen door.

He stepped inside and found himself standing in a living room that felt like a combination nest and cockpit. The small space was filled with knick-knacks, small plants, and an easy chair with an electric foot massager at the base, crusty with minerals from evaporated hard water. There was a multicolored Afghan thrown over the chair's back, and next to it a doily-covered pedestal table with a coffee mug and a spoon and an automatic tea warmer with the amber ON light glowing. Beneath a cut-glass lamp was a Bible, its worn black binding showing traces of brown lining.

At the side of the room was an upright piano with the keyboard cover down and, next to that, a sofa with a too-small Sears catalogue slipcover. In the corner, facing the chair, a television set with the volume turned low showed Sally Jesse Raphael's cherubic face staring at three fat men in tank tops and Nazi helmets. A Hoover vacuum cleaner circa 1965 sat in the middle of the room, its electric cord snaking across the floor to an outlet. The mutt curled up in the easy chair eyed Nat suspiciously: don't even think about it. Under the window, an air conditioner rattled and clicked and dripped condensed water into a puddle on the floorboards.

Vestie Viney bent over slowly, grabbed hold of the vacuum cleaner cord, and yanked the plug from the wall. 'Don't usually clean till Fridays, but when I heard you was coming, thought I better spruce up.'

Love those jungle drums.

She showed him to the sofa. 'Now, what's this about Virgil?'

'You met my fiancée three years ago,' he said, 'a pretty woman named Camilla Bissonette. Brunette, green eyes, about this tall.'

'You mean the one that shacked up with Dr Walker?'

That one, right. Fuck you very much for the positive ID. 'Yes.'

'What about her?'

'You talked to her about your husband's death and gave her some photographs and X-rays. Do you remember?'

'Nope.'

'You don't recall showing her pictures of your husband?'

'Pictures, yep, but not no X-a-rays.'

He opened the envelope and pulled out the negative. 'You don't remember this?'

She held it up to the light and tilted her head back as if she was wearing bifocals even though she wasn't. She handed it back to him. 'Don't mean nothin' to me. What'd you say your name was?'

'Hennessy. Nat.'

She strained and shook her head. 'Down here, Nat's usually a first name. That don't mean nothin' to me, Mr Nat.'

He pointed at some gray letters in the margin of the negative. 'It says the patient's initials were RAD. Do you know who that is?'

'Sounds like – sounds like Rad to me.'

'Who's Rad?'

'Don't know, never heard of him.'

'Does the name Roy Driggers ring a bell?'

He saw her face fall ever so slightly. It wasn't much, but for a detective it was enough. He'd finally hit a drum of his own.

'Don't know him,' she said, her nervous eyes and hands saying she did.

'He was in his early twenties, a former skinhead, if you know what I mean.'

'I know what a skinhead is,' she said. 'They was yellin' at each other on the TV 'fore you got here.'

'He was born and raised in northern Mississippi, picked up the nickname Sneezer, came to New Jersey and eventually got himself sent to jail for beating up people.' She stared at him. 'One of them died,' he said.

'Don't know him.' Her lips were pulled tight now. Lying obviously wasn't easy for her.

'They let him out of prison so he could take part in an experimental medical program,' he said. 'Dr Walker brought him to his clinic.'

'Don't know him, don't know him.' She leaned forward and got up out of her chair. Standing in front of him, she licked her lips and opened and closed her hands again. 'Have to go now, Mr Nat. Got to finish cleanin' 'fore Virgil gits home.'

Before Virgil gets home? She was a nervous wreck. Nat stood up slowly.

'What happened to Roy Driggers, Mrs McCoy?'

'Don't know.' She looked around the room as if she needed a life preserver, then walked to the screen door and pushed it open and held it there. ''Bye, now.'

He walked to the door. 'He's dead, isn't he?' She was looking at the ground, saying nothing. He hated tormenting her, but not enough to stop. 'I need to know what happened to him, Mrs McCoy.'

'If he's dead, sound's like good riddance, you ask me. They's killers, those skinheads. Besides, Dr Walker never would of—' She pursed her lips, catching herself.

'Dr Walker would never have what?'

'None of your business. Say, what day is it?'

'Wednesday, July ninth.'

'Lord,' she said quietly to herself, 'I done forgot the flowers.'

'What flowers?'

'None a your bees-wax. You're gettin' me all rattled, Mr Nat.' She put her hand on his chest and pushed him hard out the door. 'You got to GO now.'

He stepped onto the porch and saw her shut the screen door behind him and close the peeling wooden door behind that. Click. A dead bolt. Go away.

He stepped off the porch and looked around with his eyes watering from the scorching afternoon light. He was on to it, all right, but he didn't know what 'it' was. Hearing a noise behind him, he turned and saw the window shade on the right side drawn down, then a second later, the shade on the left side too. She was behaving as if Driggers was in her closet.

He looked toward the barn and the field beside it.

Roy Driggers, where are you?

He sat in Vestie Viney's hayloft, waiting for something to happen. He'd driven his rental car to the first stand of trees he found, parked it out of sight, and walked through a field of tall weeds to the rear of the barn, hoping that with her shades drawn she wouldn't see him. He knew payoffs came from tedious stakeouts, but this one was pathetic. Here he was in a broken-down barn in godforsaken rural Mississippi, beyond the edge of the known world, waiting for a slightly batty old woman to make a nervous move, although to what end, he had only the faintest idea. The itch of straw and chiggers and gnats, the heat rising in cartoon squiggles off the sun-parched ground . . . what was he doing here?

He waited.

And dozed.

And slept.

He woke to a noise. Must have been sleeping lightly because he recognized it as a slamming door.

He watched her leave the porch carrying flowers, two different kinds, pink and purple in one bunch, yellow in the other.

Flowers. The ones she'd talked about.

Trying not to trip over the two-by-six beams, he moved to an opening and watched her until he could see nothing of her, at which point he started down the steps from the hayloft to the first floor.

He waited, careful not to be seen. He would have left the barn and followed but the landscape was too open. After a while he saw her returning, her light-blue dress emerging against a stand of hunter-green needles. She walked back to the porch and opened the door, looking exactly as she had on her way out, a woman doing a chore. Except for one thing: she no longer had the flowers.

He'd walked about fifteen minutes when he saw a headstone. Approaching it from the rear, he circled it and bent to read. *Virgil Bascomb McCoy. 1927–1997. May God Be Merciful.* The stone was clean and the grass around it trim, and lying at its base was a bouquet of coreopsis, the yellow and maroon sunflowers he'd seen her carrying. He touched one and found it moist and fresh.

He stood up and looked around. At the foot of the grave was the handful of pink and purple meadow beauties she'd also been carrying, too few to be called a bouquet. He stepped to them and squatted. Why were they lying at the foot instead of the head?

Touching them, his eye caught a smooth, level spot beneath the flowers about the size of a saucer. He brushed away dead grass and loose debris and found a flat, gray marker aged by mildew and weather. Rubbing the surface clean, he saw the letter 'I', then knelt closer and pared away the encroaching grass. There were three letters engraved on the placard, each standing in bold relief: *R.I.P.*

He stood up slowly, staring at them. I'll be damned. He'd

heard stories about the Mafia pulling stunts like this, but he'd never actually seen one. In some cases it was two bodies in the same casket, in others a cadaver slipped into someone else's grave. Either way, it was a nice way to hide a body. What were the chances Driggers was down there? Considering how Vestie Viney had fallen apart talking about him, good enough to justify his plane ticket. He started back to his car, thinking it made sense except for one small problem: this wasn't the Mafia. Why hide him at all?

By the time he got to his car, only one thought – still undeveloped and unclear – occurred to him more than once, an instinctive form of sleuthing. Patient RAD is what he thought about. Patient RAD and his Kluver–Bucy Syndrome.

Day five, and she was still asleep.

Nat had made his nightly call to the hospital to check on Camilla's condition. He held the telephone at his ear and looked out the window of his motel room at the cracked asphalt parking lot. The NO in the neon NO VACANCY sign was flickering on and off in a visual stutter.

He made another call.

'Sally Shaw here.'

'It's me. Nat.'

'Hey, where are you?'

'Mississippi.'

'In July?'

'It's air conditioned. What's happening with Dolly?'

'She's still inside, but Jackson hasn't said anything to her about Tangerine or Angel Rico.'

'No reason he would.' Nat didn't care if he ever talked about Tangerine or Angel Rico. He didn't want evidence, he wanted Jackson.

'Remember she said she used to be a Rockette?' Shaw said. 'She's stayed in touch with some of the dancers, and she's got this knockout friend named Joanne who she says Jackson wants to meet.'

A great pair of legs? Yeah, he might come out for that. 'Why did she quit the Rockettes?'

'I don't know. Does it matter?'

'Just curious. Did she make her daily call on time?'

'Four o'clock on the nose.'

Good sign. 'You want to do me a favor while I'm gone?'

'Like what?'

'Take another ride on the Internet?'

'Not in Amerigo's office, I don't. The next time I go cat burgling, we're doing Tiffany's.'

'Maybe the library then.'

'What is it with you and that place?'

'The disease we found? KBS? I need to know if it would show up on an autopsy, what you'd see if you were looking at the brain.'

'I'll give it a shot,' she said. 'When are you going to tell me what this has to do with what we're doing?'

'Later. Shaw?'

'Yeah?'

'If you find an article on the subject, when the librarian goes to print it out, don't turn the monitor toward the printer, OK?'

'OK,' she said. 'I'll just open the CD Rom drive and put a Styrofoam cup in it.' She hung up.

The CD Rom drive? So *that's* what the cup holder was.

It was 8 a.m. and the heat was already rising as Nat walked past the flags drooped in front of the sheriff's office. He entered the cold-storage air of the reception area and stepped up to a scarred wooden counter reminiscent of a 42nd Street hotel. A middle-aged woman with roly-poly arms and a tightly coiffed hairdo stood at a desk. Even before she spoke, he knew she was the police precinct wizard who knew everyone in town.

'Be right with you,' she said, straightening papers in a folder.

He scoped out the room: neon lighting, beige walls, an old-fashioned wooden coat rack, wire baskets, train-station oak benches uncomfortable enough to discourage the most dedicated courthouse hanger-on from hanging on.

The woman waddled over to him with a pleasant, proper face.

'Detective Nat Hennessy,' he said, laying the worn leather case that held his shield on the counter. 'I'm visiting from New York City.'

'How do, Detective,' she said. 'I'm Rejuvia Miller, the assistant county clerk?' Ah, yes, a clerk who ended every sentence with a question mark. 'What can we do you for this morning?'

'I was hoping to have a minute with Sheriff Benson.'

She pointed at a door at the side of the room. 'Go on in, he's expecting you.'

Expecting me? Of course. The motel clerk, the spy satellite, the dog at the gas station – any one of them might have made

345

the call. He picked up his shield, smiled, stepped over to the door, and opened it.

Sheriff Benson sat with his feet up on his desk reading the sports section of the Jackson *Times*. A cup of coffee rested in the center of his desk blotter with no cream or sugar in sight. Seeing Nat enter, he put down the paper and stood up. Nat walked over, introduced himself, and sat in a creaky spindle chair with an uncertain wobble that made its occupant uneasy. Nice touch. He had to remember that.

The sheriff sat down in his leather-covered desk chair and leaned back with his hands behind his head. He inquired about Nat's comfort at the Log Cabin Motel, even though Nat had said nothing about where he was staying. Nat thanked him for seeing him on an unannounced visit, as if it was.

'I understand you been out to see Vestie Viney McCoy,' the sheriff said.

'I dropped by yesterday,' Nat said. It was standard courtesy for an out-of-town detective to introduce himself to the local police *before* mucking around in their jurisdiction. Too late for that now.

'Vestie Viney done something wrong?'

'Not that I know of,' Nat said. He never gave an unequivocal No to that question. You never knew.

'Woulda surprised me if you'da said she had,' the sheriff said. 'I've known Vestie Viney for thirty-five years and I've never seen her cross against a light.'

'Actually, I'm in town looking for a parole violator from the New York State Department of Corrections,' Nat said. He took the BCI photo out of an envelope. 'A fellow named Roy Driggers.'

'Roy Driggers,' the sheriff said, examining the face. 'Don't think I know him.' He laid the photo down. 'What makes you think he's in Hardy?'

'He was a prison volunteer in a medical program conducted

by NeuroPath Labs a few years ago,' Nat said. 'You do know NeuroPath Labs, I assume.'

'Oh, yes, indeed,' the sheriff said. 'Everybody in these parts knows NeuroPath and Dr Walker. Fine family, the Walkers.'

'Driggers was released in his custody for this experimental program and came down here to his clinic. After that, he disappeared.'

'Now I know who you're talking about,' the sheriff said. 'Young fellow born upstate who jumped parole.'

'That's the one,' Nat said. 'Whether he jumped parole or not is the question.'

The sheriff reached for his coffee cup. 'Did Rejuvia offer you a cup of Java?'

'Already had my quota this morning, thank you.'

The sheriff took a sip and eyed Nat over the rim of his cup. 'If he didn't jump his parole, what else you got in mind?'

Nat repositioned himself in his chair. 'I think he's keeping Virgil McCoy company.'

The sheriff looked confused. 'Company?' He opened a Havana cigar box, took out a lump of brown sugar – the only substance inside – then closed the lid and dropped the cube into his cup and stirred it with the eraser on a yellow pencil. 'I must have an old-fashioned case of the slows,' he said. 'I didn't follow how you get that.'

'I think Roy Driggers died in an unauthorized medical experiment at Dr Walker's clinic and was buried on his farm alongside Virgil McCoy.'

'Do you have some evva–dense to support that?'

'Not yet, but I think an autopsy will give it to me.'

'Maybe it will, I don't have the slightest idea. What do you want from me?'

'I want you to disinter Driggers' body and have the state medical examiner do a cause of death.'

The sheriff pushed his cup of coffee aside, picked up the

telephone, and hit a button. 'Rejuvia, would you check and see if we have a file on a fellow named Roy Driggers? That's right, D-r-i-g-g-e-r-s.'

'Also known as Sneezer,' Nat said.

'AKA Sneezer. He woulda been a fugitive in the last three years. When you're done with that, call Judge Pretty and ask if I can see him for a minute, would you?' He hung up. 'As you know, I can't just go out and dig up a body without a court order.'

'I assume you can get one if you want it.' The words came out too full of assumption, as in, I know the kind of justice you boys have down here.

'Well, now, not quite,' the sheriff said. 'We got judges on the state payroll with something to say about that, and regardless of what you see on television, they mind their manners.'

'I'm sure.' He'd asked for that.

The sheriff sat looking at him, saying nothing. His fingers beat a pent-up tattoo on his thigh.

Finally, Nat said, 'Shouldn't we be going?'

'Where to?'

'See the judge?'

'Naw, relax.' He picked up his telephone and hit a button. 'Rejuvia, it's real cream and two sugars, case you forgot.' He hung up and leaned forward and rested his forearms on his desk and twiddled his fingers. Nat sat wondering. Confusion in the air.

Nat took a breath and was looking at his watch when the door opened and a tall, gangly man with a raw, Lincolnesque face entered the room carrying a fresh cup of coffee with real cream and two sugars. The sheriff stood up as if a judge had entered the room, which he had. Nat did the same.

'Detective Hennessy, this is Judge Sumter Pretty the third, District Court, Eastern District of Mason County.'

The judge switched the coffee mug from his right hand to his left and extended his warmed palm to Nat.

'Have a seat, young man,' he said. He wore a white shirt, a narrow tie, and a light blue suit, and even without a robe there was no question about his authority. Nat thought it was unusual that he'd come to the sheriff instead of expecting the sheriff to come to him. Maybe this wasn't going to be so difficult after all: they were in a back room without a court reporter, the three of them fraternal members of the criminal justice system, all men, all white, and despite the year on the calendar, this was Mississippi.

'Detective Hennessy here is visitin' us from New York.'

'Fine city,' the judge said, pulling a chair to the side of the desk. 'Some of the folks down here think it's Sodom and Gomorrah, but not me.' He sat down and rested a foot on the edge of the desk, black shoes, white socks. 'I go up ever' year just to get my *batteries recharged*, if you know what I mean.' He grinned and winked. 'But don't get me wrong. I'm talking about my pacemaker.'

Nat felt a small prayer rising in his throat. Please, God, spare me. If the South had fought with bullshit instead of bullets, New York would be eating grits instead of bagels.

The judge produced a pair of nail clippers and went to work on his fingers. 'How can we be of help, Detective?' Another 'hep'.

Nat explained that he was looking for a fugitive from New York who he thought was buried in the grave of Virgil McCoy.

'Roy Driggers,' the sheriff said.

Nat said he was hoping the judge would issue an order disinterring the body and, if it was there, ask the medical examiner's office to do an autopsy.

The judge clipped a nail. 'You got anything on this boy Driggers?' he said to Sheriff Benson.

The sheriff picked up the phone and pushed his buzzer. 'You find anything? Mm-hmm.' He hung up. 'Nothing.'

'You say you got a suspicion,' the judge said. Clip, clip.

'He was last seen at Dr Walker's clinic. Driggers was one of his volunteers.' Nat lifted the manila envelope, opened it on the desk, and pulled out the shiny X-ray negative and handed it to the judge.

Judge Pretty held it up to the light, turned it around, and frowned. 'What am I looking at?'

Nat borrowed the yellow pencil the sheriff had used to stir his coffee and stood next to the judge's chair. 'This is a picture of Roy Driggers' brain.' He pointed to *Patient: RAD*.

'Is his middle initial A?' the judge asked.

'I assume it is, but I don't know for sure.' He added, 'Yet.'

The judge looked over at the sheriff, whose look said, don't ask me. 'Go on,' the judge said.

'If you read this memo, you'll see that something went seriously wrong with Driggers.'

'Assuming he's patient RAD,' the judge said.

'Right.' Nat held out Rodriguez's memo. 'As a result of Walker's experiment, he contracted a horrible brain disease called Kluver-Bucy Syndrome.'

'Where did you get this piece a paper?' the judge asked.

'From a woman named Camilla Bissonette.' Go ahead, tell him. 'My fiancée.'

The judge lowered the X-ray. 'Where did *she* get it?'

'From Vestie Viney McCoy.'

'Vestie Viney gave this X-ray to your fiancée?

'Along with the memo.'

'Your fiancée a detective too?'

'No, she's an architectural restorer.'

The judge handed the negative and memo back to Nat and gave him a puzzled look. 'I'm trying to get my hands around this thing, but they don't quite link up.'

'Camilla met Vestie Viney three years ago while she was a house guest of Dr Walker's,' Nat said.

'Oh, I *see*,' the judge said. 'While she was a *house guest*.'

Nat saw a smirk cross Sheriff Benson's face. The judge studiously avoided it and resumed clipping his nails. 'Her friendship with Dr Walker – that couldn't have somethin' to do with you being here today, now, could it?'

'Purely coincidental,' Nat said. He actually thought it came out reasonably convincing.

'Have you asked Dr Walker about this?'

'He knows I have the memo and negative, but I haven't talked to him about them yet.'

Clip. Silence. 'Is that it?'

'Is what it, Your Honor?'

'Is that what you've got in the way of probable cause for a disinterment order?'

Nat cleared his throat. 'When I went out to visit Mrs McCoy, I found two markers on her husband's grave instead of one, and two sets of fresh-cut flowers.'

The judge brushed fingernail clippings from his lap. 'And?'

'That's it.'

The judge dropped his foot to the ground. 'Let me get this straight. You want me to dig up the grave of Virgil Bascomb McCoy to help you hunt down a missing parole violator from the great state of New York who could be anywhere on the planet, dead or alive, and the basis for this inherently disrespectful act to the deceased and his family is: one, the strange demeanor of his wife who we all know keeps her marbles in a frying pan; two, the parolee was last seen in the lawful custody of one of the state of Mississippi's finest doctors and most respected citizens; three, an X-ray has the initials RAD on it even though we don't know Mr Driggers's middle name; and four, you saw two markers on a grave, neither one with the name Driggers on it, and two bunches of flowers. Do I have that right?'

Nat straightened up in his chair. 'The way you frame it makes it sound pretty skimpy.'

'Skimpy? Hell, boy, Oliver Stone wouldn't give this thing a look-see.'

He was right. No real court would disturb a grave on the basis of what he'd presented. It was an insult to their intelligence and the minimum standards of probable cause. He'd been hoping for a nudge and a wink and a white man's slippery justice, but what he'd got was a slap in the kisser by a card-carrying member of the Society for the Protection of Cush Walker's Ass.

OK, so he deserved it. So what? It didn't alter the relevant question, which was, is Roy Driggers buried in Virgil McCoy's grave? Nat didn't need the actual body. He needed Cush Walker to fear that sooner or later he'd *get* the actual body.

'Thanks for your help, Judge,' he said, standing up. He shook hands with the judge and sheriff and gathered up his envelope.

'Come on back any time,' the sheriff said. Nat left them sitting together waiting to talk about him as soon as he got out the door.

It was late at night, Nat's usual time for visiting Camilla, and having spent the last few hours on an airplane, he was tired. He walked to her door, knocked once, and pushed it open.

Her bed was empty.

His adrenaline woke him up.

He stepped back into the hallway and sensed energy in the air. Trouble. Crisis. Camilla.

Nurse Punt came running down the hall carrying a chart and an electronic device with jack-tipped wires trailing behind. She saw Nat but didn't slow down.

He jogged along beside her. 'What's going on?'

To a nurse sitting behind the station desk she said, 'Call Dr Cotler and tell her we've got a code ten-ten in OR three.'

'For crissake, Virginia!'

'One of her aneurysms burst,' she said.

The words punched him in the stomach. 'How bad is it?'

'You'll have to ask Dr Walker.'

Nat caught him on the fly walking down the hallway and fell into lockstep beside him.

'How serious is it?'

Cush Walker flipped the pages on the chart he was carrying and read as he walked. 'She's stabilized, but two more are ready to go.'

'What can you do?'

'Operate.' To a nurse he said, 'Tell Dr Cotler I'll brief her at nine.'

'How soon?'

'Twenty-four hours.' He turned back to the nurse. 'Tell Rod I need him now.'

'Are you going to try a nanoscan repair?' Nat asked.

'You know the answer to that.'

'What are her chances if you don't?'

'You know the answer to that, too.'

'That's not acceptable.'

'I don't make the odds around here, Detective. Virginia, ask Rod to get Sandy and her last anesthesia report together after the RL trial, will you?'

'I need to talk to you a minute,' Nat said.

'Not now.' To Nurse Punt: 'And make sure Carla's on-board.'

'It's about Camilla. You have to try a nanoscan repair,' Nat said. 'I've been in Mississippi.'

Cush stopped walking first, then Nurse Punt. He handed her his chart and asked her to tell Rod he'd be there in a minute. She continued down the hall.

Walker turned to him. 'I know. I heard.'

'Which means you know what I found.'

'I know what you *imagine* you found. Next time you want to hallucinate, come and see me and I'll give you a pill that'll save you the air fare.'

'I'm going to dig him up.'

Walker straightened and stood about eight feet tall. 'Why is it every time I see you you're threatening me?'

'I'm not threatening you, Doctor. I'm blackmailing you.'

The veins in Walker's neck stood out and his jaw muscles worked. 'What do you want?'

'Your finger on the Start button of all your fancy machinery. I'm bringing you your beta tester in the back seat of my car, cuffed and sedated. I'll put him on a gurney and wheel him onto the elevator and bring him up to Five East. All you have to do is admit him, scan him, and use the blueprint of his brain to fix Camilla.'

Walker looked at him hard. Nat saw that he was listening, sniffing the bait. Then suddenly he wasn't.

'Out of my way,' he said, lifting his hand. 'One of us has to be serious about trying to save your former fiancée.'

'His name is J.J. Jackson,' Nat said. 'If you want Roy Driggers and his messed up, KBS-riddled brain to stay in the ground, you'll sign the admitting papers.'

Walker brushed by him and walked down the hall. Nat turned and headed for the nurses' station.

Former fiancée? Fuck him.

After four rings Shaw answered the telephone. Nat could hear Miles Davis's 'Sketches of Spain' playing on her stereo, loudly.

'Can you hear me?' he asked.

'Wait a minute, I can't hear you.' She clanked the phone on a hard surface and in a second the music disappeared. 'Where are you?'

'At a pay phone at the hospital. I need you to find Dolly and meet me on the West Side in an hour. Take a cab, I'll be at the usual place in a Caprice.'

'Why the rush?'

'We're taking J.J. Jackson tomorrow.'

There was a delayed reaction. 'But he hasn't given Dolly anything we can nail him with yet. All we've got is the same old pross rap.'

'We're taking him anyway. One more thing. We have to figure out how we can do it alone, just you and me, no TAC squad, something safe and quiet.'

'I've been thinking about that since you mentioned it, and I have an idea. Want to hear it?'

'Tell me when you get there.'

'How'd you make out?' Cush asked.

He walked into the lab and found Rodriguez intent on a computer screen, analyzing the data on his latest 'reverse logic' trial. Because RL used less energy and produced less heat in the infinitesimally small nanoscanners, Cush's hope was for a breakthrough.

Rod lifted his amber-tinted glasses and stretched his aching back. 'We made some progress, but we're not home yet. They're cooler in the repair cycle because we can let them work at a reasonable pace, but when we're scanning for a blueprint, all the receptors on the Z-5s have to be working at once, which means they're still running hot.'

It was the usual dilemma. They couldn't obtain the template they needed to repair damaged brain tissue without destroying the healthy brain cells of the volunteer they were scanning.

Rod said, 'I'm not giving up.'

'Hennessy was just here,' Cush said. 'Back from Mississippi.'

'What's he want?'

'Same thing as before, a scan on the guy who shot Camilla. Somebody named J.J. Jackson.'

Rodriguez waited for the other shoe to drop. 'What makes him think you changed your mind?'

'He found Virgil McCoy's grave.'

OK,' Nat said, 'let's go over this one step at a time.'

He was in the driver's seat, Shaw in the passenger seat, Dolly in the back. It was eleven fifteen and a street lamp lit the interior of the car like a 1940s film noir. Only the cigarette butts and gray fedoras were missing.

Sitting on Dolly's lap was a hooker's nylon street bag. She'd taken a cab to a loading dock and slipped into the back seat of Nat's car as instructed, saying she was nervous and couldn't stay long.

Nat spoke to her over the back of the driver's seat. 'You and Jackson are gonna go on the Radio City tour during the matinee performance – do they have a tour then?'

'Yes,' Shaw said.

'OK, the tour group goes to a room where a Rockette in costume comes in and gives a short talk. What happens then?'

'That's my friend Joanne,' Dolly said, 'the girl he wants to meet.'

'Why isn't she going to be on stage?'

'She's not in this show,' Dolly said. 'After she gets done with her talk she poses for pictures with the group and then they move on. That's when me and J.J. hang back and I introduce him to her.'

'Then what?'

'She's gonna offer to take him backstage where he can see the show from the wings – you know, hang out together and let him put some moves on her.' She rolled her eyes. 'He thinks he's such a stud, he makes me sick.'

'Why's she doing this? The Rockettes are as squeaky clean as Mickey Mouse.'

'She's not *really* doing it,' Dolly said, exasperated with the question. 'She's playing along as a favor to me.'

'Go on.'

'After they watch the show for a while, she's gonna come on to him and ask him if he wants to see the room under the stage.'

'That's the subbasement I was telling you about,' Shaw said. 'It's enormous, a good forty feet deep. The stage itself is actually made up of three separate platforms sitting one in front of the other on these huge hydraulic elevator shafts that raise and lower them so the stage hands can load sets and props while the show is going on. The Rockettes can be dancing on one stage while one or two of the other ones are down and the audience can't even tell.'

'Sounds like an aircraft carrier elevator.'

'From the movies I've seen, I'd say it is. Dolly's friend is going to invite Jackson to see how the elevators work from down below. You know, wink, wink, in the subbasement where there are no stage hands around to see what we're up to.'

'There's nobody down there?'

'There's a hydraulics engineer in a control room below the orchestra pit, but there's still plenty of space where she can make believe they're going to fool around.'

'What if a stage comes down while they're down there?' Nat said.

Dolly said, 'You're going to nab him before Joanne has to spend any time under the elevators.'

'That may be the plan, but what happens if it doesn't go the way we expect?'

'Even if she's under the stages, they don't go all the way down except when they need to load a prop that's real tall, like Uncle

Sam's hat.' The Rockettes were performing a summer show that featured Independence Day themes: red, white, and blue sequined tights, fake fireworks, medleys of danceable patriotic music by George M. Cohan and Irving Berlin.

'So what's to keep her from getting squished if they load the hat?'

'Can't happen. The bottom of the elevators are stopped by these thick steel horses about four feet high. If somebody was below a stage when it dropped, all they have to do is sit on the floor.'

'OK, so Joanne has suckered Jackson into the subbasement. What next?'

'You and I will be waiting in the control room when they get there,' Shaw said. 'We cuff him, walk him up the back stairs and out the side door to an unmarked car.' She ate a peanut butter cup.

Nat thought about it.

'See a problem?' Shaw asked.

'I'm looking for one.' He looked at Dolly. 'Isn't Jackson going to find it strange to have this girl take him to the bottom of a huge elevator pit?'

'For some private time with a Rockette?' Dolly said. 'A tall girl with a twenty-two-inch waist, spangled tights, and three-inch heels? You kiddin' me?'

'Picture this, Nat,' Shaw said. 'To get to the subbasement from the mezzanine you have to climb down a vertical steel ladder, sort of like going down a submarine hatch. If he goes first and she follows close behind, he's going to have her tush in his face all the way down.'

Dolly lit a cigarette. 'You could have an army waiting for him down there and he wouldn't notice it.'

Maybe they were right. All this person Joanne had to do was distract him for a few seconds. But Nat knew he would have to be on top of the situation, otherwise Jackson would grab Joanne and use her as a hostage. But he had the right weapon to keep that from happening. 'You ever been down there?' he asked Dolly.

'Once, when I first joined the Rockettes.'

'How long did you dance for them?'

'Two years,' she said.

'Why'd you stop?' Shaw asked.

'This,' she said, lifting her leg and touching the outside of her thigh. 'When you're five eleven and you're doing shoulder-high kicks every day, you mess up the illial tibial bands.' She held her watch up to the window to try to catch some light.

'No offense, Dolly,' Nat said, 'but the Rockettes are like Miss America contestants. How'd you get by with hooking?'

Dolly's face turned stormy. 'I wasn't *in* that line of work in those days.'

Nat was about to follow up with another question, but Shaw gave him the evil eye – lay off the personal stuff, OK? You're going to piss her off and blow it.

'What do you think?' she asked.

'I want to go over it one more time.'

'I can't, I got to go,' Dolly said.

'I said one more time,' Nat said. 'If we do this, it's got to be right.'

'I'm, a Yankee Doodle Daaan – deee . . . Yaan–kee-Doodle-Do-or-Die . . .'

Nat and Sally Shaw stood on the red-painted observation area on the perimeter of the cavernous basement halfway between the stage above and the basement below, listening to the orchestra playing and thirty-six Rockettes dancing: clicka, clicka, click – pu-thump – clicka, clicka, click – pu-thump. Behind them were boxes of soldier hats with white feathery plumes, toy guns, and costumes hanging on racks.

'A real live nephew of my Un – cle – Sam's . . . Born on, the Fourth of, Juliiiii.'

Nat looked up at the bottom of the elevators and saw black girders seventy feet long with heavy-duty black electrical cords hanging in U-shaped bundles from the substructure. Directly in front of him, supporting three side-by-side platforms that together made up the whole stage, were three pairs of shiny cadmium pistons similar to the ones service stations used to lift automobiles, except these were the size of redwoods.

At the bottom of the shafts, spread low around the basement floor, were elevator pipes and wheel valves and gears and equipment, none of which rose above the tops of the four-foot-high yellow steel 'stoppers' Dolly had described. The anvils resembled the bumpers Nat had seen at the end of train tracks at Grand Central. Each one had a wooden railroad tie bolted to its top as a pad to cushion the stage's steel girders when it dropped all the way down. On one pad he could see the imbedded imprint of a steel wrench, testimony to the thirty tons of stage that had evidently sat on it. Everything about the place was massive, heavy, and powerful.

'*I've-got, a Yankee Doodle Sweeeet . . . heart . . .*'

Nat saw a worker moving a glittery prop to the edge of a mezzanine loading dock across from where they were standing, readying it for one of the three stages to descend and pick it up. Otherwise, there were no tourists and only a few stage hands in sight, which was good; their view of the subbasement was blocked by the stage they were loading, which meant when the time came, they wouldn't see him take Jackson. Craning his neck over the edge of the railing to get a view of the bottom floor, he saw no one down there either. Apparently the hydraulics engineer was tucked away in his office.

A red warning light began rotating near the basement floor and a horn sounded the *ank, ank, ank* of an airport baggage carousel when it starts to move. They heard the rumbling of machinery and the release of hydraulic fluid from the pistons, allowing one of the three stages to drop. It was the rear one and it fell quickly, maybe a foot a second, faster than he had expected something that massive to move. When it reached the mezzanine level, about twenty feet above the basement floor, it stopped and three men began loading props onto the stage.

'*Sheee's . . . my Yankee Doodle joy.*' Clicka, clicka, click.

Shaw led Nat across a narrow cement bridge beneath an identical narrow space that separated the stage from the orchestra pit. They reached a manhole-like opening and found the yellow steel ladder that led down to the subbasement. Shaw checked her watch. It was almost three o'clock. Thirty minutes more and Dolly's friend would be bringing Jackson down.

'I'll go first,' she said, reaching for the ladder.

Nat stopped her with his hand. She looked for an explanation.

'This is where you get off the train,' he said.

'What are you talking about?'

'I'm doing this alone.' He straightened his tie.

'Over therrrre, over therrrre . . .'

'What do you mean, alone?'

He unbuttoned his jacket to go down. He wasn't wearing his .38 special.

'Send the word, send the word, over therrre . . .'

'Where's your weapon?' she said. 'What's going on?'

'This isn't your collar.'

She flushed with disbelief and stood up straight. 'Kiss my ass, Hennessy. You want the glory, you can have it, but—'

'It's not about the glory,' he said.

'. . . the Yanks are com–ing . . .'

She didn't get it. 'Who's gonna be your backup?'

'I don't need one.'

'The drums rum-tumming ev'ry-wherrrre . . .'

'Since when are you taking a killer without a backup? Aren't you the one who told me—' Her face dropped.

'So pre-paair . . . Say a praay'r . . .'

'Jesus,' she said. 'You don't plan to arrest him, do you?'

'Don't start writing a screenplay, Shaw, we haven't got time.'

'Who is this guy?' she said. He didn't answer.

'Send the word, send the word, to be-waaare . . .'

She said, 'I knew something was up when you pulled that he–got–away crap with Rico. The busted foot, the cut on your jacket, handcuffs banging on metal. You had him and let him go, didn't you?'

'I'll see you back at the office,' he said, and grabbed hold of the ladder.

'You let him go and set him up to be killed, and now comes the payoff. What is it, drugs or money?'

'Shut up, Shaw, you're starting to piss me off.'

She took hold of his lapel to stop him. 'Is this how it works?

Make it look like a bust so you can do business with this guy Jackson?'

'When Johnny comes marching home again . . .'

He removed her hand from his jacket, careful not to let her feel the square object in his coat pocket. 'Nothing wrong with being a rookie, Shaw, as long as you don't act like one.'

'Fuck you,' she said, hoisting her bag up her shoulder. 'I may be a greenhorn and a Vice Squad hooker, but I'm not a dirty cop.'

He stepped onto the first metal rung. 'This isn't what you think.'

'Oh, yeah? Then what is it?'

'Trust me, you don't want to know.'

'Trust you?'

'We'll give him a hearty welcome then . . .'

She leaned forward and punched his chest with her long finger. 'You used me, you son-of-a-bitch, and I don't like being used!' Still, he knew she understood what he meant. When a cop broke the rules, you didn't involve your partner. If she knew what he was about to do, she'd either have to rat him out, which would wreck her career, or cover up for him, which would make her a co-conspirator and perjurer. Fortunately, she was too angry and disgusted to fight about it.

'You're right. I don't want any part of this,' she said.

'Hurrah! . . . Hurrah!'

She left.

Nat went down the ladder to the subbasement floor to acquaint himself with the lay of the land. The long, narrow engineer's room he'd come into contained gauges and switches and electrical breakers on a panel covering a large portion of the wall. Beneath it was a narrow console holding tools, a speaker box, and a microphone at the end of a flexible gooseneck. Sitting nearby was a partially eaten egg salad sandwich on salmon-colored delicatessen paper. The engineer must be close by. At the end of the control panel the room extended into unlighted space where he could barely make out rows of electrical contacts on one wall and hydraulic levers on the other. Large, painted pipes criss-crossed the floor of the unlit area with wheel-shaped manual shut-off valves rising to a level about knee high.

He stepped back from the ladder and pulled a black metal device about the size of a television remote control from his inside coat pocket and held it up to the light. It was a stun gun, a battery-charged weapon that arced three thousand volts of electricity between two shiny metal nubs at the end.

He looked up the ladder he'd just descended. If he stood off to the side, he'd see J.J. Jackson's feet coming down the metal rungs before Jackson saw him. It was the only advantage he needed. Once he touched the gun to any part of his body – his thigh or ankle or ass – Jackson's central nervous system would collapse, dropping him to the floor like a dead duck. Before he came to – and before Joanne was in harm's way – he'd be on his stomach with cuffs behind his back.

First Nat needed to find the engineer and tuck him away.

He stuck his head through the door and looked around the cavernous, well-lit basement beneath the stage. There was no one there. He looked up and saw the underside of the three elevators. They were all the way up, at performance level, their flat tops holding the Rockettes as they danced. He looked across the basement room and saw a door leading to two automobile-sized storage tanks that held the hydraulic fluid that moved the elevator cylinders. Maybe the engineer was back there. Before maneuvering through the maze of pipes on the basement floor, first he'd search the far end of the office.

He walked back into the long narrow space. Large vertical equipment blocked his view of the far end of the room where the engineer might be working. He stepped around the first column of electrical panels.

'Hello?' he said. 'Anybody here?'

The music above was going full steam.

Shaw dropped her bag on the floor next to the desk and flopped into her wooden chair. Pulling a sheaf of pink telephone messages from Donald Duck's mouth, she ran through them perfunctorily, tossing them back onto her desk, still pissed.

She stared at an orange sitting on her desk. Good cop my ass. Hennessy had really fooled her – and apparently everyone else in the station house. So he wasn't straight, and now she knew it. What was she supposed to do with that?

What in God's name would make him do business with a killer?

The orange was small, about the size of a tangerine.

Start with that. Tangerine. Dolly's brother. Daryl.

She opened a brochure she'd picked up during her tour of Radio City Music Hall and idly paged through it.

She turned to a photograph of the Rockettes standing on stage in their classic kick line and read the monograph below. The company had one hundred members who performed in New York, Las Vegas, and other locales . . . were originally a dance troupe from Missouri known as the Rockets . . . had been at Radio City since the 1930s. Any girl was welcome to become a Rockette as long as she was at least eighteen years old, proficient in dance and tap, stood between 5′ 5½″ and 5′ 9″ tall, and—

Her eyes froze. '. . . between 5′ 5½″ and 5′ 9″ tall . . .' She read it again and felt the blood in her head run for cover.

She opened her lower desk drawer, rummaged through folders and pulled out Dolly's file: photo, name, address, telephone, white, female, age – height: 5′ 11″. Her throat closed.

Holy shit.

She grabbed her bag and jumped up and ran for the door. *She wasn't a Rockette.* Which meant everything else she'd said was suspect. Tangerine wasn't her brother – Joanne wasn't her friend – Joanne probably didn't even exist. They were all bait, a story, a Brooklyn Bridge for sale, and she'd bought it.

She stopped at the desk of a detective who was talking on the telephone and scribbled on a notepad and barked at him, interrupting his conversation, 'Call this number right away – it's Hennessy's pager!' Then she ran for the door, thinking the obvious: Dolly isn't our confidential informer – she's his. J.J. Jackson's. Dolly is his shill.

The detective lowered his receiver. 'What message you want me to send?' he yelled.

'He's on to you!' she yelled back. 'Tell him, he's on to you!'

Nat saw a stool a few feet away in the semi-lit extension of the office, an open can of Coca-Cola sitting on it. He walked to the shadows and picked it up. It was still cold and mostly full. The engineer had to be somewhere close by.

'Hello?' he said again.

He drew the stun gun from his pocket and hit the Ready button and heard a quiet whistling sound as it powered up.

Turning back, he looked toward the well-lit portion of the office, the uneaten sandwich next to the microphone. Time to go back there and investigate.

He looked down to step over a hydraulic pipe and saw a brown work shoe lying in the shadows next to a metal box of switch breakers. Leaning down to pick it up, he noticed that its laces were still tied. Still tied?

This was not good.

His beeper sounded.

He pulled back his coat to look at the message window on his belt. 'He's . . . on . . . to . . . you . . .'

There was no warning, only a hand across his mouth, muscular fingers that came from his left side and jerked his head backward, exposing his neck.

His first thought was garrotte.

His second thought was knife.

With his left hand he clawed at the palm covering his mouth; with his right he curled the stun gun behind him in search of his assailant's body. Before he could make contact, an iron hand found his right wrist and grabbed it.

The iron hand forced Nat's weapon upward until it was shoulder high. *Where is he going with this thing?*

The iron hand forced the stun gun toward Nat's head.

He felt his thumb bent backward against his own shoulder – felt the tremble of muscle giving out – felt the metal prongs turning inward toward him. *Got to keep the contact points from touching me—*

A bolt of lightning ripped down the back of his neck and spine into the soles of his feet, blinding him with a burst of white. His legs turned to jelly and the room turned perpendicular. He recognized a bounce – his head hitting the floor – but felt no pain. He was still conscious but deaf and paralyzed inside his own skin.

The first of his senses that returned was the feel of his own tongue, then his back, aching from a spine-snapping spasm. His eyesight returned from the perimeters toward the pupils.

He could see a pair of black shoes standing in front of his nose . . . feel a hand pin his neck to the ground as if holding down a turkey for the kill. He tried to speak but the words came out gibberish. The iron hand suddenly let go. The gibberish had informed his attacker that he was conscious again.

The second jolt of electricity he didn't feel at all.

★   ★   ★

They were only twenty blocks away but it was midtown Manhattan on a Friday afternoon and it was raining and the cars and trucks were barely inching toward the Lincoln Tunnel. It gave Shaw time to replay her mistakes. Like believing that the telephone number on the bottle of Cheetah – Dolly's number – somehow made her a potential friend of Tangerine, not an enemy. Like not questioning why Dolly had refused to talk on the phone when she first called her, or why, fifteen minutes later, she'd called back all sweetness and cooperation. Like never guessing that Dolly might have hung up after the first call and called her boss – J.J. Jackson, Tangerine's pimp and killer – and told him the police had called and asked him what to do. Like Jackson telling her to cooperate with these two fine detectives, invite them up for an interview, play along as if she was Tangerine's bereaved, heartbroken sister. Like letting her sucker them into thinking they'd turned her into their own confidential informer when she was Jackson's CI all along. His pipeline, his snitch.

'Come on, let's go,' she said to the driver. With its siren wailing and light bridge flashing, the police car was able to break petty laws like running red lights, but not the big ones that mattered, like gravity, pedestrians, or avoiding a teenage driver speeding down Seventh Avenue with his window rolled up and his radio cranked to the max with the Rock N' Roll Madame on Z-100.

Sitting in the passenger seat, Shaw saw him coming first – 'Watch it!'

The speeding Impala went into a pirouetting skid and clipped the rear fender of the police car, breaking the seal on the rim – pop! – flattening the tire. Both cars came to a rest in the middle of the intersection at Seventh and 38th.

'Damn,' Shaw said.

She jumped out of the car and ran up the center of Seventh

Avenue looking for a cab. Sooner or later she'd find one, too, but at the moment she was still ten blocks away in midtown Manhattan on a rainy Friday afternoon.

He awoke on his back to the sound of an orchestra playing in the distance, voices singing 'Anchor's Aweigh' and the rasp of strapping tape being ripped off a roll. He tried to open his eyes, but except for a touch of light seeping through parted eyelashes, a swath of adhesive held them closed.

His lips were puckered and his cheeks tight from strips of adhesive. Under his stretched-out body he could feel something narrow and hard like a board, and he could feel his hands bound tightly to his sides.

Rip. He felt a line of stringy tape wrapped around his chest tightening him to the board. Rip. Another sticky ribbon, this one around his thighs. The tune in the distance changed. *'Over hill, over dale, as we hit the dusty trail . . .'*

Rip. A strip was wrapped around his shins. He had the picture now: he was a living mummy tied to the top of an anvil.

More tape ripped, more strands applied.

He breathed through flared nostrils with a wheeze, sweating, fighting off panic. His captor was breathing hard too, the sound of a man working. He knew who it was but couldn't bring himself to say the name even in the silence of his mind.

The ripping stopped and the medley turned to the Marine Hymn. *'From the Halls of Mont-a-zoo . . . UU-ma, to the shores of Tripo . . . leee.'*

The engineer must be unconscious or dead. Eventually someone would miss him. Eventually. Christ, how long was that?

He felt a presence nearby, warm breath, the smell of sweat.

'Motherfucker,' J.J. Jackson said, 'you making me do something I've never done before, kill a cop. Messing up my nice quiet life, shit. When they find you, it's gonna be trouble, and I don't like trouble.'

371

Nat felt fingertips prying at his face, then felt a corner of tape pried loose, gripped, and pulled, ripping the cover from his eyes.

Nat winced and blinked at the light. He could see the under-carriage of the elevator stages sitting three stories above him, masses of girders and cross beams and black electrical wires.

'Look at that,' Jackson said.

Nat rolled his eyes toward the back of the stage. A spotlight fell on a white backdrop, casting shadows of Rockettes dancing. '*Oh, how I hate to get up in the morrr . . . ning . . .*' They were up there singing and dancing in front of an adoring audience of six thousand people while he was lying here about to be killed.

Where are you, Shaw? Somebody's got to—

He heard a warning buzzer – *ank, ank, ank* – and saw the reflection of a red light twirling like a magnetic beacon on a detective's car.

A stage was coming down.

Jesus Christ.

Which one?

He heard pumps stop and reverse their flow and valves open to drain thousands of gallons of water and oil from the giant cylinders into the tanks behind the subbasement wall. The dancers must have moved onto the second and third stages because the first stage was coming down.

Yeah, that one.

The one directly above your head.

It started moving slowly at first, then, when it dropped out of sight of the audience, started coming down fast . . . a foot a second . . . thirty-two feet from the anvil stoppers . . . thirty-one feet from his face.

Sweat ran into his wide-open eyes.

Jackson squatted, keeping his head beneath the surface of the four-foot-high anvil stoppers, and watched.

The stage continued dropping, the warning horn sounding

ank, ank, ank. The dancers continued dancing and singing, *'You gotta get up, you gotta get up, you gotta get up in the morr . . . ning.'* The red light continued twirling.

Nat's eyes were focused on the descending steel beam. It looked like the bottom of an alien spacecraft coming down to land. When it did, it would crush his head like a walnut.

He heard a muffled voice from his throat fill his ears. His own voice yelling for help.

The girders slowed for landing – ten feet away, eight feet, six, five, four. He closed his eyes and waited for a quick, merciful end.

He felt it, quick and merciful. Then nothing. It had been easier than he'd imagined. Downright painless.

Then why was he feeling a spot of piss on his leg?

He opened his eyes. A cluster of rubber-coated electrical lines was draped across his chest and the girders were suspended two feet above his face. The warning buzzer had stopped and the red light was off. He heard valves close. The elevator wasn't moving.

'Shit,' Jackson said.

There was a muted rumble above them, the sound of something being rolled on or off the elevator platform, a prop requiring the platform to be stopped at this precise elevation.

Jackson rose and moved to Nat's side. Nat watched him pull a knife from his pocket, open it, and pass the blade in front of Nat's eyes. He laid it on Nat's chest as if he'd be back for it in a minute, then held the stun gun under Nat's chin and put his finger on the activator button. An act of mercy before slaughtering him? Not Jackson. Not possible.

'You'd like me to zap you out cold, wouldn't you?' Jackson said. He pulled the black box away from Nat's chin and laid it on his chest next to the knife, then lifted a roll of strapping tape and unwound a long piece, maybe ten feet of it, and twisted it into a white cord. He did it again three more times, adding layers to the first strand until he'd turned the three of them it into a rope

A rope – what's he doing with a—

Jackson ran it up through an opening in the girder on the bottom of the stage, immediately above his head, and back down, looping it around Nat's neck and tying it with a slip knot. He jerked on the line and lifted himself off the floor to see if it held. It did. Strong as a hangman's noose.

He taped Nat's ankles to the anvil, around and around, then lifted the knife off his chest and cut the other bands holding Nat's body to the frame. His hands were still taped to his sides, but except for the tape around his feet and the tape noose around his neck, the rest of him was free.

'You know what they say,' Jackson said, head tilted back. 'What comes down must go up.' He rubbed his chin pensively. 'What do you think's gonna come off first – your head or your feet?'

Jackson squatted again like a kid watching an ant hill, lowering himself below the anvil. He had his hand between his legs and was strangely rubbing his crotch. Nat pictured him squatting next to his father's head on the sidewalk. If by some miracle he got out of this alive, he would kill this guy. That was his decision. Even now, the thought of it, the certainty of it, was comforting, an emotional North Star.

'I'm saying the head's gonna come off first,' Jackson said. 'Two feet, one neck – definitely the head.' His eyes were turning glassy. 'Any second now, white boy, you gonna be lynched by a bunch of tap dancers singing "The Star-Spangled Banner". Cool.'

Ank, ank, ank. The red warning light came on signaling that the elevator was about to move. Nat's pulse hit two hundred. OK, Shaw, it's closing time, you can come and get me now.

The elevator started upward.

Nat felt the electrical cables resting on his chest start to move toward his neck, and the tape rope around his neck start to stretch out. The moving cables caught the stun gun lying on his chest and pushed it up under his chin. He tilted his head forward and caught the black box between his jaw and upper chest, and felt the tightening electrical cable squeeze it against his Adam's apple. Now it was simple: which had less slack to be taken up – the electrical cables or the rope? Which one of these nooses would hang him first? He prayed it was the electrical cable because if it was, maybe he could . . .

The stage continued to rise slowly, pulling Nat's head, chest, and torso upward like a puppet on a string. He felt the electrical cords and the tape tightening more or less together, both choking him. Taking his last breath, he held it as if under water and drove his chin toward his chest as hard as he could. The stun gun pinned under his chin kept the electrical cords from garroting him, but nothing protected his neck from the slowly tightening tape rope beneath. His hands twisted and wrenched against the strapping tape on his arms.

The rising stage lifted him up into a standing position, pulling his feet against the lines that bound them to the anvil.

He squinted in pain and used every muscle in his body to keep the electrical cords caught under his chin, begging their slack to be taken up before the noose of tape hanged him. He could feel the upward pull of both lines on his neck, hear his spine crack, feel his knees and ankles giving way. He steeled his muscles against the strain, head quivering, shoulders shaking, preparing to be drawn apart—

Zzzzt-pop! A flash of light. Either his head had come off or the electrical lines had been pulled from their socket. He felt his neck held by the tape noose alone and felt the electrical lines drop down and dangle against his chest. The elevator had stopped. His head would not be pulled off after all. Lucky him. Now he'd be hanged instead.

A disembodied voice echoed in the room with the music filtering down from the stage. 'Warren? Warren, what's happening down there?' It came from a speaker near the anvil. 'Warren, talk to me – we're showing a power failure up here. Should I override?' There was no Warren, no answer. 'Warren, we're due topside with elevator one – talk to me!'

J.J. Jackson yelled toward the microphone, 'Go ahead and override!'

A pause, waiting for the override.

The disembodied voice said, 'Who is that? Warren? Is that you?'

Nat could feel his neck muscles exhausting themselves, feel his windpipe pinched tight, holding the fire in his lungs. He opened his eyes and saw nothing except circles spiraling down to a point in the center, the remnants of his last bit of oxygen. The arteries in his neck were squeezed closed, insulating his ears from the sound of his own drumming pulse. He felt his tongue push against the back of his crushed-together teeth, trying to escape. He'd lost it. He was going under . . .

Unable to hold it any longer, he gave up. His muscles relaxed. Singing voices melted away down a long corridor in his mind – Rockettes, angels, he had no idea which. Come and get me, was his last thought, the one he'd been sending to Shaw since Jackson had grabbed him. Except this time, it wasn't addressed to her.

Shaw ran up the long, carpeted ramp at the front door of Radio City Music Hall to the doors to the auditorium, shield in hand, and entered the theater to find a heart-sinking scene: the enormous organ was playing happy music, the house lights were up, the curtain was down and people were sitting or milling about.

She worked her way down the aisle to the stage and ran up the steps two at a time, through the heavy velour curtain at the wings, past the stage manager standing at his TV monitor, down the steps to the mezzanine.

She looked over the railing into the well of the basement and saw people gathered in a circle like football players in a huddle. A pair of feet bound with white strapping tape poked out of one side of the group and a man with his shirt sleeves rolled up, looking like a doctor, knelt over a body.

She walked the rest of the way to the yellow ladder leading down to the subbasement floor. No need to run now.

There was a jam-packed split second where everything he saw and heard told him he was dead: the blinding light the TV psychics said there'd be, the whooshing sound of breathing in outer space, a faceless angel with a halo.

'Nat? Are you with us?' The faceless angel had flaming red hair haloed by a ceiling light, and Sally Shaw's voice. His fingers touched cottony sheets. Earth stuff. The mortal coil.

'What happened?' he said into an oxygen mask. His whispery voice sounded like a metal rasp on wood. Lava burned his throat.

'Don't try to talk,' she said. 'Your neck is bruised.'

At least he still had it. He struggled to sit up. His joints ached, his head, hips and ankles – every place there were ligaments. He had to be an inch taller.

He laid his head back on the gurney and drew a 'J' in the air with his finger.

'He got away through an air space below the orchestra pit.'

Nat tapped his left wrist.

'Eight thirty p.m.' she said.

My God, they'd be operating on Camilla in an hour. He struggled to sit up again, this time rising onto his elbows. Looking around, he saw a small cubicle with white curtains drawn for privacy. Outside he could hear people bustling around the emergency room, billowing the curtains as they walked by. There was a hook on the wall holding his clothes.

'Dolly?' he rasped.

'She was in it with him all along.' Her face showed pain. 'I'm really sorry, Nat—'

He waved his hand to stop her, pointed at his chest, my fault, then lay back on the bed and shivered.

'Want a blanket?' she said.

He nodded yes and made a motion with his hand as if he also wanted something to drink.

'Water?' He moved his head slightly, no. 'Coke?' No. 'With rum?' Yes. 'I'll bring you a Coke.' She went through the curtain.

He struggled to rise, one inch at a time. Reaching a sitting position on the edge of the gurney, he cradled his head in his hands, giving his neck support. He had to see how far he could go. There was no time, they were going to operate on Cam without a blueprint, her chance of surviving was nil. His eyes focused on the garment hook, then on his shoes on the floor. Inside the pocket of his jacket was his notebook . . . Dolly's telephone number . . . Jackson's address. On Howe Street.

He tested each muscle and ligament and joint. They needed oil and ice, but they worked. Placing his hands on the edge of the gurney, keeping his weight suspended, he extended a bare foot toward the floor, tentatively, like a fire walker testing the coals. His toe almost made it to the ground before the pain kicked in. But it still worked.

Shaw carried a small brown bag containing a cold drink, a straw, and a little white napkin through the commotion of the ER.

She reached out for the white curtain around Nat's cubby and drew it aside. For a second she actually considered looking under the gurney.

He was gone.

The bedroom looked soft and inviting, not sensual, but comfortable, a place to rest.

Nat stood with his hand on the light switch, breathing in the museum of his life: books stacked on the table, a tarnished silver candlestick next to the bed, a pillow propped up on Cam's side for reading, the scent of her silk, his cotton. He had already made the necessary telephone call to set up the meeting he was headed for, and had convinced Cush Walker to delay Camilla's operation for an hour. Now that his plan was set, he had to reconcile himself to it. He thought about his prayer at Camilla's bedside, his promise to do whatever it took to save her. What he was about to do wasn't what he'd had in mind at the time, but if she had any chance of making it now, it was the only course left.

He opened his address book to Jackson's entry. You got away, but it won't last. I'll find you. No matter what. Just a matter of time.

He unbuckled his belt slowly – every movement hurt, every muscle ached – and slipped off the leather holster on his right side. After buckling his belt again, he stuck the holster and .38 into his side jacket pocket. Scanning the room, his eyes fell on an old Gaelic cross made of stone, a foot-high object on the floor next to the dresser. He and Camilla had found it in an antique store in County Cork on a cold, windy October night filled with poetry and ghosts, and had brought it back to New York as a remembrance of his ancestors' lamented past. They'd both felt it beckon to them when they'd seen it, but once it was amid sunlight and car horns, it had lost its romantic appeal and been consigned to the bedroom floor. Strange, noticing it now. He didn't believe in ghosts and didn't care much for poetry, but this time he felt their relevance. Robert Frost, high-school English. *'The woods are lovely, dark and deep . . .'*

He knew what he had to do. He'd promised her he would do it.

Near the bathroom door was the fireplace screen, his doggy corral, which he picked up and returned to the hearth. He wanted to go down to Robin's loft and get the pup and bring him up and lay him on his chest with his muzzle under his chin and sleep for twelve, twenty-four hours. He wanted to wake up feeling his cold nose on his cheek . . . turn over and wake up Camilla . . . pinch her earlobe and let the dog lick her chin . . .

He looked around the room. Objects that had always been immediate now seemed strange and remotely dated. The face of the television set was cold; the clock on the table distant. The stack of newspapers in the corner heaped and forsaken. Camilla was in another world now, half in the past, half in the future, and so was he. Where had he missed the road untaken?

He hobbled to the nightstand and lifted a silver-framed picture of the two of them. He knew what he had to do. Whatever the price, he'd said. *'But I have promises to keep . . .'* He'd felt the snap of his decision the minute he'd seen J.J. Jackson stooped by the anvil. Right after he'd promised himself that if he survived, he'd kill him. Right after.

He looked at his watch. Nearly eleven o'clock. *'And miles to go before I sleep . . .'*

Pulling the bedroom door closed, he heard a long, steady creak that sounded like a violin note held by a bow at the close of a furious concerto, spun down at just the right speed. How did violinists do that? It was all so perfectly balanced – the coordination of ear and fingers, the application of resin on horse hair, the hand muscles obeying the nerves' intricate messages, carving a sunny melody out of a sodden jungle of noise. It all came from the brain. Everything that mattered came from the brain. Now it was time to use his.

He lowered himself at the knees, careful not to bend his stretched, strained back, and lifted a small canvas bag and carried it down the spiral staircase through the studio to the unlit kitchen. The message light was blinking; he pushed the Play button. It was Shaw's voice: 'Where are you, Nat? You're supposed to be in the ER. I'm on my way to your apartment. If you're not waiting for me, I'm calling for backup.'

He hit the Erase button and lifted the cookie jar off the top of the refrigerator, then pulled his holstered revolver out of his side pocket and laid it inside. What he was about to do required no gun, only nerves of steel.

He'd promised her, he'd promised himself. Whatever it took. *'And miles to go . . .'*

'Liquid carbon in?'

'All set.'

'All right. Let's start counting down.'

Cush Walker and Rodriguez took their places in the operating room, Cush at a small stand-up console next to the patient, Rod a few feet away in a chair at the master console that let him run the Z-5 nanoscanners. The Mark VII computer terminal was on-line and humming, waiting to feed the mainframe in Los Alamos. A white-smocked technician sat at a console in front of it, relaxed, drinking a soda.

In the center of the room was a huge, donut-shaped laser scanner with an operating table jutting out from the hole. Nearby was the operating paraphernalia of Cush's nanotech medicine: the cryogenic cooling system, stainless-steel tanks of liquid nitrogen, pumps, gauges, and tubes.

The room was much like any other operating room, large enough to maneuver around without being cramped, high-ceilinged to let the heat rise, criss-crossed at the top with steel beams for easy positioning of lamps, electrical lines, and mechanical gear. The biggest difference was the computer terminal, backup tapes, and electronic equipment that controlled and monitored the nanoscanners.

A radiologist sat near a bank of screens giving readings from the fast MRI, the nanoscanners, and from the electroencephalogram machine. The anesthesiologist's control panel was lit up with the patient's vital signs: brain temperature, pulse, blood pressure, respirations, and intracranial pressure or ICP. A scrub nurse stood by, and an electrical engineer moved around the maze of equipment.

Above the main console, surrounded by a nest of wires and power lines, was a bank of monitors and speakers, ready to report what was happening inside the patient's brain. The video cameras mounted on the walls aimed their snouts down, waiting for the game to begin.

What they saw on the operating table was a human figure beneath a blue cooling blanket, his or her face obscured by a molded white mask and a stainless-steel and graphite skeletal sphere that had been bolted to the cranium. Fitted to the skull was a cap with platinum terminals speckling the surface, each with colored wires running into a cable that snaked across the white tile floor to the computer terminal, and from there split into a multicolored fan that disappeared into a bank of pigtail ports.

The guidance system built into the frame around the patient's head was ready to position the molecule-sized nanoscanners inside the brain, capture the data they gathered, and transmit it to the computer. The sounds in the room were minimal: pumps were not yet operating, the hum of electrical equipment only a steady white noise, the volume on the beep-tone oscilloscopes and monitors still turned down. Conversation in the room was not clipped, but neither was it extraneous. Soft-soled shoes on the floor occasionally squeaked.

To the right of the operating table, next to Rodriguez, was a silver-lined tank with a small electric pump attached to its top containing the pink-colored serum filled with Z-5 nanoscanners. For the first time, reverse logic was guiding the on-board bio-computers with faster computing and – theoretically, at least – cooler temperatures.

Exactly how much cooler remained to be seen.

'Computation?' Cush asked.

'Looks good,' a technician answered.

'Hand me that chart, would you, Josh?'

The young engineer handed a metal clipboard across the table.

'Telemetry?' Cush said.

'Reading fine.'

'How about you, Sandy?'

'Ready when you are, Cush,' the anesthesiologist said.

'Carla?'

The radiologist said, 'All set.'

Cush slipped a Lifesaver into his mouth. 'Serum?'

'Two liters cooled and ready to pump,' Rodriguez said.

Cush moved up to the patient's head and sat on a stool. 'We're all set to go. It's not too late to change your mind.'

Two eyes opened and blinked.

'Forget it,' Nat Hennessy said. 'Give me a piece of that candy, would you?'

'Sorry, can't do,' Cush said. He sat still, waiting for a change of heart by his patient. When he heard nothing, he said, 'OK, let's start. Two ccs of epi.'

'You gonna knock me out?'

'Just the opposite, I need you to be as alert as possible. I'm giving you a small dose of adrenaline.'

'Epi's in,' the anesthesiologist said.

'Is this going to be what a person might call painful?' Nat asked.

'You'll feel some strange sensations, maybe hear a few noises and see some fireworks behind your eyes, but if we do it right, it shouldn't be serious.'

'Maybe you'd like to define "serious".'

'Just tell me what you feel.' Cush looked up. 'Start the serum.'

Rodriguez tapped a few keys and watched a cylinoid-driven valve move pink liquid toward the catheter in the base of Nat's spine.

'Talk to me,' Cush said to Nat.

'What about?'

'Whatever keeps you awake and thinking.'

'What exactly are we trying to do here?'

'What you wanted me to do with Jackson: scan the sectors of your brain that correspond to the damaged sectors in Camilla's, then use them as a blueprint to make her repairs.'

'I assumed that, what I want to know is how much do you need?'

'Remember the pictures of her brain I put on the lightboard? We need a clean picture of at least ninety-seven per cent of the brain cells in those areas, which means we haven't got much wiggle room. Tell me when we've got threshold volume, Rod.'

'Another minute.'

'Pulse, Sandy?'

'One-nineteen and rising.'

Carla said, 'The MRI is showing a lot of scatter.'

'Keep talking,' Cush said to Nat. While the Z-5s moved into his brain, the team mapped the areas they were going to scan. They'd do a static scan first, then change gears and do a dynamic profile of the brain in action.

'What did you do to Roy Driggers?' Nat asked. 'I read about the symptoms of KBS. They're hideous.'

Cush said, 'Try another subject.'

'You know why they called him Sneezer?' Nat asked.

'I need a location shift,' Rod said.

'Talk to me about BIAS,' Cush said.

'What about it?'

'Tell me what you think of it.'

'Whoa,' Rodriguez said, 'we got a good jump with that question.'

'It sucks.'

'Why?'

'I flunked it.'

'Cooling blanket, Sandy?'

'It's running.'

'You flunked it?'

'That's what they tell me.'

'So what does that tell you?'

'It tells me that deep down I guess I don't care much for certain people.'

'Cryo?'

'Going in now,' Rod said.

'Like who?'

'Like you.'

'I'm getting a new network,' Rodriguez said. 'Hold on to that line of thought if you can.'

'Tell me what you don't like about me,' Cush said.

'Don't get me started,' Nat said. 'I'll burn up your machine.'

Rod said, 'A little more and we'll have a static on all sectors.'

'Check that pump, it sounds funny, Bill,' Cush said. 'You know,' he said to Nat, 'I'm not overly fond of you, either.'

'Need a little more in the left quadrant,' Rod said.

'Maybe we should trade places,' Nat said. 'You ever been on this end of your gizmo?'

'Once,' Cush said.

'What happened?'

'What do you think?' Cush asked.

'OK, we're at threshold,' Rodriguez said. 'I'm ready to boot up for the first dynamic.'

'You survived with no problems, right?' Nat said.

'I'm here and you're there, so you tell me.'

Nat exhaled. 'Let me know when you're going to start seriously squeezing my nuts.'

'It's your brain we're working with, Detective.'

'According to my partner there's not that much difference.'

'We're at threshold,' Rod said.

'Let's boot up,' Cush said.

Rod clacked on the keyboard. 'I've got good signal.'

They waited for the programs to boot up.

'OK,' Rod said, 'we're loaded and ready to launch.'

'Listen up, everybody,' Cush said. 'We've only got one shot at this, so let's get it right first time.' He checked the monitors. An image of the interior of Nat's head was lit with different colors, and numbers appeared outlining the two major areas of the brain where the scan had to take place. Cush checked each and made his decision. 'I want a blueprint of sectors forty to eighty first, then sections two hundred to two-fifty second. Anybody not ready?'

No one spoke.

'Clocks set?'

'Clocks set.'

'OK, let's start the scan.'

Rod double-clicked on an icon and a bank of monitors offered up new pictures. The sounds in the room changed: the traditional beep tones of the patient's heart increased and the speakers transmitted the growling sounds of brain cells excited by the nanoscanners. His neurons took in the aliens – they had no choice – but they didn't like them.

Nat felt himself entering a house of horrors, waiting for the first monster to jump out. His pulse pounded like a miler's.

'I need a diversion in area two,' Rodriguez said.

'Think of a scene from a movie, Hennessy.'

'Which one?'

'Whatever comes to mind.'

'I see a coliseum and gladiators. Like in *Ben Hur*.'

'Sandy?'

'Cooling blanket's at fifty per cent.'

Nat stopped talking.

'What else do you see?' Cush said.

'I see a fat emperor sitting in the stands with a ring of asparagus around his head. He keeps pulling at his toga, and he's got fat lips. It's Charles Laughton, I think.'

'He wasn't in *Ben Hur*.'

'That's who I see.'

'What else?

'His wife, the empress. She's sitting next to him all nervous and fidgety.'

'Who plays that role?'

'Deborah Kerr.'

'Sandy?'

'Brain temp's at ninety-nine point eight. BP, pulse, respirations all green. ICPs at twenty-one.'

'Keep talking.'

'The gladiators are going at each other.'

'OK!' Rod said. 'We've got area one locked up.'

'What are they saying?'

'The guy with the pitchfork has his hands on his knees, like he's out of breath. He says . . . can I have some water?'

'Is that you or the gladiator talking?'

'Me.'

Cush placed a straw in his mouth and let him suck in a few tablespoons of water. 'What else?'

'The other guy is raising his weapon like he's going to whack him.'

'Josh?'

'No problem.'

'What kind of a weapon?'

'One of those balls with nails all over it. The first guy is holding up his hand to stop him and . . . say something . . .'

'What does he want to say?'

'It's getting hot in my head, Doc. That's me again.'

'Cryo?'

Sandy said, 'It's running.'

389

'Go on.'

'He says . . . tell me, do you prefer Mitchum's dry stick . . . or Ban Clear-Gel?'

'And?' Cush asked. No response. 'What's his answer?'

Nat struggled to talk. 'The black guy says . . .' He didn't continue.

'What's he say?'

'He says . . . I prefer Lady Speed Stick by Mennen . . . Lasts longer.' He fell silent again.

'We've captured area two.'

'Sandy?'

'Temp's up to one hundred and three point five.'

'Let's do the rest while we can.'

'Give me one second,' Rod said.

Cush turned to Nat. 'Right about now you must be wishing your friend Mr Jackson was on this table instead of you, right?'

'Yeah, but I can see how it would have been . . . a problem. He never would have . . . sat still for this.'

'I never understood how you were going get him here in the first place,' Cush said.

'Piece of cake.'

'Ready when you are,' Rod said.

Cush spoke to Nat. 'OK, this is the fun part, the blueprint that makes or breaks the repair. No more loafing, Hennessy. I want your brain on fire.'

'How?'

'Think of something that makes you angry. Redundancy, Rod?'

'Twenty per cent but it's falling fast.' The number of Z-5s would soon need to be increased.

Nat said, 'Can your computers tell what I'm thinking?'

'No.'

'That gives me . . . some real possibilities.'

Cush looked at the bank of monitors. 'I want pictures now, Carla, MRI and baseline feedback from the Z-5s.' Listening to the machine, he said, 'So, what makes you angry?'

'Other than you?'

'No reason to leave me out.'

'What happened to my father.'

'Let me know when reserves hit fifteen per cent, Rod. Why, what happened to your father?'

'None of your business. My head's getting really hot.'

'Fifteen per cent and falling,' Rod said.

'That's the serum you're feeling,' Cush said to his patient. 'It's well below body temperature, but it feels warm. How's our rate of distribution, Rod?'

'Excellent.'

'Coverage?'

'Like ants on a picnic blanket.'

Cush checked the monitors and popped another Lifesaver. Four views of Nat's frontal lobes appeared in outline, and on each screen small clouds of blue were spreading outward like a slow-moving hurricane on a Channel Four weather map. The nanoscanners were moving into the neurons from the space around the brain that held the cortical spinal fluid, exactly as they were supposed to. Whatever Hennessy was picturing – whatever he was thinking about his father – it was lighting up whole segments of his neural webbing. Intensely. Nicely. Then it trailed off.

'He's flagging,' Rod said.

'What's wrong?' Cush said.

'I can't picture it anymore.'

'Then try a new subject,' Cush said.

'Such as?'

'Try me. What pisses you off most.'

'You know.'

'BIAS?'

'That's one.'

'We've got a good picture again,' Rod said. Nat's brain cells tickled the Z-5 sensors and sent growling noises out of the speakers. On the monitors, the cells that were firing made fluorescent green sparkles in different sectors of the brain. 'Give me some more of that,' Rod said.

'What else?'

'You know.'

'Me and Camilla.'

'You got it.'

'What about us?'

'Everything.'

'Don't let him get away,' Rod said.

'Where are we, Sandy?' Cush said.

'One hundred and four point six.'

'You don't have to tell me exactly what you're thinking, Hennessy, but whatever it is, you need to keep thinking it. Give me his alpha waves.'

'Eight per second and falling,' Sandy said.

Cush said, 'Come on, Hennessy, picture it. Talk to me.'

Nat said nothing, then, 'I feel funny.'

'Funny how?'

'Sleepy.'

'No, no – I want you wide awake.'

Rod said, 'He's fading, and our reserves are down to ten per cent.'

Cush leaned down to Nat's ear and whispered. 'What about me and Camilla?'

Nat said nothing.

'Go ahead,' Cush said, 'picture the two of us together.'

'Piss off,' Nat said.

Rod said, 'Whatever you're doing over there, Cush, it's good.'

Cush said, 'You're already picturing us, aren't you?'

Nat said, 'I thought you said . . . you couldn't tell what I'm thinking.'

'Right now, a blind man could see what you're thinking.'

'More of that,' Rod said.

'Picture it,' Cush said. 'Camilla and me together.'

'Lay off, Walker,' Nat wheezed.

Cush looked over at his monitor. The oxygen uptake in Nat's frontal lobe was surging and whole hunks of his cerebral cortex were turning from greenish yellow sparkles to a constant yellow-orange glow.

'I guess we know what lives in those sectors,' Cush said. 'You always get this hot at the peephole?'

'Fuck you . . . and the horse that . . . fucks you . . .'

'That's the ticket,' Cush said. He straightened up. 'Redundancy?'

'Down to two per cent.'

'What's his pulse, Sandy?'

'One fifteen and holding.'

'IC temp?'

'One hundred and five point two,' Sandy said.

Damn. His temperature was rising too fast.

They continued scanning in silence, six white coats surrounding a human electrical generator, trying to catch lightning in a bottle.

'Your voice . . . sounds funny,' Nat said. 'I see circles and . . . pinwheels.'

'Which direction are they going?'

'Counterclockwise. Your voice . . . sounds . . . really strange.'

'We're getting serious heat, Cush,' Rodriguez said quietly.

'Keep scanning,' Cush said. 'Talk to me, Hennessy.'

'Very hot and . . . thirsty.'

Cush placed a straw from a water bottle into his mouth. 'You're fading on me, Hennessy.'

'We're getting more heat, Cush.'

'Just keep scanning,' he said. 'Where are we, Sandy?'

'One hundred and five point seven Fahrenheit.'

Whenever she added the word 'Fahrenheit', Cush knew it was bad.

'How long have we been over one hundred and four?' he asked.

'Eleven minutes.'

Not just bad, very bad. They were already maxing out and they weren't half finished. If they didn't level off soon they'd fry his brain before they got near their target. If reverse logic was helping, it wasn't enough. Cush raised his head and looked at Rodriguez. Rod caught his eye and shook his head, we're not there yet, we still need more.

Cush returned to the privacy of Nat's ear. 'Listen to me, Hennessy. We need to inject more scanners. Do you think you can handle it?'

'Go 'head . . . take your shot.'

'OK, here we go.' He gave Rod a thumbs up, signaling him to inject. Rodriguez clacked on his keyboard, opening the valve to the pump.

Nat groaned and pumped his fingers open and closed.

'How do you feel?' Cush asked.

'Like a . . . roasted . . . duck,' he croaked.

'Can you take more?'

'Stick it . . . to me.'

Cush signaled for more.

Nat's neck stiffened and his face tightened.

'One hundred and six and rising,' Sandy said.

Rod said, 'We've got plenty of Z-5s, but we need more squiggles.'

Cush understood what that meant. He had to fire up all the neurons in sectors thirty to forty he possibly could, the areas corresponding to the most damaged part of Camilla's brain. Having learned in the BIAS protocols that nothing caused a cerebral glow like a deep, genuine hate, he leaned in close again.

'Come on, Hennessy, don't crap out on me now.'

Nat didn't answer.

'We're losing him,' Rod said.

'Picture me and Camilla,' he said.

'God,' Nat rasped, grimacing. 'So frigging . . . hot.' His fingers were squeezed white.

'I still need cerebration,' Rod said loudly.

'You have to concentrate, Hennessy,' Cush said into his ear. 'Picture the two of us dancing together. Not vertically, horizontally, if you know what I mean.'

'He's rising,' Rod said.

'Go ahead, picture us together,' Cush said.

'Good uptake,' Rod said.

'Dark skin on white—'

'Shut up . . . you smoky . . .'

'Keep it going,' Rod said, 'we're getting busters and popcorn.' They were the soundbite signatures of the neurons they were scanning.

'One hundred and six point eight degrees,' Sandy said.

Cush waited for Nat to continue. 'Smoky what?' he whispered. 'Finish the thought.'

Nat exhaled deeply, searching for a way out.

'Don't hold back – I *want* you to finish the thought,' Cush said. 'I need you all fired up!'

Nat was breathing like a drowning man breaking surface. 'You smoky . . . black . . . bastard.'

Rod yelled, 'Hold that thought, whatever it is!'

'Say it again,' Cush whispered.

Nat heaved air in and out.

'One hundred and seven point two,' the anesthesiologist said.

'Say it,' Cush said. 'Say "you smoky black bastard" again.'

'Kiss my . . .' Nat was now hunting wildly for an escape, '. . . bare naked ass.'

Cush straightened up and laid his hand on the heat gauge as if to slow it down. 'Cryo?' he asked impatiently.

'It's running full bore,' Sandy said.

'We've got sectors forty to eighty in the bank!' Rod said. There was audible relief from Carla, the radiologist.

Sandy kept her eyes glued to the thermometer. 'One hundred and seven point three Fahrenheit,' she said.

Rod clacked away on the keyboard. 'I'm moving on to the occipital lobe now, Cush. Give me something long and constant and we'll finish this thing off!'

Nat was having trouble focusing. Cush took a sponge and wiped the sweat off his patient's forehead, then reached down for the cup and raised a bent straw to his mouth, feeding him another sip of water. Nat's temperature was climbing, his respirations quickening. His resting pulse was up to 126.

'How do you feel?' Cush asked.

Nat waited, slowing his breathing. 'I feel like . . . that computer in . . . *2001*.' His voice was strained and hoarse now, a godfather on his deathbed. 'What . . . was his name?'

'HAL,' Cush said.

'I feel like . . . HAL . . .' his voice labored in the fog. 'When the astronauts . . . are pulling out . . . his memory rods . . . and there's nothing . . . he can do about it . . .'

'What's the temperature, Sandy?'

'One hundred and seven point five and rising.'

'He just sits there and sings . . . while they take away . . . his brain.'

'One hundred and seven point six.'

'What's he singing?' Cush asked. No answer. 'Sing what he sang, Hennessy – I need a song.' If he got him into a thought process that was constant, where one phrase led to another, he might keep him cerebrating long enough to scan the last sectors.

'Daisy . . . Daisy . . . give me your answer do . . .'

'How much more do we need on the left hemisphere, Carla?'

'I've got seventy-six per cent of the remaining sectors.'

'That's all?'

'. . . half crazy, all for the love of you . . .'

'Temp's at one hundred and seven point seven and rising,' Sandy said.

'. . . won't be a stylish marriage . . .'

'We're red-lining.'

'. . . can't afford a carriage . . .'

'Everybody hold what you've got,' Cush said. 'Give me your increments, Carla.'

'We've downloaded seventy-nine per cent, Doctor.'

'. . . but you'd look sweet . . .'

'One hundred and eight degrees, Cush, and still rising!'

'We're at eight-one per cent of target, Doctor!'

'. . . upon the seat . . .'

'Jesus, Cush, you better take a look at this,' Rod said.

Cush looked over at the monitor. Bright red spots were popping out all over Nat's frontal lobe like little bomb bursts on a night-time target.

'He's burning up,' Cush said softly.

'Eighty-two per cent, Doctor.'

'. . . of a . . . bicycle . . .'

'More liquid nitrogen, Cush? We're over one hundred and nine degrees Fahrenheit.'

'We can't do it, we're freezing his spine as it is.'

'. . . built . . .'

'One hundred and ten degrees and still rising.'

'Eighty-four per cent completed, Doctor.'

'. . . built . . .'

Cush waited – he needed at least 97 per cent to save Camilla, but Hennessy was dying. He'd lose her if he didn't keep going, but he'd lose Hennessy if he did. He'd lose them both in a minute – she was comatose and Hennessy was about to die – but it wouldn't work if he stopped now, he needed more template to save her. But he was *killing* this guy, and there was this cliché to cope with, this thing his father had taught him about the fox – its mangled paw, the winter barn, the plumes of his father's breath, his father's hands cupped on the back of Cush's neck, telling him to make up his mind and save the fox or kill it, that silence he'd felt before he made his choice, that moment he'd become a doctor – when he was only nine years old – when he'd learned to do what was right.

'What's the temperature?' he asked.

'One hundred and ten point five.'

'What's the distribution?'

'They're all working.'

'How much have we captured?'

'Eighty-six per cent, but—'

'Shut it down,' Cush said.

'. . . *built* . . .'

'But Doctor, we haven't reached target yet—'

There was an incredulous silence, and delay. 'I said, shut it *down*!'

The room filled with the sound of a switches being snapped off, a generator winding down, pumps stopping.

'. . . *built* . . .'

Cush shone a small flashlight into Nat's open eyes, searching for burst blood vessels.

'. . . *built* . . .' His voice was a mere whisper now.

Cush turned off the light. 'Talk to me, Hennessy.'

'. . . *built* . . .'

'Say it,' Cush said in a whisper. 'Finish the song.'

'. . . *built* . . .'

The room was quiet, broken only by idling machinery and beep tones signaling the patient's heartbeat.

'Say it! "For two!"'

More silence.

'Come on, Hennessy, say it! "Bicycle built for two."'

'. . . *Fuh* . . .'

'That's it – for two!'

'. . . *Fuh* . . .'

Nothing more came out.

Cush pulled his stool closer. 'I've never heard singing as bad as yours, Hennessy, but don't worry, we're used to it.'

Silence. Beep . . . *whir* . . . beep . . . *whir*.

Nat's mouth and eyes were frozen half open in a restful pose, a snapshot of a man caught by a photographer's lens in mid-sentence.

'Come on,' Cush pleaded in a whisper. He placed Nat's hand in his own and massaged it gently. 'Talk to me, Nat.' He'd never called him Nat before; the name sounded inappropriately friendly. He waited. Except for the sound of more toggle switches, the room was quiet. 'Come on. Speak to me.'

Nat's vital signs showed on the monitor – heart rate one-twelve, respiration mid-range. But there was no sound from his lips, no movement in his hands, no twitch of relaxing muscle. His brain waves were in the theta range, down from a normal twelve per second to only five. He was on the edge of a heat-induced coma.

The whole room waited, all eyes on Cush and Nat.

Beep . . . beep . . . beep. The heart monitor sounded lonely.

'If you can hear me, Nat, give me a sign.'

Everyone waited for something to happen. Nothing happened. Finally, Rod stood up.

'Cush?' he said quietly.

Cush stayed focused on his patient. 'A squeeze or a blink. Come on.'

Beep . . . beep . . . beep.

Everyone continued waiting. Nat's brain waves had fallen into the delta range now, the slow and sluggish thought pattern of a comatose 'Q', the irreverent name interns gave to brain-damaged patients who slept with their mouths open and their tongues hanging out. Rodriguez looked at the monitor and watched them flatten to ripples on a sleepy pond.

'Cush?' Rod said gently.

Cush didn't respond.

Beep . . . beep . . . beep.

They all waited, and then waited some more.

'There's nothing more you can do, Cush.'

Cush finally heard the words. He sat up straight on his stool, regaining his self-control. After a moment he laid Nat's hand at his side, then lifted a bottle of saline and placed a drop in each of Nat's eyes and closed them gently.

Rod stared at Nat's sleeping body. 'I can't believe he did this.'

Cush could. He wanted to think he'd do it for her too. Still, he was impressed. After smearing petroleum jelly across Nat's lips, he looked over at the monitors. The patient's respirations were steady, his blood pressure normal, his pulse down to 92, the cooling blanket still running. He looked back at his patient.

'Is he going to make it?' Rod asked.

Cush waited, thinking. 'We'll know in the next twenty minutes.'

The overhead lights had been dimmed, the room soothed by the quiet whir of a hard drive workhorse. Appearing on a monitor were the three-dimensional structures of two brains: on the left, in shades of red, Hennessy's, on the right, in green, Camilla's. Working a joystick, Cush tilted and rotated the images as if they were weightless astronauts tumbling slowly in space.

'Think we got enough of Hennessy to rebuild her?' Rod asked.

Cush tapped the keyboard. 'Let's take a look.'

Slowly, the image of Hennessy's brain began drifting toward Camilla's, passing through each other like smoke until they were lined up on each other, superimposed. A click on a menu, and the colors changed, royal blue coloring parts of the brain where the scan had picked up a perfect template from Hennessy, lighter blue where it had obtained only 90 per cent of his brain cells, sky blue 80 per cent, and so on. White revealed sectors where the computer had recorded no blueprint at all.

Cush leaned forward and focused. Using the joystick again, he highlighted the white zones, then instructed the computer to simulate a repair of Camilla's damage and calculate how much of it was likely to be successful. When the sectors had been tabulated, the computer gave its tally: 84 per cent.

It was borderline. Neither one spoke.

'What do you think?' Rod finally asked. While the volume of a brain scan was important, it wasn't the whole story. Some cells were more important than others. Certain segments of unrepaired tissue could have very significant consequences. This they knew from unhappy experience.

A light blinked on the telephone. Rod lifted it, and after listening a moment, hung up. 'She's in OR two, prepped and ready to go,' he said.

'And Hennessy?'

'No change. Vital signs good, still unconscious.'

The two of them continued examining the monitor.

Rod pointed with the cursor. 'She's got massive damage here, Cush, and aneurysms ready to blow over here. What have we got to lose?'

The moment he'd said it, he wished he hadn't.

'You know the answer to that,' Cush said softly.

Yes, he did. A repair that went haywire and invaded the temporal lobes could be worse than no repair at all. Some outcomes, they'd learned, were more grotesque than death. It was the KBS factor. They didn't need to discuss it, not even in the privacy of this room.

Rod doodled on a notepad. 'What do you think?'

Cush sat back in his chair, considering his decision.

'I think we should go for it.'

FIVE

A minor operation: one performed on someone else.

—Anon.

Death is the greatest kick of all – that's why
they save it till last.

—Graffito, Los Angeles, 1981

Darth Vader was in the room. She knew because she could hear his voice.

Sweat blossomed on Camilla's neck and closed eyelids. She wanted to get up and defend herself but she was trapped in what neurologists called the 'hypnopompic moment', that brief second when you're between sleep and consciousness, when life and death momentarily merge. Darth Vader was nearby, as feathery as a dream and as real as iron.

'This . . . is sea-a-nen.'

There it was again, his voice, threatening her.

Sleeping brain cells were winking on like electricity after a summertime blackout, sweeping up the east coast of her brain like millions of synaptic dominoes. Her eyes opened wide, dry and dusty. A black figure appeared on a distant horizon where a gray wall was fused to a gray ceiling. It was Darth Vader, moving through the disordered mist, stalking her with a sea-a-nen, whatever that was.

He stopped moving. She stopped breathing. He moved in quick jerks. Her newly constructed horizon neurons – the ones that linked the old, undamaged part of her brain to the newly repaired segments – were re-establishing neural circuitry and, with it, whole hunks of personality. But not all. Not history or memory. Not normal speech or normal motor control.

She decided to attack him. He wasn't the only Spiderman on

this planet. She had a premonition that said she, too, knew how to climb.

She raised her face and felt a sheet of lightning ignite over her neck and shoulders. After lowering her head to stop the pain, she lifted it again, slowly, and fixed her eyes on the enemy. Why she was in a bed, and why she was hurt, she didn't know.

Rise slowly.

Music and voices and light flickered in the dusky room. Must be Vader's light saber, powering up. Looking for it, she found a television set on a wall with pictures of a rural flood, houses and cars and people paddling boats around rooftops somewhere in Georgia. She looked back at Darth Vader on the ceiling.

Go ahead, try it. I dare you.

She tried to rise again and felt her body pinned to the mattress by an invisible force. Pulling the covers off her torso, she still had her eyes on the enemy. He stood still, waiting.

She raised herself onto an elbow, then, breathing hard, rolled like an injured football player onto her side, then her knees, holding onto the headboard to keep from falling. Something tugged at her skin. She looked down and found lines criss-crossing her hands and arms and neck. Claustrophobia washed over her and she began pulling them away: a line marked 'IV' to a shunt in her hand, another marked 'ICP' for intracranial pressure. Seeing Styrofoam pads on her chest, she peeled them off, along with the electrocardiogram wires they held, then the EEG wire taped to her skull, then a pair of air hoses to the Venodyne pressure boots that kept blood clots from forming in her calves. The telemetry cap on her head she left alone: it felt like a helmet, and that would come in handy. She was ready to fight.

She needed a weapon. Looking at the bedside table, she found a thin bud vase holding a flower. As she reached for it, her arm felt heavy with disuse, as if she'd slept on it wrong. No pins and needles, just dead weight. She took hold of the vase and pulled it toward her, dribbling water into her pillow.

Looking up, she saw Darth Vader zipping across the ceiling toward the wall.

She tightened her grip on the vase. Here I come.

Gripping the headboard, she tried to raise herself to her feet, but nothing happened. Her right leg was on the planet Rip Van Winkle, her left somewhere else. She began dragging the right one as best she could.

The door to the room opened, flooding it with hallway light. It was Nurse Punt responding to an alarm triggered by the broken lines.

'Oh, my God,' she said.

She hustled to the bed and pulled Camilla onto her back, paying no attention to the horsefly on the ceiling or the voice of James Earl Jones – Darth Vader's voice – booming out of the television set, threatening her again with a sea-a-nen.

'This . . . is CNN.'

By the time he got there, Camilla was in her bed. There was the usual low light, the same monitoring equipment tracking her life, the IV poles with bags of saline and liquid food dripping sustenance into her body, the faint smell of medicine, the spongy hospital air. And yet everything had changed. The patient was awake.

Cush Walker closed the door behind him. The bed had been raised into a half-sitting position and she was staring at the ceiling, eerily. Nurse Punt had cleaned the bacteria from her teeth with a cotton ball soaked in mouthwash and pulled a comb through her once shiny hair. It was the least, and unfortunately the most, that she could do.

He walked to his patient and saw something he hadn't seen for three years: her open eyes. But she did nothing to acknowledge him, still staring blankly, her gaze fixed on a distant point. My God, he'd seen this before. She'd dropped back into her coma with her eyes open, a condition called being 'locked in'. Or was it worse than that? How much of the operation had worked? How many neurons were still in limbo? What side effects did she have? Three letters – KBS – repeated themselves in a sing-song.

'Camilla?' he said softly.

She didn't answer, she didn't blink.

'Camilla, can you hear me?'

She spoke: 'What the heck kind of a hospital has horseflies?' Her voice broke up like a once-purring motor trying to re-start.

A wobbly hand pointed toward the ceiling before falling back to earth.

He looked up and saw an enormous black horsefly walking upside down on the white cork panels.

Camilla turned her head toward him and they made contact at last – their rich, blackstrap-molasses, green eyes locked on each other.

It was her. She was seeing him now, recognizing him, reaching out to him to say, hello, darling.

'Who are you?' she said.

'I'm Cush Walker.' His chest hurt from her non-recognition. 'Your doctor.'

'Oh, so *you're* the one.'

He didn't like the sound of that; it had a tone of accusation about it. Was it the thing she figured out just before she was shot? He lowered the safety bar on the side of the bed. 'I'm the one what?'

'You're the one I remember who . . .' She stopped. He waited. Remembered what? It could have been anything, but there was only one thing he imagined.

'What do you remember?' he asked.

The door to the room opened and they both turned to see a man standing in the doorway, his face largely shadowed. He wore sweatpants and sneakers and a hospital T-shirt that sagged around his neck. His hair was uncombed and a hose trailed behind him like Frankenstein's feeding tube. It was Nat Hennessy, his face eager, his hope transparent: is that really you? Is my bride back from the dead?

'Camilla?'

Her face was a blank. He focused on her with his head turned slightly to the side, as if he was trying to see around the blind spots in the northwest quadrants of his eyes. He held his left arm close to his body, his side in pain, and walked in a slow, self-conscious shuffle. The extent of his neurological damage wasn't clear yet, but Walker said he'd seen similar symptoms before and thought they weren't permanent.

Nat walked to her side.

'Cam, sweetheart, are you awake?'

She raised her hand toward him, a bride recognizing her groom. Then four fingers curled to her palm, leaving the index finger pointing at him. 'Who are you?' Punching him.

'It's me,' he said, a stranger in his own home. 'Nat. Your fiancé.'

Walker gave him a disapproving stare but he ignored it, searching her face to see if she was Camilla Jekyll or Camilla Hyde. He lifted her hand gently.

Walker spoke, his voice low. 'This isn't the time, Detective.'

Nat stayed focused on his lover.

'I'm in the middle of an examination,' Walker continued.

'Go right ahead,' Nat said. He let go of her hand and turned and shuffled to a leather chair at the side of the room, next to a coffee table, and sat on the edge of the seat, elbows on knees, a spectator on the fifty-yard line. Walker turned back to his patient.

Camilla looked at her doctor and said, 'What's wrong with his eyes?'

Her mind was in a fog. She was trying to understand what these two men were doing in her room.

The one who said he was her doctor ignored her question and pulled a wooden stool to the side of the bed.

She was unbelievably thirsty. 'Can I have a drink?' she asked.

'Not yet.'

Why not? She watched him reach into a cardboard cup next to the bed and fish out an ice chip and place it between her lips. 'Do you know your name?' he asked.

That was easy. 'Vanilla.' But I don't know who I am.

'Camilla.'

'What?'

'Your name is Camilla.'

'I just said that, didn't I?' He didn't answer. 'How long have I been asleep?'

'Ten days.'

'Ten *days*? What happened to me?'

'We'll come to that in a minute. Do you know where you are?'

'New York City Hospital.'

'Very good.'

'The nurse told me.'

'Do you know what day it is?'

'Is that a trick question?'

'No, why?'

'It's night.'

'OK.' He frowned as if she'd said something wrong. 'Spell the word earth backwards.'

She pictured it, and started at the end. 'H, T . . .' The word turned around. 'E, A, R,' she said. What is this? Feels like I'm in school. Where'd I go to school?

'Can you count backward from a hundred in sevens?'

I'm in school. He's my teacher. She smelled chalk, the wax on the wooden floors, the cafeteria with mashed potatoes and deep-fried fish from . . . where? She pictured a place with water and banyan trees, a bridge where old men fished and smoked pipes.

'Camilla?'

Down by the bay. The bye. The bayou. Bye-bye, you. You, you, you. Such a funny word, 'you'. Say it over and over it gets even stranger. What's wrong with me?

'Camilla, can you hear me?'

'Yes?' He was talking to her, this man with the smooth, lovely

411

skin. The one who was her teacher. No, her doctor. Or was he her fiancé? No, that was the other one, the one sitting on the chair. Watching me. Why, I don't know.

'Can you count backwards from a hundred in sevens?'

She took a breath. 'Ninety-three.' She paused. 'Eighty-eight – no, wait, no wait. Eighty-eight – wait, wait – eighty-eight—'

'Relax,' Cush said. She was rhyming under pressure, not a good sign. It was what schizophrenics did. It was what . . . Spider did. *Don't jump to conclusions.* She was unusually literal, another sign of neurological deficit, although how deep he couldn't tell yet.

He held up a ballpoint pen. She said it was a pen. He touched his cuff; she answered shirt. He touched his wristwatch; she said clock – close enough. He tested her color perception and she got it right: yellow, green, red, blue. He checked her hearing with a tuning fork and a syringe of ice-cold water in her ears – no problem. He tested her pupils with a flashlight – they contracted – then checked her vision, watching her eyes follow a pencil. He wiggled his fingers at the sides of her head and her peripheral vision caught it.

He touched her forehead, cheeks, chin, and jaw on each side simultaneously, searching for dissimilarity. He told her to stick out her tongue and saw that it was straight, no sign of palsy of the twelfth cranial nerve. He placed a drop of liquid on it from four different vials – sweet, sour, salty, bitter – and she tasted them all. He flattened her tongue with a wooden blade and she gagged, which was good. He held the light in her open mouth and told her to swallow. She did, no trouble. Now she could have water. He handed her a glass.

'Slowly,' he said.

She gulped it. So energetic and impatient.

He loved her.

'Tell me what happened to me,' she said.

'You were in a coma.'

She looked blank. 'I don't know what that is.'

'A deep sleep.'

She stared at him and began rhyming. 'Deep sleep, deep sleep . . .' She closed her eyes, exasperated with herself. 'How did I get into a coma?'

Nat leaned forward, all ears, worried about the answer.

'You were shot,' Cush said. 'Open your eyes and raise your right hand.'

She looked at her hand but it didn't move. 'Where?'

'Toward the ceiling.'

'I mean, where was I when I was shot?'

'At the Statue of Liberty. Can you raise your hand?'

She raised it slowly, as if it was dead weight. She was still suffering from a loss of motor control on her right side.

Cush looked at Nat as he asked the next question. 'Do you remember being at the Statue of Liberty, Camilla?'

Nat glared at him, not speaking.

There he is again, getting uptight.

'No,' she said.

Cush turned back to her. 'When it's six o'clock, where are the little hand and the big hand?'

'On the six and the twelve,' she said impatiently. She was getting tired of being treated like a child.

'Close your eyes and try to move your right hand again.'

She closed her eyes and tried. Her hand moved, but only slightly. He lifted her arm and worked the joints. They felt normal.

'What's wrong with me?' Her tone was all business.

'I don't know yet,' he said. 'First I'm trying to find out what's right with you. Open your eyes.'

'I wish you would make up your mind.'

'I don't want you to go to sleep.' He reached down to the foot of the bed and pulled the top sheet from under the mattress, exposing her feet.

Nat stood up to get a better view.

Her hospital gown covered her down to her knees. Cush drew a wooden tongue depressor from his pocket and broke it in half, leaving one end round and smooth, the other splintered and sharp. Using the jagged end as a probe, he touched the bottom of her foot. She flinched.

'Feel that?' he said.

'Yes.'

'Does it feel sharp?'

'Yes.'

He turned the broken stick around and touched the smooth end to her skin, running it up her leg to her knee, looking for quivering muscle, a sign of clonus, a neurological disease. There was none.

Nat took a step forward and hovered.

Holding her ankle in one hand, Cush worked his way up her calf to her knee, touching her skin with both ends of the broken paddle. Each time he touched her she responded.

So did he.

Cush pushed her gown above her knees and folded it back. She had lost weight; the insides of her thighs were slightly concave, long and affecting.

That did it for the other man in the room. 'OK,' Nat said.

Cush looked at him and said, 'Sit down,' then reached out and pushed the call button next to the bed before returning to his exam, repeating the same test on her other leg.

Nat ran his hand through his hair and shifted his weight from one foot to the other.

The door opened and Nurse Punt walked in. '*Mr* Hennessy,' she said in a scolding, English-accented voice.

He turned to her and raised his palms defensively. 'I'm OK,' he said.

'What is *this*?' she said, lifting the dangling IV line from his hand. 'You're coming with me.' She took him by the arm.

'What's going on?' Camilla asked.

'Camilla,' he said, being pulled toward the door. He retrieved his arm from Punt and walked to the coffee table and pulled a flower from a vase he'd filled every day and carried it to the bed. When she raised her hand to take it, he lifted her fingers and kissed them, then gave her the flower. 'I'll be back before it wilts,' he said. He turned and looked at Cush, pointed his finger at him in a silent warning, and left the room with the nurse.

Camilla turned to Cush. 'Is he really my fiancé?' She held the flower and admired it, the thought behind it, the man who'd given it to her. 'What's his name again?'

Cush hated telling her. 'Nat Hennessy.'

'Nat,' she said, raising the petals as if to smell them.

Instead, she pulled three or four off the stem with her lips, and curled them into her mouth.

Cush felt hot prickles on his face.

In spite of his instructions, Camilla closed her eyes. She needed to rest a second, get control of her confusion. Her frustration.

'Don't go to sleep,' she heard Cush say. 'Talk to me.'

'I don't know what to say, I can't remember things.' Her head felt stuffed with unfinished business, splintered ideas and a sense that everything she wanted to know was slightly out of reach, on the tip of her tongue. She was experiencing a bizarre sense of *déjà vu* every ten to fifteen seconds.

'Tell me what you're thinking.'

'I keep seeing pictures that get halfway developed then disappear or turn into something else.' She imagined herself on a windswept building or mountainside, waiting for something or someone she couldn't identify. 'I'm getting a little scared.'

'Keep talking to me. This is Cush.'

She kept her eyes closed. 'Don't worry, I'm just resting.' She took a long breath, as if hoping to start over. 'Cush. Where did that name come from?'

'My great-grandfather. According to the Bible, Cush was the first black man on earth.' He pulled the sheet down over her feet and tucked it in. 'Are you hungry?'

'Yes,' she said.

He brushed the hair from her forehead. 'An appetite's a good sign.'

'What's an appetite?'

'Being hungry.'

'You seem . . . familiar to me.'

He got off the stool, walked to the side of the room and pulled one of the leather-upholstered, chrome-legged chairs to the side of her bed.

'What do you recall about me?' he asked.

'I can't tell yet. What should I recall?'

'We knew each other before the accident.'

'We did? When?'

'Three years ago.'

'Was I your patient?'

'No, we went together.'

She opened her eyes and stared at him, trying to find a link. 'Went where?'

'We were close friends. Lovers.'

'Oh? How long?'

'About half a year.'

They sat in a moment of silence that was easy for her, awkward for him. 'Then how did I become Nat's fiancée?'

'You met him after we broke up.'

She picked up what was left of the flower he'd given her, the one she'd mutilated with her mouth. 'That's why he's so concerned about me.'

'His guilt is why he's worried about you,' Cush said.

'Guilt? About what?'

'You should ask him.' He checked the monitoring equipment.

'You sound like you have a suspension but don't want to tell me.'

'Suspicion.'

'What?'

'Suspicion, not suspension.'

'Why did we break up, you and I?'

'You were upset about something,' he said.

'What was it?'

'I'm not sure. Not exactly.'

She reached for a glass of water, hand shaking. 'What a strange answer. Another suspen – suspicion.'

He got to the glass first, lifted it, and held it with her hand on his as she took a drink. Every time she touched him, he felt light-headed and surprised. How amazing to see her awake, alive, in his care.

She laid her head back on the pillow. 'What did I do with myself before I was shot?'

'You were an architectural conservator,' Cush said. The past tense struck him. 'You still are.'

'What is it?'

'You fix things like old walls and bridges and statues.'

She closed her eyes and breathed deeply. 'I don't remember any of it. When am I going to get my memory back?'

'You have to be patient.' He picked up the telephone and called Virginia Punt and asked if she could bring some apple juice.

Camilla looked perplexed. Her complexion turned sallow. 'What's that?'

'The telephone?'

Her eyes turned wild and searched the room frantically. 'No, no – that noise – what is it?'

'Describe it to me.'

417

'That whistle – can't you hear it?' She squinted in pain and covered her ears, her right hand flopping in a palsied motion toward her head.

He stood up. 'It's only tinnitus,' he said, touching her shoulder, 'an irritation in a nerve in the ear. It's nothing to be afraid of.' Another bad sign.

She crushed her eyelids closed. 'Oh, God,' she said softly, tears beading up on her black lashes. 'I'm so sick.'

He sat on the edge of the bed and stroked her hair.

'Who am I?' she said. 'What's wrong with me? It's like I'm dead.'

He said *shh* and stroked her back, telling her she'd be all right, walking the doctor's tightrope between legitimate hope and unfounded promises.

She pulled him close. 'Don't go away,' she whispered.

'I'm not going anywhere.' The feel of her in his arms – my God. He'd forgotten how much he loved her.

The door opened, startling him like a boy getting caught smoking behind the barn. He let go and turned to see who it was.

It was Nat Hennessy with a glass of apple juice on a hospital tray.

Camilla saw him and the juice. 'Is that for me?'

Nat walked to her with his crabbing gait and spot-filled eyes, and handed her the glass.

'Thank you, Nat,' she said, wiping her eyelids with her fingertips.

As she drank it, Nat turned his back to her and glared at Cush. Do that again, his eyes said, and you're going to be missing a few neurons of your own.

Sally Shaw stood in the hallway talking to Lieutenant Joe Amerigo, his hand on the doorknob to his office. She said she wanted to stay on the Bissonette shooting but he said no dice, he already had six detectives working with the FBI and Major Case, and now five more working on the attempted murder of Nat Hennessy at Radio City and the bludgeoning of the engineer. He needed her elsewhere.

Shaw wasn't buying. 'You don't take a partner off a case like this without a better reason than staff allocation, Lieu. What's the deal?'

He looked at her, opened the door, and waved her in. As she walked past him, his eyes fastened on a man wearing a baseball cap and a khaki vest coming toward them as if preparing to serve a subpoena.

'Lieutenant,' the man said, pulling a pad from his shirt pocket, 'can I have a minute?'

'How'd you get up here?' Amerigo said.

'The stairs,' the man said. He was being defensive, but Amerigo took it as smart ass.

'You gotta get permission to be up here,' he said. Reporters weren't allowed on the second floor without clearance.

'I called the DCPI,' the reporter said, referring to the Deputy Commissioner for Public Information. He unfolded a piece of wrinkled paper. 'Talked to somebody named Cook, a woman.'

'Nobody called me,' Amerigo said.

'All I want to know is if you've found a connection between

419

the shooting of Camilla Bissonette and the attempted murder of Detective Hennessy.'

'What kinda connection?'

'Like, is it somebody he put away who's out to kill him? Like maybe he's involved in something?'

'Involved in something?' Amerigo dared the reporter to say what he really meant: money, dope, pussy, rackets. Hearing no answer, the lieutenant stepped inside his office, slammed the door, walked to his desk and lifted the telephone and punched in a number. To Shaw he said, 'He asked a good question.' He handed her a piece of paper from his desk. 'That's your Five from last Friday.' It was her DD5 detailing her trip with Nat to Radio City Music Hall. 'Public information? Lieutenant Amerigo, Midtown South. I got a press pimp standing outside my door saying he cleared an interview with somebody over there named Cook. Izzat true?' Waiting for an answer, he handed Shaw Nat's Five from a couple of days before. 'According to you and Hennessy,' he said to Shaw, 'Angel Rico got himself killed a few hours after you almost collared him.' Into the telephone, he said, 'I didn't ask his name, my question is, did somebody over there clear somebody over here?'

Shaw said, 'What are you driving at?'

'I don't know, you tell me.' Into the telephone: 'Next time you send a reporter over here without telling me, I'm gonna put him on the line and you answer his fuckin' questions yourself.' He hung up and sat down at his desk and stared at Shaw.

'Why did you leave Hennessy in the basement at Radio City?'

She felt her cheeks go hot. 'It's right there,' she said, pointing at her Five. 'He told me to go back to the office.'

'Yeah, I noticed,' he said.

'If I'd had any idea he was headed for trouble I never would have listened to him.'

'So why'd he tell you to go?'

Shaw froze him with her icy street-corner stare. 'If there was something more to tell you, Lieu, I would have told you.' She said it in the voice she used to shut up johns who liked talking dirty to hookers without propositioning them.

He fished an ice cube out of a Styrofoam cup and laid it in a wrinkled handkerchief and ran it over the front of his neck, staring at her. Then he picked up some paperwork, his signal that their conversation was over.

She stood there feeling like a piece of shit. She'd done what Nat had told her to do, but the only thing anybody cared about was why she'd bailed out on her partner. And they were right. She never should have left him. Now Amerigo was homing in on Nat's leaky story about how Angel Rico got away, and she was in the middle of it. If she didn't get control of what was going on, her career would be over before it got started.

She moved toward the door. 'I got a question for you, Lieu.' He didn't look up. 'What's the deal with Hennessy's father?'

He looked up.

'You told me not to bring up the subject with him,' she said. 'I want to know why.'

'When he was a kid he saw his father killed in a street thing the night of the seventy-seven blackout.'

'What happened?'

'All I know is his father was murdered and the perp walked.'

The killer got off? An *uh-oh* appeared on the horizon. 'What was the perp's name, do you know?'

He glanced up at her. 'Come on, Shaw, it happened over twenty years ago.' A curious look. 'Why the sudden interest?'

Too curious; she had to get out of this. 'Everybody around here seems to know more about my partner than I do, that's all.'

He held her eyes, looking for a crack in the stone wall, making her sweat. Then he looked down. 'There's a mugging the sergeant needs you to look into.'

A mugging. Wow. She reached for the door.

'Shaw?' Amerigo said.

'Yeah?'

'You know what you get after thirty-five years of being a cop?' She waited, thinking promotions, medals, a big pension. 'One of these,' he said, pointing to his nose. 'Mine's so good it can smell a cow fart downwind. I suggest you bear that in mind.'

No problem, Lieu. I'll do that.

It was late, the Fifth Avenue library she'd once taken Nat to was closing, but Shaw refused to budge. She sat in front of the screen watching a blur of black-and-white *New York Times* microfiche rip past her eyes at high speed. She stopped to find the date. She was at July 14, 1977, the day after the great New York City blackout. Looting, arson, theft. Rape, robbery, assault. Six hundred and fifty fires in the city, 1,766 alarms. A riot in the Bronx House of Detention. The reopening of the Tombs, a prison so decrepit it had been closed years before. Muggings, purse snatchings, physical assault. Hospitals jammed with injuries and shootings, most of them in the backs of young men fleeing lootings. The sick and injured tended to in hallways. Doctors performing surgery on four patients at a time in operating rooms designed for one.

Acts of bravery and humor. People rescuing each other from stalled elevators, young people helping the old get home safely. Others discovering love and desire, producing, exactly nine months later, the sharpest spike of births in New York City's history. Fun and games. Death and destruction. The blackout of 1977.

She continued rolling the tape and found a man killed by a bottle thrown from a rooftop . . . a woman who died in a stalled elevator . . . a man found beaten to death near Franz Siegel Park in the South Bronx.

The South Bronx?

'Getting ready to close up shop,' an assistant librarian said.

Shaw rolled the tape slowly until she found the victim's name: Ian Hennessy, a businessman from Manhattan. On his way to Yankee Stadium with his eleven-year-old son, Nathaniel, when the lights went out.

She sat back in her wooden chair and let the tension of the last hour ease out of her back. After a drink from a bottle of water, she leaned forward again, squinting, pressing the Slow Forward button, once more bathing her face in the speckled light of the machine.

She found what she was looking for in the Metro section: the arrest of a man for the beating to death of Ian Hennessy. Not just any beating, one with a baseball bat. It gave her gooseflesh reading about it. The accused killer, a resident of the South Bronx, was named Jackson Levander James.

'You've got to turn it off now,' the woman said.

Jackson Levander James? My God, could it be? There were two Js and a Jackson in the name. Was it him, or a coincidence? She tried to stay skeptical, but her instincts and logic wouldn't let her. Nat had let Angel Rico go free to kill the man who had killed his father, and somehow Jackson had turned the tables on Rico and killed him instead. The message he had burned onto Angel's chest – BAT MAN WAS HERE – wasn't meant for the tabloids. It was for Nat. Now they both wanted each other dead. Nat had taken his shot at Jackson by using Rico as a hit man, and Jackson had taken his shot, literally, using a long-range .22. They'd both missed, and Camilla had been caught in the crossfire.

She'd just solved her first crime.

She rewound the last reel of microfiche, turned off the reader, and returned the film to the library desk. If she was going to save Nat from Jackson, and Amerigo – and from himself – she had to find J.J. Jackson before he did, arrest him, and put him on ice. Given the high profile of Camilla's shooting, the Miss Liberty case, she'd have to do it by the book.

Easy as one, two, ten.

She headed to her apartment with her goal in mind and absolutely no idea how to get there.

Take J.J. Jackson by the book? If she arrested him for pimping, he'd be out in no time. If she arrested him for murdering Angel Rico, she'd have to explain to the DA why Jackson was a suspect in the killing, which would put Nat in the frying pan. Same if she booked Jackson for shooting Camilla. Q: Tell me, Officer Shaw, why do you suppose Mr Jackson took a shot at Camilla Bissonette? A: He was aiming at Detective Hennessy and missed? Q: Very good. And why was he aiming at Detective Hennessy? A: Because Hennessy had hired a hit man named Angel Rico to kill him? Sooner or later that's where it would end up. Talk about screwing your partner. If she was going to save him, she'd have to figure out something slicker than that, and she'd have to do it on her own.

She walked with a little less bounce in her step.

Slow down, you're getting ahead of yourself. First thing you have to do is what you failed to do with Dolly.

You have to find J.J. Jackson.

The black stretch headed for LaGuardia Airport carrying a forty-something passenger in a striped gray suit, two-colored shirt, leather-tipped braces, and a yellow power tie, the uniform of Wall Street. As the limo approached the EZ Pass lane at the Triborough Bridge, the man leaned forward and asked the driver to pick up a newspaper.

J.J. Jackson swung left into the pay lane and rolled down his window and bought a *Post* from a kid with a canvas money apron around his waist. When J.J. saw the headline, he bought two, passing one through the open privacy window. He usually read only the sports section, but this story had grabbed his attention: SLEEPING BEAUTY WAKES UP.

The passenger read in silence as Jackson swung back into an EZ Pass lane and crossed the bridge. 'Looks like this girl is out of her coma but isn't out of the woods,' the man said to his driver. 'She still can't remember anything or talk right, or walk. Pretty sickening.'

Jackson said, 'Makes you wonder if she'd be better off dead.'

'Good-looking girl, too,' the passenger said. He read more. 'And now her boyfriend is all fucked up after somebody tried to kill him, too. Gotta be the same guy, right?'

'Of course, but they'll never catch him.'

'Why not?'

'He's too smart.'

'Hey, sleeping beauty.'

She opened her eyes and raised her head instinctively. 'Hello, Doctor.'

Cush sat on a stool next to the large, stainless-steel whirlpool tub. 'What are you wearing in there?'

'Nothing. Why?'

He felt a pleasant flush. 'Awake for one day and already you're getting by with murder.'

'Murder? Who?'

'It's a figure of speech.' He reminded himself that she didn't understand abstractions – metaphors, irony, sarcasm, *double entendres*.

It was only nine o'clock in the morning and having finished her first rehab session, she reclined in the whirlpool with her neck nuzzled on a towel-covered headrest, her eyes closed, her face dripping with perspiration. The buoyant water gave her body a light and heavenly feeling, suspending the paralysis on her right side.

'When am I getting out of here?' she said.

'One day at a time. Once you master the treadmill, they'll move you to the parallel bars and teach you how to walk on different surfaces – wood, tile, rubber mat, things like that. Then you'll use an aluminum walker, crutches, a cane, and before you know it, nothing.'

'How long will it take?'

On a sliding scale of neurological damage known as the

Rancho System, she'd been classified as a five after the operation – not good, but not impossibly bad. Her muscle tone and coordination made her a strong candidate to regain her motor control.

'I've seen patients do it in a week,' he said, 'and I've seen some do it in six months.' He'd also had Rancho fives who could never do it at all. What bothered him most, though, was a different set of unknowns.

Rodriguez caught Cush going out the door of the lab. 'Where you off to?' It was a question he ordinarily would not have asked his boss, but in the last two days he'd had reason.

'I'll be upstairs making rounds,' Cush said.

Making rounds? Sure he was. 'We're ready to try the new cold scan,' Rod said.

'Go ahead and get started and I'll be right down.'

'You want us to start without you?'

Cush looked at him as if he didn't understand. 'Is there a problem with that?'

Rodriguez pushed the door closed gently, saying nothing until it was shut. 'If you don't mind my asking, what's the situation, Cush? I've seen you in the lab maybe fifteen minutes since you came back from Mississippi. You're with your . . . *patients* more now than you have been in years.'

'We've just done the most extensive scans and repair we've ever tried, Rod, where else should I be?' He looked at his watch, then at Rod. 'I'll be back in twenty minutes.' He reached out and opened the door. 'I want to do another temporal lobe scan on Camilla tonight.'

'It's not going to show us anything new,' Rod said, but Cush had his back turned. As he went out, Rod said, 'The best way to save her is to get back in the lab, Cush. We're still pioneering this thing, you know?'

'Black goes first.'

She heard what he said and lifted her left hand, but he returned it and made her use her right instead. She slowly moved a checker diagonally onto a black square, getting the hang of small muscle movement.

'Do you remember how to play?' he asked.

'I think so. Do you?'

'Oh, yeah,' he said. 'One summer when I was a kid, I had scarlet fever and the county board of health quarantined me, so I played checkers all the time.' He moved a red disc. 'I slept in the hayloft, and every morning when I woke up I saw this smooth, green field in the distance that sloped on a hillside and had a forest behind it like a meadow in a fairytale book. I could only see a piece of it between a stand of pines and a barn post, which made it very mysterious.'

She moved another checker.

Cush looked over her move and continued. 'At the edge of the woods I could see a tall pine tree with reddish-brown needles that glowed in the sun as if it was on fire. Being little and superstitious, I decided it was a sign from heaven, like Moses's burning bush, telling me something important.' He moved a checker. 'I wanted to see what it had to say, so when I got well, I filled my canteen and got my dog—'

'You had a dog?'

'A yellow lab.'

'What was his name?'

'Old Blue.'

She smiled at him. 'Sarcasm, right?'

'More like irony, but you're getting the point.'

'I love dogs,' she said. She moved a checker straight ahead onto a red square. 'How do I know I love dogs?'

'Your memory's coming back,' he said. 'You have to stay on the black squares.' She corrected herself and made another move. 'Anyway,' he said, 'Old Blue and I went tramping off in search of the green field and the fire tree.' He jumped one of her checkers.

She studied the board and moved another disc. 'Did you find it?'

'No,' he said.

She looked surprised. 'Why not?'

'It wasn't there.' His hand hovered over the board. 'When I reached the place I'd seen from the loft, the whole meadow had vanished and been replaced by a rocky, untillable field I already knew, called the pebble pasture.'

'Maybe you hiked in the wrong direction.'

'That's what I thought, so I climbed back up to the loft, found the tree again, and went after it.'

'Did you find it this time?'

'No. It wasn't there to find.'

'Come on.'

He moved a checker.

'Better not do that,' she said, 'I'll jump you.'

Didn't he wish. 'I tried the next day,' he said, 'but the same thing happened. I sat down next to Old Blue, and the more I thought about it, the spookier it got. Maybe it was a ghost. Maybe it was the scarlet fever, or maybe God was playing a trick on me to teach me a lesson of some kind.' He jumped one of her checkers. 'I made the trip a few more times and gave up. For the rest of the summer I went up to the loft and watched the tree catch fire, wondering what it was all about.' He pointed at the board, your turn.

'What did you think?'

'I decided it wasn't like a burning bush after all, it was more like Noah's rainbow – you know, God's promise not to bring me so close to death again. You remember what a rainbow is, right?'

'A colored arch in the sky.'

'You can see it, but you can't actually find it, just like the fire tree. You don't want to make that move, it sets up a double jump for me.'

She looked crestfallen. 'Too late, I already let go of the checker.'

He reached out and jumped two black pieces and took them.

She reached out and jumped him one, two, three, four times. 'King me.' She'd set him up.

'I'll give you the first three, but the last one wasn't diagonal, you have to take it back.'

'I know that,' she said.

'Then why'd you do it?'

'Never mind.' She moved the last jump back.

She looked up at him and married him to her eyes, drawing a blush. 'You must have been the cutest little boy,' she said, lifting a checker off the board and running it over her lips.

'A bad boy,' he said, reaching out and taking back the checker before she could put it into her mouth. 'Every Sunday I got a swat on the butt from Mrs Farmer for refusing to take a nap on my straw mat.'

'Oh, God, I can just see it.'

What a smile. Amazing. He could see it in her eyes: she was falling in love with him all over again. He touched her cheek with his fingertips, then produced a thermometer and stuck it into her mouth and lifted her wrist to take her pulse.

'So you never found the fire tree?' she said around the thermometer.

'Actually—'

The small white light on the silent telephone next to her bed began blinking. He picked it up and heard Rod say they had a problem, he'd better get down there right away. He hung up the phone and took the thermometer from her mouth. It showed a perfect 98.6. 'I'll be back in a while,' he said, standing up. 'Can I trust you not to cheat, or do I have to memorize the board?'

She lifted another checker to her lips. 'Memorize the board.'

'I don't see any lesions,' Cush said.

He and Rod were examining digital renderings of superfast MRI pictures of the temporal lobes of Camilla's brain, looking for signs of Kluver-Bucy Syndrome. The problem was, even if they found some lesions, their existence predicted nothing specific. Like rabies, you knew the patient had the disease only when you saw certain symptoms, like exploring the environment with your mouth, or becoming sexually aggressive, or suddenly assaulting someone for no apparent reason.

Or worse.

'What makes you think she may have a problem?' Rod said.

'Small signs. Oral manipulation, counting objects in the room.'

'Could be anything.'

Cush looked at his watch. 'Could be.'

'Looks like Hennessy dodged that bullet,' Rod said. 'There are no signs of any Z–5s into the temporal lobes. Even his blind spots are improving.'

Yeah, let's hear it for Hennessy.

Cush left the room.

He sat in his chair next to Camilla's bed, laid his hand on her hip, and shook her gently. She woke with a start, blinked, and rolled onto her back with her eyelids closed.

'How are you feeling?' Cush asked.

'I was dreaming I was alone in a boat and the wind was taking me away from the shore,' she said, opening her eyes, 'and there wasn't anything I could do about it.'

He poured her a glass of water from a carafe.

'When I was nineteen, I used to fly a crop duster,' he said. 'You had to look out for telephone lines and trees when you were spraying, and I used to have this dream I was headed for a string of electrical wires at the end of a field. I'd pull up and fly over them only to see another string above those, then another and another until the plane was standing on its tail.'

'Did you crash?'

'I always woke up.'

She handed him the glass. 'Tell me what happened to the fire tree.'

He checked his watch. 'I'd given up on it until one day when a milk cow didn't come home and I had to go after her. I found her in the pebble pasture I told you about, and while I was looking around for a stick to move her along, I caught a glimpse of a dead branch low on a pine tree a few yards into the woods. Something about it looked strange, so I walked to it and saw a pink glow on the ground. When I looked up I could see the rays of the afternoon sun turning dead needles bright orange as if they were on fire.'

'That was it?'

'It was right there at the edge of the pebble field all along.'

'How did you miss it?'

He shook his head. 'Sometimes things up close looks different from a distance, and vice versa. I knew that hardscrabble field like the palm of my hand, but from the barn I could only see what looked like a slice of grass through the trees. What I couldn't see I made up in my imagination – filled in the blanks, so to speak, with a beautiful green field and a burning tree that no one else could see but me.'

'Were you happy or disappointed you found it?'

'I was happy I'd solved the mystery, but a little sad it was over.'

She touched the checkerboard lying next to her. 'Am I ever going to get out of here?'

'You'll be home before you know it.'

'You probably say that to all your patients.'

'You're not like all my patients.'

'Why not?'

'You really want to know?'

'No, I just asked for no reason.' She smiled at him. 'Irony, right?'

'Sarcasm.'

'I'll never get that right.'

'I love you,' he said.

The words came out too fast, suspending the two of them at the top of a roller coaster.

'That's – certainly special,' she said.

'Sorry,' he said. 'I shouldn't have said that.'

'Why?' She reached out and touched his hand. 'I think – I'm feeling the same way about you.'

He raised her right hand and placed his fingertips against hers, then pushed their hands palm to palm and back out again like a daddy-longlegs doing a push up on a mirror. 'Remember doing this?'

'I wish I did.'

He let go. 'Patients always fall in love with their doctors. You'll get over it the minute you walk out of here.'

'It isn't like that.' She touched his cheek. 'I can't remember anything specific, but I know I've known you before. I can't imagine why we broke up.' She ran her fingers across his lips. 'So soft.'

'You shouldn't do that,' he said. 'I shouldn't let you.'

'Why not?'

'It's not professional.'

'I don't understand.'

'Like hell you don't.'

'OK, maybe I do and don't care.' She pulled herself closer to him.

'You will if somebody walks in on us.'

'You think?' The devil in her eyes. 'What would they do?'

'They'd arrest us and put us in jail.'

'Together?' She laid her hand on his thigh.

It was warm, but a question kept cooling him off: was this really her, or was it clinical behavior she couldn't help?

She put her forehead against his. 'What would you say if I said, kiss me now or you may never get another chance?'

'I wouldn't say anything.'

'Why not?'

'I'd be too busy kissing you.' Correct that. 'Camilla, we shouldn't—'

'Be quiet.' Hand on his cheek. 'If you don't kiss me now, you may never get another—'

A single knock and the door opened – Cush snapped around expecting to see Hennessy in a rage.

This time it was a nurse with a paper cup of pills. Cush stood up while Camilla emptied the pills into her mouth and washed them down. After the nurse left, Camilla smiled at Cush and patted the bed next to her, come sit by me. When he didn't, she crumpled up the paper cup into a little ball, put it into her mouth, and began chewing it like bubble gum, still smiling at him.

Oh, God. It's happening.

Shaw entered the 144th Precinct and asked the desk sergeant where she could find an officer named Orlando Kline. She had gone to undercover school with him and they had stayed in touch from time to time while she was working Vice.

She showed Orlando a column she'd cut out of the *Daily News* about a man arrested in the Bronx following a two-year investigation into loan sharking and numbers. The columnist was outraged that a man like this could enter a guilty plea, be fined fifteen hundred dollars – 'an easy afternoon's take' – and walk out the door. What had caught Shaw's attention was the last paragraph describing the defendant as a Bronx entrepreneur who made 'pimpmobiles', a man named Joseph Romano.

Shaw handed the article to her friend and pointed at Romano's photograph. 'You know this guy?'

Orlando Kline took a look. 'Yeah, I know him, I did a stakeout on him six months ago. He stretched Caddys and Continentals.'

Interesting. 'Have you ever run into a limo driver named J.J. Jackson?'

Kline pooched out his lips and shook his head no.

Shaw wrote Jackson's name and her office telephone number on a piece of notebook paper and handed it to him. 'Ask your guys to let the girls on the street know I'm looking for him, would you? And give me a call if you hear something?'

Kline said he'd spread the word, then walked her to the door, hitting on her lightly: you look good, how about dinner sometime? She gave him a smile that said, how sweet of you, not a chance, and drove over to Romano's body shop and sat in her car across the street. Waiting for something to happen, she made a list of all the hookers she knew who might have heard the names Joe Romano or J.J. Jackson. When she finished, she dropped the car into gear and returned to Manhattan.

Back at the station house, she started tracking down the names on her list while simultaneously investigating a credit card theft she'd caught. Sometimes asking around the street worked, sometimes it didn't. If it didn't, she'd hit the corners herself and try to find what she needed. She was into this now. She had no choice.

He stood at her door the next morning like a high-school freshman on his first date, ripping through his last-second checklist: hair combed, face shaved, no cologne, two buttons open at the collar – no, make that one, you don't want to look like Zorro.

He touched his pants pocket and felt the sapphire and diamond engagement ring he'd given her a few months before. Would she remember it? He had no idea. When you were on a blind date with the woman you slept with, anything was possible.

He sniffed the flowers he held in a cellophane megaphone and debated his decision to tell her who'd shot her and why. But then the door opened and everything got wiped from his mind.

There she was. Alive and on her feet. Stunning.

She wore a cotton skirt and a simple blouse, and was without makeup or jewelry. Despite the blind spots in his eyes, he saw her face. The slight loss of weight made her cheekbones appear higher than before, her eyes larger and darker, her lips fuller. And her hair – my Lord. It was thick and shiny again, inviting his fingers up the nape of her neck. A touch of color had replaced her hospital pallor. He knew about her motor control problem, her aphasia and amnesia, but at the moment he was a kid looking for a way home, and she was the yellow ribbon on the tree.

She opened the door wide and ushered him into the room. He handed her the flowers.

'Aren't you sweet,' she said. 'What are they?'

'Freesias, your favorite.'

438

She sniffed them. 'They smell like something I've smelled before.'

'A cello,' he said.

She looked confused.

'You always said freesias smelled like harps and cellos.'

'Really?' She smelled them again. 'What a lovely idea.' She looked around for something to put them in, reminding him that he'd forgotten a vase. 'Sit down, I'll be right back,' she said.

He walked to a leather-cushioned chair facing an identical one on the other side of a coffee table. Sitting in the middle of it was a large vase of long-stemmed red roses, enormous and beautiful. Turning to sit, he saw her hobbling toward the bathroom on crutches.

My God, what had he done to her?

He looked around the room and recalled the hours he'd spent here after the shooting. The Venetian blinds were lifted now, painting the floor with bushy-tailed morning light, and the made-up bed seemed smaller and less ominous with its side rails down and its clean, crisp sheets tautly tucked. There were other signs of normalcy, too, like newspapers, get-well cards, and file folders with her grandmother's diary and papers. And the roses. He saw a card dangling on a ribbon with indecipherable handwriting on it – a doctor's scribbling, no doubt. Vintage Cush Walker, perfectly timed for Nat's visit. Classic, bold, and long-stemmed. *Longer than yours, Hennessy.*

The prick.

She opened the bathroom door and stood with the freesias in a stainless-steel urinal as a vase. He stood up as she limped back and placed the flowers on top of the electronic gear next to her bed, incongruously, like daisies sticking out of the barrel of a gun. He offered her a hand as she leaned her crutches against the back of her chair and shuffled to the front of it and sat. Even crippled, she was graceful.

He pushed the vase of roses aside to get an unobstructed view of her face.

'Well—'

'So—' They both spoke at once.

'You first,' she said.

'No, I was just going to ask how you're feeling,' he said.

'Better, thank you. How about you?'

'I'm fine, just fine, no problem,' he said.

'I understand you have blind spots and a loss of feeling on your left side.'

'Nothing that won't be gone in a few weeks,' he said. He leaned forward with his forearms on his thighs. 'I understand you have amnesia.'

'Big time. It must have come as a shock to you, seeing your fiancée with no idea who you are.'

He minimized it with a smile. 'Who knows, maybe I'll improve my chances that way.' She didn't get it. His smile disappeared. 'Do you remember anything about us?'

'Nothing.' She stared at him with the eyes of someone trying to place a stranger. 'I understand I owe you a large thank you.'

'What for?'

'The brain scan that fixed me.'

'Under the circumstances, it was the least I could do.' *Under the circumstances*. Did she have any idea what he was hinting at? That a guy who gets his fiancée shot would ordinarily try to fix it?

The room turned silent. *Tell her*.

'Camilla—'

She cocked her head and waited.

He said, 'The dog was a terrific surprise.'

'The dog?'

'Your wedding present.'

'I gave you a dog?' she said.

'Yeah. He's really cute.'

'What's his name?'

'He doesn't have one yet, just the initials WFC, Waiting For Camilla. I thought we should name him together.'

'Why would we do that?'

He flushed and reached out and broke a thorn off a rose stem.

'I'm sorry,' she said. 'Cush says I've lost the normal inhibitions people have about what they say.'

'Cush' says? Not Dr Walker? 'No, no, it's refreshing.' He set the thorn on the table top with the flat side down and the tip raked back like the dorsal fin of a shark moving through a sea of glass. 'Is your memory completely gone?'

'I remember some childhood events but not much else. I understand I was an architectural repairman before the accident.'

She's calling it an accident. Tell her what happened. 'You're an architectural restorer,' he said, 'a very good one.'

'It's so strange. I don't even know what that is and yet I have this burning desire to get it back.' She stretched her arms from side to side. 'Cush says I've got a rare form of amnesia that may not be curable. Not very attractive, is it?'

'You're attractive, trust me.' He touched the engagement ring through his pocket.

She stared at him, trying to comprehend. 'Excuse me for saying this, but you must have loved me a lot.'

'I did.' He looked at her open, available face. 'I still do.'

'That's too bad.'

'Why do you say that?'

'Because number one, I don't know you, and number two, I'm in love with my doctor.'

He drove the tip of the thorn into the sworls of his thumb deep enough to let it dangle from his skin. She couldn't be in love with her doctor. Two weeks ago she was in love with him. 'You think you know Walker well enough to say that?'

'Yes. He seems very familiar to me, very safe and warm.

When he takes my pulse it doesn't feel like it's a doctor doing it.'

Doesn't feel like a doctor. This was getting worse by the minute. 'He's your doctor, Cam, he's not supposed to be touching you that way.'

'What way?'

'Getting personal with you while you're in the hospital and your memory's gone.'

'Getting personal?'

Jesus, how literal did he have to be? 'He's trying to get into your pants!'

'What a funny idea. Why would he want to do that?'

'Sex! He wants to have sex with you!'

'Oh, that. That's not going to happen.'

He waited for her to add, *because of you.*

Instead, she said, 'I'd like to, but he says it would be unprofessional.'

He tried to swallow the whole thing, but the 'I'd like to' part just wouldn't go down.

'Frankly,' she said, 'I don't see the problem.'

Jesus Christ, who was this alien who looked like Camilla? Any second now he expected to see her head spin around.

Seeing his face, she said, 'Uh-oh. That didn't come out right, did it?'

He pulled the thorn from his thumb and set it on the glass. Stay cool, this isn't her fault. This might not even be the real her talking. He picked up a tennis ball.

'Oh, I'm glad you reminded me,' she said, reaching out to take it from him. 'I'm supposed to squeeze it for strength and coordination.' She began kneading it in her right hand. Then she saw blood on it. 'What's this?' He held up his thumb and showed her a thin red line streaking into his palm. 'You're bleeding,' she said.

'It's just a thorn.' He sucked the blood off the wound and

pressed it against the palm of his other hand. After a moment, he stood up and dragged his chair next to hers. Walker might have been a brilliant manipulator of molecules, but he didn't know shit about manipulating a cop.

'It's very common, you know,' he said.

'What is?'

'Patients falling in love with their doctors.'

She began squeezing the tennis ball again, concentrating on it like a juggler. 'He and I were in love before.'

'Do you remember that?'

'No, but I found some of his letters and photographs and things I wrote about him in my diary. And he's been telling me about us.'

I'll bet he has. 'I have some photographs of us too.'

'Really? I'd love to see them.'

'I'll bring them by.' He watched her exercise her hand. 'Has he told you why you broke up with him?'

'He says it was over a misunderstanding of some kind, but he's not exactly sure what.' She looked at him. 'Do you know what it was?'

'Not . . . exactly.' His paused to impregnate his answer.

'What does that mean?'

'I know a few things about him.'

'What kind of things?'

'Personal.'

'Things I told you?'

'Among others.'

'Oh, no – what did I say?' She brought the tennis ball to her mouth.

'Don't worry, getting you to talk about an old boyfriend was impossible. According to you, current love lives are basic, past ones are baroque.'

'That sounds vaguely familiar,' she said. She raised her eyebrows and came up empty. 'But then, lots of things do. I can never tell when I'm really remembering something or when I'm making it up. What's baroque?'

'It means superficial.'

She set down the tennis ball and reached for a pad of paper and a pencil. After writing down the word, she looked at Nat sympathetically. 'This must be very hard for you, hearing me talking about another man.'

'All things considered, I'd rather be in Philadelphia.'

'What's in Philadelphia?'

'Sorry. You still don't recall anything about me?'

She examined him with an artist's eyes. 'I'm trying. You seem . . . impatient. Jealous, maybe?'

'Jealous for sure.'

'Are you angry with me?'

'Not in the least. If I'm angry at anyone, it's myself.'

'Why?'

Because I did this to you. 'It's the nature of the Irish.'

'I don't know what that means.'

'Neither do I.' Another fine choice of words. 'Would you like me to get you a soft drink?'

'No, but a glass of water would be nice. There's some in that bottle – or did I tell you that already?'

'It's a carafe, if you're looking for new words.'

'Carafe.'

He poured them both a glass and handed her one. 'You shouldn't get involved with Cush Walker until you get your memory back, Cam. And I intend to do everything in my power to make sure he tries to cure you.'

'He's my doctor, why wouldn't he?'

'Because he's afraid of what you'll remember.'

'About what?'

'Why you're in love with me instead of him, for one thing. And what you found out about him before you were shot.'

'That sounds sinister.'

'I think it is.'

Nat stared at his glass of water, envying its clarity. Should he tell her about Spider Murphy and Roy Driggers and a disease called KBS? Should he try to remind her of what she'd unraveled before the bullet arrived? 'Ask him about Roy Driggers,' he said, breaking off another rose thorn and placing it beside the first one.

'Who's Roy Driggers?'

'That's what you should ask him. And while you're at it, ask him how Driggers managed to contract KBS.'

'What's KBS?' she asked. Too much information. She frowned and picked up the pad and pencil.

'It's a very bad brain disease.'

She took a note. 'Cush says you hate him because he's black,' she said. 'Is that true?'

'I don't know how to answer that.'

'What's wrong with yes or no?'

The old Camilla's inside her, all right. God, he missed her. 'It's more complicated than that.'

'In what way?'

'I don't hate him because he's black, I hate him because he's more powerful than I am. At least at the moment.'

'In what way?'

'He's your doctor, and he's this big deal, prize-winning scientist. And he's very arrogant.'

'I think I know what that means.' She paused. 'What's that mean?'

'He thinks he's smarter than other people.'

'But he is.'

That hurt. 'He doesn't have to act like it.' The word *uppity* wanted to come out. She was having a hard time with this, and so was he. 'The biggest problem I have is that he's trying to take you away from me.'

'He's not taking me,' she said. 'I'm going on my own.'

That hurt more.

She said, 'So his being black doesn't have anything to do with how you feel about him?'

'I wouldn't – I can't honestly say it doesn't have anything to do with it,' he said. 'I know it's not the way you're supposed to think these days, but sometimes race gives you an idea of who somebody is.'

'That's so strange,' she said.

'Not really. Everybody assumes that people they don't know have certain general characteristics.'

'Like what?'

'Oh, you know. Protestants are cold fish, Jews like money, the Irish drink too much.'

'What's wrong with the French?'

'Generally speaking, they're assholes.'

Her face went blank, then he remembered: *Bissonette*. Christ.

'Individually, of course, they can be quite wonderful,' he said.

'Nice try,' she said. She set her glass on the table, whispering a word to herself that sounded like 'sarcasm'.

'Let me ask you something,' he said. 'Do you remember solving a mystery just before you were shot?'

'No, but isn't that interesting, Cush asked me the same question.'

I'll bet he did. Nat reached out and pushed the thorn representing his shark ahead of Cush's.

She said, 'Apparently it's not unusual to forget something you learn right before a head injury.'

'Lucky for him.'

'What makes you say that?'

I'm not sure. In fact, half the time I'm sure it's about me. Now's the perfect time to tell her.

His toes curled up in his shoes. But if you tell her you caused her injury – before she knows anything else about you – forget about Cush Walker, you won't stand a chance.

'Maybe the mystery was about my grandmother,' she said. 'I've been reading her diary and it's full of interesting information.' She picked up the brown leather book from the coffee table and opened it.

The door opened and Nurse Punt stuck her head inside for a moment and said Nat's time was up.

He dropped his hands onto his knees as she closed the door. 'I should be going,' he said quietly. 'But I'll be back. I live right down the hall until they let me out of here.'

She put down the diary as he stood up, then reached for his hands so that he could help her to her feet. Finding her balance, she faced him and rested her hands on his. He drew her into a silent embrace, a sailor giving his girl a last hug as the ship's horn called. They were close enough to the bed to touch it, but it was made of stone.

She pulled back far enough to look at him. 'I'm sorry, Nat.'

'Don't say that,' he said. 'It sounds too final. I'm not giving up.'

'You have to.' She pushed him away, establishing their official distance. 'When you think of me, try thinking about the part of me that's black and it'll be easier for you.'

What a weird, cockeyed thing to say. His face must have shown it.

'Considering how you feel about black people,' she continued, 'I thought it might help you get over me.' She looked at his confused expression. 'Oh, don't tell me – you didn't know?'

'Know what?'

'That I'm part black.'

There went her head again, doing another three-sixty. 'What are you talking about?'

'My grandmother's diary,' she said, pointing. 'My biological grandfather was a black man. Didn't we talk about that before the accident?'

Now *his* head was spinning. 'No, we didn't.'

There was a firm knock at the door, Nurse Punt's last warning. Camilla reached out and put her hand on the pull. 'We'll have to continue some other time,' she said, opening the door.

My God. She was kicking him out before the mushroom cloud had begun to settle.

She was sitting at a table in the third-floor cafeteria with her cane propped against the table eating tuna fish salad with potato chips and drinking a cup of hot tea. Cush set his tray across from hers and sat down to a peanut butter and grape jelly sandwich on white bread and a Coke.

'A reporter from *Modern Behavior* magazine wants to interview you,' he said.

'About what?'

'Your recovery.'

'Good, I'm bored out of my mind.' She lifted the tea bag and watched it dangle at the end of the string – then her face went blank. 'Wait a second. I remember something.'

'What is it?'

'I remember the restaurant the night we broke up.'

'What's it look like?'

'I can see large red leather booths, candles with little lamp shades on the table, and a lavish ladies' room with lots of white marble. I remember being there and talking about – wait a minute.' She looked at him with wide, Audrey Hepburn eyes.

'Talking about what?' he asked.

'Roy Driggers,' she said. Her mind returned to the present. She tilted her head back and dropped the tea bag into her mouth as if it was a goldfish held by its tail. Chewing it slowly, she looked across the table at Cush and asked him: 'Who's Roy Driggers?'

He was in luck: there was no one in the workout room except himself and Cush Walker. He wasted no time getting to it.

After leaving Camilla's room, Nat had gone searching for the doctor, replaying his conversation with her each step of the way.

She loved the way 'Cush' took her pulse. She loved falling in love with him. She'd love to have sex with him if only he'd let her. Fuck. And then the final kick in the ass – I'm part black, Nat, and you're not, but since you don't like blacks anyway, isn't that swell? Now you can get over me in no time. Oh, man.

Walker must have loved hearing she's got a touch of black blood. The racist bastard.

By the time Nat located Nurse Punt, who said the doctor was working out in the gym, he was deeply, fully steamed. He found a baggy white hospital T-shirt and pair of basketball shorts, then put on his black street shoes – couldn't find a pair of sneakers – and headed for the gym looking like a pissed-off geek.

Entering the room, he saw Cush standing behind a slant board isolating his biceps with a twenty-five-pound weight, looking perfect in his tailored gray sweatpants, white sneakers, and a navy T-shirt. He had to have seen Nat coming, but he paid no attention.

Nat stepped in front of the board and stood watching him. When Cush still didn't respond, Nat stepped forward and pushed his shoulder, knocking him off balance and the barbell to the floor, *ka-clang*.

Cush glared at him, sweating. Saying nothing, he walked over to a counter and picked up a four-foot-long stainless-steel bar that hooked onto a pull-down chain on an exercise machine, carried it to the doors, and stuck it through the double pull handles, barring anyone from entering.

Nat took off his shoes. Cush used his toes to pull off his sneakers at the heels, then peeled off his socks. They stepped onto a large exercise pad and began circling each other.

'I should tell you I boxed in high school,' Nat said.

'I'm petrified,' Cush said. Half a circle later, he said, 'I should tell you I wrestled.'

Wrestled? Not good. Unless a boxer landed the first punch he didn't stand a chance against a wrestler, at least not once a wrestler got inside the boxer's reach.

Cush stopped circling and stood up straight. 'This is not a smart idea, Hennessy.'

'For who?'

'Either of us.'

Nat continued to circle. 'We're always on your turf,' he said. 'Why don't you get up enough guts to come onto mine?'

'It's not about guts, it's about doing something dangerous—'

Nat jabbed with his left once, twice, and hooked with his right.

Cush ducked and dropped into a squat, ran his arm and shoulder between Nat's legs, and exploded upward against his crotch, lifting him into the air like a sack of meal, then dropping him onto his back – the worst position a boxer could be in. Before Nat could move, Cush had fallen across his chest like a cowboy tying a calf and ran his left arm under Nat's chin and around the back of his neck in a half-nelson. He used his other hand to pin Nat's free hand to the mat. Nat did the only thing he could: held still and breathed hard.

'What the hell is wrong with you?' Cush huffed.

Nat didn't answer. He didn't know about competitive holds, only that if he didn't get off his back he didn't have a chance.

'I don't get into fights with my patients,' Cush said, '. . . not even the ones who need . . . their butts kicked.'

Nat bucked and wriggled until he'd worked his right hand between Cush's chest and his own. Using nothing but muscle, he twisted onto his left side, then onto his stomach, then moved onto his hands and knees in a tight, egg-shaped ball with his arms tucked hard against his chest. Cush still controlled the mat.

Nat gathered his strength and swung his legs in front of himself in a one-eighty pivot and up into a squat. Before Cush could pull him back he charged the doctor like a linebacker and slammed him onto the floor. Surprised by the move, Cush swiveled into a new position, but not before Nat had turned Cush's arm into a chicken wing. Suddenly, the doctor was in a hammer lock and a police-hold hand crunch, his fingers bent down toward his own wrist. Pain burst onto his face and his head fell backwards. They rose to their knees with Nat still behind.

Cush got one foot on the ground, pushed up, and staggered into a standing position.

They were both on their feet with Nat in control of Cush's extremities except for one: his free hand. It moved behind Nat's back and grabbed him by the balls – not with a doctor's professional touch, more with the gentleness of a blacksmith gripping a horseshoe. For a brief instant the two men stood in an equilibrium of air-sucking agony, then, almost as if by agreement, they released each other and separated, sweating like mules, massaging aching joints, trying not to show each other where they hurt. Breathing hard, they began to circle each other again.

Nat assumed a boxer's stance and bobbed and weaved, looking for an opening, careful not to try a hasty punch this time. He jabbed at Cush lightly and moved around him erratically, turning Mohammed Ali's formula on its head, stinging like a butterfly, dancing like a bee.

'I'm finished with this,' Cush said.

Before he turned away, Nat jabbed at him, once, twice. Cush grabbed his wrist; Nat, not wanting to be thrown the way he was before, pulled back to break the grip, placing himself off balance. In one motion, Cush stepped behind him, ran his hands under his armpits, and locked his fingers behind Nat's neck in a full nelson.

Nat's arms were spread out to the sides like a scarecrow's and his head was bent forward and down. He tried to sweep Cush off his feet with a backward kick but it only made matters worse, dropping him to his knees. This time Cush was taking no prisoners. Nat's head bowed forward onto the mat.

'Hang it up,' Cush panted.

'Fuck you,' Nat answered. He rested a moment, then tried to reach behind him and grab any part of Cush he could find – hair, head, face, whatever. He wasn't even close. 'Hitting on a patient with amnesia,' he said. 'You're sicker . . . than she is.'

With the top of Nat's scalp resting on the mat, he could see Cush's knees behind him, upside down. The pain was now running down his neck to the base of his spine, cramping his lats. He was in trouble. 'Ah, shit,' he groaned.

'Listen to me,' Cush said. 'Nothing is going to happen between me and her until she's well.'

'Bull . . . shit,' Nat said. 'Beautiful white girl . . . touch of black blood . . . You can't . . . help yourself.'

Nat felt Cush freeze.

Huh? He didn't know? Hell, no, he didn't know – she hadn't told him. What a *great* sucker punch!

Cush bore down.

'Ahhhhhhhh,' Nat yelled.

'We're quitting on three, understand?' Cush said.

'Why should I quit . . . when I'm winning?'

'One . . . two . . . three.'

Nat tried to rear up and buck Cush off his back.

Cush held him down again.

Nat was holding his breath and exhaling in spurts, trying to deal with the pain. They were both running down.

Cush said, 'For a detective . . . you're not all that bright . . . are you?' He let go and pushed Nat onto his side. After catching his breath, Cush got to his feet, removed the metal bar from the door handles, and laid it on the counter. 'Let me tell you something,' he said, his hand on the door. 'Roy Driggers' middle name was Montavius. He hated it so much he wouldn't have used it to collect the lottery.' He left.

Nat got to his feet a minute later and walked to the door with a limp. Now he had something else to think about: Roy Montavius Driggers.

If Roy Driggers wasn't Patient RAD, who the hell was?

'I don't know how you managed to accomplish this,' Shaw said, 'but you look worse now than you did in the basement of Radio City.'

Nat flopped onto the passenger seat of the car holding an ice cube on his lip. His face was red and swollen, his neck still aching from Cush's full nelson.

'Glad to see you, too,' he said. Actually, he was.

She started the engine. 'What in God's name happened to you? You look like you were in a street brawl.'

'I was.'

'Here's a novel idea. Try winning sometime.' She pulled away from the hospital curb. According to NYPD regulations, an injured officer was required to be examined by a police surgeon at his assigned medical unit before he could return to active duty. Nat had taken a taxi from his wrestling match with Cush to the Queens med unit in order to be examined – not for the fight, but for the injuries he'd sustained at Radio City Music Hall. Rather than tell them about Cush's overheated brain scan – how could he explain that? – he let the Health Service's physician assume that his vision problems and the deadened nerves on his left side had come from his near-hanging at Radio City. To avoid being sent to a neurologist for further tests – all those forms, all those questions – he had the examining doctor call Cush Walker – yes, *that* Dr Walker – whom Nat said he'd visited after walking out of the ER. Even without a heads-up,

Cush played along, giving the police department doctor an accurate diagnosis of Nat's problems without mentioning the brain scan.

'How is Camilla?' Shaw asked.

'Better in some ways, not in others.'

'And what's wrong with you?' she said.

'I've got minor lesions in the left parietal cortex leading to a left-side disturbance of discriminatory sensations. Specifically, sensory inattention and partial extinction.'

'Huh?'

'I've lost feeling in my left side and I have blind spots in both eyes.'

'Jackson did that to you?'

'Something like that.'

'So what's this mean? You're, like, paralyzed?'

'More like numb. They poke you in the ribs with a pin and you sit there and watch but don't care.'

'This could be useful.'

'I'm sure.'

They rode in silence, trying to imagine what the other had in mind.

'So, is this permanent?' she said.

'They say I'll get over it anywhere from a few weeks to a couple of years. Nobody knows for sure.'

'Can you work?'

'Sure, but the department's dickhead assistant surgeon doesn't think so. He put me on restricted duty in command.'

They both knew what that meant: no enforcement activity allowed, only shuffling papers and answering the telephone and going slightly crazy in detective hell.

'You gotta get back on enforcement,' she said. 'Amerigo's assigned me to Hart and Jacobs.'

Hart the Fart, what a bummer. He was a fireplug with a bald spot who passed gas and picked his teeth and acted like a regular on *NYPD Blue*. But he'd been helpful at the BIAS union meeting.

'What kind of cases are you catching?' he said.

'Oh, really big ones,' she said. 'A credit card stolen at Macys, a runaway at the Port Authority, a box of stolen jeans. Last night I interviewed a refugee from the sixties who got stoned on Drano at Madison Square Garden.'

'The tribute to the Grateful Dead?'

'That's the one.'

'Damn, I wanted to catch that.'

She gave the windshield a smile. 'I myself would rather drink Drano than admit this, but I've actually missed you the last few days.' They came out of the midtown tunnel and merged into the molasses of trucks and cars crossing Manhattan.

'So, did you tell them?' he asked.

'Of course not.' She was irritated with the question. 'You're my partner, why would I do that? Once I give them Jackson's name, Amerigo is going to ask me how I got it, and three questions later he's going to figure out you hired Angel Rico to be your hit man, whether I tell him or not. He's already highly suspicious of what's going on.'

Nat tossed the ice cube out the window.

'At the moment,' she said, 'I'm operating under the assumption that there's a meaningful difference between outright lying, which I haven't had to do yet, and staying silent, which is probably just as bad, but I'd appreciate it if you wouldn't tell me it is.'

'How'd you figure it out?'

'You keep forgetting I'm a detective,' she said. 'I found out what happened to your father.'

He didn't respond.

'Also, I owe you,' she said.

'For what?'

'Leaving you in the basement with Jackson.'

'You didn't leave me, I told you to go.'

'I didn't have to listen.'

They drove south toward his loft. 'Drop me at Vic's Billiards, would you?'

'Jesus, Nat, you come out of the hospital looking like death and you want to shoot pool?'

'I've got some personal business to tend to.'

She turned at the next corner and pulled up. 'You gotta give it up, Nat. You're going to wreck yourself trying to get Jackson. Let the guys in Major Case or the Bureau find him and prosecute him on charges that have nothing to do with you and Rico.'

'It's too late for that,' Nat said. 'If you think I'm in trouble now, what do you think's going to happen if they arrest him and start grilling him?'

'How can he tell them what you did with Angel Rico? He killed the guy.'

'He'd concoct a cover for himself and go for reduced time for ratting me out.' He looked at her seriously. 'How many months you suppose a corrupt detective is worth?'

'You're not corrupt, Nat. You made a mistake.'

'Yeah, well, don't you make one too.' He opened the door and got out.

She spoke to him through the open window. 'What are you going to do?'

What was he going to do? There was this fucked-up body to tend to, bruises on his neck and stretched ligaments from Radio City, lesions in his cortex, a blind spot in his eyes, loss of feeling on his left side, and a killer headache that came and went just for the fun of it. There was J.J. Jackson still out there roaming around like a pissed-off cowboy with an Uzi, ready to kill him if he didn't find him first, ready to give him up to the IAB if he did. And there was Camilla, his almost-bride, who in her screwed-up condition didn't even remember who he was and had fallen in love with Dr Cush Walker, egghead Superman. What was he going to do?

'First things first,' he said. He reached through the window and tapped a goodbye on the dashboard.

'Want me to wait?' she said.

'I'll grab a cab.'

'You look like hell.'

'Cab drivers don't care.'

'I think I should wait.'

'Shaw?'

'Yeah?'

'Don't wait.'

By the time it had ended, Camilla had mixed emotions about the interview. On the one hand, she thought Cush was right: Cynthia Weber was sympathetic and her magazine wasn't trying to embarrass her, although, as Cush had warned, there were the inevitable questions about her sex life. Weber said she thought Dr Walker was a real hunk – didn't she agree? To which Camilla asked, hunk of what? To which Weber said, you're putting me on, right? To which Camilla said, I'm not putting you on anything, I'm not even touching you. To which Weber said, you're scaring me, Camilla, so Camilla stopped asking questions. Weber then asked her if she was falling in love with her doctor. To which Camilla said, oh, yes, definitely, and watched Weber take a fast note. And sex? What about it? Camilla asked. Let's start with have you had any since the shooting? No, Camilla said, but she would soon. Seeing Weber scribble wildly, she thought she'd better stop talking about the subject of sex, although why it was such a hot topic to everyone but her continued to mystify her.

She liked Weber, but she also envied her. They were about the same age, but worlds apart. Weber looked like one of the women Camilla saw on television who had something to do with her life besides get well from a coma, a professional who wore interesting clothes and makeup and was nicely disheveled from working. Watching her, Camilla guessed that she herself must have once possessed some of these qualities. The thought depressed her.

Weber gathered up her gear and stood up to leave. 'I don't

know exactly how your doctor's going to do it,' she said, 'but if anyone can cure you, he can. With those eyes and hands?' She rolled her eyes. 'He can put me on his table and operate on me any day he wants.'

'Are you sick?'

There it was again, that look on Weber's face that said, you don't get it, do you?

'Good luck,' Weber said, shaking hands, 'and let me know if there's anything I can do for you.'

'Actually, there is,' Camilla said. How should she say this? 'When I get bored I read medical manuals to entertain myself, and the other day I came across something I haven't been able to find in the medical dictionary. Do you think you could look it up for me?'

'I can try,' Weber said, taking a pad and pencil from her bag. 'What is it?'

'A disease with three initials,' Camilla said. 'KBS.'

Nat squeezed the balls around the black number eight and lifted the wooden rack, leaving the set in a perfect triangle. His friend set the cue ball slightly off center, made a solid bridge with five fingers, and leaned into it, undisturbed by throbbing woofers, loud conversation, or the clatter of glass on a wooden bar. He drove the cue forward, a matador making the kill.

Smack.

The balls scattered. Just before they stopped, the fifteen dropped into the corner pocket.

His friend pulled a letter from his pocket and handed it to Nat. 'It's a little strange,' he said. He moved around the table, chalking his cue tip as he found his next shot. 'The three.' He bent forward beneath the hanging lamp and shot with the ease of a bass player using a bow, sinking the three ball without touching the cushion.

Nat finished reading the letter and looked up. At a dollar a ball, this was going to be an expensive night. His friend Tommy Kingman – 'Soft Touch Tommy' to pool players, anything but a soft touch to the guys he put in jail – was an assistant district attorney for Manhattan whom Nat had worked with for six years. 'What's so strange about it?'

Kingman leaned forward, head low, eyes at the top of the sockets, his tongue poked out between his lips. The shot was obvious; no need to call it. He stroked the cue and sunk the nine.

'Mississippi law gives the state medical examiner the right to exhume a corpse without a court order in cases of suspected homicide. That's the state ME's authorization letter you're holding in your hands.'

'Does that mean I don't have to go back to Judge Pretty for permission to disinter the body?'

'Maybe yes, maybe no. There's a wrinkle. The five,' he said, calling the pocket with a touch of the tip of his cue.

A wrinkle. If it was the law, there was always a wrinkle.

Kingman lined up the shot. 'Ordinarily, the medical examiner knows where the body to be disinterred is buried, like in a cemetery plot, so the only question is whether to perform an autopsy in order to check out the possibility of foul play.' He practiced his stroke two, three times. 'In your case, you don't know whether the body is in the grave you want to dig up or not.' He took his shot: *tap, bump, bump, crack*. The five rolled toward the pocket, touched the rubber cushion, and dropped like a perfect putt.

Nat set his beer bottle on the flat edge. Kingman stalked the table. 'The county prosecutor might try to stop you from using the law in this somewhat unexpected and novel way.'

Great. Another member of Cush Walker's Mississippi mutual admiration society to contend with. 'Where does that leave me?'

'Thirteen in the corner,' Kingman said.

'Which corner?' Nat said.

'Fuck you.'

Tap, crack . . . roll . . . ka-thunk.

'If I were you,' Kingman said, straightening up, 'I'd take that letter back to Judge Pretty and try to get him to bless it.'

'I thought you said I didn't have to?'

'I said maybe you didn't.'

'And if he doesn't agree?'

'Then you can appeal his decision, or you can listen to the best two words a prosecutor can ever hear: case closed.' He stooped down and closed an eye and measured a shot.

'No way is the county prosecutor going to support this.'

'Don't be so sure. He may not like it, but he can't just arbitrarily kiss off a state official who claims to be exercising statutory authority.'

'I thought you just said he could.'

'I said maybe he could.' Kingman stood up and bent over the table. 'Two bucks on the side says the seven drops here.'

'Go for it.'

'There's another reason you should try to get the cooperation of the county authorities down there,' Kingman said, poking his tongue between his lips again.

'What's that?'

'Who else is going to dig up the body?'

He stroked the cue ball lovingly and watched it caress the seven and drop in as advertised. Nat didn't mind. He liked it when Kingman was on target.

She had waited for him anyway.

Sally stopped in front of the loft and left the engine running.

'Thanks for the lift,' Nat said.

'You needed it.'

'Want to come up for a cup of coffee?'

Yes, she did, but she sure didn't need to get started down that road. Cut the crap, Sal, he's just talking coffee. 'I think I'd better pass.'

'I can show you the pup.'

'How's he doing?'

'Cute as a button.'

'That's dirty pool, Nat, luring me with puppy dogs when I should go home.'

She turned off the engine and got out of the car.

Shaw wandered through the shadowed recesses of Camilla's studio, looking at tools and artifacts and architectural books filled with photographs of repaired objects.

Nat sat on the chaise longue beneath a gooseneck lamp wearing a pair of jeans, a sweatshirt, and a pair of paint-speckled loafers. The dog was on his lap, eyes squinted closed as Nat rubbed him behind the ears. Shaw roamed the studio respectfully, examining a broken Victorian door here, a gold-leafed picture frame there, C-clamps and chisels and fasteners and cans. She liked the feel of the room and the lateness of the hour. She liked hanging out with a man. OK, she liked hanging out with Nat.

'What do you think we should name this guy?' he asked. The dog stretched and came to life and licked Nat on the chin, wagging his tail in a wild, puppy-dog rumba. Nat gave him his favorite stuffed animal, Petey the Parrot, a cartoonish bird with an eye patch, a three-cornered hat, and black felt boots.

Shaw set down a wooden sugar scoop and picked up a Rubik Cube. All eight sides were solid colors. The puzzle had been solved. 'This yours or Camilla's?'

'Mine.'

'You worked this thing?'

'Yeah. Three dimensional geometry, my one claim to fame. If I did personal relations the way I do spatial relations, I'd be set.'

She leaned on a bureau and watched Nat pet the dog. 'OK,'

she said, 'here's the deal. What are you thinking about at this very moment?'

He continued playing with the dog, not looking up. 'Cush Walker and Camilla. Have you ever gone out with a black guy?'

'Yeah, as a matter of fact, I have. What's this?' She held up an old wooden box.

'I think it's a Shaker dovetailed dough bin,' he said.

She turned it around and examined it. 'We lived together for a year,' she said. She put the dough bin down and carried her coffee cup to a wicker chair facing the side of Nat's chaise. The arms had been stripped and were awaiting a fresh coat of stain, but it was comfortable.

She kicked off her shoes and lifted a foot and petted the dog with her toes.

'How'd you meet?' he asked.

'On the job. I was working the street one night when this john got the bright idea he wanted some action right then and there and grabbed me and put me on my back. Somebody saw us and flagged down a radio car and my guy Clyde came to the rescue.'

'My guy Clyde,' Nat said. 'Were you hurt?'

'Only my pride.'

'And you fell in love with Clyde.'

'Love, lust, whatever.' She took a drink. 'Some of both.'

'What was he like?'

'He was a good-looking guy about your height and build, big dimples, a trim mustache – sort of a dark-skinned Clark Gable with the best-looking derrière you ever saw.' She took a sip of her coffee. 'I don't know why, but I have this thing for men with great behinds.'

'You and Camilla.'

Damn, she knew he had one.

'So the color thing wasn't a problem?' he asked.

'Oh, you know, there were the usual people staring at you, guys who looked at him like he was my pimp, liberals who fawned over us like we were the answer to their prayers.'

'Did it drive you nuts?'

'Not really. You got used to it.'

He placed the pup on her lap and took her empty coffee cup and headed for the kitchen. 'And the sex?' he asked. 'Hold your answer until I get back.'

And the sex. She remembered the first time she and Clyde spent the night together, and the never-made beds that followed. She recalled the skin games they played, the sexual stereotypes they indulged to plumb their fantasies and turn up the heat. She remembered his tenderness and selfishness, his lovingness and neediness, his generosity and bad hours on the job, his overbearing awareness of her that drove her crazy and at the same time made him sensitive to what was on her mind. She remembered how, in time, they didn't see each other's skin color at all, not even in bed. And how they both missed it.

Nat returned to the studio and handed her a fresh cup of coffee and sat on the chaise, watching her mesmerize the puppy with a finger stroke on its forehead. 'So?' he said.

'I was just thinking about how you finally tune race out, even in the sex. At first you do it because you think it's what you're supposed to do, but of course that's no more possible than sitting in a corner not thinking about the color red. But after awhile the whole subject gets boring, and while you're still vaguely aware of it, you begin to tune it out, sort of like elevator music. At least in your one-on-one private life. You don't even know you've done it until one day Clyde gets funky and says something that takes you back to your early days together and you think, how about that, I haven't thought about that stuff for months. It's sort of like getting over a cold. You can't put your finger on the exact time it goes away, you just notice one day that it's gone.'

'So why did you break up?'

'Race.' She saw confusion on his face. 'Not in the negative sense, just the opposite. As long as we were into each other's color there was this exotic thing between us, this edge to play with, but once we got to know each other for who we really were, we found out we weren't right together, at least not for the long haul. Instead of being a problem, color turned out to be the glue. It just wasn't enough.'

'What about friends and relatives?'

'They were very decent to us, actually, although looking back, I suppose they never stopped worrying about the kids thing and other people's reactions and all that. Clyde and I never wanted to admit it, but I think it wore us down a little.'

Nat took a drink of coffee. 'You're the psychologist, Shaw. What the heck it is about color that makes people crazy?'

She lifted her cup and looked at the light reflecting off the surface. 'I think it's like an enormous Rorschach test. If you're a white man who's sexually insecure, sex is going to be what bothers you about blacks. If you think you have to be cool in order to be accepted, cool is what you'll like most about blacks. If you hate your parents, having sex with an outsider is really going to stick it to them, and so on. Race isn't about the color of the other guy's skin as much as it's about your own neediness. Which means for white people, it's not about them as much as it's about us.' She lifted one of the puppy's ears.

'You think it works the same way in reverse?'

'Sure it does. You've got black people distrusting whites just because they're white, or black folks assuming you must be privileged no matter how poor or screwed up your life really is. But it's probably a little more understandable when you're holding the short end of the stick.' She lowered the dog's ear and drank some coffee. 'How about you? Did you ever date a black girl?'

'Not unless you count Camilla,' he said. 'Her grandfather was partly black.'

Shaw didn't get it. She turned to a trestle table next to her chair and picked up a framed photograph of Camilla standing with Nat on a beach. 'This girl is part black? She's as white as I am.'

'Sure looks that way, doesn't it?'

'Looks that way?' She set the frame back on the table. 'Looks is the whole point, unless you're— Jesus, Nat, don't tell me you're into race as something more important than color.'

He laid his head back on the chaise. 'I really don't know. I see a lot of crime committed by blacks, but the best partner I ever had was a black guy who took a bullet for me. I think BIAS is a load of shit, but I know we've got a race problem on the force, and for all I know, I'm a part of it. Cush Walker burns my ass, but I'd feel the same way about him if he were white – wouldn't I?' He stretched his hands toward the ceiling, then dropped them and looked at Shaw. 'Obviously, I don't know what I think.'

'Why do you need to think anything? It's not the only problem in life that doesn't have a solution.'

He got up and headed for the kitchen, mumbling something about Eskimos.

'What'd you say? I couldn't hear you,' she said.

He stopped. 'I said, do you suppose Eskimos have illegitimate babies?'

'Where the heck did that come from? Of course they do.'

Of course they do. 'I've always wondered why black people get under my skin, and now I know why.'

'Why?'

'I'm a bigot. It never occurred to me before. You don't think of yourself that way, but it's the only explanation that makes sense.'

'Maybe you are, maybe you're not.'

He continued walking. 'I'm getting the coffee pot. The Scotch is in that cabinet. It's going to be a long night.'

Standing in the shower, he reached out and grabbed the globe-shaped plastic faucet handle. The stream dwindled but didn't stop. He turned the knob harder to the right, feeling the resistance of a screwed-down metal valve against a worn-out rubber gasket. He liked the feeling of softness and firmness at odds with each other, the sense of bone straining against tissue. But the faucet continued to trickle.

He turned the globe harder and listened to it squeal in his hand. The sound of it, human and hurting, sent a pleasant tingle up his arm and down into his groin. He was enjoying this now, standing there naked and muscular, wrenching this thing off.

The faucet defied him, continuing its drizzle. Beat, beat, beat. Nothing did that to J.J. Jackson and got away with it. Nothing. Enforcing his will was basic to who he was. Violence was his nature, and if it wasn't, he would have chosen it anyway because it distinguished him and put bread on the table. Handled right, violence was a skill like any other, except more powerful. It made you hated by some people, but it made you respected with the ones who mattered.

He remembered the rabbits at the good behavior farm where he'd worked, and the prison psychologist's questions. 'Did your mother beat you? Did your father skip out? Were you sexually molested? Did you deliberately kill the white rabbit instead of the black one? Do you hate white people?' No, no, no, and no. Fuckin' fruitloops, they were dumb as concrete. *I love to kill.* Black, white, male, female – it doesn't matter, I'm an equal

470

opportunity hit man. It works. Not one guy I slumped has ever talked back to me. It's not that fuckin' complicated. Not even my old man gets credit for teaching me that.

He pictured his father reaching for the leather . . . remembered his own small hands trying to cover his naked little butt. He could still feel the power of the violence that ensued, and the strange, erotic pain that followed.

He opened and closed his fingers on the globe to get a new grip, then turned it hard to the right, very hard. It cried like a cat but the rivulet of water didn't stop. The neck of the fixture had been screwed down as far as it could go, so he gave it a violent twist and felt it snap off in his hand, popping a piece of plastic against his leg and into the porcelain tub. The fixture rotated loosely now, around and around, offering no resistance. That felt good, too. Very good.

His blood gathered in his middle. Hey, brother, what you doin' down there? Enjoying sex with a shower handle?

He tilted his head back and let the drops of water from the still-leaking shower head beat down on his face and body. His hands roamed.

Beat, beat, beat. What his spinner did to him while he was driving.

Beat, beat, beat. What his father did to him with the razor strap.

Beat, beat, beat. What a great way to start the day.

'Hey, aren't you . . . ?' The man stood in the airplane aisle pointing at Nat, trying to figure him out. 'You're the cop that got shot out on the Statue of Liberty, right?'

'That was my fiancée,' Nat said.

'The girl, right. You got hurt at Radio City, I followed it in the papers. You headed for Atlanta?'

'Jackson, Mississippi.'

The man touched Nat's shoulder, as close to fame as he'd

get today. 'Keep it up. Without guys like you, we'd be living in a jungle.'

A jungle. Nat went back to the morning paper. The front page of the Metro section had a story about the City Council rescheduling the BIAS hearings, quoting a councilman who promised to look into the tape-recording incident as a condition of re-docketing the bill. Nat turned the page.

After finishing the sports section, he leaned back, closed his eyes and thought about baseball. He must have been twelve when the coach traded him to a rival little league team, saying they needed him more, even though he knew that was bullshit. It was because he was different from the other kids on the team. Off center, which made him a little threatening. A kid whose parents were both dead, which meant they had to watch what they said.

He remembered showing up the next week to play for his new team, the former enemy, the slugs in blue satin jackets. Then he remembered how they'd beat the shit out of his old team, and how great it had felt. Good enough to remember even now. If he and Camilla had a little boy, what would they say about him?

He opened his eyes and sat up and found a glass of orange juice on his tray. Taking a drink, he turned the page, hunting for a different article.

'Steinbach's Florist.'

'Disco?'

'Yeah?'

'J.J. Jackson.'

There was silence first, then a breathy voice spoke into a hand cupped around the mouthpiece. 'Ah'm gonna have the cash for you this afternoon, J.J.'

'There you go again, breaking my heart.'

'Come on, man, ah'm gonna have it, no shit.'

'Relax, Disco, it's your lucky day. I'm going to let you work it off.'

'Doin' what?' His voice sounded nervous.

'I want you to deliver some flowers to a hospital room.' J.J. had the morning *Post* open to a story with three photographs of Camilla Bissonette: the first, walking with a cane, her doctor beside her; the second, standing in climbing gear at the Statue of Liberty; and the third, in better days, sitting in a restaurant with friends and her fiancé, Detective Nat Hennessy.

'Who's in the hospital?'

'Meet me at Dede's in half an hour and I'll lay it out.'

'Can't you tell me on the phone, man?' Disco said. 'I leave now, old man Steinbach's gonna fire my ass.'

'Fuck Steinbach, the bitch-ass punk is straight from the ghetto, know what I mean? Bring some flowers and leave your boots in the closet. I want you in sneakers.' *Click.*

Nat found his Avis Chevy in the Jackson Airport parking lot and tossed his overnight bag into the back. The sun had turned molecules of trapped oxygen into millions of hot-air balloons. He rolled down his windows and adjusted the car seat to the one-hour comfort zone and started the engine. He didn't need the courtesy road map, he knew where he was going.

He pulled out of the parking lot and headed for Interstate 20.

Think like a white man. Walk like a white man. Talk like a white man. You gotta get by.

''Scuse me, ma'am,' the young black man said. 'Can you tell me where to find Miss Bissonette's room?' He held up a bouquet of white and yellow daisies. The usual sticker that said Steinbach's Florist was nowhere on it, nor was there a receipt or delivery instructions attached, nothing that could be traced back to him.

'Miss Bissonette is in a secure area,' the receptionist said. She looked at a sign-in log, saw no indication that a delivery to Five East was expected, and picked up the telephone. 'I think she's still in the middle of a television interview,' she said, waiting for an answer.

Television interview? 'Uh, yeah, that's what these was for.'

The young man stood in front of her desk shifting his weight anxiously from one foot to another.

The receptionist spoke into the receiver and hung up. 'They can't find anybody who knows anything about a flower delivery. Sorry, but I can't let you go up to the fifth floor without authorization.' She bent forward and peered down the hallway. 'If they were for the interview, looks like you're too late anyway. They just came down.'

The young man turned and walked down the corridor and found a telephone bank in a cul-de-sac that was being used as a staging area for the television crew. Sitting on the marble floor was the equipment the receptionist must have been looking at: tripods and hand-held halogen lights and metal boxes with lids laid back, tools and electrical cords. A hefty bearded man wearing a bandana and a khaki photographer's vest was packing up while a thirty-something woman in a charcoal suit and a good haircut stood nearby fluttering a yellow pencil in her fingers, reading a checklist on a clipboard.

The young man with the flowers approached her. 'You just do an interview with Bissonette?' he said.

She didn't look up. 'You can see it tonight on Channel Six.' She turned toward the bearded man. 'I'm heading back to the studio, Gus.'

Gus was on one knee stuffing the equipment box, ignoring her.

'These are for you,' the young man said to the woman, holding out the flowers.

That got her attention. She looked at them, then at the delivery man. 'For me?'

'They was for the interview, but I got here too late.'

As she searched the cellophane package for a note, the delivery man stepped on a coiled yellow cable and slid it across the marble floor toward the wall beneath the bank of telephones. It bounced off the baseboard and came to rest against a stainless-steel wastebasket, out of sight. The woman turned back to the young man and handed him the bouquet. 'These aren't for me,' she said and walked toward the main hallway.

The young man carried the bouquet over to the waste can, dropped it in, and lifted the roll of electrical cable. After walking to a nearby elevator, he waited politely. In a moment the doors opened and a madhouse crowd pushed its way off to make room for another madhouse crowd to move in. Shuffling onto the car, he turned around and kept his eyes forward. Nobody looked at him twice.

Cush turned the sign on Camilla's door to read **DO NOT ENTER: DOCTOR ATTENDING** and walked into her room carrying a red three-ring binder loaded with papers. He found her propped up on the bed reading her grandmother's diary. She set it down and smiled as he crossed the room and laid the binder on the table. She looked good: sweatpants, sneakers, a baggy T-shirt, and uncombed hair, giving her a naturalness he liked. But there was something new as well, this radiant thing he fully understood was meaningless but powerful all the same: this touch of common ancestry, this twist of DNA that linked them someplace in the distant past, now somewhere in their souls. He loved the thought of it.

She cocked her head to the side.

'Are you busy tonight?' he asked.

'I'm having dinner with Tom Brokaw at six thirty, a special rehab session at eight, reading at nine, and lights out at ten.'

'Could you break your date?'

'That's asking a lot.'

'I'd like to have dinner with you.'

She was surprised. 'What's the occasion?'

'No occasion, just dinner.'

'I'd love to.'

He pulled a roll of candy from his pocket. 'Care for a mint?'

'No, thanks,' she said.

That was good. No compulsive oral exploration. No rhyming or counting of floor tiles or catatonic stares at the ceiling. No myoclonic jerks of the extremities. No loss of cognition. General improvement all around. No more sign of KBS. 'I'll pick you up at seven.'

'Should I reserve a table in the cafeteria?' she asked.

'Leave that to me.'

Nat sat at the counsel's table waiting for his legs to be cut out from under him.

The county attorney stood at a lectern before Judge Sumter Pretty III, his coat open and the knot in his tie pulled down just enough to let him breathe. Other than Sheriff Benson, there was no one else in the courtroom but a stenographer who stared lazily at her fingernails, waiting for argument to begin. The prosecutor was reading the legal papers Nat had brought from New York: a memorandum from the assistant district attorney and a letter from the Mississippi state medical examiner honoring the Manhattan assistant district attorney's request for a state autopsy of one Roy Driggers, AKA Sneezer. Assuming they could find him.

The problem was in the legal papers. Nat's friend, the prosecuting attorney, had written to them before Cush Walker had told Nat that Driggers' middle name was Montavius, so if Patient RAD referred to someone other than Driggers – and, of course, Nat didn't know – the application now before the court was inaccurate. If Nat didn't own up to the possibility, he could be making a false application to the court. Knowing how well Cush Walker was wired with these guys, chances were the judge already knew that Driggers wasn't RAD. What a nice way to put Nat's tit in a wringer.

The prosecutor looked up from the lectern. 'Your Honor,' he said, 'I've read the papers.'

'And?' Judge Pretty said.

Here it comes, the contempt citation, the arrest for perjury.

'They seem to be in order.'

The judge leaned forward to Nat with a frown. OK, so I got by the county prosecutor, but now the judge is on to me. Nat felt the Roto-Rooter starting to turn as the judge stared at him. Son-of-a-gun is looking right into my evil heart. Then the judge said, 'When do you want the grave opened up?'

I'll be damned. Nat stood up. 'As soon as possible, Your Honor.'

The judge turned to the sheriff. 'How about it, Ben?'

Sheriff Benson gave a nod as if his team had just struck out. 'I'll git Bobby Joe to take his back-hoe out there first thing Monday morning.'

'Is that agreeable to the great State of New York, Detective Hennessy?'

'It is unless it can be done tomorrow.'

The sheriff said, 'We can git another back-hoe out there in the morning, Your Honor, but Bobby Joe won't be working it, and he's the only one that knows what he's doing.'

'He's also Vestie Viney's nephew-in-law,' the judge said, 'which means less of a stink when she finds out somebody's diggin' up her husband's grave. Besides, tomorrow's Saturday and the coroner's office is closed. You dig up a dead body in this heat, Detective, you better have a cooler handy or the state medical examiner isn't gonna touch it with a rake.'

Nat said, 'May I have the court's permission to be at the grave site during the disinterment?'

The judge looked at the sheriff, not the county counsel. Sheriff Benson raised his eyebrows, OK by me.

'So ordered,' Judge Pretty said. He picked up his file and stepped off the dais and unbuttoned his robe as he went through the side door.

Sheriff Benson stood up to leave. 'You goin' home and coming back Monday?' he asked Nat.

Sure, Sheriff, I'm leaving for the weekend so you and Bobby Joe can take that back-hoe and find a brand new resting place for Roy Driggers. 'I think I'll kick off my shoes and stay awhile,' he said. 'Pay my respects to Vestie Viney and get me a little of that fried chicken at Ginny's Diner.' Half a day in Hardy and he was already talking like a cracker. Felt kinda good, actually.

'You like catfish?' the sheriff asked.

Nat tried not to puke.

''Cause if you do,' the sheriff said, 'ever' Friday night they got the best damn deep-fried catfish balls you gonna find south of the Mason Dixon.'

The man was serious. 'Thanks, Sheriff, I just might do that.'

'See you at the grave,' the sheriff said. He pushed through the swinging wooden gate to the spectators' gallery.

'Bright and early Monday morning,' Nat said.

A young black man who resembled an electrician stood in front of the emergency exit at the end of the fifth-floor hallway, a mere twenty feet from the patient's door, rolling a line of electrical cord in his hand like a cowboy's lasso. Watching the door, he saw a tall black doctor leave the patient's room, turn the **DO NOT ENTER: DOCTOR ATTENDING** sign to its blank side, and walk away. The young man waited until the doctor had disappeared around the corner, then moved to the door carrying the coil of electrical cord draped over his shoulder. He turned the sign back to **DO NOT ENTER** again and went into the room.

★　　★　　★

Nurse Punt was like a busy mother with sleeping children: no matter where they were or what she was doing, her patients were connected to her central nervous system. She saw Cush Walker pass the nurses' desk on the way to his office. 'How's our girl?' she asked without looking up from her papers.

'Taking a nap,' he said, and walked on.

The young man looked around the room a moment to calm himself, then walked to the patient's bed. Bissonette was lying on her side with her back to him, sleeping beneath a thin blanket. Her neck – the part of her he needed – was exposed.

Moving quietly, he laid the yellow coil of electrical cable on top of a red binder on the table next to her bed.

Pretty thing, lying there asleep. Sorry, booty, but it's you or me.

He planted his sneakered feet on the tile floor and leaned his thighs against the side of the mattress for leverage, then reached out and positioned his hands around her neck. His heart was doing triple time. One . . . two . . .

Nurse Punt was three steps from Camilla's door when she noticed something out of order. The sign on the door still read **DO NOT ENTER: DOCTOR ATTENDING** even though Dr Walker had just finished his examination. Naps did not qualify for that kind of privacy.

She turned the sign around and started to walk away when she noticed something else: there was no sound coming from the room. Camilla kept the television set on all the time, listening even when not watching, hoping for a memory catalyst.

The nurse opened the door quietly, careful not to disturb her patient's sleep.

She had difficulty understanding the picture: a woman – Camilla – stood next to the bed in her hospital gown swinging a coil of yellow-coated electrical cord at a repairman – a young black man in an electrician's coveralls who was holding Cush Walker's red binder in front of his face for protection. Camilla was in a fury, her eyes excessively angry, her lips curled with swear words, backing him toward the wall.

Camilla leaned forward and spat at him. White foam sprayed onto the intruder, some clinging to her chin.

The man saw Nurse Punt and moved before she did. All she saw were pieces of things in motion: hands, feet, the red binder, a look of fear on the man's face. She barely had time to brace herself before he knocked her into the hallway onto her back. A gong sounded in her head and cartoon planets and stars flooded the insides of her eyelids. The rest was a blur – legs churning in a workman's jumpsuit, the sound of soft-soled sneakers swooshing on a hard floor as he ran toward the emergency exit at the end of the hall and disappeared.

Breathing wildly, eyes darting, Nurse Punt rose to her feet and pushed her way into her patient's room. Camilla remained in the middle of the bed, chest heaving, eyes cold beneath matted strands of dangling hair, the yellow cord hanging from her hands like a whip.

Nurse Punt approached her gingerly, as if Camilla didn't recognize her, which, apparently, she didn't. In a few minutes, calmed by some soothing talk, Camilla was on her back again, the electrical cord draped across her legs, staring quietly toward the ceiling.

When Nurse Punt left, Camilla reached down, found the plug at the end of the line, and stuck it into her mouth, looking upward, counting the cork tiles.

Nat stood at the grave poking at the earth with the rubber toe of his New York sewer boots, trying to see if someone had already opened it up. The evening light was casting long shadows behind vertical surfaces – trees, the headstone, even the yellowed bent grass – but there were no fresh clumps of dirt to catch a dying sunbeam.

Stepping on the hardened sod around the flat marker, he smelled burning briar first, then heard a voice: 'Need a shovel?'

He turned and saw an old man approaching from the direction of Vestie Viney's barn, pipe in mouth. The gentleman needed no introduction. The coal-dusted eyes and chiseled cheeks had been stolen right off Cush Walker's face – or vice versa. Nat reached out and introduced himself.

'Oh, I know who you are,' the old man said, shaking hands. 'I'm Dr Booker T. Walker.'

'Then you probably know why I'm here,' Nat said.

'Everybody in town knows why you're here,' the doctor said.

Nat waited for Cush's grandfather to declare his intentions.

Booker T. pointed his pipe stem at the gravestone. 'Anybody tell you about Virgil McCoy?'

'Only how he died,' Nat said.

'Mmm,' the man said, puffing. 'Probably the most interesting thing he ever did.' He took the pipe from his mouth and checked the bowl. 'Short of getting dug up again, that is.'

'He's not the one I'm after,' Nat said.

'So I hear.' The old man drew air through his pipe, then crossed his foot over his knee and banged the ashes onto the ground. 'Had your dinner yet?' he said, stamping the ashes.

'I thought I'd grab a bite at Ginny's Diner.'

'Good idea,' the old man said. 'I'll take you.'

'Thanks, but no thanks,' Nat said, stepping away. 'I'll take you.'

He took a scalpel in hand, laid the tip of the blade to the black skin, made a small nick to enter, and drew it downward in an arc from the head to the bottom of the belly. The flesh opened up white and moist like a ripe, split fruit.

Next he made a clean cut around the neck, removing the head. Using a forceps, he held the loosened gray skin and slowly, carefully, peeled it downward, stripping it away from the body until nothing remained but the pinkish-white meat beneath.

Moving quickly, he turned the body over and pressed his hand on the backbone, separating the flesh from the vertebrae. After pinching the rib cage, he slid the blade of his scalpel under a bone at the top of the spine and excised it like a surgeon filleting a fish. When all the ribs had been removed, he slid his hands under the corpse and lifted it carefully, keeping its floppy, unstructured flesh intact. Then he carried it to the bed and laid it down.

My, oh, my, did that look good: catfish steamed on a bed of spinach. Simple, tasty. As good as it gets.

Cooking was the closest thing to a pastime Cush enjoyed, an oasis of relaxation even here in the private kitchen near his fifth-floor office. He turned down Charlie Parker on the stereo and set the automatic rice machine to fifteen minutes, then finished off the two catfish with a light soy marinade, julienne strips of fresh ginger, minced coriander, mushrooms, and a couple of chopped spring onions. After placing them in the center of a light-tan bamboo steamer, he rinsed his hands and dried them on the lab coat he wore in place of an apron.

A Slow Burning

He was dropping a pinch of hamburger meat into a Baggie to take home to his pets, Ike and Tina Turtle, when Nurse Punt entered the kitchen. He thought she might still be a bit shaken by what had happened that afternoon: a bump on the back of her head, interviews with hospital security, staff gossip and hubbub, reconstructing the papers stolen inside Cush's red binder – none of which, fortunately, was particularly difficult to replace, least of all his usual three-day schedule. Mostly, Nurse Punt was upset by Camilla's outburst. It was so much like one she'd witnessed once before, she said – choosing not to remind him by whom or when – and hoped never to see again. Cush nodded, and, like her, said nothing more about it.

After debriefing her on what had happened and examining Camilla during a nap, Cush had decided to cancel their dinner. But when Camilla woke up, refreshed and excited about the evening, he changed his mind. She was virtually unaware of what had happened to her that afternoon, recalling images of the man who'd attacked her as if she'd dreamed instead of lived them. Cush still wasn't sure why. Or was but wouldn't admit it.

'Your guest has arrived,' Nurse Punt said, her cheeks uncharacter-istically pink. 'Wait till you see her.'

He placed two Italian bone-white plates on a handsome wicker tray with brass fittings and horned handles, then lifted the steamer from the stove top and placed it next to the plates, condiments, and silverware, filling the air with the fragrance of ginger and soy and fresh-cooked fish. Nurse Punt reached for the tray, let me do that, and carried it toward the door leading to the hallway.

As she backed through the swinging doors, Cush removed his lab coat and eyed himself in a full-length mirror on the broom closet door. He looked Gatsby-esque in a pair of stone-colored linen slacks and a white cotton shirt open at the neck, sleeves rolled to his forearms. He evened them, checked his teeth, and touched his collar for no apparent reason.

Then he opened the door.

J.J. Jackson sat in the driver's seat of his limousine with the door open and one foot outside, tapping a rock covered with hardened cement dust in time to a dance tune blaring on the radio. It was a warm Friday night, the Harlem River sitting quietly in front of him near flood tide, reflecting the headlights of the cars on the other side as they streamed north toward the George Washington Bridge. He held his left shoe up and examined its shiny alligator leather in the ambient light, then pulled an orange utility rag from his glove compartment and wiped off the dust.

'Spooky down here,' a voice said. A tall young black man approached the limousine cautiously, looking around at the cement factory – gravel pits, piles of dirt, towers with roller-coaster rails hanging in the air, machinery, chains, gears, equipment.

'You're late, Disco,' J.J. said. 'I got a pretty little spinner waiting for me.' He motioned toward the back of the limo.

Disco opened the back door and got in, leaving it open the way J.J.'s driver's door was. The air conditioner wasn't running but J.J. motioned for him to close the door anyway.

Jackson swiveled around in the driver's seat and looked back at Disco through the open privacy window. Disco was slouched on the soft leather cushions, knees apart. 'I got to her,' he said, 'but I couldn't do her.'

'You got into her room?'

'Close enough to get my hands round her neck.' His tone of voice was cool to the point of condescending: you don't like it, J.J., you can blow me. 'The girl woke up and went after me like some crazy bitch, man.'

J.J. closed his door and turned down the volume and told Disco to talk to him. 'You let a sick girl in a hospital room whip your ass?'

Disco told him everything – how he'd talked around the

restrictions to Five East, how he'd gotten into Bissonette's room, how she went nuts on him, how the nurse walked in before he could bring the girl down. Then he handed Jackson the floppy red three-ring binder he'd grabbed off the table next to the bed.

J.J. paged through it, saying, 'What's this?' It appeared to be filled with medical reports that meant nothing to him.

'I don't know, it looked important,' Disco said.

Not to Jackson. But after putting it on the passenger seat, he noticed a salmon-colored piece of paper peeking out from inside. Pulling it away, the words 3-DAY SCHEDULE FOR DR WALKER appeared at the top. After a quick read, he folded it up and stuck it into his pocket, then got to his knees in the driver's seat and extended his arms through the window, wiggling his fingers to Disco to come close. 'You did good,' he said.

Disco struggled out of his sprawl and leaned forward to accept his boss's embrace. 'We even now, J.J.?' he said into his ear.

'Yeah, baby, we even,' Jackson said, patting Disco on the back. 'Almost.'

He held Disco's head in his hands and gave him a kiss on the cheek. Disco, not particularly fond of this Eye-talian godfather shit, tried to pull back.

J.J. held his head in place.

Disco tried to pull back again.

J.J. held Disco's head tight and turned it clockwise as if it was a large shower knob he was turning off.

Disco's fingers rose to Jackson's hands and dug beneath the skin, trying to pry them off.

J.J. held on and rotated Disco's head a quarter turn more. The gristle in the back of his neck made a grinding noise, cartilage raking vertebrae. 'Mother . . . *fuck*,' Disco said in a high voice. He reached out and pushed his hand into Jackson's face.

J.J. tightened his grip.

Disco's eyes scrunched into slits and a squeal slipped out of his mouth.

J.J. turned the boy's head a little more, screwing it down like a shower valve against a worn-out rubber gasket.

Disco's cheeks were pulled back now, taut and shiny, teeth showing, head trembling under the strain. His voice rose to the eerie screech of five fingernails drawn down a blackboard. J.J. twisted his errand boy's head beyond the limits of spinal cord, muscle and vertebrae.

Snap.

Disco's high-pitched screeching stopped like a bug hitting a windshield. His head turned fluidly in Jackson's hands. J.J.'s veins enlarged and his brain sparkled and his heart pumped fresh juice into his biceps and neck and groin.

He dropped Disco's rag-doll head and turned around and fell back into the driver's seat, spent and alive. His hands spread wide on his thighs, wiping Disco's sweat and spittle from his palms.

What a cool way to start the morning. What a bitchin' way to start the night.

'Hey, Shaw. You got a call coming in on two.'

Shaw picked up the second line. 'Hello?'

'Sal?' It was the whispered voice of someone who must have known her on the street when she was working Vice. Nobody else called her Sal.

'This is Detective Sally Shaw, who's this?'

'This is Gina. Remember me?'

She sure did. It was one of the girls she'd left a message for, Gina Marascino, a petite, pretty hooker known as – what else? – Maraschino Cherry. A couple of years earlier Shaw had busted her on a solicitation charge, but when she'd learned the girl had a two-year-old baby, instead of hauling her in she'd taken her to St Agnes Church and helped her get back on her feet, literally. She was so grateful she'd cried. Shaw hadn't seen her since.

'Cherry?'

'Yeah, listen, I gotta talk fast, I'm on a boat out here on the Hudson River, and I'm sittin' in the powder room, which for some fucked-up reason they call the head, don't ask me why.' Back on her feet? Back on her back. 'I heard your message about looking for a guy named J.J. Jackson.'

Shaw stopped doodling. 'You know where I can find him?'

'Maybe. I'm working for Paradise Escorts now, OK? We been partying all day with this high roller named Romano and some jerk named Schlitz or Schmidts or something like that, and on the way back, Romano tells the skipper to phone his limo driver and make sure he's waiting for us at the Seventy-ninth Street marina, OK? When I hear him say "J.J.", I'm thinking maybe this could be your man.'

'Good thinking, Cherry.'

'It's Gina now, OK?'

'How long will it take before you get to the marina?'

'What do you think I am, Captain Nemo?' She breathed into her cellular phone so hard it sounded as if she was blowing on it.

'Are you south of the Tappan Zee Bridge?'

'When I come into the ladies' room we could see the lights on the city buildings, that's all I know.' More blowing. 'Listen, my nails are dry now, I gotta hop.'

Just like a bunny. 'Thanks for the call, Cherry.'

'It's Gina now, OK? Gina.'

'Thanks, Gina.'

'Remember St Agnes?'

'I sure do.'

'Me, too.'

Click.

She was wearing a black dress with spaghetti straps and a short hemline and a pair of platform shoes with open toes, courtesy of an emergency delivery by her downstairs neighbor, Robin Feld, who did it without asking questions. On her ears were simple gold earrings that glinted through her silky black hair when she moved.

'My God, look at you,' Cush said. He hadn't seen her in a dress for so long he'd forgotten. 'How do you feel?'

'Like I just made a jail break,' she said. 'Now you tell me.'

'I feel great.'

'I mean how do *I* feel.' She opened her arms to him.

He drew her to him and touched the piano keys of her ribs. Feeling them made him light-headed.

'What smells so good?' she asked.

'You'll see in a minute. Take my arm.' Cush helped her up the concrete steps, through a steel door, and onto the hospital roof. She stood with her eyes closed, breathing in nature's air for the first time in memory, literally. A balmy summer breeze brought her skin alive.

She opened her eyes and saw a round dinner table with a white tablecloth and two chairs flanked by terracotta planters, each holding tall green palms. Hurricane lamps enclosed the candle flames and spread their buttery light across the table: a bamboo steamer; dishes of cold creamed corn and relish; a green salad glistening with a sheen of olive oil; fresh vine-ripened tomatoes; a basket of bread; condiments, silverware, and dishes, so much she couldn't take it all in. Twinkling goblets sat next to the dinner plates, and off to the side of the table, on a pedestal, a silver wine butler held the chill in a fresh bottle of napkin-draped Cristal, his favorite champagne. The velvet fog of Mel Tormé crept across the wooden deck, carrying Cole Porter's 'I've Got You Under My Skin'.

'What have you done?' she said.

Using her cane, she stepped forward and walked with him surprisingly well to a brick parapet at the edge of the roof. After steadying herself with a hand on his shoulder, she admired the city. The fading light tinted the dust and smog in shades of peach and amber on blue, and urban lights – neon signs, apartment lamps, industrial spotlights – blossomed like nocturnal flowers on steel and concrete. The town was alive with movement and horns, people congregating in large huts and small ant hills. In front of her was the length of the East River, and to the right, the Empire State Building.

'What a magnificent view,' she said.

He stepped behind her and steadied her back against his chest. 'Which building do you like most?'

She took her time to decide. 'That one,' she said, pointing at the Chrysler Building.

'Very good,' he said, 'it was your favorite before the accident. You're memory's coming back.'

'Not really,' she said. She put her head back on his shoulder. He stretched his arms around her waist. 'You're going to have to finish the job.'

'I can't do that yet,' he said. 'It's too dangerous.'

She watched an airliner cross the sky. 'Is that the problem, or are you afraid of what I might remember once I'm well?'

He turned her around to face him. 'Fear of your memory isn't the reason I can't use the nanoscanners, Camilla. I want your memory to return as much as you do, and there are things I'm going to do to try to get it back. Safe things.'

'Like what?'

'Like taking you back to the Statue of Liberty.'

'What for?'

'Sometimes revisiting the place of an accident breaks an amnesia.' He could see her trying to picture it.

'When are we going?'

'Tomorrow afternoon.'

'Really?' She was intrigued. 'Will Nat be there?'

'He's flying back from Mississippi in the morning.'

She looked expectant. 'Do you think it will work?'

'Maybe.'

'And you're not afraid if it does?'

'Of course not.'

She laid her head against his chest and let him hold her. 'I love you, Cush,' she said. 'Cush?'

'Yes?'

'I have to ask you something.'

'Fire away,' he said.

'And I want you to tell me the truth, OK?'

'What would you like to know?'

Shaw pulled into the parking lot at the 79th Street marina at a slow pace, trying not to make waves, hoping to see everything in a panoramic sweep. Her open windows invited in the smell of brine and waterlogged timber, the sound of gulls calling and halyards snapping against aluminum masts. This river could take you anywhere in the world. Down to South America, hang a right to the South Pacific, anyplace. Coconut palms and naked, brown-skinned boys. Smoke grass? She'd rather dance in it.

She entered the underground parking lot and drove gently down the first aisle looking for a black limousine with a black driver. After peeling off the wrapper, she popped a baby peanut butter cup into her mouth and stayed focused on the cars. The area was dreary and badly lit: Parks Department trucks, chainlink fences guarding stowed equipment, wooden horses and graffitied walls.

She hit the brakes: black limo, two o'clock high, lights off, parked at an angle near the door leading out to the dock.

She pulled into the first empty parking space she could find and turned off her engine and looked through the back window. The limo was a stretch, but there was no sign of anyone inside. She focused on the plate. New York blue on white. Maybe it was him. Maybe it wasn't.

She saw passengers coming through the door. Two went that way, three went this. She checked her watch. Ten after ten. She must have missed them.

She watched the door to the marina, but there were no more passengers. Wadding her candy's tinfoil into a little ball, she dropped it into the ashtray. Five minutes passed, still nothing. The limo must be parked there for the night.

She started the engine and pulled back and stopped to adjust her rearview mirror. Looking at it, she saw a girl come through the door. Not exactly a girl, more like a petite woman in boots, a short skirt, and an impossibly small waist. One like Gina Marascino's.

Shaw put the gear shift in park and left her headlights off.

Gina walked a few steps, turned, and waited. A second girl came through the door wearing a white leather skirt, then a tall, thin white guy came out wearing sunglasses even though it was night. They stood by the car and waited.

Another man came through the door. It was Joseph Romano, looking so much like his newspaper photograph it gave her new respect for the *News*. Then another figure: a short, stocky black man wearing a black suit, a chauffeur's cap, and a shirt so white it was luminous. He walked in front of the group of four, leading the way to the limousine.

She saw the four passengers pile into the back of the limo,

all smiles and giggles, and watched as J.J. Jackson got into the driver's seat, backed out, and glided toward the exit ramp.

She started up and followed them in her standard-issue 1997 Taurus.

Nat pulled his rental car up in front of the barn's swung-out doors and sat with the engine idling, his headlights illuminating the empty hay racks inside. Dr Booker T. Walker opened the passenger door and struggled to get out. Nat sat watching him patiently, smart enough not to patronize him with an offer of help. When the old man finally got to his feet, he closed the car door and bent down to the open window. Thank you, he said, it was a pleasure meeting you. The words floated on a cloud of Southern grace, the kind that made Northerners feel clunky. Then he stuck his finger in the window and pointed at the ignition key. 'Shut down those lights, the owls don't like them and the mosquitoes do.'

Nat did as he was told. The moist summer air wrapped them in a cottony blanket.

'Come on in for a glass of tea,' the old doctor said.

Nat said thanks, he'd enjoy that, but it was late and something had unexpectedly come up that meant he had to catch a plane to New York first thing in the morning. His answer was met with magnetic, parental silence.

He turned off the engine and got out.

'Spider Murphy,' she said. 'What happened to him?'

Cush filled her glass with champagne, then his own. 'Did Hennessy put you up to this?'

'Nat knows how to fight his own wars,' she said. 'This is me talking.'

He lifted the bamboo steamer lid and placed a catfish fillet on each plate, then spooned out the steamed spinach. After tasting the broth, he offered her some. 'Careful, it's hot.'

She tried it and pronounced it delicious.

He ladled the broth over the two portions of fish. 'What do you already know about Spider?'

'Only what Nat told me, that he's a skinhead who went to jail for beating up a married couple in New Jersey, and you gave him a lobot – low-*bot*-oh-mee – and turned him into a vegetable and taught him to peel a banana upside down, for what reason Nat doesn't know.'

Cush poured himself a glass of champagne with studied indifference, drank half of it, and set it on the table.

'Spider Murphy was a volunteer test subject in our BIAS program,' he said. 'He was a kid filled with more hate than a Klan Wizard. We located the problem and ablated it.'

'Wait a minute, wait a minute. You did what?'

'A few years ago doctors discovered how to locate the brain cells that hold emotional memory, like fear, hate, and phobias. They're called retention neurons. We used the same technology to locate his unusually strong emotional attitude on race. Not

the garden variety prejudice you see every day, but the kind of
hate that leads to violence. What we call a racial aversion.'

'How did you do that?'

'We put him under a high-intensity scanner and told him
stories that made him live through experiences he didn't like.
Once we located the right neurons – the ones that lit up like
a Christmas tree – we downloaded a picture of them into our
computer, then went back and ablated them.'

'Ablated?'

'Burned. We use the nanoscanners to cut paths across portions of his neural webbing and stop his phobic reaction from
expressing itself. Sort of like cutting fire breaks in a forest.'

'That sounds terrible. Like a lobot—'

'Lobotomy. Not really. Years ago, frontal lobotomies were
like using a telephone pole to rearrange a few flowers. We
don't do that any more. Our tools were precise, but we didn't
have permission from the internal review board to do what I
described, and we made a mistake.'

'Something bad?'

'You could say that.'

'What was it?'

'We'd been scanning a pair of monkeys named Cain and
Abel. Nothing harmful, just copying. We needed a distinctive
behavior to scan, so we taught Cain how to peel a banana
upside down.'

She ate some steamed spinach. 'I'm listening.'

'We scanned him while he was doing the trick and downloaded
it into the computer. Ordinarily, when the nanoscanners are
finished we sanitize them by erasing the data they've collected
so we can use them again.'

He offered her more champagne – she declined for the
moment – then topped up his own glass. 'A little of this stuff
goes a long way with me, if you remember.'

'I don't.'

He took a sip and held his glass in front of his eyes, watching the bubbles rise like thin lines of volcanic gas from the bottom of the ocean. 'We put Spider Murphy on the operating table to do our search-and-destroy mission. We pulled the Z-5s from the refrigerator, warmed them up, injected them into his cortical-spinal fluid and watched them go to the brain. When the coordinates looked right, we signaled them to boot up, but for some reason they didn't.'

'Boot up?'

'Start their computer programs. We knew the Z-5s were receiving our signals, so we decided to purge the boot instructions and start over, sort of the way you do when your home computer glitches out.'

'But if you purge them while they're inside his brain, where's the purged stuff go?'

'Good question. I'll tell you while we're dancing.'

'Bad answer. I'll dance with you when you tell me.'

No problem with that mind. 'A boot dump isn't harmful, it unloads about the same amount of electromagnetic garbage into your brain as you get listening to some bad rap. We programmed the nanoscanners to release their start-up instructions and try again. Then we noticed something else going on. Ordinarily, a boot dump takes about two or three seconds, but the controller indicated a continuing download. Stage one took a minute, then the scanners purged stages two, three, and so on until they'd unloaded all twenty-eight stages.' He folded his napkin. 'When we reversed our checklist we discovered we were using Z-5s that were still loaded with the experiment on Cain. For some reason, we'd failed to sanitize them, and instead of dumping in a few harmless boot instructions, we'd dumped the banana trick.'

'Was that a lot of information?'

'Uh, yeah, relatively speaking, that was a lot. A while later we did another scan on Spider and got a bigger surprise.'

'What was that?'

'His racial phobia was gone. We hadn't ablated it, but it was gone.'

'Why?'

'The neural webbing behaved as if it had been overwritten by the banana trick. So we withdrew the scanners and went back to the drawing board.' He fiddled with the glass.

She was silent. 'You cured his racial hatred by replacing it with a trick from a monkey?'

'In effect, that's what happened. But it wasn't precise. Unfortunately, we scrambled a few healthy neurons in the process.'

'With what?'

'Nothing coherent, just white noise.'

'So sometimes you can transfer a coherent thought—'

'And sometimes you transfer gibberish. Or sometimes nothing at all. About half the time, actually.'

'Only half? Those are pretty good odds, aren't they?'

'Only if you're in the right half.'

She finished her glass of champagne. 'How close are you to overwriting memory whenever you want?'

'Close.' He stood up and walked to her side of the table, took her hand and helped her to her feet. 'Time to dance.'

She got up, but her mind was still on his experiments. 'What else could you use to overwrite memory besides a banana trick?'

'Pretty much anything, I suppose. What have you got in mind?'

'I was wondering what *you* had in mind.' He didn't answer. 'You must have something interesting after all these years, right?'

'I thought we were going to dance now?'

She put her arms around him and they began their slow, romantic movement, more touching and holding than dancing.

'When we're done, I've got more questions, you know,' she said. 'One of them is about Roy Driggers.'

He drew her close and whispered in her ear. 'When we're done, I'm going to say, not now, Sweet Pea, some other time.'

She opened the glove compartment, lifted out a Ziploc refrigerator bag, and opened it. Inside was a pair of white latex gloves, standard equipment for law enforcement personnel and EMTs. Behind that she found a Slim Jim, a thin, flat piece of metal with hook-shaped cutouts that tow truck drivers used to unlock car doors.

She pulled on the gloves and opened the door. Squeezing her shoulder bag to make sure her gun was there, she got out of the car and closed the door quietly.

She walked kitty-corner to the parking lot of Muchas Muchachas, the dance club where J.J. Jackson had taken his passengers. She found his limousine – she hadn't let it out of her sight – and waited by the rear fender, checking if anyone could see her. The front door to the club was out of sight around the corner, but she saw party-goers headed in that direction.

She waited until the scene was quiet – no engines running or windows zizzing up or down, no parking lot attendants hustling by – then reached out and tried the limo's back door. No surprise: the doors were locked.

She took the Slim Jim from her bag and moved to the front door on the passenger's side where she could keep her eye on the corner. After flattening the tool against the window, she stuffed it into the door and began fishing for the lock. She'd done this before; it was simply a matter of trial and error. And time. Her hands were calm, but her stomach was a mess.

She continued fishing and worrying. There was noise from around the corner, music blaring from an open car window, people talking, car doors slamming, valets peeling rubber in cool squeaks. Commotion was her ally, business as usual her camouflage.

Thunk. She was in.

She opened the door and climbed into the passenger seat and sat still, composing herself. The cushion was soft and cool, the leather sumptuous. Another time and place and she could get used to this stuff.

She tried the glove compartment. It was locked. Must be something good in there – an unregistered handgun, a slab of crack, a deck of heroin – the thing she needed to know about but not disturb, the hook that would let the cops bust him without any indication that she or Hennessy had anything to do with it. No DD5 to file, no questions asked.

She tried the console next to the driver's seat. Same problem. Locked. She sat back and considered her options. She'd have to try the passenger area.

Closing the front door softly, she opened the one behind and slipped into the back seat. She waited a moment, listening. In front of her was a lowered jump seat, and to the left, a burled walnut bar with a television screen beneath. The door to the bar was cracked slightly.

She pulled it down and snapped on her tiny penlight, dialing the beam to its narrowest focus. Inside the bar were heavy, cut-crystal glasses and bottles of VSOP whiskey, French-labeled cognac, and a single-malt Scotch. Under the bottles was a mirrored tray, and on that – OK, what have we here? A single-edged razor blade and traces of white powder?

Now we're getting somewhere.

She searched the bar for a container, found nothing, then reached down behind the back seat. There was nothing there but the outlines of a metal compartment between the seat and the trunk. What was that?

She held the penlight in her mouth and pushed the seat down with both hands and saw part of a steel box built into the back of the trunk, its edges rippled with rivets and a long piano hinge. It must have opened from the opposite side, like the lid of the trunk.

That interested her.

She let go of the seat cushion and turned out the penlight and put it into the small pocket on the side of her leather bag. Hearing voices outside, she slouched onto her back and hid. It sounded like a young couple laughing privately, searching for an empty back seat where they could make out.

She locked the doors and picked up the single-edged razor blade from the mirror and put it between her teeth. After pushing her leather bag through the privacy window, she clambered through it and more or less fell into the driver's seat. Facing the windshield, she took the razor blade from her mouth and cut the New York State registration sticker off the glass.

She dropped the stringy remains into her bag and lowered her gloved hands down the sides of the steering column, then searched beneath the dashboard. There it was. Looking around, seeing no one nearby, she squeezed the lever and gave it a pull. *Thud.* The trunk lid popped open.

She reached through the window, laid the razor blade back on the cutting mirror, looked for anyone nearby – all clear – and exited on the less conspicuous passenger side. When she got to the trunk, she raised the deck.

The compartment was lined with gray carpeting and neatly placed contents: a wooden box of tools lashed down with bungee cords, a net hammock filled with a tow strap, flares, a halogen lamp, leather gloves, and highway emergency gear. On the side was a boot for the spare, and nestled forward of that were the outlines of the steel box she'd felt from the back seat. The side protruding into the trunk was covered with carpeting, completely unnoticeable – if she hadn't already noticed it.

She felt along its edge. Hidden beneath a flap was a steel hasp with a combination padlock holding it closed.

She pried away the carpeting and exposed the screw heads fastening the hasp to the box. Pawing through the tool box, she found a pair of pliers, a butane welding torch – Jesus, could this be the one? – and the screwdriver she was looking for. Working fast, she unscrewed the hasp from the box and lifted the lid.

Inside was a silvery aluminum briefcase sitting in a cushion of spongy plastic. She lifted it out, laid it on the trunk floor, and unsnapped the latches. My God, look at that. Nestled neatly into foam templates were pieces of a high-powered rifle: a gun stock, a bolt and chamber, two lengths of a barrel, a telescope, bullet casings. He hadn't thrown his sniper's weapon into New York Harbor after all.

Her illegal search had turned up exactly what she needed. Now, if she could find a way to get it into the hands of the police – anonymously and legally – ballistics could match it to the bullet fragment the FBI had found beneath Camilla's body on the platform floor.

It was perfect.

She heard footsteps behind her and straightened up abruptly, banging her head on the underside of the trunk lid. Before she could turn around a voice cut her through her middle.

'Hey, baby, wanna dance?'

They sat on the porch in silence, watching the fireflies romance each other in winking, luminous dances. Nat could see moonlit signs of a well-anchored life all around him: the worn spot on the railing, the rocker that talked with a creak, the small wicker table holding the old man's ashtray, the chair grooved by his body. The pace of life on this porch wasn't so much slow as it was deliberate, a daily rhythm that now included the crickets, lady bugs, and night crawlers.

The doctor lifted his pipe. 'Is your father still alive?'

'No, he died when I was eleven.'

'You don't say. Sort of like Cush's dad.'

'His father died when he was a boy?'

The old doctor leaned forward and reached for a pear-shaped pitcher. 'Care for some more tea?'

'No, thank you.'

'Think twice before you say no,' the old doctor said. 'I'm going to tell you a story that's going to use up a whole glass.'

'Have we done this before?' she asked.

'Not under the stars,' Cush said.

Camilla held tight as the two of them danced around an invisible magnet suspended between them. 'Being on a rooftop feels familiar to me,' she said.

'That's your climber's memory coming back.'

She pulled away and looked into his eyes. 'You know what? Even though I don't know why we did it, I'm sorry we broke up.'

He pulled her to him and breathed in her fragrance, a delicate perfume part shoulder, part neck. If only she were well again – her motor control restored, her memory intact. With a few selective erasures, perhaps – he still wasn't clear about that – but intact. With all signs of her KBS gone. Especially that. God, he wanted that.

They danced the way they always did, like two worn-out marathoners in a quiet embrace, barely moving. When the song ended they returned to the table and he poured them champagne and served her fresh strawberries dipped in Jimmy-and-Bobby's sauce, a mix of sour cream, a touch of lemon, brown sugar, and bitters.

He lifted his glass and looked at her through it. Her black blood was like a bead of food coloring dropped into a mixing bowl of icing and blended to invisibility. Still, simply knowing it was there closed a psychic distance he often felt between himself and white people in general. Watching her in the soft light, he imagined how their ancestral blood might have been mingled at some point in the past, perhaps during an African tribal dance, perhaps in a steamy slave quarter, perhaps between two lovers on a giddy Parisian night. His own white blood, like that of most American blacks, was far more plentiful than her touch of black, but that was beside the point. It was the mixture in her that got him and drew her close.

'Hennessy told me something interesting,' he said.

'What's that?'

'He said you have some black blood in your family.'

'Yes, on my mother's side. Want a strawberry?' She held them aloft, generously.

He took one, thanks. Mixed blood. About as interesting to her as a strawberry. One of the blessings of amnesia.

'Does it matter to you that I'm part black?' she said.

'Not at all. There's a rumor that I'm part black, too.'

She looked at him curiously, pretty sure there was a subtext in there someplace, but not certain what it was.

He set his glass on the table and stood up and walked to her chair and helped her to her feet, then led her to the deck. They began dancing again.

He lifted her face to his and started kissing her tenderly, then felt it billow into something hungry. He ignored his conscience for as long as he could, but it quickly became too stern to blow off. Breaking their kiss, he pulled her head to him and breathed in her hair. 'We'd better call it a night' – his voice sounded a little desperate – 'while I still can.'

Her fingers found his face and glided around it, exploring him as if he was a statue. She lifted her lips to his and pulled him toward her. 'Don't go yet,' she whispered.

'We have to.'

'Just one more dance.'

Of course. They continued their minimal movement with the yaw, pitch, and tilt of two hips swiveling through a storm.

She kissed his neck.

He kissed her cheek.

He placed his hand on her naked back and felt the smoothness of it, the tender licking of the hem of her dress up and down his leg. He drew her closer, tangling their breaths and limbs. Her legs slid around one of his and tensed against it like a pair of hands.

'I want . . . you,' she whispered.

'I want you, too – but we can't.' The subterranean beat of the music said, sure you can.

Suddenly, she stopped dancing.

What is it? his eyes asked.

She raised his hand to her lips and spread his fingers, then placed one in her mouth and sucked it.

Jesus. He pulled away gently.

Her fingers met at the top button of her dress, fiddled with it a moment, and pushed a button through the hole. Two phrases battled in his head: *she wants me* was one; *it's the syndrome* was the other.

He put his hand gently on hers, stopping her. 'Sweetheart.'

She dropped her fingers to the second button and opened it. Parabolic silhouettes of her breasts caught the light before disappearing into the shadows of her dress. He was breathing as if he was walking knee deep in surf.

'Cam—'

Her lips swarmed over him like a cloud of butterflies. His anchors came unstuck from the sand beneath his feet. Her mouth turned voracious. His brain went numb.

He found the strength to pull away. 'We have to stop.'

'That's right, Cush, baby. Stop me,' she said.

Stop me? Did she mean it – or had she finally figured out irony?

'I want you,' she said, 'to . . . *stop* me . . .'

Irony. Like a weapon.

He tried to hold himself together, but his senses were bouncing and zinging like ball bearings thrown down a marble staircase. She was beautiful and in love. He was in love and ready. But she was his *patient*, for God's sake, a woman who couldn't even remember her own fiancé. She was in his care, in his hospital, suffering from amnesia. For all he knew Hennessy was right: this wasn't *her* wanting him – not the real, healthy her – but a disease. The devil within.

He had to pull back and retreat. He was only one tick away from making a very big mistake.

He reached down and placed his hands behind her knees and picked her up in his arms. 'Time for you to go home.'

'That's where I want you to *take me*,' she said, redefining the meaning of *take me*. When this girl catches on, she catches on fast.

Even as he carried her across the deck to the door, he wasn't sure what he was going to do, only what he was supposed to do. When he reached the opening, still aroused, he paused as if he'd forgotten where he was, as if something inside him wanted out.

'What is it?' she asked.

He couldn't answer for the moment.

He had to sneeze.

Shaw sat in her car listening to the radio, second-guessing herself for what she'd done at the limo trunk. Turning to the voice that had startled her, what she found, instead of a gun in her face, was a good-looking guy in a charcoal Armani suit and an open black shirt leering at her through a pair of gorgeous, Latino eyes. She'd straightened up tall to give him a good look at her tumescent nipples – the only weapon she had available at the moment – and keep his eyes out of the trunk. Fortunately, his Latin blood was strong.

They flirted. To distract him, she ran the palm of her hand

up her thigh in a move she'd patented in Vice, and said, sure, she'd love to dance, but her old man was on the premises, why didn't he go in first and she'd follow, OK? Mr Armani smiled at her and cracked his gum and walked toward the club, giving her a chance to put the trunk back as she'd found it, escape to her Taurus, and hunker down for a long stakeout.

She'd moved to a new parking place in order to give herself a clear view of Jackson's limousine. From where she was sitting now, she could see the front door to Muchas Muchachas. It was approaching midnight. She'd have to be as patient as a gumshoe on a divorce case, and without a partner, it would be twice as boring. The club wouldn't get warmed up until twelve, earliest, which meant J.J. Jackson and his pals would be partying until, what – two or three? So, OK, no problem. When they finally came out, they'd be high on cigarettes, pot and vodka, tired of dancing and looking for a little fresh air, a snort, a kiss, anything other than her gray Ford.

That was the thing she liked about this most. They'd never see her coming.

The old doctor took a moment to collect his thoughts before finishing the story of his son's death. When he was done, they both sat quietly, disrupted and haunted. It had been years since Nat had experienced what his mother used to call 'a learning moment'.

He told the story of his own father's death.

'Jackson Levander James was tried for murder,' he explained, 'but he had a couple of old ladies get up on the stand and testify he'd spent the night watching over them, and that was all he needed.'

'What about your testimony? And the girl's?'

'She was painted as hysterical and confused by darkness and the rape, and I was portrayed as an eleven-year-old boy traumatized by seeing his father butchered.'

The moon was receding behind a large cloud, leaving deeper shadows on the porch, nature's scowl at the obscenities they were discussing. Nat had never told the whole, graphic story of his father's death to anyone, not even Camilla, but the story of Cush's father had punctured his defenses and left him ready to talk. Once he got started, there was no stopping him.

It was nearly midnight and the air was cooling in the hard lunar light. A stray lightning bug blinked at Nat like a tiny lighthouse signaling him that he was on course.

He heard Dr Booker T.'s rocking chair start up and saw a cloud of textured air escape his mouth from his pipe, then two more. The smell of briar mingled with the scent of honeysuckle and damp weeds, producing a musky aroma he thought he'd smelled when he was a kid. Whether real or imagined, it provoked a sense of simplicity and calm.

'You and my grandson are both confused,' Booker T. said.

Nat's silence asked, how so?

'If experience is a mother, the two of you are brothers, and yet you're both bent on destroying each other for the least justified reason in the world.'

'It's not the first time two men have fought over a woman.' Nat's voice sounded in B minor, somewhere between embarrassment and self-defense.

'It's not a woman I'm talking about,' the doctor said. His voice reminded Nat of the comforter he'd had as a boy. He was feeling something he hadn't felt since the beginning of that night in the South Bronx: the presence of his father. The old man said, 'It's what you don't see in yourselves.'

Booker T. then talked about white men in hoods and black men on crosses, black men who grew up angry and white men who didn't understand why. As he puffed and talked, Nat watched the clouds uncover the moon. Soon there was less chirping, a quieter rustling of leaves and grass, a shift in the wind and the tone of things. A learning moment. A subtle change of heart.

A silky riot swept over him, worsening his sexual turmoil. He sneezed again and felt goosebumps cobblestone his skin.

'Are you allergic to me?' Camilla said, her hands all over him.

They were standing inside the door to her hospital room. He knew he'd finished sneezing because it was always the same number: five. 'I'll see you in the morning.' He pulled away and saw her face was flushed and damp. 'Are you all right?'

'I don't know, suddenly it seems hot in here,' she said. 'And I'm so thirsty.' She breathed in and out heavily, trying to shake it off. Whatever 'it' was. 'I don't want you to go.'

'I know, but—'

'Once you go black, you never go back.'

What?

'Black, back . . . black, back . . .' Her eyes had turned glassy, her voice deep and skitzy as if it was coming from someone else inside her.

Someone like . . .

Oh, Christ. This wasn't classic KBS. This was KBS with something added. He knew what was happening now. He even knew what she was going to say next.

She closed her eyes and licked his cheek and said, 'Stick it to me, Doc. You . . . smoky . . . black . . . bastard . . .'

His heart hammered the hollow of his chest. 'Camilla, listen.'

She opened her eyes and fixed them on the wall above her bed.

'What is it?' he asked.

She blinked and shook her head. 'What's happening to me?' She was in a daze. 'Oh, my God . . .' Her eyes widened and she began trembling. 'Oh, my God, Cush – I can see it!'

'See what?'

'He's got a stick – no, no, it's a bat – a baseball bat!'

'Who does? Tell me what you're seeing!'

She grabbed her forehead and pulled back her hair, her eyes stony, her face taut. 'He's lying on the sidewalk!'

'You're having a dream.'

She looked at her hands. 'No, I'm not, I'm wide awake.' She walked to the end of the bed and stopped. 'He's trying to get up – he can't get up!'

'Camilla, let me explain—'

She stretched out her arms. 'I see him! It's my father! No, it's not *my* father – it's *his* father! Mine – his – I can't tell!'

Cush grabbed her and held tight. 'Shh.'

She pushed him away, strongly. 'No! No! He's going to – he's swinging the bat – he's swinging it up and down, and—' She screamed: 'No, no, no, no, no, no!' Her head shook and she closed her eyes and pitched forward with her face in the palms of her hands. 'Oh, my *God* – I can see it – he's hitting him with a bat – I can see it, I can see him – his head – oh, my *God* – it's so horrible – his legs are quivering and, oh, my God – his face! He – his eyes are pleading, he needs help – he needs me to help him—'

Cush reached out for her.

She reached out for something unseen. 'Put it back! Put it back—'

He slapped her face.

She stopped talking and turned toward him, her eyes cold, her voice a growl. Then she sprang at him and spat.

He grabbed her, spun her around, and held her back against his chest, pinning her arms to her sides. She trembled and grunted and tried to get free.

He turned her face to his and pulled her to him and wrapped his arms around her and smothered her in safety. She shivered like a kid in a draft. He stroked her hair and kissed her forehead and held her while she cried a normal, human cry. After a minute, he looked at her and saw that her eyes were closed, her face drenched in tears, her cheek turning red where he'd hit her.

THE NEXT MORNING, SATURDAY, *July 26*

Swollen pink air from the Atlantic was puffing like cotton candy across Queens and the East River, sugar-coating the towers and buildings of Manhattan. Cush woke up and saw her standing at the window in her hospital room, her face lit by its reflection. He sat up in his chair.

'I didn't hear you,' he said, his eyes slightly swollen. After her hallucination he'd laid her on the bed and covered her with a blanket and dozed in one of the leather chairs at the side of the room, waking every hour or so to see if she was asleep. She was still wearing her black dress from the night before, her feet bare.

He stood next to her at the window. She seemed to be somewhere out there at sea, deeply alone.

'How do you feel?' he asked. She nodded without answering. 'I'll be right back,' he said, and walked to the bathroom and splashed cold water on his face, then wrung out a washcloth and brought it back to her. She shook her head.

'What happened to me?' she said in a flat, no-nonsense tone. Coldness, he'd learned long ago, was her first stage of fury.

He refolded the washcloth. 'You remembered the death of Nat Hennessy's father.'

'That's not possible. I never met him.'

'That may be true, but his death is part of your memory. I know because I put it there.'

An incredulous look.

He took her by the hand to draw her to a chair but she

held fast, preferring to stand. Leaning over the coffee table, he picked up a carafe of water and saw an envelope marked 'FOR CAMILLA BISSONETTE, PERSONAL, from Cynthia Weber of *Modern Behavior Magazine*.' The envelope had been torn open, its contents read.

'What happened to you last night was the result of an unintentional memory transfer from Hennessy to you,' he said.

'Memory transfer? What are you talking about?'

He stood with the carafe and a glass in hand. 'I told you how we overwrote Spider Murphy's memory with the banana trick,' he said.

'I remember.'

'Well, it wasn't entirely an accident.' He poured a glass of water and handed it to her, then poured one for himself.

'I had been experimenting with memory transfer for a few years with no success. When I saw it happen with Spider, I realized that it was linked to our BIAS remedies and to rebuilding brain cells. Then the question became how to unlink it so that we could do it as a controlled, stand-alone procedure of its own.'

She held her arms as if she was cold.

'We haven't been able to do that yet, which is one of the reasons I was so reluctant to repair your brain damage. When we scanned Hennessy for a blueprint, we picked up various things he was thinking about, like the memory of his father's death. When we made your repairs, it came along for the ride, just like the banana trick did with Spider.'

'But of all his memories, why that one?'

'Because it's so strong. To get a clean picture of the brain while it's working, we need the patient to express a deep, clear memory. The death of a child, winning the lottery – emotional events in people's lives are stored by the brain with special definition. If you ask someone what he had for breakfast a month ago, he probably can't remember, but if you ask him where he was when Kennedy was assassinated a third of a century ago, he'll still be able to tell you.' Especially, he wanted to add, if your father was lynched that night.

'So you made him picture his father's death?'

'Among other things.'

'And it became part of the procedure you used to fix my brain?'

'Yes.' He took another drink of water. 'But that's not the only complication that came out of your repair.'

She picked up a sheaf of papers she'd taken from the envelope from Cynthia Weber. Sitting in a leather chair, she turned the first page. 'I know what the other one is,' she said. 'Kluver-Bucy Syndrome.'

'It's not necessarily as bad as you think, Camilla.'

'Don't tell me that, Cush. It's horrible! I just read this article!'

'Then you must know that there are varying degrees of the disease, different symptoms—'

'I've got the worst of it!'

'That's not true.'

'I spat at you!'

'You were upset about Hennessy's memory.'

'I attacked you!' She stood up.

'You attacked the man you thought was killing your father.'

'I tried to bite *you*.'

'You don't know that for sure.'

She flapped her hands at her sides in exasperation. 'For a man of science, you sure do know how to kid yourself.'

'Even if you have it, there are things that can be done. There's the possibility of remission. Full recovery even.'

'Full recovery?'

'Sometimes.'

'Rarely,' she said, leaning forward, tapping the article. 'We both know where this is headed, Cush. First I attack people the way I did last night, then I howl like an animal and try to have sex with anyone who walks. After eating my own feces, I lose my ability to read, write, speak and think, and eventually – not too long, I hope – I die in a state of extreme dementia.'

'KBS will eventually be repaired by nanoscanners just like any other neural disease. It's only a matter of time.'

'Lot of good that did Roy Driggers.'

That caught him. 'What's he got to do with this?'

'You've given KBS to someone else, Cush, stop pretending you haven't. I read the memo Rodriguez sent to you three years ago. Patient RAD?'

'It's not who you think it is, trust me.'

'Who is it, then?'

Cush rested his elbows on his knees, his chin in his hand, thinking. Then he reached out and tapped the arm of the other leather chair.

'Sit down,' he said. 'I'll tell you.'

'We have a lot of privacy up here in the NeuroPath wing, but not enough,' Cush said. 'Hospital administration and the internal review board are always looking at what we do – that's their job – but there was no way they would approve of the procedures we had in mind. To get them off our backs, I got permission from the Department of Corrections to take Driggers to the clinic in Mississippi to do a BIAS scan, nothing unusual at that point. When we got there, that's what we did. But after we located his racial aversion, we decided to take the next step, which was to overwrite it. To do that we needed a neural phrase from someone else, but getting it required a lengthy scan, which meant a dangerous amount of heat. I decided we should take it from me.'

'Why you?'

'Who else was I going to use? I couldn't ask anyone on the staff, and there were no volunteers available. Besides, if I was willing to use someone else, I had to be willing to use myself. I also thought it would be less dangerous for me because I knew what I was doing, which meant the scan would take less time.'

She waited.

'We needed a neural phrase that was distinctive enough to identify later, so that we could tell whether it had transferred over to Driggers and seated itself, so I picked a shirt buttoning exercise. When I was a boy, I used to button my shirt from the bottom up so I could pull on my jeans and finish buttoning while I was headed out the door and get moving that much quicker.' He nodded, I know, I was compulsive even then. 'It was a distinctive phrase that would be easy to trace, like peeling a banana upside down. We did the scan, stored it, and I felt fine. We were pretty excited, actually.

'The next day we downloaded it from the computer to Driggers, and everything seemed to be working fine until we were almost finished. All at once his temperature started red-lining, and before we could shut it down he took a heat spike.' He laid his head back and talked to the ceiling. 'We withdrew the Z-5s as fast as we could, but he went into a coma. A few days later he came out of it, but with some problems.'

'What kind of problems?'

'Kluver-Bucy.' He took a drink of water. 'When we recognized the early signs, I took him out of the clinic and put him on the farm, hoping it would be calming and therapeutic. He loved horses and was very good with them. But we hit a snag. One Saturday – do you remember when we drove from Hardy to the Gulf for the weekend?'

'No.'

'We did, and while we were gone Driggers hiked up to Vestie Viney's house to pay her a visit. She'd met him once before when she'd stopped by the house on her way to a bake sale to drop off a fresh pie. This particular afternoon she was playing cards with her girlfriends when he knocked on the door and said he was there to groom her horses. When she said she didn't have any horses, he said, no problem, he wasn't *really* there for the horses, he was there to have sex with her.'

'He said it just like that?'

'Actually, it was a little more earthy than that. Her mouth dropped open and she thought, oh my God, it's one of Dr Cush's crazy patients. She slammed the door and yelled if he came back she'd shoot him. He got the message and left.

'This set off a round of clucking at the card party, as you can imagine. Vestie Viney said she was mortified, hardly knew the fellow, all that, and her friends were shocked too. But by sundown, the whole town had one version or another of what had happened, with the usual people raising the usual eyebrows and deciding what had really happened. Vestie Viney, the lonely widow, had been up to no good with the farm boy.

'You and I drove back to Hardy the next afternoon, but before we got there, Driggers had returned to her house. It was Sunday, and this time Vestie Viney was alone. She peeked out the window and saw him standing on the porch bouncing up and down on his toes with his overalls and underpants off and the rest of him – as she put it – ready to go.

'She pretended she wasn't home. When the porch went quiet, she raised the blind and found his mouth pressed up against the window, foaming like a rabid raccoon, scaring her half to death. She ran for the shotgun in the bedroom closet.

'When she came back, he was gone – no sign of him or his clothes. She moved from window to window looking for him, but when she couldn't find him, she decided he must have gone back home and went back to the bedroom to put away the gun. There he was, standing by the bed naked as a jaybird, his clothes on the rocking chair and his eyes wild as a madman's.

'At this point she said he lunged at her, and I don't doubt he did. Whatever happened, she raised the gun and fired both shells. She hit him in the neck and chest, killing him instantly.'

Cush exhaled through his nose and rubbed the corners of his eyes. 'She called me instead of the sheriff, and I came right over. I can't remember exactly where you were at the time. When I got there, I saw what happened and knew that she was frightened out of her mind about what was going to happen next.'

'But if she did it in self-defense, why?'

'Picture the scene. She'd shot a young man who was standing in her bedroom with his clothes off and no sign of forced entry, the same boy her friends saw come by the day before to have sex with her. In Hardy, Mississippi, this raises some troubling questions.'

'But you knew what he'd done and why.'

'Of course. Sexual aggression is a common symptom of KBS. I explained that to her and told her she'd done nothing wrong, I'd tell that to the sheriff, but she wouldn't have it. She said she was going to jail, and just as bad, I was going with her.'

'Why you?'

'For letting the boy loose, as she put it. She may have been a little daffy, but she wasn't completely off the mark. Testifying about Driggers's disease might have taken her off the hook, but it would have put me on it.'

'But I thought you said he was a volunteer?'

'He was – for BIAS, not the procedures that gave him KBS. Those weren't even known to the internal review board, never mind approved. Even if I escaped indictment for what I'd done, the scandal would have wrecked everything that mattered – the company, the lab, our work, my reputation, you name it. On top of that, Vestie Viney was convinced I'd be out of a job and have to sell the farm, which meant she'd get kicked off her land and end up in the county poorhouse. Which, as far as she was concerned, was as bad as jail.'

'What did you do?'

'We buried him.'

'You *buried* him?'

'Vestie Viney and I buried Roy Driggers.'

'Where?'

'At the foot of Virgil's grave.'

'Why there?'

'She wanted him there so she could pay her respects when she visited her husband.'

'Her respects?'

'She felt guilty about killing him. I understood that, believe me. I agreed to bury him there as long as she didn't mark the spot.

I figured it was better to have her laying flowers and praying at her husband's known grave than at a separate place, which would have raised questions with her friends. But she marked Driggers's grave anyway, with a small, flat stone. By the time I saw it, the weeds had nearly grown over it, so instead of pulling it up and upsetting her, I let it go.' He rubbed the palm of his hand. 'That turned out to be a mistake.' He sat quietly. 'I can still see us out in that field on Sunday night, digging under a flashlight.'

'Did anyone question you about his disappearance?'

'Sure, but I handled it. I told his parole officer he'd jumped ship and disappeared, and the sheriff took me at my word and eventually closed the case. I think he pieced together what really happened a year or so later, after a couple of late-night whiskeys with Vestie Viney, but he never said a word to me.

'A couple of days later you packed your bags and left without saying goodbye. I couldn't tell if you'd found out what happened, or just suspected something, but the timing was awfully coincidental. Then when you wouldn't take my calls, I decided you'd learned enough about Driggers to be frightened off but didn't want to talk about it. Whatever the reason, we were over. I went back to work convinced I'd lost you but gotten away with Driggers.'

'So that's your secret,' she said.

He stretched, wearily. 'Unfortunately, that's only part of it.' He circled his head, trying to unkink a night spent in a hospital chair, then settled back. 'Even though Driggers was dead, we had the data from his nanoscan in the computer, which meant we had a chance to investigate the memory transfer and the KBS – what had caused it, and how we could cure it.

'We went as far as we could with computer mock-ups, but eventually we needed to make a reverse transfer in order to see what we had. In other words, we had to download Driggers's memory from the computer – or a relevant piece of it – to someone who could tell us if the shirt buttoning exercise had gone over.'

'How could you do that?'

'The same way we did the transfer to him. Find a subject and make a download.'

'But what about the heat problem?'

'We thought we could control it. Generally speaking, downloading a memory phrase or rebuilding damaged cells is cooler than scanning to capture a neural template. But you're right, even then, heat could unexpectedly spike out the way it did with Driggers, and it could cause KBS or retardation, the way it did with Spider. So we tried to construct a safety net before making the reverse transfer. We asked ourselves what would happen if we interrupted the Z-5s while they were in the middle of transferring a phrase to a patient and let them cool off before continuing. You can't do that when you're recording a memory because it would leave blind spots, sort of like turning off your tape recorder in the middle of recording a song. But in a reverse transfer, where you've already got the song and all you want to do is lay it down on another tape, pausing it during transmission shouldn't leave a gap.'

'Did it work?'

'As far as the heat problem was concerned, the lab tests looked good. We were ready to go with a human subject, which I decided should be me again. The first scan had gone fine, so why not try to duplicate it? I was learning things I couldn't have learned otherwise, and I knew the code we'd attached to the shirt-buttoning phrase, which meant I'd be able to tell quicker than someone else if it had seated itself in Driggers.'

'You were pushing your luck, you know.'

'Ego afflicts all scientists and inventors. At that point, I saw myself as Elisha Otis, the man who proved elevator brakes were safe by getting on an elevator and cutting the cable.'

'What happened to you, Cush?'

'The reverse transfer worked, but there was a glitch – what the team calls a Columbo.'

'What's that?'

'An unexpected event that trips you up. Toward the end of the transfer, a large group of Z-5s wouldn't respond to our signals and went on a frolic of their own.'

'My God, that sounds like what happened to Roy Driggers.'

'You mean Patient RAD.'

'They're the same, aren't they?'

'No. RAD stands for Research and Development, the designation we use for in-house projects.'

'In house?'

'Someone in our own lab.'

'Are you saying *you're* RAD?'

'That's right.'

'But Patient RAD has Kluver-Bucy Syndrome.' She digested the thought.

'See what I mean?' he said. 'There's some good news in this story after all. I'm living proof that KBS isn't necessarily fatal. After a few rough weeks it went into remission, and it's been there ever since.'

Come on, J.J. Come out and play. I've got a game for you you're not going to believe.

The sunrise bathed the street in an orange glow. It was nearly six o'clock in the morning now, and Shaw was still at her vigil, waiting for J.J. Jackson to make his move. She had her plan of action worked out in her head, but she couldn't get started until he was in his car and rolling.

She grabbed the steering wheel and shifted her weight in the seat. How long could these people party? Much longer and she'd have bed sores.

She turned toward the window overlooking the East River. 'Why are you doing this, Cush? Not BIAS and repairing brain cells, but transferring memory?'

'There are so many reasons I don't know where to start.'

'Start anywhere, I don't care.'

'When we talk about transferring memory, we're not just talking about passing along recollections of the senior prom or a fun vacation in France. If we can do that, there's no reason we can't capture and transfer all the functions of the brain – knowledge, experience, analytical ability, personality traits, special skills.'

'Like my climbing ability?'

'All your skills. If we had them stored in the computer, we could repair your broken neurons and give you back the memory you had before the operation. We could cure the worst diseases of the brain – Alzheimer's, stroke, even bullet wounds – and keep the person's uniqueness intact, not force him to wander around with a lobotomized stare. But it's neater than that, like fixing a sick heart valve with a new one that's better. We could fix a brain defect and give the patient more knowledge than he had before.'

'What do you mean, more knowledge?'

'Once you can capture the functions of the brain, think of the things that could be done. We could preserve the motor control of a talented surgeon, the eye of a great painter, the spatial relations of a brilliant architect or engineer and pass them on to future generations.'

'Are you sure we'll *want* to do that?'

'I hate sounding like the op-ed page, but ultimately we'll have no choice. Someday the planet's going to be exhausted and the only way to continue life will be to go somewhere else. If we get it right, we'll take our brains – the essence of what makes us human – and download them into titanium bodies that can live in four hundred degree temperatures and breathe hydrogen and sulfer gases. Then we'll travel to new places and perpetuate the human race.'

He picked a daisy from a vase on the table and twirled it between his fingers the way he did on the farm.

'But that's not what started me down this road,' he said.

'What was?'

'My father's death. I remember sitting at his funeral feeling this endless burning in my chest. I heard the preacher say my daddy was in heaven now and someday I'd join him there, but I wanted him here and now, not in the hereafter. I knew the lynch mobs could always kill his body, but what about his mind? What about the things I loved about him most, like the way he loved me and his family and patients? Everyone in Hardy loved my dad. Everyone decent. Sitting there, I tried to figure out how to get him back. When I realized I couldn't do that, I promised myself I'd do the next best thing, which was invent a way to keep the killers from taking away the best part of people like my father. Their personality and intelligence.'

She sat down and watched him play with the flower.

'Of course,' he said, 'over time the fire in the belly cools. There was school and internships, basic science and nanotech engineering. But then one day Spider Murphy showed me that it could happen, and I realized that the promise I'd made to myself at my father's funeral wasn't gone, it was just stored in the attic.' He laid the flower on the table. 'It's going to happen, Camilla. We're only at the glimmer stage now, but whether I do it first or someone else does, preserving memory after the body's wet stuff has died is going to happen. It's a dream that's haunted people since they first mourned a dead child in some godforsaken torch-lit cave. I can't control the process yet – it's only fragmentary so far – but eventually, it's going to happen.'

She walked back to the window. 'Look,' she said.

Joining her, he saw the edge of the sun peeking over the horizon like a fireball erupting out of the earth.

'What's it like,' she said, 'knowing it belongs to you?'

'What does?'

'The sun, the moon, the stars?'

He shook his head. 'I'm not God.'

'If preserving memory beyond the grave isn't playing God, what is?'

He leaned against the window, his head against his hand. 'Why does this always happen when medicine does something new? You need to make up your mind what you want, OK? Do you want nature's gift of smallpox, or do you want Dr Jenner's cure? Are you only going to listen to God when he's talking through a burning bush, or are you interested in what He has to say through Jonas Salk?'

'But this is dangerous, Cush.'

'Hell, yes, it's dangerous, what leap forward isn't? Even the polio vaccine isn't completely foolproof, it still gives the disease to a small number of kids every year.' He was warming up. 'Not long ago people said you couldn't transplant a liver or kidney, it would be violating God's law, creating a Frankenstein's monster. Well, go downstairs and tell that to the family gathered around a sickbed praying for someone else's heart. Dangerous? Satan's miracle? It's so routine people see it as a right.'

He pushed away from the window.

'Improving people's lives has never been risk-free, you just have to win the game. The history books are full of heroes whose outrageous risk-taking became acceptable when they got what they were after, and not just in medicine. How many people died making the robber barons their fortunes? Where's your moral outrage over that guy whose statue stands outside Grand Central Terminal – what's his name, Cornelius Vanderbilt? Lord, you can't *count* the number of people he killed building his canal across Nicaragua, but today Vanderbilt is one of the finest names in the country. How about Menachem Begin, a terrorist who bombed the King David Hotel? How about Yasser Arafat, a terrorist who won the Nobel Peace Prize? How about all the giants who are great because of the marvelous ends they served, regardless of what they did to get there?'

She didn't answer.

'All that hypocritical Sunday-school crap about the ends not justifying the means. Give me a break. It doesn't matter how many cities Sherman burned to the ground as long as he took the South. It doesn't matter how many Chinese railroad workers got pounded into the sand as long as they linked the Atlantic to the Pacific. It doesn't matter how many slaves died in chains as long as the men who put them there wrote a constitution preserving "freedom" and the sanctity of life. It doesn't matter how many Japanese are vaporized as long as it ends an awful war. If you're a general who killed Indians by the thousands, you get a bust of yourself in the Capitol rotunda. I know, I've been there. If you lie, cheat, and steal big enough, you get your face on coins and stamps and your name on universities and foundations. In America – everywhere, for all I know – success is a hell of a lot bigger than integrity.'

He carried the carafe into the bathroom. 'What have I done that bothers you so much?' he said through the door, filling the container. 'I'm not building a private fortune, and I'm not dropping bombs. I'm not even putting innocent people's lives at risk. I'm using killers to find ways to protect people the criminals want to kill.' He walked back into the bedroom and offered her fresh water, then poured himself a glass.

Camilla said, 'What do you want from me, Cush?'

'Right now? Your understanding. It's like what Abraham Lincoln said about the Civil War: if I win it, what they say against me won't amount to diddly-squat, but if I lose it, ten angels swearing I was a great guy won't amount to a hill of beans. If I win what I'm after, I want to be forgiven for the mistakes I've made along the way, just like every other pioneer. I want you to cut me some slack.'

'And what about Roy Driggers?' she said. 'Did you cut him some slack?'

He didn't answer. 'I'm not asking to be forgiven for that. I went too far. Like everybody who makes mistakes, I know I'm going to pay the price. I just don't want it to happen before you and other people can benefit from what I'm doing.'

'Another godly statement,' she said touching the window. 'Actually, I'm glad you're God.'

'Why?'

'You can give me back my life.'

'No, I can't. Not yet.'

'Yes, you can. You saved half my life before, and I'm grateful for it, but now I want the other half.'

He reached out and tried to draw her to him, but she wouldn't let him. 'We were amazingly lucky doing the first stage of your repair,' he said. 'Lucky with you and Hennessy both.'

'Luck is the residue of the well-prepared. I read that in the newspaper yesterday.'

'It was referring to baseball, not brain surgery.'

'Same principle. I don't know how you'll do it, but I know you can.'

'Trying could kill you.'

'I'll take the risk.'

'Why? Look at you – look at the progress you've made.'

'Look at me? OK, let's do. I can't climb, I can't walk right, I can't cook a meal or keep a diary. Never mind the physical limitations, I could probably learn to live with those, but half the time I have to ask what a simple word means. I have a degree in fine arts and engineering and have no idea what they are. I can't even remember who I am when I see myself in photographs.'

'Camilla—'

'But that's not the worst of it. On top of that, now I have this hideous disease that's going to humiliate me and torture me to death – but that's OK, until it happens at least I've got what's left of my mind. But wait, that's not *your* mind you've got there, Cam, that's' – her hands went out – 'Nat Hennessy's!'

'That's a bit of an exaggeration.'

'Not if you were in my shoes last night. Not if you were as scared as I am right now. I don't want to live a life where I'm holding the man I love and suddenly experience the death of someone's father. I don't want to be walking down a street – if I learn how – and wonder when I'll start spewing psycho-babble and spitting at my friends and trying to bite them. I can't live that way. It shocks people. It shocks me.' She stepped over to the coffee table and picked up the article Cynthia Weber had given her. 'If you have any love for me, you'll play God one more time.'

'I'm not God,' he said, standing. 'God doesn't make the mistakes I've made.' He walked to her and took her hands in his. 'Before I go, I want to know one thing. The feelings you showed for me last night – did they come from you or your . . . condition?'

She raised her hands and let him draw her to him. 'Cush,' she said, holding on, 'they came from me. I'm in *love* with you. For all I know, I have been for a long time. But I'm very frightened now.'

He kissed her hair, let her go, and walked to the door.

'Cush?'

'Yes?'

'Did you ever find out if the memory phrase got transferred from you to Driggers?'

'No, but I found one that came back to me during the reverse transfer.'

'What was it?'

'Remember when I got excited last night and started sneezing?'

'Yes?'

'Roy Driggers's nickname was Sneezer.'

They rode on the upper deck of the Liberty Island ferry just as they had three weeks earlier, Nat carrying a bottle of chilled peach champagne and glasses, Camilla carrying a small bouquet of lavender freesias tied with blue and white ribbons. Cush Walker had told them to duplicate as many details of the day as possible.

Watching the briny foam churn beneath the bow, Camilla asked Nat to tell her about the two of them, their history together, partly out of curiosity, partly because she hoped it would wake something sleeping in her brain.

He started by telling her that they'd met on the street while she was climbing, had a disastrous first date, then fell in love. She wanted to know what kinds of fun they had together, so he told her about late dinners and how they talked about everything the way Irish men and Southern women did. He described movies they'd seen and trips they'd taken and the friends they had in common, the food they enjoyed, the music they liked. Sounded pretty nice to her. But it woke no recollections.

On the eve of their wedding, he said, he'd given her a jar of pennies, one for each week he said he'd stay in love with her, enough to last a hundred years. Sounds corny, she said, smiling. Guess you had to be there, he said. I wish I had been, she said. I know I was, but I can't remember.

There were moments when he felt almost familiar to her, but mostly he still seemed a total stranger. What was it about him that had made her fall in love and want to marry him? So bizarre, not

529

having a clue. So scary. And what was he holding back? He kept acting like he wanted to tell her something but couldn't bring himself to do it.

He poured her a glass but she said she'd had too much wine the night before. He told her to hold the glass anyway because she'd done it on their last trip. When she took it, he asked her what she'd been doing the night before to drink too much wine, but then said never mind, he'd rather not know. So full of conflict, this one-time fiancé. About what?

'Is your mother still alive?' she asked.

'No, she died of cancer when I was nine.'

'I'm sorry to hear that,' she said. 'And then your father died when you were eleven?'

'Yes.'

'That must have been awful.'

'It was reasonably bad,' he said.

'Especially considering how it happened,' she said.

He looked over at her. 'You know how it happened?'

'I remembered it all last night.'

'Wow,' he said, 'your memory's not only getting better, it's already better than mine. I didn't think I'd told you that.'

'You have no idea what's coming back to me.' Why not tell him how?

'Camilla, there's something I need to tell you about the man who killed my father.'

'The one with the baseball bat,' she said.

'Yeah,' he said slowly, once again puzzled. 'His name is J.J. Jackson, but before that it was Jackson Levander James. I used to keep a copy of his ID card in my top dresser drawer. Do you remember seeing it?'

'No, but I know what he looks like. Kind of stocky and muscular.'

'How'd you know that?'

'I've seen him.' She sipped champagne and saw an expression

that said, one of us is cuckoo. 'Where is he now, in prison?'

'No, he was acquitted.'

'After what he did?'

'The jury didn't believe me.'

'But that's terrible. I *know* he did it. I saw it.'

Now he looked really worried. 'You couldn't have. It happened when I was a kid.'

'Why did they let him off?' she asked.

'The legal system doesn't always work right.' He leaned his forearms on the railing and watched the water rip past. 'That's why I tried to fix it myself.'

'What do you mean, fix it?'

He was giving her that same expression again, the one that said he had something on his mind. 'I hired someone to kill him.'

It came too fast for her. 'Kill who?'

'I let a criminal go free to kill the man who killed my father. I turned him into my hit man. A guy named Angel Rico.'

She tried to pick up what he was saying. 'Did he do it?'

'No, Jackson killed him first. Then he tried to kill me.'

'How?'

'With a rifle.'

'He took a shot at you? Where?'

'On the torch of the Statue of Liberty.' He waited. 'The afternoon before our wedding.'

A collision in her head.

He said, 'Do you understand what I'm saying?'

Memory was gone, but not logic. That's how I got *shot*? That's how I got this way? 'I – understand.'

'Saying I'm sorry is so inadequate it feels like an insult, but I don't know what else to say.'

Oh, Nat. Speaking softly, she said, 'I'm sure you didn't mean it to happen.'

'No, of course not. Reckless people never do.'

'So that's why you risked your life to bring me out of my coma.' She turned away from him and held her glass on the railing, watching the champagne jiggle.

Neither one spoke for a long time.

'I don't know why,' she said, smiling, 'but I feel like crying.' She looked down at her shoulder bag hanging at her side. 'The last couple of days have been a mess.' She handed him her glass. 'Would you excuse me a minute? I need to get myself together before we reach the statue.'

He watched her turn and walk away, limping, careful not to lose her balance on the lightly rolling deck. After she'd disappeared into the cabin he raised his glass. Congratulations, Nat, you finally did it. He downed the contents.

Now it was time to draw the next breath, the one that began life without her.

Shaw heard a metallic scraping noise and a car horn and woke up with a start, disoriented. Huh? She straightened up and looked around. The radio was on, the air conditioner still blowing, the announcer saying, 'Ten-ten WINS news time five fifteen p.m.'

Five fifteen p.m.? Holy shit, she'd been asleep for the last half hour.

She sat forward and squinted dry-eyed at Jackson's limousine, but couldn't see it. The reason was simple.

It was gone.

She leaned toward the window, disbelieving. Gone? Shit, shit, shit! She'd blown it!

She sat back in a slump and looked off. A block away to her right, a set of tail lights turned bright red, then soft red as the driver's foot came off the brake. They were on the back of a black trunk – a limousine maybe? Yeah, it was a limo, she could see the flying wing antenna on the deck.

She pieced it together quickly: the scraping noise that woke her must have been the limo's bumper hitting the cement ramp as it left the parking lot. Maybe it was J.J. Jackson driving away in a hurry, a little hung over. Whoever it was, he was standing down the street at a green light. Why wait on green? Probably turning on his air conditioner, putting in a CD, getting his wake-up coffee together or strapping on his seat belt. The only thing he couldn't have been doing, she assumed, was waiting for her to wake up and give chase.

She heard the Everly Brothers singing in her head, 'Wake up, little Sally'. Give it a shot. Instinctively, she reached for the ignition key and turned it, grinding the starter into an already running engine. She dropped the car into drive and hit the accelerator, keeping her eyes on the limo up ahead.

The traffic light turned orange. As if the limo saw her coming, it started up and went through. Closing in on it, she saw New York plates, then the letters JJJ.

She stomped on the gas, looked both ways at the intersection, and sailed through the red.

Cush stood at the base of the Statue of Liberty assessing the land, the water, the situation. It was five thirty in the afternoon, the air warm and muggy, the scene virtually indistinguishable from the Fourth of July he was trying to duplicate. He paced like a nervous groom, watching the flags flapping listlessly in a gentle southwest breeze. Would she remember Hennessy and their wedding? Would she fall in love with him all over again? Would she recall the epiphany that had made her blood run cold? Would the floodgates of her memory open?

He walked around the marble plaza at the rear of the statue's massive, fifteen-story stone pedestal, trying to envision what was happening inside. He had arranged for a gangway attendant to pull Nat aside when he and Camilla stepped off the ferry and send him to the nearby information booth where he had made sure Nat understood the ground rules, including why he himself would stay out of sight until the exercise was over.

After crossing the stone plaza, he walked through the massive brass doors and introduced himself to a Park Police guard who was working overtime, reading a book and listening to a Yankees pre-game show on a headset.

Cush looked at the ceiling. 'They on their way up yet?'

'Left a minute ago,' the guard answered, lifting the earphones.

Cush pictured them inside the tiny glass emergency elevator that rose up the statue's hollow interior, between the girders and iron beams.

The guard said, 'How long would you say they're gonna be up there?'

'Half an hour or so,' Cush said. 'Mind if I come in?'

The officer signaled him to walk through the magnetometer. When he did, an alarm sounded.

He unloaded his pockets onto a table: keys, some change, and the cellular telephone Nat had given him when he had taken him aside at the ferry landing. Following his instructions literally, Nat saw no reason to carry a phone he hadn't carried on the Fourth.

Cush walked through the metal scanner again. This time, there was no warning sound.

'Sorry for the fuss, Doc,' the guard said.

Cush walked into a room where the statue's original torch had been on display since the 1986 refurbishing. He was on his way to the mezzanine floor museum to kill time waiting for Nat and Camilla to return. Stopping at the base of the steps, he turned back and called to the guard. 'Is the construction crew out?'

The guard looked up. 'The foreman's making sure right now. He'll be down in a minute.'

Cush waved thanks and looked at the old torch. He hated waiting around with nothing to do. He'd give Nat and Camilla a few minutes to get clear of the area – he didn't want to distract

Camilla by showing himself – then he'd walk up the marble steps to the hallway that held a life-sized replica of the statue's face and hang out there. He checked his watch. It read 5:35.

He waited.

'Wait a minute. This feels familiar.'

Camilla was standing ten feet away from the copper replica of the statue's face, staring at it expectantly. Then quizzically. Then . . . blankly.

'Take your time,' he said. 'You're supposed to just let it come.'

She shook her head. 'I don't remember a thing.'

He tugged gently at her arm. 'Don't worry about it, we weren't here long enough for you to remember.'

'But *you* remember,' she said.

They walked up another flight of steps to the bottom of a spiral staircase leading to the crown and entered the small, glass-enclosed emergency elevator cab that was working after hours. A vertical monorail ran up the side, and a heavy cable drew it upward like a crystal ornament on a Christmas tree. Nat touched the Up button and a quiet whir lifted them toward the top.

'How do you feel?' he asked.

'Hopeful,' she said flatly. Desperate was more like it.

The awkwardness they'd felt on the boat coming over was worse now. Here they were – her without her memory, him partly responsible for the loss – both rising toward the re-enactment of an intimate, romantic celebration that had ended with a bullet in her brain. She couldn't tell what she dreaded more, having to relive the personal stuff or the shooting.

The elevator stopped in the statue's upper chest near her right shoulder and they got out, leaving the door ajar. A few steps later they entered a small gate at the base of a narrow, windowless stairwell leading up the inside of the statue's arm to the small platform encircling the golden flame of the torch.

'You went up first,' he said.

'OK.' She continued up the vertical steps holding a metal railing. When she reached the hatch door in the base of the flame, she turned the handle and pushed it open. The late afternoon sunlight burst over her like an ocean breaker, making her squint. She climbed onto the platform, using her hand to shield her eyes from the golden flame. Nat followed her and closed the hatch door behind him.

Where the hell was he going?

Shaw was moving down the West Side Highway with her cellular telephone in hand, waiting for a long stretch of solitary road where she could execute her plan to nail J.J. Jackson anonymously. Jackson's limousine was rolling along about ten car lengths in front of her in the right lane, nice and steady, within the speed limit, inconspicuous and law-abiding.

It was time to do it. She punched in 911 and hit Send.

A man's voice answered, 'Police operator, emergency.'

'I'm driving down the West Side Highway and a black limousine just ripped past me swerving from one lane to the other. If he's half as drunk as he looks, he's going to kill someone.'

'Which direction are you headed?'

'South.'

'At what cross street?'

'I'm coming up on . . . Ninety-sixth Street.'

'Have you got a plate number?'

'On the limousine?'

'Yes.'

'It's New York license number JJJ 696.'

'You said it's a black stretch?'

'Yes – oh, my God, there he goes again – he just swerved

into the left lane and almost crashed into a car.' She thought that sounded pretty convincing.

'All right, take it easy and tell me what you see.'

'Oh, my God, I think somebody's pointing a gun out the window!'

'Hold the line, ma'am.'

She heard the operator talk to a dispatcher as Jackson's limousine continued its smooth, uneventful trek down the West Side drive. No swerving, no speeding, no gun.

'Where are you now?' the operator asked.

'South of the Ninety-sixth Street exit. Somebody better stop him fast.'

'Stay on the line, ma'am, and don't get too close.'

'Hello?'

'Can you hear me?' the operator said.

'I lost you for a minute,' Shaw said, pretending a bad connection.

'I said stay with him as long as you can but don't get too close.'

'OK.'

The operator talked to the dispatcher again, then to Shaw. 'He isn't pointing the gun at you, is he?'

'No, he's pointing it at the car next to him.'

'Is it a handgun or a rifle?'

Careful, now – this has to be plausible. 'I think it's a rifle.'

'Can you still see him?'

'Barely.'

She knew what was happening on the other end of the line because she'd been there. The 911 dispatcher was relaying a citizen's call to police HQ, and HQ dispatch was sending out a ten-thirty – help needed – to a radio car. Another problem: what if the police car came onto the highway from the on-ramp just up ahead? They'd be looking for a wild limousine to come roaring by, but it wouldn't be wild or roaring. She'd better cover that.

'He's slowing down now,' she said.

She saw a blue police car in her lane an eighth of a mile ahead, ambling along. Jackson's limousine passed it on the left, no problem, no speeding. The police car moved into the left lane behind it, followed it a minute, and bingo! The light bridge lit up.

The limousine moved into the right lane to let the cop pass, but he stayed behind. A siren whooped and the limo pulled onto the off-ramp at 79th Street, down to a circle, the cop car following closely.

Shaw followed at a distance. At the bottom of the ramp, the limousine pulled over peacefully and so did the cruiser. Shaw came to a stop halfway around the circle and sat watching through the windshield, engine idling. Another radio car pulled up behind the first, lights whirling. A female cop got out and joined two men from the first car.

Be careful now, guys. Check the windshield and you'll see there's no registration, which gives you the right to search the vehicle. Check the computer to see if the limo's stolen, and even though it won't be, hold Jackson and do your search. Impound it if you have to – with no registration you can do that, too – but search it for the gun the caller reported seeing. Find the rifle in the trunk and match it to the riflings on the bullet fragments that ripped through Camilla's head.

You don't know it yet, guys, but you're about to be heroes, the men and women in blue who nailed the Statue of Liberty Sniper.

She only wished she could be one of them.

Camilla stood with a hand on the massive gold-leaf flame of the torch, steadying herself until she got used to the altitude. Nat set down the bottle of peach champagne, two glasses, and a pair of binoculars and kept a respectful distance from her. Pushed to the side of the platform was uncollected construction gear:

coils of climbing lines, scaffold ropes, a canvas bag of brushes, buckets of chemicals, a metal canister and, around the torch, a rubber-coated chain that anchored a winch.

'Are you all right?' he asked.

'Yes,' she said. A gentle wind lifted her hair, scribbling a black veil across her face.

He pointed at a bucket of solvent. 'You used to work with this stuff.'

She was gazing at the blue harbor and vast horizon. 'Stunning, isn't it?'

A light bulb blinked. 'That's what you said the last time we were here.'

It is? She brushed her hair from her face and stepped away from the torch to the railing, reaching for it with one hand before letting go of the flame with the other. He stepped forward to offer a hand.

'I'll bet I didn't walk like an old lady the last time I was here,' she said.

'No, but I did.'

'Why?'

'I have a thing about heights.'

'A thing?'

'I get dizzy and nauseated. Sick to my stomach.'

'I know what nauseated means,' she said. It never worked right: they either told you what you already knew, or assumed you knew what you didn't. Either way, you felt like a child.

Nat stepped up to the railing and put his hand on it close to hers. 'That was one of the differences between us,' he said. 'You had no fear of heights.' He looked at her staring out at the sea. 'Does it bother you to look down now?'

'The only thing that bothers me is not remembering anything about it.' That wasn't quite true. Looking down, she couldn't believe she'd climbed over this railing and dangled on a rope and walked down the side of this thing and did whatever she did. No wonder she was once in love with this guy. She was a whole different person back then.

God, she wished she could remember.

Nat stepped back toward the base of the torch and lifted the end of a coiled climbing rope, a half-inch-thick elasticized line marked with violet and white flame stitches. He pulled it back to the platform railing near her hand.

'You know how to use this,' he said, stretching it out in his hands. 'Do you remember what a climbing harness is?'

'It's like parachute straps, isn't it?'

'Exactly, with a hook at your belly.' He handed her the rope.

She took the line in both hands and made a small loop, the beginning of a knot.

'That's good, you're making a bowline,' he said.

She turned the loop one way, stopped, reversed it, and gave up. 'I have no idea.'

He took it from her, dropped it to the floor and pushed it aside, trying to ease her frustration.

'What else did we do?' she said.

'Well, it was the day before our wedding, so we talked about that.' He lifted the bottle of champagne.

'What did we say?'

'What did we say,' he repeated. Using his thumbs, he pried off the cork with a familiar pop. 'Do you have any recollection?'

'None whatsoever.' She looked away. 'I'm sorry, Nat, this must be as awkward for you as it is for me.'

'No problem,' he said.

'I'm a big girl, OK? If this is going to be helpful, we'd better just' – she shrugged – 'do what we did before.'

'Exactly.' He poured.

'I've noticed something,' she said, taking a glass. 'You like to say "exactly" when you're nervous.'

'Really?'

'And "really".' She lifted her glass. 'So, should we get started?'

'Exactly.'

They each took a sip and set their glasses down. She waited for the taste of peach to ignite her memory of the last time they were here, but there was nothing, not even a flicker.

Shaw stood next to the driver's seat of her car leaning on the open door, watching the cops on the other side of the circle milling around Jackson's limo like it was a beached whale. A cop opened the back door and told someone to get out. Charcoal-gray pants emerged first, then a pair of sleek alligator shoes hit the pavement. A good-looking guy stepped out who reminded her of – hey, it was Mr Armani, the stud who'd asked her to go dancing!

What was he doing in Jackson's limo?

She saw a cop talk through the open driver's window, ordering the driver to get out. Sure enough, the door opened and out stepped J.J. Jackson. His face was turned away but she could see what he was wearing: a black uniform, black cap, and black shoes. He was tall and thin and – *tall and thin?*

Wait a second.

The arresting officer turned the driver around, placed his hands on top of the limousine for a pat down, and ordered him to remove his cap. When he did, a waterfall of long, brown hair tumbled onto his shoulders. Make that *her* shoulders.

Shaw felt a torpedo hit her belly. I've been decoyed! This female driver seduced me into thinking Jackson was behind the wheel, got me to follow her from the nightclub, woke me up with a scrape of the bumper and a blast on the horn and a pause at a green light until I saw her and took chase. And Mr Armani? He wasn't asking me to dance – he was checking me out for his boss, Jackson. Told him a cop had broken into his trunk, to which Jackson said, good, keep her busy with the car while I slip away and—

And what?

Oh, my God.

As Shaw started for the driver's seat, the female driver turned and looked directly at Shaw as if she knew she was there all along. It was Dolly. Keeping her eyes on Shaw and her hands on the roof, she spoke a silent message with a gotcha-again smirk.

Hello, Foxy.

'Well, let's see. We were standing right about like this,' Nat said. He reached out and put his hands on her upper arms and guided her away from the railing. 'You were telling me about your grandmother.'

'What was I saying?'

'You were talking about something you'd read in her diary.'

'What else?'

'Cush Walker. You were trying to figure out why you'd left him, I think. Do you remember any of that?'

No, but now that you told me, I don't have to. 'What else?'

He placed the binoculars around her neck. 'We talked about us – you know, predictable romantic stuff.' He looked for a sign of recognition.

'That's a little vague.'

'I was standing right here—'

'You already said that.'

'You were—'

'Standing where I'm standing.'

'Exactly.'

'Then what?'

'We held each other.'

'Uh-huh.'

'Does that ring any bells?'

'Not even a tinkle.'

'Look, Camilla, if you'd rather not—'

'I want my memory back. You don't have to be polite.' She reached out to him.

He took a step forward and took her hands, then drew her into an embrace.

'What did you say to me?'

'Something about helicopters.'

She waited. 'What about them?'

'I said if one of them flew by they'd be able to see us.'

'So what?'

'We were considering doing something that would have entertained them greatly.'

'Really.'

'You said "really". You nervous?'

'Yes, but not as nervous as you are.' She waited, then asked the next logical question. 'In what way, "entertained"?'

'They would have seen us doing what we were talking about doing.'

'You've made that much clear.' She thought about it. 'What were we talking about doing?'

'Uh, let's take this one step at a time.'

'OK.'

He drew her closer to him.

She closed her eyes and tried to remember. 'Is that how we were?' she asked.

'It would be if you put your hands around me like this.' He positioned them.

'Tell me what you said,' she said.

'I said, "You sure you want to do that up here?"'

'Do what?'

'What we were talking about doing.'

'Oh,' she said. 'I think I'm getting the picture. What happened next?'

'You said, "Let's do it and inaugurate the statue."'

'Inaugurate?'

'Do something for the first time.'

'Mm-hm. This was getting serious.'

'Afraid so. Any recollections?'

'Not yet. What happened next?'

'I said something like, "Don't you think one of the horny little Frenchmen who built this thing must have inaugurated it already?" And you pulled me over here.'

'I pulled you?'

'I was happy to go.' He placed her hands around his belt as she had done before and made her draw him toward the torch. 'Any bells?'

'No bells.'

'We sat down here.'

'What for?'

'To . . . fool around. Know what I mean?'

'I have a pretty good idea,' she said. She liked him enough to do that? Amazing. She wanted to bring back her memory, but there were limits. 'Maybe we'll skip that part for the moment.'

'Exactly.' He sounded relieved. Or disappointed. 'After awhile, we stood up and went back to the railing.'

They stepped over to it. Nat looked over the edge, briefly, then at her.

'Did you look down like that?' she asked.

'Yes.'

'Even though you're afraid of heights?'

'Yes. Would you like to take a break?'

'No. What happened next?'

'You had your back to the railing, like this.' He positioned her. 'There were a pair of binoculars around my neck and I was looking over your shoulder toward the water. There was a boat at the dock with a man standing in the back of it.'

'In the stern.'

'You recall that word?'

'Unimportant words come back to me all the time.'

'I thought I could see him looking up at us with a telescope, so I raised the binoculars like this and looked down at him.' He raised them from her side. 'How about that. There's a man in a boat down there right now.'

'What was I doing?'

'Holding on to me.' He lowered the binoculars.

'Like this?'

'Harder.'

'Like this?'

'Harder.'

'How about this?'

'That's about it.'

'Oh, wow,' she said. 'I must have had some serious feelings for you.'

Must have had. There it was again, that killer past tense. He held her tightly with one hand, the binoculars with the other.

'How long did we stay like this?'

'About as long as we are now.'

'Then what happened?'

'We kissed each other.'

There was a lapse in conversation. 'I see,' she said. 'On the lips?'

'Mostly.'

'Where else?' Before he responded she said, 'Don't answer that.' The silence that followed was more embarrassing than the answer. 'Cush says emotional memory is the strongest,' she said.

'I know,' he said. 'Does that mean if kissing me was an emotional experience, there's a chance your recollection will come back?'

'I would think so,' she said. 'But that also means if it wasn't that good, I probably won't remember.'

He'd take his chances. If she didn't like it, he always had the railing.

'What did you do with the binoculars?' she asked.

'I held them away from your face,' he said.

'I think you should do it now.'

'Hold the binoculars away?'

'Kiss me.'

'Are you sure?'

'I think so.'

'Would you like to think it over?'

'No, I'd like to get on with it.'

Get it over with, is what he heard. 'OK,' he said. 'Here goes.'

The magnetized red light was rotating on top of the car, and so was one in the windshield. Shaw hit the siren button, moved a taxi cab into the right lane, and floored it until she had to brake behind a truck carrying lawn mowers.

She held her cellular phone in front of her face to keep her eyes more or less on the road as she dialed. What was Nat's pager number? Damn. 917, then 555, then 6897 – or was it 6987?

She punched in the first number with her thumb and hit the Send button. Static, no connection. She moved into the right lane and passed a guy cruising in the left – that always pissed her off – then streaked down the West Side Highway. She hit Redial and waited. Silence filled her telephone ear, the siren on her car filled the other.

There was a connection. 'Leave a message on my pager at the tone,' the canned voice said. She cut it off by punching in her phone number, knowing Nat would recognize it instantly. If, that is, he was carrying his pager. For good measure, she punched in a three-number code and the star button that to cops meant emergency – call back immediately!

She passed a string of cars on her left.

Even if he had his pager, was it on his belt or in his jacket? In the afternoon heat his jacket would be off. Being with Camilla, he'd turn the audible signal off too. Would he feel the vibrator?

She got on the police radio and hit transmission. 'Detective Shaw, Central, K.' K at the end of a sentence was police talk for 'over'.

'Central, K.' His transmission ended with a radio sound, *psht*.

'I'm on the West Side Highway at Thirty-fourth Street going south and I need a harbor unit to ten-eighty-five me forthwith at the old fireboat house next to Battery Park, K.'

'Where you going, Detective? K.' *Psht*.

'Liberty Island. We may have someone stalking an officer with a gun, K.'

'Ten-four, stand by.' *Psht*.

She cursed the traffic.

Nat's cellular phone. Maybe he was carrying that.

She picked up her own cellular phone and punched in his number. 'Come on, Nat,' she said aloud, praying that he could hear the ring.

Hearing a tweeting sound in the room where he was waiting, Cush turned to find it but the tone turned with him: it was coming from his own pocket, from the telephone Nat had given him before rejoining Camilla. He pulled it out and hit the green button and put it to his ear.

'Hello?'

Static, and a distant voice. '. . . Shaw here, who is this?'

'This is Dr Cush Walker.' More static. No answer. 'Hello?'

'. . . ective Nat Hennessy . . . is . . . the eye . . . copy?'

'I didn't get that,' Cush said. 'Say again.'

'. . . Tell Detective Hennessy . . .' No more words.

'I got Hennessy,' he said. 'Say the rest.'

'Jack . . . the eye . . .'

Jack the eye?

Shaw said, 'Repeat . . . J.J. . . . the island.'

Jack the eye . . . J.J. the island.

'J.J. Jackson is on the island?'

'Ten-fo . . .'

Cush's eyes turned upward toward the inside of the statue's head. He heard himself asking the guard if the construction crew was out of the building, and the guard's answer: 'The foreman is making sure everybody's out, he'll be down in a minute.'

'Good God,' Cush whispered.

Nat pulled Camilla close to him with both hands and touched his lips to hers. He felt himself falling into her once again, touching her, kissing her, feeling his center of gravity drawn to her. He wondered what she was thinking.

She was thinking: Not bad, this kiss.

He: It's Camilla.

She: I know one thing I saw in this guy.

He: Is she remembering anything about me?

She: I don't remember a thing about him, but stay with it – one little turn of the key and the floodgates could open.

After a long kiss, she signaled she'd had enough, sliding her glacial indifference across his heart, uprooting everything soft and green in its path.

He pulled back and placed his lips on the side of her neck, forgetting that he was supposed to look over her shoulder at the dock where the sniper's boat had been moored.

After a moment she pulled away. 'That was a lovely kiss,' she said.

He continued holding her. 'Any bells?'

'Sorry.'

'This is when the bullet hit.' He looked down at the dock and the boat that was still sitting there with a man in the cockpit. 'For a split second I actually saw it coming.'

'What did it look like?'

'A June bug. Remember what they are?'

'Sort of.'

'My hand was on the back of your neck where it is now, and that's when it hit.'

She drew away from his arms. 'What happened after that?'

'I cradled you to the floor and yelled for help and took you to the hospital. When I looked back at the dock, the shooter was gone.'

She eyed the water's edge where the sniper's boat had been moored, just like the boat that was sitting there now. 'I don't remember any of it.' After a few moments of silence, she said, 'Thanks for trying, Nat, I think it's time to go.'

The hatch door at the base of the torch opened and a wooden box of tools slid onto the deck followed by a man's head and torso. He sported a trim mustache, an orange jumpsuit, and a pair of sunglasses beneath the bill of a pulled-down baseball cap. On his hands were chamois gloves.

'Excuse me,' the construction worker said, looking at Camilla. 'You people mind if I gather up a few things before the boat leaves?'

Nat didn't recognize him even though he'd seen him a thousand times before – by the light of a bonfire, in a courtroom, under the stage at Radio City, and in countless bitter dreams.

The twin engines rumbled with a deep-throated growl, driving the 25-foot-long police boat through the water. Shaw peered into the July haze toward the torch but it was still too far away to see anyone on the platform. The boat slapped the top of a shallow wave, pitched up slightly, and skimmed across the top to the next one, snapping its blue canvas bimini in the wind. They were doing 35 knots, at least.

She turned back toward the boat's skipper, her red hair blown into a cocoon around her face, and formed a pair of make-believe binoculars with her hands.

The skipper pointed at a strong box at the top of the well leading to a weather cabin below. She opened the lid and lifted out a pair of rubber-coated binoculars. Placing the safety cord around her neck, she raised the lenses to her face, adjusted the focus, and searched the statue. All she could see was a copper-green blur bouncing up and down. They'd have to get closer.

She rested the binoculars on her chest, turned to the skipper, and stepped over the bulkhead, making her way back to the helm. When she reached him she leaned toward his ear and shouted above the engine noise.

'What else have you got?'

'Binoculars?' he yelled back as a question.

'Weapons,' she said.

He lifted a lanyard from around his neck with a silver key dangling from a hook at the end. 'The cabinet,' he shouted, pointing at the door.

*　　*　　*

Cush climbed the last steps to the deck in the statue's shoulder, lungs burning, breathing through his mouth. He saw the small glass elevator standing with its door partly open, unresponsive to the Call button below. Entering the inside of the statue's arm, he could hear voices shouting over each other, punctuating the air with the madness of a cockfight. Panting, moving quietly, he climbed the rungs of the ladder and cautiously cracked the hatch to the platform.

Sunlight bouncing off the torch's flame momentarily blinded him. Adjusting his focus, he saw a man he assumed was Jackson standing with a burning butane torch in his right hand, Camilla's neck in his left, her back against his chest and her fingers digging into a forearm that choked her. Her feet were nearly lifted off the ground and her eyes were wild, focused on a blue flame whooshing a few inches from her face.

He looked to his left and saw something equally bizarre: Nat Hennessy standing outside the railing that encircled the platform, the tips of his shoes barely securing a toehold on the metal lip, his hands whitening from the tension of his grip. His head was lowered as if he'd just run a mile.

Suddenly there was more shouting. Jackson was commanding Hennessy to let go of the railing and balance on his toes. It was blood sport. Sadism. The yellow insanity of an execution.

Nat raised his head and saw Jackson bring the torch closer to Camilla's face.

She screamed.

Cush opened the hatch door with a bang.

Jackson backed up a step, muscles quivering, eyes set on the intruder.

Camilla gagged out, 'Cush!' before Jackson's hand covered her mouth.

Cush stared at her captor, trying to gauge the depth of his lunacy. Foamy spittle dotted his mouth, his eyes were bloodshot, and veins stood out on his neck. Wildness was everywhere, manic spikes knifing the air.

Cush looked over at Nat and saw his face flushed and strained, surprised to see him. Everyone's breathing was short, everyone's muscles tight.

Cush climbed up to the platform and stood with his back touching the statue's golden flame, trying to remain cool.

J.J. Jackson said, 'Welcome aboard, punk.'

Nat leaned forward from outside the railing to rest his ribs on his hands and relieve the tension in his arms and back. He was literally on edge, stretched to the limit.

Jackson waved the butane torch like a music director's wand, motioning Cush to move toward Nat.

'Take it easy,' Cush said to Jackson.

'Shut up and get over there.'

Cush stepped sideways, keeping his eyes on Jackson, walking with his hands raised, palms down and open, no threat here. As he moved toward Nat he looked for an angle, an exit, an inspiration.

'Move!' Jackson said, and brought the tip of the torch closer to Camilla's head. The sound of the flame changed pitch and scorched a new pattern of air.

Nat lifted his eyes. Camilla tried to say something, but Jackson's hand muffled her voice.

Nat erupted: 'Leave her alone!'

'Over there, motherfucker!' Jackson yelled at Cush.

Cush's viscera rattled the cages of his memory. He'd felt like this only twice in his life – once visiting a state prison shortly before a riot, once in the south pasture the night of his father's lynching.

Cush raised his open palms higher, saying, take it easy, be cool, I hear you. He saw Jackson's legs trembling inside his overalls, making the orange fabric shiver.

Cush continued moving toward Nat with his eyes on Jackson.

'Take his hand,' Jackson told him.

Cush reached out and grabbed Nat's wrist.

'Not there,' Jackson said. 'There.'

Cush didn't get it.

'Outside.'

He got it. Jackson was telling him to climb over the railing and stand next to Nat and hold onto him with one hand and the railing with the other. He was telling him to put himself in Nat's shoes. He was telling him to get ready to jump.

Stall. Wait. Pretend. Maybe he could rush him – but by the time he got there her face would be a piece of seared hash, her eyes charcoal sockets. He searched Nat's face for a ploy.

Nat's eyes darted, looking for a way to exploit the momentary disruption created by Cush's arrival. If it had ever been there, it was gone now. Jackson and his torch were in control.

Jackson waved the weapon at Cush. 'Do it!'

Cush looked over the edge of the railing – paused a moment as if looking for something specific – then crossed in front of Nat, placing the detective between himself and J.J. Jackson. When he found the spot he wanted, he lifted his leg, straddled the railing, and brought his other leg over it in a slow hurdle, pushing Nat a little closer to their captor. After establishing his toehold, he turned his head and looked down again in the direction of the statue's head and spikes and Gallic nose, but mostly at her right arm, which was holding the torch they were standing on. It was raised at a sloping angle, and just below her elbow, bunched up on her biceps, was a mass of rippled copper depicting the folds in the sleeve of her Greek gown. He didn't want to look beyond, but it was unavoidable. The stone-hard plaza was distant and uninviting. He imagined keeping his eyes on it all the way down, seeing it rush up, feeling his soft cells yield to marble ones in one painless, unforgiving instant.

He turned back, hands on the railing, and waited.

'Put your arms around each other,' Jackson said. Cush looked at Nat and stood still. 'Goddamn it, I'm tired of telling you to do everything twice!'

'Tell me what you want,' Nat said.

Jackson disregarded the question, squeezing Camilla tighter around her mouth and nose, suffocating her. Tears streamed down her face.

'Do it!' Jackson screamed at Cush.

'Take it easy!' Nat yelled.

'Shut up or I'll burn her!'

'Don't hurt her!' Nat yelled. He was red-faced and furious, an animal crammed upside down into a small cage. Once again the air was filled with stretched wires, snapping and pinging into coils.

Holding onto the railing with his right hand, Cush lifted his left off the railing and placed it around Nat's shoulder. Doing likewise, Nat held the railing with his left and raised his right to Cush's back and grabbed his shoulder. The two of them stood like a pair of old buddies, two Flying Wallendas about to swing out into space without a trapeze.

Jackson pushed Camilla forward and edged up closer to the two men, careful not to come within range of Nat's cobra hand. He wanted to see them in intimate detail when they stepped off the steel footing, see whether their cheeks were trembling or frozen, their mouths open or closed, their eyes savage with the last seconds of life or already dead and gone. He'd made that inquiry before and found it high-quality erotic juice like no other, not even what he got from a spinner. He wanted a taste of it, real bad. He wanted it now.

The safety of the platform floor beckoned to Cush's eyes. It was right there inside the railing, but for all practical purposes it might as well have been a mile away.

A mile away, Shaw waved her hand at the skipper, signaling him to slow down. He pulled back on the throttle and the boat settled into deep watery troughs, rolling lightly from side to side as it quartered the harbor's swells.

Shaw raised her binoculars and found four figures standing on the torch. There was Jackson and Camilla – what were they doing? – and there was Nat and Cush Walker standing side by side – *outside* the railing? What in the world—

She understood.

She lowered the binoculars and raised a high-velocity .22 and rested the barrel on the top of the window above the cabin. The last time she'd held a rifle was at a county fair shooting lead ducks. She knew how to squeeze a trigger, not pull it, but on a rocking boat? With three innocent people in her sights? She wiped the hair from her eyes and leaned into the scope, her hands oily with sweat.

She placed the largest part of Jackson in her scope and talked to herself. 'Aim high and to the left of Camilla.' The thought of shooting her in the same way she'd been shot before, on the same platform, with the same people, momentarily froze her.

The boat was rocking in a regular rhythm. The next time the cross hairs passed over Jackson's back, she'd do it. Here it comes: ready – set – *now!*

She squeezed the trigger but nothing happened. She looked at the bolt. Problem wasn't there – problem was here, with the safety – she'd forgotten to push it off.

She reset the rifle and looked into her scope and felt her doubts start to smother her. If she'd taken the shot it might have hit any one of them – or missed them all. She lowered her weapon. 'We gotta get closer,' she yelled to the skipper.

He pushed the throttle full forward, nearly knocking her off her feet.

Their feet were growing tired from standing on their toes.

Nat's voice was deliberate now, hard and weary but rational. He was appealing to J.J. Jackson's self-interest, his sense of survival. He'd never get off the statue without being caught, Nat said. Once he and Cush hit the plaza floor, the Park Police would be up here in a second, seal the doors, and catch Jackson on his way down.

'Not with your girlfriend as my hostage,' Jackson said. He waved the torch again, changing its tone from high hiss to low. 'When I count to three, both of you take a step back and let go.'

Camilla's eyes were rebelling, her head shaking, no, don't do it! The jet of blue flame heated her cheek, turning it red.

'How do we know you'll let her go?' Nat asked.

'You don't. One . . .'

'Then why should we jump?'

'If you don't, I'll burn off her nose. Two . . .'

'You'll do it anyway!'

'Then I'll do her eyes. Three.'

Nat and Cush stood still, transfixed.

'I said three, gentlemen,' Jackson said.

They did nothing.

'OK,' he shrugged. 'Watch this.'

He lowered his left hand from Camilla's mouth to get his fingers out of harm's way, then placed his forearm across her throat and brought the blue flame close to her face. Feeling the heat, she jerked her head forward as hard as she could, placing her hair in the path of the fire. Small yellow and orange sparks flew around her head. Her eyes were crushed closed. She screamed.

Nat and Cush both leaned forward yelling, 'No! No! No! Stop!' reaching for Camilla, for Jackson, for a shred of sanity.

Camilla's hands flailed at the crackling flames in her hair, smacking them until they were out. Smoke and the stench of burning human cells rose around her like a sacrifice to this big, impassive, copper goddess. Her face was shrouded in a thick haze, her eyes closed and her mouth open in a long, rhythmic sob that turned silent like a baby crying itself into breathlessness.

Jackson coughed and waved the blue torch flame through the rising smoke to clear it from his nose and throat. He wanted the air to be still and clean when he burned her face off. He wanted to see the two men's reactions clearly. He wanted to maximize the tingly pleasure in his groin.

'Either way, you boys are going to die,' he said. 'Do it my way and at least the girl lives. Now, let's try that again.'

Cush Walker stood watching and listening, now intense and strangely silent, so calm it was almost as if he was no longer there. He lowered his left hand from Nat's shoulder, looked down his side, and edged a few steps around the platform to his right, carefully positioning himself. Standing alone now, holding the railing with both hands, he looked up and stared through an invisible wall into Camilla's eyes. Even in her frenzy, she understood what he was going to do. Once again, she shook her head and body in a frenzied no!

Without saying anything, Cush let go of the railing, stepped backward into the soft, hazy air – and fell.

Nat grabbed for him instinctively, caught his shirt, and felt it rip in his hand. Cush dropped easily, feet first, as if he was bouncing on a trampoline.

Looking down, Nat saw why he had moved so deliberately to his right before stepping into space: he was trying to fall onto the statue's up-stretched forearm. Having saved Camilla – temporarily – he was making a last-ditch effort to save himself.

His feet hit the statue's arm above the elbow after a descent of about twelve feet. The second his shoes made impact he grabbed for the copper plates, trying to break his fall. It was logical but desperate beyond hope: the angle was too steep, smacking his torso against the metal covering, knocking the wind out of him and sending a clatter up the arm. When his feet hit the copper gown gathered at the statue's biceps, it flipped him over into a half cartwheel.

Jackson pulled his hostage to the edge of the railing to get a better look. Camilla's nostrils puffed in and out and her head continued shaking a ferocious no.

Cush hit the statue's shoulder head first and came to rest against the side of her neck, a whisper away from sliding across her collarbone and down her breast to the granite floor some twenty-five stories below. He was lying on his side in a precarious perch, his legs bent at the knees as if he was a runner photographed in mid-stride, one hand on his hip, casually, the other beneath his head like a pillow. Except for a breeze that flipped his necktie onto his face, there was no sign of life.

If you're alive, don't wake up, Nat told him telepathically. *Move an inch and you'll go down.*

'Goddamn,' J.J. Jackson said, looking at his victim. 'The nigger did it.' He raised his blow torch closer to Camilla's head and spoke to Nat. 'You next, bitch.'

Nat had nothing left but rage. 'Fuck you.'

'You want to see her light up?' he said.

'Go to hell.'

'You ever seen a hole burned through a head?' Jackson gave him a knowing smile that said, I have. Then his smile disappeared. 'Move around toward me.' He pulled Camilla backward to stay out of Nat's reach. 'This time I want a clean drop all the way down.'

Nat moved away from the statue's arm as slowly as he could, holding the railing as he shuffled away from the statue's arm toward Camilla and her captor.

'That's far enough,' Jackson said. 'Now, kiss your Saxon ass goodbye!'

Nat stood speaking to Camilla with his eyes. Should I rush him? his arched eyebrows asked. Yes, her narrowing eyes answered. But he'll kill you, his furrow said. He'll kill me anyway, her closed lids answered. Nat shook his head, we don't know that. Any delay extends your life. The Park Police, a passing helicopter – anything could happen that's better than watching him burn you to death.

'Let go!' Jackson barked.

Nat looked along his left side to the ground. There was nothing between him and the marble plaza. He looked back at Camilla and spoke to her with his eyes: I have to go now, sweetheart. Time to shed the body. Time to disconnect.

'Jump!' Jackson said. 'I got business to tend to after you're gone.'

Nat heard that. 'Business?'

Jackson grabbed the front of Camilla's hair and pulled her head downward and moved his hand to the back of her head, pushing her hair out of the way, exposing the nape of her neck. 'Where's the hole where the bullet went in, baby?' He fingered her hairline. 'There it is.' He turned her to the side so that Nat had a clear view of the scar, then he stuck out his tongue and licked the wound. 'When you're a grease spot down there,' he said to Nat, 'I'm gonna open this sucker up again and get into the soft pink stuff inside. Know what I'm saying?'

Nat threw one leg over the railing.

Jackson pinched his forearm under Camilla's chin and choked her, no longer playful, then brought the torch to her head.

Nat straddled the balustrade, trembling.

Jackson lowered the flame from Camilla's head to the railing.

Nat felt the heat creep along the stainless-steel pipe toward him, heating his left hand – it turned so hot he had to let go – then felt it on his right. Any second now, he'd have to release it—

He heard a hiss above his head, followed by the delayed sound of a *crack* from afar.

Everyone froze.

They heard a second bullet arrive – no hiss this time – just

559

splintered gold leaf and copper plating where it hit the torch above their heads.

Jackson flinched instinctively, head down, shoulders hunched, looking up.

Nat hurdled the railing.

He rammed into Camilla first, pushing her into Jackson and knocking the three of them onto the platform floor in a sandwich. Straddling the lower half of Jackson's body, Nat rode him like a steer and reached over Camilla's shoulder trying to gouge out his eyes. His left hand fumbled for Jackson's right torch hand, found his wrist, and pinned it to the floor of the platform.

Jackson's free left hand rode up Nat's arm to his neck, onto his chin, and viciously drove his head up and back.

Camilla squirmed out from between them and fell against Jackson's wooden tool box, spilling its contents onto the floor. She rolled onto her hands and knees coughing, trying to open her windpipe.

With his head driven back, Nat saw nothing but sky. His hand slid off Jackson's face and felt a rope nestled beneath his neck. Grabbing it, he pushed it onto Jackson's Adam's apple, forcing a dry hack from his mouth. Then he felt the heat of the torch on his arm.

Jackson's right arm was stronger than Nat's left. Slowly, he was lifting the torch and curling it toward Nat's elbow. It was coming closer – more heat – *can't stop it* – getting hotter. He tried to look down, but Jackson's hand held his head back too far to see. He could tell that the rope in his right hand was worthless unless he could cinch it across Jackson's neck with both hands, which meant he'd have to let go of Jackson's torch hand and grab the line, which meant—

More heat. The hair on his arm was burning.

He's going to kill me unless I *go . . . for . . . it.*

He released Jackson's right hand, felt the torch flame curl into his torso, and grabbed the loose end of the rope and ran it across Jackson's neck and pushed down with all his weight. The heat of the torch pierced his side, sharp and dry like cold steel, then moved across his ribs like the tip of an icicle. It didn't hurt as much as it should have – adrenaline and the loss of sensation caused by the brain scan helped deaden the pain. So far.

He pushed the rope so deeply into Jackson's neck it disappeared, cutting off his breath. Nat instantly saw the two possibilities: if he had squeezed off Jackson's windpipe while he had a lung-full of air, Jackson would have enough oxygen to hold the torch until it was too late. But if he had caught him at the bottom of an exhale, with no breath left . . .

He had. Jackson let go of the torch, and Nat's chin, and clawed at the rope with both hands, desperately searching for air. With the trigger on the torch released, the butane flame died and the tank rolled against Camilla's foot as she was rising to one knee, coughing.

At last Nat could see what was happening. Jackson hacked out the bit of air remaining in his mouth, scratched at Nat's arm a moment, and returned his fingers to the rope.

'You're killing him!' Camilla rasped.

Yes! Yes! You got it! I'm killing him! Jackson's eyes were bulging and his tongue had popped out of his mouth, soft and pink.

Nat pushed down harder.

Jackson's eyes were turning sleepy, his eyelids closing halfway over watery pools.

'Oh, my God,' Camilla said.

That comment didn't sound like it was meant for Jackson. Nat glanced at her and found her transfixed, hand at her mouth. staring at his left side. Looking where she was looking, he saw his burned shirt and two ribs glistening beneath a streak of red and blackened flesh. A viscous liquid he'd never seen before was oozing from the wound.

Shock was starting to set in. He felt like a scaffold about to collapse.

'Help me . . . kill him,' he wheezed.

'You don't need to – you've got him!'

Don't need to? *Got* him? Was her brain that damaged? As long as Jackson had so much as a whisper in his lungs, he'd try to kill them both.

Nat was breathing with a rattle now, feeling his muscles burn out. He needed her to regain her senses. He needed his gun. He needed the police. He needed help.

Jackson managed to suck in a half lung-full of air in a reverse cough. Nat yanked the rope tight again, choking it off, but he had no strength left.

I gotta get off the tiger's back . . .

The tools that had spilled onto the floor from Jackson's tool box appeared in the visible sector of his eyes: a screwdriver, pliers, a cordless drill, a C–clamp – a cordless drill.

It was lying on its side, and tightened in the chuck was a paddle bit – an inch-wide flat hunk of steel with a razor sharp spike made to rip holes in plywood.

He pulled the rope tight with all his remaining strength and blinked away the sweat. Where in God's name were the police?

'Police!'

Shaw ran toward the entrance at the rear of the statue, went through the door, and found a guard sitting at a table with his feet up, a pair of earphones strapped over his head, reading a book. Obviously he hadn't heard the rifle shots.

She snatched off the headset. 'We got a problem!' she puffed, showing her shield.

The guard put down his book. 'What's going on?'

'I've got an NYPD detective up there,' she pointed upward and caught her breath, 'and somebody's trying to kill him!'

The chair dropped onto all fours. The guard grabbed his walkie-talkie and stood up. Shaw pulled him outside onto the plaza behind the statue. 'Look!' she said, pointing.

Cush Walker's foot dangled over the back of the statue's shoulder, and above that, at the torch, was – what *was* that? She backed up for a better angle and shielded the light from her eyes. There was one man standing on the platform, and another man – she couldn't tell who – was kneeling in front of him, head back, sucking on something the other man was holding.

He had the drill bit stuck inside his mouth. If the trigger was squeezed, the steel paddle would rip a hole through the back of his throat and sever his spinal cord. It wasn't a .38 special, but it was enough of a weapon to keep Nat's subject at bay.

Jackson's head was tilted up as if in prayer. At Nat's direction, both his hands were stuffed inside the pockets of his jumpsuit, out of the way.

Nat's left arm was worse than useless; when he moved it, pain exploded through his body. The hole burned in his side finally hurt more than the anesthesia of his nerve disorder could handle. Still, he was awake enough to experience a moment he'd dreamed of for years: a chance to dangle J.J. Jackson at the end of his slender mercy. The panic on Jackson's face, the pounding in his neck, the abject fear of impending death – Nat wanted to be awash in them, to drown twenty years of hate in their rapture. Once he triggered the drill it would be all over – no more burning in the blood, no more vengeance in the name of the father.

Fuck atonement. He wanted to see Jackson suffer.

First, with a confession.

Sweat clouded his vision. He poked the steel spike on the bit against the back of Jackson's mouth and widened his eyelids like a truck driver in need of No–Doz. Then dizziness, the world turning on a Ferris wheel.

'You killed . . . my father . . . Tell me . . . you're sorry.'

'Ah sorry.'

'Don't lie to me, asshole!'

Jackson appeared confused.

Camilla watched impassively with her hands at her throat, her eyes filling with tears.

'Give me a sign,' Nat told Jackson, 'and I'll end it for you. A blink, a nod . . .'

J.J. crushed his eyelids closed and held them tight – there'd be no blink from him, no self-immolation. He held still and waited for the drill bit to explode through his head, his face scrunched up as if it already had.

Nat's strength was falling below minimums. He saw pinwheels in what was left of his vision. 'I'm . . . losing it,' he said to Camilla.

'What can I do?' she said.

'Look away . . . while I finish it . . .'

'Wait!' She lifted a climbing rope from one of the coils that rested on the platform at their feet. 'I'll tie him up!' She racked her brain for a memory, a breach in the dam. A knot, a knot – how do you tie a knot?

Nat caressed the trigger but didn't squeeze it. This disease she had . . . and this feminine sentiment . . . this amnesia, this craziness . . . he couldn't wait any longer, he had to kill the bastard . . . now.

He sank to his knees and rested his left armpit on the railing to hold himself up. The weight of his body loosened the clots in the hole in his side and fresh blood began seeping out. The shank of the bit was slipping out of Jackson's mouth. Sweat streamed down Nat's face and neck. He caught a glint of hope in Jackson's eye . . . then fuzzy worms . . . then color, shapes, vision, disappearing.

Camilla bent down and looped the rope around J.J. Jackson's ankle and drew the end back and tied a slip knot on the line. She had it! She remembered!

Too little too late.

Jackson pulled a hand from his pocket and removed the drill bit from his mouth. Nat hit the trigger and heard the paddle whir harmlessly in mid-air. Jackson knocked the tool from his hand and Nat slumped onto his side, his left hand still holding the railing, his eyes fixed in a glassy stare.

Jackson rose to his feet and watched Nat breathing in short gasps. No problem, J.J.'s expression said. He'd deal with this piece of shit in a minute.

First, he wanted the live one. The spinner.

Camilla backed up a step. Jackson rubbed his rope-burned neck, front and back, then rolled his head in a circle like a prize fighter warming up. 'When I get done with you, you gonna wish you weren't born a girl.'

She backed up another step, circling the tiny platform to the pile of construction equipment blocking her path.

She was trapped.

Her foot hit metal and knocked it over with a clang. The object responded with a blubbery squeal, the sound of air escaping the pinched neck of a balloon. A puff of white air drifted across the platform in front of her knees . . . like smoke . . . like fog . . . like something her brain was desperate to recall. Yes! *Liquid nitrogen* . . . warming in a canister . . . bleeding off through a spring valve. Liquid nitrogen, the chemical that once burned my arm. I can see it now. I remember!

She reached down and picked up the stainless-steel canister with the diamond-shaped red warning label and drew her hand down the rubber hose to the handle at the base of the wand. Her fingers moved onto the trigger as if they'd been there yesterday. She raised the wand and pointed it at her stalker.

Jackson looked at her through half-lidded, contemptuous eyes. 'OK, bitch, put down the bug spray—'

She squeezed the trigger and shot a stream of liquid nitrogen out the nozzle – at nearly 340 degrees below zero, fluid so cold it turned soft metal into peanut brittle. The moment it touched the warm air it vaporized into a jet stream of freezing fog.

The first blast caught him on the chest, freeze-drying his jumpsuit into orange-white powder. He looked down at it, then up at her, his contempt for her now giving way to surprise.

She raised the nozzle and pulled the trigger again. This time the mist hit his face.

He screamed and covered his eyes with both palms. She hit him again. When the gaseous ice had cleared, the backs of his hands had turned to powder and the skin was cracking and sloughing off.

He dropped them away. His cheeks and forehead were a mass of red and white blisters, his eyebrows and mustache burned off. The epithelial layers of his eyeballs were peeling away like the filmy skin of a hard-boiled egg.

It wasn't good enough. She blasted him again.

He screamed and covered his eyes again and stood like a child playing hide and seek who won't stop yelling.

She stepped forward and shoved the tip of the wand into his open mouth and pulled the trigger. A stream of liquid nitrogen rippled through the hose and out the wand into his esophagus. When it hit body temperature, it expanded into a gas 850 times the volume of the fluid pumped into him.

It really didn't require that much.

When Nat's vision returned, he had difficulty understanding what he was seeing. J.J. Jackson looked like an astronaut in a punctured space suit, his body erupting with white fog from his nose and mouth like steam from a cartoon bull. Unable to vent itself fast enough, the gas was creating escape routes of its own, opening holes in the base of his neck first, then spewing pink steam out of every outlet it could find or invent: his nose, mouth, and ears, his eye sockets, sinuses, and cheeks. His head began to look like the pockmarked surface of the moon, its old craters erupting with new geysers.

He stumbled backwards in silence, his voice box frozen to dust, cold gas still whooshing from unlikely orifices. He fell across Nat's spine as he was struggling to rise from his hands and knees.

The weight of Jackson's body gave Nat new strength. 'Get . . . off . . . my . . . BACK!'

Jackson rose into the air, slid off Nat's shoulders onto the railing, and teetered there a moment, his hands flailing like a baby tossed on a blanket.

Then he fell.

Nat held onto the railing to steady himself and watched Jackson claw the air for a sky hook.

Camilla stared at the rope she'd tied to his ankle and watched it uncoil at a furious rate, listening to it *zizz* on the metal handrail as it played out. A flash of the last few feet streaked toward the sky and the sound stopped. There'd been no time to tie the end to the winch chain around the base of the torch.

Nat leaned forward, forgetting his acrophobia, and watched Jackson's body trail the rope behind him like a roll of unfurling toilet paper. His body became smaller and more distant, its destination more inevitable, until it finally pancaked on the stone surface, bounced surprisingly high, and dropped into a heap.

Nat's eyes were fixed, not yet sure what they were seeing, not yet sure they wanted to see what they were seeing. Like a hostage grown used to his captor, he felt a perverse touch of ambivalence. Jackson had escaped him for so long it seemed implausible that he wasn't doing it again. But then Nat saw a pool of crimson next to the crumpled body begin a lemming-like creep toward the sea. The image of it, the visible evidence, worked its way through Nat's eyes and down his throat into his chest.

SIX

I don't want to achieve immortality through my work ... I want to achieve it through not dying.

—Woody Allen

THE NEXT DAY, SUNDAY, *July 27*

Nurse Punt led Camilla up the last set of cement steps to a steel door, pushed it open quietly, and moved aside to let her pass. She stepped over a transom onto the deck on the roof and looked around. The East River stretched out to her right like a silk ribbon rippling toward the sea, while the air over Queens glittered with rusting urban dust. To her left, uptown apartment buildings played hide and seek with steel birds floating slowly toward LaGuardia Airport.

She saw him sitting in a wooden deck chair, one leg propped on a pillow, his right arm held close to his body by a triangular canvas sling. He wore sunglasses and a short-sleeved blue denim shirt, a pair of moss-green khakis and tan loafers, and he was reading something he held in his left hand, a memorandum or report of some kind. Always the doctor.

She approached him like a girl nearing an injured bird. He caught sight of her in his peripheral vision and lowered the report to his lap. Removing his sunglasses revealed a bandage across his brow above a partly closed eye. Below it, the skin was purple and stretched shiny from swelling.

'Pardon me for not getting up,' Cush said.

She leaned over and kissed him, wrapping her arms around his neck. 'Hello, baby,' she said as if she hadn't seen him in months. They held each other in silence.

She finally let go and dragged a chair up to his and sat next to him, leaning forward, holding his hand and examining his face. He gave her a damage report: torn ligaments in his knee, bruises on his hip and thigh, a cracked bone in his forearm, ten stitches in his left eyebrow. Nothing that wouldn't heal. It was an accurate report as far as it went, but it didn't mention the problem that mattered most. About that, not even a hint. He asked about her injuries. She mentioned her burned hair, but otherwise she was fine, no lingering damage, only the exhilaration of being alive. They replayed what had occurred on the platform, Cush amazed by her courage, Camilla stunned that he had jumped. She described how he'd been rescued from the statue's shoulder – the quick work of the Park Service, the use of the climbing ropes to get to him fast and pin him down, the rescue in a basket lowered from, guess what? A helicopter.

'Did Rod tell you we're doing your operation?' he asked.

'Yes,' she said.

He moved his leg carefully into a new position. 'If we can scan what we need, you should have your memory and motor control back very soon.'

'Will I get Nat's memories again?'

'I don't think so. We're going to scan him a little differently this time, identify coherent phrases he inserts into the blueprint and filter them before rebuilding your neurons. That way, the result should include none of his memory bias. I hope.'

'And my KBS?'

'That's another story. I don't know how serious it is, and even if I did, I'm sorry to say I don't know how to fix it.'

'How can you be sorry? I got it because you saved my life.'

'It won't necessarily get worse, you know,' he said.

'Then maybe it won't. Rod said you're planning to use Nat again for the scan. How's he feel about that?'

'He's the one who suggested it,' Cush said. 'He said we should dance with the girl we came with.'

'I think I know what that means,' she said. Then, to herself, she said, wouldn't it be nice not to have to ask?

'He survived the first scan, so he should be fine. This one will cover less ground, and with the Z-5s running a little cooler, that should help.' He brushed the hair from her face, then placed his fingertrips against hers and went palm to palm, a daddy-longlegs doing a push-up on a mirror. 'There are so many other things I want to tell you.'

'We've got plenty of time, Cush.'

'Not really.'

'Why not?'

'We're doing your scan tonight.'

'There it is,' Rod said. His voice was flat, professional, and unhappy.

He stood at a lightboard that held a positive transparency resembling a jumbled system of white highways running across a gray desert. Cush sat in an easy chair with his leg on a pillow, and Rod's pencil point rested at a place on the photo, first the left temporal lobe, then the right. The forward section of both were orange instead of blue like the rest. He slipped another transparency under a clip and examined the same data in larger detail.

'Look at those little fuckers,' Cush said.

Rod didn't need to examine it more closely, he already had.

'What does Schulman think?' Cush asked. The chief neurosurgeon's opinion was important to him. He understood the limits of nanotech medicine.

'He wants to do a lobectomy of the anterior region of one side or the other. Try to cut out the problem.'

'Tell him thanks, but it's a waste of time,' he said.

'You know,' Rod said, 'since we're seeing no symptoms yet, we could devise a search and destroy mission with a new generation of Z-5s, program them to go in and find the rogues that are causing the damage and—'

Cush cut him off. He could make the final decision without discussing it with his patient because he *was* the patient. The dormant scanners resting in his temporal lobes – the rogue Z-5s described by Rodriguez three years earlier in his *Patient: RAD* memo, warning Cush that they were sleeping in his brain – had finally come to life with the blow to his head on the statue's arm. He'd been careful not to disturb them, staying healthy, driving cautiously, keeping his distance from electromagnetic signals. The closest he'd come to trouble was fighting with Hennessy in the gym, although, foolish as it had been, he'd managed to avoid a jab to the head and gotten out in one piece. But now his luck had run out. He lifted another transparency and held it up to the light. Two bright masses of active Z-5s appeared like dual suns rising on each side of his brain.

'Just like poltergeists,' he said. 'They're back.'

Cush and Camilla sat on a bench in the park near the hospital. He was telling her the rest of the story about the fire tree.

'When I was a kid,' he said, 'one of my chores was to feed the chickens every morning and make sure they were safe at night. Once in a while a fox or a coyote would dig his way into the coop and we'd have a bloody mess on our hands. The summer before my father died, I came into the coop one morning and found what was left of two dead hens. I took some bricks and stones and filled up the hole under the fence and thought I'd solved the problem, but a week later, just like clockwork, we had two more dead chickens.

'My father was getting impatient, and I was getting furious. I took a varmint trap from the tool shed and placed it where the last hole had been dug, figuring the fox would go there first, but he outfoxed me and dug around it and ate another chicken. Except this time it wasn't just any chicken, it was my prize hen, winner of a blue ribbon at the Mason country fair. Now it was war. I set the trap again.

'A week went by and nothing happened, then one night I heard this howl and all the hens going crazy. I pulled on my jeans and got a flashlight and found the fox with his leg caught in the wire snare. He'd been trying to pull himself free – I can still see him hunkered down with slitty eyes. When I reached for him he started yanking back, trying to escape. I turned my flashlight on his leg and saw blood and ripped fur. It was the first time I'd seen a living bone, and I remember wondering what made it light blue instead of white. He was licking his chops in pain, cowering one minute, baring his teeth the next, and he had white foam all over his chin.'

'What did you do?'

'It was four in the morning, so I went back to the house and got my twenty-two—'

'Twenty-two?'

'Rifle. I woke up my father and told him what was happening and he rolled out of bed and pulled on his overalls and came with me. When we got there the fox was lying on his side, panting. My father put a canvas sack over his head to calm him down, then set the lantern by the snare and examined the bloody paw. It was messy but the tendons were still intact. He stood up and handed me a wire cutter and said, "What's it going to be?"

'I stood there with the cutter in one hand and my rifle in the other, not understanding the question. Ordinarily you shoot an injured animal, that's what the twenty-two was for, but my father was telling me I had a choice to make. We could suture the wound and bandage it up and the fox would live, or we could do away with him right then and there.

'I had to think. He'd killed my prize chicken and several other hens, and if he survived, who was to say he wouldn't be a menace all over again? I hated him. The thought of nursing him back to health and letting him go really got me. I asked my father if that's what he was telling me to do, and he said, no, he was telling me to make a choice.

'Well, now, this presented a problem. My dad ordinarily didn't resort to tricks in situations like this. If he was telling me to choose, I had to choose. He told me to take the hood off the animal and look at him and decide.

'I took the canvas bag off the fox's head and looked him in the eye, and suddenly he seemed harmless. It was the first life or death decision I ever had to make.'

'What did you do?'

'What do you think I did?'

'Knowing you, I'd say you took him to the house and nursed him back to health and set him free.'

'Good guess,' Cush nodded. 'Actually, I put a bullet between his eyes.' He stared at Camilla. She stared back. 'That's more or less the way my father looked at me.'

'What did he say to you?' she said quietly.

'Nothing. He simply took the rifle and his lantern and walked back to the house.' Cush rubbed his face. 'I've never felt the power of silence like that in all my life.'

Camilla reached out and touched the back of his hand. 'The animal was in pain. You did what anybody would have done.'

'I did the wrong thing.'

She looked at him curiously. 'You sound as if you still regret it.'

'I sat in the dark next to the fox thinking about what I'd done, picturing my father's face after I'd pulled the trigger. I finally snipped the wire and put the critter in the burlap bag and went up to the loft and sat there with my dog. After awhile the hens settled down and everyone went to sleep.' He took a drink of water. 'You've never lived on a farm, have you?'

'Not that I remember.'

'Just before first light, everything gets very quiet. The leaves stop rustling and the crickets quit chirping. That's the way it was that morning. I sat in the loft window waiting for the sun to come up and give me a glimpse of the fire tree, but when it came, the orange flame at the top had disappeared.'

'How strange.'

'That's what I thought. Actually, the sun just hadn't come up far enough yet, but I had this spooky feeling that the tree wouldn't burn for me because I'd killed the fox.'

Camilla spread her fingers onto his hand.

'I sat there trying to figure out what it all meant. I remember feeling this enormous frustration and anger at the fox, and my father, and myself.'

'Why yourself?'

'I assumed there was an answer to every problem in life, if you just looked hard enough. Now I knew that wasn't true. If I'd let the fox go, he would have come back and killed more chickens, so I killed him, which disappointed my father and was wrong. What kind of a world was that? Living on a farm you see death all the time – animals dying of sickness, chickens and hogs getting slaughtered. What was the big deal about this henhouse killer? The idea of a dilemma, a problem without a solution, had never occurred to me.'

Rubbing his hand, she said, 'Even then, you took things too much to heart.'

'I went down to the door and laid the fox in an empty feed box, then I made a cross out of two pieces of wood and put the coffin and a spade and a quart of milk into the burlap bag and set out to find a burial ground.'

'Where did you take him?' she said.

'To the fire tree. I buried him under the needles. When I was done, I sat down and tried to think what I should write on the cross. He didn't have a name, so I wrote FOX on it and pounded the stake into the ground with the spade. Then I drank the milk. Nothing ever tasted so good.'

'What did your father say when you got back?'

'Nothing.'

'Why not?'

'He didn't need to.'

'When the sun came up, did the tree catch fire again?'

He smiled at her. 'What do you think?'

'I was just wondering if you hate me because I'm black, or if my being black is your excuse to hate me.' Cush reached into the box of Ritz crackers Nat was holding out.

'It's a tough one, isn't it?' Nat said. 'Every white man's dilemma.' Nat dug into the box himself and tossed one to the pigeons. 'Not that you feel any differently about me.' For most enemies, going through what they had gone through would have made them sheathe the long knives, take a puff on the peace pipe, give it a rest for awhile. Not these two.

They sat in front of the hospital on a park bench overlooking the East River, watching a tugboat send a roiling wake toward the retainer wall. It was lunch hour with noon-time joggers moving by, office workers eating sandwiches, and mothers pushing baby strollers in the sun. Wearing a baggy pullover to cover the bandages on his rib cage, his left arm taped to his side, Nat resembled a car wreck more than a detective. Cush, bruised and swollen, didn't look that much better, except that he was better dressed.

Cush handed Nat a green binder filled with white typewritten pages. 'Read this before the scan tonight.'

'What is it?'

'Preparation.'

'For what?'

'Just read it.'

Nat fanned the pages, saying, 'What is Dr Jekyll up to now?' He laid the book by his side.

'When my grandfather told me how your father died,' Cush said, 'I thought it might create a small bridge between us, but then I came to my senses and realized there wasn't a chance.'

'Why's that?'

'You'll never know how much race played a part in your father's death, but I know race is the *only* reason my father was lynched. You'll never wonder who killed your father – matter of fact, you knocked him off – but I never saw the faces of the men who killed my dad and never will.' He tossed his cracker over the pigeons to a squirrel that sat begging on hind legs. 'Every time I see a white man who makes my palms sweat, some small part of me wonders if he was one of the guys who did it – or would do it to me, if he knew he could get away with it.' He rested his arm on the back of the bench and looked at Nat as if he was a possibility himself.

'There it is,' Nat said. 'Every black man's dilemma.' He sailed a Ritz into the air like a Frisbee and watched a seagull snap it up before it had reached its apex. 'Your subconscious thinks about race far too much.'

'I see. Like yours doesn't.' He watched Nat toss another cracker. 'You know,' Cush said, 'nothing is going to please me more than watching Camilla fall in love with me once she's well.'

'You think?' Nat said.

'If you're my competition, I know. What you don't under-stand is that before she was shot, she figured out who you really are. Your character. The essential, unchangeable you.'

'Speaking of which – the subject of fine character, that is – I assume you know what's going to happen when I dig up Roy Driggers.' The sheriff had told Nat they'd wait for him to return to disinter the body. 'It's going to put your neck on the chopping block – your laboratory, your Nobel, maybe even your freedom, depending on what the autopsy shows. But best of all, it's finally

580

going to destroy all those fuzzy-minded illusions Camilla has about you.'

'You really are something, Hennessy,' Cush smiled. 'You threaten me just before you climb onto my operating table and expect *me* to be afraid of *you*?'

'If you were going to turn me into a Spider Murphy or a Roy Driggers, you would have done it to me the last time you had me on the table. The emergency nature of the operation, all those consent forms I signed – nobody ever would have known. This time, I've written a will and made a record and ordered an autopsy if I die. Too many people will be watching.'

'But as usual, you're missing the point.'

'Which is?'

'What I can do to you that's more interesting than what I did to them.'

Cush sat at his desk reading a letter he'd just written. When he finished, he added a postscript, then folded the paper in half and slipped it into a dove-gray envelope. He was writing the name of the addressee on the front when Rodriguez entered the room.

'The OR will be ready at seven o'clock. How about you?' Rod asked.

'I'm ready now,' Cush said. He handed the envelope to Rod. 'Deliver this for me, will you? But only if it needs to be.'

Rod looked at it, then at Cush. 'How will I know?'

'You'll know,' Cush said.

Nat sat on the park bench reading the binder Walker had given him. The scenes and stories he read were curious. There was one about Thanksgiving dinners Walker spent at his home, another about a hayloft where he'd slept when he had scarlet fever, another about searching for a peculiar pine tree on his farm. There was the long and deeply wrenching description of his father's death that Nat had heard from Booker T., although not quite in the excruciating detail given here. Why would Walker do that?

Nat continued reading.

There was a story about a chicken-eating fox he had killed, stories about his prep-school days at Milton Academy, recollections about a college newspaper column he wrote about jazz and classical music. Nat read slowly, planting each scene in his mind with as much detail as he could, as he'd been instructed.

He got up and stretched and walked along the sidewalk, watching barges and white cruisers moving up and down the river, then returned to the bench and continued reading. When he'd finished a description of Walker's first year in medical school, he turned the page.

It landed him in the rough stuff. Cush and Camilla.

Walker described how he'd first seen her in a cafeteria at Columbia University, and how he'd been struck by her even at a distance. He described how he was trying to concoct an opening line when she picked up her tray and left. He wrote of the immediate sense of loss, the anxiety that he'd never see her again, and how it reminded him of a story by F. Scott Fitzgerald about a man who sees this beautiful woman waiting for a trolley. Their eyes met for only a second, Walker wrote, before she boarded the car and was gone, and for the rest of his life not a day went by that he didn't think about her. Walker feared he was doomed to be that man, that's how much she'd impressed him. He said he was in love with her before he ever met her.

Nat swallowed hard and considered what he was doing. He wasn't just a voyeur now, he was a self-torturer. What was the scientific point of this exercise? He closed the book and decided to stop reading. Then, thinking about Camilla and the scan that was only a few hours away, he opened it again.

It got worse. Much worse.

Walker wrote about the first time he and Camilla had made

love. 'It was a summer night at the farm, very quiet and hot with mosquitoes drawn to the candlelight. I tore a cotton sheet into strips and soaked them in cool water and wrapped them around her like a mummy, and massaged her through them. When her body turned the strips warm, I began unwrapping them slowly, starting with her feet, then moving up her legs to her hips and abdomen, pulling them away like ribbons off a gift box. Pretty soon we were into it and the strips were unraveling like soggy banners flying in the air. We locked hands and became an oval blur. It was like nothing I'd ever experienced before, as if I were slipping into a second mind where opposites came together – tenderness and wildness, rawness and grace. The more compressed I got, the more I sailed free. I have no exact memory of how it ended, only that I didn't want it to end. Neither, I discovered, did she.'

Nat dropped the green book next to his hip on the bench. Operation or no operation, he couldn't read this any more. He sat staring at the pigeons, listening to himself breathe. What was Walker trying to do here? If this was one of the stories they intended to tell him to get his neurons all fired up, why tip him off in advance? Wouldn't that only moderate his feelings when the time came? This wasn't preparation for a scan, this was personal torment – a branding iron stuck inside his brain.

The images wouldn't go away. Staring at the river, he could see Walker and Camilla lying on a flat, pillowless bed, see her face focused and intense, the same face she showed Nat when the two of them made love, except now it was turned up to someone else.

He felt snails of heat move across his neck. Maybe the point was to drive the images so deeply into his brain Walker wouldn't need to work as hard as he did last time to get them to ignite. Maybe it was to do the scan with speed, which meant less heat. The first few pages of the book – those poignant stories of a boy's childhood – were just come-ons to ease him into the emotional, provocative stuff, harmless pied pipers leading him down the path to a secret garden where Cush and Camilla were wallowing in the splendor of the grass. Making love in ways Nat had never thought of. Novel, imaginative ways that Walker knew would stick in his patient's mind during the scan. And afterward.

He stood up and walked to the railing overlooking the river, carrying the notebook with him. After pulling the first few pages from the book, he folded them into perfectly balanced paper airplanes – his fine spatial relations still intact – and sailed them into the river. Watching them bounce on the water with the flotsam, he decided to drop the whole book in and let the fishes have a turn.

As he prepared to toss it, his finger stuck in the place he'd been reading. Opening it, he looked at the next paragraph.

It was about a trip Walker and Camilla had taken to the sand dunes near Pensacola. Then it was about an off-Broadway play they'd seen – notes on what they'd liked about it, what they hadn't. Walker wrote about books they'd both read, movies they'd seen, dinner parties they'd gone to, who was funny, who was a bore.

The tone and content were different now. He was not only seeing Camilla through Walker's eyes, he was catching glimpses of Walker through *her* eyes, even though it was Walker reporting. He said she enjoyed visiting him at the clinic, watching him work with his patients, helping him solve an engineering problem by asking layman's questions that forced him back to basics. He said she'd liked getting up with him in the middle of the night to help him birth a calf, and that she claimed the sexiest thing he ever did was to remove a spot from her silk blouse just before she went to dinner. He said he wanted her to be proud of him when he won the Merkle Prize for Nanotechnology, and she was, but not as proud as she'd been seeing him deliberately spill a glass of water at a dinner table of awestruck sixth-graders to put them at ease. Nobility and humanity, two sides of the same coin. As much as Nat hated it, he was beginning to understand what it was about Walker that had made her fall in love with him.

But he loved her too. And she was his, not Walker's.

He continued reading, etching the words and phrases and images into his emotional memory until his hips ached from standing. Returning to the bench, he decided he'd finish reading the book after all. He would deliberately crawl inside Cush Walker's skin and experience every word, phrase, and thought he could find, exploring his life both in the lines and between them. Dull his emotions by tipping him off in advance? Not a chance. When he'd finished reading he'd have enough fire in his brain to create a dynamic template so clear and complete the nanoscanners would build perfect brain cells for Camilla. A full recovery. And once she had her memory back, the sweet irony was that Walker and his journal would give her back to him.

Cush sat at the control console in the operating room, his face lit by a monitor a few inches away. The door was locked, and except for himself, the room was deserted. They were only a few hours away from the procedure.

He read from an open manual as he typed his instructions into the computer. He'd almost finished his private business here.

A red light flashed in the lower corner of the screen as the CPU talked back to him, making sure that he really wanted to make the radical change of instructions he'd typed into the program that ran their computers.

REPEAT: IS THIS PROGRAM MODIFICATION YOUR TRUE INTENTION?

He hit Y for Yes.

THIS IS YOUR LAST CHANCE: ARE YOU SURE?

He hit Y for Yes again.

TYPE IN YOUR NEW CODE NOW.
He did.
The red warning light turned green.
YOUR PROGRAM MODIFICATION IS COMPLETE.

It was the same operating room and the same medical team, but this time the patient was in a different frame of mind. Wearing a white smock, ankle socks, and the 'hockey mask' conductor, Nat rested on an operating table raised at the torso and the knees, looking like Hannibal Lecter in a beach chair. The nanotech team was working smoothly, the petaflop computer terminal wired live to the Los Alamos mainframe. Surrounding Nat's head was the eight-foot, doughnut-shaped superfast MRI, and inside that was the skeletal, basketball-sized stereotactic frame clamped to his skull. The cryogenic cooling system was operating, and in front of his face on a metal frame was the green briefing book Walker had given him. At the doctor's direction, he was reading it for the second time.

'Any second now, I'll have the locations in his brain of everything he's read,' Rodriguez told Cush from his seat at the master control console.

Walker stood behind him examining the monitors, free to roam from station to station as the situation required.

Nat finished re-reading the material and rested quietly, eyes closed, waiting.

'OK, everybody,' Walker said, 'we've got the sites located. Let's go to the next stage.'

He pressed a switch and the operating table Nat was propped up on straightened and became flat. Nat's pulse compressed into anticipatory beats as he waited for the team to apply the cooling blanket and begin the dynamic. Sandy, the anesthesiologist, plugged a drip line into the catheter in the back of his hand, but for some reason Carla, the radiologist, didn't apply the cooling blanket. Josh, the circulating nurse, didn't talk either. Bill, the computer jock, stood by, waiting. Compared to the last time, everyone seemed almost lethargic. What was going on?

'Tell me when I have to start thinking in pictures,' Nat said.

'Ready with the Diprivan?' Cush asked Sandy.

'Ready.' She tapped her keyboard.

Diprivan? Nat knew what that was – it was the knockout drops they'd given his partner, Ben Brown, while he was in the ICU recovering from his gunshot wound, a white liquid producing a sleep so strong the nurses called it 'milk of amnesia'. His heart rate jumped. Sleep? Sleep was the enemy of a dynamic scan.

'I thought we were doing the dynamic,' Nat said.

'Start it,' Cush said to Sandy.

'What's going on?' Nat said. He tried to rise off the table but the restraining straps held him down.

Cush left the line of monitors and walked to his side. 'We already did the dynamic scan while you were reading.'

Already *did it*? Then what were they doing now? Too much Diprivan was coma-inducing. If they'd already located the neural sites of the stories he'd read in the briefing book . . .

Christ Almighty. Walker was using him as a guinea pig. But for what? *'You're forgetting what I can do to you that's more interesting than what I did to them.'*

His neck muscles tensed, then just as quickly relaxed. He exhaled smoothly and sailed right over the edge of the water-fall.

'We're pushing the envelope, Cush.' Rod's voice was unhappy. 'We gotta back off.'

'Stay with it,' Cush answered. His tone of voice was certain, leaving no room for argument.

The neurosurgical team hadn't taken a break since Hennessy had gone under. The only person in the room who was now in a different position was Cush Walker. Instead of hovering over the patient, this time he *was* the patient, stretched out on the same operating table Nat Hennessy had occupied half an hour earlier. He had a chest-high microphone attached to his hospital gown that amplified his voice.

'Where are we, Sandy?' Rod said.

'Temp's one hundred and seven and rising,' she said.

'Did you hear that, Cush?' Rod said, knowing he had.

Cush's whispered voice boomed across the room. 'Keep . . . scanning.' His eyes remained focused on his green journal, which he read intensely. He blew into his microphone, signaling that he'd finished the page and needed to have it turned, which Josh did. He was on the last few pages of the neural phrases he wanted recorded.

'One hundred and eight,' Sandy said loudly, giving warning.

Rod sweated more than Cush but said nothing. Reverse logic was running the Z-5s cooler for longer periods, but they'd exhausted the margins and were now red-lining. Once the heat began to build, it moved fast.

'Cush, we've got all we need for the procedure,' Rod said. 'For God's sake.'

'I want . . . it all . . . everything I've got . . . on the petaflop,' Cush said. His voice was sounding intoxicated from the fever.

'Everything?' Rod said. 'You're delirious, Cush.'

'One hundred and nine point five,' Sandy said.

'That's it, we're finished,' Rod said. 'I'm taking the helm.'

'No,' Cush said in a commanding whisper.

Rod disregarded him. 'OK, everybody, I don't care what he says, he's red-lining and we're winding down on three. One . . .'

Cush said, 'Not until we finish . . . Series E.'

'We've got ninety-nine per cent of the Series E scan,' Carla said.

Rod said, 'That's all we need. Two . . .'

Cush's voice was desperate. 'Wait . . .'

Rod ran his hand through his hair. 'I can't wait, Cush! You're burning up!'

'One hundred and ten degrees,' Sandy said.

Rod said. 'Three!'

'We've got one hundred per cent of E!' Carla said.

A red light flashed, signaling completion of the Series E scan. Rod hit the toggle switch to take manual control of the nanoscanners and tapped in a message to stop the scan.

Nothing happened.

He stared at the monitor. The distribution graphs were increasing instead of falling.

'What the hell?'

A message appeared on the primary monitor announcing another scan – SERIES F – followed by numbers counting down the way they did at the start of a motion picture: 5–4–3–2–1 – START SERIES F.

Rod's mouth hung slack-jawed. *Series F?* Where did that come from?

The stainless-steel pumps whirred, injecting fresh scanners to join the overheated ones and begin a new scan. According to the monitor, a larger one. Much larger.

Rod sent instructions to the controller's CPU. Nothing happened. 'We're locked out! Somebody's locked us out!'

Cush spoke into his mike. 'Relax . . . I programmed . . . it.'

'Hit the manual override!' Rod yelled. Bill reached for a red handle on the computer board and pulled it down but nothing happened. He pushed it up and back down again. 'There's no digital linkage!'

'We're running *very* hot,' Sandy said.

'Cush!' Rod said.

'Stay with it,' Cush said. 'Keep . . . Los Alamos . . . on line . . .'

Rod began clacking away on the console, searching for a way into the automatic program. 'What have you done?' he said. He tried another combination. No luck. Then another. Still nothing.

'One hundred and eleven degrees and rising,' Sandy said.

'For God's sake, Cush, what's the security code?'

Rod looked at the third monitor. The nanoscanners had saturated Cush's cortex and hippocampus and were scanning at full capacity.

'Jesus Christ,' Rod said. 'He's programmed a universal scan! On himself!' A universal scan recorded every memory phrase it could find in every sector of the brain, simultaneously.

'Except for the temporal lobes!' Carla said. 'For some reason he's not touching them.'

'That's the site of his KBS!' Rod said. He zoomed in on the injury. The Z-5s were swarming over it like molecular bees. 'They're doing a search and destroy!' Rod said. 'He's knocking out the rogue scanners by burning them up!'

'What should I do?' Bill yelled at Rod. If the power was cut they'd lose communication with the Z-5s, at which point the little viruses could do whatever they wanted – stop, go, or run amok, who knew what?

Rod tried another approach. 'I designed this thing,' he mumbled to himself, 'I can break it.'

Cush said. 'I'm having . . . a hallucination . . .'

Rod clacked on the keyboard, opening the code files. He found the last one that had been entered, assumed it was Cush's, and copied it.

'I'm seeing . . . something interesting,' Cush said.

Rod entered the code into the security field. A new window opened up on the primary monitor. OVERRIDE AUTO PROGRAM?

He hit Y for Yes.

THIS WILL DESTROY ALL SUPPORT FILES IN THIS DIRECTORY. ARE YOU SURE?

Y, Y, Y! Yes, yes, yes!

'It looks like . . .' Cush stopped in mid-sentence.

MANUAL CONTROL RESTORED. 'We're back in!' Rod yelled.

'Oh, my God!' Sandy said. 'Look!'

On the third monitor a yellow-white glow was spreading over the screen like ink spilled on a blotter. An artery in Cush's brain had burst and blood was flooding into it in a massive stroke.

'LN two, Sandy!' Rod yelled, directing more liquid nitrogen into the cooling lines. She also administered heparin and TPA, two stroke-controlling drugs. Rod continued typing on the keyboard.

Bill said, 'I've got restored linkage on the override – should I use it?'

'No!' Rod said. 'Now we need the Z-5s to repair the heat damage!'

Rod continued typing on the keyboard, trying to re-program the overheated Z-5s to seal the ruptured vessel and metabolize the blood that was running into the brain. His CPU was communicating with the devices but they were too hot to process his new instructions.

'I need more coolant!' Rod yelled.

'If I run it in any faster we'll go terminal!' Sandy said. If she froze his spinal column and brain, the freezing process wouldn't necessarily kill him but the thawing process would, cracking open his cells and bleeding out their nuclei. None of their nanotech programs could repair damage that extensive.

Cush lay perfectly still.

The heart monitor stopped spiking. His heartbeat was slowing.

'Come on, everybody,' Rod said. 'Give me what you've got!'

The harder they fought, the more ground they lost. His heart still pumped, but the EEG couldn't have cared less. His brain was dying before their eyes. Cerebration was disappearing and, with it, Cush Walker. They worked fast, trying to re-program the Z-5s to mop up after the storm and restore order in his head. They stayed with it as long as they could, and might have stayed longer, but it would have made no difference.

He was gone.

Sandy reached out and took the doctor's lifeless hand and squeezed it. Her eyes were shut and moist; everyone in the room was stricken. Except for the whir and hum of the equipment, the room was quiet as a mountain top. Eventually, everyone turned toward Rod at the console, his shoulders slumped, his fingers no longer working the keyboard. The team stood silently.

'How much did we get?' Rod asked softly, at last.

Carla checked her monitor. 'We picked up all of the charted phrases he had in his briefing book and beyond that an unknown amount of the universal.'

'Is everything we scanned on the petaflop?'

'It's all there.'

Rod rubbed his face with his hands. He turned to Sandy. 'What's Hennessy's condition?'

'He's still in recovery, sleeping like a baby.'

'Is he ready?'

'He's been ready for an hour.'

Rod consulted his monitor. 'I'm looking at the index,' he said. 'We've captured almost every one of Hennessy's target neural sites.' He leaned back in his chair. 'We've got a choice to make, everybody. I know this is the worst possible moment to have to make it, but we either finish the procedure now, or abandon it permanently.'

'How can we give up?' Sandy said. 'We know what Cush wanted.'

'Can we do this while Hennessy's sleeping?' Bill asked.

'It's the *only* way we can do a download of this size,' Rod said. 'We don't need him in an active state now that we have the sites, we need him quiet and receptive.' He looked around the room. 'Is anybody not on board? Once we start there's no turning back.'

Camilla stared at the box in her hand, answering Rod's question – 'Are you OK?' – with a nod. After a moment, she pulled the ribbon and opened it. There was a folded envelope inside, and beneath it, Cush's gold pocket watch, the one that had once belonged to his father. The sight of it, still ticking, still alive, stung her nose and blurred her eyes.

She lifted it out and slid her finger beneath the envelope flap. Inside was a piece of stationery which she opened reluctantly.

Sunday July 27

Dearest Camilla,

Last night I finally found the line of poetry Sebastian wrote to your grandmother when he left her, the one that goes, 'They that love beyond the world cannot be separated by it.'

I also found the rest of the line engraved on my father's pocket watch, 'Death is but crossing.' Of course, they both come from the same poem. How could we have missed it? It was written by William Penn in 1693, and it goes like this:

'They that love beyond the world cannot be separated by it. Death is but crossing from the world, as friends do the seas; they live in one another still.'

It was written for us, Camilla. We will love each other beyond the world we've known. We will never be separated by it. We will live in one another still.

Trust me, it is possible – and in *this* life, not just the next. Watch carefully for the signs. You'll see.

Cush.

P.S. That speech I gave you in my apartment the other night – the one about Mr Vanderbilt and how you can get away with anything as long as you do it big enough? I take it back. We pay for going too far, even when it's for something good. Besides, when you're standing outside the railing looking down, you see that success isn't the point. Love is.

TWO DAYS LATER, TUESDAY, *July 29*

There was something about the Mississippi earth that shrunk the ordinary distance between life and death. The rotting Cypres swamps that fed the tall, elegant pines, the decomposing grass that fertilized the soft summer flowers, the carrion amidst lively chipmunks, the vultures circling with robins, the mold and decay renewing beauty and life.

Nat and Camilla stood beside the open grave and listened to the last words of the Baptist minister invoke the heavenly spirit. Cush's grandfather nodded and began to sing a hymn, 'My Work Is Done', and soon other black voices joined in. The first shovel of dirt hit the top of the white birch casket, its stones and clods clattering in a wooden timpani. Ten feet away, an old black woman placed a wreath against the tombstone that marked Cush's father's grave.

An enormous gray thunderhead moved across the dead aim of the sun, cooling the sultry air for a moment, dimming the tracer lines of insects spiraling crazily above the dry yellow grass. Camilla cried. Nat drew her to him with his good right arm and watched the stand of pines at the edge of the pebble field. The singing voices, full of pain and hope, echoed the rich, soulful sound of slave ancestors as they took Cush into their own and cradled him down.

There were all manner of people standing in the field – relatives, friends, patients, Rodriguez and the staff from New York, employees of the Calvin Walker Memorial Clinic in Hardy, neighbors who knew Cush Walker, townsfolk who only knew of him, black children in white shirts and knit ties showing frightened eyes, their usual energy hushed by this large, mysterious power called death.

With the crowd beginning to disperse, Nat and Camilla started for their car, parked by the barn near Vestie Viney McCoy's farmhouse. Nat looked to his left in the direction of her husband's grave, the location, he was sure, of the body of Roy Driggers.

'You coming back tomorrow?'

The voice behind him was Sheriff Benson's. Nat stopped to let him catch up. He had seen him and Judge Pretty standing among the mourners during the Bible reading.

Wheezing from carrying the load of his belly, the sheriff said, 'We got the back-hoe up at the barn, and Jimmy's ready to go to work.' He wiped his face with a white handkerchief.

Nat introduced Camilla to the sheriff, who doffed his hat. The three of them resumed their trek up the hill.

'I'm afraid tomorrow's not a good day for me,' Nat said.

'How 'bout the day after?'

'Afraid that's not good, either.'

The sheriff looked concerned. 'I don't know how long we can keep the back-hoe up here, Detective.'

Nat stopped walking and held out his hand. 'Well, then, I guess we'll have to let it go.' The sheriff kept his eyes glued to Nat's, waiting for the other shoe to fall. 'Goodbye, Sheriff.'

Sheriff Benson took Nat's hand.

'You ever get to New York,' Nat said, 'drop by Midtown South and look me up. I know a diner on Eleventh Avenue that'll make you feel right at home.'

When he'd finished shaking hands, Sheriff Benson gave Camilla a courtly nod and said her name, then put on his hat. He gave Nat a last look, his own version of take care, now, then turned and headed for his office.

The sound of a Boeing 737 taking off deafened them and placed a pause in the conversation. Camilla welcomed it because she had nothing more to say. Nat was irritated by it because his most important words hadn't yet been spoken.

He moved their bags to the side, out of the way. They were standing at the door to the jetway leading to the flight from Jackson, Mississippi, to New York. The other passengers were boarding now; and in a few minutes the jetway door would be closed.

Camilla was not getting on board. Instead of going back to New York, she'd decided to spend time with her family in New Orleans. He knew, of course, that she was only trying to let him down gently, and that if she didn't come with him now, she never would.

'OK, I'll say it,' she said. 'I *have* thought about it, and it's just not going to work.'

They had been discussing their future for the last hour, driving from the grave site to Jackson Airport. Camilla's repair operation had been a success. Except for some loss of muscle tone, her motor control was returning to normal and her aphasia was disappearing fast. Her memory was being reclaimed at a steady rate as her horizon neurons linked the old with the new, re-establishing circuitry. Every few hours she seemed to have fresh recollections, not so much in a flood as in a series of small awakenings. Each time it happened, she felt a thrill of recognition.

Equally important, so far there were no signs of Kluver–Bucy Syndrome. Cush and his team had not found the nanotech cure they'd been looking for, but having repaired the other damage to Camilla's brain – what remained from the bullet wound – they hoped that her healthy new cells would neutralize the syndrome on their own, organically, in what doctors called a 'spontaneous' cure.

Without warning, she remembered one of the things she had wanted to tell Nat when they were on the statue's platform, just before she was shot. It wasn't the murder mystery she had unraveled. Whatever that was about, she still had no idea. What she remembered now was the thing she'd discovered two days before the shooting – that her grandfather was part black, which meant that she was, too. The problem wasn't the fact of it, or her feelings about it. The problem was his reaction to it. Whether it was visceral or conscious, she worried that it would matter too much to him, becoming a subtle, damning screen between them. Just as she couldn't imagine being married to a man who prayed for the salvation of her soul each night, believing himself saved and her damned, neither could she imagine living with a man who questioned the blood in her veins. Admittedly, it was a matter of pride and principle, not practicality, but it was a principle that mattered. Once she'd discovered her blackness, she'd begun seeing him in a different light. If she married him, in some small but relentless way she feared she'd always wonder if she was sleeping with the enemy.

Nat protested. That wasn't how he felt about her now, and wouldn't have been even if she'd told him the night she'd learned it from her grandmother's diary. He'd always loved her and always would, regardless of her blood or color or ancestry. She was flesh and blood Camilla, not an abstraction. As her memory continued to return, she'd see how he felt more clearly.

He didn't stop there. Whatever he'd done or said to make her doubt him – and he wasn't denying that he had – it was irrelevant now because he understood himself in ways he hadn't before. He'd learned how working the streets as a detective had distorted his perception and made him cynical even, in both subtle and not so subtle ways, about people of color. As irritating as it was to admit it, he'd also learned something about himself from Cush Walker, and BIAS. If she was ready to marry him before she was shot, God knows there was no reason to give up on him now that he'd grown up.

But that was the point, she said – she *wasn't* ready to marry him before she was shot. She had gone to the statue to tell him about Sebastian and her grandmother, and her biologically small – but metaphysically large – blackness. She'd decided to postpone the wedding.

'People change, you know,' he said. 'Women ask men to change all the time, then when we do, they don't believe it.'

'It happens so rarely.'

'But not never. Why else would you keep trying?'

'That's a question, not an answer.'

'Live with me awhile and see for yourself,' he said.

She fiddled with her airline ticket.

He said, 'Would you give up on me if I snored?'

'Snoring is baroque. This is basic.'

Yep, her memory was coming back. 'I didn't give up on you when you couldn't walk or talk, or when you had no memory and fell in love with another man.' It was cheap, but he was losing.

'You're making me feel guilty.'

'That's the general idea.'

The real problem was Cush Walker, who was beating him from the grave. Nat had the same feeling he'd had when she'd told him in the hospital that she didn't know who he was but it didn't matter because she was in love with her doctor anyway. Except this was worse. In the hospital she had amnesia and Walker was snowing all over her like a blizzard. Now her memory was back and Cush Walker was gone. Now she remembered who her fiancé was, and she remembered who *she* was, and still wanted out. Walker was right. It was his essential nature she was rejecting, and that was a tough nut to crack, even for him.

She took a deep breath and looked around the room for an exit from the pressure he was putting on her. Finding none, she turned to him with eyes so ambivalent he thought she must be seeing double. His argument was sensible, she said. She was close to agreeing with him, she said. But not close enough.

'I might come back after some time off,' she said. 'First I want to finish my physical therapy, do some hiking and climbing and get back in shape.' And mourn Cush, he heard her thinking.

Sure, she'd come back. Along with Santa Claus and the Easter Bunny.

The last of the passengers had boarded the plane.

'What can I do to persuade you?' he said.

'Nothing.'

He squeezed her earlobe. 'I'm going to miss you,' he said.

'Me, too,' she said. Her eyes were clouding with happy sentiment about the good times she could recall, and sadness about the bad. He could see that he was becoming past tense even as he stood there in front of her.

OK, sweetheart, this is it. I love you too much just to walk away. Desperate times call for desperate measures.

He took her into his arms and kissed her. The plane was about to leave, but so what? Her kisses were worth it. They always were. When they finished, he didn't have to say he already missed her. The physical evidence spoke for itself.

His burgeoning desire for her made her smile. 'I'm going to miss your kisses, too.'

'What should I do with the pup?' he said. His eyes closed, his face wrinkled up—

'He's yours,' she said.

—and he stifled a sneeze.

A voice on the public address system gave the last call for Flight 102 to New York's LaGuardia Airport.

'What should I name him?' Nat said. His face was still flushed from the kiss and the near sneeze.

She looked at him curiously. 'You'll think of something.' Her mind seemed to be wandering, focused on another subject.

The gate attendant rolled the ticket podium away, preparing to close up.

Nat took a handkerchief from his pocket and wiped his eyes. 'I had an idea for a name—' His nose wrinkled up again.

'What's wrong?' she said. The terminal was air conditioned, he didn't have a cold.

'I . . . don't . . .' He sneezed again. '. . . know.'

The ticket taker said, 'If you're going to New York, folks, it's now or never.'

He told the airline attendant he was coming, then gave Camilla one last embrace. This time he had no choice: 'Yee-ah-*choo*! My God.'

'See how easy this is going to be?' she said. 'You're allergic to me already.'

He wiped his watery eyes. 'Never happened before.'

He picked up his bag, left hers on the floor, and while the attendant examined his ticket folder, Camilla looked into his eyes as if she was searching for a lost contact lens. It felt eerie to him; almost as if she didn't recognize him. Almost as if she was looking for someone else.

'What is it?' he said.

She snapped out of it and shook her head – nothing, never mind.

He put out his hand for his ticket receipt – and sneezed once more. 'I've got a name for the pup that keeps coming to mind, but it makes no sense.'

'What is it?'

The airline attendant pushed him gently through the entrance to the gangway and closed one side of the double doors. Nat walked backward, still talking to Camilla. 'I mean, he's brown and black and white . . . so why would I want to call him Blue?'

He stopped, raised his hand, squinted, and sneezed for the fifth time. When he opened his eyes, he saw Camilla disappear from view as the door was closed.

She stood watching him disappear behind the door, her hand frozen in a wave goodbye.

Then her face. Oh, my God – that's no allergy – that's Cush! That sneeze is *Cush's* sneeze!

She ran to the door and knocked – 'Nat! Wait!'

'Sorry, ma'am,' an agent behind her said. 'The flight is closed out.'

ONE WEEK LATER, TUESDAY, *August 5*

Nat lay on his side in his bed, almost, but not quite, asleep. The scent of talcum powder and fresh-cut flowers lingered faintly, but his mind was elsewhere now, still reviewing what had happened.

It had been a week since he and Camilla had said goodbye at the airport, and even though his side was still healing, the pain was gone now and his mobility much improved, allowing him, in the chief surgeon's view, to go back to work. During his first day back on the job, he and Shaw had caught a particularly nasty case, a sexual assault on a young girl who'd been walking home from a Catholic girls' school early in the evening when she was grabbed from behind, pulled onto a garment center loading dock, taken up in an elevator to the rooftop, and sodomized.

Nat had a particularly strong visceral reaction to cases of this kind. Even where the physical injury was small, the emotional damage was often large and unpredictable. He'd once investigated a double rape that had taught him something about the mystery of a psyche under assault. Two working-girl roommates who were the same age and shared the same outlook on life had been sitting in their apartment watching a sitcom one night when a man broke in, tied them up, and over a two-hour period proceeded to rape them. The circumstances were virtually identical for both girls: same perpetrator, same room, same MO, same tape on the hands and mouth, same ugly threats, same everything. By the time the man was caught two months later, one of the girls had already shaken off the worst of it and returned to her job and the apartment, while the other was still in a psych ward at the hospital. You just never knew.

During their interview of the schoolgirl, Shaw, sensing a need for privacy, had asked Nat if he minded getting her and the girl a sandwich and a couple of aspirin, easing him out of the room. He was impressed with her style, her experience on the street, her way of asking the right questions and getting complete answers, her ability to put victims at ease by alleviating their shame and embarrassment. Her time working Vice had obviously given her wisdom on the subject of male perversity.

The thirteen-year-old girl described her assailant reasonably well, considering the stress. He was five-eight to five-ten, slightly built, and wore a white T-shirt, black jeans and sneakers. The problem was, the only identifying marks she could describe were a pair of socks that didn't match and a nylon 'do-rag' on his head – a tight-fitting, pirate-like bandana that black and Hispanic guys wore to keep their hairdos in place before a night on the town, or to effect a look. Still, the do-rag description was helpful because in this case it had been worn by a white guy, and that was unusual.

After interviewing the witness, Shaw and Nat canvassed the area and talked to everyone they could find – employees in the warehouse, people in the nearby shops and the luncheonette across the street, and of course the cart-pushers who ran garments up and down Seventh Avenue. Many of them fit the perp's description in a general way – jeans and T-shirts and sneakers – but when it came to actually identifying him, they had nothing.

Just as they'd reached the point detectives hate most – when they know they're plumbing a dry hole – Shaw noticed a small shop two blocks from the warehouse with a sign in the window advertising wholesale remnants: *Do-Rags Here*.

They entered the shop, showed their shields, and interviewed the manager and his female clerk, neither of whom had any recollection of anyone fitting the subject's description. Nat left his card, asked them to call if they heard anything useful, and was starting out the door when Shaw said she wanted to do a little shopping while they were there. Don't do this to me, Nat said, we've still got too much ground to cover. She gave him a sarcastic glare and suggested maybe he'd like to check out the store across the street to see if they sold non-matching socks, OK? Nat took the hint and went outside.

A few minutes later Shaw came out with a small plastic bag containing the ugliest fuchsia tank top he had ever seen. You stuck around the shop for this? he asked. No, I stuck around for this, she said, and handed him a scribbled note the woman clerk had slipped her saying she'd sold three do-rags to a white guy who pushed a cart on the early shift and drank his breakfast coffee at the shop next door.

Nice work, Shaw. They'd check it out in the morning.

Now here he was, back at the loft, lying on his side trying to get some sleep, listening to a garbage truck groaning in the distance and someone calling a dog. The clock next to the bed said one fifteen. He'd taken Shaw to dinner a few hours earlier at a cozy place with great calamari and roasted peppers. It started out with his giving her hell for having chased down Jackson by herself, with no backup. You could have been hurt, you know? Yes, boss. I don't want to see you get hurt, understand? No, boss. You mean too much to me. I doubt that, boss. When he was done, he smiled and thanked her profusely, saying he was damn lucky to have her as his partner. By the time they'd finished two bottles of wine and the evening, she knew exactly how he felt about her. Afterward, seeing it was late, he'd taken her straight to her apartment.

Sitting in his car in front of her building, relaxed and a little buzzed, they finally got around to talking about the subtext that had been nudging them all night: the romance between them that might have been. Or what Shaw, referring sarcastically to the police manual, called their 'interpersonal relations'. Timing was everything, they agreed. It simply hadn't been on their side.

'It probably never would have worked anyway,' he said.

'Why not?'

'I'm filled with too much inner conflict.'

'I love inner conflict.'

'I'm also Irish.'

'I'm a redhead.'

They sat and watched a light rain make stars on the windshield. He lowered the window on the driver's side. 'I like the smell of concrete in the rain, don't you?' he said.

'Yeah, it smells fresh,' she said. Raindrops began splattering into the car. 'Here, let me close it a little,' she said.

Reaching across his lap with her right hand, she took hold of the window crank and dropped her sea of wild hair just below his chin. It smelled clean and faintly of anise shampoo. With her left hand on his right shoulder to steady herself, she pushed her ample breasts against him and started cranking up the window, moving her head up and down above his lap with each turn, just enough to unnerve him – then drive him nuts.

He couldn't take it anymore.

He cupped her cheek in his palm and raised her head until they were nose to nose, an inch apart. Somewhere in his head he saw a warning sign: 'Tire Damage – Do Not Back Up!' Once he crossed the line, he knew he couldn't go back.

'Shaw?' he said.

'Yes, Nat?'

'I'm going to make a very big mistake now.'

'You are?'

'I am. I thought you should know before I do it.'

'What are you going to do?'

He pulled her face toward his – then moved his lips past hers and kissed her ear. 'I'm going to say goodnight.'

She held still for a moment; then said, 'I hate it when you make big mistakes, Nat. I really do.' She pulled back and watched more speckling of the windshield. 'But I'm not surprised. You've been bonkers for Camilla from the day I met you.' She looked over at him. 'Besides, you're a very controversial cop, and I wouldn't want to wreck a great career.'

'Why would going out with you wreck my career?'

'Not yours, Nathaniel. Mine.'

He smiled at her and opened his door. Now they could both leave with a clear conscience, no hint of rejection in the air. Shaw was once again in control, at least 'interpersonally' speaking.

They walked to the door of her apartment building and stood in the foyer watching the street puddles glisten, thinking about what they'd said, still wondering what might have been. Feeling a touch of seller's remorse – that moment right after you've given up something you love – Nat turned to her and gave her a hug.

HORN, HORN, HORN, HORN. This time it was a car alarm that woke him.

He turned over in bed and opened one eye to find the clock. It said quarter to two. God, he'd given Shaw that hug only two hours ago. Repositioning his head on the pillow, he told himself to go to sleep. The two of them and the schoolgirl would have to be cruising the garment district no later than six.

He was almost gone when he heard footsteps on the wooden floor.

Uh-oh. Here we go again.

He heard a whispered goodnight to the pup and felt the mattress sink behind him with the weight of a female body climbing into bed. Once more, the scent of fresh talc. She rested quietly, not moving – he could feel the curiosity building inside her, the pleasant confusion, the anticipation of doing it once more. She turned toward him and touched his arm lightly and placed her mouth near his ear.

'Nat?' a voice whispered so softly. It was almost lost in the silence. 'Are you asleep?'

He breathed smoothly, signaling his deepest slumber.

'Making love was so lovely,' she said anyway.

She rubbed his back lightly. Five minutes passed, then ten. 'Can you hear me, baby?' she said softly.

Baby was right. He had finally drifted off like one.

'Can you . . . hear me?' she said again. She wanted to catch him in that half-awake, half-asleep hypnotic state, when he spoke his mind easily.

He moved slightly and murmured but didn't answer.

After waiting a moment, Camilla pulled away and laid her head on the pillow. When she'd seen Nat become aroused by their kiss and sneeze at the airport, the thought that he might have inherited it from Cush during his brain scan was like a thunderbolt. After all, if it had happened to her with Nat's memory of his father's death, why couldn't it have happened to him? Instead of going to New Orleans, she'd boarded the next flight to New York.

In the week since she'd returned, she'd seen other signs of Cush's personality in Nat. A tenderness, a maturity she hadn't seen before, although the abstraction of it made her wonder if she wasn't just seeing what she wanted to see. But then she'd discovered another concrete chip of Cush: recollections of his first bicycle. And instead of picturing himself riding it in the streets of New York, he pictured himself – strangely, he said – on a dusty rural road in the South. And later that night, in his half-sleep, he'd called her Sweet Pea, a name only Cush had called her.

That's when she began to understand the magnitude of what had happened.

Now, slowly, she was seeing other pieces of Cush emerge

in Nat. There was the inexplicable desire he had at Jackson Airport to name their dog Blue. There were memories of the day Cush's father had died that were wrenching and specific – more so, she thought, than they could have been simply from his having heard the story from Cush's grandfather. The more she saw, the more excited she became. And intrigued. And hopeful. How far would this thing go?

Unable to contain herself, she finally told Nat what was happening. He listened politely, even intently, but skeptically. It was one thing to transfer a banana trick to someone, he said, something else to replant a whole jungle of information and emotion. He felt no other person inside him, no split personality, no ghosts in the attic. Memories, like knowledge, were transmitted from one person to another in the usual way: through pictures, letters, stories, and learning. But that night, just before he went to sleep, he rolled over and placed his fingertips on hers and pushed their palms together as if they were doing a push-up on a mirror. Her heart had stopped. She woke him fully and told him what he'd done. He agreed he'd drop by the lab the next day and talk to Rodriguez about it and see if he had an explanation.

But she didn't need one, she already knew. Not that she had a scientific understanding of it yet – how well it had worked, how deeply it had gone – but she knew what she saw and heard. Somehow, to some extent, Cush's memory was *alive* in Nat's consciousness. Somehow, he knew things that only Cush had known. In unguarded moments, they slipped out like silver arrows.

Apparently – obviously – to some extent a memory transfer had occurred. 'We will live in one another still,' Cush had written to her in his note. 'Trust me, it is possible, in this life, not just the next. Watch carefully for the signs. You'll see.' Now, for the first time, she was beginning to understand what he meant. Through his years of work he had created the first stage of a new definition of secular life – a measurable, reproducible, scientifically based way to capture the only worldly energy that truly mattered – the life of the mind – and give it over as a gift. It was the dawning of modern immortality, the continuation of life in this world, just as he said, a preservation of human experience from one generation to the next that didn't depend upon videotapes or stories or history books or psychics or learning or any other bridges to the past. And if you could do it with memories of events, why not with skills and behavior and attitudes?

She got out of bed and went to the kitchen phone and called Rodriguez. Tell me what happened to Cush and Nat, she said. After hemming and hawing and asking her what made her think that anything had happened, he relented and said there was no longer any reason she shouldn't know.

After the fall at the statue had reignited Cush's KBS, he said, rather than postpone Camilla's operation Cush decided to go forward with it and search for a KBS cure afterward. Putting Nat on the operating table and scanning him for a blueprint gave Cush a shot at an experimental memory transfer. Rod and the staff got ready for the procedure but, unknown to them, Cush switched signals and programmed a universal scan of his own memory. Apparently, having tried and failed to find a cure for KBS so often before, he had no confidence that they would find one now. Rather than accept a short, brain-damaged life and an ugly death, he saw his chance to make a huge leap forward. It was a brave attempt with a sad result, Rod said. The universal scan killed him. Afterward, Rod and the staff completed the download to Nat, but there was no indication that the transfer worked. True, transfers to monkeys normally took six to ten weeks to kick in, and no one knew how long a human transfer of this size might take, but Nat's post op MRIs showed nothing remotely similar to successful monkey transfers, and Rod knew of nothing to indicate that one had taken place.

Camilla did. She decided to keep track of what she was seeing and tell Rod when she felt the evidence was irrefutable. It was only a matter of time. In her heart, she was sure that a transfer of some magnitude had happened.

She sat imagining the unimaginable. How much of Cush had been transferred into Nat? She could hardly wait to see.

Nat and Cush. Cush and Nat. To some degree still unknown, both of them were lying beside her in one comfortable person. Which one did she love? The immortal remains of the noble scientist she'd known and loved the longest, or this mortal, passionate Irishman who lay sleeping in her bed?

In time she'd know, but at the moment, there was no choice to be made.

'I've got you both,' she said softly, and went to sleep.

Camilla sat bolt upright in bed.

'Oh, my God. He's dead.'

Nat woke up and turned toward the voice, mildly startled, half awake. He saw Camilla sitting in the gray, 2 a.m. air. 'What is it?' He patted the sheet looking for the dog, imagining a suffocated puppy. 'Blue?'

'Not Blue. Sebastian. He's dead.'

Nat flopped back onto the pillow and ran his hand through his Buckwheat-and-Spanky hair. 'Sweetie, he was twenty years older than your grandmother, and she's been dead for years. This is not exactly news. Where's the dog?'

'I don't mean he just died, I mean he was dead all along.' She bent forward and lifted the puppy from the end of the bed where he'd gone to find cool air. 'I told you I re-read Camilla Bea's diary yesterday? Well, I just remembered the mystery I figured out at the statue.'

Nat reached for the light but she asked him to leave it off, so he did.

'The poem Sebastian wrote to Camilla Bea in his goodbye letter,' she said. 'He wrote the second line of it and left out the first. I couldn't understand why, but now I know.'

'Remind me.'

'The first line goes something like, "They who love each other beyond the world cannot be separated by it." The second line – the one he didn't write – says not even death can come between them, they will live in each other's memories still.'

'So why did he leave it out?'

'He had to. Someone was watching him write the letter. If he'd written in the second line, it would have given away the message he was trying to send to Camilla Bea.'

'Wait a minute, wait a minute. Who was watching?'

'Camilla Bea's father.'

Nat tried to follow. 'Your grandmother Camilla Bea's father was with Sebastian when he wrote his goodbye letter to his daughter?'

'Not only was he with him, he made him do it.'

Nat decided to slow down and piece it together. 'I don't know how you get that, but even if her father was with Sebastian, why would he care about the missing line of the poem? The whole point of the letter was to tell Camilla Bea that he was crossing the sea to go to Paris, wasn't it?'

'The problem is in the first word of the line, "Death". Don't you see? Sebastian was telling Camilla that he was about to die. Turn on the light, would you?'

'I thought you wanted it off,' he said, turning it on.

The dog lifted his head, blinked his incomprehension, and laid it back on the sheet with an exhale.

She squinted a moment, then covered her face with her hands as she talked. 'Oh, my God, it's coming to me.' The same words she'd said at the torch. Maybe, at last, it was.

She jumped up and walked to the dresser and opened the bottom drawer and lifted out a burled cardboard box with the word LETTERS printed on the spine. Opening it, she reached in and removed a pile of papers and spread them on the bed, then pawed through them until she found a notebook with her handwritten notes in it – the questions and pieces of the puzzle she'd compiled before she was shot – and two old letters written on heavy ecru paper, Sebastian's letters to his lover, her grandmother, Camilla Bea.

She crossed her legs in front of her and put on a pair of

reading glasses, slipping into studious mode. 'Camilla Bea found Sebastian's goodbye letter pinned to the door of his apartment the day she ran away from home expecting to go with him to France. She never saw him again, but she got another letter in the mail from Paris about six months later, shortly after their baby was born.'

'OK.'

'He wrote both letters, but he didn't send her either one.'

'Why not?'

'He couldn't have. He was dead.'

Nat hated it when this happened to a detective. 'I'm not following you.'

'I think I need a drink of water,' she said, turning the pages of her notebook.

He got up and walked to the bathroom and brought her a glass. She was too busy to drink, so he set it on the nightstand and got back into bed. Pulling her pillow on top of his own, he laid his head back and closed his eyes and folded his hands on his chest and waited.

A moment later, she said, 'Ah-ha.' He watched her read the notebook, sucking the end of a pencil. 'Just what I thought.' She closed it. 'In the Dear John letter Sebastian pinned to his door, he called Camilla Bea his "little flower", but according to her diary, he hated that term because it belonged to her father, whom she despised. So why would he call her a name he hated in his tender goodbye?' She didn't wait for an answer. 'Look,' she said, lifting the second letter, the one Camilla Bea had received from Paris. 'He did it again. "Take care, little flower," he says. Something's wrong with that picture, wouldn't you say?'

'Obviously,' he said, lost.

'Same with the Eiffel Tower,' she said. 'He hated it, called it the abomination of Paris, so why would he send her an etching of it?' She paged through her grandmother's diary to a red marker, excited. 'Camilla Bea couldn't figure that one out either, at least not when she first received it. But later, when she did figure it out, she was so horrified by what it meant she couldn't bring herself to write about it.'

'What was it?'

'I'll get to that in a minute.' She turned more pages in the diary. 'If he had sent a picture of the Eiffel Tower to her willingly, he would have made some reference to it in the letter – an ironic explanation, a change of heart about it, a joke, a wish that she was with him so that they could ignore it together – something. But there isn't anything like that. You know why?'

'I don't know why,' Nat said, eyes closed.

'Because when he wrote the Paris letter, it was six months *before* his child was born, before he even left New Orleans to *go* to Paris. As a matter of fact, he wrote it at the same time he wrote the Dear John letter he stuck on the door telling her he was off to Paris to join his wife and son. Which, by the way, was a lie.'

'How do you know?'

'Because he didn't have a wife and son. The only woman he loved was Camilla Bea.'

'Wait a sec.' Nat shook his head. 'Then why did he go to Paris?'

'Don't you see? That's the point, he didn't. He couldn't have. I keep telling you, he was dead.'

Nat took a drink of Camilla's water and plumped up his pillows. 'Maybe you should start at the beginning.'

She swiveled a quarter turn and sat facing him with her legs crossed Indian style. 'OK, here's what happened. Camilla Bea comes home one night and tells her mother she's pregnant by Sebastian, her partly-black piano teacher. She says she loves him and she's going to marry him, just as she reported in her diary. Her mother freaks out, slaps her, and tells her not to say anything to her father, the stock market's crashed and he's got other problems to cope with. But according to Camilla's diary, he found out anyway, and on his way out the door to New York the next morning didn't even speak to her, which hurt her deeply. So this socially conscious, proper Southern gentleman now knows that his fifteen-year-old daughter, the light of his life, his *little flower*, is pregnant by a black man she says she's going to marry.'

'I thought Sebastian looked white.'

'Yeah, right, tell that to her father. Remember, we're talking about New Orleans in the twenties. As far as he's concerned, it's not bad enough that he's just lost most of his fortune, now he's about to lose his daughter, and in a way that's humiliating to him. It's not acceptable, so on his way to the train station he makes a detour to confront the bastard who's gotten his daughter pregnant.'

'Where, at his apartment?'

'Let's see how this would have worked.'

He handed her the glass of water; she took a drink and handed it back.

'Yeah, he goes to Sebastian's apartment and tells him he knows everything. Sebastian is never going to lay eyes on his daughter again. Sebastian probably stands up to him and says no way, Jose, I'm going to marry her. Forget it, her father says, you're not even going to be on the same continent with her. You're going back where you came from, to Paris. At that point he pulls out a wad of money to buy Sebastian off.'

'How much?'

'Nat. Please. Whatever the amount, he can't be bought off. He's in love with Camilla Bea.'

'Go ahead.'

'There's more heated argument. Sebastian says he's not walking out on her, he'll make a better father than her old man ever was, something like that that enrages her father. Now they really get into it.'

'And her father pulls a gun.'

'He pulls a weapon of some kind, probably a gun. He forces Sebastian to take out a pen and stationery and write Camilla a goodbye letter saying he's already married with a wife and child in Paris and he's skipping town to join them.'

'A fictional woman.'

'Totally. It's made up to break Camilla Bea's heart and make her forget him.'

'And Sebastian writes it.'

'This is it right here,' she said, lifting the ecru page. 'While he's writing it, he hunts for a way to tell her it's against his will, it's a lie, there's a gun pointed at his head, whatever.'

'Had to be a gun.'

'OK, I'll give you the gun. To signal Camilla Bea, he uses the phrase "little flower". He knows he can get it past the old man because it's his own favorite term for her, he has no clue Sebastian hates it.'

'That's pretty good.'

'Wait. He has to be sure Camilla Bea gets the picture, so he gives her another wink with the line from the poem, "They that love beyond the world cannot be separated by it." To her father, it looks like a soupy line cribbed from a poem. But Sebastian is counting on Camilla Bea to look it up and see what he's really talking about.'

'Which is death.'

'And she does, but not right away. Her first reaction after reading the goodbye letter is to be crushed – who wouldn't be? But then she rebounds and decides that even with wife and child in Paris, he still loves her. I'm not guessing about that, it's what she wrote.' She held up the diary. 'She still hasn't looked up the poem at this point, but her intuition is strong and eventually she does, just as Sebastian hoped.'

'Let's go back to Sebastian's apartment,' Nat said.

'OK. So now her father has the gun on Sebastian and the

Dear John letter in hand. But given Sebastian's obstinate love for Camilla Bea, the old man realizes this won't be enough to keep them apart. He needs an ace in the hole, so he makes Sebastian write a *second* letter that sounds like it's being written from Paris six months later, after Camilla Bea's baby is born.'

'Which is why it has no date on it and doesn't mention the baby's name or whether it's a boy or a girl.'

She pointed at her nose, you got it. 'The first letter is the one her father intends to pin to the door of the apartment and arrange for Camilla Bea to find. To do that, he tells her nanny to let her escape during a trip to see the doctor. Nanny deliberately turns her back in the drugstore – which Camilla Bea finds strange, according to what she wrote – and she doesn't run because she doesn't want to get her nanny in trouble. So her nanny just comes right out and gives her some money and tells her to go for it.'

'And the second letter?'

'Her father takes it with him to New York and mails it to someone in Paris with instructions to send it to his daughter after the baby is born. And send a small token with it, he says, something Sebastian would send.' She handed the second letter to Nat and he skimmed over it. 'When the baby's born, the person does what he's told and sends a picture of the Eiffel Tower, the universal symbol of Paris, to Camilla Bea. Of course, like Camilla Bea's father, he has no idea Sebastian hated it.'

'The letter has just the right tone,' he said, reading it. 'Cool without being heartless, distant but sincere.'

'Which is the tone her father forced him to affect,' she said. 'Now her dad is standing there in the apartment with two arrows in his quiver – the kiss-off letter for the door, and the letter he's going to have sent from Paris later.'

'But if Sebastian is really that much in love with Camilla Bea, what makes her father think he'll stay away from her regardless of the letters?'

'Ah, exactly. Camilla Bea's dad knows from their argument that the minute he leaves town, Sebastian is going to see her. What can he do? He has to leave to catch his train to New York. His life is a shambles. His beloved fifteen-year-old daughter is pregnant, Sebastian's black blood is coursing through her veins, his fortune is going down the tubes. Suddenly, it's too much. Another insult, another fight, and bang. Sebastian's dead.' Camilla looked over the ecru letter and set it down. 'Now her father is in trouble,' she said. 'Even if it was a crime of passion, he still went into the apartment with a gun and killed an innocent man.'

'But a black man,' Nat said. 'How much of a problem was that for a powerful, rich white guy like him?'

'I don't know, but in this case it didn't matter.'

'Why not?'

'Because of the Hammer.'

Nat's head dropped back onto the pillow.

'Camilla's father collects his wits and calls his hunting pal Hammer, the chief of police.' She fingered the documents and found a picture. 'This is him here, the chubby one with the elephant gun.'

Nat took the photograph and looked at it.

'The chief comes over to the apartment and checks out the situation. He'll have to put the furniture right side up, fill a bullet hole in the wall, wash some blood off the floor, but it can be handled. He tells her father to pin the kiss-off letter to the doorjamb and catch his train to New York and leave the rest to him.'

'For what?'

'What, for what?'

'For what price? The Hammer didn't do it for nothing. Her father lost a lot of money, but he's still a rich man, right?'

'And he knows the Hammer has him over a barrel, but what can he do? He goes to New York and assesses the situation.

If he doesn't nip blackmail in the bud, the Hammer will milk him dry.'

Nat lifted the dog off the foot of the bed and brought him up.

'Being a decisive man, an executive, a gambler,' Camilla said, 'her father pays the chief a slug of cash and says that's it, it's finished.'

'But he knows it's not,' Nat said.

'In fact, he's *counting* on the chief to come back for more because that's how he's going to neutralize him. Knowing he's a corrupt, greedy little bastard, he's going to trap him with the diplomat's paradox.'

'What's that?'

'The threat of mutual destruction.'

She took a drink of water and crossed her legs again and leaned forward. 'The Hammer makes sure there's no dead body to cope with, no homicide investigation, no coroner's inquest, nothing that hasn't been handled, then takes the first payoff and says everything is cool. As far as the world knows, Sebastian has gone off to live in Paris the way the story says he has – he's already written the letters that prove it. But a few days later, here comes the chief again, just like the sun, saying he's going to need more money to keep the lid on. How much? her father asks. A mere pittance, he says, and gives her father a number. And make it cash again, he says. In a little brown bag. Now, the big stock market crash becomes her father's ally. He says he'll make another payment, but not in cash, only assets – railroad stock, title to a piece of land, a Texas oil well – something worth far more than the chief has demanded.'

'Call it an oil well,' Nat said.

'OK. On the one hand, the Hammer doesn't like it because taking title to a piece of property creates a record of the transfer, but on the other hand, this is a huge payment and it may be the only chance he'll have to get paid, hard assets being difficult to come by after the crash. Who knows what creditors are waiting to gobble them up? With a little persuasion, the chief relents and takes it. After all, he reasons, why would Camilla Bea's father disclose it? He has far more to lose than the chief – big businessman with a reputation, political clout, social standing, a family name, assets in hand now and more to be made. But when the Hammer takes the oil well, he has no idea what's coming next.'

'Which is?'

'A trust. Camilla's father sets up a trust, but instead of putting money in it, he fills a safe deposit box with papers and documents describing the bribes and the transfer of the oil well. Then he instructs the trustee what to do.' She held it up and paraphrased it. 'It says if the maker of the trust – Camilla Bea's father – is ever charged with a felony of any kind, whether during his lifetime or for fifty years thereafter, the trustee is to release the sealed documents to the press and relevant public authorities. It doesn't describe what's *in* the safe deposit box, and it doesn't define what crime he has in mind, of course. He doesn't need to. He knows there's only one crime that matters, and so does the Hammer.' She showed him the trust document.

'Then he tells the Hammer what he's done,' Nat said.

'Better yet, he sends him a carbon copy of the documents. At least, I would have. Now the Hammer knows he's been had. If he rats out his old pal he'll be indicted for blackmail, conspiracy, and all those other good things that put corrupt sheriffs in jail, even in New Orleans.'

'So that's the end of it? A stand-off?'

'It should have been, but it wasn't. The Hammer being the Hammer, I think he decides two can play this high stakes game of chicken. Get rid of the trust and make the next payment, he tells Camilla Bea's father. And her father takes the threat seriously. He's seen this guy stand his ground in the face of charging rhinos.' She uncrossed her legs and leaned back on the pillow.

'Camilla Bea's dad has to tip the balance of power or the Hammer will drain him. He figures the angles. He can continue playing chicken, or he can do something so radical he'll win the game outright. He goes for the kill. Only problem is, it's a costly one.'

'The Hammer?'

'No, himself.' She reached out and scratched Blue on the belly. He closed his eyes and became a little ball of butter. 'Once he knows the chief won't back off, the only honorable thing he can do now is protect his family. By setting up the trust and taking a stroll out the window, that's exactly what he does. Once he's gone, the Hammer can't blackmail him anymore. If he tries it against the family or the trustee, he just puts his own neck in the noose. So now the family is spared a scandal, her father's name remains good, and what's left of his fortune is saved. And who knows? Maybe it satisfied his guilt for killing Sebastian.'

'Pretty harsh satisfaction.'

'But effective. The stock market crash was a perfect cover for jumping out a window. Camilla Bea and her mother assumed in private that it was about her black baby, but he'd fooled them about that, too. It was about Sebastian's murder and the Hammer's blackmail.'

'So when did Camilla Bea figure this out?'

'My guess is the etching of the Eiffel Tower made her rethink everything – the "little flower" endearments, Sebastian's leaving without seeing her, the works. None of it made sense to her. That's when she went to the library and found the missing line from the William Penn poem, and that did it.' She turned to the last page of her grandmother's dairy.

'Here's her last entry in her diary: "What happened is too painful to bear. I cannot write of it. Ever." I assumed she was talking about what Sebastian had done, but she wasn't. What was too much to bear was realizing that her own beloved dad

625

had killed her own beloved husband-to-be and the father of her baby.' She raised her hands, palms up. 'That's it.'

Nat stretched his arms and took a deep breath.

'This was . . .' She stopped talking and stared at the dog. 'This was the mystery I was working on when the bullet hit.'

Nat rubbed his forehead. Hard to believe. All this time, guilt and paranoia had convinced him it was about himself and Angel Rico.

'Very good, sweetheart,' he said. 'Now can we get some sleep?'

She turned out the light and they settled in.

He dozed, thinking – or feeling – that something that had needed closing had finally been closed. A pothole in the road. The door to an interrogation room. He pictured stitches in a seam. Maybe it was a wound. Whatever it was, it had ended.

SEVEN

They are aware of each other;
they live in each other;
what else is love?

—Virginia Woolf

Eternity is a terrible thought. I mean, where's it going to end?

—Tom Stoppard

TWO MONTHS LATER, FRIDAY, *October 24*

It was autumn in New York, and the leaves were at their peak. Cherrywood smoke sweetened the air from brownstone fireplaces and soft wool cuddled coolness from the skin. The heat of summer was lost in the stratosphere and, with it, the memories of July. Spring was the usual time of rebirth, but this year, for Nat, it was in the fall.

He stood at the counter of an antique jewelry store searching for a new ring for Camilla. The old one, still graceful to the eye, carried too much baggage, so he'd sold it. Superstition was one thing, memories were another. The saleswoman showed him an amethyst, her birthstone. Nice, but not right.

And it had to be exactly right. Tonight he intended to ask her – again – to marry him. Not that he was overly worried about the answer. The last two months had been a coming together for them both, and today's events in particular had touched her nicely. The City Council had passed the BIAS bill with the help of Nat's testimony. He'd acknowledged taping Cush Walker's comments and leaking them to the press, but more importantly he'd testified – with a surprising degree of specific knowledge (even Lieutenant Amerigo was impressed) – about the accuracy of the test, using himself as an example. It didn't trouble him to admit he'd failed it earlier. He'd taken it again and passed, easily this time. Rodriguez himself had administered it. It was, in Camilla's view, something to celebrate, and tonight he knew how they'd do it.

The saleswoman showed him an amber intaglio. Good, but not quite.

After Nat's testimony, Camilla had given him a kiss and told him she was proud of him – for his honesty, intelligence, and mature, even-keeled attitude. He seemed less angry than she had known him to be in the past, she said. Even his partner, Sally Shaw, had noticed a difference. Not that he'd lost his boyish charm or love of trouble or quickness, but he was far more focused than he had been, and more professional. And there was a touch of technical brightness about him now, beyond his usual genius for geometry and spatial relations, reminding Camilla of someone else she'd deeply loved and admired.

The saleswoman showed him a diamond pendant and suggested it instead of a ring. It was so gorgeous he almost went for it, but tradition clawed him back.

He'd told Camilla that it didn't bother him that he sometimes reminded her of Cush. In fact, nothing about Cush Walker bothered him anymore. On the contrary; Cush's life interested him – his boyhood, his medicine, and especially his experiences as a black man. Maybe he'd reach the point some day where he could actually look a black person in the eye and see the person first, the color second. After draining Cush's experiences as a black man for all they were worth, he would look forward to the day when the entire subject of race became so boring that it just, fucking, didn't, fucking, matter.

The saleswoman opened a black velvet case with a dozen rings resting in their slits, but Nat saw only one. It was an antique white-gold band with five sapphire stars set in a square field of white pearl. That was it. He bought it. If it did its job tonight, the day after tomorrow they'd be married.

He left the store and headed for home, stopping at a florist to pick up a bouquet of blue lilies on the way. A flat of Southern sunflowers had caught his eye and given him pause, but he overcame the urge. Funny, he'd never even noticed them before.

Sitting in the back of a taxi cab, he finally felt as if everything was falling into place. For the first few weeks after Cush died, Camilla had missed him greatly and talked about him a lot. But the adventure of discovering him in Nat's personality had taken away some of the sting. Best of all, she was well now, no speech problems, amnesia, or loss of motor control – and no signs of KBS, knock wood. Rodriguez and Dr Schulman, the hospital's chief neurosurgeon, said there was no reason to assume it would return.

But the big deal had been the notion of the memory transfer. Whenever he exhibited a trait of Cush's, she wanted to know what it felt like. He said it was difficult to explain. Do you feel like a different person? she asked. No, not at all, he said. Do you feel confused? No more than usual. Are you aware of his character traits and memories? Depends. He said sometimes a memory surprised him, but it always felt as if it had come from his own experience, not imported from someone else. He compared it to remembering that the first car he drove was blue. In fact, blue might have been the color of Cush's first car, but it felt like his own.

'Does Cush ever take over like one of the three faces of Eve?'

'No, that never happens,' Nat said. 'I think that's called schizophrenia.'

'I know, that's why I asked.'

'I don't feel a separate person living inside me,' he said. 'Whatever memory phrases came over from Walker feel integrated into my own. No pun intended.'

She liked that. It felt good to understand metaphors and puns again, even bad ones.

'I don't think I inherited as much of Walker's mind as you think I did,' he said.

'That remains to be seen. What's seven times seven?'

'Forty-eight?'

'Hm,' she said. 'Maybe you're right.'

But he wasn't right, she said. She knew what she saw with her own eyes. He was vanilla ice cream with chocolate chips inside, and she loved it. She loved him.

She loved *them*.

When the right time came, she said, she'd have one whale of a story to give to her writer friend, Cynthia Weber.

He entered the loft building carrying the bouquet and the ring in his pocket. They'd have a drink together, then they'd go to dinner at their favorite Italian restaurant where he'd pop the question. If she said yes, they'd have peach champagne – or maybe he'd break new ground and go for something great, like Cristal – and then they'd go dancing late into the night.

Dancing. Wasn't that amazing? Two months ago he couldn't even do a box step, and now here he was, ready to do a merengue.

Wonders never ceased.

When Nat came through the door to the loft, he knew something was wrong. Camilla normally wore her disposition on her sleeve the way people with open personalities did, but now she seemed unusually quiet and preoccupied. She took the lilies from him and thanked him with a perfunctory kiss and put them into a vase, but left them in the kitchen. They talked about each other's day – the case he'd caught, the building façade she'd begun repairing. Two more weeks and she'd be making her first climb. Maybe that was what was bothering her.

'Are you ready to climb again?' he asked.

'I can hardly wait,' she said.

Must be something else. 'You in the mood for Italian tonight?'

'Sounds fine.' No enthusiasm.

'Would you rather not go dancing?'

She examined him as if he'd divulged a secret. 'No, how about you?'

'I'm raring to go,' he said.

She frowned at him and turned quiet again.

'What's wrong with that?' he asked.

'I still can't believe it,' she said. 'This person who had the rhythm of a dog, wanting to go dancing. Not just dancing, but the merengue. I'm not even sure I know how.'

'It's easy,' he said. 'Come here, I'll show you.'

He turned on the stereo, slipped a Latin dance CD into the disk holder, and soon the loft was filled with the sound of egg-shaped coconuts rolling across sandy beaches and bumping into old tin cans. He pushed the chaise and a work table out of the way, then took her into his hands more than his arms – there had to be a right amount of distance between them – and began leading her. In a minute she was moving with him, smiling, catching on, improvising, swiveling her camshaft hips, stomping cockroaches in slow motion. 'Do it as if you're moving down a row of people seated in a movie theater, trying to get to your seat,' he said as they danced.

When the music ended, they fell into a warm hug. He kissed her and held her. She spoke into his ear.

'Cush hated the merengue,' she said.

He held her head close to his, saying nothing.

She said, 'He didn't like fast dances of any kind.' She pulled back and looked at him. 'As a matter of fact, he didn't care much for dancing of any kind. He did it, but it was mostly an excuse for holding me.'

Uh–oh.

He looked for help in her eyes. None showed up. 'What are you saying?' he said, knowing what she was saying.

'He hated blue lilies, too. They reminded him of his father's funeral.'

She broke their embrace and stepped over to a small table by the door to the hallway and lifted two envelopes with cellophane windows. 'The new mailman delivered some of Robin's mail to us by mistake. These are for you.' She handed him two envelopes containing invoices addressed to him in care of Robin Feld. They were unopened, but then, they didn't need to be open. The return address on the first one read Gloria's Dance Studio; the second, the Hedley School of Culinary Arts.

He gave her a confused, innocent look. 'So?'

'*So?*' she said. 'So I want to know what's going on here. But before you answer, I should tell you I spent the afternoon with Rodriguez.'

Damn. 'And?'

'He said there's no evidence the transfer worked,' she said. 'The MRI scans he's been doing on you every week – without your telling me – show nothing.'

'Did he also tell you that the scans couldn't find the banana trick in Spider? Or Cush's shirt-buttoning phrase in Roy Driggers?'

'Yes.'

'And that in the monkey trials, the transfers sometimes took months to kick in?'

'He told me.'

'Well, there you are.'

She sat down. She wasn't interested in dancing. She was in detective mode. 'But you've been telling me things have already kicked in.'

Uh, right. He felt like the husband who'd told his wife he'd spent the night on the porch swing only to be reminded that the porch swing had been gone for two years. Maybe so, the man said, but that's my story and I'm sticking to it.

'Nat?'

'What?'

'What have you done?'

'About what?'

'You know what. Why are you pretending to be Cush Walker?'

He decided to tell her the truth.

No, the transfers had not worked. No, he felt no 'otherness' inside him, no alien living within, no Cush Walker inhabiting his skin, no images of his experiences, no knowledge of his stories, no memories of his life, no words, no phrases, no likes, no dislikes, no skills, tastes, desires, or traits that were from her former doctor.

'But that's not the point,' he said. 'I've got a new outlook anyway, not from some hokey downloading of Walker's neural webbing, but from the most powerful mind-altering influence there is.'

'What's that?'

'Learning.'

He said he had learned things – about Cush Walker growing up as a black kid in Mississippi, about his experiences as a student, about his father's lynching and certain similarities to his own father's death, regardless of Walker's claim to the contrary. He had learned things about Walker's feelings for her – the passionate, tender, painful things that he begrudgingly admired about the man even if they tied his stomach in knots.

But more than that, he'd learned things about himself, in particular this quirk of prejudice that had frightened her away and made her decide not to marry him. He understood why he used to feel the way he did about black people in general. They were like a guy in a speeding car who cuts you off: as long as you don't know who it is, or why he did it – as long as you can't *see* him – you feel perfectly entitled to a small, quick case of road rage.

So, sure, he had adopted some of Cush's characteristics because that was the only way he could keep her from leaving him. If he hadn't, she would have walked out on him at Jackson Airport and never come back. That's why he'd faked Cush's sneeze, exactly as he'd described it in his briefing book. He loved her too much to let her go. He was desperate. But if appropriating pieces of Cush Walker had begun as an an act of stealth with ulterior motives, it had grown into something else far better. What he liked about the man he'd made a genuine part of himself. What she saw now was what she got. He'd changed. He'd grown. He'd matured.

She wasn't buying.

'It's fraud,' she said. 'I can't tell what part of you is really you, and what part is made-up Cush.'

'It's all me, regardless of where it came from.'

The puppy came bouncing over to Nat. He reached down and picked him up.

'How do I know that?' she said. 'How many of the things I find attractive in you – never mind if they came from Cush – how many are being faked to please me?'

'Nothing.'

'I don't believe that.'

'Try me.' He scratched the puppy behind the ears.

'What about your recently developed taste for classical music? Is that real or fake?'

He stared at the pup's face. 'Try me again.'

She threw her hands in the air.

He said, 'Ask me about something that really matters to you.'

'Like what?'

He could see that he'd scored a point. Small, but a point. Go for two. 'We're getting married the day after tomorrow,' he said, putting the dog on the floor.

'I beg your pardon?'

'I'm proposing to you at dinner tonight. You're supposed to say yes. I have the ring in my pocket. It's gorgeous.'

'Good God, Nat.' She sat on the chaise and held her forehead in her fingers. Seeing no reason to bid against himself, he said nothing.

She said, 'I feel as if I'd be marrying you under false pretenses.'

He went into an old-fashioned kneeling position at her side. 'You're irritated with how I did it – and I don't blame you for that. If there'd been any other way, I would have done it – but don't confuse the How with the What. What bothered you before was your fear of how I'd feel about your ancestry. Well, good news. It's irrelevant – actually, I think it always was, even on the chaise playing your little game. I'd like to be able to say your black blood absolutely fascinates me, tell me more, but frankly, I don't care one way or the other. You've seen that for yourself. I'm not faking it. I've reached this state of blissful neutrality on the subject of race in general. Learn, baby, learn.'

She stared him in the eyes, saying nothing.

He said, 'Marry me, Camilla.'

She didn't blink.

'I'm on my knees.'

Still no answer.

'They're starting to hurt,' he said.

She smiled at him.

He thought he had her.

'I need some time to figure this out,' she said.

He stood up. 'Why is it every time we have an argument you want time to think about whether we should split?'

'Because every time we have an argument you give me a good reason to split.' She stood up and walked past him and up the spiral staircase to the bedroom.

He called after her. 'Do you have *any* idea what it takes for a

guy with the rhythm of a dog to learn how to do the merengue?'
To Blue: 'No offense, fella.'

She disappeared up the steps. He waited a minute, then
followed.

As he entered the bedroom, he saw her pull out a dress on a
hanger, as if she was already packing.

'Do you think this would work?' she said.

'For what – a trip back to New Orleans?'

'For dancing the merengue?'

It was a great evening. They danced, talked, and touched. They drank champagne – not peach, and not Cristal – that maiden voyage would have to wait. But it didn't matter.

He proposed.

She said yes.

They came home early and made love on the chaise. No games this time – nothing psychological or edgy, nothing shallow or deep. Just two people in love making love in the here and now.

They heard a sigh under the bed, and Blue wandered out onto the rug with the gait of a tired pack mule. He extended his paws in front of him, arched his back, stretched, then walked to the side of the bed and stood on his hind legs with his paws on the edge of the mattress, wagging his tail and blinking sleepily. He wanted up.

'What's it going to be?' Nat asked Camilla. 'Dog up or down?'

'Down,' she said. 'Up gets too hot.'

Nat petted Blue's head. 'You heard what she said, boy. Go back to sleep.'

Nat laid back against the headboard. Camilla sat in the middle of the bed with her legs crossed in front, her back straight, her head moving in slow circles as she did her exercises. 'You sure you want to do this?' she asked.

'What's that?'

'Get married?' She raised her hands above her head as if she was reaching for the moon.

'Sure, I'm sure,' he said. 'Are you?' He watched her. 'Or are you still pissed?'

She lowered her arms and turned her back to him and stretched out on her right side. Then she extended her left leg and breathed deeply. 'I never stay mad.' She began raising and lowering her leg like a gate at a railroad crossing. 'Although, faking a *sneeze*? Really, Nat. It's one thing to steal mannerisms, but his sneezes were like mini orgasms.'

He didn't answer. He was in bed with a naked lady who was doing leg exercises – what was there to say?

She continued her motion. 'I mean, how would you like it if I faked an orgasm?'

He reached over the side of the mattress and lifted Blue onto the bed. The puppy licked him on the chin once, thank you, thank you, then immediately abandoned him for Camilla. She stopped moving her leg and nuzzled him nose to nose with cupped hands behind his ears. He gave her a dog kiss and lay down against the silky smooth leg. No fool, Blue.

Nat lay on his side behind her with his head propped up in his hand, watching. 'Have you?' he asked.

She began raising and lowering her leg again. 'Have I what?'

'Faked an orgasm.'

The leg kept moving but there was half a beat before she answered – just enough to make a detective stick to his line of questioning.

'With who?' she asked.

'With me.' *With who.*

'Never!' she said.

'Come on, if you're going to accuse me of faking something, you may as well own up to a little faking of your own.'

'I have never faked an orgasm with you.'

'I see,' he said.

'You don't believe me?'

'If you say so, of course I do. Although . . .'

'Although what?'

'Poker players who say they never bluff are the best bluffers of all.'

'I'm not bluffing,' she said. Leg up, leg down.

He laid his hand on her hip and felt the muscle tighten and relax with her movement. 'That's too bad.'

She digested the comment a second, then stopped exercising

and turned over and propped herself up on one hand like a mermaid sitting on a rock. 'You'd *like* it if I had faked an orgasm with you?'

He gave her an arched eyebrow. 'Since you've never done it, I guess we'll never know.'

'Why would you like it? Hypothetically speaking.'

'I look at it this way. Which is the bigger act of love – giving a man this automatic physical response you can't help, or giving him this great performance because you love him so much you want to make him happy?'

She stared at him. 'You're a strange man, Hennessy. A *very* strange man.' It had the tone of, what am I getting into?

He lowered his head onto the pillow and closed his eyes. 'I'll take your orgasms any way I can get them. Is that you or the dog?'

'Doing what?'

'Licking my foot.'

She leaned forward and stretched out her hand. 'C'mere, boy.'

Blue got up and slunk toward the dog catcher, accepting his fate on a cold, hard floor. When he came within reach of her hands, she lifted him up and laid him on the sheet between her and Nat and rubbed his head softly. He exhaled as if he'd died and gone to dog heaven. She settled back against her pillow and rested with her face up, eyes open. For some reason she was hungry, but it was too late for that, she'd eaten more than usual and danced less than she should have.

After a minute, she turned out the light and curled up behind Blue and Nat, turning them into three spoons in a drawer. A sonorous silence filled the room, the soothing clatter of street noises in New York rising from the bottom of an urban well. In another minute, they'd all be skipping down the yellow brick road.

Camilla's whispered voice broke the silence.

'Nat?'

'Mm?'

'I'm glad you're the way you are because you want to be, not because a scientific experiment made you that way.'

'Mm-hm.'

More silence. Welcome to the night.

'Nat?'

'Mm.'

'I meant it when I said I haven't.'

Silence from him.

From her, an additional, 'Faked an orgasm, that is.'

In a matter of seconds she felt his body melt into the mattress and harmonize with the void. But she waited to be sure.

'Nat?' she whispered.

There was no answer this time, only silence punctuated by the rise and fall of perpetual-motion lungs in a rhythm that couldn't be pretended.

'Did you hear me, sweetheart? I've never faked it.'

He didn't answer because he couldn't. He was out.

She made herself comfortable and let her muscles retreat in soft ripples from her neck to her feet. The last relaxed toe should have put her under, but her nagging conscience wouldn't let her go. Not until she made that one, small, final, honest confession.

'Almost never.'

It started as a simple night-time waking, a change of position before going back to sleep. Not this time. Something kept him awake. Not something – the absence of something. A presence. A heartbeat.

He turned toward Camilla and saw her side of the bed empty. He raised his torso, straining at the neck. And where was the dog?

He sat up, thinking, go back to sleep, they're fine. He waited, then gathered the sheet around his waist and Dutch-rubbed his hair. He was dressed as he always was in bed: naked.

'OW-uuuuu! OW-uuuuu!'

It was Blue, the beagle in him baying across the room.

'Hey,' Nat rasped, 'what's the problem?' No answer from the dog, no answer from Camilla.

'Ow-uuu – uu – u!' the puppy howled.

'Be quiet, Blue.' What a weird bark. 'Cam?'

He turned on the lamp and saw the dog sitting outside the bathroom door, his head tilting back for another, *'Ow-uuuuu!'*

Nat got up, walked to the door, and knocked. 'Cam? You in there?'

The dog started up again. *'Ow-uuuu!'*

Reaching down to lift him, he noticed that there was no light slipping out from beneath the door. 'Cam, are you all right?' No answer.

Maybe she was downstairs.

He opened the door a crack and set down the dog. Then he opened it all the way.

The light from the bedside lamp cast a fog onto the bathtub. What? The canvas shower curtain had been pulled off its rod into a heap in the tub.

He snapped on the light. Another growl filled the room.

This time, not from the dog.

He walked toward the pile of cloth. It quivered once.

Another growl.

He reached out and lifted the curtain. As it rose, he saw two feet on white porcelain, then shins and a pair of knees held tightly by familiar hands.

'Cam?' he said, pulling the curtain clear.

She was staring at him with scowling, bloodshot eyes, shivering, her hair wet and matted, her face lined, her lips blue.

'What in God's name—'

She leaped out of the tub, teeth bared, growling rabidly, spitting froth – and tried to bite him.

'If you can't do a nanoscan, what's the alternative?' Nat asked, jaw muscles rippling.

'Time and nature,' Rod said. 'Sedatives and Tegretol when she's awake.'

Nat looked down at Camilla and felt his heart pound. She was on her back, lightly sedated and held down in five-point restraint – cuffs on her hands and ankles, a leather strap across her forehead. A beautiful butterfly chloroformed and pinned to a board.

'Why can't you try a scan?' he said.

'We don't have a program to cure KBS,' Rod said glumly.

'Then why not get one?'

'If we weren't going out of business, maybe we could.'

'Out of business?'

'The IRB is shutting down the lab pending an investigation.'

'Christ,' Nat mumbled, rubbing his neck. 'How much do they know?'

'Only that their Nobel candidate died doing an experiment on himself, which is enough.'

Nat turned to Dr Schulman, the chief neurosurgeon. 'What about conventional surgery?'

'We could try,' Schulman said softly, 'but when you remove the temporal lobes, you have a tendency to deaden the patient's affect.'

'You mean turn them into zombies,' Nat said.

Schulman raised his eyebrows. 'I wouldn't necessarily go that far.'

He didn't have to. Nat had read all about this stuff. He couldn't imagine Camilla without her personality. Or worse, he could.

Schulman pulled Rod aside and huddled near the door. Nat turned back to Camilla and stroked her hair.

She opened her eyes.

'Cam?' he said softly.

No answer, a dead stare.

'It's me, babe. Can you hear me?'

Her neck muscles tightened; she wanted up.

Absolutely. He pulled back on the restraining strap on her forehead and unbuckled it.

Her neck muscles relaxed, her claustrophobia eased.

Schulman looked over at them. 'Hey, don't do—'

Her head jerked upward, mouth snarling, teeth bared.

Schulman ran to the opposite side of the bed.

Nat grabbed a pillow and put it under her chin. She bit into it like a crocodile taking a chicken. He put his hand on top of it and pushed her head down; Schulman grabbed the restraining strap, drew it across her forehead, and cinched it tightly. Her teeth were still showing when he removed the pillow, and her throat rumbled.

Nat's skin was numb and tingling, and he found himself short of breath. Sitting down to calm himself, he tried to imagine the chaos and fear deep in her brain, the silent, internal howling she must have been making at this very moment.

I'll never let them tie you down like this again, Cam, no matter what it takes. Anything is better than this.

Anything.

Rodriguez typed in a request and waited. The monitor gave him a status report on the repair of a test animal with KBS. Every task the Z-5s performed was marked COMPLETED in green. Rod leaned back in his chair, frustrated, and took a drink from a can of soda.

'Looks good to me,' Nat said, sitting in the next chair. They were the only people in the room.

'That's the problem. All systems are functioning right, the Z-5s are going to the damage sites and making their repairs, but when they exit, the disease persists. We've been trying to figure out what's wrong for the last two years and still don't have a clue.'

'Which leaves us with Schulman and his rusty knife.'

'Don't knock Schulman, he believes in what Cush was doing. At one time he was a member of the team.' He leaned forward and asked the computer to give him a new equation. A few more days and the symbiotic relationship he had with this computer would be history. Come on, baby, reveal yourself. 'For some reason when they're working on the temporal lobes, they seem to do something we can't see.' He was talking to himself, not Nat, his non-scientist visitor.

'Could it be a glitch in your signals?'

'No, if they weren't responding to instructions, we couldn't get them to make repairs of any kind.'

A telephone rang on the console to his left. Rod pushed his swivel chair over to it, turning his back on Nat to take the call. It was Schulman, calling to report on Camilla. She'd had another seizure and was exhausted. He thought they should operate soon.

Turning back as he talked, Rod found Nat sitting in front of the monitor, poking at the keyboard with his index finger, the only way he knew how to type. Up came a long mathematical formula of a kind you'd expect to see on a blackboard at Cal Tech or MIT.

Rodriguez hung up and rolled his chair forward. 'No offense, Detective, but unless you've had some advanced math, this is going to look like gibberish.'

'Advanced math? I can't even remember my multiplication tables. What are these things?' He pointed at strings of numbers and symbols, cyber-alphabet soup.

'Those are the algorithms that run the Z-5s.'

'What's an algorithm?'

'A decision tree. It says when you get to point A, if you find such and such, take the left fork, if you find this and that, take the right. It tells the Z-5s what to do, at the speed of light.'

'Looks like Greek to me.'

'Actually, you managed to put your finger on the problem.' He reached in front of Nat and tapped in some instructions to exit the program. The monitor quickly closed a series of windows that had been opened.

'Wait a minute, what was that?' Nat said.

'What was what?'

'Go back to that picture that came up on the screen.'

Rod stopped the exit sequence and returned to it. 'It's a three-dimensional representation of the algorithms that drive the program.' The screen showed a stack of dressmaker's wire forms piled on top of each other.

'Interesting.' Nat squinted at it, turning his head sideways to get another perspective. 'Mind if I take a look?'

Go ahead, humor him, why not? This whole program would

soon be on ice. Rod scooted to the side and let Nat take the joystick and begin turning the structure in the cyberspace of the monitor.

'For a guy who's not in this business, you're pretty good with that thing,' Rod said. 'You play computer games?'

'Not much,' he said absent-mindedly, focused. 'I seem to have this aptitude for spatial relations. Comes in handy if you have to build a jungle gym without instructions.'

He tapped some keys, this time using all ten digits, like a touch typist, and brought up a different picture on the monitor.

'You've pulled up a picture of Camilla's right temporal lobe.'

'I know,' Nat said. He rotated and spun the three-dimensional computer representation, then hit some keys and brought up another picture of the left temporal lobe. 'She has bilateral damage nearly exactly the same in both lobes.'

'You can see that?'

Nat didn't answer; he was too busy.

Rod stopped asking questions and watched.

Nat said, 'There's the problem, right there. When you programmed the repair function, you layered it.'

'Layered what?'

'For some reason, your Z-5s are rebuilding brain cells on odd-numbered latitudes at a different rate from the even-numbered.'

Rod leaned forward and inspected the screen where Nat had placed the cursor arrow. What was he talking about?

'Picture the brain in thin layers,' Nat said, 'as if it's been carved out of a fat deck of playing cards. Now watch this.'

He worked the joystick and the keyboard smoothly. After clicking on an icon of a miniature spyglass, he zoomed in on a piece of the temporal lobe by a magnification factor so large it brought them into a whole new microcosmic world.

Rod was more than impressed; he was amazed. They were

at the heart of the problem. 'Cush and I have looked at this before,' he said.

'But you didn't understand what you were seeing, OK? You weren't looking at it the way I am. See these small lines?'

'Yes?'

'Those are curls.'

'What are curls?'

'Small ripples in the layers of the temporal lobe your Z-5s have created as they do their repair. Saddle-shaped parabolas instead of true planes.'

How's a detective know that?

Nat scrolled evenly with the joystick. No Page Down button, no search for the Any key, no placement of his coffee cup in the middle of a CD Rom drive. He had the skill of a professional.

He pointed with a cursor. 'There's one right there. See it? The Z-5s are curling up every fourth card in the deck. You can't see them mathematically unless you know what to look for, but spatially, there they are. When they leave the repair site, they seem to have done their job just fine, but the neural connections they leave behind are still haywire. Result? KBS.' Back to the monitor. 'All you have to do is alter the algorithms and align the timing sequence on the fourth latitudes to correspond to the other three. Sort of like getting the timing right on your distributor.'

Wow. Rod didn't know how he was doing it, but this idiot savant was on to something incredible. Don't rock the boat. Go with it and figure out how he did it later. 'I hear you, but I can't do that,' Rod said.

'Why not?'

'When I broke the security code on the F Series scan, I destroyed the program files.'

'Walker must have backed them up, didn't he?'

'Yeah, but the override destroyed those files, too.'

'Are you sure?' Nat examined the monitor. 'Why would

a guy as smart as he was put them where they could be wiped out?'

'When he was locking us out, it was the last few hours of his life. I assume he had other things on his mind.'

'Maybe.' He didn't think so.

Nat worked the keyboard with the skill of an organist. Rod watched, mesmerized. After a moment Nat sat back. 'There they are.' An inventory of backup files appeared on the screen.

My God, he was right. Cush had backed up the files in a completely different directory. Rod took back the keyboard and tried to open them, but a warning appeared: **Access Denied. Enter Series F Code.**

'Fuck,' Rod said. 'They're in there, but they're still locked up.'

'Let me have a look.'

Nat took over the keyboard again and brought up a window that called for the security code.

'What kinds of codes has he used in the past?' he asked.

'Alpha numerics like his birthday, his Mississippi address spelled backwards, things he could remember. When I was looking earlier, I tried every one I could imagine.'

Nat tapped on the keyboard. Letters and numbers didn't appear in the code box, only asterisks masking what he typed. 'You didn't try this one.'

The monitor turned blank, then a series of files began cascading down the screen, lines upon lines of them with names and numbered extensions.

Rod's eyes widened. 'Sweet Joseph and Mary! That's them!'

Nat rolled his chair back and stood up and let Rod have the keyboard. Rod's eyes were glued to the screen as it continued scrolling through the lines. 'How did you do that?'

'I told you, I have this strange gift for geometry. That and being a detective.'

'But this is proprietary stuff only Cush knew, and you went right to it.'

'Must be a Columbo,' Nat said. 'It's the unpredictable that trips you up, and the unpredictable that saves you.'

A Columbo? Rod stopped typing and gave Nat a look reserved for the Lone Ranger. 'Who the hell are you?'

'Cut the shit, Rod, you're creeping me out.' Nat rubbed his face with his hands, and for a second Rod thought he was about to pull off a rubber mask. The thought of who was beneath it, the evidence of it, was piling up so fast it made him a little dizzy.

Nat said, 'When you get the program fixed, get some sleep. Tomorrow's going to be a big day for Camilla. If you're being shut down, we'll have to act fast and make no mistakes.' Then he started for the door.

'Wait a minute! What's the security code you found? I may need it again.'

Nat came back, stroked some keys, and turned the security code asterisks into English. There, in the box, were the four words Cush had secretly entered when he'd locked them out: *Death Is But Crossing.*

Rod felt the blood drain from his head. He'd seen that phrase only once before, on the back of Cush's pocket watch.

That had to be it, there was no other explanation. Cush's memory must have finally kicked in – right before his eyes! All the phrases transferred into Nat's brain, sitting there waiting to be triggered by an emotional event – the pressure of trying to save Camilla's life.

It must have worked after all.

My God.

'I'm telling you,' Nat said from the shower, 'it didn't work.' He turned off the water. 'At least not the way Rodriguez thinks it did.'

He stepped out of the tub, singing to himself as he toweled off. *'I'm getting married in the morning . . . ding, dong, the bells are going to chime . . .'* It was shower-stall singing not made for human consumption. Even Blue kept his distance.

Camilla stood in the bathroom combing her hair. It had been four weeks since the operation, and her recovery was still on track. 'That's not what Rod thinks. He says if it didn't work, you never would have found the answer.'

'It's a case of one and one making three,' Nat said. 'My eye for structure opened the vault, but the important stuff was already there. They just couldn't see it. Hand me those shorts, would you, honey?'

'Then how did you know how to analyze what you saw?'

'I didn't. I just took my cues from Rod.'

'That's not what he says.'

'Rod's absolutely brilliant, but for a scientist, he's also full of shit.' And now taking a long overdue vacation. Sorry, Cush, but with your lab in limbo and your research still under wraps, your posthumous Nobel will have to wait.

Camilla wasn't ready to throw in the towel. 'He says you knew exactly where to go in the program to find the flaw.'

He stepped into his briefs. 'You know those stories about how a father sees a car sitting on his kid and lifts it up so they can pull

655

him free? That was me. I had this burst of mental lifting that let Rod and Schulman pull you free. If I hadn't seen you in that room in five-point restraint, I never could have done it.'

'Then what about the way you used the keyboard and the joystick? I thought you didn't even know how to type?'

'Baby, when you're under enough pressure, you can do anything.'

She stuck her lipstick into its tube. 'And the security code? *Death is but crossing?* Where did that come from?'

'Straight out of Walker's briefing book.'

Her eyes questioned him.

'What?' he said.

She shook it off. 'I gotta read that book some time.' After snapping the waistband on his underpants, she gave him a kiss goodbye.

'Wait,' he said. 'What do you want for dinner?'

'You're the new chef around here.' He'd taken a sudden interest in cooking, and was good. 'Surprise me.' She went out the bedroom door.

Nat buttoned his shirt and grabbed a necktie from a hanger, a silk job with red measles on a field of blue. He planned to drop by the station house to pick up an envelope from Amerigo – what was in it, the Lieu wouldn't say – then talk to Shaw about the cases he'd leave behind while he was on his honeymoon. Then he'd shop for dinner. It was the eve of their wedding; they both preferred to dine in, just the two of them, simple and elegant. The last time they'd been this close to the altar, they'd gone out to celebrate and she'd been shot. He was taking no chances.

Turning to the mirror on the closet door, he slid the necktie under his collar – and stopped. *Death is but crossing?*

That's funny. I can't remember where I read it in the book.

He tied a half-Windsor and walked to the chest for a pair of socks. Opening the drawer, he saw Walker's briefing book and lifted it out. After backing up to the edge of the bed, he sat and flipped through the pages. It would just take a minute or two.

I know it's in here. He kept skimming. Walker never mentioned it to me, and neither had Camilla. It has to be here.

He riffled through a few more pages until his back hurt, then checked his watch – Christ, he was late – and closed the book. He'd finish reading it when he got back. Placing it in the drawer, he thought, oh, yeah, now I remember – I think it's near the end, where Walker wrote about his father's lynching. I'm pretty sure that's where I saw it. Must have been.

He stood at the elevator in the hallway outside the door to the loft, waiting for it to rise, thinking about what he'd cook for dinner.

Cat.

He needed a good wine. Maybe champagne. A Cristal, his favorite. His favorite? How could that be? He'd never tasted it before – had he?

And spinach. He really wanted spinach.

He pulled a handkerchief from his back pocket and wiped his forehead. It was really hot in here. And where was the damn elevator?

Fish.

They'd be on their honeymoon over Thanksgiving, but he had no interest in turkey tonight. He was in the mood for something else. Something like . . . catfish.

Catfish steamed on a bed of spinach. That's what he wanted.

He paused, feeling strange. Catfish and spinach? What was going on? He was a New York City boy; catfish was disgusting. And steamed spinach? Steamed spinach was a sorry, soggy mess that sounded like . . . something he wanted.

He pushed the Down button – wait a minute, hadn't he already done that? A second ago? Closing his eyes, he laid his forehead against the hunter-green cast-iron frame and waited for the elevator to come up and his dizziness to pass. The chains on the huge machine began clanking as the car made its way up to the fourth floor. Blinking, he watched the top of the cab rise behind the iron grating and metal mesh that surrounded the shaft. It slowed, rose flush with the floor, and stopped. The air was quiet.

He pulled the metal door open and got on.

It doesn't matter.

He pulled the gate closed. What doesn't matter? Why you change your attitude, your tastes, your likes and dislikes doesn't matter. How you do it doesn't matter. The only thing that really matters is — a touch of dizziness hit him again — the only thing in life that truly matters is . . . what condiments you use with steamed catfish. Ginger or spring onions?

Such a strange mix of thoughts.

He pushed the first floor button and the elevator clanked and moved down with a start. Shredded spring onions — and a julienne of carrots, that's what he'd use. And spinach. His taste buds were really watering for steamed spinach.

He walked down the New York sidewalk filled with awareness of the late morning sunshine, New York grit, and a vague, light-headed feeling that this was going to be a good day.

Passing an Army-Navy surplus store, he stopped to take a look at a backpack in the window. For some reason, seeing it made him slightly dizzy again.

He pulled out the envelope Amerigo had given him with instructions to open it on his honeymoon and tore it open anyway. At the top were the words BIAS TEST RESULTS. Now, why in the world would Amerigo hand him this? He'd given him the results weeks ago.

The first paragraph explained the pass-fail system. Nat's eyes dropped to a box at the bottom of the page.

It said, PASS.

Well, I'll be damned.

He looked up from the piece of paper. Yeah, of course, why didn't he see it before? Amerigo told him he'd failed in order to juice him up and try to nail Cush Walker. Now that this bit of nonsense was over, Joe was owning up to what he'd done, giving Nat his wedding present.

What a bastard.

But you gotta love him.

A man walking a dog came up the sidewalk and stood next to Nat, looking at the camping gear in the window.

'You like to hike?' the man said.

'I do today,' Nat said.

'Really. Where are you headed?'

'To the tree,' Nat said.

'The tree?' the man said.

Nat turned to face him feeling a bit exasperated. 'Yeah, you know, the tree.' It seemed obvious.

The man gave him a long face, then tugged at the leash on his dog. Come on, boy, what we've got here is another garden-variety, New York City weirdo.

Nat shook his head. What was wrong with white people, anyway? Sometimes they could be so incredibly . . . *dense*.

More dizziness. He looked at the back of his hand. What did he mean by that? Why would he think of white people as dense? It was like kicking himself, sort of, except it also felt . . . good, sort of.

Strange.

He felt a small sheen of perspiration form on his forehead. He knew so many things about Cush Walker from the briefing book, but sometimes they felt as if they'd been inside his head for years, not just for the last few weeks. In fact, sometimes he couldn't recall whether he'd read them, or heard them, or exactly how he'd got them. They just seemed to be . . . there. A part of his experience. How could that be?

It doesn't matter.

He tossed the test results into a wire wastebasket on the corner and turned back to the store window, experiencing a powerful *déjà vu* that lingered long after he thought it should have vanished. The backpack seemed familiar, as if he'd seen it or used it someplace before. Not as the 33-year-old man he was now, living amid slabs of concrete and steel . . . but as the nine-year-old farm boy he'd been years before, getting ready to head out in the early morning sun, a stick in hand, a pocket knife in his jeans, a dusty yellow lab named Old Blue at his heels, convinced that today was the day he'd finally find a hidden green pasture and a tall, mysterious pine he called the fire tree.

ACKNOWLEDGMENTS

In doing the research for this book, two people were helpful beyond measure. Dr Mary Kathryn Hammock, a neurosurgeon in Washington, D.C., educated me to the point of guiding my hand across the page. Joseph E. Lisi, actor and former captain with the New York Police Department, was so inventive he should be penning fiction of his own. I might have written a book without these two friends, but it wouldn't have been this one.

Similar thanks goes to Dr Ralph Merkle for his imagination, creativity, and good humor, and to Dr Roy Bakay, Dr Mahlon de Long, Dr Steven Flitman, Dr Eric R. Kandel, Dr Scott Rauch, and Dr Pamela Sicher for their generous help. Same to my writer pals Bill Broyles, Lorenzo Carcaterra and William Diehl, and to John and Marcia Vaughey for their marvelous hospitality. Thanks also to Fran Gale at the Center for Training, Larry Belante of the Statue of Liberty Foundation, John Bonanni of Radio City Entertainment, and to my 'beta tester' readers, Anne, Donna, Gloria, Joanne, Katie, Matt, Paul, Richard, Stephani, Susan, Tamara, and Tiffany.

Deep appreciation goes to Peter Gethers for his rare ability to keep the train on the tracks, and to Sam Vaughan, an editor who magically combines great seasoning and grace with a modern eye and vitality. He is the best.

A special tip of the hat to Tom Hedley who, knowing that on any given day a writer's emotions span the gamut from delusional self-satisfaction to justifiable self-homicide, listens patiently and says, there, there, now, time to get back to work.

To my dear colleague and publisher supreme, Sue Fletcher, and her talented associates at Hodder & Stoughton – never has so much been owed by so many (writers and readers) to so few. I offer my snappiest salute.

I want to thank my agent, Owen Laster, whose gentlemanly professionalism continues to impress me and, more importantly, impress my publisher. And finally, thanks to my friend and co-agent, Joni Evans, to whom this book is dedicated. Her contribution is the easiest to describe. Without her, none of this would have happened.